I0577344

Carl Alwin Schenck

Forest Mensuration

Carl Alwin Schenck

Forest Mensuration

ISBN/EAN: 9783741120831

Manufactured in Europe, USA, Canada, Australia, Japa

Cover: Foto ©Andreas Hilbeck / pixelio.de

Manufactured and distributed by brebook publishing software
(www.brebook.com)

Carl Alwin Schenck

Forest Mensuration

BULLETIN No. 20.

U. S. DEPARTMENT OF AGRICULTURE,

DIVISION OF FORESTRY.

Walter Mulford

MEASURING THE FOREST CROP.

BY

A. K. MLODZIANSKY,
ASSISTANT IN DIVISION OF FORESTRY.

Prepared under the direction of

B. E. FERNOW,
CHIEF DIVISION OF FORESTRY.

WASHINGTON:
GOVERNMENT PRINTING OFFICE.
1898.

LETTER OF TRANSMITTAL.

U. S. DEPARTMENT OF AGRICULTURE,
DIVISION OF FORESTRY,
Washington, D. C., June 24, 1898.

SIR: I have the honor to transmit herewith for publication a brief presentation of the methods by which measurements of felled and standing trees and of whole forest growths are best performed, together with a discussion of a method employed in ascertaining the rate of growth of trees and forest crops, developed in the Division of Forestry, by Mr. A. K. Mlodziansky.

The publication of these (with exception of the last) more or less elementary methods of procedure, selected from a large number of methods that have been developed, seems justified at the present time, as with the waning of forest supplies more accurate methods of measuring the forest crop are indicated. Moreover, the entire business arrangements of a well-conducted forest management are based upon a knowledge of the amount of product which may be had or expected from a given area. This knowledge can not be satisfactorily ascertained by mere estimates; hence mathematical methods must be employed.

Especially is this true with regard to the rate of growth at which the forest crop develops, for all financial calculations of the profitableness of forest management presuppose this knowledge. The method developed by Mr. Mlodziansky in the work of the Division, with regard to collecting and collating the data in ascertaining the rate of growth of white pine and other species, the results of which are presently to be published, will recommend itself for the rapidity with which a large number of measurements can be coordinated and summarized.

Respectfully,

B. E. FERNOW, *Chief.*

Hon. JAMES WILSON,
Secretary of Agriculture.

CONTENTS.

ILLUSTRATIONS.

MEASURING THE FOREST CROP.

INTRODUCTION.

The methods of measuring wood when cut are well known. For firewood and billets, for pulp wood, spokes, staves, etc., the cord of 128 cubic feet is employed; for telegraph poles, posts, etc., the linear foot, with diameter limits, furnishes the measure; for saw logs various standard log rules are used, which pretend to give the amount of timber that can be sawed from logs of given lengths and smallest measured diameter. We say "pretend," for in fact the amounts given in these log rules, or scalers' books, do not in most cases coincide with the amount obtained by the miller. That amount depends upon the care with which the miller handles the log and the character of the saw he employs.

It is not, however, the measuring of the cut wood that we propose to discuss here, but the measuring of the standing crop as it is found in the forest. This knowledge, not only of what amount of wood is standing on an acre at a given time, but what amount grows in a year or has grown in a given period, is of great importance with a crop which requires many years to mature, and does not, like a field crop, have a definite period when it is ripe, but with which the harvest depends on the question when it is profitable to cut the crop.

The amount which grows each year varies at different periods of the life of the crop, hence if we want to determine when it is most profitable to cut the crop we must be able to measure its growth and to determine whether the yearly or periodic increment is such as to make it desirable to let the crop stand because it increases in value in due proportion to the cost of its standing, or to cut it because the wood made per year ceases to pay interest on the cost.

In order to measure the amount of timber standing and the amount of wood growing we must know the methods of measuring (1) the contents of a single tree; (2) the contents of a stand of trees or growing stock; (3) the rate at which single trees and whole stands grow under varying conditions and at various ages.

While full knowledge of the subject may be acquired only by special study and application, familiarity with the simplest method is within the easy reach of everyone interested or engaged in lumbering or forestry operations, and only the simplest methods are to be discussed here.

MEASUREMENT OF STANDING TREES.

HEIGHT MEASURING.

There are various methods employed in determining the height of a standing tree; of these the geometrical method may be recommended for its simplicity and sufficient accuracy. At some distance from the tree (fig. 1), where both top and base are readily visible, place a pole from 4 to 5 feet long (SF) perpendicularly in the ground; put in the ground another and longer pole (DE) at some distance from the first one, so that the poles and tree are situated in the same vertical plane.

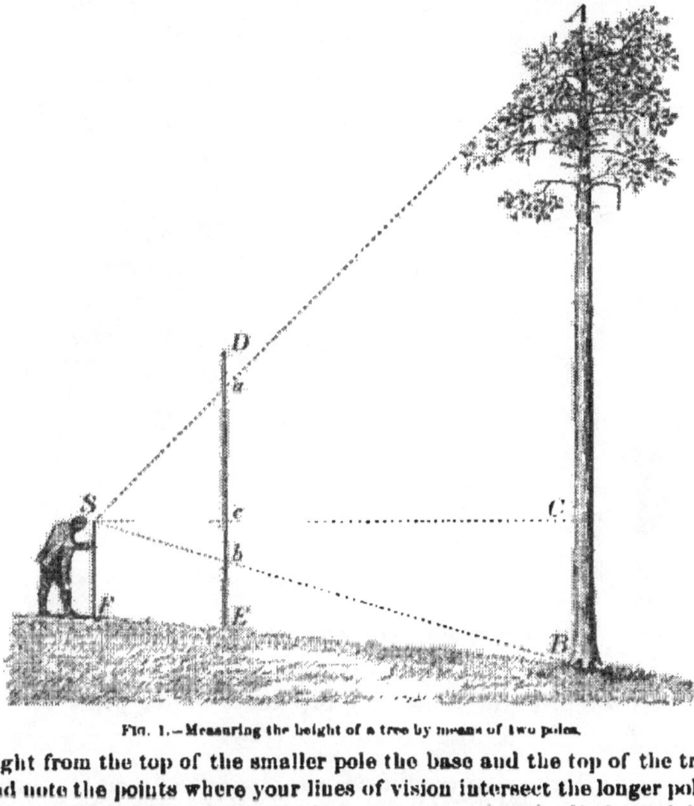

FIG. 1.—Measuring the height of a tree by means of two poles.

Sight from the top of the smaller pole the base and the top of the tree and note the points where your lines of vision intersect the longer pole; measure the distance between them; measure also the horizontal distance between the small pole and the tree and that between the two poles. Multiply the first distance by the second and divide by the third, the result being the height of the tree $\left(\frac{ab \times SC}{Sc}\right)$.

Example: Let the distance between the points where the lines of vision intersect be 6 feet, the distance between the pole and tree 30 feet, the distance between the poles 2 feet; then the height of the tree equals $\frac{6\times 30}{2}=90$ feet.

Another simple method, where possible, is to measure the shadow of the tree and of a pole or man, when the unknown height (h) of the tree is in the same ratio to the known length of its shadow (s) as the length of the pole (p) to that of its shadow (ps), both of which are also known;

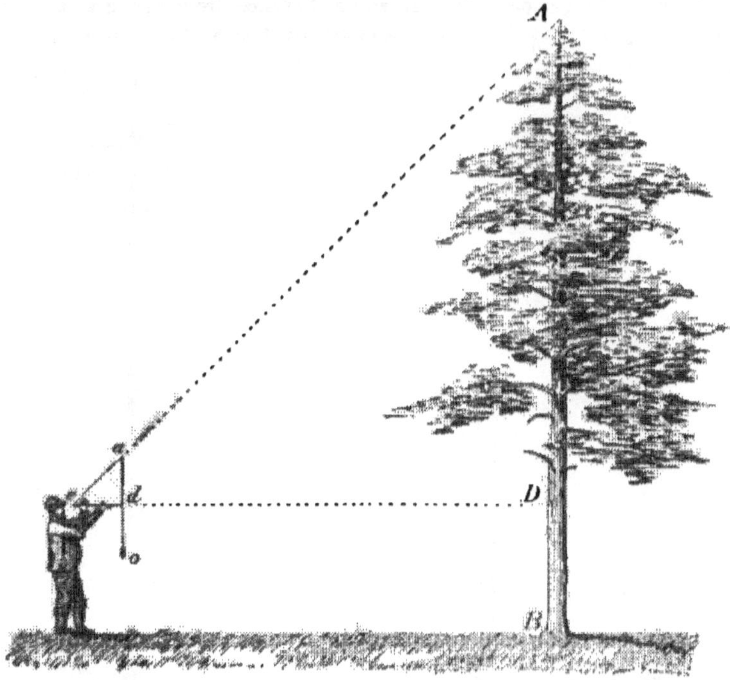

FIG. 2.—Measuring the height of a tree by means of a right-angled isosceles triangle.

that is to say, the height is equal to the product of the tree's shadow and the pole's length divided by the length of the pole's shadow $\left(h=\frac{s\times p}{ps}\right)$.

There are various instruments for measuring the height of a standing tree, based on the same principles as the first-mentioned simple method. The calculations are usually placed on the scale of the instrument and the height can be read off at once. The simplest one is a right-angled isosceles triangle, which may easily be made of pasteboard or wood. In using this triangle the observer should select a spot on the same level with the base of the tree at a distance approximately equal to the height of the tree (fig. 2).

Place the triangle to the eye so as to sight along the longer side, while holding the shorter sides (with the aid of a plumb line) so that the one is strictly vertical, the other horizontal; then shift your position forward or backward until you can just sight the top of the tree; measure your distance from the tree and add the height of your eye above the ground; the sum gives the height of the tree. After some practice with either of these two methods on trees standing in the open, one may become sufficiently expert in estimating the heights of trees to meet most requirements.

The most convenient instrument which may be recommended for measuring the height of trees is the so-called "mirror hypsometer" of Faustman.

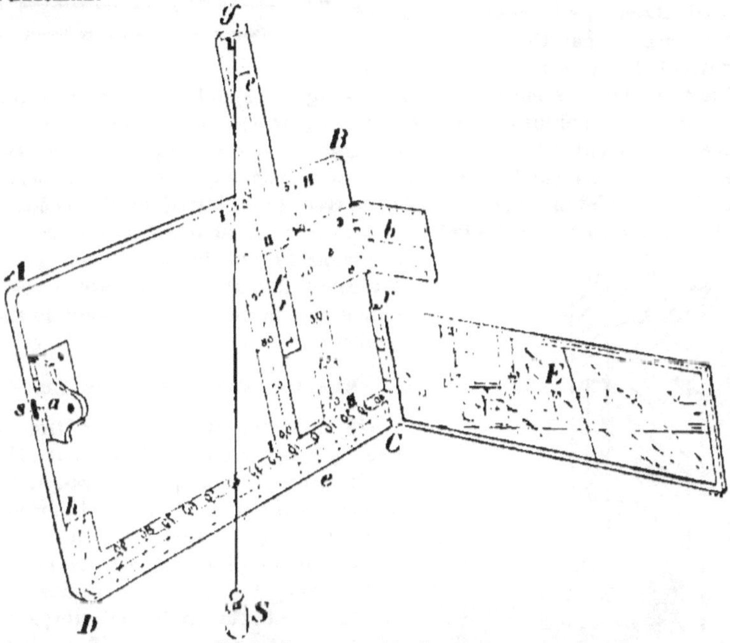

FIG. 3.—Faustman's mirror hypsometer.

The instrument (fig. 3) consists of the following parts:

ABCD—Rectangular wooden board (or brass frame), 7.3 inches long and 3.1 inches wide.

a—Eyepiece made of brass.

b—Frame with hair line.

ge—Sliding scale for registering the distance from the observer to the tree. It consists of two parts, the shifting part with the attachment of the plumb line *gS*, and the graduated part with a spring attachment (*f*) to keep the shifting part in position.

CD*h*—Height scale from which the height is read off.

E—Mirror, of similar length with the board and 1 inch wide, in which the height scale is reflected.

In using the instrument the observer should select a spot from which the top of the tree is distinctly seen; then measuring off the distance from the tree in feet, shift the sliding scale until its lower end stands opposite this distance. Thereupon sight from the eyepiece past the hair line and the top of the tree and read off in the mirror the figure which the plumb line strikes on the scale. In the same manner sight the base of the tree and find the corresponding figure. The sum of the two figures represents the height of the tree when the observer is situated above the level of the base of the tree. When the observer is situated below the level of the base of the tree the difference between those figures should be taken in order to obtain the height of the tree. The figure represents the position of the instrument when in use, the observer being supposed as on the same level with the base of the tree and as shown on the sliding scale at 100 feet distant; the height of the tree, as indicated by the position of the plumb line reflected in the mirror, is 40 feet. When the instrument is not in use all its parts are easily folded and put into a case, which can be conveniently kept in the pocket.

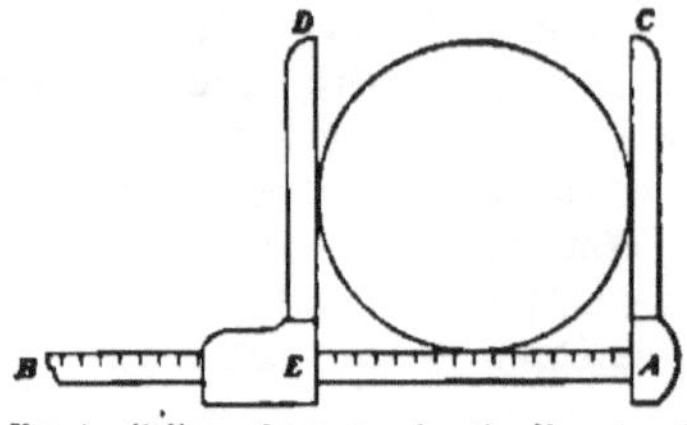

FIG. 4.—Calipers for measuring the diameter of trees.

MEASUREMENT OF DIAMETER.

The diameter of a standing tree is usually taken breast-high or above the swelling of the base and measured by a pair of calipers, the essential parts of which are a graduated rule, divided in inches and subdivisions, with two arms (fig. 4), one of which (AC) is fixed at right angles to the graduated rule (AB), while the other may be shifted along the rule, remaining parallel to the immovable arm (AC).

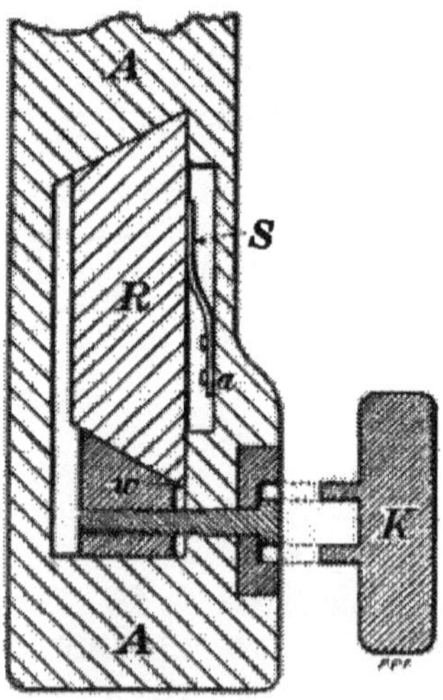

FIG. 5.—Section of the movable arm of Heyer's calipers.

In measuring, the calipers are usually placed breast-high horizontally against the trunk, so that both the rule and the immovable arm touch it; then the movable arm is shifted along the rule until it is brought in touch with the trunk, when the diameter can be read off on the rule. The length of the rule depends upon the size of the trees to be measured, and the length of the arms should not be less than half of that of the graduated rule. Calipers from 4 to 5 feet long will answer in most cases.*

Since trees are rarely cylindrical, being often larger in one direction than in the other, it is advisable to make two measurements and take the average, or else take care to measure the estimated average diameter. Instead of measuring the diameter, the circumference may be measured by a tape and the diameter determined by dividing it by 3.14, which is the ratio of the circumference to the diameter.

MEASUREMENT OF VOLUME.

In determining the volume of a standing tree the stem or bole only is considered; the cubic contents of the branches may be estimated by themselves. It is rather difficult to determine the volume of a standing tree because geometrical forms which exactly correspond to the shape of a stem are not known. Moreover, the shapes of trunks differ with age, with species, and with the soil and forest conditions under which they grow; hence we can obtain the volume only approximately by comparing it to the mathematical form which it resembles most nearly. The form of a stem of a tree is neither a cone nor a cylinder, but resembles most closely the form known as a paraboloid. The volume of a paraboloid equals the product of its base by one-half of its height. The base of the tree is taken at a distance from the ground, usually breast-high, where the irregularities of the trunk caused by the root swellings terminate. Here the tree is calipered, and the area for the corresponding diameter (found in the area table, p. 37) is multiplied by one-half of the height of the tree.

Example: Let the height of the tree be 90 feet, the diameter, breast-high, 21 inches. The area corresponding to a circle of 21 inches diameter is 2.40 square feet. The volume of the tree then equals $\frac{2.40 \times 90}{2} = 108$ cubic feet.

Another method, devised by a German forester, Mr. Pressler, may be recommended for determining the volume of a standing tree: Find a place along the stem (fig. 6) where its diameter (d) is exactly one-

* The calipers should be so constructed that the arms work strictly parallel to each other and at right angles to the rule; it should, therefore, be made of wood which is not easily affected by moisture. Air-dry pear wood may be recommended as a material least subject to shrinkage. Swelling and shrinking of the wood makes the shifting of the arm either difficult or too easy, often throwing the arm out of the perpendicular, thus destroying the required parallelism between the arms. To avoid this various constructions of calipers have been adopted. The calipers of Gustav Heyer, a section of which is given in fig. 5, may be recommended. A represents the section of the movable arm; R is the cross section of the rule; S a spring fastened at A pressing on the rule and pushing it down; *w* is the cross section of a wedge made of brass and fastened to a screw which can be moved by the key K. By moving the wedge backward and forward the rule can be tightened or released, thus enabling the observer to regulate the shifting of the movable arm without throwing it out of the perpendicular.

half of that at breast height (D); this point is called the guide point. This point can be determined by estimate after some practice or else by use of a simple instrument (fig. 7) consisting of three hollow cylinders (A, B, and C), which fit one into the other. The instrument then can be lengthened and shortened in the same way as an ordinary telescope. The cylinders may be made of stiff manila or other similar paper. Into the outer cylinder (A) two pins (*k* and *l*) are thrust 1 inch from the end; they can be moved in and out, permitting a change of distance between their heads. Cylinders A and B are of the same length, 13 inches each, while that of C is 2 inches long. The end of cylinder C is closed by a paper cover, in the center of which a hole (*y*), of one-fourth inch in diameter, is made as an eyepiece. Looking through the eyepiece (*y*), arrange the heads of the pins so that the distance between them coincides exactly with the diameter of the tree at breast height. Without changing the distance between the heads of the pins, the observer draws out the cylinders so as to double the former length, allowing for that purpose the two inside cylinders to project into each other 1 inch; then range the telescope up the trunk until a point is found where the diameter of the tree again corresponds with the distance between the heads of the pins. At this point the diameter of the tree is one-half of that at breast height. To obtain the volume of the tree, estimate or measure the height of the guide point, add 2 feet, and multiply this sum by two-thirds of the area corresponding to the diameter (D) measured at breast height.

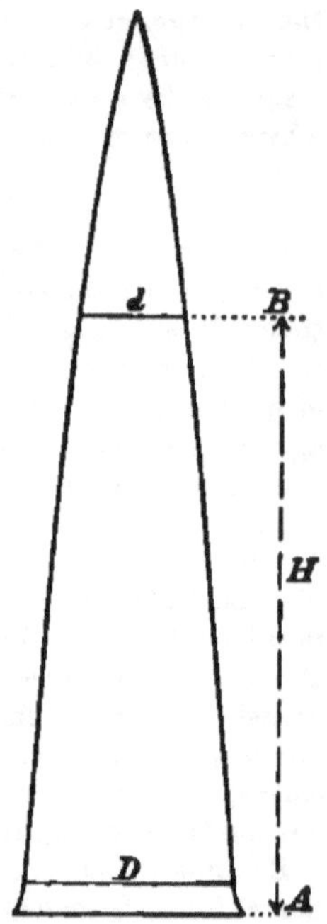

FIG. 6.—Pressler's method of determining the volume of a standing tree.

Example: A tree of 26 inches in diameter at breast height is 13 inches in diameter at a height of 60 feet from the ground—that is to say, the height of the tree to the guide point equals 60 feet. Adding 2 to 60 and multiplying by two-thirds of 3.69 (3.69 square feet represents

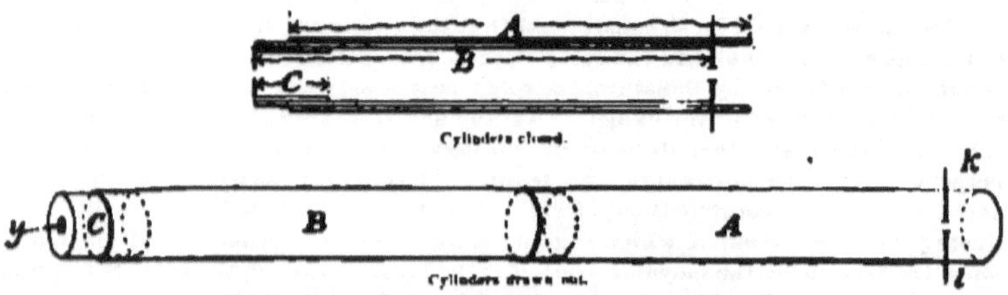

FIG. 7.—Instrument used for determining the guide point.

the area of a circle with a diameter of 26 inches), we find the volume of the tree to be 152.5 cubic feet. The merit of this method lies in its being equally applicable to trees of various geometrical forms; it is correct for trees of parabolic and conical forms; for trees representing the form of a cone with a concave surface the difference is only 1.4 per cent.

MEASUREMENT OF VOLUME OF A STANDING TREE BY EMPLOYING THE FACTOR OF SHAPE.

The trunks of trees, as has been mentioned, differ in shape. The shape of the trunk of a cypress, a spruce, or a fir is totally different from that of a pine, hemlock, or oak. The cypress, spruce, and fir, tapering rapidly toward the top of the tree, form stems resembling either a cone, as in the spruce and fir, or a neloid or conical shape with a concave surface as in the cypress. The pine, the hemlock, and most of the hard-wood trees, tapering more gradually toward the top, form stems of a conical shape with a convex surface. An oak or a tulip tree, on the other hand, may nearly approach the shape of a cylinder. As we have stated before, trees never attain a mathematical form, but only approximate more or less closely one or the other form.

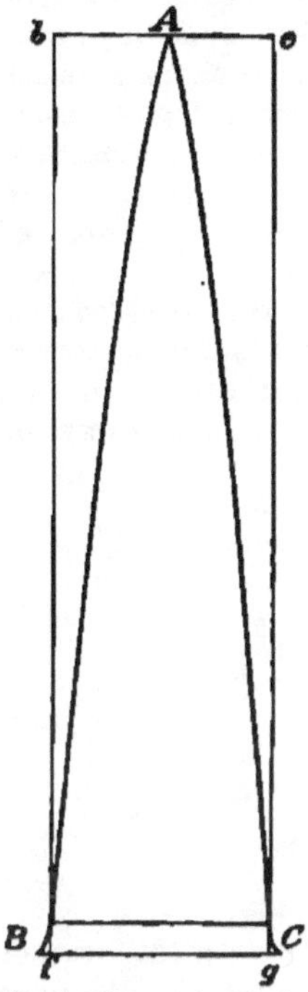

FIG. 8.—Determining the factor of shape.

The European foresters noticed long ago that there exists a relation between the actual volume of a tree and that of a regular geometrical body of corresponding dimensions. From actual calculation they learned further that this relation, varying with the kinds of trees, their dimensions, and conditions of growth, seems to be strikingly uniform. In Germany, for instance, there were measured more than forty thousand individual trees of various species and, all of them being felled, the forester was able to determine their volume in an accurate way. The actual volume of each individual tree thus obtained was compared with that of a cylinder of the same height and of the diameter at breast height. This comparison proved that the actual volume of the tree when divided by that of the cylinder of the corresponding dimensions gives a quotient which is constant for trees of the same species, approximately the same dimensions, and grown under the same forest conditions.

This quotient showing the taper of the tree, or the relation between the volume of a tree and of a cylinder of the same height and diameter breast high, is called the *factor of shape* or *form factor;* it is usually expressed in decimals and represents arithmetically the form of the stems.

For instance, if we take a tree of 22 inches diameter and 82 feet in height (fig. 8), whose volume by careful measurement we have found to be 93.1 cubic feet, we determine its form arithmetically or its factor of shape by dividing the volume of the tree by the volume of a cylinder of the same dimensions, which is 216.5 cubic feet. The factor of shape is, therefore, $\frac{93.1}{216.5}=0.43$. That means that the volume of the tree is forty-three hundredths of the volume of a cylinder of the same diameter and height. Applying this method when factors of shape have been determined by a number of previous measurements, the diameter and height of the tree are measured, the volume of the corresponding cylinder found, and that volume multiplied by the factor of shape in order to obtain the cubic contents of the tree. This method gives more accurate results than those obtained from calculations of geometrical forms which the stems of the trees are supposed to represent. The factors of shape of a species may be determined from a number of accurate measurements of the volume of felled trees.

Below we give the factors of shape for white pine when situated in a moderately dense forest. They are based upon 722 individual trees, which, being felled, were measured and the results collated in the Division of Forestry, with a view of determining the rate of growth of the species:

Diameter at breast height.	Corresponding factors of shape.	Diameter at breast height.	Corresponding factors of shape.	Diameter at breast height.	Corresponding factors of shape.	Diameter at breast height.	Corresponding factors of shape.
Inches.		*Inches.*		*Inches.*		*Inches.*	
6	0.51	17	0.46	28	0.42	39	
7	0.50	18	0.45	29		40	
8	0.50	19	0.44	30		41	
9	0.49	20	0.44	31		42	0.40
10	0.49	21	0.43	32	0.41	43	
11	0.48	22	0.43	33		44	
12	0.48	23	0.42	34		45	
13	0.48	24	0.42	35		46	0.39
14	0.47	25	0.42	36			
15	0.47	26	0.42	37	0.40		
16	0.46	27	0.42	38			

It is seen that for a pine from 29 to 36 inches in diameter the factor of shape is 0.41. Suppose we are to determine the volume of a standing white pine of 31 inches in diameter, breast high, and 130 feet in height. The volume of a cylinder of 31 inches in diameter and 130 feet high is equal to 681.4 cubic feet. Multiplying 681.4 by the factor of shape (0.41) we determine the volume of the tree to be 279.4 cubic feet.

MEASUREMENT OF FELLED TREES.

HEIGHT AND DIAMETER MEASURING.

The height of a felled tree is measured either by a tape (a steel tape measure being most accurate) or by a measuring pole from 4 to 8 feet long. The diameter of a felled tree at any given place is measured by calipers described above. It is always advisable to note the average diameter of two measurements taken at a right angle.

MEASUREMENT OF VOLUME.

The volume of a felled tree may be determined with more accuracy than that of a standing tree, for the tree on the ground may be measured in parts and the volume of each part determined separately. While the tree, taken as a whole, does not closely resemble any of the known geometrical forms, the portions of the tree, especially when they are small, may be compared to some of the known forms with less hesitation. Of the various methods which may be employed in determining the volume of a felled tree, the following are recommended:

(1) *When great accuracy is required and the volume of the stump is included.*—Divide the tree into sections, each 4 feet in length, and caliper at right angles at each section, noting the average of the two diameters, including that of the butt. Find in the table the areas corresponding to the diameters noted and add all together. Multiply the sum of the areas by 4 feet and the product will be the total volume of the tree, if the last measurement with the calipers was taken at 2 cet from the top. If the last measurement with the calipers was taken

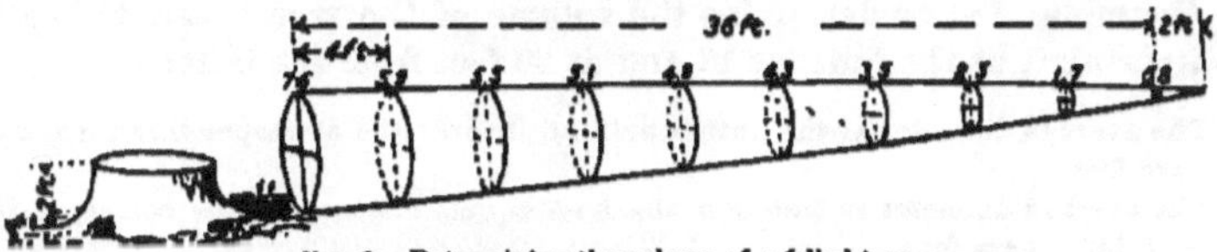

Fig. 9.—Determining the volume of a felled tree.

at a greater distance from the top, the volume of the top part must yet be added. The volume of the leader, or top, equals one-third the product of the basal area by its length. The base of the leau ,, is taken at 2 feet from the last point of measurement with the calipers. The diameter of the leader is measured and the corresponding basal area found in the area table. Example: Let the average diameter of the butt be 7.6 inches (fig. 9), and the average diameters calipered from butt for every 4 feet be, consecutively, 5.9, 5.5, 5.1, 4.9, 4.3, 3.5, 2.5, 1.7, and 0.8 inches. The last measurement with the calipers was taken at 2 feet from the top. In the area tables we find:

Location.	Diameters.	Areas.
	Inches.	*Sq. ft.*
Butt	7.6	0.315
4 feet from butt	5.9	.190
8 feet from butt	5.5	.165
12 feet from butt	5.1	.142
16 feet from butt	4.9	.131
20 feet from butt	4.3	.101
24 feet from butt	3.5	.067
		1.111
28 feet from butt	2.5	.034
32 feet from butt	1.7	.016
36 feet from butt	0.8	.003
		1.164

Multiplying the sum of the areas 1.161 by 4, we find the total volume of the tree to be 4.6 cubic feet. In case the last measurement with the calipers was 3.5 inches, i. e., it was taken at 14 feet from the top, then the volume of the leader must be added to the product of 1.111×4, which is 4.4. The base of the leader begins 2 feet above the last measurement with the calipers; the diameter measured here is 3 inches and the corresponding basal area equals 0.049 square feet; one-third the product of 0.049 by 12 (length of leader) is 0.02, which, added to 4.4, makes 4.6, the total volume of the tree, the same as obtained from previous calculations.

(2) *When less accuracy is required and the volume of the stump is excluded.*—The tree is calipered at the butt and in a few other places where it is most convenient; each log length, for instance. The volume of each portion between two measurements with the calipers equals one-half the product of its length multiplied by the sum of the areas corresponding to the diameters thus measured. The total volume of the tree is determined by summing up the volumes of all the parts thus separately calculated, including also the leader. The last measurement of the tree with the calipers is taken as the base of the leader, the volume of which is calculated in the same way as given above.

Example: Let us determine the volume of the tree taken above by calipering it at the butt, at 12 and at 20 feet from the butt:

The average diameter at the butt equals 7.6 inches; the corresponding area, 0.315 square foot.

The average diameter 12 feet from the butt equals 5.1 inches; the corresponding area, 0.142 square foot.

The average diameter 20 feet from the butt equals 4.3 inches; the corresponding area, 0.101 square foot.

The sum of the areas of butt and top of first length is 0.457; the length of first log is 12 feet; the volume then equals one-half of 12 multiplied by 0.457, or 2.74 cubic feet. The distance between the second and third measurements with the calipers is 20 feet minus 12 feet, equals 8 feet, and the volume of this portion of tree equals one-half of 8 multiplied by 0.243 equals 0.97 cubic feet. The volume of the leader equals one-third of 18 multiplied by 0.101 equals 0.61 cubic feet. The total volume of tree (stump excluded) is determined by taking the sum of 2.74, 0.97, and 0.61, which equals 4.3 cubic feet.

MEASUREMENT OF A STAND OF TREES OR GROWING STOCK OF A FOREST.*

On first thought it appears to be a very simple problem to measure the contents of a stand of trees or a forest, since a forest is an aggregate of single trees whose volume we already know how to determine. It appears as though we should need only to measure each tree and add the results. But this would be an expensive operation, and since absolute accuracy is neither necessary nor attainable, a method of averaging is employed in which the trees composing the forest are grouped into classes and only sample trees of each class are measured. The measurements are extended either over the whole forest or over only small typical areas, usually called "sample areas."

DETERMINATION OF THE GROWING STOCK BY EXTENDING THE MEASUREMENTS OVER THE WHOLE FOREST.

When the forest is not large its growing stock is usually determined by extending the measurements over the whole forest, i.e., the diameters, breast-high, of all the trees constituting the forest are measured with calipers. Of course the diameter measurements of different species are kept separate. If there exists an interdependence between the height and diameter growth, i. e., if the species grows at a uniform rate and trees of larger or smaller diameters are correspondingly taller or shorter in height, there is no necessity of measuring the heights; the average height is then determined by a sample tree, the selection of which will be discussed later. But if the height is not proportional to the diameter, i. e., if trees of the same species and equal diameters differ considerably in height, then classification by height becomes also necessary, and the scoring of trees is done not only by diameter but also by height classes. Differences in height development usually occur when the same species are found in the same forest under different soil conditions. A shallow compact clay soil for instance would produce relatively different proportions from a deep, loose, loamy sand.

* In this country it has so far been customary only to estimate the growing stock. The result necessarily is mostly far from the truth even with the most expert estimator, and as the estimator is usually employed by a purchaser, the estimate usually comes out from 10 to 30 per cent and more below the actual volume.

There are various ways in which estimators proceed. One of the most frequently used is to establish by either measurement or estimate for the district to be estimated, the average number of superficial feet per tree, then the trees are counted and their number multiplied by the figure obtained for the average tree, making allowance at the same time for breakage, defects, etc.

This method is especially in use where one species uniformly developed is to be estimated. More detailed estimates are made when several species of economic value are to be taken into account.

When the formation of height classes is not necessary, the following method of scoring may be recommended:

FORM No. 1.—*Diameter measurements.*

Diameter breast high in inches.	NAME OF THE SPECIES.									
	OAK	Total in each diameter class.	HARD MAPLE	Total in each diameter class.	HICKORY	Total in each diameter class.	ASH	Total in each diameter class.	BLACK WALNUT	Total in each diam. class.
8	[illegible]	23								
9	[illegible]	76								
10	[illegible]	87	[illegible]	25						
11	[illegible]	172	[illegible]	75						
12	[illegible]	43			[illegible]	53				
13	[illegible]	97								
14	[illegible]	115			[illegible]	18				
15	[illegible]	84								
16	[illegible]	164	[illegible]	31			[illegible]	56		
17	[illegible]	181					[illegible]	29		
18	[illegible]	46								
19	[illegible]	57	[illegible]	21						
20	[illegible]	88								
21	[illegible]	118							[illegible]	5
22	[illegible]	78							[illegible]	56
23	[illegible]	32								
24	[illegible]	84							[illegible]	11
25	[illegible]	85							[illegible]	12
	Total	1620	Total	213	Total	79	Total	85	Total	98

When the formation of height classes is necessary, the form No. 1 may be modified as follows:

FORM No. 2.—*Diameter measurements.*

Diameter breast high.	Oak. Height, Class I. Number of trees of each diameter.	Oak. Height, Class II. Number of trees of each diameter.	Hard maple. Height Class I. Number of trees of each diameter.	Hard maple. Height, Class II. Number of trees of each diameter.	Hickory. Height, Class I. Number of trees of each diameter.	Hickory. Height Class II. Number of trees of each diameter.	Ash. Number of trees of each diameter.	Black walnut. Number of trees of each diameter.
In.								
8								
9								
10								

Form No. 2 would be applicable should the oak, the hard maple, and the hickory of our hard-wood grove differ in height so as to necessitate the formation of two height classes for each of these species. Each height class then will have to be treated like a separate species. Of course only the species of economic value are measured. In the example represented by Form No. 1, five species were supposed to form the stand. In measuring, fractions of less than one-half of an inch are disregarded while those over half an inch are counted as full inches. Each tree calipered is scored in the appropriate species column on its proper diameter line by a mark, each fifth score crossing the four preceding, so that groups of five scores are made for more convenient addition. The measuring can be done more expeditiously if two or more persons divide the labor of scoring, calipering, and marking the calipered trees so as to avoid repetition in measuring; one scorer following two measurers who call out species and measured diameter, and mark the measured trees, or else one or two assistants blaze the trees to keep the work in line, preventing repetition as well as omission of trees.

When all the trees have been scored, the volume of each species may be determined either (1) by felling and measuring in detail a sample tree representing the average of all the trees of the species, or (2) by felling and measuring a number of sample trees, each representing the average of a diameter class, or (3) for the greatest accuracy, by felling and measuring a proportionate number of sample trees for each diameter, the proportion felled being a fixed percentage of the number of trees of each diameter.

DETERMINATION OF VOLUME BY MEANS OF AN AVERAGE SAMPLE TREE.

This method requires for each species (*a*) a calculation to determine the diameter of the average sample tree; (*b*) the selection of the sample tree in the forest and its measurement; and, finally (*c*) the calculation of the total volume of the species.

CALCULATION FOR AVERAGE SAMPLE TREE.

To find the diameter of the average sample tree it is first necessary to find the basal area of its cross section, breast-high. To do this, the basal areas of the cross sections, breast-high, of all the calipered trees must first be found. This is done by finding in the area table (p. 37) the areas corresponding to each diameter represented in the calipered trees, multiplying these figures by the number of trees of that diameter and adding the results.* The addition represents the total basal area of the cross sections of all the trees. If, now, we divide this by the total number of trees of the species, we get the basal area of the average sample tree, and from the area table obtain the diameter corresponding to that basal area.

Applying this method, for instance, to determine the diameter of the average sample tree for the oak, in our area table on page 37, we find that the basal area of—

	Square feet.
23 oaks of 8 inches in diameter equals	8.03
76 oaks of 9 inches in diameter equals	33.58
87 oaks of 10 inches in diameter equals	47.45
172 oaks of 11 inches in diameter equals	113.52
43 oaks of 12 inches in diameter equals	33.77
97 oaks of 13 inches in diameter equals	89.41
115 oaks of 14 inches in diameter equals	122.94
84 oaks of 15 inches in diameter equals	103.08
164 oaks of 16 inches in diameter equals	228.99
181 oaks of 17 inches in diameter equals	285.31
46 oaks of 18 inches in diameter equals	81.29
67 oaks of 19 inches in diameter equals	131.92
88 oaks of 20 inches in diameter equals	191.99
118 oaks of 21 inches in diameter equals	283.83
78 oaks of 22 inches in diameter equals	205.91
32 oaks of 23 inches in diameter equals	92.33
4 oaks of 24 inches in diameter equals	201.06
85 oaks of 25 inches in diameter equals	289.75
	2,534.16

The total basal area of the 1,020 oaks equals 2,534.10 square feet. Dividing this area by the number of trees we find that 1.56 square feet is the basal area of the average sample tree which corresponds to a diameter of 16.9 inches.

SELECTION AND MEASUREMENT OF SAMPLE TREES.

When the diameter of the sample tree has been determined, a thrifty tree of the species with such a diameter should be selected in the forest. Care should be taken that the sample tree is not situated in an opening nor on a road nor in a crowded growth; also that it have an average well-developed crown, and that it be sound, straight, and free from wind shakes. The sample tree so selected is felled, measured, and its

* The product may be obtained directly from the tables of volume, as explained.

volume determined in the way explained on page 16, where the measuring of a felled tree is discussed.

CALCULATION OF THE TOTAL VOLUME OF THE STAND.

The volume of the sample tree thus obtained represents in the average all the trees of the species. The total volume, then, of the species may be determined by multiplying the volume of the sample tree by the number of trees of the species contained in the forest. When a species is represented by a large number of trees it is always advisable to select more than one sample tree and determine separately for each its volume in cubic and superficial feet. There will be noticed a difference between the volumes of the sample trees notwithstanding their diameters and heights are the same; this is due to the difference in the tapering of the sample trees or, in other words, to the difference of the factor of shape, which though small is invariably noticed even among trees of the same dimensions. The average volume of the sample trees, whether in cubic or superficial feet, is then multiplied by the number of trees of the species in the forest, in order to obtain the total volume of the species. For the oak measured and recorded in the above example five sample trees of 16.9 inches in diameter at breast height and of the same height were selected in the grove. All of them were felled and sawed into logs. The following are their actual volumes given in cubic and superficial feet:

Sample tree.	Cubic feet.	B. M.
No. 1	46.2	180
No. 2	48.3	204
No. 3	44.8	156
No. 4	47.5	193
No. 5	42.1	148

These five sample trees give in the average 45.8 cubic feet and 176 feet B. M. Multiplying these two averages by 1,620 (number of oaks) the volume of the oak equals: (1) $45.8 \times 1,620 = 74,196$ cubic feet; (2) $176 \times 1,620 = 285,120$ B. M. The same operations and calculations are made for each species of the stand.

The following form (No. 3) shows how the measurements are finally collated for computing the growing stock of the grove:

FORM No. 3.—*Showing the computing of growing stock by means of average sample trees.*

Name of species. (Average height, 80 feet.)	Diameter at breast height.	Number of trees of each diameter.	Basal area of each diameter.	Sample tree.					Volume of growing stock.	
				Average dimensions.		Sample tree No.	Volume.			
				Basal area.	Corresponding diameter		Cubic feet.	B. M.	Cubic feet.	B. M.
1	2	3	4	5	6	7	8	9	10	11
	Inches.		*Sq. feet.*	*Sq. feet.*						
Oak	8	[illegible]	8.03							
	9	76	33.58			1	46.2	180		
	10	87	47.45							
	11	172	113.52							
	12	43	33.77			2	47.3	204		
	13	97	89.41							
	14	115	122.94							
	15	84	103.08			3	44.8	176		
	16	164	228.99							
	17	181	285.31							
	18	46	81.29			4	47.5	182		
	19	67	131.92							
	20	88	191.99							
	21	118	283.83			5	42.1	148		
	22	78	205.91							
	23	32	92.33							
	24	64	201.06							
	25	85	289.75	1.56	16.9					
Total		1,620	2,534.16						74,196	285,120
Average							45.8	176		
Hard maple	10	26	14.18							
	11	75	49.50							
	16	91	127.06							
	19	21	41.35	1.09	14.1	1	32.7	120		
Total		213	232.09						6,965	25,560
Hickory	12	63	49.48							
	14	16	17.10	0.84	12.4	1	25.5	90		
Total		79	66.58						2,014	7,110
Ash	16	56	78.19							
	17	29	45.71	1.46	16.4	1	43.8	168		
Total		85	123.90						3,723	14,280
Black walnut	21	5	12.03							
	22	68	179.51							
	24	11	34.56							
	25	12	40.91	2.78	22.6	1	93.4	336		
Total		96	267.01						8,966	32,256

Total contents, 94,904 cubic feet; 364,326 B. M.

Having recorded in columns 1 to 9 the measurements and calculations of all the trees and of the respective sample trees for each species, the volumes in columns 10 and 11 are found by multiplying the volume of the sample tree by the number of trees of each species, and to obtain the volume of the growing stock of the whole grove the last two columns are added up, which addition shows the grove to contain 94,904 cubic feet of wood, from which 364,326 feet B. M. might be obtained, the balance to be turned into slabs, sawdust, firewood, etc.

DETERMINING VOLUME BY SAMPLE TREES OF DIAMETER CLASSES.

More accurate results in ascertaining the growing stock of a forest may be obtained by arranging the trees of each species in diameter classes and then finding and measuring a sample tree of each class. The calculation to determine the basal area and, hence, the diameter of the sample tree of a diameter class, the selection of the sample tree in the forest and its measuring and the calculation of the volume of the diameter class are performed in the same way as described above. Each diameter class is to comprise trees differing not more than 4 inches in diameter at breast height. The oak of our hard-wood grove, then, would be divided into five diameter classes. The first diameter class would contain trees from 8 to 11 inches in diameter, inclusive; the second, trees from 12 to 15 inches, inclusive; the third, trees from 16 to 19 inches, inclusive; the fourth, trees from 20 to 23 inches, inclusive; and the fifth, trees from 24 to 25 inches, inclusive.

The first diameter class would then contain:

	No. of trees.	Basal area.
		Square feet.
8 inches in diameter	23	8.03
9 inches in diameter	76	33.58
10 inches in diameter	87	47.45
11 inches in diameter	172	113.52
Total	358	202.58

The basal area of this diameter class, 202.58 square feet divided by 358, the number of trees it contains, gives the basal area of its sample tree as 0.56 square foot, which corresponds to a diameter of 10.1 inches. Two sample trees of 10.1 inches selected accordingly in the forest among the oaks had in the average a volume of 16.8 cubic feet and scaled 60 feet B. M. Multiplying 16.8 and 60 each by 358 (number of trees in the class), we obtain 6,014.4 cubic feet and 21,480 feet B. M., which is the volume of the first diameter class in cubic and superficial feet respectively. The same process is repeated for the other diameter classes and species, selecting and measuring a smaller or larger number of sample trees as the diameter class contains a smaller or larger total number of trees. The final addition gives the volume of the stand. The accompanying table (Form No. 4) illustrates in detail the manner of recording and computing the growing stock of our hard-wood grove by arranging each species in diameter classes.

Form No 4.—*Showing the computing of growing stock by arranging the species in diameter classes.*

Name of species.	Diameter at breast height.	Number of trees of each diameter.	Basal area of each diameter.	Diameter classes. Class number.	Number of trees.	Basal area.	Sample tree. Average dimension. Basal area.	Corresponding diameter.	Average actual volume. Cubic feet.	B. M.	Number of sample trees of each size class.	Volume of each diameter class. Cubic feet.	B. M.
	In.		*Sq. ft.*			*Sq. ft.*	*Sq. ft.*	*Inches.*					
Oak	8	23	8.03	1	358	202.58	0.56	10.1	16.8	60	2	6,014.4	21,480
	9	76	33.58										
	10	87	47.45										
	11	172	113.52										
	12	43	33.77	2	339	349.20	1.03	13.7	30.9	120	2	10,475.1	40,680
	13	97	89.41										
	14	115	122.94										
	15	84	103.08										
	16	164	228.99	3	458	727.51	1.59	17.1	47.7	192	3	21,846.6	87,936
	17	181	285.31										
	18	46	81.29										
	19	67	131.92										
	20	88	191.99	4	316	747.06	2.36	20.8	70.8	336	2	22,372.8	106,176
	21	118	283.83										
	22	78	205.91										
	23	32	92.33										
	24	64	201.06	5	149	490.81	3.23	24.3	96.9	480	1	14,438.1	71,520
	25	85	289.75										
Hard maple	10	26	14.18	1	101	63.68	0.63	10.7	18.9	70	1	1,908.9	7,070
	11	75	49.50										
	16	91	127.06	2	112	168.41	1.50	16.6	45.0	180	1	5,040	20,160
	19	21	41.35										
Hickory	12	63	49.48	1	79	66.58	0.84	12.4	25.5	90	1	2,014	7,110
	14	16	17.10										
Ash	16	56	78.19	1	85	123.90	1.46	16.4	43.8	168	1	3,723	14,280
	17	29	45.71										
Black walnut	21	5	12.03	1	73	191.54	2.63	21.9	78.6	384	2	5,737.8	28,032
	22	68	179.51										
	24	11	34.56	2	23	75.47	3.28	24.5	98.4	480	1	2,263.2	11,040
	25	12	40.91										

Total contents, 95,834 cubic feet; 415,464 B. M.

The black walnut in the blank is divided into two diameter classes to maintain the uniformity of the diameter classification adopted for our hard-wood grove; otherwise all the trees of the black walnut could have been included in one diameter class.

DETERMINING VOLUME BY FELLING AND MEASURING A PROPORTIONAL NUMBER OF SAMPLE TREES FOR EACH DIAMETER.

Still greater accuracy of result can be obtained if instead of choosing at haphazard a number of sample trees of each diameter class, a definite proportion of the trees of each class or of each diameter is used for the computation. For instance, we may decide to measure 1 per cent of the trees of each diameter. All sizes of timber are then represented by sample trees in the proportion in which they occur in the forest; we have in the sample trees, then, an exact counterpart of the entire growth reduced in proportion. The relation between the volumes of the whole forest and the proportionately reduced forest of sample trees is exactly the same as that which exists between their corresponding basal areas; hence, dividing the basal area of the whole forest by the basal area of all the sample trees, and multiplying the quotient thus obtained by the volume of all the sample trees, the growing stock of the forest is determined. This method requires neither calculations to determine the dimensions of the sample trees nor the separate measuring of each to determine the volume. All the sample trees of the corresponding diameters are directly selected in the forest, felled and sawed into logs of desired length, which logs are piled together and the volume of the pile determined as a whole in cords or in cubic feet. Or else the number of superficial feet of all the sample trees can be accurately and directly obtained by sawing the logs into boards and other kinds of lumber.

The choice of the per cent or the proportion of trees to be taken as sample trees is influenced by the accuracy to be attained and the size of the area to be measured. If a tolerably satisfactory representation is to be had, not less than 10 to 15 trees, or at least 1 per cent, should be used.

Suppose that in order to determine the volume of the 1,620 oaks of our hard-wood grove, recorded in Form No. 1 (p. 19), it was decided to take 1 per cent, or in all 17 sample trees. If the fraction is less than one-half it is disregarded; if more than one-half it is considered as one. Then the number of sample trees for the oak would be determined as follows:

23 trees of 8 inches diameter require	$\frac{23}{100}$—no sample tree.
76 trees of 9 inches diameter require	$\frac{76}{100}$—one sample tree.
87 trees of 10 inches diameter require	$\frac{87}{100}$—one sample tree.
172 trees of 11 inches diameter require	$1\frac{72}{100}$—two sample trees.
43 trees of 12 inches diameter require	$\frac{43}{100}$—no sample tree.
97 trees of 13 inches diameter require	$\frac{97}{100}$—one sample tree.
115 trees of 14 inches diameter require	$1\frac{15}{100}$—one sample tree.
84 trees of 15 inches diameter require	$\frac{84}{100}$—one sample tree.
164 trees of 16 inches diameter require	$1\frac{64}{100}$—two sample trees.
181 trees of 17 inches diameter require	$1\frac{81}{100}$—two sample trees.
46 trees of 18 inches diameter require	$\frac{46}{100}$—no sample tree.
67 trees of 19 inches diameter require	$\frac{67}{100}$—one sample tree.
88 trees of 20 inches diameter require	$\frac{88}{100}$—one sample tree.
118 trees of 21 inches diameter require	$1\frac{18}{100}$—one sample tree.
78 trees of 22 inches diameter require	$\frac{78}{100}$—one sample tree.
32 trees of 23 inches diameter require	$\frac{32}{100}$—no sample tree.
64 trees of 24 inches diameter require	$\frac{64}{100}$—one sample tree.
85 trees of 25 inches diameter require	$\frac{85}{100}$—one sample tree.

The 17 sample trees of the corresponding diameters are then selected in the forest, felled, and sawed up into logs, which are piled together with the tops of all the sample trees. Let the pile be equal to 6½ cords, or 832 cubic feet. Let us suppose that the 6½ cords were sawed into lumber and furnished 3,360 feet B. M. From the measurements with the calipers, recorded in Form No. 1, we know the basal area of the oak to be equal to 2,534.16 square feet; the basal area of 17 sample trees we find in the area table to be equal to 27.22 square feet. Dividing 2,534.16 by 27.22 we obtain a quotient equal to 93.1. Multiplying 93.1 by 832, the volume of the sample trees in cubic feet, we determine the volume of the oak to be 77.459 cubic feet; or, multiplying the quotient, 93.1, by 3,360, the number of superficial feet furnished by the sample trees after they passed through the mill, we obtain 312,816 feet B. M., which is the total amount of merchantable lumber contained in the oak of our hard-wood grove.

The volume of the other species may be determined in the same manner, and then the growing stock of the grove is obtained by adding together the volume of the trees of all its species.

DETERMINATION OF THE GROWING STOCK BY MEANS OF SAMPLE AREAS.

It is always possible to find in a forest a small area the contents of which represent an average proportion of either the whole forest or of at least a considerable portion of it. The volume of this small area may be easily and rapidly determined by one of the methods above described. Such an area may be called a sample area, and the contents found on it per acre may be called an acre yield. If the small area represents an average condition of the whole forest, then, in order to obtain the growing stock of the whole forest, the acre yield of the sample area need only be multiplied by the number of acres in the forest; when the sample area represents only the conditions of a portion of the forest, then the acre yield multiplied by the number of acres involved in that portion gives only the growing stock of that portion, and for other portions of different conditions corresponding acre yields must be found.

Example: Let a forest containing 100 acres have three distinct forest conditions represented, each by 40, 35, or 25 acres, respectively. Let the 40 acres be represented by a sample area of one-half an acre; the 35 acres by a sample area of 1½ acres, and the 25 acres by a sample area of one-fourth an acre. Let the volumes of the sample areas determined by one of the methods given above be—

(1) The volume of the one-half acre equals 3,000 cubic feet and 12,000 B. M.
(2) The volume of the 1½ acre equals 12,000 cubic feet and 48,000 B. M.
(3) The volume of the one-fourth acre equals 2,500 cubic feet and 10,000 B. M.

The acre yields of the corresponding portion of the forest equal then—

(1) 3,000 cubic feet and 12,000 feet B. M. multiplied each by 2 equals 6,000 cubic feet and 24,000 feet B. M.

(2) 12,000 cubic feet and 48,000 feet B. M. divided each by 1½ equals 8,000 cubic feet and 32,000 feet B. M.

(3) 2,500 cubic feet and 10,000 feet B. M. multiplied each by 4 equals 10,000 cubic feet and 40,000 feet B. M.

The volume of an acre of the forest condition represented by the 40 acres equals 6,000 cubic feet and 24,000 feet B. M.; multiplied each by 40 equals 240,000 cubic feet and 960,000 feet B. M.

The volume of an acre of the forest condition represented by the 35 acres equals 8,000 cubic feet and 32,000 feet B. M.; multiplied each by 35 equals 280,000 cubic feet and 1,120,000 feet B. M.

The volume of an acre of the forest condition represented by 25 acres equals 10,000 cubic feet and 40,000 feet B. M.; multiplying each by 25 gives 250,000 cubic feet and 1,000,000 feet B. M. Adding together the volume of these three portions of the forest, we find the growing stock of the forest equals 770,000 cubic feet or 3,080,000 feet B. M.

In selecting the sample area care should be taken that—

(1) The species found in the forest be proportionally represented on the sample area.

(2) The density of crown cover of the sample area and the percentage of openings be the same as in the forest.

(3) All the sizes of timber and the corresponding number of trees of each size be found on the sample area in the same proportion as found among the trees in the whole forest or the portion to which the sample area refers. The selection of the sample area is a delicate operation and therefore requires considerable skill on the part of the estimator. The selected sample area should be staked off in the form of a square, which may contain from one-fourth to 2 acres.

HOW TO DETERMINE THE RATE OF GROWTH.

As the knowledge of the contents of a forest growth is necessary in order to determine its present valud for purposes of sale or purchase, so the knowledge of the rate at which its contents are changing, increasing or decreasing is of the highest importance in determining the profitableness of wood growth. The questions whether the annual or periodic increase is sufficient to pay interest on the investment, and whether it is proper to cut and utilize the wood crop or to allow it to grow and accumulate longer, are answered by measuring its rate of growth.

Just as the contents of a forest or acre or stand is ascertained by means of measuring one or more sample trees, the rate of growth of the stand, acre, or forest for any period may be ascertained from these sample trees. This calculation may concern itself either with the rate at which the height accretion takes place, or the diameter accretion, or the volume or mass accretion. It may also be made with reference to a longer or shorter period. If the period is taken as one year we may call it annual or yearly accretion; if for a number of years, for instance a decade, we may call it periodic accretion. Again, the annual accretion may be that of the one year for which we measure, the current annual accretion; or else it may be the average of a number of years, the average annual accretion, which is found by dividing the height, diameter, or volume by the number of years it has taken to grow. For instance, a tree 120 years old, containing 87 cubic feet, would show an average annual accretion of $\frac{120}{87}=0.72$ cubic feet, while its current annual accretion for the one hundred and twentieth year may be 1.4 cubic feet; and if we had ascertained the volume which it formed in the last ten years, as 15 cubic feet, this would be the periodic accretion for that decade.

The measurements by which the accretion, annual or periodic, is ascertained, rely upon the fact that, in all temperate zones at least, trees form annually one layer of wood, which appears on a cross section of a tree as a ring, more or less clearly defined, and on its longitudinal section made through the pith as a section of an enveloping cone (fig. 10). Hence by counting and measuring the rings appearing on cross sections taken at various heights from the ground, or by counting and measuring the enveloping cones appearing on the corresponding longitudinal sections made through the pith, not only the age, the progress in diameter, and area increase of the sections, but its height and volume development can be easily and accurately ascertained. Let us, for example, analyze the tree represented in fig. 10: A represents the longitudinal section of the tree made through its pith; B represents the tree in cross sections, made (1) at the surface of the ground; (2) at 13 feet; (3) at 25 feet; (4) at 37 feet, and (5) at 49 feet from the ground; the total height of the tree is 54 feet. Each ring of a cross section corresponds to an enveloping cone, and the number of concentric rings counted on a cross section, as seen from fig. 10, corresponds with the number of enveloping cones counted above each section.

Just as the width of the concentric rings on both sides of the center on a cross section determines the annual increase of the diameter, so the distance between the apexes of two enveloping cones determines the annual increase of the height. It is clear that the difference between the number of rings counted at the bottom and top sections of a log gives the number of years which it has taken to produce the length of the log. Or, if we take the lowest section of the tree, cut so that all the years of its growth are contained in the section (as in fig. 10), and deduct from the number of rings found on this section the number of rings found on any higher section, the difference then equals the number of years during which the tree had grown to attain the height of the higher section. Or, again, the number of rings counted on a cross section gives also the period of time during which the portion of the tree situated above has developed its height. Thus we find that during the period of forty-four years, the age of the tree, the trunk has reached 54 feet in height. The average annual growth in height is therefore equal to 54 feet divided by 44, equals 14.7 inches.

From the second cross section we find that the tree had grown 40 feet in the last thirty-one years (number of rings on that section), which means 15.8 inches annually during that period; or subtracting from the total age of the tree (44) the age of the second cross section (31) we find that the tree during the first thirteen years of its life has reached the height of the second section, i. e. 13 feet, which means that the tree

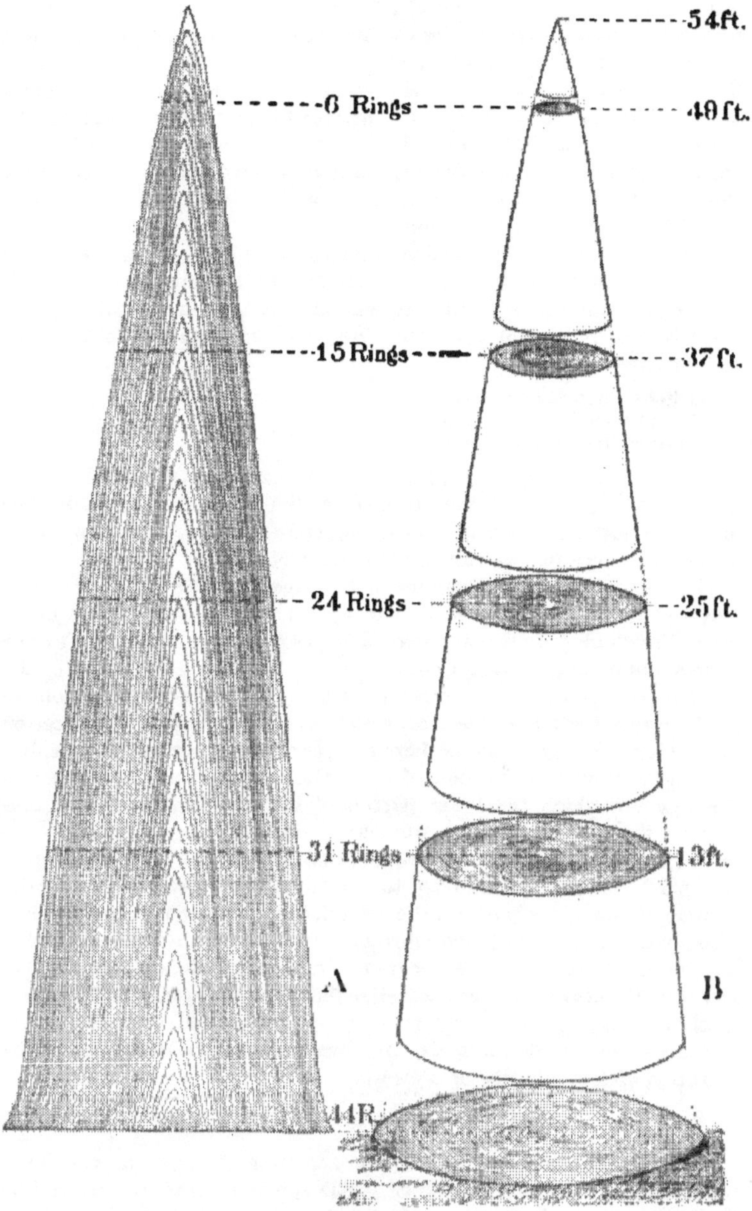

FIG. 10.—Showing the progressive development of a tree. A. Longitudinal section made through the pith and showing the sections of the enveloping cones. B. Cross-sections showing number of rings at various heights from the ground.

during this period grow annually 1 foot in height. By similar reasoning we find from the third cross section that the tree had grown 29 feet for the last twenty-four years, or 14.5 inches annually, and 25 feet for the first twenty years, or 15 inches annually; from the fourth cross section that the tree had grown 17 feet for the last fifteen years, or 13.6 inches annually, and 37 feet for the first twenty-nine years, or 15.2 inches annually; from the fifth cross section that the tree had grown 5 feet for the last six years, or 10 inches annually, and 49 feet for the first thirty-eight years, or 15.6 inches annually.

The rate at which the diameter and the area of any cross section of the tree increases can be easily ascertained by measuring the width of the rings on the various cross sections and finding in the table (p. 37) their corresponding areas. Thus we find, for instance, that on the second cross section—

The first 10 rings measure 3.9 inches.
The first 20 rings measure 6.2 inches.
The first 30 rings measure 7.9 inches.

The corresponding areas found in the table are, respectively, 0.8, 0.21, and 0.33 square feet. Subtracting either the diameters from each other or the corresponding areas, we can ascertain accurately the growth in diameter or area for the respective periods of time.

The rate at which the volume of the tree increases may be easily determined for any period of time by calculating the volume of as many enveloping cones as there are years in the period. Various methods may be employed to ascertain, for instance, the volume of the last period of years. The simplest one is: (1) To determine the volume of the upper portion of the tree, which has for its base a cross section containing as many rings as there are years in the period by considering that portion as a paraboloid; (2) determine the volume of each of the logs into which the lower portion of the tree is sawed, with and without the width of the last number of rings (number of years in the period), as explained on page 16, and deduct the sum of the last from the first volume; (3) adding to the difference thus obtained the volume of the upper portion, the growth for the desired period of time is ascertained. For the tree represented in fig. 10, the mass-accretion for the last 6, 15, 24, and 31 years could be conveniently ascertained, and thus the current annual accretion for those respective periods accurately calculated. Generally trees are not analyzed with such completeness, and simple methods have been devised for determining the accretion of a single tree or a forest.

DETERMINING THE ACCRETION OF A STANDING TREE.

In determining the average annual accretion the age and volume of the tree must be first ascertained. The age of a standing tree can be obtained only by observation, which is based on actual counting of the rings on stumps of felled trees of the same size, same species, and grown on the same site, or at least in the same locality and under the same conditions.

In determining the current accretion it is better to establish the increase of volume for the last five or ten years and assume that the current accretions were the same annually during that period; it is safer to make this assumption than to deal with a single year's increase, which is an unstable quantity changing with the season.

The current accretion of a standing tree may be conveniently expressed in per cent of volume of the tree. If the increase of actual volume is to be expressed, then it ought to be calculated with simple interest; but if the mass of a tree is looked upon as a capital, then it is proper to consider the accretions as returns on the capital represented by the amount of wood and to calculate it with compound interest in order to establish the expediency and profitableness of the investment.

MASS ACCRETION WITH SIMPLE INTEREST.

If the present volume of a standing tree is 115 cubic feet, and that of the same tree five years ago 109 cubic feet, then 115 − 109 = 6 gives the increase of volume for the last five years; the accretion for one year is $\frac{6}{5} = 1.2$ cubic feet. Dividing 1.2 by 109 and multiplying the quotient by 100 we find the current annual accretion equals 1 per cent expressed in per cent of volume. But while the present volume of the tree can be easily determined by employing one of the described methods, the volume which the standing tree had five years ago is difficult to establish. It is necessary, therefore, in order to determine the current accretion of standing trees to devise a method which should not require the determination of the present and past volumes of the tree. Suppose a standing tree, the accretion of which we are to determine, has a basal area at breast height, which we will designate for convenience sake by a letter A; let the basal area which the tree had five years ago be a, then the present and past volumes of the tree may be represented by the following products:

(1) Present volume: Base A multiplied by one-half of the height of the tree.

(2) Volume five years ago: Base a multiplied by one-half of the height which the tree had five years ago.

Suppose also that the tree is considered after it has reached its full height growth (a number of species reach it before 100 years of age), then the height accretion for five years is comparatively small. Disregarding this small difference, the proportion between the present and past volumes of the standing tree equals the proportion which exists between their basal areas A and a; in other words, the per cent of volume accretion is the same as that of the area accretion. The per cent of the area accretion may be easily determined when the diameter which the tree had five years ago is established. This can be ascertained by cutting out a chip or else by using an instrument—Pressler's increment borer,* by means of which a cylinder of wood can be extracted from the stem and the width of the rings measured. Taking twice the width of the last five rings and subtracting it from the present diameter (at breast height), the diameter the tree had five years ago is nearly enough determined.

Example: Let the present diameter of a standing tree be 22½ inches at breast height; let the width of the first five rings from the periphery, measured on the cylinder extracted by the Pressler borer, or on the chip of wood cut out, be two-eighths of an inch. Multiplying the two-eighths by 2 gives one half inch as the diameter increment for the last five years, and subtracting the half inch from 22½, we find that the diameter the tree had five years ago equals 22 inches. In the tables for areas (page 37) we find that the area corresponding to 22½ is 2.76 square feet; that corresponding to 22 inches, 2.64; the difference (2.76−2.64=0.12)

* Pressler's apparatus (fig. 11) consists of a hollow borer, slightly tapering from the handle toward the point, inserted into a handle; a flat-toothed wedge, which for convenience of measurement is graduated into centimeters; and a cradle, being of a small semicylindrical piece of tin, used to hold the chip when measuring in order to avoid its breaking; the handle also is hollow, so as to receive the borer, wedge, and cradle when the instrument is not in use. The borer is screwed in a radial direction into the tree, at right angles to its axis, to the desired depth, whereby a cylindrical column or chip of wood enters the hollow borer; then the wedge is inserted through the hollow borer between the chip and the inner wall of the borer, with its toothed side toward the wood and firmly pressed in. The borer is now screwed backward one or two turns, whereby the chip is severed at its base from the tree; a few more forward turns of the borer cause the chip to be pushed back until it can easily be withdrawn by the use of the wedge and placed into the cradle. In this way a chip of wood is obtained from 2 to 5 inches long, according to the length of the borer. The width of the concentric rings is then measured. If the rings are not distinct, a smooth surface may be prepared with a sharp knife.

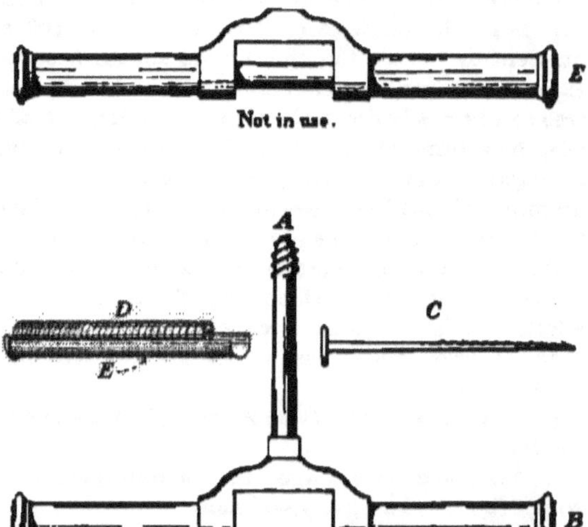

FIG. 11.—Pressler's accretion borer

divided by 5 gives 0.024 as the current area accretion for one year; dividing this one-year growth by 2.64 and multiplying the result by 100, we find that 6 is the per cent of area, and thus of volume accretion of that particular tree of 22½ inches in diameter at breast height. The per cent of volume accretion, as has been seen, may be expressed by a fraction, the numerator of which is the volume increase for one year, and the denominator is the volume of the tree previous to that year.

The difference between the successive current accretions, though increasing with age, are small in proportion to the increase of the respective volumes, which are always enlarged by one year's growth. In other words, the fraction or the per cent of accretion it represents decreases steadily with age.

Pressler gives a simple formula ($\frac{100}{A}$) which expresses the per cent of accretion of the tree when it has reached its maximum stage of growth. "A" is the age of the tree when it reaches the stage of maximum growth, i. e., when the current accretion becomes equal to the average annual accretion. If the per cent of accretion of the tree obtained from calculations is larger than $\frac{100}{A}$, it shows that the average annual accretion still increases; when it is less than $\frac{100}{A}$, the average annual accretion is on the decrease.

MASS ACCRETION WITH COMPOUND INTEREST.

In determining the mass accretion with compound interest the general formula of compound interest could be applied. To avoid calculations by logarithms Pressler gives a formula of his own, and a table of figures based on it, the practical application of which is very simple: Measure the diameter of the standing tree at breast height; extract by Pressler's borer a cylinder of wood and measure off the width of the last *n* years (*n* designates the number of years in the period for which the calculation is to be made, generally five or ten years); then divide the diameter by double the width of the last *n* rings, and the so called relative diameter is established. Finding then the relative diameter, thus obtained, in the column of the relative diameters (Pressler's table, p. 40), the corresponding number, given in the same line with the relative diameter, should be divided by *n*, and the quotient will be the per cent of accretion with compound interest.

Example: Let us take the same tree for which the per cent of accretion was determined with simple interest; its present diameter at breast height is 22½ inches; the width for the last five years is two-eighths of an inch. Dividing 22½ by double the width of the last 5 rings, we find the relative diameter equals 45: (22½÷½=45). In Pressler's table we find that 6.7 corresponds to the relative diameter of 45 when the tree is of a very thrifty growth. Dividing 6.7 by 5 we find the current annual growth equals 1.3 per cent with compound interest.

In Pressler's table on page 40, for each relative diameter two figures are given—one for an average thrifty growing tree, the other for a very thrifty growing tree. The general appearance and the crown development of the tree will indicate which one of the figures should be taken for calculations.

DETERMINING THE ACCRETION OF A FELLED TREE.

The average annual accretion of a felled tree may be determined with greater accuracy, because the volume and the age of the tree can be obtained with more exactness. The age of the tree is established by counting the rings on the stump section and adding to the number counted five or six years, which were required by the tree to reach the height of the stump.

The current accretion for any given number of years of a felled tree may be determined as follows:

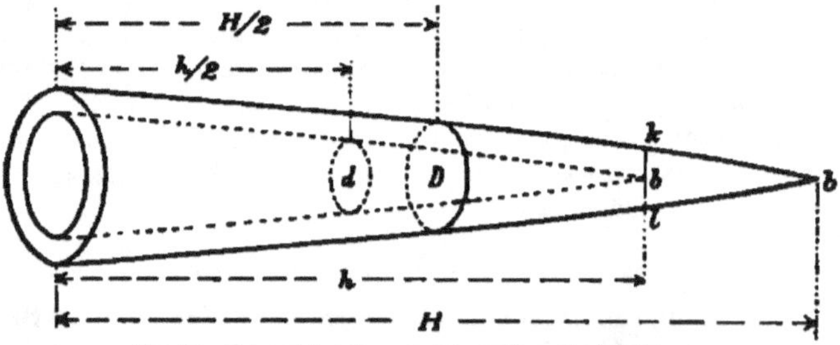

FIG. 12.—Determining the current accretion of a felled tree.

Find the volume of the felled tree by multiplying its height (H) by the basal area which corresponds to the diameter measured at the middle of the tree (D), bark excluded; then, by some trial, find a place near the top (see fig. 12) where the section (*kl*) contains as many rings as there are years in the period (*n*) for which the accretion is to be determined. Then from the middle of the topless portion (*d*) of the tree extract, with Pressler's accretion borer, a cylinder of wood; measure off on that cylinder the width of the last *n* rings and subtract twice that width from the outside diameter measured here without bark. The difference gives the diameter the tree had *n* years ago. Multiplying the basal area corresponding to that diameter by the length (*h*) of the topless portion of the tree the volume of the tree as it was *n* years ago is ascertained. The difference between the present and past volumes gives the periodic accretion for the last *n* years.

Pressler simplifies this method by measuring at the middle of the topless stem $\left(\frac{h}{2}\right)$ both the present diameter and that of the tree as it was *n* years ago and calculates the respective volumes by employing the length of the topless stem. The excess in volume which results for the present tree due to the fact that the diameter which should have been taken halfway of the full length tree $\left(\text{at } \frac{H}{2}\right)$ was measured too low, is counterbalanced by neglecting the volume of the top for the n years.

DETERMINING THE ACCRETION OF A FOREST.

There are several methods employed in determining the mass accretion of a stand of trees for a short period (from ten to twenty years), during which it may be safely assumed that the number of trees of the stand will not diminish owing to natural thinning (death). Of these the following may be recommended:

When the growing stock of a forest has been ascertained by means of an average sample tree, then the accretion of that tree for a given number of years should be multiplied by the number of trees the forest contains, in order to determine the rate of growth of the forest for that period of time. In case the growing stock of the forest was established by arranging its trees in diameter classes, the accretion of each diameter class is determined separately by multiplying the accretion of the sample tree by the number of trees involved in the class. Adding together the accretion of all the diameter classes we obtain a sum which represents the rate of growth of the forest for the period of time in question.

When the growing stock of a forest is determined by means of a proportional number of sample trees representing each diameter, the accretions of the sample trees, calculated for each of them separately, are added together and the sum is multiplied by the quotient obtained by dividing the basal area of the forest by that of all the sample trees. The product gives the rate of growth of the forest during the period for which the accretion of the sample trees was determined.

Table of areas of circles for diameters of 1 inch to 60 inches.

Diameter.	Area of circle.	Diameter.	Area of circle.	Diameter.	Area of circle.	Diameter.	Area of circle.	Diameter.	Area of circle.	Diameter.	Area of circle.
In.	*Sq. ft.*	*In.*	*Sq. ft.*	*In.*	*Sq. ft.*	*In.*	*Sq. ft.*	*In.*	*Sq. ft.*	*In.*	*Sq. ft.*
1.0	0.0055	3.0	0.0491	5.0	0.1364	7.0	0.2673	9.0	0.4418	11.0	0.6600
.1	.0067	.1	.0524	.1	.1418	.1	.2750	.1	.4517	.1	.6721
.2	.0079	.2	.0559	.2	.1474	.2	.2828	.2	.4617	.2	.6842
.3	.0092	.3	.0594	.3	.1532	.3	.2907	.3	.4718	.3	.6965
.4	.0107	.4	.0631	.4	.1590	.4	.2987	.4	.4820	.4	.7089
.5	.0123	.5	.0669	.5	.1650	.5	.3068	.5	.4923	.5	.7214
.6	.0140	.6	.0707	.6	.1710	.6	.3151	.6	.5027	.6	.7340
.7	.0158	.7	.0747	.7	.1772	.7	.3234	.7	.5132	.7	.7467
.8	.0177	.8	.0788	.8	.1835	.8	.3319	.8	.5238	.8	.7595
.9	.0197	.9	.0830	.9	.1899	.9	.3404	.9	.5345	.9	.7724
2.0	.0218	4.0	.0873	6.0	.1963	8.0	.3491	10.0	.5454	12.0	.7854
.1	.0240	.1	.0917	.1	.2029	.1	.3579	.1	.5564	.1	.7986
.2	.0264	.2	.0963	.2	.2096	.2	.3668	.2	.5675	.2	.8118
.3	.0289	.3	.1009	.3	.2164	.3	.3758	.3	.5787	.3	.8252
.4	.0314	.4	.1056	.4	.2234	.4	.3849	.4	.5900	.4	.8387
.5	.0341	.5	.1105	.5	.2304	.5	.3941	.5	.6014	.5	.8523
.6	.0369	.6	.1154	.6	.2376	.6	.4034	.6	.6129	.6	.8660
.7	.0398	.7	.1205	.7	.2448	.7	.4129	.7	.6245	.7	.8798
.8	.0428	.8	.1257	.8	.2522	.8	.4224	.8	.6362	.8	.8937
.9	.0459	.9	.1310	.9	.2597	.9	.4321	.9	.6481	.9	.9077
13.0	0.9218	16.4	1.4670	19.8	2.1382	23.2	2.9356	26.6	3.8591	30	4.9087
.1	.9360	.5	1.4849	.9	2.1599	.3	2.9610	.7	3.8882	31	5.2414
.2	.9504	.6	1.5030	20.0	2.1817	.4	2.9864	.8	3.9174	32	5.5851
.3	.9648	.7	1.5212	.1	2.2036	.5	3.0120	.9	3.9467	33	5.9396
.4	.9794	.8	1.5394	.2	2.2256	.6	3.0377	27.0	3.9761	34	6.3050
.5	.9941	.9	1.5578	.3	2.2477	.7	3.0635	.1	4.0056	35	6.6813
.6	1.0089	17.0	1.5763	.4	2.2699	.8	3.0894	.2	4.0353	36	7.0686
.7	1.0237	.1	1.5949	.5	2.2922	.9	3.1154	.3	4.0650	37	7.4667
.8	1.0387	.2	1.6136	.6	2.3146	24.0	3.1416	.4	4.0948	38	7.8758
.9	1.0538	.3	1.6324	.7	2.3371	.1	3.1679	.5	4.1248	39	8.2958
14.0	1.0690	.4	1.6513	.8	2.3597	.2	3.1942	.6	4.1548	40	8.7266
.1	1.0843	.5	1.6703	.9	2.3825	.3	3.2207	.7	4.1850	41	9.1684
.2	1.0997	.6	1.6894	21.0	2.4053	.4	3.2471	.8	4.2152	42	9.6211
.3	1.1153	.7	1.7087	.1	2.4283	.5	3.2738	.9	4.2456	43	10.0847
.4	1.1309	.8	1.7280	.2	2.4514	.6	3.3006	28.0	4.2761	44	10.5592
.5	1.1467	.9	1.7475	.3	2.4745	.7	3.3275	.1	4.3067	45	11.0447
.6	1.1626	18.0	1.7671	.4	2.4978	.8	3.3545	.2	4.3374	46	11.5410
.7	1.1785	.1	1.7868	.5	2.5212	.9	3.3816	.3	4.3681	47	12.0482
.8	1.1946	.2	1.8066	.6	2.5447	25.0	3.4088	.4	4.3991	48	12.5664
.9	1.2108	.3	1.8265	.7	2.5684	.1	3.4361	.5	4.4301	49	13.0954
15.0	1.2272	.4	1.8465	.8	2.5921	.2	3.4636	.6	4.4612	50	13.6354
.1	1.2437	.5	1.8666	.9	2.6159	.3	3.4911	.7	4.4925	51	14.1863
.2	1.2602	.6	1.8869	22.0	2.6398	.4	3.5188	.8	4.5238	52	14.7480
.3	1.2768	.7	1.9072	.1	2.6638	.5	3.5465	.9	4.5553	53	15.3207
.4	1.2936	.8	1.9277	.2	2.6880	.6	3.5744	29.0	4.5869	54	15.9043
.5	1.3104	.9	1.9482	.3	2.7122	.7	3.6024	.1	4.6186	55	16.4988
.6	1.3274	19.0	1.9689	.4	2.7366	.8	3.6305	.2	4.6504	56	17.1042
.7	1.3444	.1	1.9897	.5	2.7611	.9	3.6587	.3	4.6823	57	17.7206
.8	1.3616	.2	2.0206	.6	2.7857	26.0	3.6870	.4	4.7143	58	18.3478
.9	1.3789	.3	2.0316	.7	2.8104	.1	3.7154	.5	4.7464	59	18.9859
16.0	1.3963	.4	2.0527	.8	2.8352	.2	3.7439	.6	4.7787	60	19.6350
.1	1.4138	.5	2.0739	.9	2.8602	.3	3.7725	.7	4.8110		
.2	1.4314	.6	2.0952	23.0	2.8852	.4	3.8013	.8	4.8435		
.3	1.4492	.7	2.1167	.1	2.9103	.5	3.8301	.9	4.8760		

Table of the volumes of cylinders and the sum

Length of cylinder or number of circles.	Diameter in inches.							
	1.	2.	3.	4.	5.	6.	7.	8.
1	0.0055	0.0218	0.0491	0.0873	0.1364	0.1963	0.2673	0.3491
2	.0110	.0436	.0982	.1746	.2728	.3926	.5346	.6982
3	.0165	.0654	.1473	.2619	.4092	.5889	.8019	1.0473
4	.0220	.0872	.1964	.3492	.5456	.7852	1.0692	1.3964
5	.0275	.1090	.2455	.4365	.6820	.9815	1.3365	1.7455
6	.0330	.1308	.2946	.5238	.8184	1.1778	1.6038	2.0946
7	.0385	.1526	.3437	.6111	.9548	1.3741	1.8711	2.4437
8	.0440	.1744	.3928	.6984	1.0912	1.5704	2.1384	2.7928
9	.0495	.1962	.4419	.7857	1.2276	1.7667	2.4057	3.1419
	17.	18.	19.	20.	21.	22.	23.	24.
1	1.5763	1.7671	1.9689	2.1817	2.4053	2.6398	2.8852	3.1416
2	3.1526	3.5342	3.9378	4.3634	4.8106	5.2796	5.7704	6.2832
3	4.7289	5.3013	5.9067	6.5451	7.2159	7.9194	8.6556	9.4248
4	6.3052	7.0684	7.8756	8.7268	9.6212	10.5592	11.5408	12.5664
5	7.8815	8.8355	9.8445	10.9085	12.0265	13.1990	14.4260	15.7080
6	9.4578	10.6026	11.8134	13.0902	14.4318	15.8388	17.3112	18.8496
7	11.0341	12.3697	13.7823	15.2719	16.8371	18.4786	20.1964	21.9912
8	12.6104	14.1368	15.7512	17.4536	19.2424	21.1184	23.0816	25.1328
9	14.1867	15.9039	17.7201	19.6353	21.6477	23.7582	25.9668	28.2744
	33.	34.	35.	36.	37	38.	39.	40.
1	5.9396	6.3050	6.6813	7.0686	7.4667	7.8758	8.2958	8.7266
2	11.8792	12.6100	13.3626	14.1372	14.9334	15.7516	16.5916	17.4532
3	17.8188	18.9150	20.0439	21.2058	22.4001	23.6274	24.8874	26.1798
4	23.7584	25.2200	26.7252	28.2744	29.8668	31.5032	33.1832	34.9064
5	29.6980	31.5250	33.4065	35.3430	37.3335	39.3790	41.4790	43.6330
6	35.6376	37.8300	40.0878	42.4116	44.8002	47.2548	49.7748	52.3596
7	41.5772	44.1350	46.7691	49.4802	52.2669	55.1306	58.0706	61.0862
8	47.5168	50.4400	53.4504	56.5488	59.7336	63.0064	66.3664	69.8128
9	53.4564	56.7450	60.1317	63.6174	67.2003	70.8822	74.6622	78.5394

of circles, for diameters of 1 inch to 48 inches.

Diameter in inches.								Length of cylinder or number of circles.
9.	10.	11.	12.	13.	14.	15.	16.	
0.4418	0.5454	0.6600	0.7854	0.9218	1.0690	1.2272	1.3963	1
.8836	1.0908	1.3200	1.5708	1.8436	2.1380	2.4544	2.7926	2
1.3254	1.6362	1.9800	2.3562	2.7654	3.2070	3.6816	4.1889	3
1.7672	2.1816	2.6400	3.1416	3.6872	4.2760	4.9088	5.5852	4
2.2090	2.7270	3.3000	3.9270	4.6090	5.3450	6.1360	6.9815	5
2.6508	3.2724	3.9600	4.7124	5.5308	6.4140	7.3632	8.3778	6
3.0926	3.8178	4.6200	5.4978	6.4526	7.4830	8.5904	9.7741	7
3.5344	4.3632	5.2800	6.2832	7.3744	8.5520	9.8176	11.1704	8
3.9762	4.9086	5.9400	7.0686	8.2962	9.6210	11.0448	12.5667	9
25.	26.	27.	28.	29.	30.	31.	32.	
3.4088	3.6870	3.9761	4.2761	4.5869	4.9087	5.2414	5.5851	1
6.8176	7.3740	7.9522	8.5522	9.1738	9.8174	10.4828	11.1702	2
10.2264	11.0610	11.9283	12.8283	13.7607	14.7261	15.7242	16.7553	3
13.6352	14.7480	15.9044	17.1044	18.3476	19.6348	20.9656	22.3404	4
17.0440	18.4350	19.8805	21.3805	22.9345	24.5435	26.2070	27.9255	5
20.4528	22.1220	23.8566	25.6566	27.5214	29.4522	31.4484	33.5106	6
23.8616	25.8090	27.8327	29.9327	32.1083	34.3609	36.6898	39.0957	7
27.2704	29.4960	31.8088	34.2088	36.6952	39.2696	41.9312	44.6808	8
30.6792	33.1830	35.7849	38.4849	41.2821	44.1783	47.1726	50.2659	9
41.	42.	43.	44.	45.	46.	47.	48.	
9.1684	9.6211	10.0847	10.5592	11.0447	11.5410	12.0482	12.5664	1
18.3368	19.2422	20.1694	21.1184	22.0894	23.0820	24.0964	25.1328	2
27.5052	28.8633	30.2541	31.6776	33.1341	34.6230	36.1446	37.6992	3
36.6736	38.4844	40.3388	42.2368	44.1788	46.1640	48.1928	50.2656	4
45.8420	48.1055	50.4235	52.7960	55.2235	57.7050	60.2410	62.8320	5
55.0104	57.7266	60.5082	63.3552	66.2682	69.2460	72.2892	75.3984	6
64.1788	67.3477	70.5929	73.9144	77.3129	80.7870	84.3374	87.9648	7
73.3472	76.9688	80.6776	84.4736	88.3576	92.3280	96.3856	100.5312	8
82.5156	86.5899	90.7623	95.0328	99.4023	103.8690	108.4338	113.0976	9

Pressler's table.

Relative diameter.	Average thrifty tree.	Very thrifty tree.	Relative diameter.	Average thrifty tree.	Very thrifty tree.	Relative diameter.	Average thrifty tree.	Very thrifty tree.	Relative diameter.	Average thrifty tree.	Very thrifty tree.
2.0	144	156	6.8	42	47	13.2	21.0	24.0	33.0	8.2	9.2
2.1	138	150	6.9	41	46	13.4	21.0	23.0	33.5	8.1	9.1
2.2	133	144	7.0	40	45	13.6	20.0	22.0	34.0	7.9	8.9
2.3	127	139	7.1	40	45	13.8	20.0	22.0	34.5	7.8	8.8
2.4	123	134	7.2	39	44	14.0	20.0	22.0	35.0	7.7	8.6
2.5	117	129	7.3	39	44	14.2	19.0	22.0	35.5	7.6	8.5
2.6	113	124	7.4	38	43	14.4	19.0	22.0	36.0	7.5	8.4
2.7	109	120	7.5	38	42	14.6	19.0	21.0	37.0	7.3	8.2
2.8	105	116	7.6	37	42	14.8	19.0	21.0	38.0	7.1	8.0
2.9	101	112	7.7	37	41	15.0	18.0	21.0	39.0	6.9	7.8
3.0	98	109	7.8	36	41	15.2	18.0	20.0	40.0	6.8	7.6
3.1	95	105	7.9	36	40	15.4	18.0	20.0	41.0	6.6	7.4
3.2	92	102	8.0	35	40	15.6	18.0	20.0	42.0	6.4	7.2
3.3	89	99	8.1	35	39	15.8	17.0	20.0	43.0	6.3	7.1
3.4	86	96	8.2	34	39	16.0	17.0	19.0	44.0	6.1	6.9
3.5	84	93	8.3	34	38	16.5	17.0	19.0	45.0	6.0	6.7
3.6	81	91	8.4	34	38	17.0	16.0	18.0	46.0	5.9	6.6
3.7	79	88	8.5	33	37	17.5	16.0	18.0	47.0	5.8	6.5
3.8	77	86	8.6	33	37	18.0	15.0	17.0	48.0	5.6	6.3
3.9	75	84	8.7	32	36	18.5	15.0	17.0	50.0	5.4	6.1
4.0	73	81	8.8	32	36	19.0	14.0	16.0	52.0	5.2	5.9
4.1	71	79	8.9	32	35	19.5	14.0	16.0	54.0	5.1	5.7
4.2	69	77	9.0	31	35	20.0	14.0	15.0	56.0	4.9	5.5
4.3	68	76	9.1	31	35	20.5	13.0	15.0	58.0	4.7	5.3
4.4	66	74	9.2	31	34	21.0	13.0	15.0	60.0	4.5	5.1
4.5	65	72	9.3	30	34	21.5	13.0	14.0	62.0	4.4	4.9
4.6	63	70	9.4	30	34	22.0	13.0	14.0	64.0	4.2	4.7
4.7	62	69	9.5	29	33	22.5	12.0	14.0	66.0	4.1	4.6
4.8	60	67	9.6	29	33	23.0	12.0	13.0	68.0	3.9	4.4
4.9	59	66	9.7	29	32	23.5	12.0	13.0	70.0	3.8	4.3
5.0	58	65	9.8	29	32	24.0	11.0	13.0	72.0	3.7	4.2
5.1	56	63	9.9	28	32	24.5	11.0	12.0	74.0	3.6	4.1
5.2	55	62	10.0	28	31	25.0	11.0	12.0	76.0	3.6	4.0
5.3	54	61	10.2	27	31	25.5	11.0	12.0	78.0	3.5	3.9
5.4	53	60	10.4	27	30	26.0	10.0	12.0	80.0	3.4	3.8
5.5	52	59	10.6	26	30	26.5	10.0	12.0	85.0	3.2	3.6
5.6	51	57	10.8	26	29	27.0	10.0	11.0	90.0	3.0	3.4
5.7	50	56	11.0	25	28	27.5	9.9	11.0	100.0	2.7	3.0
5.8	49	55	11.2	25	28	28.0	9.7	11.0	110.0	2.4	2.7
5.9	49	54	11.4	24	27	28.5	9.5	11.0	120.0	2.2	2.5
6.0	48	53	11.6	24	27	29.0	9.3	11.0	130.0	2.1	2.3
6.1	47	53	11.8	23	26	29.5	9.2	10.5	140.0	1.9	2.2
6.2	46	52	12.0	23	26	30.0	9.0	10.0	150.0	1.8	2.0
6.3	45	51	12.2	23	26	30.5	8.9	10.0	170.0	1.6	1.8
6.4	45	50	12.4	22	25	31.0	8.7	9.8	200.0	1.3	1.5
6.5	44	49	12.6	22	25	31.5	8.6	9.7	250.0	1.1	1.2
6.6	43	48	12.8	22	24	32.0	8.5	9.5	300.0	0.9	1.0
6.7	42	48	13.0	21	24	32.5	8.4	9.4			

A METHOD OF INVESTIGATING TIMBER GROWTH.

When a forest is to be bought, sold, or assessed, or when its timber is to be cut, the questions which are to be solved relate either to its growing stock alone—if the forest is to be disposed of immediately—or to the progress of its growth during the period for which its standing timber is intended to be kept. The mastering of the methods discussed on the preceding pages enables one to solve these questions with ample accuracy. With additional knowledge relating to local prices on cleared land, market condition of lumber and timber, cost of labor, transportation, etc., the present value of the forest, or that which it may have at the expiration of a short period, is easily ascertained. The determination of the growing stock in such cases terminates the inquiries. But when a forest is intended for rational management, with the expectation of making it yield continual returns, the knowledge of its growing stock serves only as a guiding point from which the way toward obtaining other information of equal importance becomes clearer. The success of conducting the other inquiries relating to the forest, with a view to working out an adequate plan for its management, depends upon knowledge of the sylvicultural possibilities of the species comprising it. The question, for instance, of how far the actual annual growth of the forest differs from the annual growth possible for the locality, under the given conditions and species or the age at which the cutting should be made in order to insure that possible annual growth, can be properly answered when the requirements of the species composing the forest and the rate at which those species grow at various ages and under various situations is known. In Europe the sylvicultural requirements of forest trees have been ascertained in an experimental, or rather historical, way. The forest districts into which the state forests were divided at the beginning of the epoch of forest regulation kept records registering the results attained by their forest trees under the various situations and treatment. These records, together with the casual and experimental observations organized later on by the European foresters, have accumulated a good deal of valuable and sound data, the systematic teaching of which has attained the rank of a science known under the name of sylviculture. It has taken Europe almost two centuries to work out its sylviculture. It would take the United States, with ten times as many species of economic value as are found in Europe, considerably more time to work out its sylviculture should it ignore the progress made in forestry science, and in spite of it follow the slow historical method of investigating timber growth.

It has been shown in the preceding pages that the progressive development of a single tree may be determined in an analytical way. The European foresters apply that analytical method for the examination of the average sample trees. The analysis of a few individual trees is sufficient to enable the forester, with the general knowledge he possesses of the rate of growth of the particular species, to determine the factor of the locality, i. e., to determine in what way the locality affects the general law of growth of the species. But when the sylvicultural requirements of a species are totally unknown, an analysis of a few individual trees is scarcely sufficient even to indicate the rate of growth of the species. To be sure, by analyzing a large number of trees taken on various sites and under various situations the rate of growth of the species could be determined, but if each of the number of individual trees were to be analyzed separately, as is done usually by European foresters, the work would be too cumbersome. It was thought necessary, therefore, in the work for the Division of Forestry of ascertaining the rate of growth of our species, to modify the European analytical method so as to make it more applicable for the thorough investigation of timber growth.

According to the analytical method as employed by the European foresters, each of the trees measured for analytical purposes is analyzed separately, and for each individual tree a table of growth is prepared. Then all the tables of growth are classified according to forest conditions, ages, and degrees of dominance. Thereupon the tables assigned to a group are averaged, and a table representing the rate of growth of the group is thus obtained. Suppose, for instance, that 50 trees of a given species were measured on a site under the same forest conditions and then analyzed. Suppose further that the corresponding 50 tables of growth, each of course representing the progressive development of a single tree, have been divided into two distinct groups, according to the accepted classification, one group containing 29 and the other 21. Finding the average of the 29 tables and that of the 21 tables, the 50 analyzed trees would have been finally represented by 2 tables, each representing the rate of growth of the corresponding group.

These operations can be simplified by starting with the classification of the trees when their measurements are taken in the forest, then proceeding with the averaging of those measurements for each group separately, and finally analyzing only the average tree of each group.

The classification of trees can be performed in a more efficient and accurate way in the forest than in the office. The measurements for each group of trees can be taken separately and so arranged as to permit the entering of sets of corresponding measurements of a homogeneous nature on separate sheets, thus facilitating their averaging. For instance, all the measurements of cross sections taken at uniform heights from ground would be entered on one sheet for all the trees of the same group. By averaging, then, these homogeneous sets of measurements, figures would be obtained representing the measurements of an average tree of the group. The analysis of that average tree would determine the progressive development of the group. Thus by reversing the process of analysis the rate of growth of the 50 trees taken in our example could be determined by the analysis of only 2 trees, each being an average for one of the two corresponding groups.

While the work in the field and the averaging either of the tables of growth or the sets of homogeneous measurements will consume the same amount of time, the time required for the analysis itself of the 50 trees would differ in the two cases in the proportion of 2 to 50, i. e., the modified method would have required only one twenty-fifth of the time that would have been consumed by the analytical method as practiced by European foresters. The saving of time will be more appreciated when it is known that the complete analysis of a single tree of seven to nine cross sections, including the preparation of the table of growth, takes a day's work. Determination of the rate of growth of the 50 trees would consume 50 working days, while under the present arrangement 2 days are sufficient to arrive at the same results.

The detailed discussion of the method, accompanied by an actual example, will enable the reader to understand its working more clearly.

FIELD WORK.

Under the modified method here presented the field work constitutes the most delicate part of the tree analysis. The reliability of the tables of growth calculated in the office for various groups of trees and the deductions made from them depend not only upon the accuracy with which the measurements of individual trees are taken, but also upon the knowledge and skill employed in classifying the trees and describing the conditions under which they grow.

The field work begins with a general description of the station. Blank No. 1, given in the appendix, may be recommended for that purpose. The geographical climate of a station is determined by its latitude. Special attention must be given to ascertaining the physical or local climate, for it has a direct effect upon the rate of growth and quality of timber. The local climate depends upon the general configuration, elevation, general trend of the valleys or mountains, nature of soil, and proximity of sea. All these local features must be carefully noted. If the locality is provided with a meteorological station the record of that station for average monthly temperature, for average monthly precipitation, and monthly means of relative humidity should be procured for the greatest possible length of time.

In most cases such climatic data can not be obtained, and that is why it is advisable to carefully examine every local feature that may exert an influence upon the temperature and humidity of the atmosphere.

FOREST CONDITIONS OF STATION.

In describing the forest conditions of the station typical forms should be indicated, and, if possible, each typical form represented by one or more sample areas. Such sample areas, besides having a statistical value, furnish valuable information on which to outline the general forest conditions surrounding the species under investigation.

It is exceedingly desirable to procure trees for analysis from each typical form of forest conditions of the station, especially so when the typical forms differ considerably from each other in soil and drainage conditions or in the composition and density of the forest. The climate being thus eliminated, it becomes more easy to determine the effect of each of the various factors upon the rate of growth of the species.

In many instances the timber investigator has little choice in selecting conditions for measuring trees, because the detailed measurement necessary for analytical purposes requires the felling of the trees and their being sawed up into logs, which operation is regulated by the lumber camps. The operators of lumber camps usually confine themselves for each winter to limited forest areas, which seldom offer a wide range of forest and other conditions. A station may comprise several camps, each of which, of course, may represent distinct forest conditions. But in most cases the timber investigator will have to connect his work with the operations of the lumber camp, and direct his attention at least to such spots of the lumber area where the species is found in primeval forest conditions and not affected by natural dangers. The spots selected must be carefully and minutely described, accompanying the description by a sample area staked off exactly in the place where the trees will be afterwards felled and measured for analysis. Blank No. 2 in the appendix may be conveniently used both for description and measuring purposes of the sample area, which should be, if possible, an acre in extent. The method of taking the acre-yield measurements has been discussed in one of the preceding chapters. As regards the description of the sample area, the example given in the blank shows exactly how it should be done.

ASPECT.

In a mountainous country the aspect or exposure must be noticed, for it exerts an influence on the climate and hence upon the growth of trees. The northern aspect has diffused light, comparatively little heat, and the soil, due to low temperature, remains moist, thus favoring rapid growth. The eastern aspect is the most favorable for forest vegetation, because the sun shines obliquely and during the coolest hours of the day; the temperature and the light are moderate, permitting the soil to retain its moisture, which again favors active growth.

The southern exposure has the sun almost all day, causing intense light, heat, and high temperature, which dries the soil rapidly and, consequently, retards tree growth. On the western exposure the sun shines during the hottest hours; again the high temperature makes it difficult to retain the moisture of the soil. Of course, the nature of the prevailing winds will modify the influence exercised by the exposure upon tree growth, and it is desirable, therefore, to note the directions of the wind, its velocity, and the amount of moisture and heat with which it is charged. It should be also mentioned that on northern and eastern exposures, especially on the northern, vegetation is retarded and the trees usually escape spring frost, but are apt to suffer from early autumn frost, owing to the incomplete lignification of their shoots. On southern and western exposures vegetation begins early and young forests often fall the victim of spring frosts.

SOIL AND DRAINAGE CONDITIONS.

In describing the soil it must be borne in mind that the fertility of a soil for sylvicultural purposes is determined by its physical properties rather than by its chemical composition. Forest vegetation requires little inorganic matter. The amount of inorganic matter barely exceeds one-half of that required by agricultural products, and then a great portion of it is returned to the soil by the fall and decomposition of the leaves and branches. The mineral constituents absolutely necessary for the growth and development of trees are: Potash, calcium, iron, magnesia, phosphorus, and sulphur. Most soils contain these mineral substances in a sufficient quantity to meet the requirements of forest vegetation. The important thing to know about the soils devoted to sylviculture is the relative quantities of the principal components of the soil, i. e., of sand, clay, limestone, and organic matter which the soil contains; for the proportion in which these are mixed determines the texture of the soil, hence its physical properties. A chemical analysis of the soil can not supply this information, nor does the nature of the rocks give a clue, for the same rocks do not always form similar soils, and the products of decomposition do not always remain together; besides the soil formed from a rock varies in its properties with the stages of disintegration. The principal components of the soil can best be determined by mechanical analysis, which is recommended whenever possible. But for purposes at hand the timber investigator can attain good results by examining the soil in the field in the following manner: Take a certain quantity of soil, say a pound, and dry it thoroughly at approximately the temperature of boiling water. The difference in weight before and after it was dried gives the amount of moisture. Crumble the dry soil into powder, take a certain quantity of it and mix it with water while stirring; let the mixture stand for a while and decant carefully the turbid liquid. Repeat this process several times until the last water to be poured off becomes altogether clear. What is left at the bottom of the vessel constitutes sand; dry and weigh it. The turbid liquid contains clay, limestone, and organic matter. Add gradually to the turbid liquid hydrochloric acid until it turns litmus paper red; filter it well and dry the residue, which contains clay and organic matter. Ignite the residue in order to burn the organic matter; the difference in weight before and after it was ignited gives the amount of organic matter, the rest constitutes clay. Adding together the weight thus obtained for sand, clay, and organic matter and subtracting the sum from the original weight of the part of the dry soil taken for analysis, the amount of limestone is roughly determined. According to the proportion in which the principal components are mixed, soils are classified as sand, loam, clay, and lime.

Sandy soils contain 75 per cent or more sand; the remainder is clay. When clay constitutes from 15 to 25 per cent, the soil is called loamy sand; when the clay is found to be 10 per cent or less, the soil is considered as a sand. Loamy soils contain from 60 to 70 per cent of sand, about 5 per cent of lime, 5 per cent of iron oxides, while the rest is made up of clay. When the clay constitutes 40 per cent, the soil is considered as loam; when the clay constitutes 30 per cent, it is considered as a sandy loam.

Clayey soils are those which contain 50 per cent of clay and more. When clay and loam are mixed half-and-half, the soil is called clayey loam: but when clay constitutes more than 60 per cent, the soil is considered as a clay.

Limy soils are those which contain over 10 per cent of carbonate of lime. According to the proportion of lime found in the soils, they are subdivided into:

Marl soils, containing from 10 to 20 per cent of carbonate of lime.
Loamy lime, containing about 30 per cent of carbonate of lime.
Clayey lime, containing about 40 per cent of carbonate of lime.
Lime, containing about 50 per cent of carbonate of lime.

These are the principal classes of soil; besides, there may be distinguished two other classes of soil, namely, humus and ferruginous soil. Humus soil contains 20 per cent and more of vegetable mold. Ferruginous soil contains from 10 to 25 per cent of iron oxide. It can be easily recognized by its brown red color.

The above classification, which is commonly used in European forestry practice, is useful because at once suggestive of the physical properties of the soil.

PHYSICAL PROPERTIES OF SOIL.

The physical properties of a soil of importance to sylviculture are those which determine its moisture conditions. Upon the amount of moisture in the soil depends the chemical activity of the soil, its temperature, and the supply of water for the growth of the plant. With regard to moisture, soils are classified by European foresters as follows:

Wet, where water flows from the clod without pressure being applied.

Moist, where water drops from the clod on pressure being applied.

Fresh, where traces of moisture are felt by pressing a handful of soil.

Dry, where traces of moisture are not felt, but when rubbed the soil does not resolve into dust.

Arid, where on rubbing the soil crumbles into dust.

The chief physical properties of soil are:

(1) *Hygroscopicity.*—Hygroscopicity of soil, or the capacity with which it absorbs and retains water, depends upon the fineness of the soil particles and is, therefore, in direct proportion to the compactness of the soil. The power of absorbing rain water is the greatest in lime, then comes clay, loam, and sand. The aqueous vapors of the atmosphere are best absorbed by clay, next by lime, loam, and sand.

(2) *Tenacity.*—Tenacity, or the degree of cohesiveness between the particles of the soil, depends upon the size of the particles. Clay and sand represent in this respect two extremes. The first one, consisting of very fine grain, represents the most tenacious, while the latter, consisting of granular and coarser grain, represents the least tenacious soil. With regard to tenacity the soils may be classified as heavy, mild, light, loose, and shifting. To the class of heavy, stiff, or tenacious soils belong clays, clayey loams, limes, and marls. Heavy soils are characterized by the deep cracks they form when suddenly dried. To the class of mild soils belong loams, sandy loams, and loamy limes. Mild soils crack when suddenly dried, but are able to retain

the form of clods. Loamy sand and sandy marl are considered as light soils, which are characterized by being capable of forming clods when moist. Sand is considered as a loose soil, which is incapable of forming clods even when moist. To the class of shifting soils belong the sand drifts and dunes. Tenacious soils are unfavorable for tree growth, because, firstly, they offer considerable resistance to the penetration of roots and their ramification throughout the soil; secondly, the circulation of air and moisture in such soils is greatly impeded. Consequently, tenacious soils are either excessively moist or excessively dry. They absorb water slowly, but in large quantities. The power of soils to retain moisture is in direct proportion to their tenacity. So the power of retaining moisture is the greatest in clay; next comes lime, loam, and, finally, sand.

(3) *Permeability.*—Permeability, or the capacity of the soil to diffuse its moisture, is proportional to the size of the soil particles. It is the greatest in sand, next in loam, lime, and least in clay.

(4) *Warmth.*—The warmth of soil, or facility with which it absorbs heat, depends, aside from the atmospheric temperature, upon its color and the quantity of moisture it contains. Clayey soils do not easily raise or lower their temperature with the corresponding increase or decrease of the atmospheric temperature—they are cold soils. Sandy soils are very active and respond to even slight changes in the atmospheric temperature—they are warm soils.

(5) *Depth.*—The upper layer, which is penetrated by the roots, is spoken of as the soil; from it the trees draw the mineral nutriments. What is below the soil is considered as the subsoil, which may be of the same nature with the soil or may differ from it.

Depth of soil in sylviculture is rather a relative conception. Soils which are shallow for one kind of trees may be considered deep when applied to other kinds of trees. It depends altogether on the nature and development of the root systems of the species. Each species, then, could have its own classification of soils as regards their depth; but for practical purposes a general and uniform classification may be adopted. The classification adopted by the experiment stations in Germany, given below, may be recommended: Very shallow, up to 6 inches; shallow, from 6 inches to 1 foot; medium, from 1 foot to 2 feet; deep, from 2 feet to 4 feet; very deep, over 4 feet.

Deep soils are very favorable, even for species with shallow root systems, for they can retain the moisture longer, while the moisture conditions of shallow soils depends upon the nature of the subsoil. Usually shallow soils suffer either from excess of moisture or from drought.

Vegetable mold tends to modify extreme differences of the soils. It makes stiff soils less tenacious and binds loose soils; it warms cold and cools warmer soils; it increases the depth of soil; it is capable of holding large masses of waters, which it gives gradually to the lower layer;

it condenses aqueous vapors, carbonic-acid gas, and ammonia from the atmosphere, which, together with the carbonic acid-gas it develops, assists the decomposition of the mineral substances in the soil.

SUBSOIL.

The subsoil, if different in nature from the soil, should be described in the same manner as the soil.

SOIL COVER.

Under soil cover is meant the weedy or herbaceous forest plants that grow in the soil. It should be noted, because frequently such weeds indicate the quality of the soil.

FOREST CONDITIONS OF SAMPLE AREA.

In describing the forest conditions of the sample area it is advisable to be as concise as possible. The blanks left for the composition of forest should be filled out after the measurements of the acre yield have been taken, because then the proportion in which the species found in the forest area mixed may be accurately determined. Very small trees, such as those under 3 inches in diameter (breast high) and under 20 feet high, should be counted separately and be considered as undergrowth. All shrub forms should also be mentioned as a part of the undergrowth.

The description of the sample area is usually concluded with general remarks relating to the appearance of the stand of trees, development of crowns, quality of timber, average ages of the species composing the stand, and such other items as may for any reason be found necessary.

DENSITY OF FOREST.

The density of a forest is usually judged by its canopy or degree of contact of the crowns of the trees. When the crowns are in touch with each other, forming a close canopy, the density is considered normal and the forest fully stocked. This condition is designated by a unit. The degrees of opening of the crown cover are expressed in decimals, thus permitting the making of 10 degrees of density. The density factor is simply a short expression of the light conditions of the forest, and the 10 degrees are established not with the expectation of getting the exact mark of density, but to enable the forester to indicate it with more facility. It is not worth while to puzzle the brains over the solution as to whether the density is 0.5 or 0.6, especially when it is remembered that the method of designating the density is in itself imperfect and mostly based upon the general impression of the forester.

ACRE-YIELD MEASUREMENT.

In measuring the trees on the sample area special attention should be given to the classification of trees resulting from various stages of development which they have attained, the basis of such classification being height and crown development. For the purposes at hand it is sufficient to consider only three classes, namely, dominant, codominant, and oppressed. Dominant trees are those which overtop their neighbors and possess fully developed crowns. Codominant trees are those which, although being of the same height as the dominant trees, possess poorly developed crowns, usually compressed on all sides by neighboring trees. Oppressed trees are those whose crowns are still less developed than those of the codominant trees; they are not only compressed, but also somewhat overtopped by the neighboring trees. It is advisable to adopt a conventional system of marking the trees of each class of dominance by blazing the bark of trees below the height of the stump, when the class of dominance assigned to a tree while standing may be either verified or rejected afterwards when the tree is felled and measured in detail.

DEDUCED RESULTS.

The sample area leaves a general impression upon the mind of the timber investigator. This impression should be utilized by converting it into figures of forest economic value, which can be easily remembered. It is exceedingly desirable that the timber investigator should deduce all the results relating to the acre-yield in the manner shown in Blank No. 2 immediately after the sample area is described and measured. Thereafter, when, while the details are fresh in mind, the timber investigator meets with similar forest conditions, he is in a position to estimate the standing timber at a glance, using previous experiences as a basis of judgment.

THE MEASURING OF FELLED TREES FOR ANALYSIS.

When the trees on the sample area are felled and sawed into logs the timber investigator should begin the detailed measurements. The sawyers are followed, and as each tree is sawed into logs the measurements are made before the logs are removed from the place where the tree fell.

The tree is calipered first at breast height, and then at intervals of 8 feet from the ground, until a point on the trunk is reached where the diameter measures 5 inches or less. In keeping a record of the measurements, the entry for each tree includes its serial number; height of tree; height to base of crown; character of growth, i. e., whether dominant, codominant, or oppressed; condition of timber, i. e., whether sound, defective, crooked, wind shaken, clear, or knotty; amount of merchantable timber (determined by scaling the logs of the tree right on the spot where it is felled); the position of the tree and surrounding species, and other remarks. Blank No. 3 of the appendix gives the measurements of the trees felled on sample area described in Blank No. 2. When the calipering is completed and recorded, the measurements of growth at the stump and at the top of each log is made by counting and measuring the rings on the average radius of each cross section, as indicated in Blank No. 4 of the appendix. The most systematic results are secured if all the trees are cut into logs of equal length, say 16 feet. Each blank of set No. 4 is intended for recording the measurements of cross sections from all the trees at approximately the same height from the ground separately for each group; thus one of Blank No. 4 records the results of stump measurements for the trees of each of the three groups (dominant, codominant, and oppressed), while the other records the results of cross section at the top of first log (18 feet from ground), the third, that taken at the top of the second log (34 feet from ground), etc. In the appendix are given two blanks of set No. 4; one records the stump section, the other the cross section taken at the top of the third log (50 feet from the ground). The groups of trees in this particular instance had nine cross sections, which were recorded in nine blanks of set No. 4. The measuring of the cross sections should begin with the stump section, because the number of rings counted on this section determines the age of the tree (of course, the allowance made for the height of the stump must be added), which must be known for establishing age classes before the measurements of sections are registered. Trees either of the same age or differing not more than twenty years for old trees and ten years for younger trees, usually constitute one age class. The rings of a section are carefully counted on the average radius, and the distances for 10, 20, 30, 40, etc., rings from the center to the periphery are noted in millimeters. The entire radius is also noted. Besides, for each cross section should be noted—

(1) Number of tree to which it belongs.
(2) Exact height from ground.
(3) Thickness of bark.
(4) Number and width of rings in the sapwood.
(5) Number of rings on the cross sections.

OFFICE WORK.

TABULATION OF MEASURED TREES.

The office work begins with a concise description of the forest conditions of the trees measured for analysis, accompanied by a tabulation for each group of such measurements and calculations, as are illustrated in the following form:

FORM No. 5.

(Site: *f*. Age-class: 240-260 years. Species: White pine.)

Location.	Description of site.	Tree number.	Age.	Diameter (breast-high).	Total height.	Height to base of crown.	Rings per inch on stump.	Volume. Tree.	Volume. Merchantable timber.	Factor of shape.	Ratio of length of crown to total height of tree.	Lumber product under present practice, per cent of total volume of stem.	Remarks.
								Cu. ft.	*B. M.*				
Du Bois, Clearfield County, Pa. Latitude, 41° 8'. Longitude, 78° 45'. Altitude, 1,200 to 1,400 feet.	Hemlock, mixed with white pine, with scattering maple, beech, and birch, on a hill sloping toward southwest, where it is bordered by the left-hand branch of Narrow Creek. The moderately dense undergrowth consists of very young beech, hemlock, and occasional birch and cucumber.	1	260	35½	158	90	7.6	435.4	[illegible]	0.40	0.43	58	Dominant.
		2	260	36	157	90	7.6	481.3	[illegible]	.43	.42	59	
		3	259	33	152	81	7.8	[illegible]	[illegible]	.40	.44	55	
		4	241	32	150	62	6.9	347.7	2,023	.41	.50	60	
		10	244	31	146	90	6.5	305.8	2,081	.42	.34	54	
		12	262	28	150	88	6.0	260.8	1,846	.43	.43	47	
		18	265	39	154	88	6.0	511.1	3,218	.40	.42	56	
		19	250	34	150	78	6.3	392.6	2,307	.42	.48	49	
		20	266	44	144	100	5.7	638.4	4,398	.42	.30	57	
		21	245	34	140	92	7.8	366.7	2,248	.40	.37	51	
		23	248	34	142	90	7.2	370.4	2,318	.42	.37	54	
		33	259	33	133	91	8.0	304.8	1,779	.40	.31	48	
		34	262	33	146	90	7.4	360.2	2,299	.42	.38	56	
		35	263	31	144	82	8.5	275.2	1,858	.30	.43	46	
		36	241	31½	134	88	7.1	307.7	1,853	.42	.31	50	
		37	261	37	146	106	6.7	442.0	2,370	.41	.27	53	
	Average		255	34	147	88	7.0	391.0	2,507	.41	.39	52	
	Soil: Yellow clay loam of a medium grain (fine shales in it), deep, fresh, well drained, with 2 to 3 inch mold on top and with a surface cover of scanty leaves, fern, teaberries, and scattering dogwood (laurel in northeast corner and on north side). Subsoil: Laminated shale of an indefinite depth.	28	261	28½	138	75	9.8	[illegible]	1,551	[illegible]	[illegible]	40	Codominant.
		25	244	26½	158	107	7.2	[illegible]	1,954	[illegible]	[illegible]	54	
		24	245	25	130	81	[illegible]	[illegible]	1,102	[illegible]	[illegible]	48	
		22	240	31	130	82	[illegible]	310.8	1,731	[illegible]	[illegible]	49	
		5	264	29	140	100	8.4	[illegible]	1,905	[illegible]	[illegible]	52	
		6	264	29	140	110	8.5	[illegible]	1,631	[illegible]	[illegible]	47	
		7	262	29	152	112	9.1	[illegible]	1,854	[illegible]	[illegible]	52	
		8	235	29	142	80	....	[illegible]	1,318	[illegible]	[illegible]	44	
		9	230	32	142	81	[illegible]	[illegible]	1,648	[illegible]	.43	46	
		11	244	30	141	81	7.5	[illegible]	1,947	[illegible]	.42	50	
		13	258	23	147	103	9.0	[illegible]	1,018	[illegible]	[illegible]	42	
		14	242	25	130	98		[illegible]	[illegible]	[illegible]	[illegible]	47	
		15	262	26	136	98		[illegible]	1,289	.51	[illegible]	45	
		16	235	24½	124	103		[illegible]	815	[illegible]	[illegible]	[illegible]	
		17	262	25	128	108	....	[illegible]	[illegible]	[illegible]	[illegible]	40	
		26	245	26	136	98	9.3	[illegible]	1,021	[illegible]	[illegible]	47	
		30	259	26½	114	90	9.2	[illegible]	1,336	[illegible]	[illegible]	[illegible]	
		29	264	28	141	81	9.2	[illegible]	1,577	[illegible]	[illegible]	47	
		31	262	25½	112	88	10.0	[illegible]	863	[illegible]	[illegible]	37	
		32	261	26	112	90	9.1	[illegible]	1,322	[illegible]	[illegible]	[illegible]	
	Average		252	27	[illegible]	95	9.0	250.0	1,421	.44	[illegible]	47	
		27	259	19	[illegible]	[illegible]	11.4	138.8	681	[illegible]	[illegible]	41	Suppressed.
		38	260	21	[illegible]	[illegible]	11.1	189.6	987	[illegible]	[illegible]	[illegible]	
		39	258	20½	[illegible]	108	13.0	130.9	558	[illegible]	[illegible]	[illegible]	
		40	261	16½	[illegible]	[illegible]	13.7	80.6	350	[illegible]	[illegible]	[illegible]	
	Average		259	20	[illegible]	95	12.5	137.2	[illegible]	[illegible]	.35	37	

ANALYSIS.

The cross sections of each group are averaged in order to obtain the measurements of the cross sections of the average tree of the group, which is then constructed and analyzed in the manner discussed under caption "Rate of growth" in preceding pages.

As an example, the analysis of the dominant group is given below. It begins with averaging the widths for the groups of rings from center to periphery for each of the cross sections from which the area and accretion are calculated.

Cross section of the stump of the average tree of the group.

SITE *f*.—Dominant group of 16 trees.

CROSS SECTION: Stump.

Height from ground, 2 feet.
Width of bark, 43 millimeters.
Number of rings in sap, 35.
Width of sap, 32 millimeters.
Total number of rings, 249.

Number of rings (center to periphery).	Radius.	Diameter.		Area.	Accretion for decades	
					Area.	Diameter.
	Mm.	*Mm.*	*Inches.*	*Sq. ft.*	*Sq. ft.*	*Inches.*
10	29	58	2.3	0.03	0.03	2.3
20	64	128	5.1	.14	.11	2.8
30	93	186	7.4	.30	.16	2.3
40	119	238	9.5	.49	.19	2.1
50	143	286	11.4	.71	.22	1.9
60	166	332	13.3	.96	.25	1.9
70	193	386	15.4	1.29	.33	2.1
80	215	430	17.2	1.61	.32	1.8
90	231	462	18.5	1.87	.26	1.3
100	246	492	19.7	2.12	.25	1.2
110	269	538	21.5	2.52	.40	1.8
120	287	574	23.0	2.88	.36	1.5
130	304	608	24.3	3.22	.34	1.3
140	320	640	25.6	3.57	.35	1.3
150	334	668	26.7	3.89	.32	1.1
160	345	690	27.6	4.15	.26	.9
170	357	714	28.6	4.46	.31	1.0
180	369	738	29.5	4.75	.29	.9
190	379	758	30.3	5.01	.26	.8
200	390	780	31.2	5.31	.30	.9
210	401	802	32.1	5.62	.31	.9
220	411	822	32.9	5.90	.28	.8
230	422	844	33.8	6.23	.33	.9
240	432	864	34.6	6.52	.29	.8
249	437	874	35.0	....	....	....

Cross section at 18 feet from the ground of the average tree of the group.

SITE *f*.—Dominant group of 16 trees.

CROSS SECTION: No. 1.

Height from ground, 18 feet.
Width of bark, 22 millimeters.
Number of rings in sap, 11.
Width of sap, 32 millimeters.
Number of rings, 238.

Number of rings (center to periphery).	Radius.	Diameter.		Area.	Accretion for decades.	
					Area.	Diameter.
	Mm.	*Mm.*	*Inches.*	*Sq. ft.*	*Sq. ft.*	*Inches.*
10	43	86	3.4	0.06	0.06	3.4
20	79	158	6.3	.22	.16	2.9
30	104	208	8.3	.37	.15	2.0
40	124	248	9.9	.53	.16	1.6
50	144	288	11.5	.72	.19	1.6
60	159	318	12.7	.88	.16	1.2
70	174	348	13.9	1.05	.17	1.2
80	186	372	14.9	1.21	.16	1.0
90	199	398	15.9	1.38	.17	1.0
100	214	428	17.1	1.59	.21	1.2
110	227	454	18.2	1.81	.22	1.1
120	240	480	19.2	2.01	.20	1.0
130	252	504	20.2	2.22	.21	1.0
140	262	524	21.0	2.40	.18	.8
150	270	540	21.6	2.54	.14	.6
160	279	558	22.3	2.71	.17	.7
170	288	576	23.0	2.88	.17	.7
180	296	592	23.7	3.06	.18	.7
190	304	608	24.3	3.22	.16	.6
200	312	624	25.0	3.41	.19	.7
210	320	640	25.6	3.57	.16	.6
220	328	656	26.2	3.74	.17	.6
230	335	670	26.8	3.92	.18	.6
238	341	682	27.3	....	....	....

Cross section at 34 feet from the ground of the average tree of the group.

SITE *f*.—Dominant group of 16 trees.

CROSS SECTION: No. 2.

Height from ground, 34 feet.
Width of bark, 18 millimeters.
Number of rings in sap, 48.
Width of sap, 32 millimeters.
Number of rings, 228.

Number of rings (center to periphery).	Radius.	Diameter.		Area.	Accretion for decades.	
					Area.	Diameter.
	Mm.	*Mm.*	*Inches.*	*Sq. ft.*	*Sq. ft.*	*Inches.*
10	39	78	3.1	0.05	0.05	3.1
20	81	162	6.5	.23	.18	3.4
30	106	212	8.5	.39	.16	2.0
40	128	256	10.2	.57	.18	1.7
50	145	290	11.6	.73	.16	1.4
60	160	320	12.6	.89	.16	1.2
70	172	344	13.6	1.04	.15	1.0
80	186	372	14.9	1.21	.17	1.1
90	199	398	15.9	1.38	.17	1.0
100	213	426	17.0	1.58	.20	1.1
110	225	450	18.0	1.77	.19	1.0
120	235	470	18.8	1.93	.16	.8
130	245	490	19.6	2.09	.16	.8
140	253	506	20.2	2.22	.13	.6
150	262	524	21.0	2.40	.18	.8
160	270	540	21.6	2.54	.14	.6
170	277	554	22.2	2.69	.15	.6
180	285	570	22.8	2.83	.14	.6
190	293	586	23.4	2.99	.16	.6
200	301	602	24.1	3.17	.18	.7
210	310	620	24.8	3.35	.18	.7
220	320	640	25.6	3.57	.22	.8
228	325	650	26.0	....	....	....

Cross section at 50 feet from the ground of the average tree of the group.

SITE *f*.—Dominant group of 16 trees.

CROSS SECTION: No. 3.

Height from ground, 50 feet.
Width of bark, 15 millimeters.
Number of rings in sap, 46.
Width of sap, 33 millimeters.
Number of rings, 216.

Number of rings (center to periphery).	Radius.	Diameter.		Area.	Accretion for decades.	
					Area.	Diameter.
	Mm.	*Mm.*	*Inches.*	*Sq. ft.*	*Sq. ft.*	*Inches.*
10	40	80	3.2	0.05	0.05	3.2
20	76	152	6.1	.20	.15	2.9
30	102	204	8.2	.37	.17	2.1
40	122	244	9.8	.52	.15	1.6
50	138	276	11.0	.66	.14	1.2
60	151	302	12.1	.80	.14	1.1
70	165	330	13.2	.95	.15	1.1
80	180	360	14.4	1.13	.18	1.2
90	193	386	15.4	1.29	.16	1.0
100	204	408	16.3	1.45	.16	.9
110	214	428	17.1	1.59	.14	.8
120	223	446	17.8	1.73	.14	.7
130	233	466	18.6	1.89	.16	.8
140	241	482	19.3	2.03	.14	.7
150	250	500	20.0	2.18	.15	.7
160	257	514	20.6	2.34	.16	.6
170	265	530	21.2	2.45	.11	.6
180	273	546	21.8	2.59	.14	.6
190	281	562	22.5	2.76	.17	.7
200	289	578	23.1	2.91	.15	.6
210	294	588	23.5	....	....	....

Cross section at 66 feet from the ground of the average tree of the group

SITE *f*.—Dominant group of 16 trees.

CROSS SECTION: No. 4.

Height from ground, 66 feet.
Width of bark, 15 millimeters.
Number of rings in sap, 46.
Width of sap, 34 millimeters.
Number of rings, 203.

Number of rings (center to periphery).	Radius.	Diameter.		Area	Accretion for decades.	
					Area.	Diameter.
	Mm.	*Mm.*	*Inches*	*Sq. ft*	*Sq. ft.*	*Inches.*
10	34	68	2.7	0.04	0.04	2.7
20	64	128	5.1	.14	.10	2.4
30	93	186	7.4	.30	.10	2.3
40	112	224	9.0	.44	.14	1.6
50	128	256	10.2	.57	.13	1.2
60	143	286	11.4	.71	.14	1.2
70	158	316	12.6	.86	.15	1.2
80	171	342	13.7	1.02	.16	1.1
90	182	364	14.6	1.16	.14	.9
100	193	386	15.4	1.29	.13	.8
110	203	406	16.2	1.43	.14	.8
120	212	424	17.0	1.58	.15	.8
130	221	442	17.7	1.71	.13	.7
140	230	460	18.4	1.85	.14	.7
150	240	480	19.2	2.01	.16	.8
160	247	494	19.8	2.14	.13	.6
170	255	510	20.4	2.27	.13	.6
180	263	526	21.0	2.40	.13	.6
190	270	540	21.6	2.54	.14	.6
200	276	552	22.1	2.66	.12	.5
203	272	544	21.8	....	....	....

Cross section at 82 feet from the ground of the average tree of the group.

SITE *f*.—Dominant group of 16 trees.

CROSS SECTION: No. 5.

Height from ground, 82 feet.
Width of bark, 13 millimeters.
Number of rings in sap, 43.
Width of sap, 35 millimeters.
Number of rings, 185.

Number of rings (center to periphery).	Radius.	Diameter.		Area.	Accretion for decades.	
					Area.	Diameter.
	Mm.	*Mm.*	*Inches.*	*Sq. ft.*	*Sq. ft.*	*Inches.*
10	30	60	2.4	0.03	0.03	2.4
20	58	116	4.6	.11	.08	2.2
30	79	158	6.3	.22	.11	1.7
40	97	194	7.8	.33	.11	1.5
50	114	228	9.1	.45	.12	1.3
60	129	258	10.3	.58	.13	1.2
70	143	286	11.4	.71	.13	1.1
80	156	312	12.5	.85	.14	1.1
90	169	338	13.5	.99	.14	1.0
100	180	360	14.4	1.13	.14	.9
110	191	382	15.3	1.28	.15	.9
120	201	402	16.1	1.41	.13	.8
130	211	422	16.9	1.56	.15	.8
140	221	442	17.7	1.71	.15	.8
150	230	460	18.4	1.85	.14	.7
160	239	478	19.1	1.99	.14	.7
170	247	494	19.8	2.14	.15	.7
180	255	510	20.4	2.27	.13	.6
185	251	502	20.1	....	....	....

Cross section at 99 feet from the ground of the average tree of the group.

SITE *f*.—Dominant group of 16 trees.

CROSS SECTION: No. 6.

Height from ground, 99 feet.
Width of bark, 11 millimeters.
Number of rings in sap, 37.
Width of sap, 33 millimeters.
Number of rings, 161.

Number of rings (center to periphery).	Radius.	Diameter.		Area.	Accretion for decades.	
					Area.	Diameter.
	Mm.	*Mm.*	*Inches.*	*Sq. ft.*	*Sq. ft.*	*Inches.*
10	21	42	1.7	0.01	0.01	1.7
20	42	84	3.4	.06	.05	1.7
30	62	124	5.0	.14	.08	1.6
40	79	158	6.3	.22	.08	1.3
50	96	192	7.7	.32	.10	1.4
60	111	222	8.9	.43	.11	1.2
70	124	248	9.9	.53	.10	1.0
80	137	274	11.0	.66	.13	1.1
90	148	296	11.8	.76	.10	.8
100	160	320	12.8	.89	.13	1.0
110	170	340	13.6	1.01	.12	.8
120	181	362	14.5	1.15	.14	.9
120	194	388	15.5	1.31	.16	1.0
140	204	408	16.3	1.45	.14	.8
150	215	430	17.2	1.61	.16	.9
160	225	450	18.0	1.77	.16	.8
161	226	452	18.1	....	....	....

Cross section at 114 feet from the ground of the average tree of group.

SITE *f*.—Dominant group of 16 trees.

CROSS SECTION: No. 7.

Height from ground, 114 feet.
Width of bark, 8 millimeters.
Number of rings in sap, 34.
Width of sap, 33 millimeters.
Number of rings, 122.

Number of rings (center to periphery).	Radius.	Diameter.		Area.	Accretion for decades.	
					Area.	Diameter.
	Mm.	Mm.	Inches.	Sq. ft.	Sq. ft.	Inches.
10	18	36	1.4	0.01	0.01	1.4
20	36	72	2.9	.04	.03	1.5
30	52	104	4.2	.10	.06	1.3
40	67	134	5.4	.16	.06	1.2
50	81	162	6.5	.23	.07	1.1
60	94	188	7.5	.31	.08	1.0
70	108	216	8.6	.40	.09	1.1
80	119	238	9.5	.49	.09	.9
90	130	260	10.4	.59	.10	.9
100	140	280	11.2	.68	.09	.8
110	151	302	12.1	.80	.12	.9
120	161	322	12.9	.91	.11	.8
122	162	324	13.0			

Cross section at 129 feet from the ground of the average tree of group.

SITE *f*.—Dominant group of 16 trees.

CROSS SECTION: No. 8.

Height from ground, 129 feet.
Width of bark, 6 millimeters.
Number of rings in sap, 31.
Width of sap, 30 millimeters.
Number of rings, 91.

Number of rings (center to periphery).	Radius.	Diameter.		Area.	Accretion for decades.	
					Area.	Diameter.
	Mm.	Mm.	Inches.	Sq. ft.	Sq. ft.	Inches.
10	14	28	1.1	0.01	0.01	1.1
20	29	58	2.3	.03	.02	1.2
30	43	86	3.4	.06	.03	1.1
40	56	112	4.5	.11	.05	1.1
50	70	140	5.6	.17	.06	1.1
60	81	162	6.5	.23	.06	.9
70	92	184	7.4	.30	.07	.9
80	104	208	8.3	.38	.08	.9
90	116	232	9.3	.47	.09	1.0
91	117	234	9.4			

The preceding tabulations are used for constructing the average tree of the group, as shown in fig. 13.

HEIGHT GROWTH.

The progressive development of the height growth is determined by means of graphical interpolation, taking as a basis the heights and ages of the cross sections as explained under caption "Rate of growth." The tree under analysis reached the height of the first cross section (18 feet) in the course of 17 years (age of tree minus age of section);

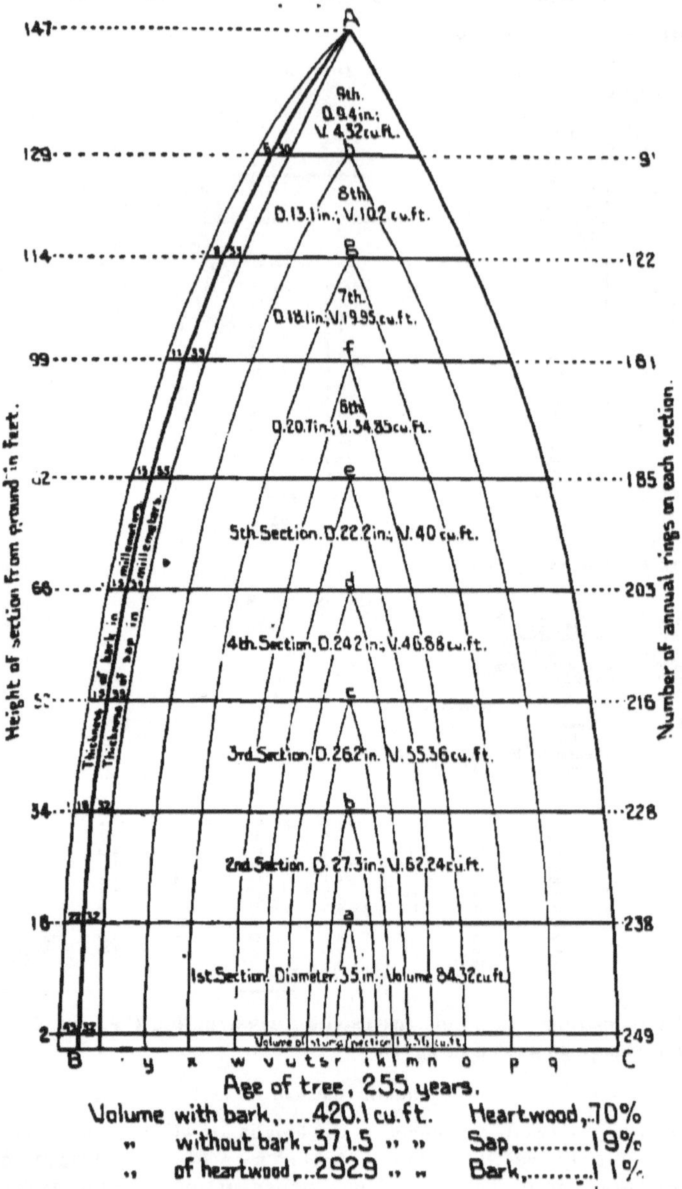

FIG. 13.—Representing average tree of dominant group dissected for analysis. The cones *cai, abk, tcl*, etc., correspond to those given in fig. 15.

it reached the height of the second section (34 feet) in the course of 27 years (age of tree minus age of second cross section), etc. Making an allowance of six years which was required by the tree to attain the height of the stump (2 feet), the following were the heights reached by the tree at corresponding ages:

A height of 2 feet in 6 years.
A height of 18 feet in 17 years.
A height of 34 feet in 27 years.
A height of 50 feet in 39 years.
A height of 66 feet in 52 years.
A height of 82 feet in 70 years.
A height of 99 feet in 94 years.
A height of 114 feet in 133 years.
A height of 129 feet in 164 years.
A height of 147 (total height) in 255 years (total age).

These figures are used for constructing a curve of height growth as follows: Take cross-section paper (see fig. 14) and let the horizontal line AB represent the age of the tree and the vertical line AC its corresponding height. Locate each of the above 10 points on the cross-section paper with reference to age and height lines and connect them. The curve thus obtained will represent graphically the height growth of the average tree of the group.

DIAMETER GROWTH.

The progressive development of the diameter on each of the cross sections can be determined in the same graphical way by plotting the age of the section on the horizontal line and the corresponding distance from the center on the vertical line. Connecting all the points thus located, a curve is obtained representing graphically the diameter growth on the particular cross section of the tree. For the tree under analysis nine curves should be constructed in order to study the diameter growth of the tree.

VOLUME GROWTH.

The detail measurements of the cross sections of the average tree of the group enables one to determine the volume the tree had when—

17 years old (age of tree minus age of first section).
27 years old (age of tree minus age of second section).
39 years old (age of tree minus age of third section).
52 years old (age of tree minus age of fourth section).
70 years old (age of tree minus age of fifth section).
94 years old (age of tree minus age of sixth section).
133 years old (age of tree minus age of seventh section).
164 years old (age of tree minus age of eighth section).

The volume the tree had when 17 years old is determined as follows (see fig. 15; cone *rai*): Calculate the diameter of the central 11 rings on the stump section and find in the tables (page 37) the area of its corresponding circle. Multiply this area by the height of the stump (2 feet); multiply also this area by one-half the length of the first section.

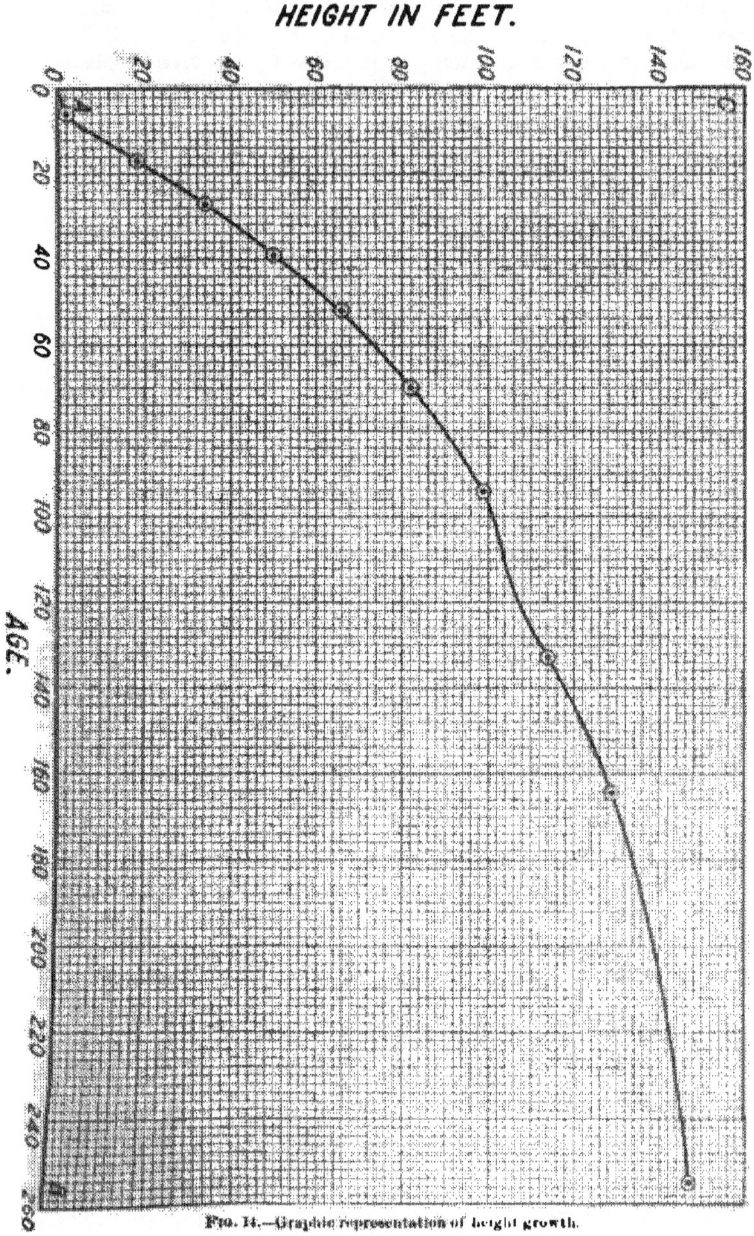

Fig. 14.—Graphic representation of height growth.

The sum of these products gives the volume of the first 17 enveloping cones, or, what is the same, the volume the tree had when 17 years old.

The volume of the first 27 enveloping cones—i. e., the volume the tree had when 27 years old—is obtained as follows (see fig. 15; cone *sbk*): Determine the diameter of the first 21 central rings on the stump section (difference between the ages of stump and second sections); determine the diameter of the first 10 central rings on the first cross section (difference between the ages of first and second sections); calculate the volume of the portion between stump and first sections, considering it as frustum of cone or as a paraboloid; calculate the volume of the portion above the first section, considering it as a paraboloid. The volume of stump the tree had when 27 years old is calculated by considering it as a cylinder, with a diameter equal to that of the first 21 central rings taken on the stump of the tree. By adding together the volumes thus calculated the volume the tree had when 27 years old is obtained. The volumes the tree had when 39, 52, 70, 94, 133, and 164 years old are determined in the same manner (see fig. 15; cones *tel*, *udm*, *ven*, *wfo*, and *xgp*)—i. e., the volume of portions of tree between two consecutive sections are calculated, considering them either as frustums of cones or as frustums of paraboloids, while the volume of the last portion of tree is calculated, considering it as a paraboloid; the volume of stump is calculated, considering it as a cylinder with the diameter taken on stump section.

The total volume of the tree is also calculated as explained above. The progressive development of volume growth may be then determined by means of graphical interpolation, as shown by fig. 16, which represents the volume growth of the average tree of the group under analysis.

The analysis is generally concluded by collating the figures relating to height, diameter, area, and volume growth in the form of the following table:

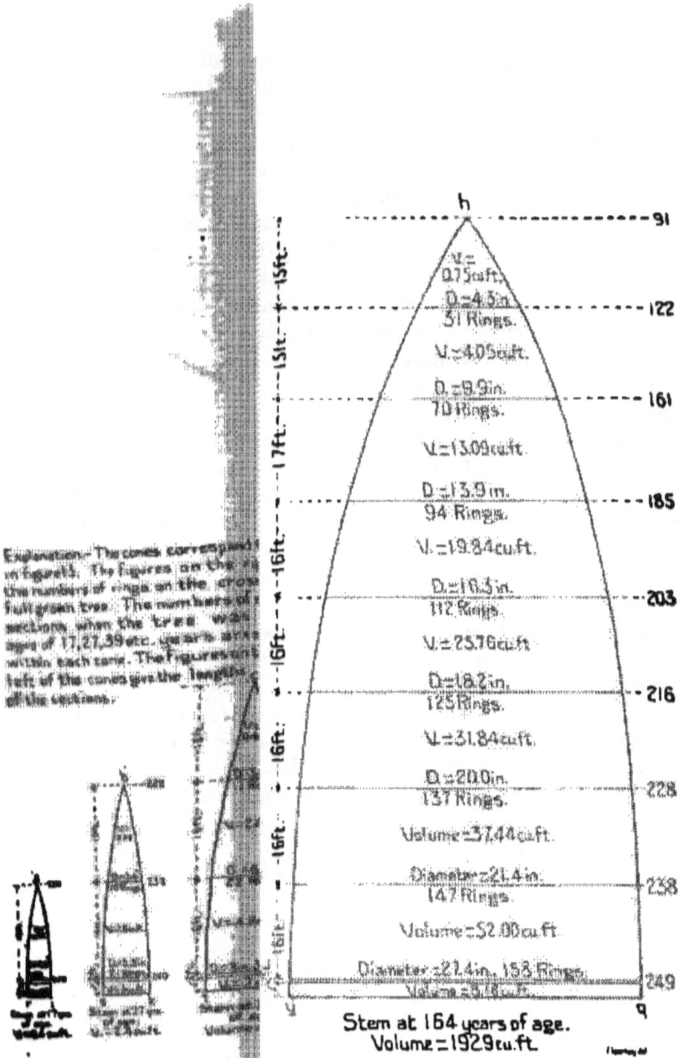
h
91
V.=
0.75cu.ft.
D.=4.3in.
51 Rings.
122
V.=4.05cu.ft.
D.=9.9in.
70 Rings.
161
V.=13.09cu.ft.
D.=13.9in.
94 Rings.
185
V.=19.84cu.ft.
D.=16.3in.
112 Rings.
203
V.=25.76cu.ft.
D.=18.2in.
125 Rings.
216
V.=31.84cu.ft.
D.=20.0in.
137 Rings.
228
Volume=37.44cu.ft.
Diameter=21.4in.
147 Rings.
238
Volume=52.00cu.ft.
Diameter=27.4in. 153 Rings.
249
15ft.
15ft.
17ft.
16ft.
16ft.
16ft.
16ft.
Stem at 164 years of age.
Volume=192.9cu.ft.

5107——Fo

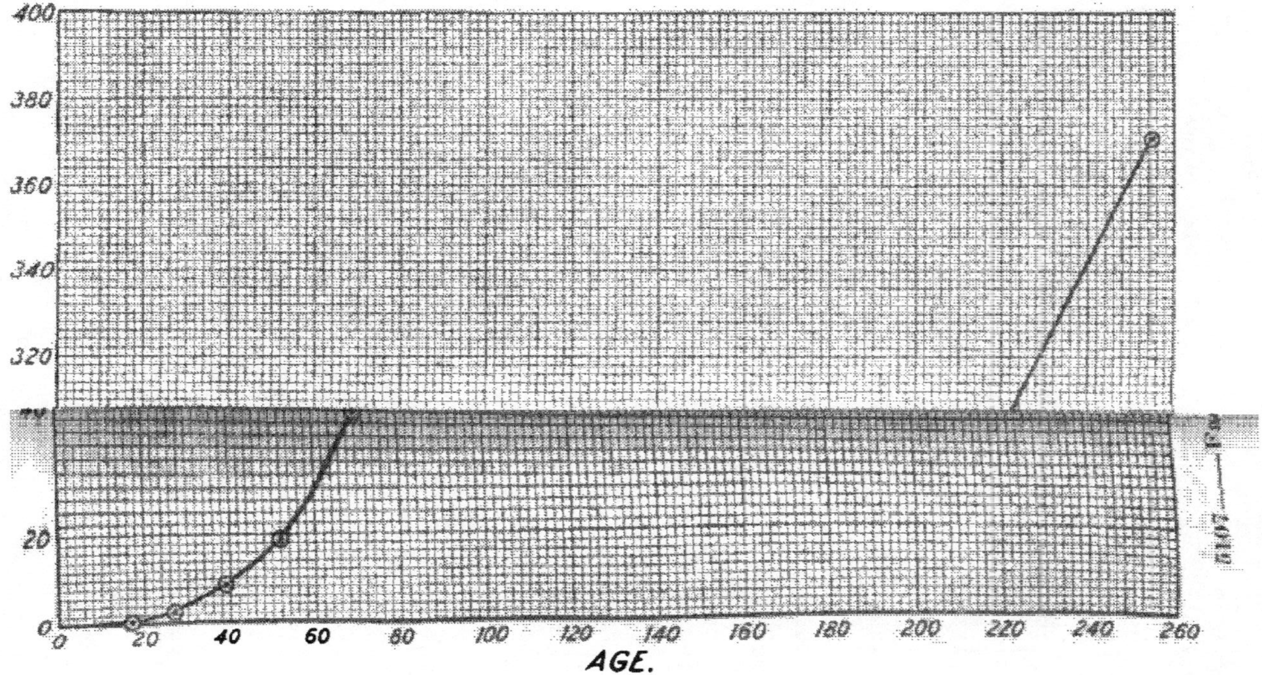

400
380
360
340
320
20
0
0
20
40
60
80
100
120
140
160
180
200
220
240
260
AGE.

Form No. 6.—*Table showing the rate of growth of the dominant group.*

Site: *f*. Species: White pine.

Dominant growth (16 trees).

Age.	Diameter at height of 4½ feet (without bark).	Total height of tree.	Volume of stem (without bark).	Relative per cent of total volume. Heartwood.	Sapwood.	Bark.	Decade.	Periodical accretion. Height.	Diameter and corresponding area on— Cross-section 1 at height of 2½ feet. Diameter.	Area.	Cross-section 2 at height of 18 feet. Diameter.	Area.	Cross-section 3 at height of 34 feet. Diameter.	Area.	Cross-section 4 at height of 50 feet. Diameter.	Area.	Cross-section 5 at height of 66 feet. Diameter.	Area.	Cross-section 6 at height of 82 feet. Diameter.	Area.	Cross-section 7 at height of 99 feet. Diameter.	Area.	Cross-section 8 at height of 114 feet. Diameter.	Area.	Cross-section 9 at height of 129 feet. Diameter.	Area.	Volume.	Average annual accretion.	Current periodic accretion.
	In.	*Feet.*	*Cubic feet.*	*Per ct.*	*Per ct.*	*Per ct.*		*Ft.*	*In.*	*Sq. feet.*	*In.*	*Sq. feet.*	*In.*	*Sq. feet.*	*In.*	*Sq. feet.*	*In.*	*Sq. feet.*	*In.*	*Sq. feet.*	*In.*	*Sq. feet.*	*In.*	*Sq. feet.*	*In.*	*Sq. feet.*	*Cubic feet.*	*Cubic feet.*	*Cu. feet.*
10	1.2	8	(?)				First	9	2.3	0.03	3.4	0.06	3.1	0.05	3.2	0.05	2.7	0.04	2.4	0.03	1.7	0.01	1.4	0.01	1.1	0.01	(?)	(?)	(?)
20	3.4	23	0.8				Second	15	2.8	.11	2.8	.16	2.4	.16	2.9	.15	2.4	.10	2.2	.08	1.7	.05	1.5	.03	1.2	.02	(?)	0.04	(?)
30	6.1	38	3.6				Third	15	2.3	.16	2.0	.15	2.0	.16	2.1	.17	2.3	.16	1.7	.11	1.8	.08	1.3	.06	1.1	.03	2.8	.12	0.28
40	8.2	53	9.0				Fourth	13	2.1	.19	1.6	.16	1.7	.18	1.6	.15	1.6	.14	1.5	.11	1.7	.09	1.2	.06	1.1	.05	5.4	.22	.54
50	10.2	61	17.0				Fifth	13	1.9	.22	1.6	.19	1.4	.16	1.2	.14	1.2	.13	1.3	.12	1.4	.10	1.1	.07	1.1	.06	8.0	.34	.80
60	12.2	73½	27.0				Sixth	9½	1.9	.25	1.2	.16	1.2	.16	1.1	.14	1.2	.14	1.2	.13	1.2	.11	1.0	.08	.9	.06	10.0	.45	1.00
70	14.2	82	40.0				Seventh	8½	2.1	.32	1.2	.17	1.0	.15	1.1	.13	1.2	.15	1.1	.13	1.0	.10	1.1	.09	.9	.07	13.0	.57	1.30
80	16.1	90	52.0				Eighth	8	1.8	.32	1.0	.16	1.1	.17	1.2	.18	1.1	.16	1.1	.14	1.1	.13	.9	.09	.9	.06	12.0	.65	1.20
90	17.8	96	64.0				Ninth	6	1.5	.26	1.0	.17	1.0	.17	1.0	.18	.9	.14	1.0	.14	.8	.10	.9	.10	1.0	.09	12.0	.71	1.20
100	19.0	102	80.0				Tenth	6	1.2	.23	1.2	.21	1.1	.20	.9	.16	.8	.13	.9	.14	1.0	.13	.8	.09			16.0	.80	1.60
110	20.4	107	98.0				Eleventh	5	1.6	.40	1.1	.22	1.0	.19	.8	.14	.8	.14	.9	.15	.8	.12	.9	.12			18.0	.89	1.80
120	22.0	110½	116.0				Twelfth	3½	1.5	.26	1.0	.20	.8	.16	.7	.14	.8	.15	.8	.13	.9	.14	.8	.11			18.0	.98	1.80
130	23.5	113½	133.0				Thirteenth	3	1.3	.34	1.0	.21	.8	.16	.8	.16	.7	.13	.8	.15	1.0	.16					17.0	1.02	1.70
140	24.8	117	150.5				Fourteenth	3½	1.3	.35	.8	.19	.6	.13	.7	.14	.7	.14	.8	.15	.8	.14					17.5	1.07	1.75
150	26.0	122	167.5				Fifteenth	5	1.1	.32	.6	.14	.8	.18	.7	.15	.8	.16	.7	.14	.9	.16					17.0	1.12	1.70
160	27.0	127	184.5				Sixteenth	5	.9	.26	.7	.17	.6	.14	.6	.16	.6	.13	.7	.14	.8	.16					17.0	1.15	1.70
170	28.0	130	202.0				Seventeenth	3	1.0	.33	.7	.17	.6	.15	.6	.11	.6	.13	.7	.15							17.5	1.19	1.75
180	29.0	132	221.0				Eighteenth	2	.9	.29	.7	.18	.6	.14	.6	.14	.6	.13	.6	.13							19.0	1.23	1.90
190	29.8	134	240.0				Nineteenth	2	.8	.26	.6	.16	.6	.16	.7	.17	.6	.14									19.0	1.26	1.90
200	30.6	136	259.0				Twentieth	2	.9	.30	.7	.19	.7	.18	.6	.15	.5	.12									19.0	1.29	1.90
210	31.6	138	277.0				Twenty-first	2	.9	.31	.6	.16	.7	.18	.7	.18											18.0	1.32	1.80
220	32.4	140	298.5				Twenty-second	2	.8	.28	.6	.17	.8	.22													21.5	1.35	2.15
230	33.2	142	320.0				Twenty-third	2	.8	.33	.6	.18															21.5	1.39	2.15
240	31.1	144	340.0				Twenty-fourth	2	.8	.29																	20.0	1.41	2.00
250	35.0	146	361.0	70	19	11	Twenty-fifth	2																			21.0	1.44	2.10

APPENDIX.

BLANK NO. 1.

UNITED STATES DEPARTMENT OF AGRICULTURE,
DIVISION OF FORESTRY.

RECORDS OF TREE MEASUREMENTS.

Name of collector: N. N.
Species: White pine.
Year: 1897.

GENERAL DESCRIPTION OF STATION: A.
(Denoted by capital letter.)

State: Pennsylvania. County: Clearfield. Town: Dubois.

Longitude: 78° 45'. Latitude: 41° 3'. Altitude: 1,200 to 1,500 feet.

General configuration: Plains hills plateau *mountainous.*

General trend of valleys or hills: (Not noted.)

Climatic features: (Meteorological tables furnished.)

General forest conditions of the region: This forest area, in 1876, extended over 20,000 acres. The lumber operations carried on for twenty years by Mr. Du Bois have left only from 1,500 to 2,000 acres of standing timber in a primeval condition.

Three typical forms of forest conditions are suggested to the observer:

(1) Hemlock and white-pine forest, with an admixture of mature hardwoods and a number of young hardwoods and young hemlock, which form the undergrowth.

(2) Hemlock mixed with white pine, with scattering hardwoods. The undergrowth, usually moderately dense, consists mainly of young hemlock with the admixture of young hardwoods.

(3) Hardwoods intermixed with white pine and scattering hemlock. The undergrowth here consists mainly of young hardwoods.

Among the hardwoods the oak, birch, and the maple form the staple of the hardwood forest, while the beech, the chestnut, the hickory, the cucumber, the ash, the cherry, and the basswood are comparatively few in number.

The region has a uniform soil and subsoil, as may be judged by the sample areas NN 5, 6, and 7, and is well provided with moisture by the many streams crossing it all over in different directions.

BLANK NO. 2.

DESCRIPTION OF SITE: *f*.

[Denoted by small letter *f*.]

Sample area, No. 5: (One acre.)

Conformation of surface: Hill sloping toward southwest, where it is bordered by the Irish Narrow Creek.

Soil and drainage conditions: Yellow clay loam of a medium grain (fine shale in it), deep, fresh, well drained, with 2 to 3 inch mold on top.

Subsoil: Laminated shale of an indefinite depth.

Soil cover: Scanty leaves, fern, and tea berries.

Origin of stand: Natural regeneration.

Form: Uniform; storied. White pine forms first and hemlock the second.

Composition: A stand of hemlock mixed with white pine, intermixed with scattering maple, beech, and birch.

Undergrowth: Absent; dense; moderately dense; scanty; consists of very young beech, hemlock, and occasional birch, cucumber, and dogwood (laurel in northeast corner).

Density of stand: 0.7 (in places 0.8).

REMARKS.—Crowns of white pine, generally well developed; clear and straight stems. Age of white pine 230 to 260 years. Age of hemlock almost the same as that of white pine.

ACRE-YIELD MEASUREMENT OF SITE: *f*.

Diameter at breast height (in inches).	White pine. Dominant, height from 140 to 160 feet.	White pine. Codominant, height from — to —.	White pine. Oppressed, height from 130 to 150.	Hemlock. Dominant, height from 90 to 120.	Hemlock. Codominant, height from 80 to 120.	Hemlock. Oppressed, height from 60 to 80.	Maple. Dominant, height from 40 to 60.	Maple. Codominant, height from — to —.	Maple. Oppressed, height from — to —.	Beech. Dominant, height from 40 to 60.	Beech. Codominant, height from — to —.	Beech. Oppressed, height from — to —.	Birch. Dominant, height from 40 to 60.	Birch. Codominant, height from — to —.	Birch. Oppressed, height from — to —.
6															
7						////////									
8													/		
9						//	/								
10						/									
11													/		
12						/							/		
13										//					
14															
15							//								
16			/				/								
17															
18															
19			/							/					
20			/												
21															
22															
23		/	/												
24															
25		///		/											
26															
27															
28															
29				/											
30		/		/											
31	//														
32	//														
33	//														
34	///														
35															
36	//														
37	/														

Undergrowth.

Name of species.	Diameter (b.h.). 3-6 inches.	Diameter (b.h.). Under 3 inches.
Hemlock.		29, 36, 43, 37, 34
Maple.		11
Beech.		47, 38, 31, 62, 28
Birch.		10

38			
39	/		4
40			
41			
42			
43			
44	/		
45			

Cucumber.

DEDUCED RESULTS.

Total number of trees on the acre: 132, of which there were—

White pine, 37. Dominant, 41 per cent; codominant, 48 per cent; oppressed, 11 per cent.

Hemlock, 84. Dominant, 32 per cent; codominant, 26 per cent; oppressed, 42 per cent.

Maple, 5.

Beech, 3.

Birch, 3.

Total yield of the acre: Volume of stems, 15,686 cubic feet; merchantable timber, 90,103 feet, B. M., of which there was a total yield of 58 per cent of white pine and 12 per cent of hemlock.

Average annual accretion: In cubic feet, 65; merchantable timber in feet, B. M., 375.

BLANK NO. 3.

MEASUREMENTS OF STEMS.

SITE: *f*. SPECIES: WHITE PINE.

Tree No.	Breast height.	Diameter (in inches) at a height from ground of— 8 feet.	16 feet.	24 feet.	32 feet.	40 feet.	48 feet.	56 feet.	64 feet.	72 feet.	80 feet.	88 feet.	96 feet.	104 feet.	112 feet.	120 feet.	128 feet.	Height to base of crown.	Total height of tree.	Character of growth: Dominant.	Codominant.	Oppressed.	Merchantable timber (B. M.).	Condition of timber: Sound.	Defective.	Crooked.	Clear.	Knotty.	Windshaken.	Surrounding species.	Remarks.
1	35½	34	29	28	28	27	26½	26	25	24	23	22	20	19	16½	15	11	90	158	×	...	...	3,090	×	...	...	...	...	...	White pine, hemlock, and small beech.	
2	36	33	31	30	29	28	28	27	26	26	25	23	21½	19½	18	15	13	90	157	×	...	...	3,401	×	...	...	...	...	...	Hemlock, pine, birch, maple, and ash.	
3	32	30	28	28	27	25½	25	24½	24½	23½	23½	21½	19½	18	15½	13½	...	84	152	×	...	...	2,637	...	...	...	...	...	...	Hemlock and pine.	
4	32	30	27½	26	26	25	24	23½	22½	21½	20½	18½	17	15	12½	10½	8	62	150	×	...	...	2,079	...	...	...	...	...	...	do	
5	29	27½	26	25	25	24	23	22	21½	21	18½	17	15½	14	11½	8	6	100	140	...	×	...	1,905	×	...	...	...	...	...	do	Crowded.
6	29	26½	23½	24½	23½	23	22½	21½	20	20	19	17½	16	15	13	9	7	110	140	...	×	...	1,611	×	...	...	...	...	...	do	
7	29	27½	25½	24½	21½	23	21½	21	21	19½	19	18	16½	15½	14	12½	9½	112	152	...	×	...	1,854	×	...	...	...	...	...	do	
8	29	26	23½	22½	22	21	20	19	18½	18½	17	16½	14½	13	11	8	6	86	162	...	×	...	1,813	Core at butt.	...	...	...	...	...	do	
9	32	28½	25½	24½	23½	23	22	21	21	18½	18	16½	15	14	11	8	7	84	142	...	×	...	1,648	do	...	...	...	...	...	do	
10	33	30½	29	27½	26½	25½	25	24	23	21½	21	19	18	15½	13½	12½	8	96	146	×	...	...	2,384	×	...	...	...	...	...	do	Crown free.
11	30	28½	27	25	24½	24	23	22½	20½	19½	18½	17½	16½	13½	11½	9	6	81	141	...	×	...	1,047	...	...	...	...	...	...	do	Somewhat crowded.
12	28	27	24½	24	23	23	22	21	20½	19½	19	17	16	13½	12	9½	8	88	156	×	...	...	1,646	...	...	...	...	...	...	do	
13	23	20½	20½	20½	20½	19½	19	18½	17	16½	15	15	14	12½	11½	9½	7½	93	147	...	×	...	1,048	...	...	...	...	...	...	do	Crowded.
14	25	23½	22½	22	21	20½	19½	18½	18	17½	16	14½	13	11½	9	6½	...	98	139	...	×	...	1,233	Core at butt.	...	...	...	...	...	do	Do.
15	26	24½	23½	22½	21½	21	21	20½	20½	18½	17½	17	16	14	12½	10	7	98	136	...	×	...	1,389	do	...	...	...	...	...	do	Top killed, somewhat crowded.
16	24½	21½	19½	19	18½	17½	17	16½	16	14½	14	12	10½	8	4½	...	...	93	124	...	×	...	815	do	...	...	...	...	...	do	Crowded.
17	25	23½	22	21	20	20	19	19	18	17½	16½	15	14	12½	8½	...	...	106	128	...	×	...	1,183	do	...	...	...	...	...	do	Do.
18	39	36	33	32½	30	29½	28½	28	26	26	23	22½	21½	18½	18	14½	11½	86	153	×	...	...	3,318	...	...	...	...	...	...	do	
19	34	32	30	29	28	27½	26½	25	24½	23	22	19½	18	16½	13	16½	8	78	134	×	...	...	2,397	...	...	...	...	...	...	do	At 134 feet top lost. Free crown (about 16 feet).

20	44	30	30	30½	35½	31	32½	31½	30½	28	27	26	23	21½	20	14½	10½	100	144	×			4,288	×						do	Crown free.
21	34	31½	29	27	29½	25½	31½	27½	22½	21½	21	19½	18	16½	14½	11½	8	92	146	×			2,348	×						do	Crown free—sound
22	31	29	27	27	25	24	23	23	21	19½	19½	17	14½	12	9½	....	....	82	130		×		1,731	×						do	Crown somewhat crowded
23	34	31½	29	28	27	25½	25	24	23½	22	20½	20½	18	16½	13½	9½	6	90	142	×			2,316	×						do	Crown free.
24	25	23½	22	21	20	19	18½	17½	16½	15	14	13	12	10	7	....	....	84	140		×		1,102	×						do	Somewhat crowded.
25	29½	26½	25½	24½	24½	24	22½	21½	21	20½	19	18	16	15½	13	11	5	107	138		×		1,854	×						do	Do.
26	26	24	21½	21	20½	19	18	17	16½	16	15	14	12½	11½	9	6	....	88	136		×		1,021	×						do	
27	19	18	17½	17½	16½	16	15½	15	14	14	13	12	11½	9½	8½	6½	....	94	132			×	683	×						do	Crown very crowded
28	29½	26	24	24	22½	22	21½	21	20	19	18	17	15	13½	10½	7	....	75	138		×		1,551	×						do	
30	26½	24½	23	22½	21	20½	20	19½	19	18	16½	13	13	11	9	6	....	90	134		×		1,336	Core at butt						do	Somewhat crowded.
33	33	30	27½	25½	25½	24½	22	22	21	20	18	16½	13½	12½	9	5½	....	91	133	×			1,770	×						do	Free exposure.
34	33	30	27½	27	26	25	25	24½	23½	22½	21	20	19	15½	15½	12	9	90	148	×			2,230	×						do	Do.
35	31	27	24½	23½	23	22½	21½	20½	20	19½	19	16½	14½	13	11	8	5½	82	136	×			1,458	×						do	Top about 18 feet, not found.
36	31½	28½	26½	26	25	24	24	23½	21½	21	19	16½	15	13	10	7½	....	88	134	×			1,865	×						do	Do.
37	37	35	32½	32	31	30	28½	28	26½	28	23½	22½	21½	17	14	11½	8	106	146	×			2,970	×						do	Do.
38	23	22	21½	20	19½	19	18	17½	17	16	15	14	12½	11	9	5	....	98	137			×	987	×						do	Crown very crowded
39	20½	18½	18	17½	17	16	15	14½	13½	12½	12	11½	10½	9½	5	....	....	100	123			×	558	....						do	Do.
40	16½	16	15½	15	14	13½	13	12½	12	11	10	8½	7½	4½	....	....	....	82	120			×	339	....						do	Crown very small.

SECTION, Stump.

SITE: *f*. AGE CLASS: 240 to 260 years. SPECIES: White pine.

Tree No.	Height from ground.	Thickness of bark.	Sap-wood. No. of rings.	Sap-wood. Width.	No. of rings.	Radius at age of— 10	20	30	40	50	60	70	80	90	100	110	120	130	140	150	160	170	180	190	200	210	220	230	240	250	260	270	280	290	300	Entire radius.	Remarks.
		mm		mm																																	
1	2	49	36	38	254	36	80	105	135	139	157	178	198	218	244	273	292	306	320	329	336	341	348	359	367	370	385	395	406	410	....	....		....	....	415	Dominant.
2	2	35	33	37	254	21	54	71	85	96	109	139	163	180	213	235	250	261	298	325	336	346	364	386	397	408	418	429	444	452	....	....		....	....	454	
3	2	55	33	35	283	34	72	98	119	135	156	177	192	209	228	250	267	287	300	312	319	326	335	343	351	363	373	385	389	400	....	....		....	....	405	
4	2	55	26	25	238	25	50	107	133	178	200	221	256	276	304	313	330	345	357	369	377	388	396	407	417	426	435	442	....	....	....	....		....	....	447	
10	2	40	47	30	238	36	78	116	145	180	205	244	248	257	276	295	309	322	337	350	362	370	389	398	404	415	422	430	....	....	....	....		....	....	434	
12	2	30	45	28	256	32	61	80	99	123	138	150	178	186	200	214	229	240	253	268	275	284	294	303	310	319	329	334	339	345	....	....		....	....	350	
17	2	50	26	38	259	24	46	74	102	121	142	175	201	224	246	266	295	321	349	375	391	409	426	441	457	464	481	498	513	528	....	....		....	....	541	
19	2	50	35	30	244	27	53	73	103	129	134	182	199	212	202	230	263	282	301	311	322	336	349	364	392	417	432	453	472	....	....	....		....	....	477	
20	2	50	38	18	260	37	80	139	185	200	231	292	345	372	392	409	426	444	461	477	488	500	509	516	525	537	547	544	561	567	571	....		....	....		
21	2	40	37	30	239	25	56	82	102	121	139	158	175	186	208	225	245	270	294	315	334	347	359	389	378	385	395	406	....	....	....	....		....	....	416	
23	2	40	24	22	242	19	53	77	99	123	144	167	180	210	244	257	274	288	302	311	324	342	354	359	366	374	383	413	420	....	....	....		....	....	421	
30	2	25	35	45	235	26	56	77	92	108	120	139	138	150	180	200	225	246	265	278	292	305	316	331	350	378	398	406	....	....	....	....		....	....	416	
34	2	40	46	35	256	23	60	87	133	160	187	222	261	275	280	302	316	328	336	348	357	367	376	382	390	398	408	415	423	429	....	....		....	....	432	
31	2	48	33	25	255	27	57	83	116	141	168	191	220	229	241	251	265	282	293	307	319	330	342	349	358	360	378	385	390	395	....	....		....	....	397	
35	2	30	41	28	252	34	74	110	138	161	182	209	232	229	237	246	253	265	276	289	293	304	318	329	336	345	352	358	365	373	....	....		....	....	378	
37	2	30	46	27	255	28	76	106	162	178	201	234	267	286	303	323	341	358	370	386	398	411	422	432	439	445	452	458	466	473	....	....		....	....	476	
28	2	39	48	28	253	36	72	104	135	169	176	195	207	211	216	225	237	251	262	270	274	279	285	289	293	298	306	312	320	325	....	....		....	....	328	Codominant.
25	2	40	38	35	236	15	41	58	71	89	104	114	133	157	173	198	220	237	249	261	276	288	303	319	335	350	365	375	....	....	....	....		....	....	381	
24	2	37	25	25	234	15	45	73	94	110	123	131	136	140	146	155	165	173	181	189	197	208	218	237	255	277	293	314	....	....	....	....		....	....	320	
22	2	40	43	30	240	32	71	111	127	156	195	218	241	254	263	275	293	306	316	324	332	343	356	365	375	385	396	407	412	....	....	....		....	....		
5	2	43	35	23	258	36	53	76	86	104	128	140	156	168	176	191	204	219	236	251	263	277	294	309	324	337	347	356	363	373	....	....		....	....	382	
6	2	40	28	25	253	23	71	102	122	146	166	183	202	218	227	239	253	264	276	288	293	299	306	316	327	338	349	358	365	372	....	....		....	....	377	
7	2	30	35	24	236	25	53	92	114	128	141	155	167	177	189	204	225	236	244	255	263	269	278	287	295	302	312	319	323	334	....	....		....	....	337	
8	2	....	....	....	229	Core for 8 inches.																															
9	2	....	....	....	230																																
11	2	32	30	37	234	31	55	80	87	106	121	132	147	166	183	199	221	245	256	270	284	300	314	327	342	357	371	384	....	....	....	....		....	....	396	

13	2	43	27	20	253	20	61	93	114	131	144	158	173	185	198	214	226	238	246	255	264	272	282	290	295	300	309	316	321	326	.....	.....		.....	.....	327
14	[illegible]		.....	.....	236							Core for 4½ inches.																								
15	[illegible]	.....	.....	.....	258							Core for 5 inches.																								
16	[illegible]	.....	.....	.....	320							Core for 3 inches.																								
17	[illegible]	.....	.....	.....	256							Core for 6 inches.																								
28	[illegible]	37	29	40	280	25	60	81	91	112	121	125	132	143	150	164	176	181	193	200	211	222	234	247	266	281	295	310	.....	.....	.....	.....		.....	.....	321
30	[illegible]	27	40	42	253	28	58	89	102	121	143	162	175	183	198	205	217	229	240	252	262	272	281	289	297	303	300	313	320	326	.....	.....		.....	.....	329
37	2	25	45	24	253	30	66	89	106	125	141	158	173	178	183	187	193	203	209	217	224	231	236	239	242	246	252	259	264	270	.....	.....	Up-pressed.	.....	.....	271½
38	2	36	47	29	251	35	73	97	119	137	152	165	170	185	192	201	210	221	231	237	244	250	256	261	264	269	272	277	281	284	.....	.....		.....	.....	285
39	2	32	54	24	252	37	81	102	122	137	148	150	163	167	170	176	183	191	196	200	203	205	208	214	220	226	230	235	238	241	.....	.....		.....	.....	241½
40	2	22	35	16	255	29	64	81	101	117	131	141	151	155	158	162	170	177	183	186	191	195	200	205	206	211	215	221	225	229	.....	.....		.....	.....	232

BLANK NO. 4.

SECTION No. 3.

SITE: *f*. AGE CLASS: 240 to 260 years. SPECIES: White pine.

Tree No.	Height from ground.	Thickness of bark.	Sap-wood. No. of rings.	Sap-wood. Width.	No. of rings.	Radius at age of— 10	20	30	40	50	60	70	80	90	100	110	120	130	140	150	160	170	180	190	200	210	220	230	240	250	260	270	280	290	300	Entire radius.	Remarks.
		mm		mm																																	
1	50	15	49	32	221	36	76	98	115	136	143	150	180	193	205	214	224	230	235	242	249	256	262	269	275	282	287	...	...	...	...	...		...	...	288	Dominant.
2	50	17	45	35	214	33	67	84	102	118	135	151	169	195	201	219	231	242	253	265	277	288	297	307	317	324	...	...	...	...	...	...		...	...	327	
3	50	17	47	42	227	33	72	97	112	125	138	150	164	176	185	196	204	210	217	226	234	243	253	263	272	280	288	...	...	...	...	...		...	...	293	
4	50	11	50	30	208	40	74	107	129	148	162	175	188	200	210	219	228	237	245	253	258	260	272	278	283	...	...	...	...	...	...	...		...	...	286	
10	50	14	50	30	210	42	80	110	130	144	158	172	183	196	205	217	225	234	245	253	259	265	272	278	283	290	...	...	...	...	...	...		...	...	....	
12	50	12	35	32	228	26	76	95	116	130	142	153	169	178	189	198	205	209	214	219	225	230	235	241	247	252	256	...	...	...	...	...		...	...	264	
15	50	19	41	40	223	35	64	86	106	127	136	157	176	195	213	228	241	257	263	275	288	292	306	318	328	337	346	...	...	...	...	...		...	...	349	
19	50	20	39	38	200	46	67	90	106	124	132	146	165	180	194	207	217	230	241	253	265	279	290	302	311	...	...	...	...	...	...	...		...	...	317	
20	50	20	50	30	219	66	123	164	193	213	231	246	262	278	288	297	306	313	320	327	334	340	347	355	363	366	...	...	...	...	...	...		...	...	371	
21	50	16	40	31	202	33	69	91	108	126	132	147	163	176	189	201	211	221	231	241	249	258	268	276	284	...	...	...	...	...	...	...		...	...	286	
23	50	15	40	40	204	29	62	91	109	122	134	148	163	177	190	200	212	223	233	242	250	259	270	280	295	...	...	...	...	...	...	...		...	...	300	
36	50	15	45	38	192	25	37	58	67	78	90	115	134	150	167	176	190	201	211	221	228	236	245	251	261	...	...	...	...	...	...	...		...	...	263	
31	50	15	41	30	223	45	82	110	135	153	164	177	190	208	210	216	225	234	242	246	256	265	276	283	290	298	304	...	...	...	...	...		...	...	307	
33	50	15	48	30	224	48	78	103	124	142	149	158	167	174	181	187	196	204	213	218	225	231	238	243	248	254	258	...	...	...	...	...		...	...	260	
35	50	15	47	20	226	47	84	114	135	148	155	161	168	176	183	190	198	204	210	217	222	226	233	239	242	247	251	...	...	...	...	...		...	...	254	
37	50	12	44	30	217	51	107	145	173	195	214	229	232	244	253	261	268	277	289	295	302	309	314	321	328	331	...	...	...	...	...	...		...	...	340	
28	50	12	63	29	238	44	81	109	127	142	153	160	167	175	184	195	204	208	214	220	225	230	235	240	243	248	253	...	...	...	...	...		...	...	257	Codominant.
25	50	15	50	40	188	38	69	82	117	133	156	172	184	194	204	215	226	238	245	253	261	268	278	...	...	...		...	...	...	...	...		...	...	284	
24	50	12	38	25	193	13	18	25	36	54	75	89	101	111	118	126	137	147	160	173	188	202	214	220	...	...	...	...	...	...	...	...		...	...	221	
22	50	15	43	27	203	34	74	107	129	148	161	174	187	197	208	216	224	230	235	241	247	254	260	266	271	...	...	...	...	...	...	...		...	...	273	
17	50	15	50	30	226	27	64	88	104	117	128	137	146	155	164	169	173	175	178	182	186	192	196	205	212	217	223	...	...	...	...	...		...	...	226	
5	50	15	43	33	220	34	66	83	97	107	116	125	136	148	158	170	182	193	203	212	225	233	241	250	258	265	272	...	...	...	...	...		...	...	....	
6	50	17	45	30	222	40	72	94	108	120	128	137	148	159	170	180	190	200	207	215	221	229	236	243	250	255	261	...	...	...	...	...		...	...	262	
7	48	13	60	30	212	40	73	93	107	120	130	140	150	160	170	180	187	197	205	214	222	229	237	244	250	255	260	...	...	...	...	...		...	...	263	
8	50	16	45	35	188	23	46	52	75	87	102	116	129	140	151	164	172	180	189	198	207	214	221	...	...	...	...	...	...	...	...	...		...	...	226	
9	50	15	42	35	192	35	56	78	96	113	131	150	162	177	189	198	206	214	230	241	250	257	264	273	...	...	...	...	...	...	...	...		...	...	275	
11	50	20	44	44	200	37	62	78	89	102	115	127	141	158	166	176	187	200	214	226	239	248	259	262	270	...	...	...	...	...	...	...		...	...	....	
13	50	12	53	33	223	31	57	74	90	99	110	119	128	135	143	149	155	162	168	174	181	188	195	201	208	215	221	...	...	...	...	...		...	...	223	

14	53	12	34	25	204	30	50	80	69	76	84	93	102	112	127	130	137	143	150	167	170	186	196	205	216	...	...	...	...	...	...	...		...	...	230
15	50	13	39	30	219	35	62	78	88	100	107	115	123	134	142	151	158	164	172	180	189	198	200	217	228	230	...	...	...	...	...	...		...	...	248
16	50	15	45	37	188	27	55	72	85	106	112	122	132	140	148	153	161	169	179	168	195	206	211	...	...	...	...	...	...	...	...	...		...	...	218
20	50	16	35	25	194	21	46	65	83	89	97	107	117	122	129	137	146	135	166	170	189	199	210	220	...	...	...	...	...	...	...	...		...	...	223
30	48	16	51	30	220	38	71	98	114	125	134	141	150	161	171	179	187	192	198	203	210	215	230	225	233	239	244	...	...	...	...	...		...	...	...
27	50	14	40	12	223	43	71	80	103	113	117	120	122	125	129	133	138	143	148	150	153	158	160	163	167	171	174	...	...	...	...	...		...	...	179½
28	50	18	53	19	223	46	60	98	111	121	129	136	145	153	160	166	172	178	183	188	192	196	201	204	207	210	212	...	...	...	...	...	Op-pressed	...	...	213
29	50	15	52	16	226	30	66	86	99	108	113	116	120	127	134	139	143	146	146	151	155	160	165	169	173	176	170	...	...	...	...			...	...	181
40	50	19	52	19	222	30	55	70	79	84	89	94	99	105	109	113	116	120	122	126	130	135	137	140	145	149	151	...	...	...				...	...	156

FOREST MENSURATION

Walter Mulford

By

C. A. SCHENCK, Ph.D.

Director Biltmore Forest School, and Forester to the Biltmore Estate

MCMV

THE UNIVERSITY PRESS
of SEWANEE TENNESSEE

PREFACE

Dear Readers:

In the following pages an attempt is made to treat "Forest Mensuration" from a scientific-mathematical standpoint as well as from the view point of practical application.

Naturally, pamphlets of as restricted a character as this treatise on forest mensuration address themselves to a very restricted circle of readers; and the expense of printing is never covered by the returns from sales.

Thus it becomes necessary, in order to reduce the expense of publication, to omit all, or practically all, lengthy explanation of a mathematical nature which the teacher at a forest school can easily supply in the course of his lectures.

The present Biltmore pamphlet on Forest Mensuration is intended, above all, to assist the students enlisted at the Biltmore School. It contains the teacher's dictation which the students, in former years, were compelled to take down in long or shorthand, to the annoyance of both teacher and students.

It cannot be expected that a present-day lumberman will take a direct and personal interest in any of the following paragraphs. Still, in conservative forestry, in destructive forestry, and in any other business enterprise, the truism is worth remembering that *"knowledge is the best of assets."*

Knowledge certainly forms the only unalienable factor of production.

With the advent of high stumpage prices, the owner of woodland will be inclined to consider, under many circumstances, the advisability of forest-husbandry—an idea which was as preposterous in past decades of superabundance of timber as the raising of beef cattle, some sixty years ago, in the prairies then abounding in buffalo.

Financially considered, a proper outcome of forest-husbandry is and must be based on a proper application of the theories and principles involved in forest mensuration.

I shall be deeply grateful to a kind reader who, discovering mistakes or incongruities in the following paragraphs, will take the trouble of sending me a timely hint.

Most truly,

C. A. SCHENCK,

Director Biltmore Forest School, and
Forester to the Biltmore Estate.

August 1, 1905.

LECTURES ON FOREST MENSURATION

SYNOPSIS OF CONTENTS BY PARAGRAPHS.

CHAPTER III.—INCREMENT OF TREES AND OF FORESTS.

SECTION I.—INCREMENT OF A TREE.

SECTION II.—INCREMENT OF A WOOD.

CHAPTER IV.—LUMBER.

CHAPTER V.—STUMPAGE-VALUES.

FOREST MENSURATION

PARAGRAPH I.

DEFINITION AND SUBDIVISION.

Definition: By "Forest Mensuration," the forester ascertains the volume, the age, the increment and the stumpage value of trees, parts of trees and aggregates of trees. As a branch of forestry, forest mensuration may be divided into the following five parts:

I. Determination of volume of trees cut down, of standing trees and of forests.
II. Determination of age of trees and of forests.
III. Determination of increment of trees and of forests.
IV. Determination of sawn lumber.
V. Determination of stumpage value.

Circular 445 of the Bureau of Forestry defines mensuration as "the determination of the present and future product of the forest."

American literature is found in Bulletin 20, Division of Forestry; Bulletin 36, Bureau of Forestry; S. B. Green, page 132; Lumber & Log Book and Lumberman's Handbook, edited by the "American Lumberman."

CHAPTER I.—VOLUME.

SECTION I.—VOLUME OF TREES CUT DOWN.

PARAGRAPH II.

UNITS OF VOLUME.

The volume of a tree or of a tree section is expressed:

1. For scientific purposes, on the basis of exact measurements, in cubic feet or cubic meters.
2. For practical purposes, by estimates according to local usage, often assisted by partial measurement, in local units (feet board measure; standards; cords; cubic feet; cord feet; etc.).

PARAGRAPH III.

MATHEMATICAL FORM OF TREES.

Trees do not grow, like crystals, according to purely mathematical laws. Tree growth is deeply influenced by individuality, by surroundings, by accidental occurrences, etc.

The body of a tree, considered as a conoid (a solid body formed by the revolution of a curve about an axis), is very complicated, being formed by a curve of high power. This is the case even in straight and clear boled conifers. The tree bole shows, however, in certain sections of its body frequently a close resemblance to a truncated neilloid, cylinder, paraboloid and cone.

The longitudinal section of conoids is outlined by a curve corresponding with the general equation

$$y^2 = px^n$$

in which *y* is the ordinate (corresponding with the radius of the basal area), *x* the abscissa (representing the height of the conoid), *n* the power of the curve; whilst *p* is merely a constant factor. The volume *v* of the conoid is obtained by integral calculus:

$$v = \frac{y^2 \pi x}{n+1}$$

It is equal to sectional area, *s*, times height, *h*, over $(n+1)$.

The truncated volumes are developed by deducting a small top conoid from a large total conoid.

$$\text{vol. tronc.} = \frac{s_1 h_1 - s_2 h_2}{n+1}$$

In the general curve equation

$$y^2 = px^n$$

we find represented:

A. For *n* equal to 0, the cylinder;

B. For *n* equal to 1, the Apollonian paraboloid, wherein the ratio between sectional area and height is constant;

C. For *n* equal to 2, the cone, wherein the ratio between radius of sectional area and height is constant;

D. For *n* equal to 3, Neill's paraboloid, the truncated form of which is found at the basis of our trees.

The top of the tree resembles a cone or Neilloid; the main bole resembles the cylinder or the Apollonian paraboloid.

The cross section (see Par. XIII.) through a tree taken perpendicular to its axis shows a more or less circular form. Near sets of branches and near the roots, however, the outline is irregular. The center of the circle usually fails to coincide with the axis of the tree.

PARAGRAPH IV.

CYLINDER.

The cubic contents *v* of a cylinder are equal to the height *h* of the cylinder, multiplied by the sectional area *s* of the cylinder.

$$\text{vol. cylinder} = h.s$$

PARAGRAPH V.

APOLLONIAN PARABOLOID.

The volume v of the Apollonian paraboloid is equal to height multiplied by ½ sectional area, or equal to ½ of a cylinder having the same height and the same basal area.

$$\text{vol. apol.} = \frac{h.s}{2}$$

The volume t of the truncated Apollonian paraboloid may be ascertained as:

A. Height of trunk times arithmetical mean of top sectional area and base sectional area.

$$\text{t. apol.} = h\frac{s_1 + s_2}{2}$$

B. Height of trunk times sectional area in the midst of the trunk.

$$\text{t. apol.} = h.s_{\frac{1}{2}}$$

PARAGRAPH VI.

CONE.

The volume of the ordinary cone is equal to height of cone times 1/3 sectional area at the base.

$$\text{vol. cone} = \frac{h.s}{3}$$

The volume t of the truncated cone is equal to 1/3 height of trunk times sum total of top sectional area s_1, basal sectional area s_2, and $\sqrt{s_1 s_2}$

$$\text{t. cone} = \frac{h}{3}(s_1 + s_2 + \sqrt{s_1 s_2})$$

PARAGRAPH VII.

NEILL'S PARABOLOID.

The volume of the Neilloid equals ¼ of its height times sectional area at the base.

$$\text{vol. neil.} = \frac{h.s}{4}$$

The volume of the truncated neilloid t equals

$$\text{t. neil.} = \frac{h}{4}\left(s_1 + s_2 + \sqrt[3]{s_1 s_2}\left[\sqrt[3]{s_1} + \sqrt[3]{u_2}\right]\right)$$

wherein h denotes the height of the trunk; s_1 and s_2 the top sectional area and the basal sectional area of the trunk.

PARAGRAPH VIII.

RIECKE'S, HUBER'S AND SMALIAN'S FORMULÆ.

Formules of practical and scientific application, used here and abroad, to ascertain the contents of logs, are those published by Smalian, Riecke and Huber.

Riecke's formula holds good for n equal to 0, 1 and 2, and is almost correct for the neilloid.

Smalian over-estimates and Huber under-estimates the actual contents of the truncated cone and of the truncated neilloid.

$$\text{Riecke—Vol. of trunk} = \frac{h}{6}(s_1 + 4s_{\frac{1}{2}} + s_2)$$

$$\text{Huber—Vol. of trunk} = h.s_{\frac{1}{2}}$$

$$\text{Smalian—Vol. of trunk} = \frac{h}{2}(s_1 + s_2)$$

$S_{\frac{1}{2}}$ designates the sectional area in the midst of the trunk, whilst s_1 and s_2 represent basal sectional area and top sectional area.

PARAGRAPH IX.

HOSSFELD'S FORMULÆ.

The formule given by Hossfeld is:

$$\text{Vol. of trunk} = \frac{h}{4}(3\,s_{\frac{1}{3}} + s_2)$$

It holds good for cylinder, cone and paraboloid. $S_{\frac{1}{3}}$ designates the sectional area at $\frac{1}{3}$ of the height of the trunk.

PARAGRAPH X.

SIMONY'S FORMULÆ.

Simony's formule requires measurements of sectional areas at ¼, ½ and ¾ of the height of the trunk, thus avoiding the irregularities caused by the roots at the base and by the branches at the top of a tree-trunk.

$$\text{Vol. of trunk} = \frac{h}{3}(2\,s_{\frac{1}{4}} - s_{\frac{1}{2}} + 2\,s_{\frac{3}{4}})$$

This formule holds good for the four standard conoids.

PARAGRAPH XI.

SECTIONAL MEASUREMENT.

The formules given in Paragraphs III. to X. have, in C. A. Schenck's opinion, a historic interest only when applied to whole trees. It is much safer to ascertain the volume of a tree bole by dissecting it into (imaginary) log sections of equal length, considering each of such sections as a cylinder or as a truncated paraboloid. The shorter the length of the sections, the greater the accuracy of the result. In scientific research, the length of a section varies from 5 feet to 10 feet. Obviously, at the top of the bole an uneven length is left, which it might be wise to ascertain as a cone (or paraboloid—Bulletin 20). The volume of the total bole, from stump to tip, equals, if the length of such full section is "l," and that of the top cone is "b," and

1) if sectional areas $s_1, s_2, s_3, \ldots\ldots s_n$ are measured at the big end of each section:

$$\text{vol. bole} = \frac{l}{2}(s_1 + 2\,s_2 + 2\,s_3 \ldots\ldots + s_n) + \frac{b.s_n}{3}$$

2) if sectional areas $s_I, s_{II}, s_{III}, \ldots\ldots s_m$ are measured in the midst of each full section, and sectional area s_n at the basis of the top cone:

$$\text{vol. bole} = l\,(s_I + s_{II} + s_{III} \ldots\ldots + s_m) + \frac{b.s_n}{3}$$

The former formula is based on Smalian and the latter on Huber.

In a similar way, and with still greater accuracy, the more complicated formulas of Riecke, Hossfeld and Simony might be adapted to sectional measurements.

Remark: If the diameter in the middle of a log is larger than the arithmetical mean of the end diameters, then the log contains more volume than the truncated cone, and *vice versa*.

If the sectional area at the midst of the log is larger than the arithmetical mean of the end sectional areas, then the log contains more volume than the truncated paraboloid, and *vice versa*.

PARAGRAPH XII.

MEASURING THE LENGTH OF A LOG.

The length of a log is measured with tape, stick or axe handle. In American logging, logs are usually cut in lengths of even feet, increased by an addition of two inches to six inches, which addition allows for shrinkage, for season checks, for damage to the log ends inflicted by snaking or driving, and for the trimming in the saw mill required to removed such end defects.

In Continental Europe, the standard log lengths are multiples of even decimeters. An excess-length of up to eight inches is neglected.

Crooked logs are made straight by deductions either from the length or from the diameter. Crooked trees should be dissected into very short logs.

The standard length of a New England log is 13 feet.

In the case of big logs, great care must be taken by the sawyers to obtain end-cuts perpendicular to the axis of the log.

The sum of the lengths of logs cut from a tree is termed "used length." The total length of that portion of a bole which is merchantable under given conditions is called "merchantable length."

PARAGRAPH XIII.

MEASURING THE SECTIONAL AREA.

The sectional areas are ascertained with the help of measuring tape, caliper, tree shears, tree compasses, Biltmore measuring stick, etc.

The sectional area is thus derived from the measurement either of the diameter or of the circumference.

For exact scientific investigations the planimeter or the weight of an even-sized piece of paper may be used.

It is best to consider the sectional area of a tree as an ellipse, the surface of which is:

$$\text{surface} = \frac{\pi}{4} D.d,$$

the big diameter D being measured vertically to the small diameter d.

Usually, however, the average diameter of the tree at a given point is found as the arithmetical mean of the big and small diameter at that point measured crosswise and not as the square root of the product of such diameters. Since

$$\frac{D+d}{2} > \sqrt{D.d},$$

the average diameter is invariably, though slightly, over-estimated by crosswise measurement. Hence it is wise to drop, as an arbitrary offset, the excess of fractions of inches over full inches.

The arithmetical mean of the sectional areas belonging to diameters measured crosswise leads to still greater mistakes.

PARAGRAPH XIV.

INSTRUMENTS FOR MEASURING DIAMETERS.

Log calipers are made of pyrus wood or of metal. American make (Morley Bros., Saginaw, Mich.) cost $4.00 each. The moving leg of the caliper is kept in place by a spring or a screw or a wedge.

The best European makes are the "Friedrich" and the "Heyer and Staudinger." Wimmenauer's "addition-caliper" counts the trees and adds their sectional areas automatically.

Short legged calipers, named "Dachshunds" by C. A. Schenck, can be used for trees the radius of which exceeds the length of the legs. The diameter is, in that case, indirectly found by the help of the secant joining the tips of the legs, which are about 5" long.

"Tree compasses," opening from six inches to thirty-six inches, and made of nickel-plated steel, cost (at Morley Bros.) $7.50. "Tree shears" (Treffurth) find the angle formed by the shear-legs when pressed against the tree and directly derive therefrom the diameter or the sectional area of the tree.

The "diameter tape" slung around the tree usually yields too large a diameter, since the circle embraces the maximum of surface by the minimum of length.

The "Biltmore Measuring Stick" can be well used in timber cruising. It requires the exact adjustment of distance between eye and fist of observer (usually 26 inches), and gives directly the diameter at the point of the stick where the sight line passes the tree tangentially. The stick is held horizontally against the tree.

26-INCH BILTMORE MEASURING STICK.

Length on the stick.	Diameter with bark.	Contents of butt log.	Contents of two logs.	Contents of three logs.
2.8"	3"	Allowing three inches for bark and three inches for taper, per log; assuming that all logs are 14' long.		
5.4"	6"			
7.7"	9"			
9.9"	12"			
11.9"	15"	22 ft. b. m.	29 ft. b. m.	39 ft. b. m.
13.8"	18"	56 " "	78 " "	85 " "
15.6"	21"	106 " "	162 " "	184 " "
17.3"	24"	171 " "	277 " "	333 " "
18.9"	27"	253 " "	424 " "	530 " "
20.4"	30"	350 " "	603 " "	774 " "
21.9"	33"	463 " "	813 " "	1066 " "
23.3"	36"	591 " "	1054 " "	1404 " "

Mr. Snead recommends to measure the circumference outside the bark at the big end and to divide the result by 4. He claims that the quotient yields the diameter at the small end inside bark in such a way as to offset mistakes made by Doyle, who under-estimates small logs and over-estimates big logs. Snead's suggestion is good, provided, that the cross section of the log is fairly circular, and that the difference between the small diameter inside bark at the small end and the big diameter outside bark at the big end, amounts to about 7 inches.

Diameter at small end inside bark.	Contents of 16 foot logs, in feet b.m.		
	Doyle.	Snead.	Actual saw cut.
10 inches................	36'	81'	70'
15 "	121'	169'	157'
20 "	256'	289'	279'
25 "	441'	441'	436'
30 "	676'	625'	628'
35 "	961'	841'	856'

The multiples of sectional area (derived from the diameter in inches, but expressed in square feet) by length of log are readily obtained from cylinder tables published by various authors. The log scale or log rule used by the lumbermen (Lufkin rule) gives at a glance the contents of logs 8 to 20 feet long, according to their diameter.

PARAGRAPH XV.

UNITS OF LOG MEASUREMENT IN THE UNITED STATES.

The units of log measurement used in the United States differ greatly. Graves' Handbook gives 43 "rules." The rules can be subdivided into three main grops:

Board feet group (Par. XVI.);
Standard log group (Par. XVII.);
Artificial cubic foot group (Par. XVIII.).

PARAGRAPH XVI.

BOARD-RULES.

A foot board measure is a superficial foot one inch thick, in boards one inch or more in thickness. It is a superficial foot, irrespective of thickness, in boards less than one inch in thickness.

The "board rules" merely guess at the number of feet board measure obtainable from logs of a given diameter. The guess is based upon either graphical considerations, circles of specified diameters being subdivided into parallelograms 1¼ inch thick (diagram method), or else on mathematical considerations, with a view to the fact that a cubic foot of timber should theoretically yield 12 board feet of lumber, whilst the actual loss for slab, saw kerf, etc., will reduce the output by 30% to 50%. In the Biltmore band saw mill, by over one thousand tests, the actual loss for logs 12 inches to 40 inches in diameter has been found to amount to 30%, or close to 1/3. Consequently, it is safe to say that the band saw obtains from a cubic foot of log 8 board feet of lumber.

The number of board feet which a log actually yields depends on:

1. The actual cubic volume of a cylinder having the length and smallest diameter inside bark of the log.

2. The defects of the log (heart rot, wind shake, bad knots, crooks), which are usually eliminated by edger or trimmer.

3. The gauge of the saw, on which the saw kerf depends. The kerf of band saws amounts to ⅛ inch, of circular saws to usually ¼ inch, of inserted tooth saws (of large diameter) to 5/16 inch, of resaws to 1/16 inch.

4. The exactness of the work, especially depending on trueness of saw, proper lining of saw and sawyer's skill; further, on the exactness of the setworks.

5. The thickness of boards obtained; the minimum width of boards permitted; the amount of lumber wasted in the slabs; shrinkage in drying.

The following table compares the contents of logs in cubic feet with their contents in feet board measure as found by C. A. Schenck through a thousand tests of actual yield in yellow poplar, as given by Doyle's rule and by Lumberman's Favorite rule.

The figures given in columns c, f and i show the contents of a log in feet board measure after Schenck's findings, Doyle's and Favorite rules. They are converted into cubic feet (columns d, g, and j) by dividing by 12. The loss incurred in sawing is shown by percentages (columns e, h, k) representing the ratio between the actual cubic contents of a log (as given in column b), and the cubic contents of inch boards (columns d, g, j) obtained from such log.

It will be observed that the loss in the actual yield according to Schenck forms a nearly constant proportion of the cubic contents of a log in the case of all diameters, whilst, according to Doyle's and Favorite rules, the figures of loss vary greatly.

The table refers to logs 12' long sawed into 1-inch boards.

Diameter of Log. Inches.	Contents. Cubic Feet.	Schenck.			Doyle.			Favorite.		
		Feet b. m.	Cubic Feet.	Loss %	Feet b. m.	Cubic Feet.	Loss %	Feet b. m.	Cubic Feet.	Loss %
a.	b.	c.	d.	e.	f.	g.	h.	i.	j.	k.
8	4.2	....	....	....	12	0.9	76	....	....	....
9	5.3	....	....	....	19	1.6	70	....	....	....
10	6.5	....	....	....	27	2.3	65	....	....	....
11	8.0	....	....	....	37	3.1	61	....	....	....
12	9.4	78	6.5	31	48	4.0	57	49	4.1	56
13	11.0	96	8.0	27	61	5.1	54	62	5.2	53
14	12.8	112	9.3	27	75	6.3	51	74	6.2	52
15	14.7	129	10.7	27	91	7.6	48	90	7.5	49
16	16.8	146	12.2	27	108	9.0	46	107	8.9	46
17	18.9	162	13.5	29	127	10.6	44	125	10.4	45
18	21.2	180	15.0	29	147	12.3	42	148	12.3	42
19	23.6	197	16.4	30	169	14.1	40	170	14.2	39
20	26.2	212	17.7	32	192	16.0	39	186	15.5	41
21	28.9	230	19.2	34	217	18.1	37	214	17.8	38
22	31.7	248	20.7	35	243	20.3	36	243	20.3	36
23	34.6	266	22.2	36	271	22.6	35	268	22.3	36
24	37.7	298	24.8	34	300	25.0	33	294	24.5	35
25	40.9	331	27.6	32	331	27.6	32	326	27.2	33
26	44.2	362	30.2	32	363	30.3	31	358	29.8	33
27	47.7	394	32.9	31	397	33.1	30	390	32.5	32
28	51.3	422	35.2	31	432	36.0	30	422	35.2	31
29	55.0	456	38.0	31	469	39.1	29	448	37.3	32
30	58.9	488	40.7	31	507	42.3	28	474	39.5	33
31	62.9	518	43.2	31	547	45.6	27	509	42.4	33
32	67.0	556	46.3	31	588	49.0	27	544	45.3	32
33	71.3	596	49.7	30	631	52.6	26	589	49.1	31
34	75.7	634	52.8	30	675	56.3	26	634	52.8	30
35	80.2	670	55.8	30	721	60.1	25	662	55.2	31
36	84.8	710	59.2	30	768	64.0	25	690	57.5	32
37	89.6	755	62.9	30	817	68.1	24	734	61.2	32
38	94.5	806	66.7	29	867	72.3	23	778	64.8	31
39	99.5	850	70.8	29	910	75.8	24	824	68.7	31
40	104.7	901	75.0	28	972	81.0	23	870	72.5	31

From column e it is evident that the bandsaw wastes close to 1/3 of the cubic contents of a cylindrical log, or 4' b. m. out of every cubic foot.

Consequently, from hardwood logs 12 feet to 16 feet long, the bandsaw will obtain the following *actual* number of feet b. m. (in 4/4" thickness):

(a) from 12 foot logs: $\frac{D^2 \times 0.78 \times 12 \times 8}{144}$, almost equal to $D^2 \times .5$

(b) from 14 foot logs: $\frac{D^2 \times 0.78 \times 14 \times 8}{144}$, almost equal to $D^2 \times .6$

(c) from 16 foot logs: $\frac{D^2 \times 0.78 \times 16 \times 8}{144}$, almost equal to $D^2 \times .7$

Hence it can be stated generally, for logs of medium length "L," that their contents in band-sawed inch lumber approximate

$$\frac{D^2}{10} \times \frac{L-2}{2} \text{ feet b. m.}$$

PARAGRAPH XVII.

STANDARD RULES.

The standard rules do not estimate the contents of a log according to output in board feet, but compare the log with a local average log. Such average logs used to have, in the Northeast, formerly, a diameter of either 19 inches (Adirondacks) or 22 inches (Saranac River) or 24 inches, and were in all cases 13 feet long.

The 19 inch standard log rule is known as Dimick's rule. Here the "standard" or "market" is a log 13 feet long and 19 inches thick. On a 22 inch base it is 13 feet long and 22 inches thick. On a 24 inch base it is 13 feet long and 24 inches thick.

The standard contents of a given log are found by dividing the cubic volume of the standard log into the cubic volume of the given log.

$$v \text{ (in standards) equals: } \frac{d^2 \times h}{19^2 \times 13}$$

Scientifically and mathematically the standard rules are superior to the board rules. One market, at a 19 inch base, is generally considered equivalent to 200 board feet; at a 22 inch base, to 250 board feet; at a 24 inch base, to 300 board feet.

It is easily shown that the output of small logs is not as badly under-estimated, and the output of big logs not as badly over-estimated on the basis of standard rules, as is the case when Doyle's rule alone is applied.

PARAGRAPH XVIII.

CUBIC FOOT-RULES.

In a third group of rules, a new unit, the "artificial cubic foot," is introduced. This group of rules is established by law in Maine and New Hampshire. (See Graves' Handbook, page 45.)

The artificial cubic foot corresponds with a log 12 inches long and 16 inches thick, which naturally contains 1.4 cubic feet. The rule assumes that 40/140 or 28.5% of a log goes to waste in the sawing process as dust or slab.

To quickly transform artificial cubic feet into board feet, the laws prescribe certain arbitrary equivalents, instead of allowing 12 board feet to equal one artificial cubic foot of timber. In New Hampshire, 10 board feet equal one artificial cubic foot. In Maine, 11.5 board feet equal one cubic foot. The rules might be used in connection with a cylinder table, deducting 28.5% from the table data and multiplying the remainder by 10 or by 11.5.

REMARK: According to the Forest Reserve Manual, logs over 24 feet long are treated as 16 foot logs and fractions thereof.

PARAGRAPH XIX.

EQUIVALENTS.

One cubic meter equals 35.316 feet or 1.308 cubic yards.

1,000 board feet of sawn lumber, 1 inch and more thick, correspond with 2.36 cubic meters of sawn lumber.

A product of one cubic meter per hectar (2½ acres) equals a product of 14 cubic feet per acre.

One gallon equals 231 cubic inches in liquid measure, or 268.8 cubic inches in dry measure (which is also ⅛ peck).

One liter equals 1.0567 quarts; one cubic foot equals 7.4805 gallons or 28.3 liters.

Logs yielding when split one cord of wood, will yield, when sawn:

For log diameter:	Feet board measure:
20″	515′
25″	566′
30″	605′
35″	629′
40″	649′

The Forest Reserve Manual adopts 2 cords as equivalent to 1,000 cubic feet b. m., provided that the wood is split from timber 10 inches in diameter and over.

TABLE SHOWING RELATIVE CONTENTS OF LOGS WITHOUT BARK.

Log diameter.	5″	10″	15″	20″	25″	30″
1 cubic foot equals ft. b. m. Doyle	......	4.12	6.2	7.3	8.09	8.64
1 cubic meter per hectar corresponds with ft. b.m. Doyle per acre:........................	......	57.68	86.8	102.2	113.26	120.96
1 cubic meter of log yields ft. b. m. Doyle:...................	44.8	145.5	218.2	258.8	285.7	303.7
1000 ft. b. m. Doyle equal cubic ft:........................	787.4	242.7	161.8	136.4	123.6	116.3
1000 ft. b. m. Doyle equal cubic meters....................	......	6.87	4.39	3.86	3.5	3.29
Artificial cubic feet per 1 ft. of log	......	.4	.9	1.56	2.45	3.51
No. of legal N. H. feet b. m. per 1 ft of log:..................	......	4.	9.	15.6	24.5	35.1
Ft. b. m. Doyle per 1 ft. of log...	......	2.3	7.5	16.	27.5	42.5

PARAGRAPH XX.

XYLOMETRIC METHOD.

The so-called "physical methods," by which the volume of a (particularly irregular) piece of a tree may be accurately found, require either the submersion of the piece in water (xylometric method) or the weighing of the piece after finding its specific gravity (hydrostatic method, § XXI.).

The xylometric method can be applied in three ways, thus:

a. Submerge the wood in a graded cylinder partly filled with water and find the water level before and after submersion.

b. Submerge the wood in a barrel partly filled with water; dip out the water with a gallon measure until the water is as low as it was before submersion. The number of gallons dipped out equals the volume of the wood submerged. One gallon equals 231 cubic inches.

c. Place a piece of wood in an empty barrel of known contents; fill to the rim with water by the gallon. The difference between the known contents and the number of gallons required gives the quantity of wood in gallons.

In *a*, *b* and *c* it is necessary to use wood dry on the outside, to leave the wood in the water a short time only, and to stir it up while in the water so as to remove air bubbles.

PARAGRAPH XXI.

HYDROSTATIC METHOD.

The hydrostatic method deals with specific gravities. Specific gravity is weight of an object divided by the weight of an equal volume of water. In the metric system, it equals weight in kilograms over cube-decimeters of volume. The specific gravity is found by weighing a given body, and then weighing it again immersed in water. It equals weight outside water over loss of weight submerged in water. The division of the metric weight of a large body by the specific gravity of a sample piece yields the volume of the body in cubic decimeters.

Since wood is lighter than water, usually, a piece of lead must be attached to the wood in order to submerge it. There must be ascertained:

1. The absolute weight of the piece of lead, H;
2. The weight of the same piece submerged in water, h;
3. The absolute weight of the wood and of the lead, G;
4. The weight of wood and lead submerged in water, g.

The weight of the wood alone is, consequently, (G—H).

The specific gravity of the wood is

$$s = \frac{G - H}{(G - g) - (H - h)}$$

The volume, in cubic feet, of a quantity of wood weighing *n* pounds, and having the specific gravity *s*, is

$$\text{volume} = \frac{n}{s} \times \frac{1}{63} = \frac{16n}{1000s}$$

The figure 63 represents the weight in pounds of one cubic foot of water.

The specific gravity of wood is greatest close to the stump and in the branches. For some species the outer layers show the greatest specific gravity; for others the inner layers.

Species.	Spec. gravity, air dry.	Weight of lumber per 1000 ft. b. m. in lbs.	Weight of one cord in lbs.
White oak......	.75	3900	3985
Beech..........	.71	3692	3767
Hard maple....	.66	3432	3510
Yellow pine....	.52	2704	2761
Spruce.........	.45	2340	2391
White pine.....	.39	2028	2069

Rules to convert specific gravity into weight per 1,000 feet board measure or into weight per cord read as follows:

1. Multiply specific gravity by 5,200. The result is the weight of lumber per 1,000 feet board measure in pounds.

2. Multiply specific gravity by percentage of solid wood contained in a stacked pile; then multiply the product by 8,050. The result gives the weight per cord in pounds.

PARAGRAPH XXII.

FACTORS INFLUENCING THE SOLID CONTENTS OF CORDWOOD.

The solid contents of wood stacks depend on the size and the form of the pieces composing them and on the method of piling. The solid contents of a cord can be found only by the methods described in Paragraphs XX. and XXI. The European experiment stations have collected data to that end on a very large scale, and have established the following laws:

a. The bigger the pieces of wood in a stack, the larger are the solid contents of the stack.

b. The longer the pieces of wood, the smaller are the solid contents of the stack.

c. Pieces piled parallel and tightly greatly increase the solid contents of the stack.

d. During the drying process, hardwoods shrink approximately by 12%, and soft woods by 9%. The shrinkage is partly offset by the cracking of wood.

These rules are important in the pulp, tanningwood and firewood trade.

PARAGRAPH XXIII.

REDUCING FACTORS FOR CORDWOOD.

The countries using the metric system pile wood in space cubic meters. One space cubic meter equals .274 cord. The pieces contained therein are 3.28 feet long. For such conditions the following figures hold good:

a. First class split wood, obtained from sound pieces 12 inches in diameter, contains per cord 102.4 cubic feet of solid wood (reducing factor 80%).

b. Composed of inferior split wood, obtained from round pieces having a diameter of 6 inches, a cord contains 96 cubic feet of solid wood (reducing factor 75%).

c. In heavy, round branch wood (diameters of about 6½ inches) 87 cubic feet of solid wood are found in a cord (reducing factor 68%).

d. In round pieces of branch wood, 4 inches in diameter, 77 cubic feet are found in a cord (reducing factor 60%).

e. In faggots, 25 to 51 cubic feet make a cord (reducing factor 20% to 40%).

The percentages for broad leafed species are smaller than those for conifers, owing to the latter's straight growth.

At Biltmore, one cord of 8 foot split oak contains about 80 cubic feet; one cord of kindling finely split about 90 cubic feet; one cord of blocks 12 inches long about 100 cubic feet of solid wood.

In the sale of tannin wood it is well to sell 5 foot sticks finely split rather than heavy blocks 4 feet long.

In the sale of pulp wood, 12 foot sticks yield much higher returns than 4 foot sticks, if sales are made by the cord.

PARAGRAPH XXIV.

LOCAL PECULIARITIES WITH REFERENCE TO STACKED WOOD.

Tannin and pulp wood industries sometimes figure at a cord containing 160 stacked cubic feet, equal to 1¼ ordinary cords of 128 stacked cubic feet.

After Graves (page 65), a cord of firewood is in certain sections understood to be 5 feet long, 4 feet high and 6⅖ feet wide.

Under "a cord foot" is understood a stack 1 foot by 4 feet by 4 feet (⅛ cord or 16 stacked cubic feet).

Under "a cylindrical foot" is understood a stacked cubic foot equal to 1/128 cord. The number of such feet (a misnomer for stacked cubic feet) in a stick is

$$\frac{d^2 \times l}{144}$$

(*l* equals length of stick in feet; *d* equals its diameter in inches).

In New England, a cord of pulp wood is sometimes measured by calipering the round sticks composing it, and tables are constructed to facilitate calculation. Proceed as follows:

Ascertain diameter of sticks in inches, square them singly, total the results and divide by 144. Multiply the quotient by length of sticks in feet and divide by 128.

PARAGRAPH XXV.

BARK.

Bark is usually sold and bought by the cord. The tanneries, however, instead of measuring a cord of 128 cubic feet, apply the misnomer "one cord" to a weight of 2,240 lbs. (the long or European ton).

Twelve cords of bark fill one common (old) freight car.

A stack of bark contains from 30% to 40% solid bark. The specific gravity of fresh oak bark is 0.874; dried, it is 0.764.

The bark of white oak has been found (at Biltmore), to comprise:

In trees 20 years old, 55% of the wood, or 35% of the whole bole;
In trees 60 years old, 41% of the wood or 28% of the whole bole;
In trees 100 years old, 29% of the wood or 22% of the whole bole;
In trees 140 years old, 21% of the wood or 17% of the whole bole.

Chestnut oak peeled at Biltmore yields the following results per tree, arranged according to the diameter of the trees 4½ feet above ground:

Diameter of tree chest high in inches.	Dry Bark in Kilogram = $\frac{1}{1000}$ cord, per Tree.		
	Minimum	Average.	Maximum.
6	5	13	27
7	6	17	36
8	8	24	48
9	12	33	61
10	18	45	77
11	26	60	95
12	37	73	114
13	50	88	135
14	65	105	158
15	81	126	180
16	98	150	204
17	116	172	234
18	136	195	266
19	159	224	314
20	181	250	365
21	205	275	...
22	230	305	...
23	265	336	...
24	275	375	...

If the percentage of bark in a log or tree (scaled with the bark) is *p*, then the bark percentage in ratio to the solid wood alone is:

$$\frac{100 \times p}{100 - p}$$

According to thickness of bark and diameter of logs, the following percentages can be given for the ratio:

$$\frac{\text{bark}}{\text{bark plus timber}}$$

Diameter with bark—inches.	Thickness of bark.			
	½"	1"	1½"	2"
10	19 %	36 %	51 %	64 %
15	12 %	24 %	36 %	46 %
20	9 %	19 %	27 %	36 %
25	7 %	15 %	22 %	29 %
30	6 %	12 %	19 %	24 %

SECTION II.—VOLUME OF STANDING TREES.

PARAGRAPH XXVI.

METHODS OF OBTAINING THE VOLUME OF STANDING TREES.

The volume of standing trees may be ascertained

By estimating it (Par. XXVII.);

By measuring heights and diameters (Par. XXVIII.);

By the form factor method, which combines estimates and measurements (Par. XXIX. f. f.).

By these means can be obtained the volume of the bole (from roots to top bud), or the volume of saw timber in any of the 43 log scales, or the volume of firewood in cords, etc., or the total volume, including brush and roots.

Under "used volume," Circular 445 of the United States Bureau of Forestry understands the sum of the volumes of logs cut from a tree; under "merchantable volume" the total volume of that portion of the tree which is merchantable under certain conditions.

PARAGRAPH XXVII.

HELPS AND HINTS TO FIND THE VOLUME OF STANDING TREES.

It is difficult to estimate the cubic contents, wood contents or lumber contents of a standing tree. In the case of estimates in board feet, the result depends on the exclusion or inclusion of crooked and defective pieces, on the taper of the bole, on the soundness of the heart, and on the minimum diameter admissible in the top log. Compare end of Paragraph XXXII.

Most hazardous is the volume estimate of over-aged trees, especially in the case of hardwoods (chestnut).

The following helps might guide the novice:

1. The volume of a sound tree bole, in cubic meters, is equal to

$$\frac{1}{1000} D^2$$

for example, diameter (breast high) 30 c. m.; contents 0.9 cubic meters.

2. The contents of a standing tree, in cubic feet, are about

$$\frac{2}{10} D^2$$

for example, diameter (breast high), 25 inches; contents (from butt to tip), 125 cubic feet.

3. The number of feet Doyle in a tall sound tree equal

$$\frac{3}{2} D^2$$

for example, diameter (breast high), 20 inches; contents 600 feet board measure.

4. The contents of a tree in feet Doyle approximate, assuming that the bole is cut into 16 foot logs, and that the tree tapers 2 inches per log:

$$N \times D\,(D - 12)$$

wherein *N* represents the number of logs obtainable; *D* the diameter of the butt log without bark at breast height.

5. The cordwood contained in a sound bole is:

$$\frac{D^2}{1000} \times C$$

wherein *C* amounts to:

1.5 in the case of trees 8" through;
2.0 in the case of trees 16" through;
2.5 in the case of trees 24" through.

PARAGRAPH XXVIII.

SCIENTIFIC METHODS OF ASCERTAINING THE CUBIC CONTENTS OF STANDING TREES BY MERE MEASUREMENT.

The cubic volume of the bole, on the basis of diameter measurement and height measurement, in the case of a standing tree, may (with the help of climbing iron, ladders, camera or instruments constructed for the purpose) be figured out:

1. According to the formulas of Hossfeldt, Riecke and Simony. In this case, the upper diameters must be measured indirectly.

2. According to Huber's and Smalian's formulas, the diameters of equal sections of the trees being indirectly measured.

3. According to Pressler's formula, which is, for the volume of the bole lying between chest height and top bud, 2/3 of sectional area "S" at chest height times "rectified" height of bole. The rectified height "r" is the distance of chest height from that point of the tree bole which has ½ of the chest height diameter (from the "guide point"). The equation 2/3 r x S holds good for paraboloid, cone and, at a slight mistake, for the neilloid.

The volume of that part of the tree bole which lies below chest height is ascertained (as a cylinder) as being equal to sectional area chest high times 4.5.

REMARK: 4.3' is the chest height usually recognized by the authors; Pinchot adopts 4.5'.
The Pressler formula does not hold good for truncated boles.

PARAGRAPH XXIX.

FORM FACTOR METHOD.

The form factor or form figure method relies on the measurement of the sectional area—usually the one at breast height,—the measurement or the estimation of the total height and the estimation of the form figure.

The form factor is a fraction expressing the relation between the actual contents of a tree, in any unit, and the ideal contents which a tree would have if it were carrying its girth (like a cylinder) up to the top bud undiminished.

The form factor may be given in reference to the volume of the entire tree, inclusive of branches in cubic feet; or in reference to the volume of the bole only; or in reference to the merchantable part of the bole; in the latter case either in feet board measure or in standards or in cords.

Historic Remarks: Some of the older authors on mensuration saw in the cone and not in the cylinder the ideal form of the tree, basing their form factors on the ideal volume $\frac{s \times h}{3}$.

PARAGRAPH XXX.

KINDS OF FORM FACTORS MATHEMATICALLY.

Scientifically we distinguish between:

1. The absolute form factors which have reference only to the volume standing above chest height. They can be readily ascertained with the help of Pressler's formula. Generally speaking, V equals S x H x F. After Pressler, V equals S x 2/3 x r; thus $\frac{\frac{2}{3}r}{H}$ equals F.

For the cone the absolute form factor is one-third; for the neilloid one-fourth; for the paraboloid one-half, whatever the height of the tree may be. Hans Rienicker, the author of these form factors, finds for trees up to 50 years old a form figure of 35% to 43% (in regular, dense German woods); in trees 50 to 100 years old, F increases up to 50%; thereafter occurs a slight decrease below 50%.

2. The normal form factors which were recommended by Smalian, Pressler and other old-time authors. They have reference to the entire volume and necessitate the measurement of the diameter at a given fraction (usually 1/20) of the total height of the tree. Frequently, in case of tall trees, the point of measurement cannot be reached from the ground. The bole form factor for diameters measured at 1/20 of the height is: For a paraboloid, 0.526; for a cone, 0.369; for a neilloid, 0.292. These form factors, like the absolute form factors, are independent of the height.

3. The so-called "common form factors" which do not express, as a matter of fact, the form of the tree, since they do not bear any direct ratio to the degree of the tree curve. They should be termed, more

properly, "reducing factors." These form factors alone are nowadays practically used. They are based on diameter measurements, chest high, and have reference not merely to the bole of the tree, but as well to any parts of the bole, to root and branch wood, to saw logs, etc. These form factors depend entirely on the height. If, for instance, a paraboloid is one rod high, the form factor is 0.673; and if it is 8 rods high, the form factor is 0.517.

PARAGRAPH XXXI.

KINDS OF COMMON FORM FACTORS IN EUROPEAN PRACTICE.

The following kinds of form factors may be distinguished:

1. Tree form factors. The tree is considered as bole plus branches.

2. Timber form factors. The term timber, in Europe, includes all parts of the tree having over 3 inches diameter at the small end.

3. Bole form factors. Bole is the central stem from soil to top bud. For America, form factors would be of great value ascertained by exact measurements and arranged according to diameter, height and smallest log diameter used.

Tables of form factors may be constructed, for instance, for shortleaf pine, on the basis of Olmsted's working plan, pages 17-33.

PINUS ECHINATA.

Diameter.	Merchantable length of bole.	Cubic feet Ideal cylinder.	Form fig.	Contents b. m. Doyle.
16"	36'	50.3	3.6	180'
18"	47'	83.1	3.6	300'
20"	51'	112.1	4.0	440'
22"	56'	147.8	4.0	600'
24"	59'	185.3	4.2	780'
26"	61'	224.9	4.4	980'
28"	62'	263.1	4.5	1190'
30"	62' 6"	306.7	4.6	1420'
32"	63'	351.8	4.7	1680'
34"	63' 6"	400.3	4.8	1930'
36"	64'	457.3	4.9	2200'

The influence of age, soil, density of stand, height, diameter and species on the various form factors, with cubic measure as a basis, has not been fully ascertained.

For the tree form factor, the most important influence, in the case of trees less than 150 years old and raised in a close stand, seems to be that of the height of the tree; with increasing height the tree form factor decreases—*e. g.*, for Yellow Pine:

One pole high	.93
Two poles high	.65
Four poles high	.53
Six poles high	.49

The timber form factor, based on cubic measure of a tree, rises with increasing age and increasing height up to a certain point (for Yellow Pine at 3 poles), provided that the term timber includes all stuff over 3 inches in diameter. The timber form factor is a function more of the diameter than of the height. Timber form factors of Yellow Pine are:

Trees 1 pole high	.07
Trees 2 poles high	.36
Trees 3 poles high	.48
Trees 4 poles high	.46
Trees 7 poles high	.45

The timber form factor in shade bearers is a little higher than that in light demanders (within an age limit of 150 years, for trees in close stand).

The bole form factor can be found, in fact, only for species forming a straight bole free from large branches (hence especially for conifers). The bole form factors, to begin with, are large; with increasing height, they decrease gradually to a par with the timber form factors—*e. g.*, for Yellow Pine:

1 pole high	.70	3 poles high	.49
2 poles high	.55	4 poles high	.47
7 poles high	.45		

European common form factors are collected by thousands of measurements taken in a large variety of localities. It must be remembered that a form factor read from a table is never applicable to an individual tree, and is only applicable to an average tree amongst thousands.

For trees less than 120 years old, the branch wood (stuff less than 3 inches in diameter) comprises from 15% to 28% of the entire tree volume; this figure, in the case of broadleaved species, rises from 25% up to 33%. For trees as now logged in America, the branchwood percentage is naturally very much smaller.

$$\text{The tree form factor equals } \frac{\text{stump plus bole plus branches}}{\text{ideal cylinder}}$$

$$\text{The timber form factor equals } \frac{\text{all stuff having over 3'' diameter}}{\text{ideal cylinder}}$$

$$\text{The bole form factor equals } \frac{\text{bole from ground to tip}}{\text{ideal cylinder}}$$

By form height is meant the product of height (total height of tree) times form factor, or else that much of the height of the ideal cylinder which the tree volume, poured into the ideal cylinder, would fill. Since the form factor on the whole decreases with increasing height, the form height is a fairly constant quantity; at least for trees of merchantable size. Hence the helps and hints given in Paragraph XXVII (to quickly find the volume of standing trees from mere diameter-measurement) may lay claim to correctness in many cases. For instance: The cubic contents of a tree are supposed to be equal to

$$\frac{\pi}{4} \times \frac{D^2 \times H \times F}{144}$$

After Paragraph XXVII., 2, these contents are also

$$\frac{2}{10} \times D^2$$

$$\frac{D^2}{5} = D^2 \times 78 \times H \times F$$

$$H \times F = \frac{288}{7.8} = 37$$

As a matter of fact, the form height of trees 1 foot to 2 feet in diameter is close to 37. And for such trees the equation holds good.

The form height may also be defined as "volume (standards, cords, bark, etc.) per square foot of sectional area chest-high."

PARAGRAPH XXXII.

MEANS FOR EXACT MENSURATION OF STANDING TREES.

The means used to find the exact solid volume of standing trees are instruments for measuring the total height of the merchantable length of a tree; instruments for measuring the diameter at given heights; further tables based on scientific research and experience, or tables merely meant to facilitate calculation. Instruments for measuring diameters far above ground are needed for the use of the formulas given by Riecke, Hossfeldt, Pressler, etc.

The six paragraphs following next dwell upon these topics.

PARAGRAPH XXXIII.

MEASURING THE HEIGHT OF A STANDING TREE.

The height of a tree can be measured by comparing its shadow with the shadow of a stick, say 10 feet long. The "Lumber and Log Book" gives another old method (page 133) of height measurement. If the observer places himself in such a way that a small pole stands between him and the tree at a distance e, and if he marks on the pole two points where his sight, directed towards the top and base of the tree, touches the small pole, and if he further ascertains the distance *E* separating him from the tree, then the height of the tree H equals

$$\frac{E}{e} \times h$$

wherein h represents the number of feet between the two points marked on the pole.

Instruments (hypsometers) for height measuring are sold in many forms. The following are frequently used: Rudnicka's instrument; Pressler's "Measuring Jack;" Faustmann's "Mirror Hypsometer;" Weise's Telescope; Kœnig's "Measuring Board;" Brandis' "Clinometer;" Klausner's instrument; Christen's "Non plus ultra."

Compare Woodman's Handbook, pages 136 to 137, for staff method; page 138 for Faustmann's; page 140 for tangential clinometer; page 143 for mirror clinometer.

Christen's stick is not accurate enough for the measurement of trees over 100 feet high. It does not require the measurement of distances. Its form is improved by Pinchot.

PARAGRAPH XXXIV.

FACTORS INFLUENCING THE EXACTNESS OF HYPSOMETRICAL OBSERVATIONS.

The best results are obtained if the distance between tree and observer equals the height to be measured. In sighting towards the spreading top of a hardwood tree, the observer is apt to overrate the height, the tip being buried in the spreading crown. The line of sight strikes the edge of the crown instead of striking the apex of the crown.

Timber cruisers are usually satisfied to determine the number of logs obtainable from the bole instead of determining the length of the bole. As a matter of fact, where the tree furnishes saw logs only, the total height of the tree is a less reliable indicator of the total contents than the length of the merchantable bole.

Instruments like Faustmann's, Kœnig's and Pressler's cannot be used in windy and rainy weather. Dense undergrowth and dense cover overhead render exact measurement impossible.

PARAGRAPH XXXV.

INDIRECT MENSURATION OF DIAMETERS.

The following instruments are used to measure the diameter of the tree at any point of bole:

a. Winkler, an addition to Kœnig's measuring board.

b. Klausner.

c. An ordinary transit.

d. Wimmenauer's telescope.

PARAGRAPH XXXVI.

PRESSLER'S TELESCOPE.

Pressler's telescope is used to find the "guidepoint" and the "rectified height," as defined in Paragraph XXVIII., 3. The diameter chest-high is taken between the nails at the end of the instrument. Then the telescope is pulled out to a length double the original, divided by the cosin of the angle found between the horizon and the probable sight to the "guidepoint" (at which the observer expects to find one-half the diameter chest-high). Thus, actually, the instrument merely examines the correctness of an original estimate.

The Pressler telescope can be used for finding the merchantable length of any bole. Merely place a stick, equal in length to twice the minimum diameter permissible in a merchantable log, at the foot of the tree, catch it between the nail points and proceed as described.

PARAGRAPH XXXVII.

AUXILIARIES FOR CALCULATION.

Auxiliaries for calculation are:

1. Sectional area tables (Schlich, Vol. III.); engineering books like Haswell's; Bulletin 20; also Green.)
2. Ideal cylinder tables (Schlich and Bulletin 20).
3. Multiplication tables and logarithm-tables.
4. Tables showing contents of logs in any of the 43 rules, according to length and diameter.

PARAGRAPH XXXVIII.

TREE VOLUME-TABLES.

Tree volume tables have been constructed on a very large scale for the leading species in the old country. In the United States, the Government is now beginning to make such tables. The tables give the cubic, lumber and cord wood contents of trees, according to species, diameter and sometimes according to total height and merchantable height (number of logs).

Bulletin 36 reprints the following tree volume tables:

A. According to diameter measure merely.

Page 92. Adirondack White Pine, volume in standards.
Page 94. Pennsylvania Hemlock, volume in feet, b. m., Scribner.
Page 94. Adirondack Hemlock, in standards.
Page 95. Adirondack Spruce in standards.
Page 96. Adirondack Birch, Beech, Linden, Sugar Maple in Scribner, feet, b. m.
Page 96. Adirondack Balsam, in standards.
Page 97. Adirondack White Cedar, in standards.
Page 98. Arkansas Shortleaf Pine, in feet, b. m., Doyle.
Page 98. Missouri Ash, Elm, Maple, Cypress, Gum, Oak, Hickory, Poplar, in feet, b. m., Doyle.
Page 99. Western Yellow Pine, in feet, b. m., Doyle (Black Hills), distinguishing between the volume of first and second growth.
Page 99. Yellow Poplar in Pisgah Forest in feet, b. m., Doyle, distinguishing between good, average and poor conditions of growth.

All tables, except Yellow Poplar tables, are based on the measurement of a large number of trees. The Yellow Poplar tables are based on stem analyses of a small number of trees.

B. According to measurement of height and diameter combined.

Page 93. Wisconsin White Pine (height expressed by the number of logs obtainable from merchantable bole) in feet, b. m., Doyle.

Page 103. Adirondack Spruce expressed in feet, b. m., Scribner, the total height of trees being measured.

Page 104. The same in cubic feet.

Page 105. The same in cords for pulp wood.

Page 106. New Hampshire Spruce in feet, b. m., in New Hampshire cubic feet sanctioned by law.

Pages 108 and 111. Adirondack White Pine with bark, expressed in cubic feet.

Page 110. Adirondack White Pine in feet, b. m., Doyle.

Monographic investigation into the growth of the leading American species is of great importance. The trees of virgin forests are very defective, however, and tree tables can never be constructed giving the contents of defective trees.

—

SECTION III.—VOLUME OF FORESTS.

PARAGRAPH XXXIX.

SYNOPSIS OF METHODS FOR ASCERTAINING THE VOLUME OF FORESTS.

The methods used to find the volumes of entire forests, of forest compartments, tracts, quarter sections, coves, etc., are:

1. Estimating (Par. XL.).
2. Exact calculation after measurements (Par. XLI., f. f.).
3. Combined measuring and estimating (Par. IL., f. f.).

Obviously, measuring without estimation is possible only in forests containing little unsound timber.

PARAGRAPH XL.

ESTIMATION OF FOREST VOLUME.

In primeval woods, where a few assortments only are salable and where stumpage is cheap, the estimation of stumpage necessarily takes the place of the measurement. If any measurements are taken, they are merely meant to back the estimation of the cruiser. The more defective the trees are, the more preferable is judgment and local long experience in the mill and in the woods on the side of the cruiser to mere measuring.

The volume of a wood is ascertained by cruisers' estimates in the following ways:

a. By estimating the number of trees and the volume of the average tree with due allowance for defects.

b. By counting the trees and estimating the volume of average trees with allowance for defects.

c. By estimating the volume of each tree separately, sounding it with an axe, when necessary, and judging its soundness from all sides.

The above methods (*a, b, c*) are applied either to sample plots or to sample strips or to the entire area.

A blazing hammer is often used to prevent duplication; the revolving numbering hammer might be used in case of scattering trees, so as to allow of control of the estimates by the owner, his forester or the prospective purchaser of stumpage.

In irregular forests—hardwood forests of the United States—the only safe way is separate estimating of each individual tree after careful inspecting. Incredible errors result from wholesale and rapid estimates.

In the case of even aged woods, a look at the height growth and a knowledge of the age gives a good idea of the forest's volume. Under very poor conditions of growth, the annual timber production per acre and year is as little as 15 cubic feet; under the best conditions it is as much as 250 cubic feet per acre and year. On an average (on absolute forest soil), 50 cubic feet per acre and year may be considered as the production of healthy and densely stocked forests.

PARAGRAPH XLI.

PRINCIPLES UNDERLYING THE EXACT MENSURATION OF FOREST VOLUME.

The basis of any exact measurement of volume is formed by a survey of the sectional area, combined with an account of the number of stems; sectional area and number are found by calipering (valuation survey). Whatever rule of log measurement may be at stake, the total sectional area of the forest is always of first importance for a survey of forest volume. Next in importance is the calipering of sample trees, followed by an exact survey of their volume. The ratio *r* existing between the volume of the sample trees (expressed in any unit or mixture of units) and the sectional area of the sample trees is identical with the form height (compare Par. XXXII., towards end) of the sample trees. The form height of sample trees properly selected is the form height of the forest. The sample trees are usually cut and worked up into logs, cordwood, tannin wood, etc., for the purpose of volume survey.

$$\frac{V}{S} = \frac{v}{s} = \frac{f.\,h.\,s.}{s} \quad \text{and} \quad V = S.\,f.\,h$$

If the trees of the forest are defective, the sample trees should exhibit average defects.

PARAGRAPH XLII.

FIELD WORK FOR EXACT VALUATION SURVEYS.

The valuation survey requires:

1. Calipering of all trees; the diameter is taken in inches or in multiples of inches. Each species and each height class or age class are or may be taken separately.

2. Entering the takings on tally sheets, arranged as follows:

Diameter.	Spruce.		Beech.	
	Height classes.		Height classes.	
	I	II	I	II
10"				
11"				
12"				
13" etc.				

The larger the trees are, the bigger is the permissible interval of calipering. If trees average two feet in diameter, an interval of 3 inches is permissible, provided that a large number of trees are calipered.

It is a strange fact that the diameter measured from east to west is larger on the whole than the diameter from north to south.

PARAGRAPH XLIII.

BASAL ASSUMPTIONS.

The only assumption made in calculating the volume of the forest after Paragraph XLI. is that the form height of the sample trees equals the form height of the forest. No other estimate or assumption is being made. This premise is much safer than the assumption that the volume of the forest bears the same ratio to the volume of the sample trees which the number of trees in the forest bears to the number of the sample trees. More unsafe is the assumption that the volumes of forest and sample trees bear the ratio of the acreage occupied by the forest on the one hand and by the sample trees on the other hand.

PARAGRAPH XLIV.

SELECTION OF SAMPLE TREES.

Sample trees are selected either irregularly or after a regular plan. In the latter case, it is best to distribute them equally among the diameter classes composing the forest (Draudt-Urich method and Robert Hartig method), instead of selecting sample trees of average diameter.

It is more important that the sample trees should have proper average class-form height (and average defects) than that they should have exact average class-diameters.

PARAGRAPH XLV.

DRAUDT-URICH METHOD.

The Draudt-Urich method is in common use abroad for measuring the forest. The trees of the forest are divided into a number of classes (usually five). Each class contains an equal number of trees, class 1 containing the largest and class 5 the smallest trees. In each class an equal number of sample trees, having about the average diameter of the class, are felled and worked up into logs, cordwood, ties, poles, etc. The form height of all sample trees is obtained as the quotient of their volume (in any unit or mixture of units) divided by their sectional area. Multiplying the sectional area of the forest with this form height, the exact volume of the entire forest and its composition (logs, poles, cords, etc.) are given by one operation.

Sample trees of the average diameter of a class are found by dividing the sectional area of the entire class by the number of trees per class. It is wrong to find the average diameter by dividing the sum total of the diameters by the number of trees.

Diameter Breast High.	Number of Trees.	Diameter Classes of Trees.	Number of Sample Trees.	Average Diameter of Sample Trees.
40″	310	I	11	29″
35″	240			
30″	506			
25″	1226			
(25″)	9	II	11	17″
20″	1040			
15″	1233			
(15″)	1847	III	11	14″
10″	435			
(10″)	2282	IV	11	10″
(10″)	2282	V	11	10″

The advantages of the Draudt-Urich method are:

1. All sample trees can be worked up in a bunch.

2. Not only the entire volume but as well the different grades of timber, fuel, ties, etc., composing the volume are found by one operation.

A large number of sample trees are, however, required, and, since the volumes of the various classes are unequal, a negative mistake made in establishing the volume of one class is not apt to be counter-balanced by a positive mistake made in finding the volume of another class.

PARAGRAPH XLVI.

ROBERT HARTIG METHOD.

Robert Hartig's method forms tree classes containing equal sectional areas—not equal numbers of trees. An equal number of sample trees is cut in each class and worked up separately for each class. The volume of the forest is also obtained separately for each class. Otherwise, the manner of proceeding is identical with that of Paragraph XLV.

Preferable it would seem to cut in each class a number of sample trees having, in the aggregate, the same sectional area. This scheme, however, would represent the big-diameter class by an absurdly small number of samples.

PARAGRAPH XLVII.

AVERAGE SAMPLE TREE METHOD.

If average trees of the entire forest are taken as samples, then the volume of the forest is obtained with smaller accuracy.

The proportion which the different assortments of timber, wood, bark, etc., form in the entire output is not clearly shown by such sampling.

In a normal, even-aged wood the tree of average cubic volume is found by deducting 40% from the total sectional area, beginning with the deduction at the biggest end. The largest tree then left is, or happens to be, *the* average tree of the wood.

PARAGRAPH XLVIII.

EXACT MENSURATION WITHOUT CUTTING SAMPLE TREES.

Frequently the cutting of sample trees for the purpose of a valuation survey is not feasible. The volume of the forest in cubic feet—but not the assortments composing the volume—may then be ascertained as follows:

a. Take the total sectional area of the forest according to diameters and species and, if necessary, according to height classes.

b. Ascertain the bole volume of some available trees with the help of Pressler's tube or by indirect measurement of heights and diameters.

c. Proceed as indicated in the last three paragraphs, keeping in mind, however, that only the cubic volume of the boles is thus obtainable. The branch-wood-percentage or the timber-percentage of the bole must be estimated.

The Hartig method (Paragraph XLVI.) might be combined with the use of Pressler's telescope, and the bole volume of a wood above breast height might be ascertained as 2/3 of the total sectional area of the forest, multiplied by the arithmetical mean of the rectified heights of the sample trees representing the various diameter classes.

$$V = \frac{2}{3} \times \frac{S(r_1 + r_2 + r_3 + r_4 + r_5)}{5}$$

The bole volume below breast height in cubic feet is equal to the sectional area of the wood times 4½.

PARAGRAPH XLIX.

COMBINED MEASURING AND ESTIMATING.

If measuring and estimating are combined, the following typical methods may be used to ascertain the volume of woods:

1. The form factor method (Paragraph L.).
2. The form height method (Paragraph LI.).
3. The volume table method (Paragraph LII.).
4. The yield table method (Paragraph LIII.).

These methods might be used in connection with the so-called "distance figure" of Paragraph LIV.

In applying these methods, one or the other of the three factors of volume (sectional area, height and form factor) are obtained by estimation.

The paragraphs following Paragraph LVIII. give a number of methods practically used and also based on combined measuring and estimating.

PARAGRAPH L.

FORM FACTOR METHOD.

The form factor method ascertains the sectional area by calipering, according to species, and, if necessary, according to height classes. The average height of the wood (by species, classes) is obtained by actual hypsometric measurement. The form factor is read from local form factor tables.

The average height is obtained—not as the arithmetic mean of a number of heights measured, but much more—correctly from the ratio existing between the sum total of the ideal cylinders and the sum total of the sectional areas of the trees hypsometrically measured. The form factors appearing in form factor tables must be averages obtained by many hundreds of local measurements.

Mistakes amounting to up to 25% in the sum total of the volume obtained by the form factor method are not impossible, since average form factors appearing from a form factor table are often at variance with the actual form factor.

Form factor tables for American "second growth" are still lacking. In primeval woods the form factor method seems out of place.

PARAGRAPH LI.

FORM HEIGHT METHOD.

The form heights of merchantable trees are, generally speaking, subject to only small variations. Those, *e. g.*, for Adirondack White Pine scaling from 18" to 36" in diameter breast-high are (for standard rule) close to 1.25.

Multiplying the sectional area of a White Pine woodlot (say 100 square feet) by the form height previously obtained through official measurements (like those by T. H. Sherrard), the volume of the woodlot—in the present example about 125 standards—is easily obtained.

Form height tables based on feet b. m., Doyle, are not as simple as those based on the standard rules and cubic foot rules, owing to the mathematical inaccurary of Doyle's rule, which causes the form heights to be pre-eminently dependent on the diameters.

Form height tables should be constructed for the leading merchantable species in the United States. Of course, such tables are more readily applicable to second growth than to first growth.

The form height tables should exhibit the number of standards, cords, ties, etc., obtainable per square foot of sectional area in each diameter class. In case of defective trees, proper allowance must be made for defects—rather a hazardous risk in primeval hardwoods.

PARAGRAPH LII.

VOLUME TABLE METHOD.

In Paragraph XXXVIII. a number of volume tables have been enumerated, from which the volume of trees of given species and diameter (and height) can be readily read.

A valuation survey of the forest (or of a woodlot or of a sample plot) yields the diameters of the trees stocking thereon. The number of trees found for each diameter class is multiplied by the contents of a tree of that diameter appearing from the volume table. The sum total of the multiples is the sum total of the volume of the forest.

SAMPLE.

Diameter.	Yellow Pine.			Hickory.			Oak.		
	No. trees.	Average volume.	Total volume.	No. trees.	Average volume.	Total volume.	No. trees.	Average volume.	Total volume.
12	30	60	1.800	7	140	980	14	160	1.400
15	42	120	5.040	9	240	2160	5	200	1.000
18	17	300	5.100	18	370	6600	23	350	8.050
21	36	520	18.720	5	500	2500	22	520	11.440
24	33	780	25.740	12	660	7920	22	730	16.060
27	20	1080	21.600	6	840	5040	7	940	6.580
30	10	1420	14.200	3	1050	3150	10	1150	11.500
33	1	1800	1.800	.....	....	....	5	1400	7.000
36	1	2200	2.200	.....	....	....	5	1800	9.000
Totals.			96.200			28.350			72.030

Grand total....................................196.580' B. M.

The volumes of the column "Average Volume" are taken from tables published by the Bureau of Forestry.

PARAGRAPH LIII.

YIELD TABLE METHOD.

All over Europe local yield tables are used to quickly ascertain the volume of pure, sound, even aged woods. For America, such yield tables —normal local yield tables—exist only in the white pine tables given in Pinchot and Graves' pamphlet, "The White Pine."

The method of construction of yield tables appears from Paragraph XCII. and following.

Under yield tables are understood "acre-volume-tables," whilst under volume tables are understood "tree-yield-tables."

Normal yield tables specify the age of even aged and pure woods, the height of such woods and the volume (by assortment) of such woods, according to the productiveness of the soil. An indication for the latter is found in the height growth.

Such yield tables hold good only for woodlots normally stocked. A woodlot is normally stocked "when all local factors of wood production have pronounced themselves unhampered in the annual production of fibre." Normal woods, even of small extent, are extremely rare. In Germany the average wood lacks 25% of being normal. Since the normal yield tables give the yield for normal conditions only, a deduction must be made from the volume indicated by the yield table when applied to a given woodlot, according to the abnormality of the same.

Proceed as follows:

Ascertain age and average height of the trees; find the yield table which gives a similar height for the same age; reduce the volume indicated by this yield table and for this age, by estimating the deficiency of the growing stock.

Obviously, there is much room for guessing, since neither height nor form figure nor sectional area in woodlots abnormally stocked can lay claim to normality.

Schuberg, denying a truism otherwise generally acknowledged, claims that the height alone does not indicate the productiveness of the soil.

At present, normal yield tables are of little use in American forestry.

PARAGRAPH LIV.

DISTANCE FIGURE.

Under "distance figure," an invention of Kœnig's, is understood the quotient *a* formed by the side *l* of the average growing space of a tree (considered as a square) and by the diameter of the average stem *d*.

$$a = \frac{l}{d}$$

The average distance from tree to tree and the average diameter of a number of trees is obtained by a number of measurements in the forest. If the area of the forest is *F* square feet, then the sectional area of the forest is

$$= \frac{\pi}{4} \times \frac{F}{a^2} \text{ square feet.}$$

The actual test proves the fallacy of Kœnig's assumptions. The explanation lies in the fact that the average diameter of a wood is not the arithmetical mean of the diameters composing it. Further, the growing space of a tree is not a square.

The actual growing space per tree can be correctly ascertained by laying a sample strip through the forest, counting at the same time the trees within the strip. The sectional area of the forest is obtainable, however, without greater trouble and with much greater accuracy, from the product calipered sectional area of trees in the sample strip times area of the forest over area of the sample strip.

On an acre of average soil, there is on an average room for the following numbers of healthy trees, according to age:

At 20 years 1,600 specimens.
At 50 years 600 specimens.
At 100 years 240 specimens.
At 150 years 150 specimens.

PARAGRAPH LV.

ALGON'S UNIVERSAL VOLUME TABLES.

So-called "universal volume tables" have been constructed by H. Algon, a Frenchman. For a description of these tables see "Indian Forester" of July, 1902.

The volumes given for each diameter of trees, whatever the species be, are presented on a number of tables as follows:

Diameter.	Volume in Cubic Feet.				
	Table 1.	Table 5.	Table 10.	Table 15.	Table 20.
6"	2.	3.	4.	6.	8.
9"	5.	8.	10.	16.	18.
12"	9.	15.	21.	27.	33.
15"	19.	28.	39.	50.	61.
18"	27.	39.	59.	69.	84.
21"	43.	60.	83.	109.	128.
24"	54.	78.	108.	138.	168.
27"	72.	107.	147.	188.	228.
30"	87.	129.	177.	228.	276.
33"	111.	163.	221.	288.	349.
36"	129.	189.	258.	333.	405.

The tables are used as follows:

1. Caliper the entire forest according to diameters and species.

2. Measure a number of type trees, selected at random, after felling them.

3. Find that volume table amongst the 20 tables given which best corresponds with the diameters and volumes of the type trees. Apply the volume table, which is found to be the proper one, to all diameter classes calipered in the woods.

Objections to the method are:

a. The danger of mistakes is very great. In an absolutely even aged wood, one tree of 15 inches diameter may easily show 50% more volume than another tree of the same diameter, the latter being more tapering and shorter.

b. In an uneven aged wood the tables are necessarily wrong because the form height is a function of age as well as of height and diameter.

c. The method does not give any idea of the proportion of logs, fuel, bark, etc.

Algon calls these tables "universal" assuming that they hold good for all species of the universe.

PARAGRAPH LVI.

SCHENCK'S GRAPHIC METHOD.

This method, as well, can be used only for sound woods. No calculation is required. The procedure is:

1. Caliper the whole wood.
2. Cut sample or type trees of small, big and average diameters, find the contents of each tree separately, together with the composition of contents as logs, fuel and bark.
3. On a piece of cross section paper, use as many units along a horizontal line as there are trees (or tens or hundreds of trees) calipered.
4. Mark the unit which each sample tree, according to its diameter, would occupy if the biggest tree were placed to the right and the smallest to the left of the horizontal line.
5. Enter over the marked units the volume of the type trees (according to the composing factors, if required) in square units. A square unit might correspond with ten feet board measure, or with 1/100 of a cord, etc.
6. Draw a line joining the ends of the columns, adjusting it by an average curve.
7. Measure the space (in square units) between the curve and the horizontal line with the help of a planimeter; the number of square units giving directly the number of feet Doyle, or of cords, etc.

If there are several assortments of volumes, several curves must be drawn. This method allows of separating the volumes of trees allotted to the several diameter classes. Mathematical errors are, practically, excluded.

PARAGRAPH LVII.

FACTORS GOVERNING THE SELECTION OF A METHOD OF VALUATION SURVEY.

In the case of a valuation survey ("stock taking") in the woods, the following points must be considered:

a. The degree of exactness required, which depends on the purpose at stake (*e. g.*, scientific investigations, or preparation for logging, or taxation).

b. The regularity, uniformity and soundness of the growing stock.

c. The minimum diameter of logs; assortments; marketability of species.

d. The possibility of cutting sample trees.

e. The expense permissible.

The question usually arises whether the entire forest or sample plots only must be surveyed. The answer depends on the configuration of the ground, uniformity of the growing stock as to size, age, species and quality of its components; further on the value of stumpage, on the accuracy required, on the available time and on the available funds.

The following *METHODS OF VALUATION SURVEYS* might be distinguished:

I. *Cutting sample trees.*

a. Sample trees selected for about five diameter classes, each class containing about one-fifth of the number of trees present (Draudt-Urich method).

b. Sample trees selected for about five diameter classes, each class containing about one-fifth of the sectional area of all trees present (Robert Hartig method).

c. Sample trees selected as average-diameter-trees of the entire forest (Old Bureau method).

d. Sample trees selected at random—*e. g.*, from dead and down trees (C. A. S. method—applied in the Balsams; Algon Universal tables; Graphic method).

e. Stem analysis, together with investigations as to thickness of bark.

II. *Without cutting sample trees.*

a. Measuring height and diameter and estimating form figure of sample trees.

b. Measuring rectified heights and diameters.

c. Measuring merely diameters and estimating form heights.

d. Photographing sample trees, having a scale—say a stick 6 feet long—on the picture.

III. *With the help of volume tables.*

IV. *With the help of yield tables.*

PARAGRAPH LVIII.

FACTORS INFLUENCING THE SELECTION OF SAMPLE PLOTS.

If sample plots are taken, there must be determined:

a. The number, situation and distribution of the sample plots.

b. The absolute and relative size of the sample plots. The Bureau of Forestry prescribes sample plots equalling from 1 to 4½% of the forest. The "Forest Reserve Manual" prescribes 5% or more.

c. The form of the sample plots and the manner by which the size of the sample plot is ascertained.

In Europe an ordinary workman calipers, on an average, 5,000 trees (in maximo 12,000 trees) per day. In Pisgah Forest 500 trees is a good day's work for one estimator and one helper.

PARAGRAPH LIX.

SIR DIETRICH BRANDIS' METHOD.

The Brandis method is indicated where the object at stake consists in a rapid survey of the stumpage on large tracts, like the vast Teak and Bamboo forests of upper Burmah.

Traversing existing trails of known length on horseback, the estimator records the diameter of each tree within a given distance (say 200 yards) on either side of the trail.

The widths of the strips traversed multiplied by the length of the trail yields the area of the sample plot. The number of the trees of the various diameters found on the sample strip appears from the records.

PARAGRAPH LX.

PINCHOT-GRAVES METHOD ADOPTED ON DR. WEBB'S ESTATE.

1. Sample acres, measuring 4 x 40 poles, are irregularly laid into swamps, hardwood slopes and spruce slopes. The sum total of the sample acres is 3½% of the total acreage.

2. The length of a sample acre is actually chained off, whilst the width is ascertained (two poles to the left and two poles to the right of the chain) by tape, by pacing and by estimating.

3. The sites of the sample acres are not marked on maps.

4. All trees on the sample acres are calipered; a number of heights are taken on each sample acre; for each sample acre the average diameter, the average height and the number of trees are ascertained.

5. From these averages is deduced, for all sample acres, the average diameter, the average height and the number of trees. All these data, of course, must be given for the various species separately.

6. From volume tables previously constructed the volume of the trees having average height and average diameter is obtained and is multiplied by the average number of trees.

7. This multiplication yields the volume of the average sample acre.

Objections to this method of valuation survey are:

a. The tree of average diameter has neither average volume nor average height.

b. The average diameter should be obtained from the fraction "total sectional area over number of trees." It cannot be obtained correctly from the fraction "sum total of diameters over number of trees." Similar objections hold good for average height.

c. Guessing at the width of a strip, in dense growth, is rather risky.

REMARK: Bulletin 36, page 125, states that volumes are now computed by the Bureau either by averaging the volumes found for the sample acres, thus obtaining the volume of a model acre as

$$\frac{v_1 + v_2 + v_3 + \ldots\ldots + v_n}{n}$$

(wherein *n* equals the number of sample acres); or by summing up all trees of each diameter class, by dividing each sum by the number of sample acres, and by thus finding for a model acre the average number of trees for each diameter class. In both cases the volumes for each diameter class are read from volume tables.

Allowance for defects is made according to local experience, all trees being calipered as if they were sound.

PARAGRAPH LXI.

THE GRIDIRONING METHOD.

1. Work with compass (if a topographical map is required, also with barometer or clinometer) and with several tapes or ropes. These ropes are meant to denote the sides of a strip; within the strip the sectional areas are taken with calipers or Biltmore sticks.

2. The tapes move continuously with the caliper men, and there is no stopping. The compass man keeps ahead of the measuring crew. One of the outside "tapers" has the correct length desired for a section. His tape must be run straight. The inner tapes may make snake lines. The tally man uses a fresh tally sheet for each section.

3. All strips lie parallel and are equidistant. The width of the strips depends on the density of growth, smallest diameter calipered, available help and accuracy required.

4. The distance between two parallel strips depends upon accuracy required, width of strip and variety of configurations.

5. Each strip is divided into sections of equal length. The tally sheet gives for each section the diameters (with bark) of the trees in that section; further, remarks on the run and altitudes of ridges and creeks traversed, on roads, settlements, existing surveyor's marks, forest fires, forest pasture, previous lumbering and regeneration. The number of seedlings in a section might be approximately given under the same head.

REPORT ON , bgg at for C. A. SCHENCK & CO., Biltmore, N. C.

	Strip.........				Sectio n No...				.....feet long			Grade							
	1	2	3	4	5	6	7	8	9	10	11	12	13	14	15	16	17	18	19
6																			
9																			
12																			
15																			
18																			
21																			
24																			
27																			
30																			
33																			
36																			
39																			
42																			
45																			
48																			

Compass Course:

Farms: whose
Reached at.................ft.

Trail or road. g. m. b. N) •
Called
Reached at.................ft.

Creek.................ft. wide
Called W) • (E
Reached at.................ft.

Ridge, sharp, flat
Called • (S
Reached at................. ft.

Few, some, many seedlings of...............
Few, some, many saplings of...............
Few, some, many poles of...............
Few, some, many fireshoots of ....

Ending at:

Advantages of the gridironing method are:

a. A topographical map is obtained at a slight extra expense. The original survey is controlled and the area of the tract is re-ascertained.

b. Cruisers are forced to traverse all sorts of country and are not allowed to skip swamps, cliffs, etc.

c. The proportion of flats, ridges, slopes, swamps, farms, or farm soil, pastures, etc., is found at the same time.

d. The strips may be used as permanent statistical sample plots, if they start from definite points (corners) and run in definite directions.

e. The procession of the cruisers is uninterrupted by stops; hence no loss of time.

For a picture of a convenient tally sheet holder see Graves' Handbook, page 123.

The gridironing method has been adopted by the working plan division in a somewhat altered form as follows (Bulletin 36, page 120):

1. Strips are always one chain (66 feet) wide. A section invariably comprises one acre equaling 1 x 10 chains.

2. The measuring tape is trailing in the center of a strip; two caliper men (proceeding one at the left, the other at the right hand of the tape) caliper a belt one-half chain wide, estimating the width at either side of the central tape.

3. The compass man or tally man with the front end of the tape attached to his belt goes ahead and stops at the end of every chain, allowing the calipers to catch up.

4. Thus there are ten stops for every acre; after 10 chains the tally man enters general notes.

5. Heights may be measured by a separate crew.

A crew of four men calipers in merchantable timber 20 to 40 acres per day; in small and merchantable timber from 15 to 25 acres per day; in longleaf pine up to 65 acres per day.

PARAGRAPH LXII.

FOREST RESERVE METHODS.

Roth's Forest Reserve Manual gives three methods of valuation survey, No. 1 and No. 2 being sample-area-methods, and No. 3 an entire-area-method.

1. Sample circles with a radius of 20 yards, the circle containing ¼ acre; the radius is estimated, or paced from a central stick. Two sub-methods are permitted, namely:

a. Count the number of trees of merchantable size; estimate the average tree according to log length, taper and thickness of bark; estimate the percentage of defectiveness (from 10% to 40% after Manual, page 49).

b. Caliper the trees in the circle into two-inch classes; estimate the average tree for each class and allow for defects as before.

In both cases a map must show the site of the sample circles. The circle method is not allowed in scattering timber. At least 5% of the entire area must be sample-circled.

2. Sample strips. Strips should be four rods wide, should run across ridges, should be shown on a map. Otherwise proceed as under 1.

3. The "forty" method is used on surveyed land. It is an entire-area method applied to 40 acres. The sides of a "forty" are 80 x 80 rods, equal to 440 x 440 yards. Prescriptions:

a. Traverse each "forty" on lines about 100 yards apart, thus crossing 4 times.

b. Halt at every 100 yards and estimate the trees within a square of 100 yards surrounding the stopping place.

c. If possible, have a compass man control the length and the direction of your runs.

PARAGRAPH LXIII.

SAMPLE SQUARES.

Sample squares containing about one acre are used in Maine and in Northern New York. The side of a sample square is 14 rods. A cruiser, from the center of the square, under the density of the growth existing in Maine and New York, can overlook a circle of 7 poles radius surrounding him. Hence, as a matter of fact—or rather of theory—he skips the corners of the square, counting only the trees in a circle which has the side of the square for its diameter. The square contains 196 square rods, whereas the circle of 7 poles radius contains 155 square rods. The cruiser estimates the contents of all trees within the "square" from his central standpoint.

PARAGRAPH LXIV.

PISGAH FOREST METHOD OF 1896.

1. The diameters of all trees promising to yield a log are measured in diameter classes of ½ foot interval by a crew of 4 to 5 helpers armed with Biltmore sticks.

The diameters are measured (or often estimated if beyond reach) at the point above which the tree is supposed to be sound.

2. Each tree measured is marked by a blaze. The foreman enters on a tally sheet the species and the diameters called out by the helpers. A special tally sheet is used for each cove.

3. The average contents of the diameter classes are estimated with the help of sample trees selected for each species and each diameter—a very uncertain estimate owing to the unsoundness of the trees.

4. Each cove is numbered or lettered to correspond with the tally sheet on a tree standing at the outlet of the cove.

PARAGRAPH LXV.

PISGAH FOREST METHOD FOR STUMPAGE SALE, BARK SALE AND LUMBERING OPERATIONS.

1. Each tree is approached individually, its diameter measured and its defects, especially its hollowness, examined by "sounding." The diameter measure and the estimated volume are entered on a tally sheet opposite the number of the tree, which is inserted in the stump of the tree by a stroke of the "revolving numbering hammer."

2. One cruiser and one helper tally 400 trees per day.

3. The method allows of ready control by the owner, the forester and the buyer. It is adapted to hardwood forests in a rough mountainous country where the merchantable trees per acre are few; and where no tree is, practically, free from defects. (Compare Graves' Bulletin No. 36, page 115).

PARAGRAPH LXVI.

HENRY GANNETT'S METHOD, ADOPTED FOR THE TWELFTH CENSUS.

1. Base the estimate on the cruising reports obtainable from the local lumber companies and railroad companies.

2. Control the applicability of the estimates to huge tracts by traversing them and by overlooking them from a mountain top.

Mr. Gannett expects that mistakes made in one county will be offset by those made in another.

PARAGRAPH LXVII.

A "FORTY" METHOD USED IN MICHIGAN.

1. A "forty" (a square of 80 x 80 poles) is subdivided into 10 rectangles of 4 acres each, measuring 16 x 40 rods.

2. The cruisers estimates when entering a rectangle. He counts the number of trees on every 4 acres and multiplies the number by the size of the average tree.

3. For each "forty" the cruiser records in a memorandum the factors influencing the logging operations or the timber values, notably the swamps, ridges, forest fires, degree of defectiveness, facilities of transportation.

A central line traversing the "forty" in a north and south direction is sometimes kept by a compassman assisting the cruiser. The outer lines of the "forty" are plain from the official survey marks.

A number of variations of this method exist, according to the custom of local cruisers and according to the predilections of the lumbermen, largely governed by the value of stumpage. Compare Graves' Bulletin 36, page 116.

PARAGRAPH LXVIII.

DR. FERNOW'S "FORTY" METHOD USED AT AXTON.

1. Each "forty" is subdivided into 16 squares of 2½ acres each, the sides of a square being 20 x 20 poles.

2. The head estimator, stepping from the corner of the square 10 poles east (or west) and 10 poles north (or south) places himself in the center of the square.

3. Helpers (students) are sent out, four in number, towards the northeast, northwest, southeast and southwest, each helper reporting the diameter and species of the trees found in that one-quarter of the 2½ acres which is allotted to him.

4. The "forties" are carefully surveyed and surrounded by carefully trimmed lines. The outlines of the 2½ acre sections are merely paced.

CHAPTER II.—AGE

PARAGRAPH LXIX.

AGE OF TREES CUT DOWN.

The age of trees cut down is found by counting the annual rings on a cross section (preferably an oblique cut) made as low above the ground as possible. Allowance must be made for the "stump years," by which is understood the number of years required by the top bud of the seedling, after sprouting, to reach the stump height ("cutting height," after Circular 445).

Ring-counting in the case of even-porous hardwoods requires the use of a lens and of some coloring liquid (aniline and ferro-chloride) on a disc planed with a knife, a chisel or a hollow planer.

The difference of the ring-numbers on the stump and the ring-numbers at any place higher up indicates the number of years used by the top bud of the tree to traverse the intervening distance. Endogenous trees do not form any rings.

False rings are formed under the influence of late frost, early frost, drought, fire and insect pests. They do not run all around the tree.

As long as the tree lives, it must annually form a ring of growth (or rather an additional coat, the sleeves of which cover the branches), the outside of which becomes a layer of bark, the inside of which is a layer of wood. In tropical countries this rule does not hold good provided that there is no change of season.

The formation of rings in the branches is regular. Branch-rings are, however, eccentric and elliptical. The formation of rings in the roots is said to be irregular, not representing the age of the root, possibly because there is no or little change of seasons in the soil.

PARAGRAPH LXX.

AGE OF STANDING TREES.

The age of standing trees can be estimated only when regular annual whorls of branches can be counted.

The records of seed years and the history of the forest kept by many forest administrations usually give an idea of the age of the trees.

PARAGRAPH LXXI.

AGE OF A FOREST.

The age of a forest is the average age of the trees composing it.

In the case of a thicket suppressed for a long time by the superstructure of a leaf canopy overhead, a so-called "economic age" is frequently substituted for the actual age. In the case of Adirondack spruce, for example, a diameter of 1 inch in the center of the trunk had better be counted, as, say, 15 years, although it may contain as many as 60 rings.

The mean age of an uneven-aged wood is defined as follows:

1. That number of years which an even-aged wood would require on the same soil, in order to produce the same volume as is now at hand.

2. That number of years which an even-aged wood would require in order to produce at the time of maturity the same volume which the uneven-aged wood is likely to produce.

The latter definition is scientifically more correct. Unless it is adopted, an uneven-aged wood may get over 20 years older in 20 years, owing to the fact that the trees dying in the meantime are mostly minors in age.

CHAPTER III.—INCREMENT

SECTION I.—INCREMENT OF A TREE.

PARAGRAPH LXXII.

THE KINDS OF INCREMENT.

The following kinds of increment must be distinguished:

a. Increment of height, diameter, sectional area and volume.

b. Current annual increment, current periodic increment and total increment.

c. Average annual increment, average periodic increment and average increment at the age of maturity.

d. Increment of the past and increment of the future.

e. Absolute increment and relative increment.

The increment of stems cut down is found by counting and measuring the annual rings on several cross sections.

The term "stem" or "tree analysis" designates an investigation into the past height growth, diameter growth and volume growth of a tree.

Circular 445 of the Bureau of Forestry defines the term "increment," somewhat narrowly, as follows: "The volume of wood produced by the growth in height and diameter of a tree or of a stand."

For definition of the term "tree analysis," see Circular 445 of Bureau of Forestry.

This circular distinguishes between:

1. Stump-analysis, being a tree analysis which includes measurements of the diameter growth at given periods on the stump only, no matter what other measurements it may comprise;
2. Section-analysis, being a tree analysis which includes measurements of the diameter growth at given periods upon more than one section of a tree;
3. Partial tree (stump or section) analysis, wherein the measurement of the diameter growth at given periods covers a portion only of the total diameter growth.

PARAGRAPH LXXIII.

HEIGHT INCREMENT.

The height increment, from the silvicultural standpoint, is of interest to the forester dealing with mixed woods.

The difference between the number of rings found on two separate cross sections through the bole indicates the number of years which the tree has required to grow through the distance lying between these two sections. By counting the number of rings at several cross sections, one of which is made as close to the ground as possible, the current and the average height growth (increment) may be obtained by arithmetical or by graphical interpolation.

A dense cover favors height increment. In rare instances, however, the stand of saplings or poles is so close that the height increment of the individual suffers from lack of food.

PARAGRAPH LXXIV.

THE CURRENT HEIGHT INCREMENT.

In the high forest the current annual height increment reaches a maximum at an early age; passing this maximum, it sinks more or less rapidly. The culmination of the current annual height increment occurs the much earlier and its slackening after said culmination goes on at a more rapid rate if

1. the species is fast growing and light demanding;
2. the tree observed belongs to the dominant class;
3. the soil is good.

For yellow pine the culmination of the current annual height increment occurs amongst dominant saplings between the 10th and 15th years; for spruce at about the 20th year; for beech and fir between the 25th and 30th years. Suppressed trees show the maximum of current height growth much later than dominant trees.

As a general rule for all species, in case of dominant trees, the longest shoot is made 10 to 15 feet above ground. Slow growing species, shade bearers and trees stocking on poor soil reach that level at a later date than trees and species growing under reversed conditions.

In the case of coppice forest, the maximum of the current height growth lies in the first three years of the life of the shoot. For oak coppice, the following table may serve as an illustration of height growth:

GROWTH IN FEET.

Age in years	10	20	30	40	50
Actual height	13′	23′	30′	37′	43′
Current annual increment	1.3′	1.0′	0.7′	0.65′	0.63′

PARAGRAPH LXXV.

THE AVERAGE HEIGHT INCREMENT.

The average annual height increment culminates later than the current annual height increment, and, after the culmination, it decreases at a less rapid rate than the current annual height increment. The average annual height increment culminates at the very age at which it is equal to the current annual height increment.

As long as the average increment increases the current increment is larger than the average. The average increment still rises during a period of decrease of current increment.

These laws hold good not only for height growth, but also for the growth of diameter, sectional area and volume. They are based merely on mathematical principles and are, for that reason, independent of species, climate and soil.

If "a" denotes the current annual increment, and if "d" denotes the average annual increment, whilst the indices 1, 2, 3, etc. (up to *n*), indicate the year of increment, then the following five equations hold good:

$$n \times d_n = a_1 + a_2 + a_3 \ldots\ldots + a_n$$

$$(n + 1)\, d_{n+1} = a_1 + a_2 + a_3 \ldots\ldots a_n + a_{n+1}$$

$$(n + 1)\, d_{n+1} = n \times d_n + a_{n+1}$$

$$n \times d_{n+1} = n \times d_n + a_{n+1} - d_{n+1}$$

$$n\,(d_{n+1} - d_n) = a_{n+1} - d_{n+1}$$

PARAGRAPH LXXVI.

RELATIVE INCREMENT OF THE HEIGHT.

The percentage of height increment forms, from the start on, an irregularly descending progression.

If the height is *h* at the beginning of a period of *n* years of observation and *H* at the end of that period, then

$$h \times 1.op^n \text{ equals } H$$

and

$$p \text{ equals } 100\sqrt[n]{\frac{H}{h}} - 100$$

Pressler substitutes for this formula in case of short periods of observation the following:

$$p = \frac{200}{n} \times \frac{H - h}{H + h}$$

This formula is derived as follows: Imagine that we are in the midst of the period of *n* years. At that time, the increment is apt to be $\frac{H - h}{n}$, whilst the height at that time is apt to be $\frac{H + h}{2}$; hence, for that middle year, the equation is:

$$\frac{p}{100} = \frac{H - h}{n} \times \frac{2}{H + h}$$

PARAGRAPH LXXVII.

DIAMETER INCREMENT.

The current diameter increment is obtained by counting and measuring the rings on a disk through the tree. It is generally best to count from the bark towards the center, along two radii standing perpendicular to each other.

The general laws of diameter growth are identical with those of height growth relative to culmination, decrease and increase of absolute (Paragraph LXXV.) as well as of relative (Paragraph LXXVI.) increment.

If we exclude the butt-piece below chest-height, the annual rings along the tree bole measured at various elevations above ground show a gradual increase of width with elevation, provided that the leaf canopy of the forest is complete and uninterrupted—*e. g.*, the width of the ring 50 feet from the ground, formed in 1903, is greater than the width of the ring formed 20 feet above ground in the same year.

For trees standing in open crown-density, the width of the ring decreases with the elevation above the ground, especially within the crown itself.

A tree standing in a thin crown-density may show an even width of ring all over the tree bole.

For very old trees in closed stand it is sometimes found that the diameter, say 40 feet above ground, is larger than the diameter, say, 20 feet above ground.

The rings on a disk are not actually circles; they more closely approach the form of eccentric ellipses (see Paragraph XIII.).

PARAGRAPH LXXVIII.

SECTIONAL AREA INCREMENT.

The increment of the sectional area is obtained from the increment of the diameters. Where greater exactness is required, and especially in case of irregular rings, the planimeter or the weight of a piece of paper having the form of the sectional area may be used for measuring to good advantage (Paragraph XIII.).

The increment of the sectional area at chest height depends on the crown density overhead; further, on the quality of the soil. At chest height the culmination of the current annual sectional area increment takes place, in the case of dominant trees, fast growing species and complete cover overhead, between the years 40 and 70.

The culmination of the current annual sectional area increment occurs always later than the culmination of the current height and diameter increment. After culmination it remains uniform for a long time.

The absolute increment of a sectional area higher up on the bole, compared with the absolute increment at chest height, is found to be equal to it in the case of dominant trees; larger in the case of suppressed trees; and smaller in the case of isolated trees.

Pressler establishes as the "law of bole formation" the following rule: "The absolute increment of the sectional area at any point of a bole is directly proportioned to the leaf surface above that point."

This rule is, on the whole, correct. An unexpected swelling, however, is often found at 9/16 of the height of the tree. Within the crown of the tree, the decrease of sectional area increment is rapid.

PARAGRAPH LXXIX.

RELATIVE INCREMENT OF DIAMETER AND OF SECTIONAL AREA.

The increment percentage at any point of the bole, like all increment percentages, forms a constantly but irregularly descending progression.

At any point of the bole the increment percentage of the sectional area is the double of the increment percentage of the diameter.

Schneider gives a handy formula for the sectional area increment percentage, viz.:

$$P \text{ equals } \frac{400}{nd}$$

wherein d represents the diameter at the beginning of the period of observation, and wherein n indicates the number of rings per inch at the time of observation.

The percentage of the sectional area increment increase along the bole with increasing height of the disk measured, excepting, however, possibly, the case of very isolated trees.

The average sectional area increment percentage of the bole is found at a point a little below one-half of the total height, namely, at about 0.45 of the total height from ground.

PARAGRAPH LXXX.

VOLUME INCREMENT.

The (current and future) volume increment of standing trees is of great interest to forest financiers; it can be estimated only, and cannot be measured exactly.

The volume increment of trees cut down may be ascertained as follows:

1. By the sectional method, or by "section analysis" (Paragraph LXXXI.).

2. From the increment of sectional area chest high, height increment and form figures (Paragraph LXXXIV.).

3. From the increment of sectional area in the midst of bole (Paragraph LXXXV.).

4. On the basis of the average annual increment (Paragraph LXXXVII., last 4 lines).

PARAGRAPH LXXXI.

SECTION ANALYSIS.

The section-method is a complete tree analysis by sections. The entire bole is divided into a number of sections, preferably of even length, at both ends, or, better, in the midst of which the periodical increment of the sectional area is ascertained (compare Paragraph XI.).

In the latter case, multiplying such sectional areas (in square feet) as belong to the same age of the tree by the length (in feet) of the sections, the volumes (in cubic feet) of the different sections at given ages are obtained.

The "top pieces," however, must be figured out separately, their length differing from the even length of the sections. These top pieces are usually considered as cones, and their volumes are ascertained as one-third height times basal area of top piece. The basal area of the top piece is identical with the upper area of the uppermost full section of a given age.

EXAMPLE FOR HUBER-SECTIONS TEN FEET LONG.

Total height	25 feet.	40 feet.	67 feet.
Total age	20 years.	40 years.	60 years.
Sectional area of Section 1	0.34 sq. ft.	0.78 sq. ft.	1.23 sq. ft.
Sectional area of Section 2	0.15 sq. ft.	0.45 sq. ft.	0.87 sq. ft.
Sectional area of Section 3	...	0.25 sq. ft	0. 64 sq. ft.
Sectional area of Section 4	...	0.03 sq. ft.	0.53 sq. ft.
Sectional area of Section 5	...	...	0.25 sq. ft.
Sectional area of Section 6	...	...	0.04 sq. ft.
Summary of sectional areas	0.49 sq. ft.	1.51 sq. ft.	3.56 sq. ft.
Summary sectional areas x 10	4.90 cu. ft.	15.10 cu. ft.	35.60 cu. ft.
Volume of top piece	0.05 cu. ft.	0.09 cu. ft.	0.08 cu. ft.
Total volume	4.95 cu. ft.	15.19 cu. ft.	35.68 cu. ft.

The volume of the top pieces forms in the older age columns an insignificant part of the total volume.

If the logs as cut in the woods are used as sections, then each section has a separate length and its volume must be separately ascertained for every decade of age of tree.

REMARK: It is wise to first ascertain the full age of the tree, allowing for stump years. It is further wise to throw off that number of years which exceeds full decades—*e. g.*, in case of a tree 117 years old, 7 years.

At the stump the rings had best be counted from the inside out, allowing for stump years. Instance: Age of tree, 117; stump years, 4 years; counting on the stump, from the inside, 6 rings establishes the ring formed in the year 10. Continuing, the rings of the years 20, 30, 40, 50, etc., up to year 110, are pencil marked. The outside seven rings are thrown off.

At all other disk-sections, count and measure from the outside in, after discarding the 7 years exceeding full decades of tree life.

PARAGRAPH LXXXII.

NOERDLINGER'S PAPER WEIGHT METHOD.

The total length of the tree is divided into 8 Huber sections, and cuts are made in the midst of these sections, at the height of 1/16, 3/16, 5/16, 7/16 and up to 15/16 of the bole. On each cross section the radii are measured, not with the rule, but with dividers.

On a piece of paper folded 4 times and thus divided into 8 sectors the measurements are entered with the help of the dividers, one sector being allotted to the first cross section, the next sector to the next cross section, etc. Multiplying the total weight of the zone indicating, say, the year 70, by height of the tree and dividing the product by the weight of a square foot of paper, the volume of the tree when 70 years old is directly obtained in cubic feet. Similarly the zones corresponding with the year 50, 60, etc., are cut out, weighed and multiplied.

If the volume increment percentage p alone is to be obtained, then it is enough to divide, say, the "weight" of the year 70 by the weight of the year 60, and the 10th root of the quotient will equal 1.0p.

PARAGRAPH LXXXIII.

SCHENCK'S GRAPHIC TREE ANALYSIS.

Graphic tree analysis offers the following advantages:

1. Mistakes are impossible, being at once noticeable on the diagram paper.

2. The volume in feet Doyle can be readily obtained for any stated minimum diameter.

3. The graphical sketch is adaptable to any of the 43 scales in use in the United States, as well as to the metric system.

4. The thickness of heart wood and sap wood and bark readily appears.

5. It is immaterial whether measurements are taken in meters or in feet, the graphical sketch readily allowing of transfers into other units.

6. Height growth and diameter growth appear at the same time, and from the same entries.

7. The length of the sections taken need not be uniform.

The method of proceeding is as follows: On millimeter paper a system of co-ordinates is established; heights are entered as ordinates, diameters or radii as abscissas. The scale for the height entries should be much smaller than that of the diameter entries.

Diameter points, at the different section-heights, corresponding to a given decade of years are joined (beginning at the outside), by which procedure the outline of the tree at that decade is established.

Th top cones are obtained by prolonging such outlines arbitrarily until they intersect with the height-axis.

The merchantable bole for each decade is dissected, on the diagram, into logs the length and diameter of which are measured on the diagram.

PARAGRAPH LXXXIV.

WAGENER'S METHOD AND STUMP ANALYSIS.

Wagener recommends a partial stem analysis for cases in which a knowledge of the absolute increment, not a knowledge of the absolute tree volume, is required. Tree volume is sectional area chest high times height of tree times form factor.

Wagener analyses:

a. the height growth by counting the rings at various altitudes along the bole;

b. the growth of the sectional area at chest height by measurement in decades in the usual way.

Wagener then estimates the form factor according to form factor tables. In the latter proposition, obviously, lies the danger of mistakes. Since, however, increment is a difference of volumes, merely the difference of mistakes—a comparatively small item—enters into the problem.

Age in years	60		80		100		120
Diameter b. h	14.		17.		19.		21.
Sectional area b. h	0.25		0.35		0.50		0.71
Height in feet	75.		85.		93.		105.
Form factor	0.50		0.50		0.50		0.50
Volume in cubic feet	9.4		13.		23.		36.
Increment in cubic feet		3.6		10.		13.	

The "stump analysis" (compare Paragraph LXXII.) introduced by the Bureau of Forestry rests on premises similar to those proffered by Wagener.

If the form height for the stump-diameters (or the number of feet b. m. per square foot of stump area for given stump diameters) is known, the rate of volume increment can be quickly ascertained by mere stump analysis.

It is, however, a well known fact that the diameter growth at the stump—especially at a low stump—is particularly unreliable as an index of volume growth, owing to the exaggerating influence on stump growth exercised by light, by water, by depth of soil and by superficial roots.

Stump analysis as a means to bring a volume in reference to a sectional area at the stump is permissible only as a necessary evil.

PARAGRAPH LXXXV.

PRESSLER'S METHOD.

Frequently the task before the forester is merely that of ascertaining the increase of bole volume during the last 10 or 20 years. Then after Pressler, one single investigation into the growth of the sectional area is sufficient when made with the help of the accretion borer in the midst of the "decapitated" bole. The volume increment in cubic feet equals the sectional area increment in question multiplied by the height of the tree.

The bole is decapitated by that number of top shoots which have been formed during the period of observation. This operation corresponds very well with the usual practice of judging the bole increment percentage from the sectional area increment ascertained at 0.45 of height of tree.

Pressler measures the sectional area at the end of the period of observation too large, measuring it at too low a point. He multiplies this sectional area, however, by too small a height—namely, the decapitated height; thus a mistake made in the positive sense is apt to be eliminated by a mistake made in the negative sense.

The axe can be used to better advantage frequently than the accretion borer.

PARAGRAPH LXXXVI.

BREYMANN'S METHOD.

Breymann gives the following formula:

1. For the current annual volume increment T:

$$T = V\left(2\frac{\delta}{d} + \frac{\lambda}{l}\right)$$

wherein "δ" and "λ" denote the annual increase of diameter "d" and length "l" respectively.

2. For the corresponding increment percentage P:

$$P - 100\left(2\frac{\delta}{d} + \frac{\lambda}{l}\right)$$

It appears that for trees of old age and hence of little height growth the increment percentage is merely dependent on the diameter increase.

Breymann, however, neglects:

1. The change of form figure, during the period of observation;

2. A number of small factors which ought to be embraced in the formula.

For stopping height growth or for $\lambda = 0$, the term given for P can be easily reduced to the term given by Schneider for the sectional area increment percentage.

PARAGRAPH LXXXVII.

FACTORS INFLUENCING THE CUBIC VOLUME INCREMENT.

The culmination of the current annual volume increment takes place at a later year than the culmination of the sectional area increment at breast height. Naturally so, because with increasing age of a tree, its root system as well as the branch system, the feeders of the body, show continuous increase.

Big and long branches, of course, require a great deal of wood fibre to increase and maintain their own strength, like levers increased in length. Hence, from a certain size of branch on, all wood fibre produced by the branch is used up within the branch itself, for its own purposes, instead of being added as increment to the merchantable bole.

After Dr. Metzger, the crown of a tree yields the maximum of bole increment if its crown diameter is, and if the number of trees per acre are:

Quality of soil.	Diameter of crown, in feet.	No. of trees per acre.
Very good.	16.5	203
Good	14.7	256
Medium	12.7	343
Poor	9.3	640
Very poor	8.3	807

From the theoretical standpoint it seems wise, consequently, to force the lower branches of a tree to die, with the help of proper tension and friction within the leaf canopy, when they exceed a length of 8.25, 7.35, 6.35, 4.65 and 4.15 feet respectively (the halves of the diameters).

Metzger's investigations are interesting, but his conclusions seem to be too sweeping.

P. P. Pelton recommends the lopping of branches in order to shorten the length of the branch-levers.

The average annual volume increment of dominant and sound trees culminates at a very high age only, if ever, owing to the late culmination of the current annual average increment.

The volume increment percentage forms—as in all cases of increment—a steadily but irregularly decreasing progression. This percentage is invariably equal to or higher than the sectional area increment percentage at chest height.

Roughly speaking, the volume increment percentage amounts to from 1 to 1.75 times the sectional area (at chest height) increment percentage, or, as Pressler gives it, to from 2 to 3½ times the diameter (at chest height) increment percentage.

Crown covers part of bole	Height Growth.			
	Seemingly nil.	Medium.	Good.	Excellent.
½ or more.	2.33	2.67	3.00	3.17
½ to ⅓.	2.50	2.83	3.17	3.33
Less than ⅓.	2.67	3.00	3.33	....

Since the average volume increment of a tree is equal or closely equal to the current annual increment at a high age only, it is usually not permissible to substitute the average increment, which is easily ascertained, for the current annual increment.

PARAGRAPH LXXXVIII.

VOLUME-INCREMENT PERCENTAGE OF STANDING TREES.

In the case of standing trees the volume increment percentage cannot be measured, owing to the impossibility of ascertaining a change of form height.

The Pressler data given in the preceding paragraph allow of estimating the volume increment percentage of standing trees on the basis of a diameter-increase, measured at breast height.

The Pressler "accretion borer" is used for the purpose, or an axe.

Stoetzer, Director of the Forest Academy at Eisenach, modifies the Schneider formula for sectional area percentage, writing it

$$p = \frac{C}{nd}$$

wherein *n* indicates number of years (rings) required to form one inch; *d* represents the diameter at the beginning of the period of investigation, whilst *C* (the so-called "constant factor of increment," which is not a constant factor at all) must be ascertained for a given species, soil, diameter, age and position by actual tests on felled trees.

In old dense beech woods *C* is, e. g., 540. After a seed cutting in the same woods during the final stage of regeneration *C* is only 450 (observation by Dr. Wimmenauer).

Trees growing as cones would grow, have C equal to 600; trees growing as Apollonian paraboloids would grow, have C equal to 800; after Stoetzer, C might amount to as much as 930, in case of suppressed trees. The minimum possible (in sound trees) for C is 400.

The Pressler values given in the table of the preceding paragraph closely correspond with the constant factors of increment ascertained after Stoetzer. In the case of the Pressler table (at end of Paragraph LXXXVII.) we find, for medium height growth and very small crown, a factor 3.00 by which the diameter increment percentage is to be multiplied. This factor 3.00 corresponds with 600 for a constant factor of increment.

If the diameter in the midst of the bole is ½ of the diameter at the end, then the tree, it seems, is conical, and an increment factor of 600 might be assumed. If the sectional area in the midst of the bole equals ½ the sectional area at the end, then the tree is a paraboloid, and the increment factor seems apt to be 800.

It must be remembered, however, that a tree forming a paraboloid grows as a paraboloid only, if its percentage of height growth is equal to its percentage of growth of sectional area—a rare case in merchantable trees.

Similarly, a tree growing as a cone must have the height increment percentage equal to its diameter increment percentage.

If n and ν represent the number of rings per inch added to original diameters d and δ at chest height and at 0.45 of the height of the tree respectively, then the "constant factor of increment C" is found as follows:

$$p\ (\text{volume}) = \frac{400}{\nu\delta} = \frac{C}{nd}$$

$$C = 400\frac{nd}{\nu\delta}$$

PARAGRAPH LXXXIX.

INTERDEPENDENCE BETWEEN CUBIC INCREMENT AND INCREMENT IN FEET B. M. DOYLE.

Doyle's rule under-estimates the contents of small logs and over-estimates those of big logs.

Consequently, the growth of a tree bole in feet b. m. Doyle is (for small trees yielding logs under 28" diameter) relatively faster than the growth of a tree bole expressed in cubic feet. The figures of Column D denote, in the following table, this excess rate of growth:

A Diameter of logs without bark.	*B* No. of ft. b. m. per one cu. ft. of timber estimated after Doyle.	*C* Differences of consecutive figures in Column B.	*D* "Extraordinary" percentage of increment Doyle co-inciding with 1" growth.
12"	5.09		8.1
		0.41	
13"	5.50		6.4
		0.35	
14"	5.85		5.7
		0.33	
15"	6.18		4.2
		0.26	
16"	6.44		4.3
		0.27	
17"	6.71		3.3
		0.22	
18"	6.93		2.1
		0.14	
19"	7.07		3.2
		0.26	
20"	7.33		2.5
		0.18	
21"	7.51		2.2
		0.16	
22"	7.67		2.0
		0.15	
23"	7.82		1.7
		0.13	
24"	7.95		1.8
		0.14	
25"	8.09		1.4
		0.11	
26"	8.20		1.5
		0.12	
27"	8.33		1.1
		0.09	
28"	8.41		1.1
		0.11	
29"	8.52		1.0
		0.08	
30"	8.60		

For the standard rules, the increment percentage of a tree can be ascertained by cubic measure as well as by standard measure.

If *n* years are required to form one additional inch of diameter, then the extraordinary percentage of Doyle-increments amounts annually to $\sqrt[n]{1.0\,D}$, wherein D represents the values of Column D in the foregoing table.

By this factor $\sqrt[n]{1.0\,D}$, the cubic volume increment percentage of a bole may be converted, *ceteris paribus*, into Doyle increment percentage, provided that

1. The cubic increment percentage of the total bole coincides with the cubic increment percentage of the merchantable bole;

2. The merchantable bole does not increase in length during the period of observation.

PARAGRAPH XC.

CONSTRUCTION OF VOLUME TABLES.

Volume tables are "tree yield tables" from which the volume of a tree of given species, given age, given diameter breast high or stump high, given height, given merchantable bole, given position (suppressed, dominant, etc., or isolated, crowded, etc.), given locality and so on can be readily read. The units of volume are cubic feet, board feet, standards, cords, etc., according to the requirements of the case.

Obviously, volume tables give, or should give, the volumes of average trees; they may give, in addition, the maximum and minimum volume possible in a tree of stated description.

Volume tables are constructed either on the basis of hundreds (thousands) of measurements taken from trees actually felled in the woods (possibly also sawn at a saw mill, to ascertain the grades) or on the basis of a smaller number of complete section analyses.

The rapidity of volume growth of a species and the development of its form height depend on many local factors—notably on climate, soil, sylvicultural systems at hand, influence of fires, fungi, insects, etc.

Owing to the multitude of local factors influencing the volumes and the changes of volumes, local volume tables alone are entitled to a place in exact mensuration.

Volume tables for second growth are more reliable than volume tables for first growth.

Circular 445 of Bureau of Forestry defines volume table as "a tabular statement of the volume of trees in board feet or other units upon the basis of their diameter breast high, their diameter breast high *and* height, their age, or their age *and* height."

The method of construction of volume tables is either mathematical or graphical.

1. *Mathematical method.*

The volumes ascertained for trees of a given diameter (breast high or stump high with or without bark), a given merchantable length or total length, a given age or a given quality or locality are added up.

The sum total of these volumes divided by the number of trees forming it yields the average volume of the tree of stated description.

These averages are shown, for the various diameters, lengths, ages and localities, in tabular form.

The volumes corresponding with such diameters, lengths, ages and localities, for which sample trees were not cut and measured, are found by arithmetic interpolation.

Finally, the differences in volume shown by average trees of similar description (*i. e.*, differing but slightly in diameter, length, etc.) are formed and rounded off in a manner causing the volumes to show a more steady mathematic progression.

2. *Graphic method.*

The volume of each tree measured is entered as the abscissa on a diagram-system of co-ordinates, whilst the diameters of the trees (or the age, etc.) are registered on the ordinate axis. Similarity of length is indicated by color of mark representing the tree; similarity of locality is indicated by the form of the mark (square, triangle, cross, circle, etc.).

Corresponding marks are then joined by chains (having square, circular, triangular links) of the proper color.

Finally, average curves as well as maximum and minimum curves are drawn for the various colors and forms of marks.

Maximum and minimum curves should not represent the very best and the very worst possibilities; they should represent the average of very good and very bad trees.

The graphic method is more reliable, because less depending on mere figures, than the mathematical method. Both methods are frequently combined.

A number of complete tree analyses furnishes more reliable results than a large number of mere volume measurements because it yields more reliable curves (guide-curves) of development for one and the same locality, and because it prevents the forester from drawing curves of growth at random.

If the sample trees (or sample logs) are sawn up at a saw mill where the lumber is properly graded according to the inspection rules prevailing for the species in question, the volume tables may also give the actual average output of specified trees in lumber of the various grades.

SECTION II.—INCREMENT OF A WOOD.

PARAGRAPH XCI.

INCREMENT OF FORESTS.

The volume increment of the virgin forest is on the whole nill.

In America the value increment of a primeval forest is based more on a price increment of stumpage than on a volume increment of trees. The volume increment, in addition, can scarcely be ascertained with sufficient accuracy for a given piece of forest at a reasonable expense.

In second growth forests, on the other hand, say in Virginia, an absolute knowledge of the productiveness of the forest renders forestal investments safer in the eyes of the owner; and the safety of the investment it is which alone can tempt the capitalist to invest in forestry. A knowledge of the increment in second growth woodlands can be obtained from tabulated statements ("yield tables") showing the rate of growth for woodlands of a given species in a given locality. Under normal yield tables are understood such tables which give the rate of growth for even-eged, pure, normally stocked, well thinned woodlots for given localities (compare Paragraph LIII. and XCIV..).

Such normal yield tables are constructed abroad for beech, pine, spruce, fir and oak. In this country they exist only in Pinchot's and Graves' yield tables for white pine. In America, pure even-aged woods are found in rare cases only (taeda, echinata, rigida, jack and longleaf pines, tamarack, coppicewood).

In the construction of normal yield tables the following points require consideration:

1. The different methods of construction (Paragraph XCII.).

2. The combination, interpolation, adjustment and correction of the results (Paragraph XCIII.).

3. The contents and use of yield tables (Paragraph XCIV.).

PARAGRAPH XCII.

METHODS OF CONSTRUCTION OF NORMAL YIELD TABLES.

Normal yield tables may be based on:

A. Repeated survey of some typical woodlots during their entire lifetime.

B. Repeated survey of different woods standing on an equal quality of soil, during a period of years equal at least to the longest difference in age found amongst them.

C. One-time, simultaneous survey of a very large number of woods of different ages standing on different qualities of soil. Missing links are here obtained by graphic or mathematical interpolation (Paragraph XCIII.).

If tables are constructed by repeated survey of several woods (B), it is often found that the links cross one another for unexplainable reasons.

PARAGRAPH XCIII.

GATHERING DATA FOR NORMAL YIELD TABLES.

In order to see whether or not two woods, in the case C of the preceding paragraph, belong to the same chain of growth, two methods are in use:

a. The horn or curve method, after Baur.

b. The stem analysis method.

Remarks on *a:*

The contents and age of all woods (normal) surveyed are plotted in a diagram, the age forming the abscissa and the volume the ordinate of the system.

Curves are then drawn outlining the maxima and minima of growth observed.

The horn-shaped space between these curves is divided into a number of sectors equal to the number of yield classes to be distinguished. The middle line of each sector illustrates the productiveness of its class.

The average height growth is obtained in a similar way, the height data forming the ordinates in a system of co-ordinates.

Baur finds that the allotment of a given plot to a volume-sector corresponds with its allotment to a height sector. In other words, the height is, after Baur, an absolutely reliable indicator of the quality of the soil, or, what is the same, of the yield class.

The growth of sectional area, height and volume being known, the development of the form factors for the various sectors is readily obtained from the fraction $\frac{v}{s \times h}$.

Remarks on *b:*

An analysis of the average stems in lots surveyed would not throw any light on their connection as members of one and the same chain of observation. After Robert Hartig, the 200 strongest trees are analyzed. After Wagener, the ideal cylinders merely of these 200 strongest stems are analyzed by ascertaining their height growth and their diameter growth at breast height. Weise and Schwappach are satisfied with an analysis of the heights merely of the 200 best stems.

The selection of sample plots is not easy, even in second growth raised under forestal care. A valuation survey establishes for each plot the number of stems and the sectional area for each diameter class of stems (usually divided into 5 classes); further, the average age and the average height of the plot. The volume is then figured out, usually, according to the Draudt-Urich method.

The experiment stations maintained by the European Governments control the growth of a large number of experimental plots, which should not be smaller than ½ acre each.

The sample plots are corner marked, and, more recently, the individual trees contained therein are numbered consecutively. Surveys of these plots are made every five years. The point of measurement is indicated by a chalk line.

In America normal sample plots have not been established as yet by the Bureau of Forestry in second growth. The sample plots at Biltmore do not represent a normal second growth.

PARAGRAPH XCIV.

NORMAL YIELD TABLES, THEIR PURPOSES AND CONTENTS ABROAD.

Normal yield tables are especially used for the following purposes:

1. To ascertain the quality of the soil (*e. g.*, for taxation).

2. To ascertain the volume of the growing stock.

3. To ascertain future yields of the forest.

4. To solve problems of forest finance, especially those of forest maturity (length of rotation).

German normal yield tables have the following contents:

A. Tables for the main forest—the secondary forest comprising such trees on the same lot as are about to be removed by way of thinning:

(1) Age, graded at five year intervals.
(2) Number of trees.
(3) Sectional area at chest height, inclusive of bark.
(4) Average diameter.
(5) Average height and height increment.
(6) Volume in cubic measure arranged according to assortments as logs, fuel, bark, etc.
(7) Periodical and average annual volume increment.
(8) Increment percentage.
(9) Form factor.
(10) Normal growing stock.

B. Tables for the secondary forest, giving merely its volume, which, as stated, is to be removed by way of thinning.

Circular 445 of the Bureau of Forestry defines "future yield tables" as follows: "A tabular statement of the amount of wood which, after a given period, will be contained in given trees upon a given area expressed in board feet or some other unit."

PARAGRAPH XCV.

RETROSPECTIVE YIELD TABLES.

In "retrospective" yield tables an attempt is made to rebuild the growing stock as it was before lumbering from the stumps found on the ground and from stem analyses of the trees now standing. Prerequisite is a knowledge of the year in which lumbering took place and of the conditions of growth since prevailing.

Method of proceeding:

1. Make stem analyses and construct tree volume tables, showing the probable contents of trees for stumps of a given diameter and for given diameters b. h.

2. On land cut over *n* years ago, find by valuation survey and stem analyses:

a. The present volume "F."

b. The volume "y" of the trees now standing as it was "n" years ago with the help of tree volume tables.

c. From the stumps the volume "x" of the trees logged "n" years ago.

3. A product of "F" units (with an undergrowth not fit for logging) has been derived in "n" years from an original stand aggregating "y" plus "x" units of volume.

4. Grouping hundreds of sample plots together, yield tables for local use are obtained. Misleading is, of course, the multiplicity of conditions (mixture of species, soils, original stands, pasture and fire) surrounding a second growth which check the applicability and the combination of the tables found.

The tables are way signs, not ways, toward a true knowledge of the productiveness of cut-over woodlands.

PARAGRAPH XCVI.

YIELD TABLES OF THE BUREAU OF FORESTRY.

Bureau yield tables are meant to show the growth on cut-over land occurring within the next 10, 20 or 30 years, if a tract is logged to a 10", 12" or 14" (or any other) limit. Bureau yield tables are based on tree volume tables and on an account of the numbers of tree individuals found in the various age classes of forest, viz., diameter classes of trees.

The influence of the different qualities of soil on tree growth is not given, only one average volume table being constructed. The volume tables show the number of years which a tree requires to increase its diameter b. h. by one inch. The volume tables record, in addition, the volume increase corresponding with such diameter increase. Applying these findings to the stumpage presumably left after logging, the volume can be ascertained which is expected to be on hand 10, 20 or 30 years later. The volume growth is forecasted, as if it were taking place under primeval conditions.

The Bureau neglects entirely the death rate of trees, due to natural causes and especially high amongst seedlings and saplings, or else due to the logging operations themselves. The results forecasted in this way must be invariably too high.

Pinchot's Spruce Tables (The Adirondack Spruce, p. 77) are based on similar premises:

a. Construct volume tables by stem analysis (stump-analysis) on land cut over for a second time, thus showing rate of growth for trees left standing at the first cut.

b. Construct tables, by actual measurements in the woods, giving the number of trees of the various diameters, composing a stumpage of from 1,000 to 12,000 feet board measure.

c. Predict the number of trees and their exact diameters to be found 10, 20 or 30 years after logging, according to severity of logging (diameter limit).

d. With the help of the volume tables, give the contents of these trees.

In these tables as well, the death rate amongst trees is disregarded. For normal death rate, compare Pinchot's "White Pine," p. 80, ff; also remarks at end of Paragraph LIV.

PARAGRAPH XCVII.

THE INCREMENT OF A WOODLOT.

The current as well as the annual average increment of normal, even-aged woods culminates at a much earlier date than the increment of the trees composing such woods. The explanation lies in the death rate of the trees.

Under a close crown density in even-aged, normal woods, the stronger half of the trees yield, from the pole stage on, practically all the increment, the weaker half of the trees being almost inactive.

The better the quality of the soil, the earlier occurs the culmination of the increment; consequently, on good soil, shorter rotations are apt to be advisable than on poor soil.

Light demanding (intolerant) species show an earlier culmination than shade bearers (tolerant) species.

For white pine woods, after Pinchot, the years of increment culmination are as follows:

Culmination of	For entire volume with bark in cu. ft.			For volume Doyle in ft. b. m.		
	I.	II.	III.	I.	II.	III.
Current incrt....	40th	50th	60th yr.	70th	70th	110th yr.
Average incrt...	60th	80th	100th yr.	135th	160th	210th yr.

I denotes best; II denotes medium, and III denotes poorest quality of soil.

The increment of a woodlot, whether normal or abnormal, can be obtained:

a. With the help of yield tables.

b. By special investigations made into the rate of growth of sample trees (Paragraph XCVIII.).

c. With the help of the average annual increment of the woodlot (Paragraph XCIX.).

The increment of a past period is never exactly equal to that of a future period, unless the age of the woods is close to that year at which the increment culminates. The increment percentage during a past period is always larger than the increment percentage during a coming period (aside of temporary increase due to light-increment).

The general laws (Paragraph LXXV.) relative to the culmination, increase and decrease of increment hold good for the volume increment of woodlots as well as for that of trees.

PARAGRAPH XCVIII.

ASCERTAINING THE INCREMENT OF WOODLOTS BY SAMPLE TREES.

The current annual volume increment and the volume increment percentage of a wood, from which its maturity largely depends, can be correctly found only by a valuation survey, combined with an investigation into the present rate of growth exhibited by a number of sample trees.

Borggreve recommends to gauge the increment of the sample trees by the Schneider increment percentage. This is usually insufficient.

The correct volume increment percentage p of a woodlot is obtained from the volume increment percentage p_1, p_2, p_3, p_4 and p_5 of the class sample trees—which represent class-volumes v_1, v_2, v_3, v_4 and v_5—as

$$p = \frac{v_1 p_1 + v_2 p_2 + v_3 p_3 + v_4 p_4 + v_5 p_5}{v_1 + v_2 + v_3 + v_4 + v_5}$$

Where the form heights of the classes differ slightly only, the sectional areas of the classes may be substituted for the volumes of the classes.

Again, where classes of equal sectional area are formed (after Robert Hartig), there the volume increment per cent. of the woodlot equals the arithmetic mean of the volume increment percentages of the sample trees, so that

$$p = \frac{p_1 + p_2 + p_3 + p_4 + p_5}{5}$$

PARAGRAPH XCIX.

CURRENT INCREMENT ASCERTAINED FROM AVERAGE INCREMENT.

Within certain limits, a short time previous and a short time after the culmination of the average annual increment, the annual average increment equals the current increment and can be used in its place as a basis for yield calculation. European Governments frequently prescribe this *modus operandi* for yield forecasts in working plans.

CHAPTER IV.—LUMBER

PARAGRAPH C.

UNITS OF LUMBER-MEASUREMENT.

For rough lumber one inch thick, or thicker, the unit of measure, known as one foot board measure, is a square foot of lumber one inch thick. This unit is the 1/12th part of a cubic foot.

For rough lumber thinner than one inch, the unit of measure, also known as one foot board measure, is the superficial square foot, and the thickness of the lumber is here entirely disregarded.

All dressed stock is measured and described as if it were the full size of the rough lumber necessarily used in its manufacture. "Inch flooring," *e. g.*, is actually 13/16 inch thick; and "3/8 inch ceiling" is actually 5/16 inch thick.

Standard thicknesses are:

3/8, 1/2, 5/8, 3/4, 1, 1 1/4, 1 1/2, 2, 2 1/2, 3 x 4".

Standard lengths are:

in hardwoods 6 to 16 feet;
in softwoods 10 to 24 feet.

In both cases, lengths in even feet (not in odd feet) are required.

A shortness of 1" or 2" in the length of hardwood boards is disregarded.

Standard defects are:

I. In hardwoods: one sound knot of 1 1/4" diameter;
one inch of bright sap;
one split, its length in inches equalling the contents of the board in feet b.m.

II. In softwoods: sound knots, viz.:
(a) pin-knots of not over 1/2" diameter:
(b) standard knots of not over 1 1/2" diameter;
(c) large knots of over 1 1/2" diameter;

pitchpockets, viz.:
(a) small pitchpockets 1/8" wide;
(b) standard pitchpockets up to 3/8" wide and up to 3' long;

pitchstreaks, viz.:
(a) small pitchstreaks not wider than 1/12 the width and not longer than 1/4 the length of board;
(b) standard pitchstreaks with dimensions up to twice as large as given under (a);

sap, viz.:
(a) bright sap;
(b) blued sap;

splits, wane, scant width, tongues, less than 5/16" long.

The point at which a defect is located greatly influences its effect on the grade of the lumber.

The two faces, the two edges and the two ends of a board must be parallel. In case of unevenness, the thinnest thickness, the narrowest width and the shortest length are measured.

Lumber is measured with the help of a lumber rule (Lufkin rule) which yields for inch boards of given lengths and given width the corresponding contents in feet b. m.

In measuring the widths, fractions of an inch are neglected in rough lumber.

PARAGRAPH CI.

INSPECTION RULES AND NOMENCLATURE.

The lumber inspection prevailing in a given market is governed by local custom or by agreement within the body of local associations of lumbermen.

The tendency of all inspection rules is directed toward a gradual lowering of rigidity.

The wholesaler's inspection is generally stiffer than that of the manufacturer. Diversity of rules is a sadly demoralizing element in lumber circles.

Lumber sawn for special purposes (*e. g.*, wagon bolsters) must be inspected with a view to its adaptability for such special purpose.

A. *Hardwood.* The grade of a board depends on

1. Its width and length;
2. Its standard defects;
3. The percentage of clear stock contained therein;
4. The number of cuttings yielding such clear stock.

The following table shows average specifications prevailing for the various grades of hardwood lumber in the U. S. markets.

The defects specified invariably indicate the coarsest stock admissible in a given grade.

Hardwood Lumber Specifications.

Designation of Grade.	Minimum Len'h feet.	Minimum Wi'th inches.	Actual Length feet.	Actual Width inches.	Allows of No. of standard defects.	Allows of Rate of clear stock.	Allows of Con'd in c't'ngs not more than
Firsts.......	10	8	10 & over	8 & 9	none	Practically all.	Practically one.
	..	..	10 & over	10 & over	one		
Seconds.....	8	8	8	8 & 9	none		
	..	..	8	10 & over	one		
	10	6	10 & over	6 & 7	none		
	..	..	10 & over	8 & 9	one		
	..	..	10 & over	10 & 11	two		
	..	..	10 & over	12 & over	three		
No. 1 Com...	6	6	6	6 to 8	none	all	1
	..	..	6	9 & over	one	all	1
	8	4	8	4	none	all	1
	..	..	8	5	one	all	1
	..	..	8 & 10	6 & over	....	2/3	2
	..	..	12 to 16	6 & over	....	2/3	3
No. 2 Com...	6	3	6 to 10	....	....	1/2	3
	..	..	12 to 16	....	....	1/2	4
No. 3 Com...	4	3	....	....	....	1/3	..

B. *Softwoods.* Softwood lumber is inspected from its best side Under "edgegrain" is understood lumber the face of which forms an angle of less than 45 degrees with the plain of the medullary rays contained in the board. All other lumber is termed "flat grain" or "slash grain," also "bastard grain."

I. *Finishing Lumber*, 1" to 2" thick, dressed one or two sides.

1. First and second clear,
   up to 8" wide; absolutely clear;
   10" wide; one small defect permitted;
   12" and over wide; 1/4 of stock may have one standard knot or its equivalent.

2. Third clear,
   allows of twice as many defects.

II. *Flooring*, 1" thick and 3" or 4" or 6" wide before dressing; either with hollow back or with solid back;

1. A, B and C flat grain flooring; wherein "A" is clear and "B" allows of one or two standard defects;

2. A, B and C edgegrain flooring; with the same allowance;

3. No. 1 and No. 2 fence flooring.

III. *Ceiling*, $\frac{3}{8}$, $\frac{1}{2}$ and $\frac{3}{4}$ inch thick; 3, or 4, or 6 inches wide.

1. "A" ceiling and "B" ceiling, with small defects only;
2. No. 1 and No. 2 common ceiling, with one and two standard defects, or their equivalent.

IV. *Drop Siding*, which is either "shiplapped" or "tongued and grooved;" it is $\frac{3}{4}$" thick and $3\frac{1}{4}$ or $5\frac{1}{4}$ inches wide. Grades A, B and No. 1 common.

V. *Bevel Siding*, which scales $\frac{3}{16}$" at the thin edge and $\frac{1}{2}$" at the thick edge, resawn from stock dressed to $\frac{11}{16}$" x $5\frac{1}{4}$". Grades as under IV.

VI. *Partition*, measuring $\frac{3}{4}$" x $3\frac{1}{4}$" or $\frac{3}{4}$" x $5\frac{1}{4}$". Grades as under IV.

VII. *Common Boards*, graded as No. 1, No. 2 and No. 3 common boards, 8", 10" or 12" wide, dressed one or two sides, or rough.

VIII. *Fencing*, graded as No. 1, No. 2 and No. 3 fencing, 3", 4" or 6" wide. The grade "No. 3" includes defective lumber with knot-holes, red rot, very wormy patches, etc., on $\frac{1}{4}$ of the length of the board. Fencing is either dressed or rough.

CHAPTER V.—STUMPAGE VALUES

PARAGRAPH CII.

STUMPAGE VALUES.

Forestry is a business; the forest largely represents its business investment; its purpose is the raising of money, of dividends.

Thus it is with investments and the dividends therefrom that the forester is concerned; and it is the task of "forest finance" and "forest management" to ascertain the factors and to regulate the components of such investments.

Forest mensuration, as a subsidiary to forest management, may well devote a chapter to the measurement of the stumpage value of trees.

Stumpage value is the price which a tree brings or should bring if it were sold on the stump.

The stumpage-value of a tree depends on the value of the lumber contained therein and obtained therefrom, deducting the total expense of lumber production (logging, milling, shipping, incidentals.)

Since the value of lumber fluctuates, as well as the cost of production, stumpage values are subject to continuous variation. The tendency of stumpage prices, all over the world, is a tendency to rise—especially so in countries of rapid development, rapid increase of population and inadequate provisions for re-growth.

The cost of production is composed about as follows:

1. Expense of logging and log transportation, varying locally between \$2 and \$5 per 1,000' b. m.
2. Expense of milling, varying between \$1.50 and \$5 per 1,000' b. m.
3. Expense of freightage of lumber to the consuming market, amounting per 1,000' b. m. to \$1.50 for very short hauls; to \$12 for a haul from Atlanta to Boston; to \$21 for a haul across the continent from Portland (Oregon) to New England.

Freight rates have, in the long run, a decided downward tendency. Still, with a majority of the lumber produced in the U. S., the item "freight" forms the chief expense of production.

For Pisgah Forest a reduction of freight rates equalling 1 cent per 100 lbs. involves a net gain for the owner of approximately \$60,000. In this possibility lies one of the strongest arguments for conservative lumbering.

An increase of the price of lumber from \$20 to \$21 at the place of consumption endears the lumber to the consumer by 5%; the owner of the forest now valuing his stumpage at \$5 will eventually experience this increase as a 20% increase of stumpage values.

The only factors of stumpage-values, which the owner himself—unaided by the development of the country—may influence, consist in the expense of logging and log freighting, and in the expense of milling, the former largely depending on the quality of available means of transportation, the latter governed by the quality of the sawmill.

In ascertaining the stumpage-value of a tree the forester considers:

a. The cost per 1,000' b. m. of logging it, of milling it and of freighting its timber;

b. The volume of timber contained in the tree, by grades;

c. The value of such lumber, by grades.

If a tree contains

45% of lumber worth \$31 per 1,000' b. m.

It is necessary to find Stoetzer's constant factor of increment or to ascertain the relative increment of the sectional areas of the sample trees at 0.45 of their heights.

35% of lumber worth \$21 per 1,000' b. m.
15% of lumber worth \$16 per 1,000' b. m.
5% of lumber worth \$8 per 1,000' b. m.

then the lumber value of the tree, per 1,000' b. m., is

$$\frac{45 \times 31 + 35 \times 21 + 15 \times 16 + 5 \times 8}{100} = \$24.10$$

Deducting from this figure the expense of logging, milling and freighting, the actual stumpage-value, per 1,000' b. m., is derived.

The actual prices paid for stumpage in the U. S. fall deeply below the figures which a test-calculation is apt to yield.

This discrepancy may be explained, above all, by

Ignorance of owners of stumpage;
Agents' and dealers' profits;
Incidental expenses overlooked.

Stumpage-values show a rapid decrease with the increase of the distance separating the tree from the nearest railroad or stream.

The grades of lumber and their proportion obtainable from logs of given species, diameter and soundness (including presence and location of defects) can be ascertained only by test-sawing in the mill.

This has been done in 1896 for yellow poplar at Biltmore (bandsaw mill). The stumpage-values then ascertained are shown by the following table:

Market Value of Poplar Stumpage in Western North Carolina, Per Tree, in Cents.

At the age of years.	Under good conditions.				Under average conditions.				Under poor conditions.			
	Diam. inches.	Logging and Milling expenses being per 1000 feet B. M.			Diam. inches.	Logging and Milling expenses being per 1000 feet B. M.			Diam. inches.	Logging and Milling expenses being per 1000 feet B. M.		
		$9	$10	$11		$9	$10	$11		$9	$10	$11
100	....	Negative.	Negative.	Negative.	....	Negative.	Negative.	Negative.	....	Negative.	Negative.	Negative.
120	18.8	8	"	"	....	"	"	"	....	"	"	"
140	21.3	40	25	"	18.2	4	"	"	....	"	"	"
160	23.5	105	72	2	20.4	22	5	"	....	"	"	"
180	25.7	265	170	98	22.4	67	35	"	....	"	"	"
200	27.7	445	325	230	24.3	160	103	30	18.5	"	"	"
220	29.6	620	465	350	26.0	287	200	109	20.0	7	"	"
240	....	...	...	...	27.5	430	330	210	21.3	27	3	"
260	....	...	...	...	....	...	460	330	22.1	60	25	"
280	....	...	...	...	....	...	...	...	....	...	45	"
300	....	...	...	...	....	...	...	...	....	...	...	5
320	....	...	...	...	....	...	...	...	....	...	...	30

Footnote: Dots below a column of figures indicate higher values, not specifically ascertained.

The values above the columns of figures are all negative and were not ascertained specifically either.

It is to be hoped that similar tests will be made for our leading species on a large scale by the U. S. Forest Service or by the various associations of lumber manufacturers. Conservative forestry as a business badly requires data allowing to estimate the actual value of logs, and hence of trees, if the uncertainty of financial results now checking the progress of conservative forestry in America is to be definitely reduced.

MANUAL

FOR

Timber Reconnaissance

1914

FOR USE OF FOREST OFFICERS ONLY

District One, Missoula, Mont.

F. A. SILCOX, District Forester

MISSOULIAN JOB ROOMS, MISSOULA, MONTANA

MANUAL FOR TIMBER RECONNAISSANCE

CONTENTS.

MANUAL FOR TIMBER RECONNAISSANCE

CONTENTS.

APPENDIX.

MANUAL FOR TIMBER RECONNAISSANCE

CONTENTS.

INTRODUCTION.

The following instructions give in detail the methods of reconnaissance which have been authorized by the Forester and by the District Office for District 1. They are based on the conduct of intensive projects by standard crews. They should also be applied, however, to extensive projects and to cases where circumstances make it necessary that very small parties or even individuals examine bodies of timber in preparation for a sale. In intensive projects of standard size, deviations from these instructions should be made only with the consent of the District Office.

EXTENSIVE RECONNAISSANCE.

For the intelligent selection of areas which will make attractive logging chances and which later may need to be covered by intensive reconnaissance, and to make possible a fair division of reconnaissance funds between Forests to secure data for use in a rough calculation of the annual growth and also of value for other purposes in the administration of the forest, a systematic cataloging of timber resources is of vital importance. Supervisors should, therefore, take advantage of every opportunity to complete extensive reconnaissance over their Forests. This work can be done in many cases for each ranger district by the Ranger in charge, but should be directed by some one man on each Forest who is responsible for assembling and checking all the data received.

The data which should be obtained in connection with extensive reconnaissance is as follows:

1. A type map usually on the scale of one mile to the inch, the typing being on a rather broad basis.
2. An age class map similar to the type map.
3. An approximate estimate by species for each watershed.

Considerable variation in methods will be necessary due to differing local conditions. In general much cruder and more rapid methods than those described in these instructions will be necessary. Under normal conditions one man working alone should cover about a township a week. The details of these instructions for intensive reconnaissance will obviously be merely suggestive as to the methods to be used.

INTENSIVE RECONNAISSANCE.

Object and Scope—The object of all intensive reconnaissance is to secure data for (1) timber sales and (2) working plans. While the former object is immediate and the latter may be postponed, the reconnaissance data collected should be sufficiently inclusive so that no subsequent field work is necessary except to secure estimates of logging cost for stumpage appraisals and to determine the exact sale boundaries after applications have been received.

The data required for these two purposes are, first, a map showing topography, culture, Forest types, age classes and other information; second, estimates by convenient subdivision in such form as to be of use both for sales and for regulating cut; and third, descriptive notes covering the silvicultural conditions and the factors affecting logging.

Selection of Areas to Be Covered—The following principles will govern the order of selection of areas to be covered:

1. Areas for which formal or informal sale applications have been received and where sales are desirable.

2. Areas within which desirable sales can undoubtedly be made in the near future if reconnaissance data are available.

3. Divisions in which there is danger of overcutting either in large or small sales, (a) in excess of the amounts which should be reserved for local needs and in guaranteeing a reasonable operating life for improvements constructed in connection with sales, and (b) in excess of sustained yield.

For the present it will be necessary to limit reconnaissance strictly to areas of the first class.

PRELIMINARY FIELD EXAMINATION.

To insure that a proposed project falls into this first class, a preliminary field examination should be made. The mere fact that an application has been received does not always mean that a sale is possible or advisable. This preliminary examination should be made well in advance of the beginning of actual field work and, if possible, by the man who will have charge of the project.

POINTS TO BE COVERED.

1. The desirability and probability of an immediate sale.
2. That portion of the area which should be covered by reconnaissance.
3. The maps and other data available for present use.
4. The plan of topographic control.
5. The per cent of the area which should be estimated.
6. The size and organization of the party.
7. The equipment needed, transportation facilities, trail construction necessary, possible camp sites, etc.
8. A tentative division of the area into logging units.
9. Deviations, if any, considered advisable from these instructions.

EXTENSIVE RECONNAISSANCE MAP.

If not already in existence, an extensive reconnaissance map should be prepared in connection with the preliminary field examination. On this, much of the above mentioned information can be entered.

PRELIMINARY PLAN.

As the result of this examination the preliminary plan will be prepared in co-operation with the Supervisor by the man examining the area, for the approval of the District Forester, and should be a solution of the above points under examination. Unless modified by the District Forester in writing, this plan of work will remain in effect until the project is completed. Subsequent projects on the same division or Forest should be carried on as far as possible along similar lines.

DISTRICT OFFICE SUPERVISION.

The preliminary plan will be checked, where considered advisable, by one or more representatives from the District office, including, if possible, the logging engineer, who will ultimately appraise the timber. As soon as practicable after the actual field work has commenced, a representative of the District office will visit the crew to assist in lining up the work and in standardization of methods.

METHOD OF WORK.

The reconnaissance field work is to be done by what is known as the strip system. The principle of this is that parallel strips located at definite intervals are estimated carefully and taken as samples representing the whole area. These strips are usually one chain in width. The distance between strips depends on the character of the timber and varies from one-eighth to one-half mile. While the strips of each series are run parallel to each other, the general direction chosen is that which cuts the drainages most nearly at right angles (as better averages are thus obtained) and at the same time gives the shortest distances between control lines. In surveyed country, however, the cardinal direction most nearly satisfying this condition is chosen. The estimating of the strips is done by crews of two men, consisting of an estimator and a compassman. The data obtained are a tally of each tree standing on the strip by diameter, in inches breast high, and by height, in 16-foot logs. Computation of this data is by means of volume tables which show the average contents in board measure, by species, of trees of each given diameter and height. Since these volume tables are based on sound timber, a deduction must be made for defect if any is present. The estimate for a 40 or other unit is obtained by multiplying the volume of the timber on the strips run within that unit by a "Correction Factor," which represents in the judgment of the estimator the ratio between the timber on the unit and on the strip.

ORGANIZATION.

The standard crew is as follows:

Chief of party.
Draftsman.
Four estimators.
Four compassmen.
Cook, packers, or teamsters, etc., as needed.

The Chief of Party should be a man thoroughly trained in reconnaissance work and of sufficient executive ability to secure accurate and effective work from his crew.

The draftsman should be not only an efficient draftsman, but also sufficiently acquainted with topographic sketching to be able to check and instruct the field men along this line and to adjust intelligently conflicting field sheets. Experience with the transit and other instruments is also a desirable qualification.

The estimators and compassmen should, if possible, have had previous experience or training in reconnaissance. At least 50 per cent should have had previous training in Forest Service reconnaissance crews. A Forest school education is an asset. Previous experience in timber cruising alone, while extremely valuable in the right type of man, is not so great a qualification as a knowledge of reconnaissance methods and a ready adaptability to woods work. This is because in reconnaissance more than a mere cruise of the timber is being secured.

RESPONSIBILITY FOR THE PROJECT.

The Chief of Party is responsible directly to the Forest Supervisor, who, in turn, is, of course, responsible to the District office. While it is often found convenient that the crews be organized by the District office and transferred from Forest to Forest in accordance with the needs of the work, yet each crew, while on a given Forest, should be considered as much a part of that Forest's organization as a crew engaged in any other line of work.

DUTIES OF THE CREW MEMBERS.

Following is a brief summary of the duties of each member of the above listed organization. The details of their work are explained on later pages.

CHIEF OF PARTY.

1. Prepare the preliminary plan.
2. Have direct charge of the personnel of the party; maintain its efficiency; have full authority in consultation with the Supervisor in releasing unsatisfactory men, in hiring and in fixing the rate of pay of temporary employees.
3. Assume direct responsibility to the Supervisor for all work done on the project. This responsibility can be properly assumed only when the Supervisor delegates ample authority to the Chief of Party.
4. Select and train one of the members of the crew as an Assistant Chief of Party to act as Chief of Party in his absence.
5. Delegate authority when necessary to permit himself ample time for acquiring familiarity with the country to be covered, for checking the character of the field work done, etc.
6. Provide for systematic recording and filing of the data collected, so that they can be turned over to a successor, if necessary, for completion.
7. Be responsible for the compilation and final completion of the field data and of the summaries.
8. Submit a brief monthly progress report in duplicate to the Supervisor, the extra copy to be forwarded to the District office.

9. Keep records of the cost of the work and submit cost reports as hereinafter described.

ESTIMATOR.

1. Estimate the timber (Form 494).
2. Note the silvical data (Form 494).
3. Assist the compassman in determining the boundaries of types, age classes and of the merchantable timber, and the density of the stand, and determine the age class by use of the axe where necessary.
4. Assist the compassman by consultation in noting the logging data.
5. Compute the estimate sheets.

COMPASSMAN.

1. Direct the course of the line by compass.
2. Obtain distances by pacing.
3. Obtain elevations by barometer or Abney level.
4. Notify the estimator at the end of each 40 or other unit determined and leave a mark to designate this point, which may be easily picked up by anyone wishing to check the work.
5. Check his line for distance and direction on section corners or established control points.
6. Map in the field the area traversed (Form 493) including topography, culture, types, boundary of the merchantable timber, density of timber or normality.*
7. Note the logging data (Form 493).
8. Assist the estimator by consultation on the silvical data.

DRAFTSMAN.

1. Check, and correct, if necessary, the compassman's field maps.
2. Compile these maps into a base map.
3. Be custodian of the camp property and records.

CONTROL METHODS.

The principles governing the selection of a system of control and the field methods involved in running the control lines are covered in the instructions for topographic survey.

THE ESTIMATE.

The per cent of the area to be covered by the strips depends upon the character of the timber. In timber of small size, where the stand is essentially uniform, where comparatively little underbrush is present, or where the timber is of relatively small value, a 5 per cent estimate is sufficient. Where the timber is large, uneven in distribution, or considerable value, and where underbrush is dense, a 10 per cent estimate is necessary. In extensive areas of grass land, brush, etc., a 2½ per cent estimate is sufficient. A 10 per cent estimate requires two strips

*See Appendix under "Normality Description."

through each 40 or its equivalent; a 5 per cent estimate, one; while for the 2½ per cent two strips through each section or its equivalent is required. In general, 5 per cent is considered standard for the lodgepole region, and for the smaller and more uniform timber of the white pine region, while 10 per cent should be used in most cases in the more valuable white pine stands. The more intensive estimate is also necessary in the case of isolated government forties, surrounded by alienations. The unit of estimate should be the 40 on surveyed ground, while on unsurveyed, the unit should be adopted by the Chief of Party usually on the basis of logging units. On surveyed ground, a single sheet (Form 494) should be used for each 40 except where the 40 lies within two distinct logging units, when separate sheets should be used for each. Similar principles should govern the use of sheets on unsurveyed projects, but timber on not to exceed two acres should be tallied on a single sheet.

ESTIMATE SHEET FORM.

Form 494 should be used for securing the estimate. In the case of surveyed land the township, range, section, forty, and meridian should be entered at the head of each sheet and the 40, with the direction in which the strip or strips are run, also noted by means of an arrow in the block of 16 squares. In unsurveyed areas the location of the sheet should be identified by township and range, if possible, and by such numbers and letters as will clearly correlate the estimate sheets with the draftsman's base map. The initials of the compassman and estimator, and the date should also be entered in the proper space. A vertical column should be used for each species. Use of a miscellaneous column should be avoided. The horizontal columns should be numbered by one-inch classes in the lodgepole region and by two-inch classes in the white pine region. The minimum diameter to be estimated is 8 inches. The tallying of the trees is by numbers expressing their height in merchantable logs, i. e., a 4 entered in the vertical column headed "White Pine," and in the horizontal column headed headed "20" represents the white pine tree 4 logs in height and 20 inches in diameter. In case the number of trees to be tallied is so great that the space for a given size will obviously be insufficient, a condensed form of tally is made possible by the use of the dot system, following the number or numbers expressing the height. In tallying, the d. b. h. (diameter breasthigh) is obtained by ocular estimate, checking the eye frequently by the Biltmore stick (or diameter tape or calipers, if Biltmore sticks are not available.) The height of the trees is obtained by ocular estimate, checking the eye by pacing windfalls wherever available and by the use of the hypsometer, if not. The width of the strip should be frequently checked by pacing out to doubtful trees. In types where a large number of unmerchantable trees are present (as in the case of white pine with its defective cedar, hemlock and white fir) a column should be reserved for a tally of these unmerchantable trees. A column should be also used for any special products present. In a cedar pole column, for example, the d. b. h. figures should be disregarded and the column should be divided into four parts headed respectively "25 feet," "30 and 35 feet," "40 and 45 feet," and "50 and 55 feet." A column for cedar logs is usually necessary to take care of the butts of trees from which a pole can be secured from the tops. The logs should be tallied by top diameter opposite the proper figure of the d. b. h. column. A column for ties may be used where considered advisable, but the use of the regular form of tally supplemented by the volume tables when separate tie estimates are advisable, is preferable.

CULL.

Since the volume tables are prepared on the basis of sound trees, it is necessary to estimate the percentage of the cull for each species found on the strip. Defect of all sorts should be entirely handled by this method rather than by reducing the diameter or the height of individual trees tallied. The cull figures estimated for each species should be entered on Form 494. Trees which are absolutely unmerchantable should be tallied in an unmerchantable tree column and the cull factors therefore need not take these into consideration. In the case of very defective species, as hemlock and white fir, where practicable, a separate tally should be made of apparently sound and unsound merchantable trees.

CORRECTION FACTOR.

The correction factor is the figure by which the estimate for the strip or strips within a given 40 or other unit must be multiplied to give the estimate for the whole unit. It is usually obtained by dividing the acreage of the timbered area within the unit by the acreage of the timbered area upon the strip or strips. If the unit is solidly timbered, the correction factor in the case of a 10 per cent estimate is ordinarily 10 and of the 5 per cent estimate, 20. A further discussion of less obvious cases is to be found in the appendix.

COMPUTATIONS.

Each estimator may be held responsible for the computation of his estimate sheets, or such other arrangement made for handling this part of the work as seems best to the Chief of Party. The volume of each size of tree tallied is obtained from the proper volume table and multiplied by the number of trees of that size as shown by the tally sheet. This step in the operation may be eliminated by the use of the multiple volume tables given in the appendix. An addition of each species column separately gives the "Volume on strip" of that species. This figure should be entered in the proper space at the bottom of Form 494. These figures are then reduced by multiplying by one minus the cull per cent, the result being the "Volume on strip net." Multiplication by the correction factor then gives the "Volume on 40."

The column for cedar poles is merely totaled by height classes and the column for cedar logs is handled similarly to the regular species estimates, using the Scribner Log Rule in place of a volume table. The number of logs and the number of trees by species is obtained by a simple count and entered in the appropriate spaces: ("Logs No." and "Trees No."); the "Logs per tree" results from dividing the number of logs by number of trees, and the "logs per M" from dividing the number of logs by the "Vol. on strip net." The "Volume to cut" need not be calculated by the reconnaissance men, but may be filled in, if desired, by the Supervisor. (Omit if this heading is eliminated from the form).

The heading on the back of this Form, **"Location of Timber,"** should be used to indicate any conditions covered by this heading not satisfactorily shown by the map. Notes such as "all cedar is within 2 rods of creek" or "80% of white pine is on north slope" are of immense value, and should be freely entered.

THE SILVICAL DATA.

The purpose of the silvical data notes is a description of the timber and of the site from the standpoint of silviculture. Its use is primarily to aid in determining the advisability of a sale and the silvicultural method applicable.

The silvical data which is to be noted is indicated by the headings on the back of Form 494. Observations should be made constantly while passing through the 40, and entries should be made before leaving it. If two strips are taken in a given 40, the entry should be made at the end of the first strip and these entries should be checked at the end of the second, any differences found being noted. The use of initials E. and W. (east and west) and N. and S. may be used to indicate varying conditions on the two strips.

The conditions of the stand is described by the use of one of the three words, thrifty, mature or decadent. Mature timber is that which has passed the point of rapid growth, but has not yet commenced to retrograde. In general, the age of mature timber is from 120 to 160 years. The words thrifty and decadent are sufficiently limited by this definition of the word mature.

Notes on **damage** include that by fire, by insects and by other agencies. The points to be noted are sufficiently indicated on the Form.

The average **clear length** of the timber should be noted for each species in 16' logs and half logs. By "clear length" is meant that portion of the bole of the tree which is practically free from branches, live or dead, and is not included in the crown.

Under **"Reproduction"** on the back of Form 494 is included only that reproduction which is of importance from the standpoint of future timber crops. Young hemlock, white fir, for example, standing beneath mature white pine, will undoubtedly be largely destroyed in logging and is not here to be considered. Such worthless reproduction is treated merely as "brush" under logging factors. The notes to be taken on young stands, and on the young individuals in these selection stands are fully indicated by the headings on the Form.

Soil is described by composition, degree of moisture and depth. The word **loam** should be used to indicate any mixture of sand and clay, silt and clay, or either sand, clay or silt with humus which results in the crumbly consistency commonly indicated by this term. By **silt** is meant siliceous material so pulverized as to have no gritty feeling; that is, it is simply an exceedingly fine sand. It lacks the characteristic odor of clay and will not remain in suspension in still water more than a few hours. Silt is not necessarily confined to alluvial deposits, although there is its most common occurrence. **Sand, clay and gravel** need no definition. By **fresh** soil is meant soil containing sufficient moisture to be damp to the touch, but not sufficient so that drops can be expelled by pressure of the hand. **Moist and dry** are sufficiently limited by this definition of the word **fresh.**

By soil of moderate depth is meant that between **six inches and two feet**, with the words **shallow** and **deep** limited accordingly.

Under the heading **"Rock"** should be entered the character of the underlying formation if it can be determined, as granite, shale, limestone, etc.

Under **undergrowth** should be entered (1) the species in their order of abundance; (2), the density of the patches of brush, etc., as **open, medium** or **close,** and (3), the percentage of area covered by the patches.

Type, age class and density or normality, although indicated only on the map, are strictly silvical characteristics, and it should be the estimator's duty to keep these factors in mind and to assist the compassman in making the proper entries on his map.

THE FIELD MAP.

The field map should be made on Form 493, using the scale 4 inches to the mile to which this Form is adapted.

On this map should be entered topography and culture in accordance with the instructions for topographic work. **Types** and **age classes** and the density or the normality of the stand should also be indicated. The type and age class is of importance from the standpoint of marking which in turn directly influences the stumpage value, and also from the standpoint of yield studies. Density figures are chiefly of descriptive value. The boundaries of these types, etc., should be indicated by dotted lines and within each boundary symbols expressing the type, age, class and density or normality should be entered. The minimum area to be distinguished as a separate type or age class is 5 acres. Smaller areas, however, which are important by reason of special features of topography or culture, such as small bodies of water, swamps, and barren or grass patches occurring in great contrast to the surrounding area, should be shown on the map. In the appendix can be found a definition of the types and the symbols used to indicate each. The boundary of the merchantable timber should also be determined as closely as possible by the crew, and checked by the Chief of Party. When at all practicable this work will be checked by the appraiser during an early part of the field work. This may be indicated on the map

N. M

by the following symbol: --, --, —. Unless the line is very distinct and

M.

certain, the estimate should always be carried some little distance into the unmerchantable area. It is usually sufficient to merely complete the "40." For definitions of types and age classes see Appendix (Pg.). In estimating crown density in a given case, the part of the total canopy space normally occupied by a full stand which is occupied by trees of all species whether merchantable or unmerchantable, of the same general age class, is designated by a figure—1 to 10; 10 representing a full stand. In the case of a broken stand with the vacant spaces stocked with seedlings, the density figure will apply to the older stand and not to the reproduction.

LOGGING DATA.

The purpose of the notes described under the term "Logging Data" is a description of the surface conditions of each unit from the standpoint of logging. These notes should be secured even if there is no merchantable timber at the present time upon the unit, since it is probable either that merchantable timber upon other areas may have to be removed across this unit or that at some future date logging operations will have to be planned on the basis of the present notes. This data is noted on the back of Form 494. For the purpose of description, the area is divided into three heads: general surface, major, and minor transportation routes. The general surface is what affects the cost of logging in place, including felling, swamping, brush disposal, skidding, etc. The minor transportation factors influence such operations as chuting. The major transportation factors bear upon the feasibility of road construction, flume building, etc. Notes are also taken on streams and stream flow from the standpoint of fluming and driving.

Under each main division the various factors to be considered are entered on the sheet. Beneath each factor are two or more description terms. Beneath each of these terms is a block of 16 small rectangles which correspond by location with the 16 forties of the Section map on the front of the sheet. The notes are taken by entering a check mark in the proper rectangle beneath the proper term. If it is desirable to distinguish between the east and west or north and south part of a 40, the initials E. and W., etc., can be appropriately entered.

Under such headings as "Rock" where the space available does not permit an adequate description, numerals can be entered which refer to references made on the blank lines on the bottom of the sheet.

The stream flow in cubic feet per second need be taken only at the lowest point at which a main stream or any of its forks is crossed by any strip.

TRAINING OF CREW.

It is essential that each crew be thoroughly trained in every detail of the work of a given project before the data secured shall be considered reliable. Such training is necessary in spite of previous experience which the crew members may have had and alone can insure the desired degree of accuracy and uniformity in the data secured. In such training it is necessary for the Chief of Party to spend more or less time in the field with the crew as a whole and with each member of the crew separately in the practice of each detail of the work. It must be assured, that is, not only that the estimate is accurate, but that each member of the crew means the same thing when he states that the underbrush is moderate in density, etc. As complete a standardization as is possible within each crew of the terms used is of far more importance than standardization between crews working on different forests. It is, however, desirable that as nearly as possible the same standards be used for all work done on a given forest, even if covering a period of years. This can only be accomplished by the Forest Supervisor keeping in close touch with the work of each crew which may be assigned to him.

CHECKING.

Two forms of checks are possible; a check of the method used and a check of the men themselves. The former can best be obtained by having men who through experience are considered absolutely reliable and accurate judges of timber cruise 40's already covered by reconnaissance.

Since, however, the methods described in these instructions have been given thorough trial, this form of check can usually be omitted. The second form is much more important, as it serves an additional purpose in instructing the men and raising their standards of accuracy. Details of a method which has been found of considerable value are given in the Appendix. The results of all checks made should be included in the Monthly Progress Report.

SUMMARIES.

The field data gathered by a reconnaissance crew is so voluminous that it is of little value unless carefully summarized. The responsibility for this summation rests on the Chief of Party. Separate summaries of the four classes of data above described should be made, preferably by logging units. The form which each should take follows:

1. **Estimate Data**—The summary of the estimates can be most conveniently put in the form of a tabulation. For this tabulation the estimates for each logging unit will be transferred from the 40 sheets involved to a summary sheet for this unit. For each probable timber sale chance the summary sheets of the logging units involved will in turn be summarized for that chance by type and age class as explained in the Appendix. On certain areas where the proportion of very small or very large timber (such as 40 per cent of the white pine on a given chance being over 30 inches d. b. h.) can be anticipated as a factor in making the appraisal and sale, these sizes should be separately summarized from the start, and each 40 sheet computed with this in mind. Not only the total stand but also the logs per tree and per M. and the cull per cent should be shown. The average acre should also be given by logging units. Notes on the young growth, while strictly a portion of the estimate, can best be handled by including them under silvical data. For sample summary see Appendix page.

2. **Silvical Data**—The summary of the notes on silvical data should take the form of a concise, but precise description of the logging unit from the standpoint of each heading on Form 494. In addition the silvical data from the map should be calculated and stated, including such information as the area within each type and age class, the density figures, etc. For sample summary see Appendix page.

3. **Map Data**—The base map is the only summary of the map data which is necessary. Full instructions for compiling this are given in the instructions for topographic mapping. This base map should be kept strictly up to date. Adjustments of type lines, etc., where the field sheets of two different compassmen disagree should be made immediately, while both men still have a definite recollection of the area.

4. **Logging Data**—The summary of the notes on logging data should take the form of a brief description of each logging unit from the standpoint of the headings on the back of the Form 493. The description can often be best made by means of rough percentages. For sample form of summary, see Appendix page.

In addition to the above summaries for the logging units, additional summaries should be made for each major drainage covered by a specific project. Further summaries by divisions or for the forest as a whole are not to be made by the reconnaissance parties, but can be compiled, if thought desirable, by the Supervisor.

EMPIRICAL YIELD TABLE DATA.

Data on yield is essential in the prediction of future growth, so that in the preparation of the working plan for the management of the Forest it is quite as essential that yield data be collected as that a reconnaissance of the present resources of the Forest be made.

The summarization of estimate data by type and age class as outlined in these instructions will make all such data collected available for empirical yield studies. It is therefore very important that the several age classes be accurately mapped and continual use of the ax for making age determinations will be necessary.

APPRAISAL OF TIMBER.

The appraisal of the timber examined is not a part of the duties of the reconnaissance crew. Figures on the cost of logging can best be collected by competent logging engineers after the reconnaissance data is summarized.

MONTHLY PROGRESS REPORT.

At the end of each month the Chief of Party should submit a progress report in duplicate to the Supervisor; the original being forwarded by the latter to the District office. This report should be a concise statement of the progress made and should mention any unusual features of the work or unexpected problems met. It should also contain the results of the check estimates made during the month.

MISCELLANEOUS.

All equipment should be obtained through the Supervisor's office in the usual manner. The District office endeavors to keep on hand, however, a small supply of barometers, compasses and similar instruments so that in case of emergency time may be saved by wiring to Missoula for additional equipment needed. In the Appendix will be found lists of the necessary equipment for the standard crew.

In certain instances modifications from the form of reconnaissance herein described may be desirable. These should be adopted by members of the party only with the consent of the Chief who should restrict them to unusual instances. Methods which are authorized in such emergencies are described in the Appendix.

Cost-keeping records should be carefully kept. The forms which should be used are given in the Appendix. Copies may be obtained from the District office. The nature of the cost records and the detail in which the figures are desired are definitely indicated by these forms.

The original field data should in all cases be considered as a permanent record and should be filed in the Supervisor's office.

APPENDIX

CRUISER STICK.

The Forest Service Cruiser Stick has four sides: (1) Biltmore stick, (2) Merritt hypsometer, (3) Scribner Decimal C scale for 16-foot logs, (4) Inch scale. The last two are for convenience in finding the approximate contents of fallen trees. Detailed instructions for the construction and use of the Biltmore stick and Merritt hypsometer follow:

BILTMORE STICK.

To use the Biltmore stick, the observer holds it in his right hand horizontally against the tree 4½ feet (breasthigh) from the ground, and 25 inches from his eye, which should be on a level with the stick. If necessary the head should be lowered till the eye is at the proper height. The distance from the tree can be measured by placing the zero end of the stick against the tree and holding the eye at the 25-inch point marked on the back of the stick.

FORM AND CONSTRUCTION.

In the absence of the standard Cruiser stick a Biltmore stick may easily be made. It should be similar to a scale stick in both material and size, except that its length need be only 36 inches or less, if intended for trees 60 inches or less in diameter. Three methods of graduation are possible.

1. One edge may be beveled and the graduations entered on this edge.

2. The edges may be left square and the graduations entered on the broad faces.

3. The edges may be left square and the graduations entered on the broad faces as lines radiating from a series of points representing the successive positions of the eye for trees of various diameters. Center lines corresponding to each radial line should also be entered crossing the stick at right angles. A stick of this pattern should be held with its edge rather than its flat surface against the tree. The radiating lines are useful to a certain extent in keeping the eye at the proper distance.

In either case it is helpful to enter the arm length on the narrow edge.

FORMULAE.

(A) $S = \sqrt{\dfrac{d^2 a}{a + d}}$ (B) $S = \dfrac{d(a - t)}{a\sqrt{(a + d)}}$

Where S = Graduation distance on stick.
d = Diameter of tree.
a = Arm length or distance stick is to be held from eye.
t = Thickness of stick.

Formula A is to be used for patterns of sticks which are so arranged that the graduations are in a line strictly tangent to the tree. This is true in the construction described in 1 and 3 above. In construction 2 the visible graduations are separated from the tree by the thickness of the stick and Formula B should be used.

TABLE.

Diameter, breast high (d) Inches	Distance (a) from eye to tree—Inches. 23		24		25		26		27	
	Actual distances (s) in inches to be marked on stick.									
	A.	B.	A.	B.	A.	B.	A.	B.	A.	B.
6	5.34	5.29	5.37	5.31	5.39	5.34	5.41	5.36	5.43	5.38
8	6.89	6.82	6.93	6.86	6.96	6.90	7.00	6.93	7.03	6.96
10	8.35	8.26	8.40	8.31	8.45	8.36	8.50	8.41	8.54	8.46
12	9.73	9.67	9.80	9.69	9.86	9.76	9.93	9.83	9.99	9.89
14	11.03	10.02	11.13	11.01	11.21	11.09	11.29	11.17	11.37	11.25
16	12.29	12.15	12.40	12.26	12.50	12.36	12.59	12.46	12.68	12.56
18	13.49	13.34	13.61	13.47	13.73	13.59	13.84	13.70	13.95	13.81
20	14.63	14.46	14.77	14.61	14.91	14.75	15.04	14.89	15.16	15.02
22	15.72	15.55	15.89	15.72	16.05	15.89	16.19	16.05	16.34	16.19
24	16.79	16.60	16.97	16.79	17.14	16.95	17.30	17.11	17.46	17.30
26	17.81	17.62	18.01	17.82	18.20	17.99	18.38	18.20	18.55	18.38
28	18.80	18.59	19.02	18.82	19.23	19.04	19.43	19.24	19.62	19.44
30	19.76	19.55	20.00	19.79	20.22	20.02	20.44	20.24	20.65	20.46
32	20.69	20.47	20.95	20.72	21.19	20.97	21.42	21.21	21.65	21.45
34	21.59	21.36	21.86	21.64	22.13	21.91	22.38	22.16	22.63	22.42
36	22.47	22.23	22.76	22.52	23.04	22.81	23.30	23.08	23.56	23.35
38	23.32	23.07	23.64	23.38	23.94	23.69	24.23	23.99	24.49	24.27
40	24.17	23.91	24.49	24.24	24.80	24.56	25.10	24.86	25.40	25.16
42	24.98	24.71	25.32	25.05	25.65	25.38	25.96	25.71	26.27	26.03
44	25.78	25.50	26.13	25.87	26.48	26.23	26.81	26.55	27.13	26.89
46	26.55	26.26	26.93	26.65	27.29	27.01	27.64	27.36	27.89	27.72
48	27.31	27.01	27.71	27.41	28.09	27.80	28.46	28.17	28.80	28.54
50	28.07	27.76	28.48	28.18	28.86	28.57	29.24	28.96	29.61	29.34
52	28.79	28.48	29.22	28.91	29.63	29.32	30.02	29.72	30.40	30.11
54	29.51	29.18	29.95	29.63	30.38	30.06	30.79	30.48	31.18	30.89
56	30.22	29.88	31.11	30.35	31.53	30.79	31.94	31.22	32.33	31.64
58	30.90	30.56	31.38	31.04	31.88	31.49	32.27	31.94	32.69	32.38
60	31.58	31.23	32.07	31.73	32.54	32.20	33.00	32.67	33.43	33.12

Values headed "A" and "B" are calculated from the formulae correspondingly lettered. In B "t" is assumed as ¼ inch.

CORRECTIONS IN USE.

For absolute accuracy the following conditions must be fulfilled. The tree must be circular in cross section; the stick must be held against the tree at a point 4½ feet from the ground; the stick must be horizontal; the line of sight from the eye to the stick at the point of contact with the tree must be perpendicular to the axis of the tree, i. e., horizontal if the tree does not lean; the stick must be perpendicular to this line of sight; the eye must be at the proper distance from the tree. If any of these conditions are not strictly fulfilled an error will result. The various sources of error are not, however, of equal importance. The following table will show how serious a variation from the above named conditions will produce an error of 1% in diameter for 10 inch, 30 inch and 60 inch trees; also the direction of the error:

Sign	Cause	Resulting in error of 1% in Diameter D. B. H. of Trees.		
		10"	30"	60"
—	Eye above or below stick by	9.2"	7.3"	7.1"
+	Stick not horizontal—one end higher than other by	4.6"	4.2"	4.1"
+	Stick not perpendicular to line of sight—one end nearer the eye than the other by..	4.9"	4.9"	5.1"
±	Eye too near to or too far from tree by	1.4"	.45"	.65"

The error resulting from taking the measurement at a point which is too high or too low varies of course greatly with the species and form of the tree. In general, however, it will be negative owing to the inconvenience of stooping to the proper height. The above table shows conclusively that the only dangerous source of error is in the distance of the eye from the tree. Fortunately, this is apt to be more or less compensating. Furthermore, the errors constant in sign may offset each other to a certain degree.

It should be further noted, however, that particular care should be taken in the case of irregular trees. Measurements of a smaller diameter will be reduced and of a larger diameter will be increased by use of the Biltmore stick. This exaggeration of the errors of the caliper in this case makes it particularly important that either two measurements, or a measurement of an average diameter be taken where an accurate measurement of a single tree is desired.

MERRITT HYPSOMETER.

The Merritt Hypsometer is designed for measuring height in 16.3-foot logs at two different distances from the tree, namely, 1 chain and 1½ chains. It is used as follows:

(1.) Pace a distance of one chain, or a chain and a half, measured horizontally, from the tree.

(2.) Hold the stick vertically, squarely in front of the eye, and as nearly plumb as possible. After some practice it can be plumbed with a fair degree of accuracy by holding at the lower end and balancing: if the tree is downhill it can sometimes be held near the upper end and plumbed by its own weight. The hypsometer side should be at right angles to the observer's line of sight.

(3.) Raise or lower the stick until its lower end, or any convenient mark for the proper distance, intersects stump height on the tree.

(4.) Holding it in this position, read on the proper scale the distance intersected by the top of the last log. If the observer is at one chain from the tree the height will be shown by the left hand scale, or large figures, if at one and a half chains, by the right hand scale, or small figures.

Height may be measured with this hypsometer on the level or on any slope, either above or below the tree, provided the distance from the observer to the tree is the horizontal distance. For very tall trees, double the distance will give double the number of logs.

Any straight stick may readily be made into a Merritt hypsometer. The following table gives measurements to be used for the different reach intervals.

For use one chain from tree.		For use 1½ chains from tree
Distance from eye to stick.	Interval on stick for measuring one log (16.3') on tree.	Interval on stick for measuring one log (16.3') on tree.
23"	5.68"	3.78"
24"	5.93"	3.95"
25"	6.18"	4.11'
26"	6.42"	4.27"
27"	6.67"	4.44"

CHECKING.

The importance of an adequate checking system can hardly be overemphasized, particularly in the case of less experienced men. The method often employed formerly, of handling this question by having some lumberman cruise occasional forties after the reconnaissance, has seldom proven entirely satisfactory, since even at best, this system merely measures the error without determining its cause.

SYSTEM FOR ANALYSIS.

The following system has been tried with considerable success, and has the advantage of giving an analysis of each man's errors as well as determining their amount. One of the most experienced estimators is chosen as a check estimator. This man, with a compassman, re-runs forties already covered by the various estimators. In every detail his work is identical with the regular reconnaissance work, except that he works very slowly and with maximum accuracy. All diameters are actually measured by Biltmore stick or calipers; the width of strip is paced out in all cases of doubt, and heights are constantly checked by measuring wind-fall or by hypsometer. Furthermore, the strips are run as nearly as possible over exactly the same ground as that covered by the original estimate, a mark being left at the end of each forty by the original compassman.

A comparative analysis is then made of the original sheet and of the check sheet on some such form as follows;

SAMPLE ANALYSIS SHEET—CHECK ESTIMATE

NE¼ SW¼, S. 13, T. 50, N. R. 4E. B. M.

Estimator, J. Smith

Species	Estimate	Check	Error	Pct. Error
W. Pine	298 M	260 M	-38 M	-14.6
D. Fir	56 M	49 M	- 7 M	-14.3
Total - -	354 M	309 M	-45 M	-14.5

White Pine

Diam. Group	No. of Trees		No. of Logs		Logs per Tree	
	Est.	Check	Est.	Check	Est.	Check
15" and over	33	31	59	68	2.1	2.2
16" -20"	20	21	82	81	4.1	4.0
21" -25"	6	5	35	29	5.8	5.8
26" -30"	3	2	24	15	8.0	7.5
30" -	1	2	9	16	9.0	8.0
Total -	63	61				

Douglas Fir

Diam. Group	No. of Trees		No. of Logs		Logs per Tree	
	Est.	Check	Est.	Check	Est.	Check
15" and over	20	18	56	50	2.8	2.8
16" -20"	17	20	76	89	4.5	4.4
21" -25"	10	8	60	49	6.0	6.1
26" -30"	6	7	51	56	8.5	8
30" -	3	3	29	24	9.7	8
Total	56	56				

Comment.

This check indicates:

Width of strip, O. K.
Diameter, O. K.
Height O. K. up to about 25 inches, **for larger trees too high.**

8-16-12 H. JONES, Check Estimator

APPLICATION OF SYSTEM.

Checks should be made at intervals depending on the experience of the crew. During the first two or three weeks after the training periods the check estimator should be kept continually at this work. Later, he may be used for the greater part of the time in routine estimating. Time may be saved by selecting for checking two forties cruised by different estimators which lie adjacent. The speed of check estimating, (including the analysis work), is about one-half that of the regular estimating work. Silvical data, logging data, cull per cents, etc., should be checked at the same time with the estimate and the compassman accompanying the check estimator should check for topographic detail.

CORRECTION FACTOR.

The application of a correction factor based upon the estimator's general impression that the strips run are a certain per cent above or below the general average of the 40, is very dangerous except in the case of the most experienced men. Even the more inexperienced estimators, however, can use it with advantage when its determination is arbitrary and mathematical, as in the following cases:

1. When the timbered area of a forty is broken by parks, burns, and other openings, the correction factor is the direct ratio between the timbered area in the forty and the timbered area covered by the estimate strip or strips

2. When different types containing nearly pure stands are traversed by the estimate strip, but when it is evident that the strip does not include an area within each type proportionate to the acreage of the type, the correction factor may be calculated in a manner similar to 1, separately for each species.

3. When the compassman makes gross errors in pacing the correction factor may be mathematically adjusted to compensate

Example 1: The compassman's map shows that 11 acres of a forty are grassland and 29 acres timbered, and that 15 chains of the double strip was run in the grassland and 25 chains in the timbered; timber area within strip 2.5 acres.

$$\text{Correction factor. } \frac{\text{Acreage timber on forty}}{\text{Acreage timber on strip}} \; \frac{29}{2.5} = 11.6$$

Example 2: The compassman's map shows that 5 acres of the forty is spruce type and 35 acres is lodgepole pine type, and that 8 chains of the single strip run was in spruce, and 12 chains in lodgepole pine. Area of spruce type in strip .8 acres; area of lodgepole pine type in strip 1.2 acres; correction factor spruce $= \frac{5}{.8} = 6.2$; correction factor lodge pole pine $= \frac{35}{1.2} = 29.2$

Example 3: A compassman falls 5 chains short of the section line on the far side of a section covered. The estimator tallies on through to the line. Obviously, the sheet for the last forty run contains too much timber at the expense of the first three forties Assuming the error in pacing to be equally distributed, we have 85 of the compassman's chains equal to 80 true chains. Each of the first three sheets then covers $\frac{80 \times 20}{85}$ chains in length and the last is $\frac{80 \times (20+5)}{85}$ chains in length.

Area of strip first 3 forties $= \frac{85}{80 \times 2}$

Area of strip last forty $= \frac{85}{80 \times 2.5}$

Correction factor (in case of one strip to forty) $= \frac{40}{\frac{80 \times 2}{85}} = 21.3$ for first 3 forties, and $\frac{40}{\frac{80 \times 2.5}{85}} = 17.0$ for last forty.

In case two strips are run to the forty the actual area of each strip should be calculated separately and the two added, the sum being divided into 40. The following table gives the area of the sample strips in each of the first three and the last 40 in the case of various errors in pacing:

Chains paced per mile	Acres in each of first three 40's	Acres in last 40
90	1.75	2.62
89	1.77	2.57
88	1.80	2.52
87	1.83	2.46
86	1.85	2.40
85	1.87	2.34
84	1.90	2.28
83	1.93	2.21
82	1.95	2.14
81	1.97	2.07
80	2.00	2.00
79	2.03	1.92
78	2.05	1.84
77	2.07	1.76
76	2.10	1.68
75	2.13	1.59
74	2.15	1.50
73	2.17	1.41
72	2.20	1.32
71	2.23	1.22
70	2.25	1.12

COST KEEPING SYSTEM AND FORMS.

The following special forms will be used for cost keeping on reconnaissance projects. These may be requisitioned from the District Office. In addition to these the standard Form 21 may be kept in the field. This will be totaled at the end of each month, and the food supplies on hand will be entered in red ink and deducted, a similar amount being carried forward to the next month. The special forms should be totaled and completed as soon as possible after the end of each month and filed in the Supervisor's office, a copy of the final summary sheet for the month only being forwarded to the District office.

CULL.

Cull is a very difficult matter for inexperienced men to handle. They may be largely assisted by the preparation of a table showing the average maximum and minimum cull per cent characteristic of a given region for each species, further divided by site, etc., if necessary. This table should be prepared from the best available information. An observant scaler who has worked in the region in question is probably best qualified to prepare it. The following table which was used on the Coeur d'Alene Forest will indicate the form such data may take.

FLAT.

Average Cull.

Extreme maximum	White Pine	*Hemlock	Tamarack	*White Fir	Red Fir	Spruce	Cedar
Extreme maximum	65	100	35	85	25	25	60
Average maximum	30	50	20	45	10	10	40
Average minimum	10	30	10	25	5	5	15
Extreme minimum	5	20	5	15	0	0	0

SLOPE.

	White Pine	*Hemlock	Tamarack	*White Fir	Red Fir	Spruce	Cedar
Extreme maximum	35	50	20	40	20	20	20
Average maximum	15	30	15	30	10	10	10
Average minimum	8	20	7	20	5	5	0
Extreme minimum	3	10	0	10	0	0	0

These cull per cents include both breakage and defects

*Trees obviously defective not tallied.

DESCRIPTIONS OF TYPES.

Following are the descriptions of the types for which symbols are given in the instructions. In these descriptions the percentages given are percentages of the numerical proportion of the trees and not of the volume. The trees considered for this numerical proportion should in mature stands include all age classes which have definitely established themselves as a part of the stand and which therefore indicate its type. Ordinarily this will include pole and sapling growth but not seedlings.

The classification hereafter outlined is based upon the present composition of the stand, regardless of whether this composition is the ultimate cover of the site or merely a temporary cover resulting from some interference with natural conditions. Where a succession of types is known to occur, either the ultimate type, or one of the stages in the succession which, as far as can now be foreseen, will be perpetuated in forest management, may, if desired, be mapped or used for purposes of management in addition to the present cover.

TREELESS LAND.

There is no clear line of demarcation between trees and shrubs, and in this classification, which is purely for practical purposes, no attempt is made to draw a fine distinction between them. Accordingly, under "Treeless Land" are included two types, "Brush" and "Sagebrush," which are often composed partly or entirely of individuals having tree form, but so small and stunted that the types in which they occur are ordinarily classed as treeless.

Barren—An area too rocky, too exposed, too arid, or at too high an elevation to support trees or grass or more than a very scattering growth of herbs and shrubs; and temporary barrens, areas repeatedly burned containing neither reproduction, grass, nor brush in appreciable quantities.

Grass—An area such as parks and mountain meadows, whose principal vegetation is grass and other herbs.

Cultivated—An area now under cultivation or lying fallow.

Sagebrush—An area whose principal vegetation is sagebrush.

Brush—All other areas the present cover of which is a stand of shrubs or stunted trees.

WOODLAND.

An area, usually at the lower altitudinal limits of tree growth, whose crop when mature is a stand of trees, ordinarily open, usually short, branchy, and crooked, most of which are fit only for cordwood, fencing, etc.

Juniper—A stand composed of approximately 80 per cent or more of any species of juniper, with very little or no pinion. Rocky mountain juniper is the chief species, usually with some limber pine, Western yellow pine, or Douglas fir.

TIMBERLAND.

An area whose crop when mature is a more or less dense stand of trees which may furnish sawlogs, ties, telegraph poles, etc.

Yellow Pine—A stand containing approximately 50 per cent or more of Western yellow pine. Usually on dry well-drained sites at the lower altitudinal limit of timberland or exposed south and southwest slopes at higher altitudes. The principal species in mixture are Douglas fir, Western larch, and lodgepole pine.

Western White Pine—A stand in which Western white pine is the key tree, forming approximately 15 per cent or more of the stand. In the northern part of the range of this type, at medium elevations, hemlock is the predominant tree, frequently outnumbering the white pine even in young stands; at higher elevations in the same region Engelmann spruce and Alpine fir are the chief associates. In the middle of its range white pine occurs nearly pure or with Douglas fir as its chief associate, and with hemlock, white fir, larch and sometimes lodgepole pine in mixture. In the southern part of the range of this type white pine is less important numerically than further north. Here in young stands white pine occasionally forms as much as 50 per cent of the stand or more, but usually the predominant trees of the type are white fir and cedar, with Douglas fir and larch in mixture, a little yellow pine on the drier knolls, and sometimes in young stands lodgepole pine.

Cedar-White Fir—The stand is composed of cedar and white or grand fir, the former nearly pure in patches, the latter predominant throughout with a considerable amount of Douglas fir, some yellow pine in groups on the knolls and as scattered individuals throughout and rare Western white pine individuals. The type occurs on the Selway and southern portion of the Clearwater National Forest south of the commercial range of white pine

Cedar-Hemlock-White Fir—Stands composed of cedar, hemlock and white or grand fir in varying proportions, with a little white pine, also Engelmann spruce, Alpine fir and rarely Douglas fir, areas which under management could be made to produce white pine in commercial quantities.

Lodgepole Pine—A stand containing approximately 50 per cent or more of lodgepole pine, usually nearly pure, but sometimes in mixture with other species. The principal species in mixture are Douglas fir, Engelmann spruce, Alpine fir and Western larch.

Douglas Fir—A stand containing approximately 60 per cent or more of Douglas fir, sometimes follows a temporary type of aspen. The principal species in mixture are yellow pine, lodgepole pine and Western larch. Usually at the lower or medium altitudes either at the lower limit of timberland or just above the yellow pine type. Occurs also on north slopes above the white pine type.

Larch-Douglas Fir—A stand containing approximately 60 per cent or more of Western larch and Douglas fir, with white or grand fir in mixture. Larch is the key tree. The proportion of larch varies greatly from very little to practically pure. The principal species in mixture is yellow pine, but occasionally with lodgepole pine, Western white pine, lowland fir, Western red cedar, or Western hemlock. Usually at medium elevations about the same as Douglas fir, but with more favorable site conditions. On less favorable sites than white pine.

Engelmann Spruce—A stand containing approximately 50 per cent or more of Engelmann spruce. Sometimes follows a temporary type of aspen. Engelmann spruce may be pure, but is more often in mixture with Alpine fir, lodgepole pine, limber pine and Douglas fir. Usually at the higher elevations and on the more moist sites.

Mountain Hemlock—A stand containing approximately 50 per cent or more of mountain hemlock (**T. mertensiana**). The principal species in mixture are Alpine fir, Engelmann spruce and Western white pine. Other species common in the mixture are whitebark pine, lodgepole pine, Alpine larch (**L. lyallii**) amabilis fir and Shasta fir. At the higher elevations usually near the upper limit of tree growth, areas of mountain hemlock not capable of producing merchantable stands should be included in the subalpine type.

Subalpine—A stand containing a varying mixture of subalpine species no one of which is abundant enough to throw the stand into any of the types already described or rarely pure stands. At the upper limit of tree growth, usually unmerchantable because of poor form and small size, and of value for protective purposes only. The principal species are Alpine fir, Engelmann spruce, lodgepole pine, white-bark pine, limber pine, mountain hemlock, and Alpine larch.

Legend—In designating land types, land classification, forest types, age classes and cut-over lands on the base map prepared by the field draftsman, symbols as given below will be used. In the preparation of land type, land class, forest type, age class, stand class and other maps to meet a specific need or for the administration of a particular phase of Forest business colors as given below will be used. The latter maps will be prepared on reproductions made by the District office from the base map. Size of areas to be shown on map as separate type covered under Map Data.

Standard Legends. (Using Color Tints).

Date of Origin	Tint No.	Classification and Stand. Maps (Atlas Legend)	Timber Type Maps	Timber Age-Class Maps
	2	Grassland	Grassland (G)	Grassland
1891-1910	10	New burn	Juniper (J)	2-21 yrs. (20)
1711-1750	15	Light 10-25 MBF	Yellow Pine (YP)	162-201 yrs. (200)
Prior to 1711		Dark 25-50 MBF		Over 200 yrs. (200+)
	Indigo	Special	Mountain Hemlock (MH)	Special
1871-1890	23	Special	Cedar-white fir (C-WF)	22-41 yrs. (40)
	5	Special	Cedar-hemlock-White-fir (C-H-WF)	Special
1751-1790	29	Light 2-5 MBF Dark 5-10 MBF	Douglas Fir (DF)	122-161 yrs. (160)
	37	Sage Brush	Sage Brush (SB)	Sage Brush
	46	Cultivated Land	Cultivated Land (C)	Cultivated Land
1911-1930	58	Water	Engelmann Spruce (ES)	Present and next decade (0)
1851-1870	62	Mineral Land	Larch-Douglas Fir (L-DF)	42-61 yrs. (60)
1811-1830	63	Woodland, poles, etc.	Lodgepole pine (LP)	82-101 yrs. (100)
1791-1810	69	Less than 2 M.B.F.	White Pine (WP)	102-121 yrs. (120)
1831-1850	72	Old Cuttings	Subalpine (SA)	62-81 yrs. (80)
	87	Brush	Brush (Bh)	Selection Forest all ages (Z)
	300	Barren	Barren (Bn)	

OLD CUTTINGS.

Less than 1-3 of merchantable timber removed	Higgins' red Vertical hatching
1-3 to 2-3 merchantable removed	Higgins' red 45° NE-SW
More than 2-3 merchantable timber removed	Higgins' red 45° NW-SE

(Cutover symbols are to be used only in case timber left in cutting still constitutes the predominant age class, not being applicable to areas where the reproduction is more important than the mature timber).

Cultivable Land	Higgins' red Horizontal hatching
Doubtful cases may be indicated by	Higgins' red Horizontal broken hatching
Burns	Higgins' black Vertical hatching

(This symbol applicable only where merchantable dead timber is the material present of predominant importance. Where reproduction of a merchantable remnant of the mature stand is of predominant importance the area should be classed as the corresponding age class of the proper timber type).

Boundaries of Types and Age Classes, dotted lined . . . .

Boundaries of areas of merchantable timber, dash and dotted lines, as

M
- -.—.—.—.—.—.—.—
NM

Reservoir Sites, Cultural Features, etc.—See "Signs, Symbols and Colors, 1912," issued in small booklet form.

Example: For a stand of timber in the white pine type 70 years old with .5 crown density the map would show this as follows: .5-WP—80. (The density is placed before type to avoid possible confusion in figures.)

Normality Description—Normality is the present condition of a stand discounted into terms of its expected yield at the end of the rotation. The term is most useful in such pure stands as lodgepole pine. Here it is considered that 1,000 seedlings per acre, well distributed, will result in the maximum production per acre. Less than this number results in reduced yield. More than this number has the same effect, through overcrowding and consequent reduction in growth.

The standard normality is 1.0. By a stand of .5 normality is meant one which is so understocked that it will by the end of the rotation, yield but half of what it could if properly stocked. By +.5 is indicated a stand which will yield the same amount but with this reduced yield the result of overcrowding. The following figures are indicative:

.3	300 per acre	+.9	1500 per acre
.5	500 " "	+.7	2000 " "
.7	700 " "	+.5	3000 " "
.9	900 " "	+.3	4000 " "
1.0	1000 " "		

These figures refer to good distribution. Uneven distribution will lower the figures on understocked and raise them on overstocked areas. Uneven height growth will raise the figures on overstocked areas. All these figures are for the youngest age class and allowance must be made for older stands.

Determination of Streamflow in Cubic Feet per Second—The flow of a stream in cubic feet per second is easily obtained with sufficient accuracy for the purpose for which it is to be used as follows.

(a) Estimate the average width and the average depth of the stream in feet.

(b) Multiply the average width by the average depth to obtain the cross section area in square feet.

(c) Estimate the velocity in feet per second at a point where the cross section area is approximately the average for some distance.

(d) A product of (b) and (c) is the flow in cubic feet per second.

Filing System—The first essential is a moisture and rodent proof box. The Forest Service metal filing case with its three card-board transfer cases serves admirably. The filing may be done in letter mail envelopes, five series of these to be kept as follows:

1. Incomplete work, arranged alphabetically by names of estimators and compassmen.

2. Completed work.

a. Maps arranged by township and section usually one envelope for each township is sufficient.

b. Estimate and description sheets arranged by logging units. One envelope for each unit.

c. Summaries filed in separate envelopes by logging units

3. Blank forms, etc.

Assignment of forties to the several estimators may be recorded on blank township plats by entering in each forty a key letter identifying the estimator to which it is assigned. When completed the estimate sheet is turned in, the total estimate shown should then be entered under the key letter. Key letters without estimates thus indicate incompleted work.

The above system applies to surveyed areas, but may be easily modified to apply to unsurveyed projects.

Equipment—The following lists of equipment and provisions have been planned for the average ten-man crew.

LIST OF EQUIPMENT.

Instruments—

1 Transit, Gurley, Mountain, (Not always needed).
1 Level, Locks. " " "
8 Barometers, Aneroid.
8 Levels, Abney.
6 Compasses, F. S. Standard.
6 Compasses, box pocket.
6 Registers, tally.
6 Cruisers sticks.
5 Tapes, diameter.
1 to 4 Tapes, steel, (preferably 2½ chains).
1 Slide Rule.
1 Sketching case.
1 Adding Machine.
"T" Square, 24.
2 12' Scales, engineers'.
1 set drawing instruments.
1 Triangle, 45°.
1 Triangle, 30° and 60°.
1 Protractor.
Drawing ink—black, blue, red, orange.
Ink, fountain pen.
Pens, quill.
Pens, Gillott's No. 303.
Thumb Tacks, solid head, 6 doz.
Rubber bands.
Clips.
Blotters, small.
Wire No. 12, small amount, for setting up camp.
Nails.

Boards for Drafting—

24"x24" }
36"x36" } 1"x12"x16' Matched

Forms and Stationery, etc.—

Map books, Form No. 493.
Estimate books, Form 494.
Time slips.
Time books.
Summary Sheets.
1 case, ranger filing.
1 tatum folder.
1 file, collapsible.
Office note.
Yellow paper.
Envelopes.

Envelopes, Manila, 6"x8½" for estimate sheets.
Envelopes, Manila, 9½"x12".
Ranger notebooks No. 289.
Pencils 4H.
Pencils No. 2.
Drawing paper. Cloth back.
Tracing cloth.
Tracing paper, thinnest grade.

Tentage—

1 10"x12" (high wall) cook tent.
1 7"x9" commissary tent.
1 fly (large) mess tent.
1 10"x12" (high wall) drafting tent.
3 to 5, 7"x9" (wall tents) sleeping quarters

Miscellaneous Equipment—

1 Map case, 10"x40"x6".
3 table tops (canvas on bed of 2½ inch slats closely laid).
2 Baldwin lamps, (acetylene).

Provision List—Taken from Trail Manual 1913.
10 men for 10 days (100 rations).

Flour	100	lbs.
*Cured Meats	75	"
Potatoes	100	"
Beans	20	"
**Sugar	40	"
***Lard	10	" in 5 lb. pails.
Butter	10	" Creamery, 1 lb. cartons.
Dried Fruits	20	"
Coffee	10	" Good grade, ground 1 lb.
Rice	5	" sealed tins.
Tea	1	"
Cocoa	2	" ½ lb. cans.
Cheese	5	"
Macaroni	2	"
Milk	48	cans. Carnation grade.
Corn Beef	5	" 2 lbs.
Tomatoes	8	" 2½ lbs. solid pack.
Peas	5	" 2 lbs. solid pack.
Corn	10	" 1 lb. solid pack.
Sauer Kraut	4	" 3 lbs.
Rolled Oats	10	lbs.
Onions	10	"

*If fresh meat is available use 50 lbs., cured, 25 lbs. fresh.
**If syrup is preferred, reduce sugar accordingly.
***If fresh meat is used, increase lard to 15 lbs.

Corn Meal	5	lbs.
Graham Flour	5	"
Pan Cake Flour	5	"
Salt	3	"
Baking Powder	3	"
Soda	1	"
Yeast Cake	1	Package.
Eggs	10	Doz.
Catsup	2	Bot.
Pickles, sour	1	kit 2 gal.
Mustard, ground	4	oz. can.
Pepper, ground	8	" "
Cinnamon, ground	4	" "
Allspice, ground	4	" "
Lemon Ext	4	oz. Bot.
Vanilla Ext.	4	" "
Vinegar	1	qt. Bot.
Soap, laundry	5	lbs.
Matches	3	five cent packages.
Candles	2	lbs.
****Coal Oil	4	1 qt. bottles.

Dehydrated fruits and vegetables may be substituted for fresh fruits and vegetables in the ration of one pound of dried to seven pounds of fresh. The following dehydrated products are sometimes of great value in side or main camps:

Potatoes (riced).
Cabbage.
Spinach.
Carrots.
Onions.
Turnips.
Sweet corn.
Green peas.
String beans.
Cranberries.
Rhubarb.
Blueberries
Raspberries.
Strawberries.
Celery (ground).
Leeks (ground).

It may be advisable to add certain articles to the above list to provide for the cold lunch feature of reconnaissance work.

Approximate total weight, 560 lbs.

" " cost, $65.00.

****Coal oil will be replaced by carbide if Baldwin lamps are used.

Kitchen Outfit—(Taken from Trail Manual 1913).

Crew of 10 men, including foreman and cook.

1 Lantern.
2 S. B. Axes.
1 Sheet steel cook stove No. 8, with 6 joints pipe.
4 Fry pans, assorted sizes.
2 Granite kettles, 12 qt., with covers
4 " " 6 " " "
2 " stew kettles, 6 qt., with covers.
1 Granite coffee pot, 8 qt.
1 Granite tea pot, 3 qt.
2 Dishpans, 14 qt.
1 Granite rice boiler, 6 in.
2 Dripping pans to fit oven of stove.
1 Can opener.
1 Rolling pin.
4 Tin wash basins.
4 Tin water pails, 10 qt.
3 Tin dippers, 1 qt.
1½ doz. Granite plates.
1½ doz. " cups and saucers.
½ doz. " dish up basins, 2 qt.
½ doz. " " " " 1 qt.
1 doz. Mush bowls.
1 Granite syrup pitcher, 1 qt.
1 " cream pitcher, 1 qt.
2 Butcher knives, 1-10 in., 1-12 in.
1 " steel.
1 Meat fork.
2 Granite stirring spoons.
1 Meat saw.
4 Tin milk pans, 6 qt.
1½ doz. Wood handled steel knives and forks.
1½ doz. Teaspoons.
1½ doz. Tablespoons.
5 1-Gal slop cans, galvanized iron.
*5 yds. 12 oz. ducking or light canvas, 36 in. wide.
½ lb. 10 oz. tacks.
10 lbs. Assorted nails.
1 Carpenter's hammer.
1 " hand saw.
1 Alarm clock.
10 yds. Crash towling.
10 yds. Unbleached muslin.

Approximate total weight 325 lbs.

Approximate total cost $62.00.

*This item is intended to be used for tops for table frames built of light poles and is already covered under miscellaneous equipment.

The tin pails may be replaced by canvas pails, and one pitcher each for milk and syrup added.

SUMMARY SHEET FORMS.

The sample summaries here given are adopted in the effort to secure direct utilization of all data collected in the field.

In case of the sample summary of silvical data the first table only is prepared with mathematical accuracy, the acreage figures under type and age class being accurately obtained from the map. The other figures of this summary and of the logging data summary are comparatively rough approximations, the field sheets and maps being used to check and supplement the personal knowledge of the chief.

Summaries of estimate data by logging units and probable timber sale chances will be made as indicated in the sample summary sheet form.

It is evident that it will be necessary to determine the average stand per acre by species for certain type and age classes, within the logging chance for use in connection with appraisal and marking. The estimates should therefore be further summarized in the following manner:

When such demands can be anticipated the estimates should be further summarized in the following manner:

A certain number of estimate sheets within each age class of each type will be selected, and the estimates for the average sample acre obtained in each case. The special age classes and types here distinguished must be determined with reference to the marking plans for the logging chance under consideration.

These results may be tabulated as below (j—r) together with acreage figures (a—i). Figures representing total calculated volume (aj—ir) are then directly obtained and the ratio between this total for the whole chance and the actual total estimate for the whole chance $\frac{S}{S'}$ easily secured. This ratio applied as a correction factor to the separate calculated total volumes for each species of each age class of each type will give the stand by species for age class and type of the logging chance with sufficient accuracy to meet the needs of the marking plans. Figures for the average acres may be then obtained by division. In the tabulation given below it is to be noted that several species will normally appear under each age class of each type.

LOGGING CHANCE.

Type	Age Classes (By species)	Acres summary from silvical data	Volume per A. From representative estimate sheets	Total cal. vol.	Actual Est. From est. summary of unit	Calculated estimates corrected	Stand per A.
A	1	a	j	aj		$\frac{aj.S}{S'}$	$\frac{js}{S'}$
	2	b	k	bk		$\frac{bk.S}{S'}$	$\frac{ks}{S'}$
	3	c	l	cl		$\frac{cl.S}{S'}$	$\frac{ls}{S}$
B	1	d	m	dm		$\frac{dm.S}{S'}$	$\frac{ms}{S'}$
	2	e	n	en		$\frac{en.S}{S'}$	$\frac{ns}{S'}$
	3	f	o	fo		$\frac{fo.S}{S'}$	$\frac{os}{S'}$
C	1	g	p	gp		$\frac{gp.S}{S'}$	$\frac{ps}{S'}$
	2	h	q	hq		$\frac{hq.S}{S'}$	$\frac{qs}{S'}$
	3	i	r	ir		$\frac{ir.S}{S'}$	$\frac{rs}{S'}$
Total for chance				S'	S		

SAMPLE SUMMARY OF ESTIMATES

(To be used for each logging unit and also for the probable timber sale chance as a whole.)

Logging Unit **Smith Creek**

Species	Total stand M. bd. ft.	Cull %	Stand per A. M. b. ft.	%	No. Logs	Logs per M.	No. Trees	Logs per Tree	Poles 25	Poles 30	Poles 35
White Pine											
10"-28"	12,000	10	4.0	16	48,000	4	6,000	8			
30" and over	8,000		6.0	24	80,000	10	16,000	5			
Cedar	5,000	15	2.5	10	40,000	8	10,000	4	10,000	5,000	6,000
West. Fir											
Sound	10,000	10	5.0	20	100,000	10	20,000	5			
Defective	15,000	40	7.5	30	150,000		30,000				
Totals - -	50,000		25.0	100	418,000	8.4	82,000	5	10,000	5,000	5,000

SAMPLE SUMMARY.

Logging Data, Smith Creek.

Cutting and Skidding Factors—Surface: 80% smooth: 20% rough. (concentrated in section 18, north of creek).

Soil: 100% firm.

Rock: Continuous ledges about 20 feet high are found on north side of creek in sections 18 and 19. Small areas of slide rock in section 7, not affecting logging seriously.

Underbrush: W. P. 200+. Hemlock, white fir, and yew of moderate density, averaging 10 feet in height, covering 40% of area. W. P. 80-160, inc., hemlock and white fir, density, light, covering less than 10% of area. (Etc. for other types and age classes).

Windfall: Light, 10% of area (section 7) average diameter 6", moderate, 70% of area average diameter 10". Heavy, 20% of area average diameter 10".

Transportation Factors—Draws—Soil 100 % firm.

Rock: Lower 100 yards of draws coming into creek from north in sections 18 and 19 become narrow canyons cut 20 feet into the ledge rock; some slide rock in section 7. Not a factor elsewhere.

Underbrush—60% moderate. 40% light. Of little importance as transportation factor.

Windfall—Moderate and of 20" material. 50% of area; heavy and of 12" material. 50% of area.

Streams—Main Smith Creek has a flow of approximately 10 cubic feet per second. A regular gradient of about 2%. Its average width varies from 7 to 8 feet at the Forks to 20 feet at its confluence with Jones Creek. The banks are good for driving. (Important branch streams to be treated in similar manner).

Stream Bottoms—Soil: 70% firm. 30% soft. (In section 19, S¼).

Rock. None that hinders road building.

Underbrush: Heavy, 50%; moderate, 50%.

Windfall: Heavy and of 15" material, 60%; moderate and of 10" material, 40%. Min. width of main stream bottom 70 feet. North branch 30 feet for 1½ miles, south branch 20 feet for 1 mile then 10 feet for ½ mile.

Miscellaneous—There is an excellent dam site in section 7, requiring about 100 feet of wing construction.

SAMPLE SUMMARY SILVICAL DATA FLAT CREEK.

Types and Age Classes.

Type	Av. Density	Age Class	Area	
W. P.	.7	20	100	
" "	.5	60	200	
" "	.3	160	400	
" "	.1	200+	1800	
" "		All		2500
D. F.	.3	120	400	
" "	.3	160	200	
" "		All		600
L. P.	.4	120	300	300
		Total.		3400

CONDITION OF STAND.

Thrifty: W. P. 20 & 60.
D. F. 120 (about 50%).
Mature: W. P. 160.
D. F. 120 (about 50%).
D. F. 160.
L. P. 120.
Decadent: W. P. 200+

Total acreage, thrifty, 500; mature, 1100; decadent, 1800.

DAMAGE.

Fire: About 200 acres in W. P. 200+ and 50 in D. F. 160, 80% of trees damaged.

Insects: Bark beetles reported generally throughout W. P. 160 and 200+. Special examination urgent.

Clear Length.

Type	Age	Species	Clear Length
W. P.	160	W. P.	2
		D. F.	1
		L.	3
	200+	W. P.	5
		D. F.	2
		L.	6
D. F.	120 & 160	D. F.	1
L. P.	120	L. P.	1

Soil

Type	Age	Soil.
W. P.	All	Sand-loam, fresh; moderate to deep.
D. F.	All	" dry, shallow to moderate.
L. P.	All	" " " " "

Rock.

Granite formation underlies almost whole area. About a section of limestone at extreme north end, in W. P. Type.

Undergrowth.

Type	Age	Density	Per Cent Area
W. P.	20	Open	5
	60	Open	5
	160	Open	5
	200+	Open	50
D. F.	120	Medium	15
	160	Close	25
L. P.	120	Open	5

Young Growth.

Type	Age	No. Per. A.	Species	Per Cent	Distribution
W. P.	20	2,000	W. P. 20;	L. 40; W. P. 40.	Singly
W. P.	60	600	W. P. 50;	L. 30; W. F. 20.	Singly

VARIATION IN METHODS.

The Chief of Party may find the following suggestions helpful when special conditions are encountered.

THE QUARTER ACRE CIRCULAR PLOT.

In stands of timber of small value scattered over large areas, a one-man crew may be used to good advantage for mapping and estimating. The estimating may be most effectively done in such a case by the taking of one quarter acre circular plots approximately 60 feet in radius at two and one-half chain intervals. The area covered by such a tally will be equivalent to a strip one chain in width.

GROUP TALLYING.

In timber which is characteristically uniform in size within one or two ranges of d. b. h. each range having differences limited to 6-10 inches and where few species are concerned the following method has been found of value in increasing the speed and conserving the judgment of the estimator. All the trees on the strip are counted, but only a certain proportion (as one in five) of them are individually sized up and tallied. The first 20 trees on a strip may be counted without tally and the next five trees nearest the estimator tallied five times each by species d. b. h. and log length. If there are two distinct sizes they may be treated separately, two counts being carried simultaneously by the estimator, or each tree of the larger size may be tallied and the smaller size tallied by groups.

Broken Tally—The tally on a strip is sometimes taken only at regular intervals arbitrarily determined. This rectangular plot method results in relief to the estimator and has some of the advantages of the circular plot method. It is considered preferable to making a reduction in the width of the strip below the minimum of one chain but is seldom, if ever, to be used by any but one-man crews.

Variation in Width of Strip—In open stands of valuable timber it is sometimes possible to secure the best results by the use of a broad strip, perhaps two chains in width. In certain cases this will double the per cent of the stands tallied with little or no reduction in the length of strip which can be run per day. The advisability of using a strip of width greater than one chain should be carefully considered before estimating open stands of yellow pine and larch.

The Use of Chain by Estimating Crew—When it is found impracticable to have control lines within reliable pacing distance of each other and when the Abney is used for elevation control, it will be found necessary to use the chain. A steel tape two or two and one-half chains in length is recommended.

MULTIPLE VOLUME TABLE—WESTERN WHITE PINE

Values from 40" to 60" D. B. H. assumed.

(Constructed by the Frustum Form Factor method. Based on 306 trees from the Coeur d'Alene, St. Joe and Lolo National Forests.)

Scribner Decimal C Rule.

Number of Trees.

DBH	Logs	1	2	3	4	5	6	7	8	9
8	1	2.5	5	8	10	12.5	15	17.5	20	20
	2	5	9.5	14.5	19	24	29	33.5	38.5	43
	3	7.5	15	22.5	30	37.5	45	52.5	60	67.5
10	1	2.5	5.5	8	11	13.5	16	19	21.5	24
	2	5	10.5	15.5	21	26	31	36.5	41.5	47
	3	9	17.5	26.5	35.5	44.5	53	62	71	79.5
	4	12.5	24.5	37	49	61.5	74	86	98.5	111
12	1	3	6	8.5	11.5	14.5	17.5	20	23	26
	2	6	12	18	24	30	36	42.5	48.5	54.5
	3	10.5	21	31	41.5	52	62.5	73	83	93.5
	4	15	30	45	60.5	75.5	90.5	106	121	136
	5	19.5	39	59	78.5	98	118	137.5	157	177
	6	24	48.5	72.5	96.5	121	145	169.5	193.5	218
14	1	3	6	9	12.5	15.5	18.5	21.5	25	28
	2	7	14	21	28	35	42.5	49.5	56.5	63.5
	3	13	26.5	39.5	53	66	79	92.5	105.5	119
	4	18.5	37	56	74.5	93	111.5	130	149	167.5
	5	25	49.5	74.5	99	124	149	173.5	198.5	223
	6	31	61.5	92.5	123	154	185	216	246.5	277
	7	36.5	73	109.5	146	182.5	219	255.5	292	328
	8	42.5	85	127.5	170	225	255	298	340	383
16	1	3.5	7	11	14	17.5	21	24.5	28	31.5
	2	8.5	17	26	34.5	43	51.5	60	69	77.5
	3	16	32	47.5	63.5	79.5	95.5	111	127	143
	4	23.5	46.5	70	93	116.5	140	163	186	210
	5	30.5	61	91.5	122	152.5	183	213.5	244	275
	6	38.5	77	116	154.5	193	231.5	270	309	347
	7	46	92.5	139	185	231.5	278	324	370	417
	8	54	108	162	216	270	324	378	432	486
18	1	4	8	11.5	15.5	19.5	23.5	27.5	31	35
	2	10	20	30	40	50	60	70	80	90
	3	19	37.5	56	75	94	112.5	131	150	168.5
	4	29	57.5	86.5	115	144	173	202	230	259
	5	38	75.5	113.5	151	189	227	265	302	340
	6	46.5	93	139.5	186	232.5	279	325	372	420
	7	57	113.5	170.5	227	284	341	397	454	510
	8	66	132.5	199	265	331	398	464	530	596
20	1	4.5	8.5	13	17	21.5	26	30	34.5	39
	2	12	24	35.5	47.5	59	71	83	95	106.5
	3	23.5	46.5	70	93	118	141.5	165	189	212
	4	34	68.5	102.5	137	171	205	239	273.5	308.5
	5	46	91.5	137.5	183	229	275	321	367	412
	6	58	115.5	173	231	288	346	404	462	520
	7	68.5	137	205.5	274	343	412	480	548	616
	8	81	162	243	324	405	486	567	648	730

MULTIPLE VOLUME TABLE—WESTERN WHITE PINE

Number of Trees.—Continued.

DBH	Logs	1	2	3	4	5	6	7	8	9
22	1	5	9	14	19	24	28	33	38	43
	2	13	27	41	54	68	81	95	109	122
	3	27	54	82	109	136	163	191	218	245
	4	41	81	122	163	203	244	285	326	366
	5	55	110	165	220	275	330	385	440	495
	6	69	138	207	276	345	414	473	552	620
	7	84	168	252	336	420	504	587	670	755
	8	97	195	292	390	487	584	682	780	876
	9	112	224	336	448	560	672	784	896	1008
24	1	5	10	15	21	26	31	36	42	47
	2	16	33	49	66	82	99	115	132	148
	3	32	64	96	127	159	191	223	255	287
	4	48	97	145	193	242	291	339	388	436
	5	65	131	196	262	327	392	475	524	588
	6	82	164	246	328	410	492	574	657	738
	7	97	195	293	391	488	586	684	782	879
	8	116	232	348	464	580	696	812	928	1045
	9	132	264	396	527	659	791	923	1052	1185
26	1	5	11	17	22	28	33	39	45	50
	2	18	36	54	72	90	108	127	145	163
	3	37	74	111	148	185	222	259	296	333
	4	55	111	167	223	278	334	390	445	500
	5	77	155	232	310	387	465	542	620	695
	6	94	189	283	378	472	566	662	755	850
	7	115	230	345	460	575	690	805	920	1035
	8	133	266	399	532	665	798	931	1065	1200
	9	153	306	459	612	765	918	1070	1225	1375
28	2	20	41	62	83	103	124	145	165	186
	3	42	85	127	170	212	255	298	340	383
	4	61	129	193	258	322	387	451	516	580
	5	87	174	261	348	435	522	609	696	783
	6	109	218	328	438	547	656	765	875	985
	7	132	264	396	528	660	792	924	1065	1189
	8	156	312	468	624	780	936	1092	1248	1404
	9	179	358	537	716	895	1074	1253	1432	1611
30	2	23	46	69	93	116	139	162	186	209
	3	47	94	141	188	235	282	329	376	423
	4	72	144	216	288	360	432	504	576	648
	5	100	200	300	400	500	600	700	800	900
	6	124	248	372	496	620	744	868	992	1116
	7	152	304	456	608	760	912	1064	1216	1368
	8	176	354	530	706	883	1060	1235	1410	1590
	9	201	402	603	804	1005	1206	1407	1610	1810
32	3	55	111	166	222	277	333	388	444	499
	4	83	167	250	333	416	500	583	666	750
	5	113	226	338	452	564	676	790	902	1015
	6	142	284	425	567	710	851	993	1135	1275
	7	170	340	510	680	850	1020	1190	1360	1530
	8	198	397	595	794	993	1190	1390	1588	1785
	9	229	458	687	916	1145	1375	1605	1835	2060
	10	258	515	773	1030	1288	1545	1800	2060	2320

MULTIPLE VOLUME TABLE—WESTERN WHITE PINE

Number of Trees.—Continued.

DBH	Logs	1	2	3	4	5	6	7	8	9
34	3	60	121	182	243	303	364	425	485	546
	4	94	188	283	377	472	566	660	755	850
	5	124	248	373	496	621	745	870	994	1118
	6	157	315	472	630	786	945	1100	1258	1415
	7	188	378	566	755	944	1132	1320	1510	1700
	8	223	446	670	893	1115	1340	1560	1785	2010
	9	255	510	765	1020	1275	1530	1785	2040	2300
	10	288	577	866	1152	1440	1730	2020	2305	2600
36	3	67	134	201	268	335	402	468	536	603
	4	101	202	303	404	505	606	707	808	909
	5	136	272	408	544	680	816	952	1089	1225
	6	174	348	522	695	870	1042	1216	1390	1562
	7	210	420	630	840	1050	1260	1470	1680	1890
	8	241	482	724	965	1205	1445	1685	1930	2170
	9	279	558	836	1115	1395	1675	1950	2230	2510
	10	316	632	950	1265	1580	1895	2210	2530	2840
38	3	74	147	221	295	369	443	516	590	664
	4	110	220	330	440	550	660	770	880	990
	5	150	300	450	600	750	900	1050	1200	1350
	6	189	378	567	756	945	1135	1325	1512	1700
	7	226	452	678	905	1130	1355	1580	1810	2035
	8	261	522	784	1045	1305	1565	1825	2090	2350
	9	306	613	920	1225	1530	1840	2140	2450	2760
	10	346	692	1038	1385	1730	2075	2420	2770	3110
40	4	122	244	366	488	610	732	854	976	1100
	5	165	330	495	660	825	990	1155	1320	1485
	6	204	410	614	818	1022	1228	1432	1636	1840
	7	251	505	755	1005	1255	1505	1755	2010	2260
	8	294	588	885	1175	1470	1760	2060	2345	2640
	9	336	672	1015	1345	1680	2015	2350	2690	3025
	10	382	764	1145	1530	1910	2290	2675	3060	3440
42	4	132	264	396	528	660	792	924	1056	1188
	5	179	359	539	718	897	1078	1258	1435	1615
	6	225	450	675	900	1125	1350	1575	1800	2025
	7	276	552	828	1105	1380	1655	1930	2205	2480
	8	320	640	960	1280	1600	1920	2240	2560	2880
	9	365	730	1090	1460	1825	2190	2555	2920	3280
	10	417	834	1250	1665	2080	2500	2915	3330	3750
44	5	194	388	582	776	970	1165	1360	1550	1745
	6	245	490	735	980	1225	1470	1715	1960	2205
	7	298	596	894	1195	1490	1785	2085	2380	2680
	8	346	692	1040	1385	1730	2075	2425	2770	3115
	9	396	792	1188	1585	1980	2375	2770	3170	3560
	10	452	904	1355	1805	2260	2710	3160	3610	4060
46	5	209	418	628	838	1048	1258	1465	1675	1885
	6	264	528	792	1055	1320	1585	1850	2110	2375
	7	323	646	970	1290	1615	1935	2260	2580	2905
	8	370	740	1110	1480	1850	2220	2590	2960	3330
	9	427	855	1285	1710	2135	2560	2990	3420	3850
	10	490	980	1470	1960	2450	2940	3430	3920	4410
48	6	282	564	846	1128	1410	1690	1975	2255	2540
	7	348	696	1045	1390	1740	2090	2435	2785	3130
	8	400	800	1200	1600	2000	2400	2800	3200	3600
	9	456	912	1370	1825	2280	2735	3190	3650	4100

MULTIPLE VOLUME TABLE—WESTERN WHITE PINE

Number of Trees.—Continued.

DBH	Logs	1	2	3	4	5	6	7	8	9
	10	526	1050	1580	2100	2630	3160	3680	4210	4740
50	6	320	640	960	1280	1600	1920	2240	2560	2880
	7	372	744	1115	1490	1860	2230	2600	2975	3350
	8	427	855	1280	1710	2140	2565	2990	3420	3850
	9	495	990	1485	1980	2470	2970	3460	3960	4450
	10	562	1125	1685	2250	3810	3380	3940	4500	5060
52	6	326	652	978	1305	1630	1955	2280	2610	2925
	7	398	792	1190	1585	1980	2380	2775	3175	3560
	8	460	920	1380	1840	2300	2760	3220	3680	4140
	9	529	1060	1590	2120	2650	3180	3710	4240	4770
	10	606	1210	1820	2425	3030	3635	4240	4850	5450
54	6	350	700	1150	1400	1750	2100	2450	2800	3150
	7	423	846	1270	1695	2120	2540	2960	3390	3810
	8	497	994	1490	1985	2480	2980	3480	3970	4470
	9	570	1140	1710	2280	2850	3420	3990	4560	5130
	10	649	1298	1945	2600	3240	3890	4540	5190	5840
56	6	373	746	1120	1490	1865	2240	2610	2985	3360
	7	450	900	1350	1800	2250	2700	3150	3600	4050
	8	527	1055	1580	2110	2640	3160	3690	4225	4750
	9	605	1210	1815	2420	3025	3630	4240	4840	5450
	10	690	1380	2070	3760	3450	4140	4825	5525	6200
58	8	560	1120	1680	2240	2800	3360	3920	4480	5040
	9	639	1278	1915	2550	3190	3830	4470	5100	5750
	10	729	1460	2180	2910	3640	4370	5100	5830	6560
60	8	592	1180	1770	2360	2960	3550	4140	4730	5325*
	9	672	1345	2010	2690	3360	4030	4700	5375	6050
	10	770	1540	2310	3080	3850	4625	5400	6160	6940

WESTERN YELLOW PINE

Bitterroot, Blackfeet, Kootenai, and Missoula National Forests, Montana.

Curved. **Scribner Decimal C.**

Diameter Breast High	Number of 16-Foot Logs								Basis
Inches	1½	2	3	4	5	6	7	8	Trees
	Volume—Board Feet.								
8	2.0	3.5	5.6						7
9	2.5	4	6						17
10	3	4.5	7	10					30
11	3.5	5	8	12					88
12	4	5.5	9	13	18				183
13	4	6	10	14	20				201
14	4.5	7.0	12	16	23				262
15	5	8	13	19	26				254
16	6	9	15	22	29	38			223
17		10	17	25	33	42			230
18		11	19	28	37	47			211
19		12	21	31	41	53			184
20		14	23	35	46	59	72		176
21		15	26	38	52	65	79		151
22		17	29	43	57	72	87		128
23		19	32	47	64	79	95		94
24			35	53	70	86	104	124	86
25			39	58	76	94	114	136	79
26			42	64	84	103	125	149	76
27			46	70	92	113	137	161	51
28			52	78	101	124	149	174	40
29			59	85	110	136	162	188	26
30			65	93	121	148	175	203	18
31			72	102	132	160	188	218	15
32			80	112	143	172	201	234	15
33				122	154	185	216	250	13
34				133	165	198	230	266	5
35				145	177	211	245	282	8
36				157	189	224	260	298	3
37				170	201	238	275	314	1
38				183	214	252	290	330	4
39				196	227	266	306	346	1
40				210	241	280	322	362	3
									2813

Top diameter inside bark 6 inches throughout.

Stump height one foot.

Scaled from taper curves, mostly in 16.3 foot logs, with a few shorter logs where necessary.

MULTIPLE VOLUME TABLE—LARCH

(Constructed by the Frustum Form Factor method. Based on 233 trees.)
Scribner Decimal C Rule.

Number of Trees.

DBH	Logs	1	2	3	4	5	6	7	8	9
8	1	2.5	4.5	7	9.5	11.5	14	16.5	19	21
	2	4.5	8.5	13	17	21.5	26	30	34.5	39
	3	7	13.5	20	27	34	40.5	47	54	61
	4	9.5	18.5	28	37	46.5	56	65	74.5	84
10	1	2.5	5	7.5	10	12	14.5	17	19.5	22
	2	4.5	9.5	14	19	23.5	28	33	37.5	42.5
	3	8	16	24	32	40	48	56	64	72
	4	11	22	33	44.5	55.5	66.5	77.5	89	100
12	1	2.5	5	8	10.5	13	15.5	18	21	23.5
	2	5.5	11	16.5	22	27	32.5	38	43.5	49
	3	9.5	19	28	37.5	47	56.5	66	75	84.5
	4	13.5	26	41	54.5	68	81.5	95	109	122.5
	5	18	36	53.5	71.5	89	107	125	143	161
	6	22	44	65.5	87.5	109.5	131.5	153.5	175.5	197.5
14	1	3	5.5	8.5	11	14	16.5	19.5	22.5	25
	2	6.5	13	19	25.5	32	38.5	45	51	57.5
	3	12	23.5	35.5	47.5	59	71	83	95	107
	4	17	33.5	50.5	67	84	101	118	134.5	151
	5	22.5	45	67	89.5	112	134.5	157	179	202
	6	28	55.5	83.5	111	139	166.5	195	222	250
	7	33	66	99	132	165	198	231	264	297
	8	38.5	77	115	153.5	192	230	269	307	346
16	1	3	6.5	9.5	13	16	19	22.5	25.5	29
	2	8	15.5	23.5	31	39	47	54.5	62.5	70
	3	14.5	29	43	57.5	72	86.5	101	115	129.5
	4	21	42	63	84	105	126	147	168	189
	5	27.5	55	82.5	110	137.5	165	192	220	247
	6	35	69.5	104.5	139	174	209	244	278	313
	7	42	84	125.5	167.5	209	251	293	335	376
	8	49	97.5	146	195	243	292	341	390	438
18	1	3.5	7	10.5	14	17.5	21	24.5	28	31.5
	2	9	18	27	36	45	54	63	72	81
	3	17	34	51	68	85	101	118	135	152
	4	26	52	78	104	130	156	182	208	234
	5	34	68	102	136	170	204	238	272	306
	6	42	84	126	168	210	252	294	336	378
	7	51	102	153	204	256	307	358	410	460
	8	60	120	180	240	300	360	420	480	540
	9	68.5	136.5	205	273	342	410	478	546	615
	10	77	153.5	230	307	384	460	538	615	690
20	1	3.5	7.5	11	15	19	22.5	26	30	34
	2	10	20.5	31	41	51	61.5	72	82	92
	3	20	40.5	60.5	81	101	121	141.5	161.5	182
	4	29.5	59	89	118	148	177.5	207	236	266
	5	39.5	79	119	158	198	238	277	317	356
	6	50	100	150	200	250	300	350	400	450
	7	59	118	177.5	236	296	355	414	473	532
	8	70	140	210	280	350	420	490	560	630

MULTIPLE VOLUME TABLE—LARCH

Number of Trees.—Continued.

DBH	Logs	1	2	3	4	5	6	7	8	9
	9	80	160	240	320	400	480	560	640	720
	10	90	180	270	360	450	540	630	720	810
22	1	4	8	12	16	20	23	27	31	35
	2	11	22	34	45	57	68	79	91	102
	3	23	45	68	91	114	137	160	182	205
	4	34	68	102	136	170	204	238	272	306
	5	46	92	137	184	229	275	321	367	413
	6	57	115	173	230	288	346	404	462	518
	7	70	140	210	280	350	420	490	560	630
	8	81	162	243	324	405	486	568	650	730
	9	93	187	281	374	468	562	655	750	842
	10	105	210	315	420	524	630	735	840	944
24	2	14	27	41	55	69	82	96	110	124
	3	26	53	80	106	133	159	186	213	239
	4	40	81	121	162	202	243	283	323	364
	5	54	109	163	218	273	327	382	436	490
	6	68	137	205	274	342	410	480	548	616
	7	81	163	245	326	408	490	570	683	735
	8	96	193	290	386	483	580	676	773	870
	9	110	220	330	440	550	660	770	880	990
	10	124	249	374	498	623	748	772	996	1120
26	2	15	30	45	60	75	90	105	120	135
	3	34	78	102	136	170	204	238	272	306
	4	46	93	139	185	232	278	324	371	418
	5	62	124	186	248	310	372	434	495	558
	6	79	158	237	316	395	474	553	630	710
	7	95	191	287	382	478	574	670	765	860
	8	111	222	333	444	555	666	777	888	999
	9	127	254	381	508	635	762	890	1015	1140
	10	143	286	430	573	715	860	1000	1145	1290
28	2	17	34	51	68	85	102	119	136	153
	3	35	70	105	140	175	210	245	280	315
	4	53	106	159	212	265	318	371	424	477
	5	71	143	214	286	357	430	500	572	644
	6	90	180	270	360	450	540	630	720	810
	7	109	218	327	436	545	654	763	872	981
	8	128	257	385	513	642	770	900	1030	1155
	9	147	294	440	590	735	883	1040	1175	1325
	10	165	330	495	660	825	990	1155	1320	1485
30	3	39	78	117	157	196	235	274	314	353
	4	60	120	180	240	300	360	420	480	540
	5	83	166	249	332	415	500	580	664	746
	6	103	206	310	413	516	620	723	825	930
	7	126	252	378	504	630	755	880	1010	1135
	8	147	294	440	587	735	880	1030	1175	1320
	9	168	346	504	682	840	1010	1175	1345	1510
	10	189	378	567	756	945	1135	1320	1510	1700
32	3	44	88	132	176	220	264	308	352	396
	4	67	135	203	270	338	405	473	540	608
	5	91	183	274	366	457	550	640	733	824
	6	115	230	345	460	575	690	805	920	1035
	7	138	276	414	550	690	830	965	1105	1240
	8	161	322	484	645	805	967	1130	1290	1450
	9	186	372	558	744	930	1115	1300	1490	1675

MULTIPLE VOLUME TABLE—LARCH

Number of Trees.—Continued.

DBH	Logs	1	2	3	4	5	6	7	8	9
	10	209	418	627	835	1045	1250	1460	1670	1880
34	4	74	149	223	298	372	446	520	596	670
	5	98	196	294	392	490	590	686	785	883
	6	124	248	372	496	620	745	870	990	1115
	7	149	298	446	595	745	895	1045	1190	1340
	8	176	352	528	705	880	1060	1230	1410	1585
	9	202	404	605	806	1010	1210	1410	1610	1815
	10	227	454	682	910	1135	1360	1590	1820	2040
36	5	107	214	321	428	535	642	749	856	963
	6	137	274	410	548	675	823	960	1100	1370
	7	165	330	495	660	825	990	1150	1320	1480
	8	191	382	574	765	955	1150	1340	1530	1720
	9	220	440	660	880	1100	1320	1540	1760	1980
	10	248	497	745	994	1240	1490	1740	1985	2480
38	5	117	234	350	467	584	700	818	935	1050
	6	146	293	440	585	733	880	1025	1170	1320
	7	175	350	525	700	875	1050	1225	1400	1575
	8	203	406	610	810	1015	1220	1420	1625	1830
	9	238	476	714	955	1190	1430	1665	1900	2140
	10	267	535	800	1065	1330	1600	1870	2140	2400
40	5	126	252	378	504	630	756	882	1010	1135
	6	157	314	470	628	785	940	1100	1250	1410
	7	192	384	575	770	960	1150	1345	1540	1730
	8	225	450	675	900	1125	1350	1575	1800	2020
	9	257	514	770	1030	1285	1540	1800	2060	2310
	10	292	584	875	1170	1460	1750	2040	2340	2630

MULTIPLE VOLUME TABLE—DOUGLAS FIR

(Constructed by the Frustum Form Factor method.) Scribner Decimal C Rule.

Number of Trees.

DBH	Logs	1	2	3	4	5	6	7	8	9
8	1	2.5	5	7	9.5	12	14.5	17	19	21.5
	2	4.5	8.5	13	17.5	22	26	30.5	35	39
	3	7.0	13.5	20.5	27.5	34	41	48	55	61.5
10	1	2.5	5	7.5	10	12	14.5	17	19.5	22
	2	4.5	9.5	14	19	24	28.5	33	38	43
	3	8.0	16	24	32	40	48	56.5	64.5	72.5
	4	11.0	22.5	33.5	45	56	67	78.5	89.5	101
12	1	2.5	5.5	8	10.5	13	16	18.5	21	24
	2	5.5	11	16.5	22	27.5	33	38.5	44	49.5
	3	9.5	19	28.5	38	47.5	57	66.5	76	85.5
	4	14.0	27.5	41.5	45	69	83	96.5	110.5	124
	5	18.0	36	54	72	90.5	108	126	144	162
	6	22.0	44	66.5	88.5	111	133	155	177	199
14	1	3.0	5.5	8.5	11	14	17	19.5	22.5	25
	2	6.5	13	19	25.5	32	38.6	45	51	57.5
	3	12.0	23.5	35.5	47.5	59.5	71	83	95	107
	4	17.0	33.5	50.5	67	84	101	117.5	134.5	151
	5	22.5	45	67.5	89.5	112	134.5	157	179	202
	6	28.0	55.5	83.5	111	139	166.5	191.5	222	250
16	1	3.0	6	9.5	12.5	16	19	22.5	25.5	29
	2	8.0	15.5	23.5	31	39	47	54.5	62.5	70
	3	14.5	29	43	57.5	72	86.5	101	115	144
	4	21.0	42	63	84	105	126	147	168	189
	5	27.5	55	82.5	110	137.5	165	192.5	220	248
	6	35.0	70	105	139.5	174.5	210	244	280	314
	7	42.0	84	125.5	167.5	209	251	293	335	378
	8	48.5	97.5	146	194.5	243	292	340	389	438
18	1	3.5	7	10.5	14	17.5	21	24.5	28	31.5
	2	9.0	18	36	45	54	63	72	81	99
	3	17.0	34	51	67.5	84.5	101.5	118	135	152
	4	26.0	52	65	78	104	130	156	182	208
	5	34.0	68	102	136	170.5	204.5	239	273	307
	6	42	84	126	168	210	252	294	336	378
	7	51	102	153	204	257	307	358	408	460
	8	60	120	179.5	239	299	359	418	478	538
20	1	4	7.5	11.5	15.5	19	23	27	31	35
	2	10.5	21	32	42.5	53	63.5	74	85	95.5
	3	21	40.5	62.5	83	104	125	146	166.5	187.5
	4	30.5	61	92	122.5	153	183.5	214	245	276
	5	41	82	123	164	205	246	287	328	369
	6	51.5	103	155	206	258	310	361	413	464
20	7	61	122	183.5	244	306	367	428	488	550
	8	72.5	145	217	290	362	435	506	580	651
22	1	4	8	12	16	21	25	29	33	37
	2	12	23	35	47	59	71	82	94	106
	3	24	48	71	95	119	143	167	191	214
	4	35	71	107	142	178	214	249	285	321
	5	48	96	144	192	240	288	336	384	432
	6	60	121	181	242	302	362	423	484	543
	7	73	146	219	292	356	439	512	585	659
	8	85	170	255	340	425	510	595	680	765

MULTIPLE VOLUME TABLE—DOUGLAS FIR

Number of Trees.—Continued.

DBH	Logs	1	2	3	4	5	6	7	8	9
24	1	4	9	13	18	22	27	31	36	40
	2	14	28	42	56	70	84	99	113	127
	3	27	54	82	109	136	164	191	218	247
	4	41	83	124	165	207	248	290	331	373
	5	56	111	167	223	279	335	391	446	502
	6	70	140	210	280	350	420	490	560	630
	7	83	167	250	334	418	501	585	668	752
	8	98	195	293	391	490	586	685	782	880
26	1	5	9	14	19	24	29	33	38	43
	2	15	31	46	61	77	92	108	123	139
	3	31	63	94	126	157	189	220	252	284
	4	47	95	142	190	238	285	333	380	428
	5	63	126	190	253	317	380	444	506	570
	6	80	161	242	322	403	484	565	645	725
	7	98	196	294	392	490	589	686	785	883
	8	113	227	340	454	568	680	796	908	1025
28	2	17	35	53	70	88	106	123	141	159
	3	36	72	108	145	181	217	253	290	326
	4	55	110	165	220	275	330	385	440	495
	5	74	148	222	296	370	444	518	592	665
	6	93	187	280	374	468	560	655	748	840
	7	113	226	339	452	565	678	790	904	1020
	8	133	268	399	532	665	800	930	1065	1197
30	2	20	40	60	80	100	120	140	160	180
	3	40	81	121	162	202	243	284	324	361
	4	62	124	186	248	310	372	434	496	558
	5	86	172	258	344	430	516	602	688	774
	6	107	214	321	428	535	642	750	856	963
	7	131	262	393	524	655	786	918	1050	1180
	8	152	304	156	608	760	912	1065	1215	1360
32	3	46	93	140	186	233	280	326	373	420
	4	72	143	215	287	359	430	503	574	646
	5	97	194	291	388	485	582	680	775	875
	6	122	244	366	488	610	732	853	975	1100
	7	146	293	140	586	733	880	1025	1170	1320
	8	171	342	513	684	855	1025	1200	1370	1510
34	3	52	105	158	210	263	316	368	421	474
	4	82	164	246	328	410	492	574	656	738
	5	108	216	324	432	540	648	756	864	972
	6	137	274	412	548	685	822	960	1096	1230
	7	164	328	492	656	820	985	1150	1310	1475
	8	194	388	582	776	970	1165	1360	1550	1745
	9	222	444	666	888	1110	1330	1550	1775	2000
	10	251	502	753	1004	1255	1506	1757	2008	2260
36	3	59	118	177	236	295	354	414	472	530
	4	99	198	297	396	495	594	694	793	890
	5	119	238	357	470	595	715	835	953	1070
	6	152	305	458	610	762	915	1168	1220	1370
	7	184	368	552	735	920	1100	1285	1470	1650
	8	213	426	610	850	1065	1280	1490	1700	1915
	9	245	490	735	980	1230	1470	1720	1965	2210

MULTIPLE VOLUME TABLE—DOUGLAS FIR

Number of Trees.—Continued.

DBH	Logs	1	2	3	4	5	6	7	8	9
	10	278	556	835	1110	1390	1865	1945	2220	2500
38	3	65	131	196	262	328	393	458	524	590
	4	97	195	293	390	488	586	684	782	880
	5	133	267	400	534	667	800	935	1070	1200
	6	167	332	502	670	837	1005	1170	1340	1510
	7	200	401	601	802	902	1203	1403	1604	1804
	8	234	468	700	946	1170	1405	1640	1870	2100
	9	271	542	813	1080	1350	1625	1895	2160	2440
	10	306	612	918	1225	1530	1840	2140	2450	2760
40	4	108	217	326	434	543	650	760	868	977
	5	146	293	440	586	734	880	1025	1170	1320
	6	182	364	546	730	910	1090	1275	1455	1640
	7	222	445	667	890	1110	1335	1560	1780	2000
	8	261	522	783	1040	1300	1565	1825	2080	2350
	9	298	597	896	1190	1485	1790	2090	2390	2690
	10	340	680	1020	1360	1700	2040	2380	2720	3060

MULTIPLE VOLUME TABLE—SPRUCE

(Constructed by the Frustum Form Factor method. Based on 189 trees from the Blackfeet and Lolo National Forests.) Scribner Decimal C. Rule.

Number of Trees.

DBH	Logs	1	2	3	4	5	6	7	8	9
8	1	2.5	5.5	8.0	11.0	13.5	16.0	19.0	21.5	24.5
	2	5.0	10.0	13.0	17.5	22.0	26.5	31.0	35.0	39.5
	3	7.5	15.5	23.0	31.0	38.5	46.0	54.0	61.5	69.5
	4	10.5	21.0	32.0	42.5	53.0	63.5	74.0	85.0	95.5
10	1	2.5	5.5	8.0	11.0	14.0	16.5	19.0	22.0	25.0
	2	5.5	10.5	16.0	21.0	26.5	32.0	37.0	42.5	47.5
	3	9.0	18.0	27.0	36.0	45.0	54.0	63.0	72.0	81.0
	4	12.5	25.0	37.5	50.0	62.5	75.0	87.5	100.0	112.5
12	1	3.0	6.0	9.0	12.0	15.0	17.5	20.5	23.5	26.5
	2	6.0	12.5	18.5	24.5	31.0	37.0	43.0	49.0	55.5
	3	10.5	21.0	32.0	42.5	53.0	63.5	74.0	85.0	95.5
	4	15.5	31.0	46.0	61.5	77.0	92.5	108.0	123.0	139.0
14	1	3.0	6.5	9.5	12.5	15.5	19.0	22.0	25.0	28.5
	2	7.0	14.0	21.5	28.5	36.0	43.0	50.0	58.0	64.5
	3	13.0	26.5	39.5	53.0	66.0	79.0	92.5	105.0	119.0
	4	19.0	37.5	56.5	75.0	94.0	113.0	131.5	150.0	169.0
	5	25.0	50.0	75.0	100.0	125.0	150.0	175.0	200.0	225.0
16	1	3.5	7.0	10.5	14.0	17.5	21.0	25.0	28.0	32.0
	2	8.5	17.5	26.0	35.0	43.5	52.0	61.0	69.5	78.0
	3	16.0	32.0	48.5	64.5	80.5	96.5	113.0	129.0	145.0
	4	23.5	47.0	70.5	94.0	117.5	141.0	164.5	188.0	211.0
	5	31.0	61.5	92.5	123.0	154.0	185.0	216.0	246.0	278.0
18	1	4.0	8.0	12.0	16.0	20.0	23.5	27.5	31.5	35.5
	2	10.0	20.0	30.0	40.5	50.5	60.5	70.5	81.0	91.0
	3	19.0	38.0	56.5	75.5	94.5	163.0	132.0	151.0	170.0
	4	29.0	58.0	87.0	116.0	145.0	174.0	203.0	232.0	261.0
	5	38.0	76.0	114.0	152.0	190.0	228.0	266.0	320.0	342.0
	6	47.0	94.0	141.0	188.0	235.0	282.0	329.0	376.0	423.0
20	1	4.5	8.5	13.0	17.0	21.5	26.0	30.0	34.5	38.5
	2	12.0	24.0	35.5	47.5	59.0	71.0	83.0	95.0	107.0
	3	23.5	46.5	70.0	93.0	116.5	140.0	163.0	186.0	210.0
	4	34.0	68.5	102.5	137.0	172.0	205.0	239.0	274.0	308.0
	5	46.0	92.0	137.5	183.5	229.0	275.0	321.0	367.0	413.0
	6	57.5	114.0	172.0	228.0	285.0	342.0	400.0	456.0	514.0
22	1	4	9	14	19	24	28	33	38	43
	2	13	27	41	54	68	81	95	109	122
	3	27	54	82	108	136	164	191	218	246
	4	40	81	122	162	203	244	284	325	365
	5	55	110	165	220	275	330	385	440	495
	6	69	138	207	276	345	414	483	552	620
	7	84	168	252	336	420	504	588	670	755
24	1	5	10	15	21	26	31	36	41	47
	2	16	32	49	65	81	98	114	130	147
	3	31	63	95	126	158	190	221	253	284
	4	48	96	144	192	240	288	336	384	432
	5	64	129	193	258	323	387	452	516	581
	6	81	162	243	324	405	486	568	650	730
	7	97	194	290	287	484	580	677	765	870

MULTIPLE VOLUME TABLE—SPRUCE

Number of Trees.—Continued.

DBH	Logs	1	2	3	4	5	6	7	8	9
26	2	18	36	54	72	90	108	126	144	162
	3	37	74	110	147	184	221	258	295	332
	4	55	111	167	222	278	334	390	445	500
	5	74	149	223	298	372	446	520	595	670
	6	94	189	284	378	472	566	660	755	850
	7	115	230	345	460	575	690	805	920	1035
28	3	42	84	126	168	210	252	294	336	378
	4	64	127	191	255	319	383	447	510	574
	5	86	174	258	344	430	516	600	688	774
	6	108	217	325	434	543	650	760	868	978
	7	131	262	393	524	655	786	917	1050	1180
	8	154	308	462	616	770	925	1080	1230	1390
30	3	46	94	140	186	233	279	326	373	420
	4	71	143	214	286	357	430	500	572	644
	5	99	198	297	395	494	594	692	790	890
	6	123	246	368	492	615	740	860	983	1100
	7	150	300	450	600	750	900	1050	1200	1350
	8	175	350	524	700	875	1050	1225	1400	1750
32	3	53	106	159	212	266	319	372	425	478
	4	81	167	245	327	409	490	570	650	735
	5	110	220	330	440	550	660	770	880	990
	6	139	278	417	556	695	834	973	1110	1250
	7	167	334	500	670	836	1000	1170	1335	1500
	8	195	390	585	780	975	1170	1365	1560	1750
34	3	57	114	171	228	285	342	400	456	513
	4	88	177	266	354	443	530	620	710	796
	5	117	234	350	466	584	700	816	934	1050
	6	148	296	434	593	740	890	1035	1186	1330
	7	177	354	530	710	885	1060	1240	1420	1590
	8	210	420	630	840	1050	1260	1470	1680	1890
36	3	61	123	185	246	308	369	430	493	554
	4	93	186	279	372	465	558	650	745	836
	5	125	250	375	500	625	750	875	1000	1250
	6	160	320	480	640	800	960	1120	1280	1440
	7	192	384	575	770	960	1150	1345	1540	1730
	8	224	448	670	895	1120	1340	1560	1790	2010
38	3	67	134	201	268	335	400	470	536	604
	4	100	200	300	400	500	600	700	800	900
	5	136	273	410	545	583	820	955	1090	1225
	6	171	342	514	685	855	1025	1190	1370	1540
	7	205	410	615	820	1025	1230	1435	1640	1845
	8	239	480	720	955	1190	1430	1670	1910	2150
40	4	111	222	333	444	555	666	777	888	999
	5	150	300	450	600	750	900	1050	1200	1350
	6	186	372	558	745	930	1115	1300	1490	1675
	7	228	456	685	910	1140	1370	1600	1820	2025
	8	267	534	800	1170	1330	1600	1865	2130	2400

MULTIPLE VOLUME TABLE—BALSAM

(Constructed by the Frustum Form Factor method. Basis: 33 trees from the Blackfeet National Forest.) Scribner Decimal C Rule.

Number of Trees.

DBH	Logs	1	2	3	4	5	6	7	8	9
8	1	2.5	5	7.5	10	12.5	15	17.5	20	22.5
	2	5.0	10	15.0	20	25.0	30	35.0	40	45.0
	3	8.0	16	24.0	32	40.0	48	56.0	64	72.0
	4	9.0	18	27.0	36	45.0	54	63.0	72	81.0
10	1	3.0	6	9.0	12	15.0	18	21.0	24	27.0
	2	5.5	11	16.5	22	27.5	33	38.5	44	49.5
	3	9.5	19	28.5	38	47.5	57	66.5	76	85.5
	4	13.0	26	39.0	52	65.0	78	91.0	104	117.0
12	1	3.0	6	9.0	12	15.0	18	21.0	24	27.0
	2	6.5	13	19.5	26	32.5	39	45.5	52	58.5
	3	11.0	22	33.0	44	55.0	66	77.0	88	99.0
	4	16.0	32	48.0	64	80.0	96	112.0	128	144.0
14	1	3.5	7	10.5	14	17.5	21	24.5	28	31.5
	2	7.5	15	22.5	30	37.5	45	52.5	60	75.0
	3	14.0	28	42.0	56	70.0	84	98.0	112	126.0
	4	19.5	39	58.5	78	97.5	117	136.5	156	175.0
	5	26.0	52	78.0	108	135.0	162	189.0	216	243.0
16	1	3.5	7	10.5	14	17.5	21	24.5	28	31.5
	2	9.0	18	27.0	36	45.0	54	63.0	72	81.0
	3	17.0	34	51.0	68	85.0	102	119.0	136	153.0
	4	22.5	45	67.5	90	112.5	135	157.5	180	202.5
	5	32.0	64	96.0	128	160.0	192	224.0	256	288.0
18	1	4.0	8	12.0	16	20.0	24	28.0	32	36.0
	2	10.5	21	31.5	42	52.5	63	73.5	84	94.5
	3	20.0	40	60.0	80	100.0	120	140.0	160	180.0
	4	30.5	61	91.5	122	152.5	183	213.5	244	274.5
	5	40.0	80	120.0	160	200.0	240	280.0	320	360.0
20	1	4.5	9	13.5	18	22.5	27	31.5	36	40.5
	2	12.5	25	37.5	50	62.5	75	87.5	100	112.5
	3	25.0	50	75.0	100	125.0	150	175.0	200	225.0
	4	36.0	72	108.0	144	180.0	216	252.0	288	324.0
	5	49.0	98	147.0	196	245.0	294	343.0	393	441.0
	6	66.5	133	199.5	266	333.0	399	466.0	532	599.0
22	1	5	10	15	20	25	30	35	40	45
	2	14	29	43	58	72	87	101	116	130
	3	29	58	87	116	145	174	203	232	261
	4	43	87	130	174	218	261	305	348	391
	5	58	117	175	234	293	351	410	468	526
	6	73	147	220	294	367	441	514	588	661
24	2	17	35	52	70	87	105	122	140	175
	3	34	68	102	136	170	204	238	272	306
	4	51	103	154	206	258	309	360	412	464

MULTIPLE VOLUME TABLE—SALSAM

Number of Trees.—Continued.

DBH	Logs	1	2	3	4	5	6	7	8	9
	5	70	140	210	280	350	420	490	560	630
	6	87	175	263	350	437	525	612	700	788
26	2	19	39	58	78	97	117	136	156	175
	3	40	80	120	160	200	240	280	320	360
	4	60	120	180	240	300	360	420	480	540
	5	80	160	240	320	400	480	560	640	720
	6	102	204	306	408	510	612	714	816	918
	7	124	248	372	496	620	744	868	992	1116
	8	143	287	430	573	716	860	1005	1150	1435
28	3	46	92	138	184	230	276	322	387	414
	4	69	139	208	278	348	417	486	586	625
	5	94	188	282	376	470	564	658	752	845
	6	118	236	354	472	590	708	825	944	1060
	7	143	286	429	672	715	858	1000	1145	1285
	8	168	336	504	672	840	1010	1175	1340	1510
30	3	51	102	153	204	255	306	357	408	459
	4	78	196	235	314	392	472	550	628	706
	5	109	218	327	436	545	654	763	872	981
	6	135	270	405	540	675	810	945	1080	1215
	7	165	330	495	660	820	990	1155	1320	1480
	8	192	385	576	770	962	1155	1345	1540	1730

MULTIPLE VOLUME TABLE—WESTERN RED CEDAR

(Based on 186 trees from District I. Diameters are D. I. B. at the top of the 1st log.) Constructed by the Frustum Form Factor Method. Scribner Decimal C Rule.

Number of Trees.

D.I.B. Top 1st Log Inches	Logs	1	2	3	4	5	6	7	8	9
10	1	5.0	10.0	15.0	20.0	25.0	30.0	35.0	40.0	45.0
	2	8.5	17.0	25.5	34.0	42.5	51.0	59.5	68.0	76.5
	3	12.5	25.0	37.5	50.0	62.5	75.0	87.5	100.0	112.5
12	1	8.5	17.0	25.5	34.0	42.5	51.0	59.5	68.0	76.5
	2	11.5	23.0	34.5	46.0	57.5	69.0	80.5	92.0	103.5
	3	16.5	33.0	49.5	66.0	82.5	99.0	115.5	132.0	148.5
	4	21.5	43.0	54.0	64.5	107.5	129.0	150.5	172.0	193.5
14	1	12.0	24.0	36.0	48.0	60.0	72.0	84.0	96.0	108.0
	2	15.0	30.0	45.0	60.0	75.0	90.0	105.0	120.0	135.0
	3	21.5	43.0	54.0	64.5	107.5	129.0	150.5	172.0	193.5
	4	28.0	56.0	84.0	112.0	140.0	168.0	196.0	224.0	252.0
16	1	16.5	33.0	49.5	66.0	82.5	99.0	115.5	132.0	148.5
	2	20.0	40.0	60.0	80.0	100.0	120.0	140.0	160.0	180.0
	3	26.5	52.0	79.5	106.0	132.5	159.0	185.0	212.0	238.0
	4	36.5	73.0	109.5	146.0	182.5	219.0	255.0	292.0	328.0
	5	45.0	90.0	135.0	180.0	225.0	270.0	315.0	360.0	405.0
18	1	22.5	45.0	67.5	90.0	112.5	135.0	157.5	180.0	202.5
	2	25.5	51.0	76.5	102.0	127.5	153.0	178.5	204.0	229.0
	3	35.5	71.0	106.5	142.0	177.5	213.0	248.0	284.0	320.0
	4	46.5	93.0	139.5	186.0	232.0	279.0	326.0	372.0	419.0
	5	57.0	114.0	171.0	228.0	285.0	342.0	399.0	456.0	513.0
	6	67.5	135.0	202.0	270.0	338.0	405.0	472.0	540.0	607.0
20	1	29.0	58.0	87.0	116.0	145.0	174.0	203.0	232.0	261.0
	2	31.5	63.0	94.5	126.0	157.5	189.0	220.0	252.0	283.0
	3	44.5	89.0	133.5	178.0	222.0	267.0	311.0	356.0	400.00
	4	57.5	115.0	172.5	230.0	288.0	345.0	403.0	460.0	518.0
	5	70.5	141.0	211.0	282.0	352.0	423.0	494.0	564.0	635.0
	6	84.5	169.0	254.0	338.0	423.0	506.0	590.0	675.0	706.0
	7	96.5	193.0	290.0	386.0	483.0	580.0	675.0	772.0	870.0
22	1	35	70	105	140	175	210	245	280	315
	2	38	77	115	154	192	231	269	308	346
	3	53	107	160	214	267	321	375	428	482
	4	68	137	205	274	343	411	480	548	616
	5	84	169	254	338	423	506	591	676	760
	6	104	208	312	416	520	624	728	832	936
	7	117	234	351	468	585	702	819	936	1053
24	1	42	85	127	170	212	255	297	340	382
	2	46	92	138	184	230	276	322	368	414
	3	62	125	187	250	312	375	437	500	562
	4	81	163	245	326	407	489	570	662	734
	5	101	202	303	404	505	606	707	808	909
	6	120	240	360	480	600	720	840	960	1080

MULTIPLE VOLUME TABLE—WESTERN RED CEDAR

Number of Trees.—Continued.

D.I.B. Top 1st Log	Logs	1	2	3	4	5	6	7	8	9
	7	138	276	414	550	690	828	965	1105	1240
	8	157	314	470	628	785	942	1100	1255	1410
26	1	52	105	157	210	262	315	367	420	472
	2	56	112	168	224	280	336	392	447	504
	3	76	152	228	304	380	456	533	608	685
	4	98	197	296	394	493	592	690	789	887
	5	120	240	360	480	600	720	840	960	1080
	6	142	284	426	568	710	852	994	1136	1278
	7	165	330	495	660	825	990	1155	1320	1485
	8	187	374	560	748	935	1120	1310	1495	1680
	9	210	420	630	840	1050	1260	1470	1680	1890
28	1	61	122	183	244	305	366	427	488	549
	2	65	130	195	260	325	390	455	520	585
	3	88	176	264	352	440	528	616	704	792
	4	116	232	348	464	580	696	812	928	1044
	5	134	268	402	536	670	804	938	1070	1205
	6	166	332	498	664	830	996	1160	1330	1490
	7	192	384	576	768	960	1150	1345	1535	1730
	8	217	434	650	868	1085	1300	1520	1735	1950
	9	245	490	735	980	1220	1470	1715	1960	2020
	10	270	540	810	1080	1350	1620	1890	2160	2430
30	1	69	138	207	276	345	414	483	552	621
	2	73	146	219	292	365	438	510	584	657
	3	98	197	296	394	493	592	690	789	887
	4	129	258	387	516	645	774	903	1030	1160
	5	159	318	477	636	795	954	1110	1270	1430
	6	189	379	568	758	947	1140	1330	1515	1705
	7	222	444	666	888	1110	1330	1550	1775	1995
	8	251	502	753	1004	1255	1505	1755	2010	2260
	9	278	556	835	1110	1390	1665	1945	2220	2500
	10	311	622	933	1244	1556	1866	2177	2488	2799
32	1	77	155	233	310	388	465	543	620	697
	2	81	163	244	326	408	490	570	652	734
	3	113	226	339	452	565	678	791	904	1017
	4	147	294	441	588	735	882	1030	1175	1320
	5	182	365	548	730	912	1095	1280	1460	1640
	6	205	410	615	820	1025	1230	1435	1640	1845
	7	249	498	746	995	1245	1495	1740	1990	2240
	8	282	564	845	1130	1410	1690	1975	2260	2540
	9	318	636	954	1275	1590	1910	2225	2550	2860
	10	352	704	1056	1410	1760	2110	2460	2820	3170
34	1	84	168	252	336	420	504	589	672	756
	2	88	176	264	352	440	528	616	704	792
	3	123	246	367	369	492	615	738	860	984
	4	162	324	486	648	810	972	1135	1296	1458
	5	199	398	597	796	995	1194	1393	1592	1790
	6	239	478	717	956	1195	1435	1673	1912	2152
	7	278	556	834	1110	1390	1670	1945	2225	2500
	8	318	636	954	1272	1590	1910	2225	2545	2860
	9	357	714	1070	1430	1785	2140	2500	2860	3210
	10	415	830	1245	1660	2075	2490	2900	3320	3735

MULTIPLE VOLUME TABLE—WESTERN RED CEDAR

(Based on 186 trees from District I. Diameters are DBH.) Constructed by deriving volumes from DIB (top 1st log) volume curves.
Scribner Decimal C. Rule.

Number of Trees.

DBH Inches	Logs	1	2	3	4	5	6	7	8	9
10	1	3.0	6.0	9.0	12.0	15.0	18.0	21.0	24.0	27.0
	2	6.5	13	19.5	26	32.5	39	45.5	52	58.5
	3	9	18	27	36	45	54	63	72	81
	4	10.5	21	31.5	42	52.5	63	73.5	84	94.5
12	1	5	10	15	20	25	30	35	40	45
	2	8	16	24	32	40	48	56	64	72
	3	11.5	23	34.5	46	57.5	69	80.5	92	103.5
	4	15	30	45	60	75	90	105	120	135
14	1	7.5	15	22.5	30	37.5	45	52.5	60	67.5
	2	10.5	21	31.5	42	52.5	63	73.5	84	94.5
	3	15	30	45	60	75	90	105	120	135
	4	21	42	63	84	105	126	147	168	189
16	1	10	20	30	40	50	60	70	80	90
	2	13.5	27	40.5	54	67.5	81	94.5	108	121.5
	3	18.5	37	55.5	74	92.5	111	129.5	148	166.5
	4	25	50	75	100	125	150	175	200	225
	5	31.5	63	94.5	126	157.5	189	220	252	284
18	1	13	26	39	52	65	78	91	104	117
	2	16.5	33	49.5	66	82.5	99	115.5	132	148.5
	3	23	46	69	92	115	138	161	184	207
	4	30	60	90	120	150	180	210	240	270
	5	37.5	75	112.5	150	187.5	225	262	300	337
20	1	16	32	48	64	80	96	112	128	144
	2	19	39	57	76	95	114	133	152	171
	3	26.5	53	79.5	106	132.5	159	185	212	238
	4	35	70	105	140	175	210	245	280	315
	5	44	88	132	176	220	264	308	352	396
22	1	19	39	58	78	97	117	136	156	175
	2	22	45	67	90	112	135	157	180	202
	3	31	63	94	126	157	189	220	252	284
	4	41	82	123	164	205	246	287	328	369
	5	51	103	154	206	258	309	361	413	464
24	1	22	45	67	90	112	135	157	180	202
	2	26	52	78	104	130	156	182	208	234
	3	36	72	108	144	180	216	252	288	324
	4	46	93	139	186	232	279	326	372	418
	5	58	117	175	234	292	351	410	468	526
	6	70	140	210	280	350	420	490	560	630
26	1	26	53	79	106	132	159	185	212	238
	2	29	59	88	118	147	177	206	236	266
	3	40	81	121	162	202	243	284	324	364
	4	53	106	159	212	265	318	371	424	477
	5	66	132	198	264	330	396	462	528	594
	6	79	158	237	316	395	474	554	632	711
	7	92	184	276	368	460	552	644	736	829
28	1	30	60	90	120	150	180	210	240	270
	2	33	66	99	132	165	198	231	264	297
	3	45	91	136	182	228	273	318	364	410
	4	59	118	177	236	295	354	413	472	531
	5	73	147	220	294	368	441	515	588	661
	6	87	175	262	350	437	525	613	700	788

MULTIPLE VOLUME TABLE—WESTERN RED CEDAR

Number of Trees.—Continued.

DBH	Logs	1	2	3	4	5	6	7	8	9
	7	101	203	304	406	507	609	710	812	913
30	1	33	66	99	132	165	198	231	264	297
	2	36	73	109	146	182	219	256	292	328
	3	50	100	150	200	250	300	350	400	450
	4	65	130	195	260	325	390	455	520	585
	5	80	161	242	322	403	483	564	644	725
	6	95	191	286	382	478	573	669	764	860
	7	111	222	333	444	555	666	777	888	999
32	1	37	75	112	150	187	225	262	300	337
	2	41	82	123	164	205	246	287	328	369
	3	56	112	168	224	280	336	392	448	504
	4	72	145	217	290	362	435	508	580	653
	5	90	180	270	360	450	540	630	720	810
	6	106	213	320	426	532	640	745	852	960
	7	124	248	372	496	620	744	868	992	1116
34	1	41	83	124	166	208	249	291	332	374
	2	45	90	135	180	225	270	315	360	405
	3	61	123	184	246	307	369	431	492	554
	4	80	160	240	320	400	480	560	640	720
	5	99	198	297	396	495	594	693	792	891
	6	117	234	351	469	585	702	820	936	1053
	7	136	272	408	544	680	816	953	1090	1225
	8	155	310	465	620	775	930	1085	1240	1390
36	1	46	92	138	184	230	276	322	368	414
	2	49	99	148	198	247	297	346	396	446
	3	67	134	200	268	335	400	469	536	600
	4	87	175	262	350	437	525	613	700	788
	5	108	217	326	434	543	651	760	869	978
	6	127	255	382	510	638	765	893	1020	1148
	7	149	298	447	596	745	895	1042	1190	1340
	8	169	338	506	676	845	1015	1185	1351	1520
38	2	54	109	163	218	272	327	382	436	490
	3	74	148	222	296	370	444	518	592	666
	4	96	193	290	386	483	579	676	772	870
	5	119	238	357	476	595	714	833	952	1071
	6	140	280	420	560	700	840	980	1120	1400
	7	163	326	490	653	815	980	1140	1305	1465
	8	186	372	558	744	930	1115	1300	1440	1675
	9	210	420	630	840	1050	1260	1470	1680	1890
40	2	58	117	176	234	292	351	410	468	526
	3	79	159	238	318	397	477	556	636	716
	4	104	208	312	416	520	624	728	832	936
	5	128	256	384	512	640	758	896	1025	1150
	6	150	300	450	600	750	900	1050	1200	1350
	7	176	352	528	704	880	1055	1230	1410	1585
	8	201	402	603	804	1005	1208	1407	1608	1809
	9	226	452	678	904	1130	1355	1580	1810	2040
42	3	86	172	258	344	430	516	602	688	774
	4	112	225	338	450	563	675	788	900	1015
	5	139	277	416	554	693	830	970	1110	1245
	6	162	324	486	648	810	972	1135	1295	1460
	7	190	380	570	760	950	1140	1330	1520	1710
	8	218	435	653	870	1090	1305	1520	1740	1960
	9	244	488	732	976	1220	1460	1710	1950	2200

MULTIPLE VOLUME TABLE—WESTERN RED CEDAR

Number of Trees.—Continued.

DBH	Logs	1	2	3	4	5	6	7	8	9
	10	269	538	807	1075	1345	1615	1880	2150	2420
44	3	94	187	280	374	467	561	655	748	841
	4	122	244	366	488	610	732	854	976	1100
	5	150	300	450	600	750	900	1050	1200	1350
	6	176	351	527	702	878	1052	1230	1400	1580
	7	206	412	618	824	1030	1236	1442	1648	1854
	8	235	471	706	942	1178	1412	1650	1885	2120
	9	265	530	794	1060	1320	1590	1850	2120	2380
	10	291	583	874	1160	1450	1745	2040	2330	2620
46	3	100	201	302	402	503	603	704	804	905
	4	131	262	393	524	655	785	917	1050	1180
	5	161	322	483	645	805	966	1130	1290	1450
	6	188	376	564	752	940	1120	1315	1500	1690
	7	222	444	666	888	1110	1330	1550	1775	2000
	8	253	506	.760	1010	1265	1520	1770	2020	2280
	9	284	568	850	1135	1420	1700	1990	2270	2560
	10	315	630	945	1260	1575	1890	2200	2520	2840
48	3	118	236	354	472	590	710	826	945	1060
	4	140	280	420	560	700	840	980	1120	1260
	5	172	344	516	678	860	1030	1205	1375	1550
	6	202	404	606	808	1010	1212	1404	1616	1818
	7	237	474	711	948	1185	1420	1660	1895	2130
	8	271	542	823	1080	1356	1625	1895	2170	2440
	9	305	610	915	1220	1525	1830	2135	2440	2745
	10	341	682	1020	1360	1700	2025	2385	2730	3070
50	4	148	296	444	592	740	888	1040	1185	1330
	5	181	363	544	726	908	1090	1270	1450	1630
	6	215	430	645	860	1075	1290	1505	1720	1935
	7	251	502	753	1004	1256	1506	1757	2008	2259
	8	288	575	863	1150	1435	1725	2005	2300	2590
	9	322	644	966	1290	1610	1930	2260	2580	2900
	10	368	736	1105	1470	1840	2210	2580	2940	3310
52	4	155	311	389	467	622	778	1009	1245	1400
	5	191	381	572	763	953	1140	1335	1525	1905
	6	228	455	684	910	1140	1365	1590	1820	2050
	7	264	528	792	1055	1320	1585	1850	2110	2380
	8	304	607	910	1210	1515	1820	2120	2430	2730
	9	342	685	1025	1370	1710	2050	2400	2740	3080
	10	396	792	1190	1585	1980	2380	2770	3170	3560

MULTIPLE VOLUME TABLE—LODGE POLE PINE

(NOTE—Trees 10 inches and up over two logs, based on 1808 trees in Gallatin County. Other measurements taken in Deer Lodge County, Montana.)

No. of Trees.

DBH	Logs	1	2	3	4	5	6	7	8	9
7	1	1	2	3	4	5	6	7	8	9
8	1	2	4	6	8	10	12	14	16	18
	2	4	8	12	16	20	24	28	32	36
9	1	2.5	5	7.5	10	12.5	15	17.5	20	22.5
	2	5	10	15	20	25	30	35	40	45
10	1	3.5	7	10.5	14	17.5	21	24.5	28	31.5
	2	6	12	18	24	30	36	42	48	54
	3	9	18	27	36	45	54	63	72	81
	4	12.5	25	37.5	50	62.5	75	87.5	100	112.5
11	1	4.5	9	13.5	18	22.5	27	31.5	36	40.5
	2	7	14	21	28	35	42	49	56	63
	3	10	20	30	40	50	60	70	80	90
	4	14	28	42	56	70	84	98	112	126
12	1	5	10	15	20	25	30	35	40	45
	2	8	16	24	32	40	48	56	64	72
	3	11.5	23	34.5	46	57.5	69	80.5	92	103.5
	4	16	32	48	64	80	96	112	128	144
13	1	6	12	18	24	30	36	42	48	54
	2	9	18	27	36	45	54	63	72	81
	3	13	26	39	52	65	78	91	104	117
	4	18	36	54	72	90	108	126	144	162
14	1	7	14	21	28	35	42	49	56	63
	2	10.5	21	31.5	42	52.5	63	73.5	84	94.5
	3	15	30	45	60	75	90	105	120	135
	4	21	42	63	84	105	126	147	168	189
	5	28	56	84	112	140	168	196	224	252
15	1	8	16	24	32	40	48	56	64	72
	2	12	24	36	48	60	72	84	96	108
	3	16.5	33	49.5	66	82.5	99	115.5	132	148.5
	4	24	48	72	96	120	144	168	192	216
	5	32.5	65	97.5	130	162.5	195	227.5	260	292.5
16	1	9	18	27	36	45	54	63	72	81
	2	13.5	27	40.5	54	67.5	81	94.5	108	121.5
	3	19	38	57	76	95	114	133	152	171
	4	27	54	81	108	135	162	189	216	243
	5	36.5	73	109.5	146	182.5	219	255.5	292	328.5
17	1	10.5	21	31.5	42	52.5	63	73.5	84	94.5
	2	15	30	45	60	75	90	105	120	135
	3	21.5	43	64.5	86	107.5	129	150.5	172	193.5
	4	30.5	61	91.5	122	152.5	183	213.5	244	274.5
	5	40.5	81	121.5	162	202.5	243	283.5	324	364.5
18	1	12	24	36	48	60	72	84	96	108
	2	16.5	33	49.5	66	82.5	99	115.5	132	148.5
	3	24	48	72	96	120	144	168	192	216
	4	34	68	102	136	170	204	238	272	306

MULTIPLE VOLUME TABLE—LODGE POLE PINE

Number of Trees.—Continued.

Number of Trees.

Logs	1	2	3	4	5	6	7	8	9
5	44.5	89	133.5	178	222.5	267	311.5	356	400.5
1	13.5	27	40.5	54	67.5	81	94.5	108	121.5
2	19.5	39	58.5	78	97.5	117	136.5	156	175.5
3	27	54	81	108	135	162	189	216	243
4	37.5	75	112.5	150	187.5	225	262.5	300	337.5
5	48.5	97	145.5	194	242.5	291	339.5	388	436.5
1	15	30	45	60	75	90	105	120	135
2	22	44	66	88	110	132	154	176	198
3	30	60	90	120	150	180	210	240	270
4	41	82	123	164	205	246	287	328	369
5	52.5	105	157.5	210	262.5	315	367.5	420	472.5
1	17	34	51	68	85	102	119	136	153
2	24.5	49	73.5	98	122.5	147	171.5	196	220.5
3	33	66	99	132	165	198	231	264	297
4	45	90	135	180	225	270	315	360	405
5	56.5	113	169.5	226	282.5	339	395.5	452	508.5
3	36.5	73	109.5	146	182.5	219	255.5	292	328.5
4	48.5	97	145.5	194	242.5	291	339.5	388	436.5
5	60.5	121	181.5	242	302.5	363	423.5	484	544.5
3	40	80	120	160	200	240	280	320	360
4	52.5	105	157.5	210	262.5	315	367.5	420	472.5
5	65	130	195	260	325	390	455	520	585
3	44	88	132	176	220	264	308	352	396
4	56.5	113	169.5	226	282.5	339	395.5	452	508.5
5	69	138	207	276	345	414	483	552	621

I

29, 1907.

INE.

Walter Mulford

Issued November 29, 1907.

U. S. DEPARTMENT OF AGRICULTURE,
FOREST SERVICE—Circular 126.
GIFFORD PINCHOT, Forester.

FOREST TABLES—LODGEPOLE PINE.

Compiled by
E. A. ZIEGLER,
FOREST ASSISTANT.

WASHINGTON : GOVERNMENT PRINTING OFFICE : 1907

14568—Cir. 126—07——1

ORGANIZATION OF THE FOREST SERVICE.

GIFFORD PINCHOT, *Forester.*
OVERTON W. PRICE, *Associate Forester.*

PHILIP P. WELLS, *Law Officer.*
HERBERT A. SMITH, *Editor.*
GEORGE B. SUDWORTH, *Dendrologist.*

Operation.—JAMES B. ADAMS, *Assistant Forester, in Charge.*

Maintenance.—HERMON C. METCALF, *Chief.*
Accounts.—GEORGE E. KING, *Chief.*
Organization.—C. S. CHAPMAN, *Chief.*
CLYDE LEAVITT, *Assistant Chief.*
Engineering.—W. E. HERRING, *Chief.*
Lands.—GEORGE F. POLLOCK, *Chief.*

Silviculture.—WILLIAM T. COX, *Assistant Forester, in Charge.*

Extension.—SAMUEL N. SPRING, *Chief.*
Silvics.—RAPHAEL ZON, *Chief.*
Management.—E. E. CARTER, *Chief.*
W. G. WEIGLE, *Assistant Chief.*

Grazing.—ALBERT F. POTTER, *Assistant Forester, in Charge.*

Products.—WILLIAM L. HALL, *Assistant Forester, in Charge.*

Wood Utilization.—R. S. KELLOGG, *Chief.*
Wood Preservation.—CARL G. CRAWFORD, *Chief.*
Publication.—FINDLEY BURNS, *Chief.*

CONTENTS.

FOREST TABLES—LODGEPOLE PINE.

INTRODUCTION.

In its general investigations the Forest Service has gathered, in tabular form, a great deal of miscellaneous data on tree growth, form, and volume. Much has been published, yet much more has been submitted in routine office reports, which are not widely available. Many of these tables are to be assembled, collated, and edited. While they represent the results of many investigations, and are the best that can be had, they must not be regarded as final, but as suggestions for further investigations, by which they must be tested. Criticism of them is desired, for only through criticism can they be corrected or verified.

The various subjects considered are: Stand tables, by well-recognized types and localities; reproduction; height and diameter growths; volume, by feet and by products; taper measurements; and present and potential yields.

The measurements for lodgepole pine tables were made by field parties in Wyoming in 1901 and 1905 and in Montana in 1902.

STAND TABLES.

The stand tables show the variations in lodgepole pine forests in the northern Rocky Mountain region. They illustrate the forest conditions to which all the tables in the circular apply and are not averages for use in estimating or cruising. They are grouped according to the two broad divisions into which the forests of the northern Rocky Mountain region naturally fall. In the northern section, from the Yellowstone National Forest north through western Montana and eastern Idaho, Douglas fir is an important tree associated with lodgepole pine. In the southern section, from the Big Horn and Medicine Bow Mountains in Wyoming south into northern Colorado and Utah, there is less Douglas fir and the associated tree is Engelmann spruce. The types sometimes blend almost imperceptibly and occur in varying combinations; but the stands given prevail over considerable areas.

NORTHERN SECTION.

The types of the northern section are represented by the following tables: Table 1, lodgepole pine flat; Table 2, lodgepole pine slope; Table 3, Douglas fir slope; Table 4, Alpine or transition type.

The lodgepole pine flat or creek type, as shown in Table 1, contains about 50 per cent pine and 30 per cent Engelmann spruce; the rest is Alpine fir and Douglas fir. This type grows on limited areas along creeks and on other moist situations below 8,000 feet.

TABLE 1.—*Lodgepole pine flat or creek type in Gallatin County, Mont.*

[Trees 6 inches and over in diameter breasthigh on 28 acres.]

AVERAGE TREES PER ACRE.

Diameter breasthigh.	Lodgepole pine.	Engelmann spruce.	Alpine fir.	Douglas fir.	Limber pine.	Total of five species.
Inches.	*Number.*	*Number.*	*Number.*	*Number.*	*Number.*	*Number.*
6	9.04	7.07	5.46	1.86	....	....
7	13.75	8.30	4.71	1.21	....	....
8	14.07	6.43	4.54	1.21	....	....
9	15.07	5.36	3.50	1.29	....	....
10	11.93	5.61	2.43	.93	....	....
11	11.07	3.86	2.04	.96	....	....
12	9.32	4.07	1.46	.82	....	....
13	7.79	3.46	1.25	.71	....	....
14	5.43	2.89	.93	.54	....	....
15	4.18	2.57	.61	.64	....	....
16	2.46	2.14	.39	.54	....	....
17	1.75	1.86	.39	.54	....	....
18	1.25	1.29	.39	.32	....	....
19	.89	1.21	.11	.32	....	....
20	.46	1.32	.07	.36	....	....
21	.21	.96	.04	.14	....	....
22	.18	1.00	.14	.14	....	....
23	.21	.79	.04	.07	....	....
24	.04	.50	.11	.18	....	....
25	....	.43	....	.11	....	....
26	.07	.39	.04	.04	....	....
27	.04	.39	....	.04	....	....
28	.04	.21	....	....	....	....
29	....	....	.04	....	....	....
30	....	.11	....	.07	....	....
31	....	.04	....	.04	....	....
32	....	.04	....	.07	....	....
33	....	....	....	.04	....	....
34	....	.04	....	....	....	....
37	....	.04	....	....	....	....
Total........	109.85	62.44	28.69	13.19	....	214.17
Per cent.....	51.29	29.15	13.40	6.16	....	100.00

TREES 10 INCHES AND OVER IN DIAMETER BREASTHIGH.

Total........	57.32	35.22	10.46	7.62	....	110.64
Per cent.....	51.81	31.83	9.47	6.89	....	100.00

Table 2 shows the lodgepole pine slope type, which, in many places, approaches the pure pine stand (75 per cent) and comprises the larger part of the forest up to 8,000 feet.

TABLE 2.—*Lodgepole pine slope type in Gallatin County, Mont.*

[Trees 6 inches and over in diameter breasthigh on 80 acres.]

AVERAGE TREES PER ACRE.

Diameter breasthigh.	Lodgepole pine.	Douglas fir.	Engelmann spruce.	Alpine fir.	Limber pine.	Total of five species.
Inches.	*Number.*	*Number.*	*Number.*	*Number.*	*Number.*	*Number.*
6	28.30	4.12	2.82	2.90	0.22	....
7	29.36	2.90	2.70	2.64	.11	....
8	25.09	2.47	2.10	2.17	.11	....
9	21.16	2.16	1.74	1.55	....	....
10	18.03	1.80	1.90	1.19	.02	....
11	15.22	1.35	1.18	.69	....	....
12	11.82	1.03	1.20	.69	....	....
13	8.60	.88	1.28	.52	.02	....
14	5.29	.67	.84	.32	....	....
15	3.66	.58	.78	.27	.01	....
16	2.06	.48	.73	.17	....	....
17	1.25	.39	.40	.10	.01	....
18	.82	.33	.40	.18	.01	....
19	.55	.34	.39	.05	....	....
20	.30	.24	.42	.02	.01	....
21	.16	.17	.24	.02	....	....
22	.13	.15	.36	.03	....	....
23	.09	.12	.20	.01	....	....
24	.02	.15	.15	.05	....	....
25	.01	.10	.13	....	....	....
26	.05	.09	.09	.02	....	....
27	.01	.03	.11	.01	....	....
28	.01	.07	.07	....	....	....
29	.01	.02	.02	.01	....	....
30	....	.08	.03	....	....	....
31	....	.01	.02	....	....	....
32	....	.05	....	....	....	....
34	....	....	.01	....	....	....
35	....	.01	.01	....	....	....
36	....	.02	....	....	....	....
37	....	....	.01	....	....	....
38	....	.01	....	....	....	....
50	....	.01	....	....	....	....
Total........	171.90	20.83	20.39	13.01	.52	227.25
Per cent.....	75.64	9.17	8.97	5.99	.23	100.00

TREES 10 INCHES AND OVER IN DIAMETER BREASTHIGH.

Total........	67.99	9.18	11.03	4.35	0.08	92.63
Per cent.....	73.40	9.91	11.91	4.69	.09	100.00

Table 3 shows the average number of trees per acre of the Douglas fir slope type, which grows on southern and exposed western slopes in the Gallatin Mountains of Montana. In the Yellowstone region it occurs on protected northern and eastern exposures. The type is of limited extent, and occurs below 8,000 feet.

TABLE 3.—*Douglas fir slope type in Gallatin County, Mont.*

[Trees 6 inches and over in diameter breasthigh on 14 acres.]

AVERAGE TREES PER ACRE.

Diameter breasthigh.	Douglas fir.	Lodgepole pine.	Alpine fir.	Engelmann spruce.	Limber pine.	Total of five species.
Inches.	*Number.*	*Number.*	*Number.*	*Number.*	*Number.*	*Number.*
6	17.64	10.21	0.43	0.21		
7	15.50	6.79	.29	.14		
8	15.14	6.15	.29	.14		
9	8.50	5.50	.36	.07		
10	9.79	3.57	.21	.07	0.07	
11	6.86	2.57				
12	5.57	2.43	.07			
13	3.64	1.29				
14	4.00	1.29				
15	2.07	1.14		.07		
16	1.50	.64				
17	2.50	.36				
18	.86	.29				
19	1.07	.07				
20	.86			.07		
21	.71	.07				
22	.36	.21				
23	.57	.14				
24	.36	.07	.07			
25	.50					
26	.43					
27	.29					
28	.43					
29	.29					
30	.43					
31	.07					
32	.21					
33	.29					
34	.14					
38	.14					
40	.07					
42	.07					
48	.07					
Total	101.01	42.79	1.72	.77	.07	146.36
Per cent	69.01	29.24	1.17	.53	.05	100.00

TREES 10 INCHES AND OVER IN DIAMETER BREASTHIGH.

Total	44.23	14.14	0.35	0.21	0.07	59.00
Per cent	74.97	23.97	.59	.35	.12	100.00

Table 4 shows the Alpine or transition type, which occurs at 8,000 feet, and changes from the predominating lodgepole pine to Engelmann spruce with Alpine fir, and finally to limber pine or mountain pine. It is a type less important than the other.

TABLE 4.—*Alpine or transition type in Gallatin County, Mont.*

[Trees 6 inches and over in diameter breasthigh on 14 acres.]

AVERAGE TREES PER ACRE.

Diameter breasthigh.	Lodgepole pine.	Douglas fir.	Alpine fir.	Engelmann spruce.	Limber pine.	Total of five species.
Inches.	*Number.*	*Number.*	*Number.*	*Number.*	*Number.*	*Number.*
6	18.93	10.29	2.43	1.43	1.43	....
7	15.64	8.36	1.79	.86	.57	....
8	9.36	6.57	1.71	1.00	.71	....
9	8.07	5.64	.64	.50	....	....
10	3.86	4.29	.64	.29	.14	....
11	2.29	3.29	.36	.21	....	....
12	1.43	2.07	.14	.21	....	....
13	.43	1.21	.14	.07	.29	....
14	.50	.64	.07	....	....	....
15	.07	.43	....	.07	.07	....
16	.07	.71	....	....	....	....
17	....	.29	....	....	.07	....
18	.14	.50	....	....	.07	....
19	.14	.43	....	....	....	....
20	....	.71	....	....	.07	....
21	....	.21	....	....	....	....
22	....	.36	....	....	....	....
23	....	....	....	.07	....	....
24	....	....	....	....	....	....
25	....	.07	....	....	....	....
26	....	.07	....	....	....	....
27	....	....	....	....	....	....
28	....	.07	....	....	....	....
29	....	....	....	....	....	....
30	....	.14	....	....	....	....
31	....	....	....	....	.07	....
Total........	60.93	46.35	7.92	4.71	3.49	123.40
Per cent.....	49.38	37.56	6.42	3.81	2.83	100.00

TREES 10 INCHES AND OVER IN DIAMETER BREASTHIGH.

Total........	8.93	15.49	1.35	0.92	0.78	27.47
Per cent.....	32.51	56.39	4.91	3.35	2.84	100.00

SOUTHERN SECTION.

The southern section is represented by tables for the Douglas Creek watershed, covering almost 30,000 acres of the Medicine Bow National Forest. The types are: Engelmann spruce type, Table 5; lodgepole pine type, quality I, Table 6; lodgepole pine type, quality II, Table 7; lodgepole pine type, quality III, Table 8.

The Engelmann spruce type (Table 5) grows in bottoms and swales, or in the moister locations generally. Its area is limited, and includes 6 per cent of the Douglas Creek watershed.

TABLE 5.—*Engelmann spruce type in the Medicine Bow National Forest, Wyoming.*

[Trees 4 inches and over in diameter breasthigh on 85 acres.]

AVERAGE TREES PER ACRE.

Diameter breasthigh.	Engelmann spruce.	Lodgepole pine.		Alpine fir.	Aspen.	Total of four species.
		Sound.	Cull.			
Inches.	*Number.*	*Number.*	*Number.*	*Number.*	*Number.*	*Number.*
4	7.42	2.51	0.16	8.31	0.22	....
5	8.54	3.59	.28	8.12	.19	....
6	10.31	5.01	.45	7.49	.13	....
7	8.87	5.44	.68	5.93	.12	....
8	8.86	6.16	.68	4.05	.08	....
9	7.54	6.00	.78	3.87	.18	....
10	6.61	5.80	.79	2.61	.07	....
11	5.47	5.73	.76	1.81	.07	....
12	6.16	5.05	.85	1.32	.06	....
13	4.56	4.46	.72	.72	.07	....
14	3.52	3.44	.55	.51	.02	....
15	3.74	2.45	.52	.33	....	....
16	2.52	1.53	.38	.16	.02	....
17	2.15	1.06	.29	.20	....	....
18	1.70	.61	.19	.07	....	....
19	1.34	.38	.08	.04	....	....
20	1.25	.24	.07	.04	....	....
21	.01	.08	.05	....	....	....
22	.80	.07	.01	.01	....	....
23	.48	.06	....	....	....	....
24	.36	.05	.01	.02	....	....
25	.21	....	....	....	....	....
26	.20	.01	....	....	....	....
27	.15	....	....	....	....	....
28	.13	....	....	....	....	....
29	.07	....	.01	....	....	....
30	.11	....	....	....	....	....
31	.11	....	....	....	....	....
32	.04	....	....	....	....	....
33	.01	....	....	....	....	....
35	.01	....	....	....	....	....
36	.01	....	....	.02	....	....
40	.01	....	....	....	....	....
41	.01	....	....	....	....	....
Total........	94.24	60.33	8.31	46.53	1.23	210.64
Per cent.....	44.74	28.64	3.95	22.09	.58	100.00

TREES 10 INCHES AND OVER IN DIAMETER BREASTHIGH.

Total........	42.70	31.62	5.28	7.86	0.31	87.77
Per cent.....	48.65	36.03	6.02	8.96	.35	100.00

Table 6 shows the lodgepole pine type, quality I, which includes the best part of the lodgepole pine land, with trees from 75 to 90 feet high. It comprises 3 per cent of the Douglas Creek watershed.

TABLE 6.—*Lodgepole pine type, quality I, in the Medicine Bow National Forest, Wyoming.*

[Trees 4 inches and over in diameter breasthigh on 23.6 acres.]

AVERAGE TREES PER ACRE.

Diameter breasthigh.	Lodgepole pine.		Engelmann spruce.	Alpine fir.	Total of three species.
	Sound.	Dead.			
Inches.	*Number.*	*Number.*	*Number.*	*Number.*	*Number.*
4	4.96	0.13	1.57	3.18	....
5	7.88	.50	2.67	2.54	....
6	10.76	.64	2.71	2.08	....
7	13.64	.68	2.46	1.44	....
8	17.33	1.19	2.50	1.48	....
9	15.93	.93	2.03	.68	....
10	19.53	1.61	1.99	.76	....
11	17.12	1.14	1.82	.38	....
12	18.00	1.53	2.37	.25	....
13	13.60	1.19	1.53	.13	....
14	11.27	.85	1.31	.38	....
15	7.84	.42	.51	.08	....
16	5.64	.51	.47	.04	....
17	4.24	.55	.42	.04	....
18	2.80	.38	.21	....	....
19	1.40	.13	.42	....	....
20	.81	.13	.17	....	....
21	.38	.21	.38	....	....
22	.25	.04	....	....	....
23	....	.08	.08	....	....
24	....	.04	.08	....	....
26	....	....	.04	.04	....
29	....	....	.04	....	....
Total........	173.98	12.97	25.78	13.50	226.23
Per cent.....	76.90	5.73	11.40	5.97	100.00

TREES 10 INCHES AND OVER IN DIAMETER BREASTHIGH.

Total........	103.48	8.81	11.84	2.10	126.23
Per cent.....	81.98	6.98	9.38	1.66	100.00

Table 7 gives the lodgepole pine type, quality II, which includes the typical pure lodgepole slopes, on which the trees are 55 to 75 feet high. This type comprises the largest part of the forest—61 per cent in this case—and may be regarded as the average stand.

TABLE 7.—*Lodgepole pine type, quality II, in the Medicine Bow National Forest, Wyoming.*

[Trees 4 inches and over in diameter breasthigh on 800 acres.]

AVERAGE TREES PER ACRE.

Diameter breasthigh.	Lodgepole pine. Sound.	Lodgepole pine. Cull.	Engelmann spruce.	Alpine fir.	Aspen.	Cottonwood.	Total of five species.
Inches.	*Number.*	*Number.*	*Number.*	*Number.*	*Number.*	*Number.*	*Number.*
4	13.32	0.30	0.73	1.57	0.01	....	....
5	18.13	.78	1.01	1.21	.01	0.01	....
6	24.40	1.24	1.25	1.25	.01	....	....
7	29.37	1.53	1.03	.97	.01	....	....
8	31.46	1.98	.94	.80	.01	....	....
9	28.06	1.90	.74	.40	....	....	....
10	24.21	2.07	.67	.38	....	....	....
11	18.80	1.78	.56	.27	....	....	....
12	16.26	1.62	.51	.19	....	....	....
13	10.48	1.34	.33	.09		....	....
14	7.00	1.07	.32	.07			
15	4.73	.85	.21	.04			
16	3.00	.57	.21	.02			
17	1.65	.37	.13	.02			
18	1.09	.28	.11	.02			
19	.57	.18	.08	.01			
20	.28	.12	.07	.01			
21	.16	.08	.05	....	....	....	
22	.11	.04	.03	....	....	....	
23	.05	.01	.02	....	....	....	
24	.03	.01	.02	....	....	....	
25	.02	.01	.01	....	....	....	
26	.01	....	.01	....		....	
27	.02	....	.01			....	
28	.01	....	....			....	
29	....	....	.01	....			
Total...	233.40	18.29	9.06	7.40	.05	.01	268.18
Per cent...	87.03	6.79	3.38	2.78	.02		100.00

TREES 10 INCHES AND OVER IN DIAMETER BREASTHIGH.

Total........	88.57	10.38	3.36	1.12	....	....	103.43
Per cent......	85.63	10.04	3.25	1.08	....	....	100.00

Table 8 gives the lodgepole pine type, quality III, which is found on the higher ridges and slopes. The trees are usually under 55 feet in height and of inferior quality. The type comprises about 30 per cent of the Douglas Creek watershed.

TABLE 8.—*Lodgepole pine type, quality III, in the Medicine Bow National Forest, Wyoming.*

[Trees 4 inches and over in diameter breasthigh on 467 acres.]

AVERAGE TREES PER ACRE.

Diameter breasthigh.	Lodgepole pine.		Alpine fir.	Engelmann spruce.	Total of three species.
	Sound.	Cull.			
Inches.	*Number.*	*Number.*	*Number.*	*Number.*	*Number.*
4	26.97	1.68	1.18	0.27	....
5	33.50	3.38	1.07	.46	....
6	36.47	4.41	.98	.48	....
7	34.20	4.51	.02	.33	....
8	30.40	4.37	.58	.37	....
9	21.09	3.43	.27	.25	....
10	16.14	2.98	.23	.21	....
11	11.05	2.17	.17	.18	....
12	8.92	2.02	.10	.18	....
13	5.38	1.35	.06	.11	....
14	3.37	.93	.05	.11	....
15	2.24	.71	.03	.09	....
16	1.47	.45	.01	.06	....
17	.82	.24	.01	.05	....
18	.55	.17	....	.02	....
19	.26	.10	....	.01	....
20	.13	.03	....	.01	....
21	.08	.03	....	.01	....
22	.06	.03	....	....	....
23	.03	.01	....	....	....
24	.02	....	....	....	....
25	.01	....	....	....	....
29	.05	....	....	....	....
Total........	233.90	33.00	5.36	3.20	275.46
Per cent.....	84.91	11.98	1.95	1.16	100.00

TREES 10 INCHES AND OVER IN DIAMETER BREASTHIGH.

Total........	50.58	11.22	0.66	1.04	63.50
Per cent.....	79.65	17.67	1.04	1.64	100.00

REPRODUCTION.

Seedling stand tables are misleading, since they apply only to small areas and do not show general reproduction. They indicate the reproductive possibilities of a tree under certain conditions only. Thus, Table 9 gives the number of seedlings on an area 20 feet by 20 feet, the average of five plots of those dimensions.

TABLE 9.—*Seedling lodgepole pine stand, Gallatin County, Mont.*

Height.	Average trees 20 feet by 20 feet on plot.
Feet.	*Number.*
0.5	6
1.0	19
1.5	18
2.0	61
2.5	79
3.0	128
3.5	70
4.0	46
4.5	26
5.0	18
6.0	4
Total....	475

This would give a stand of more than 50,000 trees per acre, but an acre of such reproduction might not be found in one continuous area. The fact that lodgepole pine reproduces vigorously after fires and in openings where the soil is favorable is well illustrated by the dense mature stands.

Seedling growth varies greatly, and is influenced most by relative light and shade. Table 10 gives the average height attained by 463 seedlings from 2 to 20 years old growing in openings, in Gallatin County, Mont. No trees over 8 feet high were measured; yet some trees from 10 to 20 feet high may have been only 20 years old, or less. Had these been included the average would have been much higher than the arbitrary 8 feet.

TABLE 10.—*Seedling height growth of lodgepole pine in openings, in Gallatin County, Mont.*

Age.	Height.	Basis.	Age.	Height.	Basis.
Years.	*Feet.*	*Trees.*	*Years.*	*Feet.*	*Trees.*
1	0.3	....	12	3.9	77
2	.6	4	13	4.5	75
3	.8	2	14	5.1	51
4	.9	1	15	5.6	28
5	1.0	1	16	6.1	12
6	1.2	5	17	6.6	18
7	1.5	5	18	7.0	13
8	1.8	11	19	7.5	23
9	2.3	30	20	8.0	7
10	2.8	41			
11	3.3	59	Total..............		463

HEIGHT.

According to the explanations of the stand tables, the different types should show varying heights for a given diameter. A tree of 10 inches breasthigh diameter may be 71 feet high on a lodgepole slope in Montana, and 64 feet high in the creek type, where the stand is not so dense. The Alpine or transition type would show a much smaller height for the same diameter. Unfortunately, stem analyses have not been taken on each type, and it is impossible to illustrate each one. However, the lodgepole pine slope of the northern section and lodgepole pine, quality II, of the southern section, which together represent the average types and much the larger areas, are well represented in Table 11, and are directly comparable. The tree in Montana seems to have a slightly greater height for a given diameter than in Wyoming. Trees 13 inches and more in diameter vary little in height for average types in the different sections.

TABLE 11.—*Comparison of average heights of lodgepole pine.*

Diameter breast-high	Lodgepole pine, quality II, Medicine Bow National Forest, Wyoming.		Lodgepole slope, Gallatin County, Mont.		Flat or creek type, Gallatin County, Mont.	
	Height.	Basis.	Height.	Basis.	Height.	Basis.
Inches.	*Feet.*	*Trees.*	*Feet.*	*Trees.*	*Feet.*	*Trees.*
2	....	....	21	4	....	....
3	....	....	31	10	34	1
4	....	....	41	12	40	3
5	....	....	50	6	45	2
6	....	....	57	12	50	1
7	....	....	62	13	54	....
8	59	3	66	94	57	13
9	62	6	69	74	60	14
10	64	34	71	265	63	84
11	67	220	73	248	66	88
12	69	203	74	150	68	69
13	71	239	75	76	71	27
14	73	88	76	82	73	29
15	74	23	77	71	75	34
16	76	1	78	43	77	16
17	....	....	79	25	79	16
18	....	....	79	16	80	7
19	....	....	80	10	81	4
20	....	....	81	11	82	3
21	....	....	82	2	....	....
22	....	....	82	7	....	....
Total	....	907	....	1,231	....	396

GROWTH.

Table 12 gives rates of growth for different regions. The first three columns are types that may be compared. Gallatin County, Mont., shows the best rate of growth, the Bighorn region next, and the Medicine Bow region shows an exceedingly slow growth. These figures apply to the greater proportion of the lodgepole forests. The creek type of the Gallatin, Mont., district shows a comparatively rapid growth and may be accepted as a maximum applicable to less than 5 per cent of the forest.

These tables are very general and show that in this region lodgepole pine growth is very slow, though on exceptionally favorable situations like the creek type it is fairly rapid. The degree to which the climatic factors and the varying densities affect the growth is not discernible in these figures.

TABLE 12.—*Comparisons of average diameter growth of lodgepole pine.*

Age.	Slope type.						Creek type, Gallatin County, Mont.	
	Gallatin County, Mont.		Bighorn National Forest, Wyoming.		Medicine Bow National Forest, Wyoming.			
	Diameter breast-high.	Basis.	Diameter breast-high.	Basis.	Diameter breast-high.	Basis.	Diameter breast-high.	Basis.
Years.	*Inches.*	Decade measurements on about 2,000 stumps of various heights, 80 to 175 years old.	*Inches.*	Decade measurements on 40 stumps of various heights, 72 to 340 years old.	*Inches.*	Decade measurements on 430 1-foot stumps, 150 to 300 years old.	*Inches.*	Decade measurements on 193 stumps of various heights up to 175 years old.
20	2.2		1.5		0.3		2.5	
30	4.0		3.0		1.6		4.6	
40	5.4		4.4		2.8		6.4	
50	6.6		5.7		3.7		8.0	
60	7.7		6.7		4.4		9.4	
70	8.7		7.6		5.0		10.7	
80	9.6		8.4		5.6		11.8	
90	10.5		9.1		6.2		12.8	
100	11.2		9.7		6.7		13.8	
110	11.9		10.3		7.2		....	
120	12.5		10.7		7.7		....	
130	13.0		11.1		8.2		....	
140	13.5		11.6		8.6		....	
150	14.0		12.1		9.1		....	
160	....		12.5		9.6		....	
170	....		12.8		10.0		....	
180	....		13.2		10.4		....	
190	....		13.5		10.8		....	
200	....		13.8		11.1		....	

The increased diameter growth through openings made by logging is shown in Table 13, which compares the diameters that trees may attain in ten, twenty, and thirty years after logging with those of the unopened stands. Readings were made on 395 stumps on land cut over ten, twenty, and thirty years ago in the Medicine Bow National Forest. A growth rate was calculated excluding the ten, twenty, and thirty year readings, and from this the virgin growth shown in the third, fifth, and seventh columns was obtained. By tabulating the increase in growth covered by the last ten, twenty, and thirty years the figures in the first column were obtained. The first ten years after logging is seen to make little difference, and is evidently needed in recovering from suppression, but in thirty years there is considerable difference for the smaller trees. For instance, a 2-inch tree after thirty years reaches a diameter of 4.65 inches in a logged stand, but only 3.85 inches in the dense stand—a gain of 0.8 of an inch in thirty years. This increase of growth diminishes in the larger trees, so that a 9-inch tree in a logged stand shows an advantage of only 0.05 of an inch in thirty years. Evidently the larger, mature, and dominant trees have little to gain by the opening up of the stand.

TABLE 13.—*Increase of diameter growth due to logging, Medicine Bow National Forest, Wyoming.*

Diameter breasthigh at present time.	Diameter after 10 years.		Diameter after 20 years.		Diameter after 30 years.	
	If logged.	Not logged.	If logged.	Not logged.	If logged.	Not logged.
Inches.	*Inches.*	*Inches.*	*Inches.*	*Inches.*	*Inches.*	*Inches.*
2	2.70	2.70	3.65	3.35	4.65	3.85
3	3.65	3.55	4.30	4.05	5.10	4.50
4	4.55	4.45	5.20	4.90	5.90	5.35
5	5.55	5.40	6.20	5.85	6.90	6.30
6	6.55	6.45	7.20	7.00	7.90	7.30
7	7.55	7.50	8.20	8.05	8.90	8.55
8	8.55	8.55	9.15	9.05	9.85	9.65
9	9.55	9.55	10.15	10.15	10.80	10.75
10	10.55	....	11.15	....	11.80	....
11	11.50	....	12.10	....	12.75	....
12	12.50	....	13.10	....	13.75	....
13	13.45	....	14.00	....	14.65	....
14	14.45	....	15.00	....	15.60	....
15	15.40	....	15.95	....	16.55	....
16	16.40	....	16.90	....	17.45	....
17	17.35	....	17.80	....	18.35	....
18	18.30	....	18.70	....	19.20	....

For accurate rates of height growth, measurements must be taken at uniform heights from the ground to the top and accurate ring counts made on each cross section. Unfortunately, in the lodgepole pine analyses these counts were not made above the stump section. This difficulty is sometimes bridged by the indirect method of reading across the age-diameter and diameter-height curves; for example, a 60-year old tree in a specified type has a diameter of 7.7 inches breasthigh and the height corresponding to a 7.7-inch diameter is 65 feet; therefore a tree 60 years old should be 65 feet high. A growth-height table may be constructed in this way, but since its silvicultural accuracy is questionable, it is not included.

VOLUME.

BOARD FEET.

Table 14 gives the volume in board feet, Scribner log rule, for trees of various diameters and heights, with a top cutting limit of 6 inches inside bark. The table was constructed from trees cut in the Gallatin region of Montana, but the height class division makes it applicable to any region or type where the height is known.

The 1,817 trees measured for this table were cut and scaled as 16-foot and 10-foot logs. A uniform 10-foot log would give a slightly higher board foot volume.

TABLE 14.—*Volume of lodgepole pine, board measure, Gallatin County, Mont.*

[Cut into 16-foot and 10-foot logs to a top diameter of 6 inches inside bark and scaled by Scribner log rule.]

Diameter breast-high.	Height of tree in feet—						Basis of trees.
	50.	60.	70.	80.	90.	100.	
Inches.	*Bd. ft.*	*Bd. ft.*	*Bd. ft.*	*Bd. ft.*	*Bd. ft.*	*Bd. ft.*	*Number.*
10	50	65	75	90	105	125	495
11	60	75	90	105	125	155	478
12	75	90	105	125	150	185	296
13	90	105	125	145	180	215	146
14	105	125	145	170	215	250	120
15	....	140	170	200	250	285	113
16	....	160	195	230	285	315	60
17	....	....	225	260	315	350	44
18	....	....	250	290	350	385	25
19	....	....	275	320	380	420	17
20	....	....	300	345	415	460	14
21	....	....	....	375	450	495	2
22	....	....	....	400	490	530	6
23	....	....	....	430	525	565	....
24	....	....	....	455	560	600	1
Total....	....	....	....	....	....	....	1,817

CUBIC FEET.

Table 15 gives the total volume of the stem in cubic feet. To reduce this to merchantable wood an allowance of 12 per cent must be deducted for bark, stump, and a 4-inch top. The bark alone forms about 6 per cent of the total volume. The allowances for top above 4 inches inside bark and for a stump 1 foot high vary greatly with the diameter and only slightly with the height. The allowance for a 10-inch tree is 6 per cent, which was taken as the average. This, added to the 6 per cent bark allowance, gives the total allowance of 12 per cent. The variation in the allowance for stump and top is as follows:

Diameter breasthigh of tree.	Ratio of 1-foot stump and 4-inch top to total volume.
Inches.	*Per cent.*
6	18
8	7
10	6
12	5
14	5
16	5

TABLE 15.—*Volume of lodgepole pine, cubic contents, Gallatin County, Mont.*

Diameter breast-high.	Height of tree in feet— 30.	40.	50.	60.	70.	80.	90.	Basis.
Inches.	*Cu. ft.*	*Cu. ft.*	*Cu. ft.*	*Cu. ft.*	*Cu. ft.*	*Cu. ft.*	*Cu. ft.*	*Trees.*
4	1.2	1.7	2.3	2.8	......	......	....	10
5	2.4	3.0	3.8	4.7	......	......	....	11
6	....	4.5	5.6	6.9	8.2	9.4	....	14
7		......	7.6	9.3	11.0	12.8	....	13
8		......	10.0	12.0	14.0	16.5	19.0	54
9			12.5	15.0	17.5	20.5	23.0	71
10			15.5	18.0	21.0	24.5	27.5	136
11			18.5	21.5	25.0	28.5	32.5	73
12			21.5	25.0	29.0	33.0	37.5	71
13			......	29.0	33.0	37.5	42.5	34
14			......	32.5	37.5	43.0	48.5	34
15			......	36.5	42.0	48.0	54.5	27
16					47.0	54.0	61.0	22
17					52.0	59.5	67.5	18
18					57.0	65.5	74.0	19
19					62.5	71.5	81.0	13
20					68.0	77.5	87.5	11
21					73.5	83.5	94.0	3
22						89.5	101.0	3
Total....	....					......		644

BOX BOARDS.

Since the box board industry now uses lodgepole pine, a table of the contents of trees in "wany" and round-edged boards would be convenient. Such a table can be constructed from Table 15 by converting the cubic feet into board feet of wany-edged boards, according to the following relation, which holds for second-growth white pine in New Hampshire, cut with a one-fourth-inch circular saw, and which will apply to lodgepole pine closely utilized:

Diameter breast-high.	Board feet per cubic foot of total volume.	Diameter breast-high.	Board feet per cubic foot of total volume.
Inches.		*Inches.*	
6	4.0	15	6.1
7	4.6	16	6.2
8	5.0	17	6.2
9	5.4	18	6.3
10	5.6	19	6.3
11	5.8	20	6.4
12	5.9	21	6.5
13	6.0	22	6.5
14	6.1		

The board feet given in this tabulation are actual saw cut and not Scribner rule. The relation is per cubic foot of total volume, stump, top, and bark included. Thus, to find the actual contents in board feet of a 6-inch tree when sawed into round-edged box boards, its volume in cubic feet (see Table 15) must be multiplied by 4. This factor increases with the diameter of the tree and reaches 6.5 for a 22-inch tree. It also increases very slightly with the height of a tree, but for practical purposes the figures apply to all heights.

TIES AND PROPS.

Two tie and prop volume tables are given. Table 16 was constructed from taper curves, and only first-grade ties, 6 inches by 8 inches by 8 feet, are included. The rest of the stem to 6 inches is regarded as mine props. This table should be used where tie inspection is very rigid, and second-grade and cull ties are not merchantable. It allows a large part of the tree to go into props.

TABLE 16.—*Average number of first-class railroad ties and mine props in lodgepole pine, based on taper curves, Gallatin County, Mont.*

Diameter breast-high.	Height in feet— 60.		70.		80.		90.	
	Ties.	Props.	Ties.	Props.	Ties.	Props.	Ties.	Props.
Inches.	*Number.*	*Feet.*	*Number.*	*Feet.*	*Number.*	*Feet.*	*Number.*	*Feet.*
10	1.2	27.0	1.3	31.0	1.4	30.0	....	....
11	2.2	20.0	2.4	25.0	2.8	27.5	....	....
12	2.6	17.5	3.1	22.0	3.6	23.0	4.4	24.5
13	3.0	16.0	3.6	19.0	4.3	19.0	5.2	20.0
14	3.5	13.0	4.1	16.5	4.7	17.5	5.7	19.0
15	3.9	11.5	4.5	14.5	5.1	15.5	6.1	17.0
16	....	....	4.8	13.0	5.4	14.0	6.4	15.5
17	....	....	4.9	12.5	5.5	13.5	6.6	14.0
18	....	....	5.1	12.0	5.8	12.5	6.8	13.0
19	....	....	5.3	11.0	5.9	11.5	6.9	12.5
20	....	....	5.4	10.5	6.0	11.0	7.0	12.5
21	....	....	....	....	....	....	7.1	12.0
22	....	....	....	....	....	....	7.2	11.0

Table 17 is based on a study of trees actually cut for ties in the Medicine Bow National Forest in Wyoming. Trees above 15 inches are more valuable for lumber, and were not cut for ties in this forest. Second-grade and cull ties were worth more than mine props; so the number of ties does not refer to first grade alone, but includes about 25 per cent of second-grade ties. For the smaller diameters the percentage of second-grade ties is much larger.

The length of props in both tables is given in linear feet, in order to facilitate the calculation when props of varying lengths are desired.

TABLE 17.—*Average number of first and second class railroad ties and of mine props in lodgepole pine, based on actual cutting, Medicine Bow National Forest, Wyoming.*

Diameter breast-high.	Height of tree in feet— 50.		60.		70.		80.		90.		Basis.
	Ties.	Props.	Ties.	Props.	Ties.	Props.	Ties.	Props.	Ties.	Props.	
Inches.	*No.*	*Feet.*	*No.*	*Feet.*	*No.*	*Feet.*	*No.*	*Feet.*	*No.*	*Feet.*	*Trees.*
10	2.0	17	2.3	21	2.5	25	3.0	29	....	....	32
11	2.4	13	2.7	18	3.0	21	3.6	25	4.0	28	219
12	2.8	12	3.2	15	3.5	19	4.1	21	4.5	24	292
13	3.3	11	3.6	14	4.0	17	4.7	19	4.9	21	239
14	3.7	11	4.0	13	4.5	15	5.1	17	5.4	19	89
15	4.0	11	4.4	13	5.0	14	5.5	15	5.8	17	23
Total...	....	....	....	....	....	....	....	....	....	....	894

APPLICATION OF VOLUME TABLES TO STANDING TIMBER.

In applying the volume tables to standing timber in the estimate of yield for the Douglas Creek watershed of the Medicine Bow National Forest, Wyoming, the following percentages were deducted for cull trees, defects, and open spots:

Pine forest.	Per cent.
Quality I	25
Quality II	30
Quality III	35
Spruce forest.	
Pine	30
Spruce	15

This deduction is ample for ties, props, and lumber. For box boards and pulpwood the deduction would probably be much less.

FORM.

BUTT TAPER.

Table 18 gives the diameters outside bark, at 1 foot intervals, from the ground to a height of 5 feet, for trees of a given diameter breasthigh. It can be used for estimating the breasthigh diameter when stumps only remain. It also gives an idea of the height and amount of the root swelling.

TABLE 18.—*Butt taper of lodgepole pine as shown by diameter outside bark, Medicine Bow National Forest, Wyoming.*

Diameter breast-high.	Height from ground in feet— 1.	2.	3.	4.	5.	Basis.
Inches.	*Inches.*	*Inches.*	*Inches.*	*Inches.*	*Inches.*	*Trees.*
5	5.5	5.4	5.2	5.1	4.9	5
6	6.6	6.4	6.2	6.1	5.9	18
7	7.8	7.4	7.2	7.1	6.9	25
8	8.9	8.4	8.2	8.1	7.9	69
9	10.0	9.4	9.2	9.1	8.9	99
10	11.1	10.4	10.2	10.1	9.9	122
11	12.2	11.5	11.2	11.1	10.9	136
12	13.3	12.5	12.2	12.1	11.9	104
13	14.4	13.6	13.2	13.1	12.9	75
14	15.6	14.7	14.2	14.1	13.9	45
15	16.8	15.8	15.3	15.1	14.9	22
16	18.0	16.9	16.4	16.1	15.9	9
17	19.3	18.1	17.5	17.1	16.9	6
Total						735

TAPER OF STEM.

Table 19 gives the comparative diameters inside the bark of lodgepole pine trees of various diameters and heights. This table was prepared from data collected in Gallatin County, Mont., but the form does not vary materially in other regions.

The table may be used in finding the probable number of various sized poles with a specified top diameter that may be cut from a given stand, provided the average height is known. For example, if it is desired to know the number of poles with a 7-inch top that may be got from a stand in quality II in Wyoming with an average height of 60 feet, the taper table for 60 feet will show that a 10-inch tree will yield a 30-foot pole, allowing for a reasonable stump; an 11-inch tree will yield a 30-foot pole; a 12-inch tree a 35-foot pole, and so on. By multiplying by the number of trees of each diameter in the stand and making the proper allowance for cull trees and defects, the estimated yield in poles of different sizes may be obtained. To insure accuracy this table, as all other forest tables, should be applied to a number of trees.

TABLE 19.—*Stem taper of lodgepole pine, as shown by diameter inside bark, Gallatin County, Mont.*

TREES 60 FEET IN HEIGHT.

Diameter breast-high.	Height from ground in feet— 5.	10.	15.	20.	25.	30.	35.	40.	45.	50.	Basis.
Inches.	*Inches.*	*Inches.*	*Inches.*	*Ins.*	*Ins.*	*Ins.*	*Ins.*	*Ins.*	*Ins.*	*Ins.*	*Trees.*
10	10.0	9.2	8.8	8.5	8.0	7.3	6.6	5.9	......	......	50
11	10.8	10.0	9.5	9.0	8.4	7.6	6.8	6.0	5.2	4.5	50
12	11.6	10.8	10.2	9.6	8.8	8.0	7.1	6.2	5.4	4.6	51
13	12.6	11.6	11.0	10.3	9.4	8.5	7.3	6.5	5.6	4.7	17
14	13.5	12.5	11.8	11.1	10.3	9.3	8.1	7.0	5.9	4.9	9
15	14.5	13.4	12.7	12.0	11.1	10.0	8.8	7.5	6.3	5.1	9
Total...	......	......	......	......	......	......	......	......	......	......	186

TREES 70 FEET IN HEIGHT.

Diameter breast-high.	Height from ground in feet— 5.	10.	15.	20.	25.	30.	35.	40.	45.	50.	55.	60.	Basis.
Inches.	*Ins.*	*Ins.*	*Ins.*	*Ins.*	*Ins.*	*Ins.*	*Ins.*	*Ins.*	*Ins.*	*Ins.*	*Ins.*	*Ins.*	*Trees.*
10	10.1	9.3	8.8	8.5	8.1	7.7	7.1	6.5	5.8	5.1	4.5	3.8	50
11	11.1	10.1	9.6	9.2	8.7	8.2	7.7	7.0	6.3	5.5	4.8	4.0	50
12	12.1	11.0	10.3	9.8	9.3	8.7	8.2	7.5	6.8	5.9	5.1	4.1	49
13	12.9	11.9	11.1	10.5	9.9	9.3	8.7	8.0	7.2	6.3	5.4	4.3	50
14	13.8	12.7	11.9	11.2	10.5	9.9	9.2	8.5	7.6	6.6	5.6	4.5	50
15	14.8	13.5	12.6	11.9	11.2	10.5	9.7	8.9	7.9	6.9	5.8	4.7	42
16	15.8	14.5	13.5	12.7	11.9	11.2	10.3	9.4	8.4	7.2	6.1	4.9	16
17	16.9	15.5	14.4	13.5	12.6	11.8	10.9	9.8	8.7	7.5	6.3	5.1	12
18	17.9	16.4	15.3	14.3	13.3	12.4	11.3	10.2	9.0	7.7	6.5	5.2	7
19	18.8	17.3	16.0	15.0	14.0	13.0	11.9	10.7	9.4	8.0	6.7	5.4	3
20	19.8	18.1	16.8	15.7	14.6	13.5	12.4	11.1	9.7	8.2	6.8	5.5	2
Total...	......	......	......	......	......	......	......	......	......	......	......	......	331

TREES 80 FEET IN HEIGHT.

Diameter breast-high.	Height from ground in feet— 5.	10.	15.	20.	25.	30.	35.	40.	45.	50.	55.	60.	65.	Basis.
Inches.	*Ins.*	*Ins.*	*Ins.*	*Ins.*	*Ins.*	*Ins.*	*Ins.*	*Ins.*	*Ins.*	*Ins.*	*Ins.*	*Ins.*	*Ins.*	*Trees.*
10	9.7	9.1	8.8	8.6	8.3	7.9	7.5	7.1	6.6	6.0	5.4	4.8	4.3	50
11	10.7	10.0	9.7	9.4	9.0	8.6	8.1	7.6	7.0	6.4	5.7	5.1	4.4	50
12	11.8	10.9	10.5	10.1	9.7	9.2	8.7	8.1	7.5	6.8	6.0	5.3	4.6	50
13	12.7	11.8	11.3	10.8	10.4	9.9	9.4	8.7	8.0	7.2	6.3	5.5	4.8	47
14	13.7	12.7	12.1	11.5	11.0	10.5	9.9	9.2	8.4	7.6	6.7	5.8	4.9	41
15	14.7	13.6	12.9	12.3	11.7	11.1	10.5	9.7	8.9	8.0	7.0	6.0	5.1	38
16	15.8	14.6	13.7	13.0	12.4	11.8	11.1	10.3	9.4	8.4	7.3	6.2	5.2	28
17	16.8	15.4	14.5	13.8	13.1	12.4	11.0	10.7	9.8	8.7	7.6	6.4	5.3	20
18	17.8	16.3	15.3	14.5	13.8	13.0	12.2	11.2	10.2	9.1	7.9	6.7	5.5	10
19	18.7	17.1	16.0	15.1	14.3	13.5	12.6	11.7	10.6	9.4	8.2	6.9	5.6	10
20	19.6	17.9	16.7	15.7	14.8	14.0	13.1	12.1	11.0	9.7	8.4	7.1	5.7	2
Total...	......	......	......	......	......	......	......	......	......	......	......	......	......	346

TABLE 19.—*Stem taper of lodgepole pine, as shown by diameter inside bark, Gallatin County, Mont.*—Continued.

TREES 90 FEET IN HEIGHT.

Diameter breast-high.	Height from ground in feet— 5.	10.	15.	20.	25.	30.	35.	40.
Inches.	*Inches.*	*Inches.*	*Inches.*	*Inches.*	*Inches.*	*Inches.*	*Inches.*	*Inches.*
12	11.8	10.9	10.6	10.4	10.1	9.8	9.4	8.9
13	12.8	11.9	11.5	11.2	10.9	10.5	10.1	9.6
14	13.8	12.9	12.4	12.0	11.7	11.3	10.8	10.3
15	14.8	13.8	13.2	12.8	12.4	12.0	11.5	10.9
16	15.8	14.7	14.1	13.6	13.2	12.7	12.2	11.5
17	16.8	15.6	14.9	14.4	14.0	13.5	12.9	12.2
18	17.7	16.5	15.7	15.2	14.6	14.1	13.5	12.7
19	18.7	17.2	16.4	15.8	15.2	14.6	13.9	13.1
20	19.7	18.1	17.2	16.4	15.8	15.1	14.4	13.5
21	20.6	18.9	17.8	17.0	16.3	15.6	14.8	13.9
22	21.6	19.7	18.5	17.6	16.9	16.1	15.3	14.3
Total								

Diameter breast-high.	Height from ground in feet— 45.	50.	55.	60.	65.	70.	75.	Basis.
Inches.	*Inches.*	*Inches.*	*Inches.*	*Inches.*	*Inches.*	*Inches.*	*Inches.*	*Trees.*
12	8.4	7.8	7.2	6.5	5.7	4.8	....	16
13	9.1	8.4	7.8	7.1	6.3	5.3	4.3	10
14	9.7	9.0	8.3	7.5	6.7	5.8	4.7	3
15	10.3	9.5	8.8	8.0	7.1	6.1	4.9	21
16	10.8	10.0	9.2	8.3	7.4	6.3	5.2	13
17	11.3	10.4	9.6	8.6	7.6	6.4	5.3	8
18	11.8	10.8	9.9	8.9	7.8	6.6	5.4	6
19	12.2	11.2	10.2	9.1	8.0	6.7	5.5	4
20	12.6	11.5	10.4	9.3	8.1	6.8	5.6	7
21	12.8	11.7	10.6	9.4	8.2	6.9	5.6	2
22	13.2	12.0	10.8	9.6	8.3	7.0	5.7	3
Total								93

YIELD.

PRESENT.

As a general index of the yield in board feet, the following estimates are given:

Yield per acre in board feet, Gallatin County, Mont.

[Cutting to a diameter breasthigh of 11 inches.]

Type.	Lodgepole pine.	Douglas fir and Engelmann spruce.
	Board feet.	
Creek	5,000	No yields computed.
Eastern slope	7,200	
Western slope	3,800	
Northern slope	7,000	

any matter which can be shown by map, although they may not always be desirable for small explanatory sketches sent in with correspondence.

The Grazing Map legend is not for use on the 1 inch to 1 mile Atlas sheets. Data relating to grazing will be drawn on a smaller scale map, which will form one page of the Atlas. It will be colored with crayons, so that alterations may easily be made when changes occur in the areas open to any kind of stock or when areas are closed against grazing.

Any data forwarded to the Service on township plats, or otherwise, if of permanent value, will be entered upon the Forest Atlas. Whenever sufficient data are received for a group of townships a standard map will be prepared, to be included in the Atlas, and a copy will be sent as soon as possible to the supervisor to replace less complete maps. In this fashion, by the cooperation of all concerned, the mapping of the National Forests can go on systematically, until a complete system of detail maps has been completed. When a Forest is completely mapped the map will be lithographed so as to be generally available.

Approved:

James Wilson,

Secretary.

Washington, D. C., *March 5, 1907.*

O

THE DETERMINATION OF TIMBER VALUES.

BY

EDWARD A. BRANIFF,

Forest Assistant, Bureau of Forestry.

[REPRINT FROM YEARBOOK OF DEPARTMENT OF AGRICULTURE FOR 1904.]

CONTENTS.

THE DETERMINATION OF TIMBER VALUES.

By Edward A. Braniff,
Forest Assistant, Bureau of Forestry.

INTRODUCTION.

In the past it has been customary to base estimates of probable profits from the management of lands for the future production of timber in the United States upon the increase of the timber in quantity. Everyone familiar with the lumber business knows, however, that the lumber which comes out of large trees is worth more per thousand feet than that which comes from small trees, because the large trees turn out a higher proportion of the choice grades. It is apparent that estimates of profits through careful forest management should take into account this factor of quality increase; but, in the absence of an accurate determination of what this quality increase is, it has hitherto been impossible to do more than state in general terms the fact that such an increase would take place and that its effect would be to make the profit from deferred operations greater than that actually shown by the figures indicating the future yield to be expected.

DESCRIPTION OF THE EXPERIMENTS.

During the winter of 1903–4, and the following spring and summer, experiments in sawmills in different parts of the country were conducted by the Bureau of Forestry. This article will be confined to a statement of how the experiments were performed, to extracts from some of the tables and the printing in full of others, and to a brief discussion of their application.

The experiments completed so far have to do with longleaf pine in Alabama and in Louisiana, and with yellow birch, sugar maple, and beech in the Adirondacks of New York. The results here reported were obtained mainly from Adirondack hardwoods. Further experiments are now progressing in the Appalachians of West Virginia with yellow poplar, white oak, chestnut, ash, and other hardwoods typical of that region.

The main question which the experiments were to answer was: Exactly how much more valuable is a particular kind of tree of a certain size than another tree of the same kind and of smaller size? Clearly, the matter could be got at only by following the logs from trees of all diameters through the sawmill and finding out what each sawed out in amounts and grades of timber. And since the experiment was concerned not with individual logs, but with whole trees, all the logs from each tree had to be traced in such a way that the aggregate product might be known. So men were placed in the woods who followed the saw crews, scaled each log, and marked it on the ends. Each tree was given a number and each log in that tree an additional figure, as 1, 2, etc., to indicate the first log, second log, etc. For example, 576² indicated the second log from tree 576. The logs were scaled according to the log rule locally used, as a check for their identification and in order to compare their contents according to the log rule with what they actually sawed out in the mill.

In the mill a man was stationed next to the slab carrier, and as each piece of siding from a marked log dropped on the live rollers this man chalked on it while it went by the number of the log from which it came. When a marked siding had passed through the edger and trimmer and had come out at the end of the mill a piece of manufactured lumber, it was graded by a competent inspector, and its log number, dimensions, and grade were tallied. By these means the contents of each log, both in grades and in quantities of lumber, were absolutely determined.

This, in brief, was the method used for all species except longleaf pine. In the case of longleaf pine the number of men available for the work was not sufficient to trace each piece of siding through the mill to see what it actually made in lumber. Instead, it was graded as it dropped from the saw and its contents were estimated.

In working up the results, the logs that had passed through the mill were first combined to form complete trees. If a log were missing, the results for all the rest of the logs from that tree had to be thrown out. An exception was made in the case of Adirondack hardwoods, when the missing log was an 8-foot top cut of just sufficient diameter to make a railroad tie and one or two boards of the inferior grades. In such cases the missing log was graded like a top log of similar dimensions and species from another tree. In no instance was this substitution used for any but small, knotty, 8-foot top logs, and then only when it could safely be done.

The trees were next divided into diameter classes varying by 1 inch, and all the lumber from each class was tallied by separate grades. The total number of feet of each grade was then divided by the number of trees tallied for that class, and the result was the average amount of lumber of that grade. Finally, the figures for each grade were rounded off by curves to reduce irregularities.

RESULTS OF EXPERIMENTS.

The results of these measurements were two tables for each species, one showing the number of feet of each grade of lumber sawed from a tree of given diameter, the second showing the money value of the lumber yielded by a single tree of each size, and the average value per thousand feet of the lumber. The tables showing money values were made by applying to the tables of grades the average selling price of the lumber at the mill.

YELLOW BIRCH.

The following table gives the grades for yellow birch:

Graded volume of yellow birch.

Diameter breast-high.	Firsts and seconds red.	Firsts and seconds.	No. 1 common.	Shipping culls (No. 2 common).	Mill culls (No. 3 common).	Sound 7" by 9" by 8' ties. (a)	Total.	Number of trees tallied.
Inches.	*Bd. ft.*	*Bd. ft.*	*Bd. ft.*	*Bd. ft.*	*Bd. ft.*	*Bd. ft.*	*Bd. ft.*	
13	....	3	5	6	20	25	59	7
14	....	7	7	7	37	37	95	16
15	....	11	10	8	41	55	125	23
16	....	16	12	8	38	72	146	32
17	....	22	14	8	35	84	163	32
18	2	28	17	9	36	94	186	67
19	4	36	20	10	45	102	217	50
20	8	44	24	11	55	108	250	30
21	23	54	28	13	65	114	297	40
22	26	66	31	15	74	119	331	46
23	36	78	33	16	82	118	363	25
24	48	86	36	18	88	112	388	37
25	62	92	38	19	93	104	408	30
26	81	97	42	20	98	96	434	24
27	101	103	47	22	106	91	470	28
28	116	110	53	22	118	86	505	16
29	128	120	59	23	134	81	545	4
30	139	132	64	24	155	74	588	12
31	150	144	68	25	180	52	619	4

a To obtain number of ties divide board feet in this column by 42.

This table shows the yield of choice grades of birch advancing rapidly with the growth of the tree. The choice grades are firsts and seconds red and firsts and seconds. The amount of red birch in a tree under 18 inches in diameter is too small to consider. An 18-inch tree contained 2 board feet of this high-priced lumber, a 19-inch tree only 4 feet of it, a 20-inch tree 8 feet, but in a 21-inch tree the amount rose to 23 board feet, showing a gain of almost 200 per cent over the product of the previous diameter. The explanation for the exceptional increase is that the rules of the National Hardwood Lumber Association, under which the lumber was inspected, require red birch 4 or 5 inches wide to show one face all red; over 5 inches, one face must be not less than 75 per cent red. Red birch is heartwood, and it happens that the heartwood is not wide enough to pass the severe inspection in considerable quantities in trees under 21 inches in diameter. The increase of red birch goes on steadily from the 21-inch to the highest diameters. The next best grade, firsts and seconds, not graded by color, is contained in practically all sizes of merchantable trees. The increase of this grade goes on steadily, but is greatest between 18-inch and 23-inch trees, because the inspection rules, which favor wide boards, show their greatest effect here. Narrow boards from small trees grade lower than wide boards from large trees.

When we compare the choice grades (firsts and seconds red, and firsts and seconds) with the common ones (No. 1 common, shipping culls, and mill culls) we find that the choice grades increase, on the whole, much more rapidly with the growth of the tree than do the latter. In the case of firsts and seconds red there was a rise between a 13-inch and a 31-inch tree from 0 to 150 feet; and in the case of firsts and seconds from 3 to 144 feet. Contrast this with No. 1 common, which rises from 5 to 68 feet; with shipping culls, which rise from 6 to 25 feet; and with mill culls, which rise from 20 to 180 feet, and the tendency of the better grades to outstrip the poor ones becomes apparent. The fact must not be overlooked, however, that a considerable amount of what would have made inferior grades went, in this instance, into railroad ties.

The following price list for hardwoods was made up after inquiry among hardwood jobbing houses in New York and Boston:

Prices of different grades of lumber from birch, maple, and beech trees.

Grade.	Price per thousand board feet.		
	Birch.	Maple.	Beech.
Firsts and seconds red	$33		
Firsts and seconds	23	$20	$14
No. 1 common	14	14	10
No. 2 common (shipping culls)	8	8	7
No. 3 common (mill culls)	6	6	6

In most instances the lowest price quoted was used. The value of the railroad ties was assumed to be 40 cents for a 7 by 9 inch tie 8 feet long, equivalent to $9.52 per thousand feet—a reasonably low price.

The figures given afford a basis for calculating the value of yellow birch trees. For example, take a birch 21 inches in diameter. Turning to the table of grades we find that such a tree contains 23 feet of firsts and seconds red, worth, according to the price list, $33 per thousand; 54 feet of firsts and seconds at $23; 28 feet of No. 1 common at $14; 13 feet of shipping culls at $8; 65 feet of mill culls at $6; 114 feet of railroad ties at 40 cents per tie of 42 feet—in all, 297 feet, worth $3.97, or $13.37 per thousand feet, at the mill.

It must not be supposed, however, that as a matter of fact the exact value of a tree of a given diameter can be calculated with absolute accuracy on the basis of the figures herewith presented. The purpose of the present article is to give an indication of the rate at which the timber value of a tree increases with its diameter growth, in consequence of the higher quality of lumber which it will yield. The number of yellow birch trees tallied for the various diameters in the above table of grades ranged from 4 to 57, and, as has already been stated, the figures of yield of the several grades given in the table do not represent the actual product sawed out, but were obtained by constructing curves to round off the inequalities shown by the actual individual averages in order to secure a nearer approximation to the general average. That the inequalities thus rounded off were in some cases considerable goes to prove that it would be unsafe to rely too closely on calculations from this table of the exact yield to be expected.

Further, the judgment of both the sawyer and the grader enters into the determination of the amount of lumber of each grade which a particular log will yield. Had the logs tallied been sawed at another mill, or even at the same mill at another time, the figures would have varied slightly. Under no circumstances is it possible to construct a table which will enable one to tell infallibly how much lumber of different grades a single tree will saw out. It is, however, possible for an owner to calculate pretty closely from the above table what he may expect to saw from a considerable body of timber of known size. From this again it is possible to construct a table of values like the following:

Value of yellow birch.

Diameter breast-high.	Graded volume.	Value per tree.	Value per 1,000 bd. ft.	Diameter breast-high.	Graded volume.	Value per tree.	Value per 1,000 bd. ft.
Inches.	*Bd. ft.*			*Inches.*	*Bd. ft.*		
13	59	$0.58	$9.82	23	363	$5.19	$14.30
14	95	.89	9.37	24	388	5.80	14.95
15	125	1.22	9.76	25	408	6.39	15.66
16	146	1.52	10.41	26	434	7.15	16.48
17	163	1.78	10.92	27	470	8.03	17.09
18	186	2.13	11.45	28	505	8.80	17.43
19	217	2.56	11.80	29	545	9.57	17.56
20	250	3.06	12.24	30	588	10.34	17.59
21	297	3.98	13.40	31	619	10.99	17.75
22	331	4.51	13.63				

SUGAR MAPLE AND BEECH COMPARED WITH YELLOW BIRCH.

Similar tables were constructed for sugar maple and for beech in the Adirondacks, and for longleaf pine in Alabama and in Louisiana. The following extract from the hardwood tables gives a comparison of the value of the lumber sawed from birch, maple, and beech of different diameters.

Value per thousand feet board measure of lumber from Adirondack hardwoods.

Diameter breast-high.	Yellow birch.	Sugar maple.	Beech.	Diameter breast-high.	Yellow birch.	Sugar maple.	Beech.
Inches.				*Inches.*			
13	$9.32	$9.75	$8.29	23	$14.80	$12.77	$9.71
14	9.37	9.83	8.70	24	14.95	12.88	9.68
15	9.76	9.93	8.94	25	15.66	12.93	....
16	10.41	10.37	8.98	26	16.48	13.07	....
17	10.92	10.71	9.10	27	17.09	13.26	....
18	11.45	11.11	9.24	28	17.43	13.58	....
19	11.80	11.47	9.33	29	17.56	....	....
20	12.24	11.84	9.45	30	17.69	....	....
21	13.40	12.30	9.52	31	17.75	....	....
22	13.63	12.57	9.61				

According to this table lumber from a 24-inch birch tree is worth $5.63 a thousand feet more than from a 13-inch tree; from a sugar maple, $3.13; and from a beech, $1.39.[a] The difference is more marked in the case of birch largely because of the presence in the high diameters of the high-priced grade, firsts and seconds red. The table for birch gives values up to 31 inches. A lumberman in cutting all sizes of birch would get, according to these figures, $8.43 per thousand feet more from his 31-inch trees than from his 13-inch trees.

The increase in value of the lumber with the growth of the tree was found to be much more rapid in the case of Adirondack birch and maple than in that of longleaf pine. The difference in value per thousand feet of the lumber from 14-inch and from 24-inch pine was $1.72, while the difference between the same diameters of birch was $5.58, and of maple $3.05. This is accounted for partly by the fact that the inspection of narrow boards is more severe with hardwoods than with pine, partly because the difference in value between poor and choice lumber is more marked in the case of birch and maple than in that of pine. The comparison is, however, not strictly a fair one, for the reason that in the experiments with longleaf pine very defective trees were rejected, while in the hardwood experiment the run of the forest at McKeever, N. Y., was taken.

PRACTICAL VALUE OF THE RESULTS.

The practical uses to which such tables might be put are apparent. With due allowance for slight changes in the character of his timber, any Adirondack lumberman could use them as a basis for figuring out, with his own price list, the values of his hardwoods. If he knows what the expenses of stumpage, logging, and manufacture amount to, he would be able to determine within close limits what trees he could cut at a profit and what trees he had better leave in the woods. In

[a] Beech over 23 inches shows a falling off in quality due to decay.

brief, he would have at hand an excellent guide to assist him in lumbering and in fixing a value on his timberlands.

Wherever surveys have been made which show the number of trees of various diameters of each species on the average acre, the tables of value could be used with peculiar effectiveness. Such surveys have been made on a number of tracts in the Adirondacks by the Bureau of Forestry. In a working plan for a tract at McKeever, N. Y., the lands were divided into six types, and the number of trees of each diameter for each species on the average acre was determined for each type. In a working plan made for a tract at St. Regis, N. Y., the number of trees of each diameter of each species on the average acre was determined for all types combined. On virgin hardwood land on the McKeever tract there were, on the average acre, of 17-inch trees, 0.80 yellow birch, 0.70 sugar maple, and 1.34 beech; of 18-inch trees there were 0.66 birch, 0.68 maple, and 0.98 beech, and so on. If all expenses of stumpage, logging, and manufacture should be as low as $10.50 on 17-inch trees there would be a profit of 42 cents per thousand feet on birch and 21 cents per thousand feet on maple. And the larger the tree cut the higher the profit. Should all birch and maple be cut down to and including 17-inch trees, there would be, with expenses at $10.50, a profit of $11.32 per acre, of which $9.82 would be from birch and $1.50 from maple. The average profit per thousand feet on all trees cut would be $4.15 from birch and $1.49 from maple.

But the profits from small trees are so slight as to make it hardly worth while removing them; certainly inadvisable if a future timber crop is to be considered. Calculating again, we find that the profits from birch and maple, if cut down to and including 18 inches, would be $11.26; cutting to 19 inches, they would be $11.06; cutting to 20 inches, they would be $10.72 per acre, etc. It will be noted that, while the smaller the cutting limit the higher the profit per acre (unless trees are taken so small as to cause an actual loss), the lower is the profit per thousand feet on the timber removed; on the other hand, the higher the cutting limit the lower is the profit per acre, but the higher the profit per thousand feet on the timber removed. Cutting birch and maple trees 17 inches and over, the profit per thousand would be $5.64; trees 18 inches and over, $6.04; trees 19 inches and over, $6.46; 20 inches and over, $6.91. "Profit per acre" and "profit per thousand feet" work in opposite directions.

Expenses vary according to distance of the timber from the means of transportation, conditions in the woods, topography, cost and quality of labor, etc. An expense of $10.50 for logging and manufacture, including stumpage, is generally considered low for hardwood lumbering in the Adirondacks, and when the expense is more than $12.75 operations are, in many cases, scarcely practicable. The profits per acre and per thousand feet in lumbering birch and maple when expenses are $10.50, $10.75, $11, $11.25, $11.50, $11.75, $12, $12.25, $12.50, and $12.75 per thousand feet were calculated for the tracts mentioned above, and the results do not encourage indiscriminate cutting of hardwoods in the Adirondacks; on the contrary, they furnish the strongest possible argument against careless lumbering. Hardwood lumbering in the Adirondacks is so expensive that as a rule it does not pay to cut any but the larger trees for lumber. It is highly to the advantage of the lumberman to know just at what diameter limit his profits are turned into losses, and it is equally to the advantage of the future productive capacity of the forest that he should know this. These figures prove that the lumberman who would make the highest profits out of the Adirondack hardwoods must cut within certain diameter limits and leave, in most cases, a considerable stand of timber uncut. The argument is based not at all on what is best for the forest, but entirely on present expediency for the lumberman. It happens, however, that what is best for the lumberman turns out, in this case, to be excellent for the forest. Hardwood lumbering in the Adirondacks is not yet on a large scale, but with the growing scarcity of timber and the advancing prices of lumber there is little doubt that it soon will be. Every effort should be made to induce Adirondack lumbermen to regulate their cutting and to show them that in taking small trees they are working directly against their own interests.

STEM ANALYSES.

BY JOHN BENTLEY, JR.

From the experience gained in instructing several classes in the subject of volume growth in individual trees, it is apparent that the method described in the text books in use in this country is difficult of comprehension by the average student of forest mensuration. As a general rule, the problems of *height growth* and *diameter growth* are handled by the majority of students quite readily, but they frequently have difficulty in mastering the subject of *volume growth* as exemplified in "stem analyses." In searching for the cause of this trouble, it appears that much of it arises from the *form* in which stem analyses are usually recorded in this country; and the object of this discussion is to recommend a more logical tabulation of the data usually included on a stem analysis blank.

It will be remembered that the blanks provided for stem analysis by the Forest Service (Form 334, "Tree Measurements") include a page in which the measurements on each cross-section of the tree are recorded in columns numbered 1, 2, 3, 4, 5, etc., (which represent decades), the values showing the "distance on average radius from heart to each tenth ring." If, as is generally the case, there is not an even multiple of ten annual rings on the section, the measurement of the odd years is recorded under column 1, (since the measurements begin with the innermost period and proceed outward), and from that point on, the difference between the values in any two adjacent columns represents a decade's growth. So far, so good; but when the measurements for the second and subsequent cross-cuts are recorded, the measurements in each case are tabulated beginning in column 1 again; and since there is almost always at least ten years difference in the total ages of successive cross-cuts, and sometimes twenty, or more, the measurement for the *last*, or *current* decade, falls, *not* in the column for the corresponding decade on the previous cross-cut, but in a column *to the left*. Glancing down the numbered columns, then, we find a series of measurements each one of which represents a different decade in the tree's life-

*Reprinted from FORESTRY QUARTERLY, Volume XII, No. 2.

history. An example of this method of tabulation is shown in Professor Graves' well known book on "Forest Mensuration," page 264, where the age of the tree at cross-section number 1 (stump) was 60 years, and the last measured radius was consequently recorded in column 6. The age of the second cross-cut was 50 years, and the last measured radius was recorded in column 5, etc. When the volumes of the several sections are computed for different decades there is a very large chance that the wrong pairs of values for cross-sectional dimensions will be selected, because, instead of being arranged one under the other in the same column, the dimensions of the cross-cuts belonging to any particular age of the tree are found in *different* columns, and they must be selected by counting *backward* from the last recorded measurement. This is one point at which the average student has difficulty, and one which can be obviated entirely by the use of a more logical method of tabulating the measurements.

A second point at which there is usually some difficulty is in the *doubling* of the measurements given for *radii*, so as to obtain the corresponding diameters. The form already referred to reads: "Distance on average radius from heart to each 10th ring — inches" and the student not infrequently forgets to double the value recorded for the radius, in order to obtain the diameter. While this may seem like a trivial point, it is, nevertheless, one which often leads to slight errors in doubling, or neglecting to double at all; and when the use of a scale reading 2 : 1 would obviate the necessity of recording radii, and permit the recording of diameters directly, it seems wise to take simple precautions and eliminate the chances of errors, by recording diameters instead of radii. Stem analysis rules as now made by instrument-makers, usually make readings of this kind easy by supplying two scales,—one graduated to inches and tenths, for measuring diameters, and the other for measuring radii graduated to half-inches and twentieths, but reading as *doubled inches and tenths*, so that radii may be read directly as diameters. The stem analysis blank would therefore read, preferably, over the columns provided for the measurements: "Average diameter of section, by decades," instead of "Distance on average radius from heart to each 10th ring."

A third point,—and one which is a source of frequent errors

in computing the volume of the tree at different periods—is the somewhat laborious and involved method of determining the dimensions of the tops (above the last cross-cut), in preceding decades. These tops are generally regarded as cones (see Graves' "Mensuration," page 292), and their volumes computed as such. The difficulty arises in obtaining the heights of the several cones as they appeared further and further within the top, or down the stem, with each preceding decade. The method described by Professor Graves, namely, to take a distance *proportional* to the number of years required to grow the distance between the two sections in question, thus assuming a regular rate of growth for the period, is quite accurate, but it is likely to confuse the student, and has been the cause of more errors in computation than any other one factor, according to my observation.*

In German text books the method described for obtaining the volumes of the tree in preceding decades frequently disregards these small cones, or tips, because the sections into which the tree is divided for analysis are short,—rarely more than 2 meters. The volumes are therefore relatively insignificant. In this country, however, where we have to compute stem analyses from trees where a top of 15, 20, or even 30 feet is left, it becomes necessary to include these tops, and their dimensions at different periods, otherwise the calculated volumes would be inaccurate to such a degree that they would be of no scientific value. Some way must be devised, therefore, which will yield accurate results, and at the same time will be readily understood and applied by the student.

In the hope of simplifying the work of making and recording stem analyses, and eliminating some of the obvious causes for mistakes in the calculations, the following suggestions are made. Nothing new or original is claimed for these suggestions; on the contrary, they have all been prompted by a perusal of the standard German text books. They are presented here simply for the purpose of showing how the work may be made more logical, and

* It has even led to an error in the very example chosen to illustrate the method (page 291 in "Forest Mensuration"), where, in the computations for the tree as it was 30 years old, the length ascribed to the tip is 4.75 feet. Since the tip at that age comprised 10/16 of the length of the section (10 feet) it should evidently be 6.25 feet, and not 4.75 feet, as printed.

at the same time more comprehensible to the mind of the average student of forest mensuration.

First, as to the methods of tabulating the measurements taken in the field. Figure 1 (page 162) shows a revised form filled in with data from a White Pine, in which the usual measurements are recorded, together with a few additional ones which will render the computations in the office less liable to error. For convenience, the spaces in which the measurements are recorded are both named and lettered, to correspond with the following list; and in the discussion which follows the several columns will be referred to by letter.

(a) The number of the section; the stump being considered No. 1, the top of the first log section No. 2, etc.
(b) The age of the section, i. e., the age up to that section, and the number of annual rings on that section.
(c) The length of the section, expressed in feet and tenths.
(d) The diameter, outside bark, of each section, in inches and tenths.
(e) The diameter, inside bark, of each section, in inches and tenths.
(f) The width of the bark at each section.
(g) The width of the sapwood at each section.
(h) The average diameter of the several sections, by decades, as explained in the following paragraphs.
(j) The diameter, breast-high.
(k) The total age, obtained as explained in the following paragraphs.
(l) Clear length.
(m) Used length.
(n) Merchantable length.

FIGURE 1.

SAMPLE FORM OF STEM ANALYSIS BLANK.

No.........

Locality ....*Date*.....................................*Species* (White Pine) *D. B. H.* (j)
Age 85 (k)

No. of section (a)	*Age* (b)	*Length* (c)	*D. o. b.* (d)	*D. i. b.* (e)	*Width of bark* (f)	*Width of sap* (g)	(h) *Average Diameter of Sections, by Decades.* 1	2	3	4	5	6	7	8	9	10	11	etc.
															85			
1	5+80	1.0	22.5	20.5	1.0	1.5	1.3	3.8	6.8	10.9	14.0	16.6	18.9	20.3	20.5			
2	15+70	16.2	18.1	17.3	0.4	1.5		2.4	5.8	9.2	12.0	14.6	16.2	17.1	17.3			
3	29+56	16.2	14.9	14.3	0.3	1.6			0.6	4.7	7.8	10.6	12.5	14.0	14.3			
4	37+48	12.2	12.4	11.8	0.3	1.6				1.6	5.1	7.6	9.7	11.5	11.8			
5	47+38	12.2	9.5	9.0	0.25	1.6					0.9	4.1	6.8	8.7	9.0			
6	52+33	4.0	7.8	7.4	0.2	1.5						2.6	5.3	7.1	7.4			
7	57+28	4.0	5.8	5.6	0.1	1.5						0.8	3.0	5.2	5.6			
8	64+21	4.0	4.2	4.0	0.1	1.2							1.5	3.6	4.0			
9	69+16	4.0	2.4	2.2	0.1	1.1							0.4	1.9	2.2			
(top)	85+0	7.2																
		81.0																

Clear length, ...(l)
Used length, ...(m)
Merchantable length, ...(n)

It must be remembered that the object of stem analyses is to secure figures of volume growth for a given species which will enable us, after compiling a large number of values and averaging them together, to construct a table showing the average increase in volume by decades. That is, it is desired to know what the volume of White Pine, or any other species, will be, under average conditions, at an age of 10 years, and again at 20 years, 30 years, 40 years, etc. Since the age at the stump (cross-section 1) is always slightly less than the true age of the tree, (from 2 to 10 years, often, depending on the stump-height, and the rate of growth of the seedling of the species), and a number of years,—usually determined by a study of seedlings—has to be added arbitrarily to secure the total age of the tree, it is suggested that these years be added *before* the stem analysis is recorded, instead of *afterward*, thereby making it possible to secure results which can ultimately be averaged together with a smaller degree of error. For example, it is known that White Pine seedlings attain an average height of one foot at an age of 5 years; a height of 2½ feet at an age of 6 years, etc. (*); if the stump of the White Pine being analysed is one foot high, it is then determined that 5 years must be added to the age of the stump to secure the total age of the tree, which is entered on the blank form at ("k"), the space provided for it.

Now, as each section is analysed, the rings are counted backward from the bark to the center, beginning at the outside and designating the outermost ring with its proper number, *viz.*, *the total age of the tree*, and *not* the number of rings which happen to be found on that section. Thus, if the total number of rings at the stump is 80, and 5 years are to be added for a stump one foot high, then the outermost ring on the stump will be counted "85" and the next one inside "84", etc., counting backward, and placing a mark at the even decades, 80, 70, 60, 50, etc. In like manner, the outermost ring on all subsequent sections will be called "85," and the counting proceed backward, until the center is reached, marking each decade as before.†

* Values are taken from U. S. Forest Bulletin 22, "The White Pine," by V. M. Spalding and B. E. Fernow, page 28.

†If it is preferred by some to count from the center outward, the number of rings on the section can be subtracted from the total age, and the counting begun at the age obtained. For example, on section 5 there are 38 annual rings; this subtracted from 85 = 47, and the counting may begin

In the column marked "Age" (Column "b") the age should be entered as composed of two values, the first expressing the number of years required to grow to the height of that particular section, and the second, the number of annual rings on that section.

This method of entering the age enables the reader of the form to determine the rate of height-growth very quickly, by simply glancing at columns lettered "b" and "c" respectively.

The form, it will be noticed, is practically the same as that formerly in use. The method of entering the values under "h," however, is quite different from that generally described in text-books, in this respect,—the measurements for all the sections at a corresponding age of the tree *fall in the same column.* That is, if the tree is 85 years old, showing 80 rings at the stump, the last measured diameter,* representing the size of that section in 1914, will fall in column 9, and the size at 80 years of age, in column 8. This is entirely logical, for the measurements of each decade's growth fall in the column bearing the corresponding number. The measurement of the odd years, representing an incomplete *decade*, fall in the *last* column, instead of in the *first* column, as was the case in the method formerly used. If the number of annual rings at the top of the first log (Section No. 2) is 70, the age at that section will be expressed as "15+70," in column "b." and the last measured diameter will be placed, not in column 7, but in column 9, directly under the corresponding measurement for section 1. Similarly, the measurements for the last section, although it shows only 15 annual rings, will be entered so that the diameter of the stem at that point in the year 1914 will fall in column 9. To find the volume of the tree in the year 1914, the dimensions of the several sections are read directly from column 9, where they appear one under the other in their logical order. There is now no chance of selecting the wrong pairs of values in computing the volumes of the several sections, and no chance for errors in doubling the radii, for diameters have been recorded directly. It would appear that one of the great stumbling-blocks to students in computing volumes from

---

at the pith (center), counting "48," "49," "50," etc., and a mark placed on the even decades, 50, 60, etc. This accomplishes precisely the same result, and obviates the necessity of counting backward, which may be objectionable to some.

*Diameters are recorded instead of radii.

stem analyses could thus be removed by tabulating the data in the manner described. The advantages of recording the data and measurements in this form are obvious, and at the same time the whole arrangement is much more logical, since the measurements for any particular decade all fall in the same column.

The second point,—namely, the recording of diameters directly instead of radii, which will necessarily be doubled later, has already been sufficiently explained, and the advantages are self-evident.

For the determination of the dimensions of the several "tips" or "tops" or "cones," which appear as we trace the history of the tree from decade to decade, (which was the third source of trouble mentioned), it is recommended that the graphic method be employed. It is a simple matter to plot the height on age by taking the values given in columns "b" and "c"; and once a curve has been drawn connecting the several points plotted, the height of the tree at an age of 10 years, 20 years, 30 years, etc., etc., can be read directly from the curve. For example, the data in columns "b" and "c" give the curve shown in *Figure 2*, (page —), and from this curve it is easily learned that the height of the tree at the age of 50 years was 60 feet. The top of the tree, then, at the age of 50 years, fell between sections 5 and 6; and the length of the cone which had a base of 0.9 inches diameter (column 5, under "h," and opposite section 5) at that period, is obtained by subtracting the height of section 5 from the total height of the tree at that age,—that is, 60-57.8 feet, or 2.2 feet In like manner, the heights of the other small tips, or cones, can be just as readily found for any and all other decades.

As a test of the accuracy of this method when compared with the old method, the calculations were carried out for the volume of the tree at every decade, by both methods, and the results are shown graphically in figure 3. It will be observed that the plotted values fall at different ages,—those by the new method falling at the ages of 10, 20, 30, 40. 50. 60, 70, 80 and 85 years, while by the old method they occur at the ages of 5, 15. 25, 35. 45, 55, 65. 75 and 85 years. When the two curves are drawn, they are found to coincide throughout their whole course. This proves the accuracy of the new method, and its adaptability to any age tree.

While the introduction of any departure from a method which has long been in general use is almost always regarded with more or less skepticism, it should be remembered that any innovations tending to simplify the work of the student, especially if they are very obviously more logical, should be acceptable. It is hoped that this method of recording a stem analysis, and the method used for obtaining the dimensions of the tree at different decades, will lead to a clearer understanding of the principles of volume growth in individual trees.

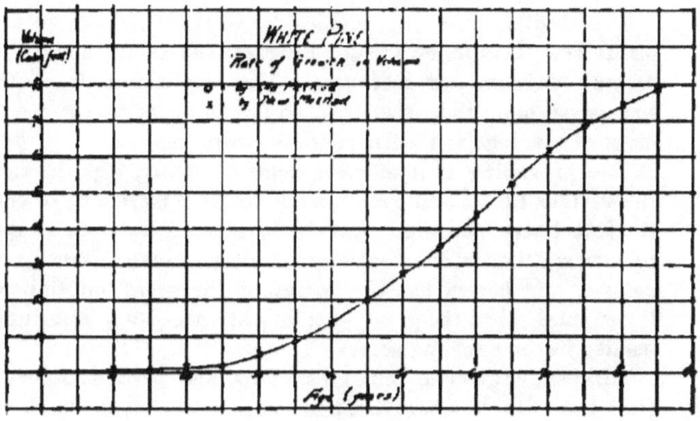

Figure 3.

Comp. of Writer.

Walter Mulford

THE MEASUREMENT OF SAW LOGS.

The English speaking peoples the world over have earned an unenviable distinction for non-progressiveness in matters concerning weights and measures. This reputation is, I think, somewhat more than sustained so far as concerns the measurement of saw logs and other round timbers.

The prevailing unit of measurement for saw logs throughout the various States and Provinces of North America is, of course, the foot board measure. But the foot board measure as applied to unsawn timber is essentially a unit of *product*, not a unit of *volume*, and herein lies the secret of the great multiplicity of "log rules" and the great—one might indeed say amazing—diversity in their scaling scores.

Millmen, engineers, mathematicians, and perhaps others have from time to time endeavored to compute log rules which would forecast with accuracy the lumber product (as inch boards) which could be sawn from logs of various dimensions. Their efforts have resulted in the production of some forty odd log rules all giving essentially, and in many cases radically, different scaling scores.

Notwithstanding the great variety provided, there is, sad to relate, no satisfactory log rule before the public, and it remains for the forester who should combine the requisite knowledge of logs, mills, and mathematics, to compute a rule that shall be equally fair to buyer and seller with logs of all dimensions. This paper has to do with an attempt along this line, and the rule which has been computed and is here discussed is submitted to the public with some confidence as being in advance of any previous effort. It is hoped that if any flaws in the reasoning be detected, some other forester will take up the task of making another forward step.

Before proceeding to discuss the principles on which the proposed International Log Rule is based, I shall pause to remark for the benefit of those outside the profession, that if the forester had his own way, he would discard the product unit in all log measurements, substituting a volume unit with a classification of the logs measured into three or four diameter classes. The purchaser could then saw his logs into boards or deals with thick or thin saws, unroll them as veneer, pulp them, or burn them, and in all cases be equally without ground for complaint as to the measurement. For the present, however, we bow to usage and content ourselves with evolution where we would gladly see revolution.

The Natural Taper of Logs. From the sides of logs there may be sawn square-edged boards of merchantable dimensions which do not reach to the small end at all and are consequently disregarded by the ordinary log rule which makes no allowance for the natural taper of the log in its scaling score. Naturally, the longer the log the greater the advantage to the buyer from this defect. It is, of course, ridiculous to assume that because the log on the saw carriage measures 19 feet in length, the sawyer cutting it will cut only such boards of even width as will be free from wane the full log length. That no modern milling business is conducted on such wasteful lines goes, of course, without saying.

Heretofore it has been customary on the part of log rule makers to compute the scale for the logs of various diameters for a *single log length*, finding the scale for logs of other lengths by simple proportion as with true cylinders. This method of rule making discriminates in favor of the seller in the case of all logs of less length than the computed length (usually 12 feet) and in favor of the buyer in the case of the longer lengths. In other words, if the scale for the computed length be correct, all shorter logs will be over-scaled and all longer logs under-scaled. The longer the log and the smaller the diameter, the larger will be the percental error. The absurdity of this method of getting the scaling score for the different log lengths may easily be demonstrated practically by cutting long logs into sections and comparing the scale given for the entire log with the sum of the scales given by the same rule for the parts after being cut into shorter lengths. For example, 4-inch logs, 19 feet long, scale by the Champlain Rule *nine* feet board measure. Cut such logs into two sections of 8 and 11 feet, respectively, and the parts will be found to give an average scale of four and ten feet board measure, respectively, or an average total of *fourteen* feet for the logs after sectioning. Or, to take a more extreme case: 6-inch logs, 40 feet long, scale by Doyle *10 feet board measure.* Cut to 8-foot sections and again scaled by Doyle the parts will be found to give an average scale of *55 feet board measure* per log, or an increase of some 400%. These results were demonstrated by measurements of the taper shown by over four thousand pine and spruce logs.

As is well known, trees of the same species, age, and stand differ greatly in the amount of taper shown. Individual logs from the same tree differ widely also. Here as elsewhere in forest measurements, the forester falls back on the great law of averages. The average taper in any given locality for any particular species may be easily determined with sufficient accuracy for practical purposes by the measurement of a few hundred logs. If greater accuracy be required for scientific purposes, a few thousand will be ample. Measurements of the average taper shown by logs representing the commercial trees of Northeastern America have revealed the welcome facts: (1) That the *average taper* does not differ greatly in different localities or with different species; (2) That it is less in good straight clean sawing timber and greater where the logs are rougher, the larger taper in the latter case compensating largely for the increased waste in edging the lumber from the inferior logs; and (3) That it never falls below one inch in eight feet when the logs are taken as they come in modern logging operations. Below are summarized the results of a few such studies:

No. of Logs measured.	*Species.*	*Diameter of Logs measured.*	*Taper in in per 8 ft. lineal.*
1070	White pine	6 to 33	1.22
3000	Spruce	7 to 18	1.30
300	Balsam Fir	6 to 14	1.26
——	Chestnut[1]	11 to 25	1.42
——	Loblolly Pine[2]	10 to 20	.96 to 1.20
——	" "	over 20	1.20 +

A mixed lot of Adirondack hardwoods gave an average taper of 1.17 inches. On page 87 of Bulletin No. 22, Bureau of For-

[1] Chestnut in Southern Maryland, R. Zon. Bulletin No. 53, Bureau of Forestry, p. 28.

[2] Loblolly Pine in Eastern Texas, R. Zon. Bulletin No. 64, Bureau of Forestry, p. 21.

estry, is recorded a series of measurements on 165 white pine trees cutting 894 16-foot logs. These measurements give a taper of 1.62 inches per 8 feet, bark inclusive, for the merchantable portion of the trees above breast height. This would indicate a taper exclusive of bark of fully 1.40 inches. This is a very high average for white pine and is doubtless due to the large size of the trees, the average diameter being 25 inches breasthigh. It is a general rule that the taper shown increases with the diameter after trees have passed the pole stage. This is especially marked in the case of dominant trees.

The Baxter rule gives an allowance for taper in its scaling score in the case of logs 18 feet long and over, the New Brunswick rule for logs 27 feet long and over, and the British Columbia rule for logs 50 feet long and over. The International rule allows for an average taper of one inch per eight feet in the case of all logs regardless of length. This is safely conservative for all diameters and all species.

Allowance for Shrinkage in Seasoning. A point that has been overlooked by some rule makers is that the scale given should refer to the amount of *seasoned* inch lumber which can be sawn from the logs scaled. Inasmuch as logs are ordinarily scaled green, it becomes necessary to allow for the shrinkage of the boards in thickness and in width which accompanies the seasoning. The margins of safety adopted by different mills vary considerably, but usually run from 1/8 to 3/8-inch in the width of the boards and from a scant 1/16 to 3/32-inch in the thickness.

In computing the International Rule a sixteenth of an inch was uniformly allowed for shrinkage in thickness and all fractions met in measuring the widths of the boards were disregarded which is equivalent to a shrinkage allowance in width of nearly half an inch.

The waste incident to sawing any log into lumber is of two distinct kinds: (1) *the saw kerf* and (2) *that lost in square-edging the boards*. The deduction for saw kerf must in all cases be a proportion of the *area* of the cross-section of the log, and hence increases as logs increase in size in direct proportion to the *square of the diameter*. The deduction for square-edging the boards is, on the other hand, in proportion to the *bark surface* of the log. But the bark surface of logs increases as the logs increase in size in direct proportion to the increase of diameter (not squared). To illustrate: a 12-inch log has 1/4 of the bark surface of a 48-

inch log, and will, if they be similar in form, have ¼ the waste in square-edging the lumber. But the area of the small end of the 48-inch log is 16 times as large as that of the 12-inch log, and if both be cut into inch boards by the same saw, there will be 16 times as much loss due to saw kerf in the larger log. To repeat in other words, the 48-inch log has *four* times as much waste in square-edging the boards as the 12-inch log, the increase being in direct proportion to the increase in diameter. The 48-inch log has *sixteen* times as much waste from saw kerf as the 12-inch log, the increase being in proportion to the increase in the *squares of their diameters*. If a rule is to be equally fair to large and small logs, it is evident that the deductions to be made for waste due to saw kerf and to square-edging the lumber, respectively, must be kept absolutely separate and distinct in the computation of the rule. In any rule where, as in the Doyle, but a single uniform deduction is made, the rule can give correct values for any given width of saw kerf at *one point only*, above and below which the logs must be over and under-scaled, respectively, or *vice-versa* as the case may be.

The first log rule maker to recognize this fundamental principle in the computation of a rule must have been a Mr. Baxter, for the Baxter rule is the oldest of the four rules so computed. The allowance for edging given by the Baxter rule is .5 inch beneath the bark. The British Columbia rule followed with an edging allowance of .75 inch beneath the bark. The only other log rules similarly computed are the recently produced Universal and Champlain rules in which the edging allowance is made proportional to the top end diameter (or circumference).

Allowance for Saw Kerf. The relation between the different amounts of lumber which may be sawn from logs by saws cutting different widths of kerf is a *percental* one. That is, if the product that can be sawn out by a saw cutting any particular width of kerf be known, the product that can be sawn out by saws cutting narrower or wider kerfs may be got by simply adding or subtracting the necessary percentage to or from the known scale. This implies that the sum of *a*, *b*, and *c* as follows is practically the same regardless of the diameters of the logs manufactured or the width of the saw kerf cut by saws used in their manufacture.

a = Waste due to square-edging the boards.

b = Allowance for shrinkage in width of boards.

c = Proportion of saw kerf waste which goes with *a* and *b*.

With narrow saw kerfs *a* and *b* increase with the increase in the amount of lumber produced, but *c* decreases sufficiently to compensate for the increased loss from *a* and *b*. Likewise with wider kerfs *a* and *b* decrease with the decreased production of lumber but their decrease is offset by the increase in *c*.

Perhaps a concrete case will illuminate this somewhat. Suppose a certain log contains 125 cubic units; that 25 units be lost in kerf; that 20 units be necessarily allowed for edging waste and shrinkage (*a* and *b* above); and that the remaining 80 units be lumber. The lumber is to edging (*a* and *b*) as 80 is to 20, therefore of the 25 kerf units 20 go with the lumber and 5 with the edging (*c*). In other words, the total allowance $(a+b+c)=25$ units. With different widths of kerf *a*, *b*, and *c* necessarily vary individually, but their total remains practically constant for the same log regardless of the thickness of the saw used in its manufacture.

This interesting and most important fact solves one of the difficulties in the way of producing a universal log rule in that it makes it possible to adapt a correctly computed rule to saws cutting different widths of kerf.

The standard scaling score of the International Rule is computed for a 1/8-inch kerf and may be adapted to saws cutting the various standard widths of kerf as follows:

			100,000 feet as scaled by the rule will cut out:
For 7/64 inch kerf	*add*	1.3%	101,300 ft. B. M.
" 3/16 " "	*subtract*	5.0%	95,000 " "
" 1/4 " "	"	9.5%	90,500 " "
" 5/16 " "	"	13.6%	86,400 " "
" 3/8 " "	"	17.4%	82,600 " "
" 7/16 " "	"	20.8%	79,200 " "

Most modern band saws cut a 1/8-inch kerf. Some 16-gauge band saws cut as low as 7/64-inch kerf. Gang saws ordinarily cut from 1/8 to 3/16-inch kerf. Rotary saws of the dimensions now commonly in use cut a kerf of about 1/4-inch. Large rotary saws cut kerfs varying from 5/16-inch to 3/8-inch. The old-time "3/8 and 7/16" inch kerf is now happily practically obsolete.

Allowance for Edging. It has already been noted that with logs of varying dimensions but similar form the amount of wood necessarily wasted in square-edging the lumber is in direct proportion to the bark surfaces of the different sized logs. The allowance to be made for neglecting the fractions of inches in measuring the widths of the boards sawn from logs is likewise in proportion to the bark surface and may most conveniently be grouped with the edging waste in computations.

Edging waste is due (1) to the *circular form* of logs, (2) to the minor crook (irregularity of surface), and (3) to major crook or "sweep" in logs. In the case of perfectly straight smooth logs the allowance for edging need provide for waste in trimming the wane from sawn boards only. Few logs, however, are either perfectly straight or free from superficial irregularities. It is therefore necessary that in the computation of any practical log rule due provision be made for these normally occurring defects in the form of the average log.

The allowance for edging the lumber from logs of various diameters and degrees of crook was first determined theoretically by mathematical computation aided by draughting. The amount to be added to this theoretical allowance to provide for the additional loss due to human and mechanical imperfections was next determined by sawing out very carefully measured (white pine) logs having all degrees of crook. I shall not here go into the details of this interesting study but content myself with a statement of my results.

1. The discovery that the edging waste remains practically constant regardless of the width of kerf cut by the saw has been already noted and fully explained.

2. It was found that the waste due to crook (major and minor) of all degrees was in direct proportion to the circumference of the logs sawn; *i. e.* the waste due to any particular degree of crook in a 20-inch log was practically double that caused by a similar amount of crook in a 10-inch log.

3. When provision is made in the scaling score for an average taper of 1 inch per 8 feet lineal, and when the logs show an average major crook of 1½ inches per 12 feet, the necessary allowance for edging waste as above defined was found to be .8 *foot board measure per square foot of bark surface* for white pine logs of all dimensions.

The effect of increasing major crook on the product of sawn lumber was also studied. The results of such a study depend directly on the size of the smallest board which is regarded as merchantable by the investigator, for with increasing crook there is a greatly increased out-put of short lengths sawn from the heavy slabs. The rules of the National Hardwood Lumber Association, the Louisiana Cypress Association and other similar bodies, have set the minimum dimensions of boards entitled to pass inspection and measurement in the case of most species at 3 inches in width by 4 feet in length. Using a minimum unit of just double this size I found that as logs were cut for ordinary commercial purposes in the mill in which I made my tests, an increase in the average major crook of one inch per twelve feet increased the allowance required for edging .1 foot board measure per square foot of bark surface. With a minimum unit of 3 inches in width by *12 feet* in length the additional waste in edging for the same increase in average crook was just three-fold or .3 foot board measure per square foot of bark surface.

As already noted, there have been four log rules—Baxter, British Columbia, Universal, and Champlain—which have had the allowance for edging provided for in a rational way. In computing the International Rule the allowance for edging was in all cases made proportional to the circumference at the *middle* of the logs and hence is strictly proportional to the bark surfaces. This differs somewhat from the method adopted in the computation of the Universal and Champlain rules, where the allowance is proportional to the top end circumference, and somewhat more from that used in the computation of the Baxter and British Columbia rules, where the allowance is a certain depth beneath the bark. Both these latter methods—and more particularly the last—give a relatively higher scale for the smaller logs.

Re Computation and Formula. The simplest mathematical formula for the International ⅛ Rule is $(D^2 \times .22) - .71D$ for 4-foot sections. Taper ½-inch per four feet lineal. The scaling score has been computed for logs from 3 to 60 inches in diameter and from 8 to 20 feet in length, longer logs to be measured as two or more logs. After computation the scale for the individual logs was, at the suggestion of Mr. Price of the Forest Service, rounded off to the nearest 5 or 0. The saving thus affected in the clerical labor of computing tallies is from ⅓ to ½, while the liability to error in multiplying and adding is reduced to a minimum. Any error due to the rounding off is of course absolutely negligible where more than a dozen logs are measured.

The Adapting of Log Rules to Universal Conditions. The product in merchantable lumber which may be sawn from a sound log of given length and top diameter depends on the skill of the sawyer, the quality of the mill equipment, the width of the saw kerf, the straightness of the log, and the amount of taper present. No log rule could or should concern itself with the varying skill of sawyers or the quality of mill equipments. It is, however, quite necessary that a log rule intended for general use be adaptable to the different widths of kerf cut by saws of various thicknesses and perhaps to the varying qualities of logs in different districts as regards straightness and taper.

Variations due to varying widths of saw kerf have been shown to bear a *percental relation* to the *scale* of logs of the various dimensions, and a table has been given above by means of which any total scale as given by the International ⅛ Rule (*i. e.*, rule for saws cutting a ⅛-inch kerf), may be adapted to saws cutting other widths of kerf. It remains to be shown how a standard scaling score which has been computed with special reference to white pine as it is logged and sawn to-day may be adapted so as to be equally satisfactory for the scaling of logs of radically different taper and sawing qualities.

That the edging waste, whether great or small, is in proportion to the bark surfaces of logs of all diameters has been stated. It is equally true that any increase or decrease in the amount of merchantable lumber that may be sawn from logs because of increased or decreased average taper is also directly proportional to the bark surfaces of the logs concerned. The reason for this will be evident if the portion of the log represented by the taper be thought of as forming a ring about the cylindrical portion and thus being practically proportional to the circumference. These two conditions being granted it follows that any variation in the sawn product of sound logs due to roughness of surface, crook, or taper, must bear a *percental relation to the bark surface of the logs sawn*.

Fortunately a discount or a premium directly proportional to the bark surface of the logs measured may be very simply added to or deducted from the scale given by a rule by using a scaling stick which shall measure the diameters of all logs scaled scant or full as may be desired. Thus, should the necessary edging waste be unusually large—due to excessive average crook or roughness—the scale may be correctly discounted by using a scaling stick on which the 0 point is placed somewhat more than 1 inch from the 1-inch graduation on the stick. Likewise should the logs cut in any locality prove to saw out a larger amount of lumber than called for by the rule, the scale given by the rule may be correctly bonused by using a scaling stick on which the 0 point of the measure is somewhat less than 1 inch from the 1-inch point on the stick. The amount of adjustment necessary to meet any given set of local conditions can only be determined by a careful investigation by a competent person of the sawing qualities of logs cut in the locality. It is fortunate that increased roughness in logs is all but invariably accompanied by increased taper and that while the former tends to decrease the lumber product from logs, the latter has the opposite effect. In most cases the one will be found to offset the other more or less completely, and herein lies an advantage of a top-end measuring rule computed for a conservative taper allowance as compared with a caliper rule which being applied at the middle of the log credits the full amount of taper.

Mill Tests with the International Rule. In making mill tests with the International Rule it must never be overlooked that the standard scaling score (published herewith) is computed for a kerf allowance of 1/8-inch and a factor of safety in the thickness of the boards of 1/16-inch (for uneven sawing and shrinkage) or a total allowance of 3/16-inch. The first step in making a test is to determine accurately the corresponding margin for kerf and shrinkage being made by the mill in which the logs are to be sawn. This can be most conveniently and accurately done by observing the loss in width of square timbers (*i. e.* logs after slabbing all four sides) from cutting any particular number of inch boards from their sides. The larger the number of boards sawn in this test the better will be the average figure for the total allowance. For example, let it be assumed that the cutting of 40 "inch" boards cost the square timbers under measurement a total of 52.5 inches, thus giving an average of 5/16-inch total allowance, which corresponds with a 1/4-inch kerf + 1/16-inch for shrinkage. The 40 boards cut under the standard conditions (*i. e.* 1/8-inch kerf + 1/16-inch shrinkage) would cost the timbers but 47.5 inches. Therefore the total scale given by the rule for the logs tested must be reduced for that particular mill in the proportion of 52.5 to 47.5, or in other words 9.5 per cent.

The next step in the test is to measure the logs sawn together with their product in square-edged lumber after manufacture. In my work I have measured the log diameters, top and butt, twice at right angles correct to tenths of inches, the mean being taken. The crook in the twelve feet towards the small end of the log was also measured by applying a straight-edge to the side showing the greatest curvature. Unless it is desired to discover the *cause* of any variation from the rule scale the measurement of the crook and the butt diameter may of course be omitted.

Further procedure can perhaps be more easily made clear by assuming a concrete case. For this purpose let the task be to determine the correction to be made—if any—in adapting the rule for specially accurate work with, say, Adirondack spruce. Let the assumed conditions be as follows:

Logs sawn (16 feet long)	1000
Average diameter at top	10 inches
Kerf cut by saw used	$\frac{3}{16}$ inch
Allowance for shrinkage	$\frac{1}{16}$ inch
Scale by International $\frac{1}{8}$ Rule	71,585 ft. B.M.
Scale adapted for $\frac{3}{16}$-inch kerf (see page 84)	68,006 " "
Actual product after manufacture	69,606 " "
Over-run of scale by saw cut	1,600 " "
Average over-run per log	1.6 " "

By using the rule formula it will be found that with a $\frac{3}{16}$-inch kerf it takes an increase of just .1 inch in the diameter of a 10-inch log to increase the scale 1.6 feet board measure. In other words, if the above supposed case were a real one, the saving in the edging waste of 1.6 feet B.M. per log on account of the greater straightness of the logs would have as great an effect on the product in sawn lumber as an increase of .1 inch in the diameter of all the logs would have on the scale. The application is obvious. If it be desired to adapt the International Rule for logs sawing out as economically as in the supposed case above, the zero point of the graduations on the scaling stick must be moved .1 inch to the right so that from 0 to the 1-inch mark on the scale, the actual distance will be but .9 inch. So adjusted, the scaling stick would be a local rule for the species or the locality giving as favorable results from actual mill tests as have been assumed for illustration purposes.

Mill Test with White Pine. The results of a test with white pine logs made in the summer of 1905 on the Ottawa under ordinary commercial conditions will be of interest. In scaling the logs for the following comparative statement, all fractions of inches in the measured diameters were disregarded if of the even half inch or less, while all greater than the half were counted as full inches, except in the case of the Champlain scale where *all* fractions were disregarded as directed by the maker of the rule. The logs were cut almost entirely to inch boards (1 1/16 inches thick) by a band saw cutting a 1/8-inch kerf :

Diam. of Logs	No. of Logs	Over-run (+) or under-run (—) of Saw Cut as compared with scale by Doyle	Scribner	Champlain	International 1/8 Rule
6–8	28	+143%	+33%	+10.3%	+2.6%
7–9	54	+115%	+35%	+8.8%	+2.3%
8–12	101	+72%	+34%	+7.1%	+0.0%
10–17	104	+45%	+23%	+4.7%	—1.1%
18–20	90	+24%	+14%	+6.7%	+0.5%
21–24	126	+18%	+14%	+5.2%	+1.1%
25–33	31	+10%	+9%	+3.3%	—0.5%

The groups of smaller logs are over-lapped somewhat to show intermediate steps in the decreasing error of the Doyle scale as the logs grow larger. The 10–17-inch group of 104 logs represents the average log as cut on Ontario public lands in 1904, the scale of the average log being 61 feet according to Doyle. The Doyle rule is of course increasingly unsatisfactory as a measure of log values as the average log milled grows smaller. The decrease in the size of the average pine log cut in Ontario has been 35% during the last 12 years. The Scribner rule is much less extreme than the Doyle but is quite out of touch with modern conditions. The theoretical allowance for edging used in the computation of the Champlain rule was a 1-inch board from the centre of the logs sawn. This is equivalent to about .3 foot board measure per square foot of bark surface, and is much too low even for the straightest, smoothest logs. The absence of any allowance for taper in the scaling score is equivalent to adding at least .5 ft. B.M per sq. ft. of bark surface when 16-ft. logs are sawn. Where the fractions of inches are all disregarded in measuring the diameters in scaling, this edging allowance is further bonused to the extent of about .22 ft. B.M. or a total edging allowance of a trifle over one foot board measure per square foot of bark surface, which is larger than necessary. Were the Champlain rule a 1/4-inch kerf rule as intended by its author, the band saw cut should have over-run its scale 10 per cent. throughout. Its kerf allowance is really $\frac{3}{16}$-inch when the boards are cut plump to allow for shrinkage, as is always done. The test proved very satisfactory for the International $\frac{1}{8}$ Rule. The total scale given the 403 logs sawn was 82,920 feet, board measure, as compared with a product of 83,288 feet measured after manufacture, an over-run of the scale of four-tenths of one per cent. It will be noted that the scale proved equally satisfactory for small and large logs.

JUDSON F. CLARK.

THE INTERNATIONAL LOG RULE.

Formula: $(D^2 \times .22) - .71D$ for 4-foot sections.
Taper allowance: ½ inch per 4 feet lineal.
Standard scale for saws cutting a ⅛-inch kerf.

Dia	Length of Log in Feet.													Dia
	8	9	10	11	12	13	14	15	16	17	18	19	20	
3	--	--	--	--	--	--	--	--	--	5	5	5	5	3
4	--	--	5	5	5	5	5	5	5	10	10	10	10	4
5	5	5	5	5	10	10	10	10	15	15	15	15	20	5
6	10	10	10	15	15	15	20	20	20	25	25	30	30	6
7	15	15	15	20	20	25	25	30	30	35	35	40	45	7
8	20	20	25	25	30	35	35	40	45	45	50	55	60	8
9	25	30	30	35	40	45	50	50	55	60	65	70	75	9
10	30	35	40	45	50	55	60	65	70	75	85	90	95	10
11	40	45	50	55	65	70	75	80	90	95	105	110	115	11
12	50	55	65	70	75	85	90	100	105	115	125	130	140	12
13	60	65	75	85	90	100	110	120	130	140	145	155	165	13
14	70	80	90	100	110	120	130	140	150	160	175	185	195	14
15	80	90	105	115	125	140	150	160	175	185	200	215	225	15
16	95	105	120	130	145	160	170	185	200	215	230	245	260	16
17	105	120	135	150	165	180	195	210	225	245	260	275	295	17
18	120	135	155	170	185	205	220	240	255	275	295	310	330	18
19	135	155	175	190	210	230	250	270	290	310	330	350	370	19
20	150	170	195	215	235	255	275	300	320	345	365	390	410	20
21	170	190	215	235	260	285	305	330	355	380	405	430	455	21
22	185	210	235	260	285	315	340	365	390	420	445	475	500	22
23	205	230	260	285	315	345	370	400	430	460	490	520	550	23
24	225	255	285	315	345	375	405	440	470	500	535	565	600	24
25	245	275	310	345	375	410	445	475	510	545	580	615	650	25
26	265	300	335	370	405	445	480	520	555	595	630	670	705	26
27	290	325	365	405	440	480	520	560	600	640	680	725	765	27
28	310	350	395	435	475	520	560	605	645	690	735	780	825	28
29	335	380	425	470	510	560	605	650	695	740	790	835	885	29
30	360	405	455	500	550	600	645	695	745	795	845	895	950	30

THE INTERNATIONAL LOG RULE.

Formula: $(D^2 \times \cdot 22) - \cdot 71D$ for 4 foot sections.
Taper allowance: ½ inch per 4 feet lineal.
Standard scale for saws cutting a ⅛-inch kerf.

Dia.	Length of Log in Feet.													Dia.
	8	9	10	11	12	13	14	15	16	17	18	19	20	
31	385	435	485	540	590	640	695	745	800	850	905	960	1015	31
32	410	465	520	575	630	685	740	795	850	910	965	1025	1080	32
33	440	495	555	610	670	730	790	850	905	970	1030	1090	1150	33
34	470	530	590	650	715	775	840	900	965	1030	1095	1160	1225	34
35	495	560	625	690	755	825	890	955	1025	1095	1160	1230	1300	35
36	525	595	665	735	800	875	945	1015	1085	1160	1230	1305	1375	36
37	560	630	705	775	850	925	1000	1075	1150	1225	1300	1380	1455	37
38	590	665	745	820	895	975	1055	1135	1210	1295	1375	1455	1535	38
39	620	705	785	865	945	1030	1110	1195	1280	1365	1450	1535	1620	39
40	655	740	825	910	995	1085	1170	1260	1345	1435	1525	1615	1705	40
41	690	780	870	960	1050	1140	1230	1325	1415	1510	1605	1700	1795	41
42	725	820	915	1010	1100	1200	1295	1390	1490	1585	1685	1785	1885	42
43	760	860	960	1060	1155	1260	1360	1460	1560	1665	1770	1870	1975	43
44	800	900	1005	1110	1215	1320	1425	1530	1635	1745	1855	1960	2070	44
45	835	945	1055	1160	1270	1380	1490	1600	1715	1825	1940	2050	2165	45
46	875	990	1100	1215	1330	1445	1560	1675	1790	1910	2030	2145	2265	46
47	915	1035	1150	1270	1390	1510	1630	1750	1870	1995	2120	2240	2365	47
48	955	1080	1205	1325	1450	1575	1700	1830	1955	2085	2210	2340	2470	48
49	1000	1125	1255	1385	1510	1645	1775	1905	2040	2170	2305	2440	2575	49
50	1040	1175	1310	1440	1575	1715	1850	1985	2125	2265	2400	2540	2680	50
51	1085	1225	1360	1500	1640	1785	1925	2070	2210	2355	2500	2645	2790	51
52	1125	1275	1420	1565	1710	1855	2005	2150	2300	2450	2600	2750	2905	52
53	1170	1325	1475	1625	1775	1930	2085	2235	2390	2545	2705	2860	3015	53
54	1220	1375	1530	1690	1845	2005	2165	2325	2485	2645	2810	2970	3135	54
55	1265	1430	1590	1755	1915	2080	2245	2410	2580	2745	2915	3085	3250	55
56	1315	1480	1650	1820	1985	2160	2330	2500	2675	2850	3025	3200	3375	56
57	1360	1535	1710	1885	2060	2240	2415	2595	2770	2955	3135	3315	3495	57
58	1410	1590	1775	1955	2135	2320	2505	2685	2870	3060	3245	3435	3620	58
59	1460	1650	1835	2025	2210	2400	2590	2780	2975	3165	3360	3555	3750	59
60	1510	1705	1900	2095	2290	2485	2680	2880	3075	3275	3475	3680	3880	60

MARKETING OF WOODLOT PRODUCTS

OHIO
Agricultural Experiment Station

WOOSTER, OHIO, U. S. A., AUGUST, 1916

BULLETIN 302

The Bulletins of this Station are sent free to all residents of the State who request them. When a change of address is desired, both the old and the new address should be given. All correspondence should be addressed to EXPERIMENT STATION, Wooster, Chio

OHIO AGRICULTURAL EXPERIMENT STATION

BULLETIN

OF THE

Ohio Agricultural Experiment Station

NUMBER 302 AUGUST, 1916

MARKETING OF WOODLOT PRODUCTS

J. W. CALLAND

Usual selling methods.—The average woodlot owner has but an indefinite idea of the contents of his woodlot, or of how best to market his woodlot products. Instances of woodlots selling for less than one-half their true value are common in most communities. Usually the farmer sells his timber "by the lot" to a portable-sawmill owner or timber buyer, receiving a lump sum for all the timber on the area. Being unfamiliar with timber values and of how they are determined he has, at best, but a vague idea of what the timber standing in his woodlot is worth. The buyer being experienced in timber-estimating and marketing can go through the woodlot and determine the amount and value of the timber before making his offer. This condition of affairs naturally leaves the owner on unequal terms with the buyer, and he frequently sells his timber for a price decidedly unfavorable to himself.

Another serious objection to the method of selling timber "by the lot" is that no provision can be made to save any desirable trees for a second crop. The buyer paying a fixed sum for everything on the area will cut every stick that offers a chance for profit and will naturally take no care of what he cannot use. What is left to the owner is, indeed, a decidedly poor tract of woods.

Such mistakes should be avoided. Woodlot owners should abandon the practice of selling the entire lot for a lump sum. The principles of forestry should be applied when timber is cut. The manner in which cutting is done determines the future condition of the woodlot.

Better selling methods.—Sales should be based upon an accurate knowledge of values. The stumpage value, which is the price that can be obtained for standing timber, depends upon the quality of the material and its nearness to market. In order to arrive at a fair stumpage value for timber, the owner must determine what the logs or other products would sell for delivered at some factory or shipping point, what it would cost to cut and deliver them, and what amount of each product can be cut from the area. The most satisfactory method, in nearly every case, is to sell by the unit; that is, so much per thousand feet of lumber; so much per tie, pole, cord, linear foot, etc., based on the amount actually cut or estimated to be in the lot, with a definite agreement as to what trees are to be left standing and the extent to which reproduction and young growth are to be protected. For the best results the owner should do the work in the woods himself, or at least have it done under his direct supervision. When the work is done by contract, careful provisions should be made to prevent careless operations and unnecessary injury to the future stand.

Many times it is not necessary for the farmer to sell the products of his woodlot to a portable-sawmill operator or to the local timber buyer. If he secures some special market for his material; does the cutting, logging, hauling, etc., with his own help and teams, he not only receives the value of his timber, but also saves for himself the profit of the buyer who generally figures on at least 20 percent margin. To be able to sell his products in some form which pays not only a fair stumpage value but also day wages for himself and team is often a great advantage to the farmer. But in order to determine the most profitable form into which his trees may be worked, he should consider every available special market for his products.

It is therefore well worth while for the woodlot owner to familiarize himself with the ordinary methods of timber-estimating, and to inquire carefully into the matter of timber values and markets before disposing of his product.

METHODS OF MEASURING WOODLOT PRODUCTS

Lumber.—Lumber is almost always sold by the thousand feet board measure (M feet B. M.). The board foot, the unit of board measure, is the equivalent of a board 1 foot wide, 1 foot long and 1 inch in thickness. Dimension timbers, planks and other pieces more than 1 inch in thickness are also measured by the board foot. The rule for finding the board-foot contents of any regular stick or sawed timber may be stated as follows: *Multiply the width of the stick by its thickness in inches; multiply this product by the length, in feet, and divide the result by* 12. Thus a plank 2 inches thick, 6 inches wide and 8 feet long, contains $\frac{2 \times 6 \times 8}{12} = 8$ board feet.

Lumbermen generally use a "scale stick" for measuring lumber. This stick is so made that it shows at a glance the contents in board feet of any regular piece of sawed lumber when the length, width and thickness are known.

Wood for paper pulp, excelsior, fuel, handles and similar products.—Wood for paper pulp, excelsior, fuel, handles, etc., is usually worked into a form too small to be scaled by the board foot. Such material as this is measured by the cord. A cord may be defined as 128 cubic feet of stacked wood. It is generally understood to be a pile of wood cut into 4-foot lengths and stacked 4 feet high and 8 feet long. Frequently, however, wood is worked into shorter lengths. When this is done it is piled 4 feet high and 8 feet long and passes as a "short cord."

Crossties, posts, poles, piles and mine props.—Such products as ties, posts, poles, piles and mine props are sold by the single piece. The market calls for these materials to be of different sizes and the value per piece is determined by the size and quality. Specifications for these products will be given later.

Logs.—The contents of logs are measured in board feet. The entire contents of a log are not measured, however, but only the amount of lumber which can be sawed from it.

FACTORS INFLUENCING THE CONTENTS OF LOGS IN BOARD FEET

The number of board feet which can actually be cut from logs of a given size will vary under different circumstances because of variation in the several factors which determine the amount of waste. These factors are as follows:

1. *Thickness of the saw.*—The thickness of the saw used at the mill will affect the actual amount of lumber that can be cut from a log. The ordinary circular saw in use at small portable-sawmills is from one-fourth to five-sixteenths of an inch thick and may cut from 10 to 20 percent less from a log in inch boards than could be cut from the same log with a band saw, because the waste in saw kerf with the band saw is only one-half as great.

2. *Width of smallest boards.*—If no boards less than 6 inches wide are sawed from a log, the number of board feet obtained will be less than if boards 3 inches wide are sawed. When a log is slabbed for sawing boards 6 inches wide, material is thrown away which would produce four 3-inch boards. The percent of loss is of course greatest with small logs.

3. *Skill of sawyer.*—A skillful sawyer by taking advantage of the irregularities of logs and carefully sawing each log in such

a manner as to get the maximum amount of lumber from it can secure a greater yield in board feet than if the logs are cut through carelessly with little regard to form and shape.

4. *Condition of logs.*—The logs cut from the average woodlot are not usually perfect. There is certain to be more or less waste due to decayed spots, crooks, knots and other defects.

5. *Thickness of boards.*—If logs are sawed into boards 1 inch or less in thickness, there will be a greater loss in saw kerf than if 2-inch planks or other thick material is sawed. Hence, the number of board feet obtained will be less when logs are sawed into thin material.

6. *Efficiency of machinery.*—If saws are properly filed and set, and good, well-regulated machinery is used about the mill, the total cut from a given lot of logs is, of course, greater than could be obtained with a poor saw and inferior machinery.

TABLE I.—COMPARISON OF THE DOYLE AND SCRIBNER RULES

Doyle Rule					Scribner Rule					
Diameter of log at small end (Inches)	Board feet when log length is				Diameter of log at small end (Inches)	Board feet when log length is			
	10 feet	12 feet	14 feet	16 feet		10 feet	12 feet	14 feet	16 feet
6	2.5	3.0	3.5	4	6	10	12	14	18
7	5.6	6.8	7.9	9	7	16	18	24	28
8	10	12	14	16	8	20	24	28	32
9	16	19	22	25	9	25	30	35	40
10	23	27	32	36	10	31	40	45	50
11	31	37	44	49	11	40	50	55	63
12	40	48	56	64	12	49	59	69	79
13	50	61	71	81	13	61	73	85	97
14	62	75	88	100	14	71	86	100	114
15	75	91	106	121	15	88	107	125	142
16	90	108	126	144	16	100	119	139	159
17	106	127	148	169	17	115	139	162	185
18	122	147	171	196	18	133	160	187	213
19	141	169	197	225	19	150	180	210	240
20	160	192	224	256	20	175	210	245	280
21	181	217	253	289	21	190	228	266	304
22	202	243	283	324	22	209	251	292	334
23	226	271	313	359	23	235	283	330	377
24	250	300	350	400	24	252	303	354	404
25	276	331	386	441	25	287	344	401	459
26	302	363	423	484	26	313	375	438	500
27	330	397	463	529	27	343	411	479	548
28	360	432	504	576	28	363	436	509	582
29	391	469	547	625	29	381	457	533	609
30	422	507	591	676	30	410	493	575	657
31	456	547	638	729	31	443	532	622	710
32	490	588	686	784	32	460	552	644	736
33	526	631	736	841	33	490	588	686	784
34	562	675	787	900	34	500	600	700	800
35	601	721	841	961	35	547	657	766	876
36	640	768	896	1,024	36	577	692	807	923
37	681	817	953	1,089	37	643	772	901	1,029
38	723	867	1,011	1,156	38	667	801	934	1,068
39	765	919	1,072	1,225	39	700	840	980	1,120
40	810	972	1,134	1,296	40	752	903	1,053	1,204

LOG RULES

Tables have been prepared which show the estimated number of board feet that can be cut from logs of different sizes. Such tables are called log scales, log tables or log rules. There are a number of these log rules in use in various sections of the country, but in Ohio the Doyle rule is generally employed. This rule is accurate only for logs of medium size, or from about 20 to 30 inches in diameter. It gives an extremely small scale for logs of small diameter, and woodlot owners selling small-sized logs by this scale will give much more material than they are paid for. For large logs, however, it gives too large a scale. A comparison is given between the Doyle and Scribner rules in Table I. The Scribner rule gives a more just scale for small logs.

For use in the actual work of scaling logs, scale sticks are made for each of the common log rules. The scale stick has printed on it numbers which show the board-foot contents of logs of different sizes.

SCALING

Scaling consists in determining, with the aid of a scale stick, the contents in board feet of a given log. If all logs were regular and perfect, scaling would be a simple process; but since very few logs are perfect the scaler must make allowance for all sorts of defects. The knowledge of how to allow for defects can be acquired only by practice and observation. The figures on the scale stick show the contents of straight, sound logs, according to diameter and length. The stick should be applied to the average diameter inside the bark at the small end of the log.

No hard and fast rules can be given for scaling, but the following are some of the visible defects in logs for which the scaler must make allowance:

1. *Crooks.*—Generally a certain percent is deducted for crooks, but for a specified log the scaler may sight along the log and calculate how much the small end must be reduced so as to contain just the largest square stick which can actually be cut from the log.

2. *Shakes.*—By "shakes" is meant cracks in timber, generally caused by wind or frost. These may either follow the annual rings of growth or cross them. If such shake cracks are confined to the heart of the log and the grain is straight, only the center need be thrown out. Still, shaky logs are usually worthless for lumber if the crack is extensive.

3. *Dote.*—This term is generally employed by lumbermen to denote decay, or rot, in timber. This may occur in any part of the

log, but is often at the center. Sometimes the sapwood is decayed or wormy while the heartwood is good. In this case only the heartwood is scaled. If a doty or rotten spot appears at one end of a log, it is generally safe to deduct that area through the entire length of the log.

4. *Cat-face.*—Cat-face is a term generally applied to partly healed scars on the trunk of a tree caused by fire, sun scald or mechanical injury. Unless decay has developed, a cat-face is not usually considered a serious defect. However, it may cause the removal of a wide slab.

5. *Mechanical injury and other defects.*—Splits and other injuries may be caused by careless felling. Checks may occur while the log is seasoning. Insect injury and various other defects are frequently encountered. For all of these the scaler must make allowance according to his best judgment.

If it is desired to find the board-foot contents of a log by the Doyle rule, without the aid of a scale stick or log table, the rule may be stated as follows: *Deduct 4 inches from the diameter of the log; square one-fourth of the remainder, and multiply the result by the length of the log in feet.*

Example: A 16-foot log is 24 inches in diameter. 24—4 = 20; ¼ of 20 = 5; 5 squared = 25; 25 x 16 = 400. Therefore, a 16-foot log 24 inches in diameter contains 400 board feet by the Doyle rule. In scaling long logs by this rule either the diameter should be taken at the middle of the log or the average diameter of the two ends should be used.

ESTIMATING THE AMOUNT OF TIMBER IN THE WOODLOT

It is quite possible for the woodlot owner to estimate his own timber fairly well. The average woodlot is not large and much more thorough methods of estimating may be employed than would be practicable on large timber tracts. However, the owner must remember that to make an accurate estimate of standing timber requires skill and experience. Therefore, if his woodlot is large and contains considerable valuable material, it will pay best to secure the services of an experienced estimator, preferably a forester who can at the same time make out a plan for the future management of the woodlot.

Only a few practical methods of estimating will be described here. They are not intended for large areas where it would be impossible to count all the trees.

The single-log method.—A method frequently used is that of estimating the entire merchantable portion of the tree as one log.

Proceed as follows: Estimate the entire length of the merchantable section of the tree; then estimate the top and bottom diameters; average these diameters, and find the contents by the Doyle rule. For example, if the length of the merchantable portion of the tree is 42 feet, the top diameter 12 inches, and the bottom diameter 20 inches, the average diameter would be 16 inches, and the board-foot contents of the log would be, by the Doyle rule, 378 feet.

The tree-to-tree count.—This method involves the use of a "tally sheet" and a log table, and requires the ability to judge diameters at different places on the tree. It is one of the best methods for the inexperienced estimator, provided he does his work carefully. By this method the estimator approaches each tree, determines the lengths of the various logs which should be cut from it, estimates the top diameter inside the bark of each log and enters it in the proper place on the tally sheet according to diameter and length.

TABLE II.—SAMPLE TALLY SHEET FOR ESTIMATING LUMBER

Diameter at small end of log inside the bark (Inches)	Length of logs in feet: 10		12		14		16	
	Log tally	Total board feet	Log tally	Total board feet	Log tally	Total board feet	Log tally	Total board feet
8		30		....				64
10		135		54		63		36
12		[illegible]		336		445		128
14		[illegible]		675		792		700
16		150		324		378		720
18		122		147				1176
20		640				224		512
Total.....		[illegible]		[illegible]		[illegible]		1136

The "dot and line" system of tallying used here is one which enables the estimator to record a large number of logs on a single sheet. The value of each symbol is shown by the following:

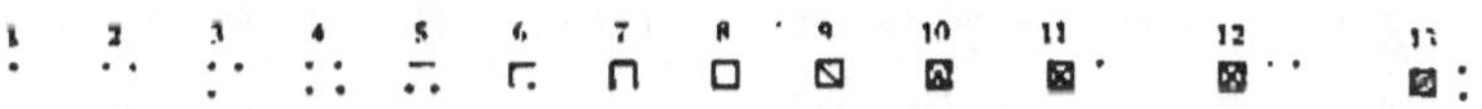

Since they are arranged in blocks of ten, they are quickly and easily read.

After all the logs have been entered on the tally sheet, the board-foot contents of each sized log is found in Doyle's log table and multiplied by the number of logs of that size, and this product entered in the next column to the right. The total at the bottom of the right-hand column is the board-foot contents of all the logs of that length, and the sum of the totals for the different length logs gives the entire estimate. With this form of tally sheet a separate page must be used for each species estimated, and the totals of all the species are added for the complete estimate of the woodlot.

If the estimator uses but one standard log-length, he will be able to lessen greatly the number of computations necessary to arrive at the final estimate, and a single tally sheet will serve for several species. The single tally sheet is generally used by experienced estimators because it greatly simplifies the tallying and scaling of the logs. The 16-foot log is the standard length commonly used. However, the inexperienced worker in a small woodlot will generally find it more satisfactory to use two or more log-lengths. Table III shows a tally sheet for use with the single log-length.

TABLE III.—SAMPLE TALLY SHEET FOR ESTIMATING TIMBER

(16-foot logs)

Diameter at top of log inside bark (Inches)	Oak	Maple	Beech	Ash	Elm	Totals		
						Total logs	Scale	Total board feet
8							16	32
10							36	72
12							64	256
14							100	400
16							144	288
18							196	196
20							256	256
Totals	3	3	3	5	2	16	....	1,500

N. B. If desired extra columns may be inserted in the tally sheet for recording the number of trees of each species.

Considerable skill is required to judge the top diameters of logs. Thus it is necessary for the inexperienced estimator to use either a pair of calipers[1] or a tape to measure the diameter of the tree at a point breast high, or about 4½ feet above the ground. This measurement will be above the root swellings and will afford a

[1]Tree calipers may be purchased from Keuffel & Esser Co., 127 Fulton Street, New York, N. Y. 18-inch size for $3.15 and 36-inch size for $4.50.

valuable check in judging the top diameters of the logs to be taken from the tree. If a tape is used, the distance around the tree is read and multiplied by 7/22, or divided by 3.1416, to get the diameter. If calipers are used, the diameter is read directly from the graduated arm. It is also a good plan to use a light 10-foot pole having attached across one end a small stick marked off in inches by prominent notches, which an assistant can hold against the tree with the cross-stick at the point where the first log would come. The diameter can be determined with fair accuracy from the notched rule. After taking a diameter measurement at a point breast high with the calipers, and another at the top of the first log, as just explained, the top diameters of the other logs in the tree may be estimated by comparison.

The average thickness of the bark at different heights on the tree must be allowed for. Taking a few measurements of the bark on felled trees will give the operator a good idea of the amount to deduct to get the inside diameter.

The advantage of this method of timber-estimating is that the operator can make allowance for all such physical defects as crooked, diseased and defective portions of the tree, and allow for excessive taper and thickness of bark before making his entries on the tally sheet.

The average-tree method.—Another method which is sometimes used is to go through the woodlot and count all the trees, determine the board-foot contents of the average-sized tree and multiply this by the total number of trees in the lot. It is important that particular care be used in selecting the average-sized tree and in determining its contents.

The diameter-class method.—A method generally more practicable than the average-tree method is to take the breast-high diameters of all the trees in the lot and tally them in inch diameter-classes, keeping the different species separate if desired. Then determine the contents of the average tree in each diameter-class; multiply the contents of the average tree of each diameter-class by the number of trees in that class, and add the results obtained for each class to secure the total volume of the entire lot. The diameters should be measured with calipers or tape, and trees should be marked in some way in order to avoid counting any of them more than once. Plain chalk or crayon may be used for marking the trees as they are counted.

MARKETS

The principal markets for the products of the farm woodlot are for lumber, building and construction material, logs, crossties, poles, piling, posts, firewood, and frequently for round cord-wood for use in paper-pulp plants, pail factories, box factories, excelsior plants and handle works. But for such woods as white oak, yellow poplar, walnut, cherry, elm, hickory and ash, there are a great number of special markets, as veneer mills, furniture factories, vehicle factories, etc. These special markets generally demand a certain quality of material, and the price paid for it is considerably above the "log run" value of lumber. Therefore, owners are again reminded that they should inquire with particular interest into all available special markets, not only to locate markets for the different species but also to determine the most profitable form into which the various trees may be worked.

However, the woodlot owner must bear in mind that a market for rough forest products, as logs, ties, poles, etc., will be more to his advantage than one for sawed material to be sold on grades, unless he is able to secure the services of an exceptionally good portable mill with a sawyer who thoroughly understands how best to saw such material from the different logs.

PRINCIPAL PRODUCTS AND PRICES

Lumber.—The principal uses of each kind of wood are given later in this bulletin. Large quantities of the lumber sawed by small sawmills is not sold on grades, but by the "log run," which is the average value of all the products sawed from the log. The prices given later are the "log run" values, under average woodlot conditions. The average "log run" value of the lumber cut from woodlots of Ohio is about $20 per thousand feet board measure.

Logs.—In this State large quantities of logs are purchased annually by sawmill companies, veneer mills, lumber companies, etc. The price paid by these firms for logs delivered at their yards depends largely upon the size and quality of the material. Generally logs are graded according to quality, as "firsts," "seconds" or "thirds." Frequently the price of a log falling in one of these grades is determined by its diameter, the large logs bringing a higher price per thousand feet than the smaller ones.

The price of logs varies over the State, depending largely upon the nature of the industries and the available supply of suitable material. However, the following values may serve as a guide. The prices given here are for a thousand board feet delivered at the yard of the purchaser.

Green hardwood logs frequently average 10 pounds in weight per foot board measure, and, therefore, cannot be profitably shipped when the market is too far distant. From 3,000 to 7,000 feet make an average carload. Logs should be cut 10, 12, 14 or 16 feet in length unless otherwise specified. They are usually cut 4 inches over the specified length to allow for trimming.

TABLE IV.—PRICES OF DIFFERENT KINDS OF LOGS (per M bd. ft.)

Wood	No. 1 Grade	No. 2 Grade	No. 3 Grade
Ash	$40 to $ 45	$30 to $40	$25 to $30
Basswood	25 to 35	20 to 25	18 to 20
Chestnut	30 to 35	20 to 30	16 to 18
Elm	25 to 30	20 to 25	15 to 18
Oak	25 to 50	20 to 40	16 to 25
Yellow poplar	35 to 45	30 to 35	20 to 25
Maple	20 to 30	18 to 25	14 to 16
Walnut	50 to 100	35 to 75	20 to 50
Beech	20 to 25	18 to 20	12 to 15

Poles.—Most telephone, electric light, power and traction companies, and railroads buy chestnut poles on their own specifications. Telephone companies carrying only a few wires often accept small poles. Poles should be made from sound, live chestnut, squared at both ends, reasonably straight, well proportioned from top to butt, peeled, and with knots trimmed close to the surface.

The following specifications and prices are about the average for a good grade of chestnut poles.

TABLE V.—CHESTNUT POLE SPECIFICATIONS AND PRICES

Length	Diameter 6 feet from butt	Diameter at top	Price delivered at pole yard
Feet	Inches	Inches	Dollars
25	10	7	2.75
30	10	7	3.25
35	12	7	4.50
40	14	7	5.75
45	14	7	6.50
50	18	7	8.75
55	18	7	10.50
60	22	7	11.00
65	22	7	15.00

Piling.—Most companies classify piling as permanent or temporary. The following specifications will show the usual requirements for piling.

Permanent piles must be white oak and must be peeled. Temporary piles may be red or black oak, beech, sycamore, black gum, maple, elm, hickory or chestnut, and need not be peeled. The diameter at the middle of the pile shall be not less than 12 inches, and the maximum diameter at the butt 20 inches. The minimum diameter at the top shall be 9 inches for piles up to 30 feet in length, 8 inches for lengths between 30 and 50 feet and 7 inches for lengths over 50 feet. A line from the center of the butt to the center of the top shall lie within the body of the pile.

Permanent piles usually bring from 14 to 18 cents per linear foot delivered at the railroad, while the average price for temporary piling is not more than 8 to 10 cents per linear foot.

Crossties.—The market for crossties is generally steady. Ties are purchased by most railroads and traction companies at any point along their right of way. Specifications and prices given by the different companies vary somewhat, but the following specifications are perhaps typical.

All ties shall be made from live timber, and shall be straight and free from soft or decayed knots, wind shakes, worm holes, checks or splits and other imperfections which impair the usefulness of the tie.

Ties may be manufactured out of the full-sized log by sawing or hewing parallel slabs from it to give the required thickness making pole ties; or by sawing or splitting sticks of the requisite size out of larger logs. If they are split out the top and bottom faces must be dressed parallel and smooth afterward in the same manner as pole ties.

All ties must be made of approximately straight grain timber; all ties except cedar must be entirely clear of bark before delivery; all cutting, sawing, hewing, splitting and barking must be done thoroughly and in a workmanlike manner.

CLASS A OR No. 1 TIES, 7 in. x 9 in. x 8½ ft.

All ties of this class whether sawed, split or pole ties, shall not be less than 9 inches wide through the body of the entire length of the tie, by not less than 6¾ inches nor more than 7¼ inches in thickness between parallel faces, which faces must be at least 8 inches wide under the rail and for 1 foot each way from the rail bearing.

CLASS B OR No. 2 TIES, 7 in. x 9 in. x 8½ ft.

All ties of this class shall be similar to Class A ties in every respect except that the parallel faces must be at least 7 inches wide under the rail and for 1 foot each way from the rail bearing.

CLASS C OR No. 1 TIES, 7 in. x 8 in. x 8½ ft.

All ties of this class whether sawed, split or pole ties, shall not be less than 8 inches wide through the body of the entire length of the tie, by not less than 6¾ inches nor more than 7¼ inches in thickness between parallel faces, which faces must be at least 7 inches wide under the rail and for 1 foot each way from rail bearing.

CLASS D OR No. 2 TIES, 7 in. x 8 in. x 8½ ft.

All ties of this class shall be similar to Class C ties in every respect except that the parallel faces must be at least 6 inches wide under the rail and for 1 foot each way from rail bearing.

CLASS E OR No. 1 TIES, 6 in. x 8 in. x 8 ft.

All ties of this class whether sawed, split or pole ties, shall be not less than 8 inches wide through the body of the entire length of the tie, by not less than 6 inches nor more than 6¼ inches in thickness between parallel faces, which faces must be at least 7 inches wide under the rail and 1 foot each way from rail bearing.

CLASS F OR No. 2 TIES, 6 in. x 8 in. x 8 ft.

All ties of this class shall be similar to Class E ties in every respect except that the parallel faces must be at least 6 inches wide under the rail and for 1 foot each way from rail bearing.

None of these ties are to vary in length more than 1 inch either way.

The following kinds of timber will be classed with white oak:

Post oak	Overcup oak
Bur oak	Black walnut
Chestnut oak or rock oak	Black or wild cherry
Chestnut oak or chinqunpin	Yellow or black locust
Swamp white oak	Red mulberry
Cow oak or basket oak	Sassafras

The following kinds of timber will be accepted for creosoting:

GROUP No. 1

Red oak	Scarlet oak
Pin oak or swamp Spanish oak	Shingle oak or laurel oak
Black oak or yellow oak	Willow oak
Spanish oak	Honey locust
Water oak	

GROUP No. 2

Beech	Sweet, red or black birch

GROUP No. 3

Sugar maple or rock maple	Mockernut hickory
White ash	Pignut hickory
Bitternut or swamp hickory	Hackberry or sugarberry
Shellbark hickory	Pecan hickory

GROUP No. 4

Yellow birch or gray birch	Cork elm, rock elm or hickory elm
Slippery elm or red elm	

The 7" x 9" x 8½' ties contain 44.6 board feet apiece and make about 22.4 ties to the thousand board feet. At 75 cents apiece they bring about $17 per thousand feet.

The 7" x 8" x 8½' ties contain 39.6 feet each and run about 25 to the thousand feet. White oak ties at 75 cents each bring about $19 per thousand feet. Treatment ties at 55 cents each bring about $14 per thousand feet.

The 6" x 8" x 8' ties contain about 32 feet each and run 31¼ to the thousand feet. White oak ties at 65 cents each bring about $20 per thousand feet. Treatment ties at 45 cents each bring about $14 per thousand feet.

Cordwood.—In Ohio cordwood has a small market value. Except near a few large towns, a haul of 5 miles makes cordwood cutting unprofitable. For fuel it usually brings from $2 to $5 per cord delivered to the consumer. Hickory, oak and chestnut are preferred for firewood. Cordwood for pulp or excelsior is worth from $5 to $7 at the mill.

Posts and mine props.—Posts are usually either 7 or 8 feet in length and, if round, from 4 to 6 inches in diameter at the small end. If posts are split, the faces are usually required to be from 4 to 5 inches across. They must be free from shakes, rotten knots and bark. Chestnut posts frequently sell for 10 cents each at the woods. First-grade locust posts delivered to a shipping point bring from 13 to 17 cents each.

Mine props may be made from any kind of sound hardwood. If round they must be 4 inches or more in diameter at the small end. If split they must contain 16 square inches of material at the small end. Props are from 2½ feet up in length. The price for props up to and including the 5-foot length varies from ½ to 1 cent per linear foot. For props from 5 feet to 8 feet in length the price is usually 1 cent per linear foot plus 1 cent per prop. These prices vary greatly over the State, depending largely on the distance from the mines where they are to be used.

COST OF LUMBERING

The cost of lumbering as used here will mean the entire cost of converting standing trees into the various products, such as lumber, poles, ties, etc., and delivering them to a market or shipping point. The determination of lumbering cost is a problem into which a great many factors enter, such as the distance of the timber from the mill and market, the ease with which trees can be felled, cut into logs and hauled to the mill, the nature of the haul to market and the cost of team hire and labor.

Hauling.—The cost of hauling must necessarily vary with the distance, with the amount of material which can be hauled at a load, and with the rate of wages. The amount of material which can be hauled at a load, in turn, depends upon the condition of the roads, the topography of the country, and whether the material is seasoned or green.

It is ordinarily assumed with such figures that $4.50 per day is the average wage for a team and driver; that on ordinary roads the average load for a team is 1,000 board feet of lumber, 500 board feet of logs, thirty-two 8-foot ties, two 35- to 45-foot poles, four 30 to 35-foot poles, six 25- to 30-foot poles, or one cord of 4-foot wood: and that the ordinary team of draft horses on country roads will not average more than a 16- to 18-mile trip per day—loading, hauling and returning with the empty wagon.

Cutting.—The cost of felling trees and cutting them into logs varies with conditions in the woods, labor costs and the nature of the timber to be cut, but usually will average about $1.50 per thousand feet.

Skidding.—The cost of skidding necessarily varies with the distance to the mill, nature of the ground, rate of team hire, etc., but in case of a portable-sawmill in the average woodlot should not average more than $1.50 per thousand feet.

Sawing.—The greater part of the timber cut from the woodlots of Ohio is sawed by small portable-sawmills. The cost of moving one of these mills is not large, and from 50,000 to 75,000 board feet will warrant a "set-up." Often where the lots are quite small, two owners or more will combine to have a portable mill move in and saw their material. The price charged by such mills for sawing will vary from $3.50 to $4.50 per thousand feet, with $4 per thousand about the average. Where logs are hauled to a stationary mill, the price for custom sawing is frequently as high as $5 per thousand feet.

Piling.—Many times when sawing is done in the winter and the lumber delivered green, the piling cost is quite small, but if the lumber is to be loaded on cars at the railroad, a cost of at least 75 cents per thousand feet must be expected for piling and loading.

Production of lumber.—Assuming that the distance of a given woodlot from market is 8 miles, that the wage rate is $4.50 per day for team and driver, that 1,000 feet of lumber can be hauled at a load and that the sawing is to be done by a portable mill, the cost of operations will be about as follows:

	Per M bd. ft.
Cutting	$ 1.50
Skidding	1.50
Sawing	4.00
Piling	.75
Hauling	4.50
Total	$12.25

However, should the distance from the woodlot to the market be but 4 miles, the team could make two trips per day and the hauling cost would be but $2.25 per thousand feet, thus reducing the cost of operations from $12.25 to $10 per thousand feet. The owner must, of course, adapt these figures so as to apply to his particular case.

Production of logs.—At the same cost for cutting and skidding logs as has been given above for the production of lumber, and for a hauling distance of 7 to 9 miles, the probable cost of putting logs on the cars at the shipping point is indicated below.

	Per M bd. ft.
Cutting	$ 1.50
Skidding	1.50
Hauling	9.00
Loading on cars	1.50
Total	$13.50

If the hauling distance is short enough to permit of two loads per day, the hauling cost will be only one-half as large, thus reducing the cost of operations from $13.50 to $9 per thousand feet.

Production of poles and piling.—Pole cutting is a simple process. It consists in felling the tree, sawing off the top at a point which will give the specified top diameter inside the bark, trimming the branches close, and peeling. Usually the cost is 1 cent for each foot in length for poles up to 35 feet long, and 35 cents for poles from 35 to 50 feet long. The cost is less if poles are cut in the spring and early summer when peeling is an easy task. However, some companies specify winter-cut poles.

The cost of making piles is about the same as for poles, since they must be peeled if they are for permanent use. But temporary piling can often be cut at a cost of ½ cent per foot of length when peeling is not required. The hauling cost for poles or piles will usually be ½ cent per linear foot for each mile of haul.

Production of ties.—The cost of making ties will run from 10 cents per tie upward. To hew ties will usually cost from 10 to 12 cents for chestnut and from 12 to 14 cents for oak. One thousand board feet of ties make a good load and the hauling cost will depend upon the distance.

Ties should be sawed at less cost per thousand feet than lumber, since there is less labor and less waste involved. Assuming 33 ties to be the equivalent of 1,000 board feet, the cost of cutting and skidding to be $3, and the sawing $3.50 per thousand feet, we find that the cost of making ties will be about 21 cents each at the mill.

Production of cordwood.—The cost of cutting 4-foot cordwood varies from 80 cents to $1.20 per stacked cord. When oak or other tough wood predominates, the cost is higher than for wood more easily worked. One dollar per cord is the average cost for most cordwood contracts. One cord of wood makes a good wagonload, and the hauling cost will depend upon the distance.

Production of posts and mine props.—The contract price for cutting posts is usually from 2½ cents to 3 cents for each post. The cost of cutting is generally a little less for chestnut posts than for locust. From 60 to 80 posts can be hauled per load. So for a 2-trip haul it will cost about 3 cents per post to deliver them at the shipping point or market. This makes a total lumbering cost of 6 cents per post.

Mine props can be profitably cut only under favorable conditions. Most mine props are cut at the completion of lumbering operations and from material of small value. The hauling cost for mine props is about the same as as for posts. The owner can generally expect to realize nothing more on mine props than good wages for himself and team, unless his haul to market or shipping point is unusually short.

DETERMINING THE STUMPAGE VALUE OF TIMBER

After the owner has determined the cost of lumbering his material and knows the market value of the products, he is in position to determine the amount of money he may realize on his standing timber by doing his own lumbering and marketing. If, for example, the market value of his lumber is $25 per thousand and the cost of lumbering $12.25 per thousand, the amount which he may realize on his standing timber is the difference between these two amounts, or $12.75 per thousand board feet.

This amount, however, cannot be considered the real stumpage value. The real stumpage value of timber is the sum for which the standing timber will sell, and not the amount which the owner can realize on it by doing his own lumbering and marketing. The purchaser is entitled to a fair profit on his investment. If the purchaser had to pay the amount for stumpage which is shown in the example above, he could not market his timber for more than enough to pay the costs of lumbering and stumpage. It is generally considered that 20 percent is a fair profit for the operator. Therefore, the real stumpage value is the difference between the market value of the product and the total lumbering costs, less a reasonable profit on the lumbering and stumpage. This is usually expressed by the equation: $S = \frac{M}{1.\,Op} - C$, in which S represents stumpage value; M, market value; C, cost of logging; and Op, percent of profit. Thus, the real stumpage value of the timber in the example given above would be computed as follows: $S = \frac{\$25}{1.20} - \$12.25$. And the real stumpage value thus found would be $8.58 per thousand, instead of $12.75. If the owner does his own lumbering, the stumpage value and the profit on the lumbering and stumpage will both be his. The following examples showing the results obtained by farmers who did their own lumbering may prove of interest in this connection.

In the first case the sale was for sawed material to be loaded on cars at the nearest shipping point, which was 4 miles from the woodlot. The stand was mostly oak with a sprinkling of hickory and other hardwoods. The owner hired a portable-sawmill and did his own lumbering. The woodlot presented rather favorable conditions for lumbering, and the 4-mile haul to the railroad was over average country roads. The teams made two trips per day and averaged 1,000 feet per load. Lumbering costs were as follows:

	Per M bd. ft.
Cutting	$ 1.50
Skidding	2.00
Sawing	3.50
Hauling	2.25
Piling and loading on cars	.75
Total	$10.00

TABLE VI.—AMOUNTS OF MATERIAL SOLD AND PRICES RECEIVED

Materials	Amount (per B. M.)	Price per M bd. ft.	Total
Heading stock	8,600	$32	$275.20
Car stock	16,400	21	344.40
Ties	46,200	19	877.80
Side lumber	8,800	13	114.40
Total	80,000		$1611.80

At $10 per thousand the total lumbering cost for the operation amounted to $800. The total market value of the products was approximately $1,600. Thus, the market value of the products less the cost of lumbering left the owner $800, $10 per thousand, for stumpage and profit.

In the second example the woodlot was located but 3½ miles from the shipping point. The stand was largely maple and beech, but contained some oak, elm, yellow poplar and white ash, together with scattering trees of a few other species. The owner wished to sell his timber standing but was unable to get a stumpage price above $4 per thousand feet.

He found markets in the nearby city for his ash, elm and yellow poplar delivered in the log. Below are shown the amounts of the different woods sold and the prices received.

TABLE VII.—AMOUNTS OF MATERIAL SOLD AND PRICES RECEIVED

Wood	Amount (ft. B. M.)	Market price	Total
Elm	40,000	$22	$880
Poplar	12,000	40	480
Ash	4,000	40	160
Total	56,000		$1520

Logging costs were as follows:

	Per M bd. ft.
Cutting	$ 1.40
Skidding	1.60
Hauling (2 trips per day, 500 feet per load)	4.00
Total	$ 7.00

He then had a portable-sawmill move in and saw the remainder of the stand. Below are shown the amounts of sawed material of the different kinds sold and the prices received.

TABLE VIII.—AMOUNTS OF MATERIAL SOLD AND PRICES RECEIVED

Wood	Amount (ft. B. M.)	Market price	Total
Oak	30,000	$22	$ 660
Maple, beech and other hardwoods	314,000	13	4,082
Total	344,000		$4,742

Lumbering costs were as follows:

	Per M bd. ft.
Cutting	$ 1.40
Skidding	1.50
Sawing	3.50
Hauling (2 trips per day, 1,000 feet per load)	2.00
Loading on cars	.50
Total	$ 8.90

It is readily seen that at $7 per thousand the total lumbering cost for the 56,000 feet sold in the log was $392. Likewise, at $8.90 per thousand the total lumbering cost for the 344,000 feet of sawed material was $3,061.60. The sum of these two amounts, or $3,453.60, represents the entire cost of the lumbering operations. The total market value of all the products sold was $1,520+$4,742=$6,262. Taking the cost of lumbering from the market value of the products leaves approximately $2,800, or $7 per thousand feet, for stumpage and profit.

This owner not only realized $1,200 more for his timber than he was offered for it as it stood in his woodlot, but he also received good day wages for himself and teams through the winter. Moreover, there were left in parts of the woodlot fine stands of selected young growth which had been protected from careless logging operations, and which will insure a future stand of timber in his woodlot.

USES OF PRINCIPAL KINDS OF WOODS AND PRICES

The most important uses of our principal woods and the average "log run" value for each kind, under average woodlot condition.

are given below. The reader should remember that the average "log run" values are generally considerably below the value of material for special uses.

Oak.—Oak is the most abundant of Ohio timber trees. The users of this wood recognize two kinds, white and red; but botanists divide these into a large number of species. The principal species included in the white oak group are white oak, bur oak, swamp white oak, chestnut oak, chinquapin oak and post oak. In the red oak group are red oak, black oak, scarlet oak, pin oak and shingle oak. There are a few other species of each group found in Ohio, but they occur only scatteringly and are not important commercially. White oak is first in utility and is generally superior to red oak, although the latter makes the more rapid growth. The average price of red oak lumber is below the price paid for white oak, but for certain special uses it is much in demand. Red oak is more easily worked and kiln dried, and on account of its porous structure takes stains and varnish more rapidly. This accounts for its being preferred by the furniture makers, including those in the chair industry. For vehicles, ship building, agricultural implements, machine construction, etc., white oak is preferred on account of its greater strength, hardness and density.

The average price of oak is about $20 per thousand feet, although good clear plank can generally find a ready market at $45. Large oak logs suitable for quarter-sawing often bring $50 per thousand feet when delivered at the veneer mills. Large quantities are disposed of as rough forest products, such as posts, crossties, piling and cooperage stock. These products are usually sold by the piece. In some localities as much as 75 percent of the oak goes into railroad material.

PRINCIPAL USES OF OAK

Planing-mill products	Furniture
Vehicles and vehicle parts	Car construction
Building and general construction material	Agricultural implements
	Boxes and crates
Crossties	Fixtures
Sash, doors, blinds and general mill work	Chairs
	Plumbers' woodwork
Handles	Ship and boat building
Refrigerators and kitchen cabinets	Cooperage stock

Machine construction

Yellow poplar.—Next to oak, yellow poplar is perhaps the most important timber tree in Ohio. In different localities this wood is called whitewood, tulip poplar, yellow poplar and poplar; but yellow poplar is the most common name used for it in the market. For many purposes it is a highly valuable wood. It seasons well, takes an excellent polish, possesses a fine grain and is unexcelled for painting. There is no better wood on the market for carriages and automobile bodies, and it has few rivals for panel work. In some localities the wood of yellow poplar, particularly in young and immature trees or second growth, is inclined to be white and hard, somewhat resembling hickory. Wood cut from such trees is generally called "hickory poplar" by mill men. No doubt the color and texture of the wood of the tulip tree is affected not only by age, but also by soil, rate of growth and climatic conditions.

The average price of yellow poplar is about $30 per thousand feet, but there is usually plenty of demand for good clear plank at $50. Veneer mills generally offer an excellent market for large clear logs.

PRINCIPAL USES OF YELLOW POPLAR

Planing-mill products	Boxes and crates
Sash, doors, blinds and general mill work	Bungs and faucets
	Vehicles and vehicle parts
Car construction	Furniture
Agricultural implements	Fixtures
Pumps	Refrigerators and kitchen cabinets
Plumbers' woodwork	Caskets and coffins

Musical instruments

Elm.—There is usually no distinction made in the market between the four species of elm growing in Ohio. The white, or American, elm and the red, or slippery, elm are the most abundant; of these the former is the most important commercially. Rock elm is tougher than the others and is usually desired by vehicle makers. There is very little rock elm found in this State, but lumbermen often apply the term "rock elm" to tough wood cut from any of the species. The terms "hard," "soft," "red," "gray" and "swamp" are often applied to elm by lumbermen in different localities without much regard to species. Being heavy, hard, dense, tough and elastic, elm is well fitted for a number of special uses. It is preeminently the best wood for patent barrel hoops and bicycle rims. The average price for elm is about $20. It will generally pay well for the owner to look up a special market for his elm.

PRINCIPAL USES OF ELM

Vehicles and vehicle parts	Handles
Dairymen's, poultrymen's and apiarists' supplies	Furniture
	Planing-mill products
Trunks and valises	Fixtures
Hoops	Musical instruments
Chairs	Playground equipment
Agricultural implements	Machine construction
Saddles and harness	Brushes
Refrigerators and kitchen cabinets	Woodenware and novelties

Boxes and crates

Maple.—Lumbermen recognize two kinds of maple, hard and soft, although there are five species growing in Ohio. Sugar and black maple supply the hard maple, while the soft is contributed by red, silver and box elder, or ash-leaf maple. Sugar maple is commercially the most important and supplies practically all the hard maple sawed in Ohio. Its wood is called for by a greater number of users than any other wood grown in the State with the exception of white oak. The wood of the soft maple is softer than that of sugar maple and not so strong, but is strong enough for most purposes and is hard compared with such woods as basswood, yellow poplar and buckeye. The white, clean appearance of soft maple makes it desirable for furniture making, where it is sometimes stained in imitation of expensive cabinet woods. In many cases soft maple goes along with sugar maple and both are listed as hard maple, except when the strength and hardness of sugar maple is demanded as in the manufacture of vehicle parts, agricultural implements, etc. Basket manufacturers in northeastern Ohio employ maple extensively, maple and beech being the principal woods used. These two woods also supply much of the car blocking used by steel mills. Basket makers pay from $12 to $14 per thousand for logs delivered at their factories. Blocking generally brings from $13 to $15 loaded on the cars. The average price for maple lumber is about $15, with good clear plank bringing $25.

PRINCIPAL USES OF MAPLE

Boxes and crates	Elevators
Planing-mill products	Laundry appliances
Furniture	Agricultural implements
Handles	Vehicles and vehicle parts
Fixtures	Musical instruments
Woodenware and novelties	Car construction
Machine construction	Chairs
Sash, doors blinds and general mill work	Refrigerators and kitchen cabinets
	Pulleys and conveyors

Plumbers' woodwork

Ash.—There are five different kinds of ash growing in Ohio, but it is difficult to distinguish them in the wood. Lumbermen generally separate them into two general classes, white ash and black ash. Some manufacturers use both kinds indiscriminately, but for many purposes white ash is considered superior to black ash and commands a better price. The sawmills of Ohio report cutting annually 12 million feet of ash lumber, but much goes directly from the forest to the factories without passing through the sawmills. Much of the second-growth white ash used for handles is cut into logs, bolts or billets in the forest and shipped directly to the factories.

The average price of ash is less than $25 per thousand feet. The owner should look carefully into the matter of special markets for his ash before sawing it into lumber. Good clear ash logs frequently bring $40 per thousand feet when delivered at handle factories.

PRINCIPAL USES OF ASH

Handles	Vehicles and vehicle parts
Car construction	Planing-mill products
Dairymen's, poultrymen's and apiarists' supplies	Agricultural implements
	Furniture
Woodenware and novelties	Ship and boat building
Sash, doors, blinds and general mill work	Saddles and harness
	Musical instruments
Boxes and crates	

Hickory.—The woods of the different hickories are similar and hard to distinguish. Consequently, lumber dealers and manufacturers generally make no effort to keep the species separate. Hickory products are cut in Ohio from shellbark, shagbark, pignut, bitternut, mockernut and the small fruited hickory. The hardness, strength, toughness and flexibility of hickory make it highly valuable for a variety of special uses. It possesses these qualities to a greater extent than any other of our domestic woods, and no substitute has been found for it in a number of its special uses. This fact combined with the growing scarcity of hickory makes the wood a valuable one.

Hickory is primarily a vehicle and handle wood and fully eleven-twelfths of the amount used by Ohio manufacturers goes into these products. Other things being equal, wood which has grown rapidly is best; such stock with its broad annual rings is called second growth. The heartwood is reddish and the sapwood white. Formerly there was a decided prejudice against heartwood or "red hickory." This prejudice still exists to some extent, but it has been proved by Forest Service tests that, weight for weight, heart is as strong as sap. Like white ash much hickory in the form of butts, bolts and billets goes from the woods directly to the factories without passing through the sawmills. The average price of hickory is about $18 per thousand feet, but good clear logs frequently bring $35 per thousand feet delivered at the factories.

PRINCIPAL USES FOR HICKORY

Vehicles and vehicle parts	Handles
Agricultural implements	Sporting and athletic goods
Planing-mill products	Professional and scientific instruments
Boxes and crates	
Furniture	Brushes
Woodenware and novelties	Car construction

Basswood.—Lumbermen often refer to the basswood tree as linden and call the lumber "linn," but it generally goes under the name of basswood in the market. There are two species in Ohio, but the wood is so much alike that it would be exceedingly difficult to tell them apart in a lumberyard, and no practical purpose would be served. Basswood is the softest hardwood and has many qualities in common with yellow poplar. It is stiff, light and easily worked, does not stain, and is without taste or odor. These qualities put it in demand by manufacturers of kitchen furniture and shipping containers intended to hold food. Basswood is a favorite with woodenware manufacturers.

Most Ohio basswood is sawed into inch boards which sell for about $23 per thousand feet.

PRINCIPAL USES FOR BASSWOOD

Boxes and crates
Trunks and valises
Furniture
Sash, doors, blinds and general mill work
Handles
Agricultural implements
Car construction
Professional and scientific instruments
Woodenware and novelties
Dairymen's, poultrymen's and apiarists' supplies
Planing-mill products
Musical instruments
Fixtures
Frames and molding
Vehicles and vehicle parts
Refrigerators and kitchen cabinets

Chestnut.—The largest demand for chestnut is for rough forest products, as posts, crossties, telephone and telegraph poles, mine props and tanning extracts. Its attractive grain and beautiful figure have lately brought it into popularity for inside finish of houses and buildings, exterior trim and store and office fixtures. Being cheaper than oak it is frequently found in finish where oak was formerly demanded. The chestnut tree is subject to attacks by boring insects, which makes the wood usually defective and accounts for the presence on the market of the low-grade chestnut lumber known as "sound wormy." It is this grade which is used in such large quantities by the box makers and casket makers, and it is also this grade which the piano builders and furniture manufacturers use above any other wood for veneer backing and cases. Being light and porous, holding its shape well and having a special affinity for glue, it is admirably adapted for these purposes.

The most serious enemy of the chestnut tree and one which may cause its ultimate extinction in this country is the chestnut-bark disease or chestnut blight. This disease has already destroyed enormous quantities of chestnut in the eastern states but so far has not spread to Ohio, with the exception of one or two small infestations.

The average price for chestnut lumber is about $20 per thousand feet with good clear plank readily bringing $35. The average for sound wormy is about $12. Posts usually bring 10 cents at the woods. Poles are bought by the pole, or by the linear or "running" foot. A first-class 35-foot pole is generally worth $4.50 at the shipping point.

PRINCIPAL USES OF CHESTNUT

Boxes and crates
Caskets and coffins
Furniture
Sash, doors, blinds and general mill work
Agricultural instruments
Dairymen's, poultrymen's and apiarists' supplies
Plumbers' woodwork
Sporting and athletic goods
Car construction
Musical instruments
Planing-mill products
Fixtures
Crossties, poles and posts
Trunks and valises

Beech.—There is but one species of beech growing in this country, although users often speak of "white beech and "red beech." Both kinds come from the same tree, one being the sap and the other the heartwood. Some trees have a large percent of sapwood and others a large amount of heart. The beech tree seems disposed to decay as it gets older; much of the mature timber in this State is not sound. Until within recent years beech was considered of little value by manufacturers, and this, together with its tolerance of shade and rapid reproduction, accounts for the fact that it is found standing in nearly every Ohio woodlot, often to the exclusion of more important timber trees. Recently, however, beech has come into considerable favor as a flooring wood, and with the development of preservative treatment is becoming prominent in the production of "treatment" timbers, ties, posts, etc.

The average price of beech is about $14 per thousand feet.

PRINCIPAL USES OF BEECH

Boxes and crates
Handles
Planing-mill products
Woodenware and novelties
Machine construction
Musical instruments
Professional and scientific instruments
Vehicles and vehicle parts
Agricultural implements
Sash, doors, blinds and general mill work
Chairs
Playground equipment
Pulleys and conveyors
Furniture
Brushes

Walnut.—Black walnut is the most costly wood native to Ohio. Most of the available large trees have been cut, and the future supply must come largely from "second growth"—that is young trees which will grow up about farms and in the woods, as well as those planted in woodlots. The dark color of the heartwood gives the tree its name. The sapwood is white and not nearly as valuable as the heart. It should be remembered by those having walnut trees to sell that it is the heartwood which is valuable and that the heart forms slowly. A tree must be of considerable size and age before the heart is sufficiently developed to be worth much as lumber. Black walnut is not generally highly figured, but often the junction of roots with the trunk, crotches and burls yield fine figures from which is cut the best of veneer. The average price for black walnut lumber is about $40. Much walnut is shipped in the log to veneer mills or for export trade and does not pass through the sawmills. Large logs cut from old mature trees frequently bring $75 to $100 per thousand feet.

PRINCIPAL USES OF BLACK WALNUT

Planing-mill products	Musical instruments
Vehicles and vehicle parts	Furniture
Sash, doors, blinds and general mill work	Bungs and faucets
	Caskets and coffins
Machine construction	Fixtures
Plumbers' woodwork	Car construction

Sycamore.—Sycamore is found along banks of rivers and streams and along the edges of swamps and lowlands throughout Ohio, but is not an important tree commercially. Formerly it was used almost entirely for butcher blocks and lining for refrigerators, but now the largest demand is for veneer in built-up lumber. Quarter-sawed sycamore has a striking grain and is growing in popularity, being used largely for making sewing machine tables, cabinet work, furniture and interior finish. The trunk of this tree often attains an enormous size, but those more than 3 feet in diameter are generally hollow.

The average price for sycamore is about $16. but it frequently brings considerably more for some special use.

PRINCIPAL USES OF SYCAMORE

Planing-mill products	Boxes and crates
Agricultural implements	Sash, doors, blinds and general mill work
Musical instruments	
Furniture	Refrigerators and kitchen cabinets
Vehicles and vehicle parts	Brushes

Cottonwood.—Owing to the difficulty in seasoning cottonwood, it is better adapted for veneer than lumber. In trade two classes of cottonwood lumber, yellow and white, are often distinguished. The former refers to the heartwood and the latter to the light-colored sapwood. Cottonwood lumber has qualities similar to basswood and yellow poplar and is often used as a substitute for these higher-priced woods. In the form of veneer it is used largely by the manufacturers of built-up lumber which is used for trunks, vehicle bodies, drawer bottoms, veneer boxes, etc. A large quantity of cottonwood is used for making boxes and crates. There is an increasing demand for cottonwood in the form of cordwood to be used in making paper pulp, and since it is an exceedingly rapid growing tree, easy to propagate and can be made to utilize waste places along streams and lowlands, it offers a favorable opportunity in many localities for commercial planting. The average price of cottonwood lumber is about $16 a thousand feet.

PRINCIPAL USES FOR COTTONWOOD

- Boxes and crates
- Vehicles and vehicle parts
- Planing-mill products
- Fixtures
- Laundry appliances
- Dairymen's, poultrymen's and apiarists' supplies
- Agricultural instruments
- Car construction
- Sash, doors, blinds and general mill work
- Refrigerators and kitchen cabinets
- Trunks and valises
- Paper pulp

Black cherry.—Several species of cherry are found in Ohio, but only one, the black or wild cherry, is important as a timber tree. Black cherry is one of America's finest cabinet woods. Its principal demand has always been for furniture, finish and trimming. It holds its shape well and works easily, which, together with its other excellent qualities, make it a favorite with the manufacturers of electrotype backing and account for its demand by makers of musical instruments, electrical appliances, etc. The forest-grown tree usually develops a long trunk free from limbs and knots, but trees growing in the open generally have too many limbs to be valuable for timber. Like other valuable trees, cherry is usually not present in sufficient amounts to enable the woodlot owner to market it to the best advantage. The average price is about $25 per thousand feet, with good clear lumber bringing $50 and better.

PRINCIPAL USES FOR BLACK CHERRY

- Car construction
- Machine construction
- Sash, doors, blinds and general mill work
- Fixtures
- Musical instruments
- Furniture
- Plumbers' woodwork
- Ship and boat building
- Vehicles and vehicle parts
- Planing-mill products

Table IX shows approximately the amount of material cut by Ohio sawmills in 1913 from each of our principal timber trees.

TABLE IX.—OHIO TIMBER PRODUCTION IN 1913

Species	Amount cut (B. B. M.)
Oak	207,500,000
Yellow Poplar	47,900,000
Maple	36,300,000
Beech	33,800,000
Elm	19,300,000
Hickory	15,500,000
Ash	13,000,000
Chestnut	12,000,000
Basswood	8,800,000
Walnut	7,100,000
Sycamore	2,000,000
Cottonwood	700,000
Cherry	500,000

COOPERATIVE MARKETING

Farmers may well interest themselves in the question of community cooperation in the marketing of their woodlot products. There is in Ohio more than 4,500,000 acres of woodland. Fully 3,000,000 acres of this is in farm woodlots. With an average stand of only 3,000 board feet to the acre, these farm woodlots contain 9,000,000,000 board feet of lumber. Surely marketing the yield from our farm woodlots is a problem of importance. The farmers who own this timber want to make the most of it.

Many owners now feel that it is less important for them to learn how to make their woodlots yield greater crops of timber than it is to learn how to be sure of getting what their timber crop is worth. Generally the owner is not in a position to harvest and market his own timber. Lumbering is a business which requires expensive machinery, efficient operation, a knowledge of markets and ability to dispose of the product advantageously. The competition among local buyers and mill men is seldom active enough to afford the owner much protection against a losing bargain if he disposes of his timber on the stump.

A lumbering operation in the average farm woodlot is not on sufficiently large scale nor is the work done with adequate equipment to enable the owner to get their true value for his products. The ordinary portable-sawmill operation is likely to produce boards or dimension material of uneven thickness. Various sorts of lumber may be sawed in such a manner as to make grading and sorting for market almost impossible. A purchaser receiving a shipment of this sort finds it highly unsatisfactory compared with the standardized product of the large mills. The woodlot frequently contains different kinds of wood each of which would be quite valuable if it were present in sufficient quantity to be marketed advantageously, but due to the limited quantity present must be disposed of at a greatly reduced figure. These facts have caused many woodlot owners to wonder if by collective bargaining they cannot be able to secure decidedly better terms than when each sells independently of the rest.

The cooperative marketing of timber presents many of the same difficulties which are encountered when farmers organize to market other farm crops. But unlike most other farm crops, the timber crop need not be marketed in a hurry. Plenty of time may be used to investigate markets and determine what it should bring.

An association of farmers holding sufficient forest land to make a good working forest would be in a position to market a high-grade product and dispose of their timber to much greater advantage than they could do as individuals. Material demanded for special uses and bringing a high price could be harvested and marketed in carload lots. Such cooperation would permit of the best class of portable-mill operation, insure better utilization and should result in better prices to the owners of stumpage.

Such an association could secure the services of a trained forester who would act as advisor in the matter of lumbering and marketing, and who could also outline proper plans of woodlot management based on localized conditions. It must be recognized that a full utilization of the productive value of the farm woodlot can come only after those forestry principles intended to make the woodlot produce timber of the highest quality possible have been adopted and put into practice.

More and more it is going to pay the farmer to have high-grade woodlot products to market; and in order that the area devoted to the growing of timber may be producing the greatest amount possible of those kinds of wood that are most salable in his particular region, it must be managed and cared for according to the recognized principles of forestry.

Under such a system of cooperation which would include not only the harvesting and marketing of the woodlot products but also placing the woodlot under a sound plan of farm management much of good should come to Ohio woodlot owners.

UNITED STATES DEPARTMENT OF AGRICULTURE

FARMERS' BULLETIN

WASHINGTON, D. C. 715 JUNE 29, 1916

Contribution from the Forest Service, Henry S. Graves, Forester.

MEASURING AND MARKETING WOODLOT PRODUCTS.

By WILBUR R. MATTOON and WILLIAM B. BARROWS, *Forest Examiners.*[1]

CONTENTS.

AIM.

Lack of familiarity with the business of timber selling usually puts the owner of a small woodland at a disadvantage, and in many regions material from the woodlot is sold for considerably less than its real value. The loss to the farmers is, in the aggregate, very large. In order to stop this loss, it is necessary that the farmer inform himself about the different kinds and grades of woodlot products, the methods of estimating and measuring them and ascertaining their value, the methods of selling, the markets, and the current market prices. Especially does he need reliable information about the amount and real value of his standing timber and the location of good markets. It is the aim of this bulletin to assist woodlot owners in getting information of this kind, so that they may market their woodlot products at fair prices.[2]

PRINCIPAL WOODLOT PRODUCTS.

LOGS.

Many wood-manufacturing industries obtain their raw material in the form of logs and bolts. Logs may be sold by sizes and grades

[1] Mr. Barrows's contribution deals with the subject of measuring, and is found on pp. 12 to 26, inclusive.

[2] Information in regard to the best methods of improving and growing timber in the farm woodlot is given in Farmers' Bulletin 711, "The Care and Improvement of the Woodlot."

or without classification by the lot. Selling "log run" is simple and direct, but offers good opportunity for speculation, usually to the advantage of the buyer, whose knowledge of timber is better than that of the seller. The method is advisable only after the owner has made a careful estimate of the amount and quality of the standing timber. Selling by sizes and grades, when these are defined in the contract, often results in larger money returns.

The quality of a log depends upon its dimensions and grade. Logs are inspected for the number and character of standard defects, which determine the grade, and are measured by taking the length and the average diameter at the small end. Large logs are more valuable than small ones of the same grade.

For example: In one market medium-grade 10-foot red-oak logs from 16 to 30 inches in diameter were worth $19 per 1,000 feet; logs from 31 to 36 inches in diameter, $23; and logs 37 inches and over in diameter, $25. Logs with only slight defects or none were worth from $6 to $10 more, and logs with more defects were worth from $3 to $5 less than these prices.

GRADING.

The grade of a log depends upon the number and character of its defects. Among those recognized by the lumberman as standard are knots, rot, shakes, season checks, frost cracks, sun scald, fire scars, seams, wormholes, stain, spiral or crooked grain, cat faces, and crook in the log. Standard grading rules may be applied to all species collectively for the purposes of rough grading, but usually there are different specifications for different species. In general, grading is more common and the number of grades larger for the more valuable woods than for the inferior kinds of timber.

Unfortunately, there are no standard specifications for log grades. Rough local grades are in quite general use, but are not defined. They are of only limited aid to the seller because they are subject to differences of interpretation.

The adoption by some acknowledged authority and the recognition throughout a State or region of a few standard grades and sizes for logs of various kinds of trees would be of very great assistance in the marketing of woodlot timber. It would afford common ground on which buyer and seller might meet.[1] Some of the various lumber manufacturers' associations publish specifications for the grading of logs of the more important trees, copies of which are available upon application to the secretaries.

Three rough grades are in use in many parts of the eastern United States. These are commonly known as "No. 1," "No. 2," and

[1] There is an opportunity for the various State forestry organizations in cooperation with lumber associations to work for the adoption of standard log grades in their States.

"No. 3," or as "good," "common," and "cull." In some regions a No. 1 log must cut its full scale in No. 1 common lumber or better, a No. 2 log must saw out two-thirds of the scale in No. 1 common or better, and a No. 3 log must cut one-half of its scale in No. 2 common with a little of the better grades. Two small limb knots are allowed in a No. 1 log, but two large knots or body knots make it a No. 2 grade, and if they occur at each end, a cull log. Exterior checking and shallow cat faces are not defects, since they go into the slab only.

In practice, the second grade sells for about two-thirds and the third grade for about one-half, or less, the price of the first grade. In some localities only two grades are used.

Other forms of grading used in different regions are: Grade No. 1, logs 10 inches and over in diameter with surface and ends clear

F-1ll1-A

FIG. 1.– High-grade logs from farm woodlots, such as these, can be profitably shipped by rail to outside markets. (White oak, yellow poplar, ash, and basswood.)

of defect, and sap wood bright in color; grade No. 2, logs having not more than three standard defects, or slightly wormy; and grade No. 3, logs falling below the No. 2 grade, chiefly because of worm and rot defects.[1]

The veneer industry secures most of its raw product in the form of logs and flitches (large-sized pieces sawed from logs). Both are sold by the thousand board feet. The specifications are not uniform. The essential points refer to the species, the size of the logs, and the grade of the wood. Diameters for hardwoods run mostly from 14 inches up, and lengths from 6 to 16 feet. Logs must be cut 4 inches over the specified length to allow for trimming. The rules for yellow poplar given below[2] will serve as an illustration of the manner of grading, although to make the specifications complete the defects would have to be defined. Very few logs meet the requirements of

[1] The National Hardwood Manufacturers' Association of the United States, Cincinnati, Ohio, issues grading specifications for grades of logs for several kinds of wood.

[2] Specifications from forthcoming bulletin, "The Veneer Industry in the United States."

the No. 1 grade, and the buyer exercises discretion in departing more or less from this standard.

No. 1 yellow poplar logs must be straight-grained and free from knots, cat faces, wind-shakes, rotten center, double hearts, hearts grown to one side, and other defects. These specifications apply to logs up to and including 12 feet in length; logs 14 feet and 16 feet long may have one defect not over 6 inches in diameter; logs over 16 feet long may have two defects not over 6 inches in diameter; also a log may have a hole in the center not greater than one-fifth of the diameter of the log.

No. 2 yellow poplar logs must be the same as No. 1, except they may have defects not to exceed one-third of the circumference.

Cull logs are those that grade poorer than No. 2.

Logs will command full price when freshly cut, but logs that have suffered from exposure are not desirable under any circumstances and will at no time bring any but low prices. Diameters will be taken the small way across the small end and the contents scaled by the log rule agreed upon.

WEIGHT.

A knowledge of the average weights of logs of different species in a green and a dry state is useful in calculating the cost of handling the material and making shipments by rail. Table 1 shows these weights for logs, bolts, cordwood, and rough lumber.

TABLE 1.—*Approximate weights of various woodlot products.*[1]

Species.	Lumber (per 1,000 board feet).			Logs (per 1,000 board feet log scale, Doyle rule).[3]						Cordwood, bolts, butts, etc., per cord.[3]	
	1 inch thick.		[illegible] (classed as 1 inch thick).[2]	Diameter inside bark at small end.							
				12 inches.		18 inches.		24 inches.			
	Green.	Air-dry.		Green.	Dry.	Green.	Dry.	Green.	Dry.	Green.	Dry.
	Lbs.	Lbs.	Lbs.	Lbs.	Lbs.	Lbs.	Lbs.	Lbs.	Lbs.	Lbs.	Lbs.
Ash, white	4,[illegible]	3,[illegible]	3,[illegible]	11,100	9,700	7,700	6,800	6,600	5,700	4,300	3,800
Basswood	3,[illegible]	2,100	2,[illegible]	9,[illegible]	5,900	6,600	4,100	5,400	3,500	3,700	2,300
Beech	[illegible]	3,[illegible]	[illegible]	12,700	10,100	8,900	7,000	7,500	6,000	5,000	3,800
Birch, yellow	4,[illegible]	[illegible]	4,000	[illegible]	10,200	9,200	7,200	7,800	6,100	5,100	4,000
Cherry, black	[illegible]	3,[illegible]	4,000	10,[illegible]	8,[illegible]	7,[illegible]	5,800	6,200	4,900	4,100	3,200
Chestnut	4,[illegible]	2,[illegible]	2,[illegible]	12,[illegible]	7,[illegible]	8,[illegible]	4,900	7,500	4,100	4,900	2,700
Cottonwood	[illegible]	2,[illegible]	2,[illegible]	10,700	6,300	7,[illegible]	4,100	6,300	3,700	4,200	2,500
Elm, soft	4,[illegible]	2,[illegible]	3,[illegible]	11,200	8,000	7,800	5,600	6,600	4,700	4,100	3,100
Elm, rock	4,[illegible]	3,[illegible]	3,[illegible]	12,[illegible]	9,200	8,[illegible]	6,100	7,500	5,500	4,800	3,600
Gum, red	[illegible]	2,[illegible]	3,[illegible]	10,700	7,800	7,[illegible]	5,900	6,900	4,600	4,200	3,100
Hickory	[illegible]	4,[illegible]	5,[illegible]	13,700	11,[illegible]	10,[illegible]	8,200	8,700	7,000	5,700	4,600
Locust, black	4,800	4,100		13,[illegible]	11,100	9,[illegible]	7,900	7,900	6,700	5,200	4,400
Maple, sugar	4,700	3,[illegible]	4,[illegible]	12,[illegible]	10,[illegible]	9,[illegible]	7,000	7,600	5,600	5,000	3,900
Maple, red	4,[illegible]	3,000	3,000	11,[illegible]	8,200	8,[illegible]	5,700	7,100	4,900	4,700	3,200
Maple, silver	[illegible]	2,[illegible]	[illegible]	10,[illegible]	7,[illegible]	7,[illegible]	5,400	6,200	4,600	4,100	3,000
Oak, red	[illegible]	[illegible]	3,[illegible]	11,800	10,100	10,[illegible]	7,000	8,800	6,000	5,800	3,900
Oak, white	[illegible]	4,[illegible]	[illegible]	14,[illegible]	11,000	10,000	7,700	8,500	6,500	5,100	4,300
Sycamore	4,[illegible]	2,[illegible]	3,[illegible]	12,[illegible]	8,500	8,300	5,[illegible]	7,100	4,900	4,700	3,200
Yellow poplar	[illegible]	2,[illegible]	2,[illegible]	8,[illegible]	6,500	8,[illegible]	4,500	5,200	3,900	3,400	2,500
Tupelo[4]	5,[illegible]	[illegible]		13,100	8,[illegible]	[illegible]	5,[illegible]	8,[illegible]	5,000	5,000	3,300
Walnut	4,[illegible]	[illegible]	4,[illegible]	11,[illegible]	8,[illegible]	8,[illegible]	[illegible]	7,100	4,900	4,700	3,200
Willow	4,[illegible]	2,[illegible]		[illegible]	5,900	8,200	4,100	7,000	3,500	4,600	2,300

[1] These weights and those in Tables 2, 3, and 5 are not the shipping weights prescribed by any railroad or any State railroad commission.

[2] Weights of rough lumber in this column are official standard weights of the Hardwood Manufacturers Association of the United States. Rough lumber is usually cut more than 1 inch thick, to allow for shrinkage in seasoning.

[3] Weights of logs and cordwood computed from A. K. Armstrong's weights of hardwood per cubic foot (90 cubic feet per cord).

[4] Figures for tupelo may be used for black gum or pepperidge.

BOLTS AND BILLETS.

Bolts are short sections of logs. Billets are obtained by halving, quartering, or otherwise splitting or sawing bolts lengthwise. The split pieces of cordwood are good examples of billets. Sawed billets include flitches, squares, and other forms of partly manufactured products. Because splitting causes a great deal of waste, it has been largely superseded by sawing. For example, a cord of average-sized hickory bolts that will yield only about 700 rived spoke billets may be sawed into 900 billets. Bolts and billets are used for cooperage, wood pulp, excelsior, wooden ware (pails and tubs), handles, vehicle parts, some agricultural implements, fruit and vegetable packages, athletic goods, pencils, etc.

F-1 W8U

FIG. 2.—Stave bolts and billets of white and red oak, cut 36 inches to make 34-inch staves.

Cooperage plants consume very large quantities of material which comes from the woods in the form of bolts and billets. Wood pulp is made from pieces of many shapes and sizes. Much of the raw material used by the handle and wagon-wheel industries is ash and hickory bolts and billets, the hickory going into ax and hammer handles and wagon spokes and the ash into hoe, rake, and shovel handles.

Bolts are measured and sold by the cord, by linear feet, and by board feet. If they are 12 inches or over in diameter, they are usually sold by board measure. Billets are frequently sold by the piece or count, particularly if sawed and of uniform size, or are stacked and measured in cords, either standard or short cords of specified width. Table 2 gives the weight per stack of bolts of different kinds of wood and of different lengths and diameters.

The grades and specifications used in slack cooperage are very numerous, but the forms and qualities for tight-cooperage stock, including staves, hoops, and heading, are much restricted. Specifications refer to the species, length, width, thickness, and soundness of timber. The white oaks are practically the only woods used in the manufacture of tight cooperage; but many different kinds of wood may be made into barrels for flour, sugar, vegetables, salt, cement, lime, etc. One representative specification for stave bolts for tight cooperage reads:

Stave bolts must be made from sound white or post oak; must measure 4 inches and up from inside of sap to heart edge; must be free from worm holes, season checks, knots, shake, and dote; and must be full 37 inches long, sawed square on end to equalize 36 inches.[1]

For handle stock, the specifications call for second growth, straight, sound bolts or billets of specified length. Ash bolts for farm-tool handles are mostly from 30 to 60 inches in length. For hammer, ax, and other handles, hickory is bought under similar conditions but including shorter lengths. Material which is inferior to that called for is frequently accepted, especially when the users are in urgent need of supplies.

TABLE 2.—*Approximate weights per stack of bolts, green and dry, of different kinds of wood and of different lengths and diameters.*

Species.	Diameter.	Length of bolt—feet.								Weight per cubic foot.
		2½ (⅝ cord.)	3 (¾ cord.)	3½ (⅞ cord.)	4 (1 cord.)	4½ (1⅛ cords.)	5 (1¼ cords.)	5½ (1⅜ cords.)	6 (1½ cords.)	
		Weight per stack—pounds.								
	Inches.									
Ash, white:										
Green	6	2,600	3,200	3,700	4,200	4,800	5,300	5,800	6,300	48.2
	9	2,800	3,300	3,900	4,400	5,000	5,500	6,100	6,600	
	12	2,900	3,400	4,000	4,600	5,100	5,700	6,300	6,900	
Air dry	6	2,300	2,800	3,200	3,700	4,200	4,600	5,100	5,600	42.1
	9	2,400	2,900	3,400	3,900	4,300	4,800	5,300	5,800	
	12	2,500	3,000	3,500	4,000	4,500	5,000	5,500	6,000	
Basswood:										
Green	6	2,300	2,700	3,200	3,600	4,100	4,500	5,000	5,500	41.3
	9	2,400	2,800	3,300	3,800	4,300	4,700	5,200	5,700	
	12	2,500	2,900	3,400	3,900	4,400	4,900	5,400	5,900	
Air dry	6	1,400	1,700	2,000	2,300	2,600	2,800	3,100	3,400	25.8
	9	1,500	1,800	2,100	2,400	2,700	3,000	3,300	3,600	
	12	1,500	1,800	2,100	2,500	2,800	3,100	3,400	3,700	
Cottonwood:										
Green	6	2,600	3,100	3,600	4,100	4,600	5,100	5,600	6,100	48.5
	9	2,700	3,200	3,700	4,300	4,800	5,300	5,900	6,400	
	12	2,800	3,300	3,900	4,400	5,000	5,500	6,100	6,600	
Air dry	6	1,500	1,800	2,100	2,400	2,700	3,000	3,300	3,600	27.3
	9	1,600	1,900	2,200	2,500	2,800	3,100	3,500	3,800	
	12	1,600	1,900	2,300	2,600	2,900	3,200	3,600	3,900	
Elm, rock and white:										
Green	6	2,700	3,200	3,700	4,300	4,800	5,300	5,900	6,400	48.6
	9	2,800	3,400	3,900	4,500	5,000	5,600	6,100	6,700	
	12	2,900	3,500	4,000	4,600	5,200	5,800	6,300	6,900	
Air dry	6	1,900	2,300	2,700	3,000	3,400	3,800	4,200	4,600	34.6
	9	2,000	2,400	2,800	3,200	3,600	4,000	4,400	4,800	
	12	2,100	2,500	2,900	3,300	3,700	4,100	4,500	4,900	
Hickory, shagbark:										
Green	6	3,500	4,200	4,900	5,600	6,300	7,000	7,700	8,400	63.8
	9	3,700	4,400	5,100	5,900	6,600	7,300	8,100	8,800	
	12	3,800	4,500	5,300	6,100	6,800	7,600	8,300	9,100	
Air dry	6	2,800	3,400	4,000	4,500	5,100	5,700	6,200	6,800	51.8
	9	3,000	3,600	4,100	4,700	5,300	5,900	6,500	7,100	
	12	3,100	3,700	4,300	4,900	5,500	6,100	6,700	7,300	

Stacks are 4 feet in height by 8 feet long, made up of bolts of different sizes. Bolts 4 feet long make a standard cord, while shorter lengths make "short cords," and longer lengths a cord and over.

[1] Tentative specifications by the Forest Service for sales on National Forests in Arkansas.

POLES.

Chestnut and eastern white cedar furnish the bulk of the eastern pole timber. Specifications for chestnut poles generally require material to be of the best quality second-growth live chestnut (cut during the winter), of specified dimensions, butt cut, squared at both ends, reasonably straight, well proportioned from tip to butt, peeled, and with knots trimmed close. Defects looked for in inspection are crookedness, split tops and butts, sap and butt rot, checks, and shakes. Poles are assigned to two or three classes, according to their length, top circumference, and circumference measured at 6 feet from the butt. Poles of the 40-foot class, for example, are required by one representative pole company to be 24 inches in top circumference[1] and 48 inches in basal circumference, while second-class poles of the same length measure only 22 and 46 inches, respectively, at the two points.

The dimensions shown in Table 3 for classes A, B, and C, with only slight modifications, are used by most telegraph and railroad companies and other purchasers of poles. The corresponding cubic contents and weights shown will be useful in making shipments. The figures are too low by from 10 to 20 per cent for full-bodied trees with small butt swell and likewise too high for trees with a marked basal swell.

As poles season they become lighter and in one year lose about 20 per cent of their weight when green. Table 4 shows the loss in weight in chestnut poles due to seasoning for monthly periods up to 15 months. To determine the approximate weight of chestnut poles after partial seasoning, apply the percentage of loss in weight shown in Table 4 to the green weight in Table 3.

TABLE 3.—*Approximate weights of green chestnut poles of different sizes.*[2]

CLASS A.

Length.	Circumference.			Diameter.			Volume.	Weight.[3]
	Top.	6 feet from butt.	Butt.	Top.	6 feet from butt.	Butt.		
Feet.	*Inches.*	*Inches.*	*Inches.*	*Inches.*	*Inches.*	*Inches.*	*Cu. ft.*	*Pounds.*
30	24	40	43	7.6	12.7	13.7	20.0	1,100
35	24	43	46	7.6	13.7	14.6	26.0	1,430
40	24	45	48	7.6	14.3	15.3	31.5	1,730
45	24	48	51	7.6	15.3	16.2	39.1	2,150
50	24	51	54	7.6	16.2	17.2	47.8	2,630
55	22	54	58	7.0	17.2	18.5	56.5	3,110
60	22	57	61	7.0	18.1	19.4	67.0	3,680
65	22	60	64	7.0	19.1	20.4	79.3	4,370
70	22	63	67	7.0	20.1	21.3	91.1	5,010
75	22	66	71	7.0	21.0	22.6	107.4	5,930
80	22	70	74	7.0	22.3	23.6	127.4	7,010
85	22	73	78	7.0	23.2	24.8	145.1	8,000
90	22	76	81	7.0	24.2	25.8	165.9	9,120

[1] Equivalent to 7.6 inches in diameter.

[2] Sizes conform to standard specifications of the National Electric Light Association.

[3] Based on a weight of 55 pounds per cubic foot.

TABLE 3.—*Approximate weights of green chestnut poles of different sizes*—Continued.

CLASS B.

Length.	Circumference.			Diameter.			Volume.	Weight.
	Top.	6 feet from butt.	Butt.	Top.	6 feet from butt.	Butt.		
Feet.	*Inches.*	*Inches.*	*Inches.*	*Inches.*	*Inches.*	*Inches.*	*Cu. ft.*	*Pounds.*
30	22	36	38	7.0	11.5	12.1	18.5	910
35	22	40	42	7.0	12.7	13.4	22.7	1,220
40	22	43	46	7.0	13.7	14.6	28.5	1,570
45	22	47	50	7.0	15.0	15.9	36.9	2,030
50	22	50	53	7.0	15.9	16.9	45.0	2,480
55	22	53	57	7.0	16.9	18.1	54.7	3,010
60	22	56	60	7.0	17.8	19.1	65.1	3,580
65	22	59	63	7.0	18.8	20.1	77.2	4,250
70	22	62	67	7.0	19.7	21.3	90.1	4,960
75	22	65	70	7.0	20.7	22.3	104.9	5,770
80	22	69	74	7.0	22.0	23.6	124.6	6,850
85	22	72	78	7.0	22.9	24.8	142.1	7,820
90	22	75	81	7.0	23.9	25.8	162.2	8,920
CLASS C.								
30	20	33	35	6.4	10.5	11.1	13.7	750
35	20	36	38	6.4	11.5	12.1	18.3	1,010
40	20	40	42	6.4	12.7	13.4	24.4	1,340
45	20	43	46	6.4	13.7	14.6	30.9	1,700
50	20	46	49	6.4	14.6	15.6	38.0	2,090
55	20	49	53	6.4	15.6	16.9	46.7	2,570

TABLE 4.—*Weights of chestnut poles during seasoning, expressed in per cent of green weight, for poles cut in the different seasons.*[1]

Duration of seasoning.	Season when cut.				Duration of seasoning.	Season when cut.			
	Spring.	Summer.	Autumn.	Winter.		Spring.	Summer.	Autumn.	Winter.
Months.	*Per cent.*	*Per cent.*	*Per cent.*	*Per cent.*	*Months.*	*Per cent.*	*Per cent.*	*Per cent.*	*Per cent.*
0	100	100	100	100	8	82	85	85	82
1	94	93	96	98	9	82	85	84	81
2	90	89	94	95	10	82	84	83	80
3	87	88	93	93	11	82	83	82	79
4	86	87	92	90	12	81	82	81	79
5	85	87	91	88	13	80	81	80	79
6	84	86	89	85	14	80	80	79	78
7	83	86	87	84	15	79	79	79	78

[1] Based on weights reported for 600 poles cut in Thorndale, Pa. (See Forest Service Circular 103, Seasoning of Telephone and Telegraph Poles, p. 11; also, Bulletin 84, Preservative Treatment of Poles, p. 51.) Apparent irregularities, like the percentages shown for the eighth to tenth months in the column headed "Spring" and the fifteenth month under "Autumn" are seemingly due to local conditions in relative humidity of the atmosphere.

PILING.

The classification or grading of piling depends largely upon its use, whether in fresh water, salt water, or on land, and upon its form and size. Very often the kind of wood is not specified, and the requirements refer to straightness, length, and butt diameter measured 3 feet from the end. Specifications are sometimes rather brief and simple, and piling then becomes one of the easiest classes of timber to grade for the market. Important construction work often calls for specifications more or less similar to the following.[1]

All piling shall be cut from sound, live trees of slow growth and firm grain, and free from ring heart, wind-shakes, decay, large or unsound knots, or any

[1] Based upon standard specifications of The Panama Canal.

other defects that will impair their strength or durability. The trees shall be butt cut, above the ground swell, and shall taper uniformly from butt to tip. Piles shall be so straight that the line joining the centers of the ends will fall entirely within the pile, and that in the opinion of the inspector they can be subjected to hard driving without injury. No short or reverse bends will be allowed. Bark shall be peeled from the entire length of all piles, and all knots shall be trimmed close. No pile will be accepted with a top measuring less than 6 inches diameter. The allowable diameter shall be as follows: Butts of piles under 30 feet in length to be from 12 to 16 inches, and butts of piles from 30 to 50 feet in length to be from 12 to 18 inches.

Piling is sold at a stated price per linear foot for specified dimensions and kinds of wood. The price increases rapidly with increase in length and in desirability of form or taper. Handling and transportation costs are large because of the heavy weight of sticks of this size. Table 5 shows the approximate weight of piling of different sizes and of different kinds of wood in both green and dry condition.

TABLE 5.—*Approximate weights of piling of different sizes, green and dry, for different kinds of wood, also weight per cubic foot of each.*

Length.	White oak.		Black oak.		Sugar maple.		
	Green.	Air-dry.	Green.	Air-dry.	Green.	Air-dry.	
	Weight—pounds.						
Feet.							
20	610	470	620	480	530	460	
25	770	590	770	580	660	530	
30	920	700	930	690	810	640	
35	1,080	820	1,080	770	900	750	
40	1,580	1,200	1,500	1,140	1,410	1,100	
45	1,780	1,350	1,700	1,280	1,590	1,210	
50	1,980	1,500	1,880	1,430	1,770	1,370	
	Weights per cubic foot used above—pounds.						
	62.7	48.0	62.5	47.6	55.9	44.4	

Length.	Chestnut.		White elm.		Black gum.		Increase with top diameter of 8″.
	Green.	Air-dry.	Green.	Air-dry.	Green.	Air-dry.	
	Weight—pounds.						
Feet.							*Per cent.*
20	540	290	490	340	440	350	15.3
25	670	370	600	430	550	430	15.1
30	810	440	730	510	660	520	15.6
35	940	520	860	600	770	620	15.7
40	1,390	790	1,290	880	1,150	920	12.3
45	1,590	880	1,380	990	1,270	1,030	11.9
50	1,770	980	1,540	1,090	1,410	1,140	12.3
	Weights per cubic foot used above—pounds.						
	54.8	30.2	48.8	34.6	41.7	36.2	

Top diameter, 6 inches; butt diameter, 12 inches for piling 20 to 35 feet inclusive; 14 inches for piling 40 to 50 feet inclusive.

CROSSTIES.

The specifications for railroad ties in most cases are for sound timber of good quality, stripped of bark, and free from imperfections that would impair their strength and durability, such as shakes and loose or decayed knots. The ties must be sawed or hewed smooth on two parallel faces, and the ends must be cut square. Pole ties are made of round timber on which are hewed two parallel faces; square ties are hewed or sawed into rectangular shape.

Ties are classified according to the species of wood, on the basis of its wearing and lasting qualities and need for preservative treatment. They are further classified into two or more grades, depending upon their thickness and width of face.

Class A ties consist of the more durable woods, and generally include white oaks, black walnut, black cherry, chestnut, sassafras, and red mulberry. Class B is made up of such woods as red oaks, beech, hickories, maples, sycamores, black gum, elms, and several others of the less durable woods requiring preservative treatment before using. Standard ties are either 8 or 8½ feet in length. No. 1 ties, for example, on some railroad schedules, if they are sawed ties, must be 7 inches thick by 8 inches wide on the face; if hewed on all sides or sawed on the faces, they must be 7 inches thick and not less than 7 inches nor more than 12 inches wide at any place on the face. No. 2 ties are between 6 and 9 inches thick and not less than 6 inches wide on the face. Variations in length of 1 inch under or 2 inches over the specifications and in thickness of ½ inch under or 1 inch over are allowed by many purchasers. Mine ties run from 3 to 6 feet in length and down to 4 by 6 inches in cross dimensions.

Prices are exceedingly variable in different parts of the country, depending upon the kind of wood, size, grade, and distance of the producing point from the larger trunk-line railroads. In middle Tennessee, for example, farmers receive from 40 to 50 cents for class A white oak ties of large size delivered along the track, while in Ohio a similar tie nets the farmer from 60 to 70 cents. Chestnut ties of the largest size bring about 70 cents each in New England.

MINE TIMBERS.

The kinds and forms of timbers in demand for mines are many, and, as a rule, many kinds of wood are usable. The principal forms of round or rough material, other than lumber, follow:

Mine props are round timbers used as main supports for the roof and sides of tunnels: in diameter they vary from 4 to 14 inches, and in length mostly from 3 to 12 feet. For chestnut, prices are from 1 to 2 cents per linear foot at the mines in Pennsylvania.

Lagging is round timber about 3 inches in diameter and 7 feet in length, used to fill in behind the props and caps to form the sides and roofing of the tunnels. Bars are extra long lagging. The mines in Pennsylvania pay about 3 cents apiece for lagging.

Caps are hewed or sawed pieces of timber of different sizes laid across the tops of pairs of props as a support for the roof lagging, which runs lengthwise of the tunnel.

Sills as foundation for props are from 8 to 14 inches in diameter. Although these are often of sawed material, square hewed timbers are much used.

Mine ties, including tramroad, motor, and heading ties, are ordinary track ties, 4 inches on the face and varying in length mostly from 3 to 5 feet.

Rough lumber goes into mine rails, collar timbers, brattice or partition boards, stringers, and sills.

Prices for round or hewed timbers in the Pennsylvania coal regions range mostly from 1 to 4 cents per linear foot, depending upon diameter; the larger sizes, above 8 inches, are commonly sold by log scale at prices of from $8 to $14 per thousand board feet.

CORDWOOD.

Any kind of wood measured by the cord and in the form of either round or split sticks is called cordwood. Firewood is measured in

F-1811-A

FIG. 3.—Chestnut wood and chestnut-oak bark at an acid or extract plant. (The wood is worth from $4 to $5 per cord at the factory, and the bark from $8 to $10 per cord.)

standard cords, mostly of 4-foot lengths,[1] or short cords of stove wood and other material varying from 12 to 20 inches in length. Materials for distillation, extract wood, excelsior, pulp, handles, cooperage, and woodenware are frequently sold by the rick or cord. The lengths vary mostly from 22 inches for heading to 5 feet for extract and handle stock. Specifications, if given, refer to the kind of wood, length, average size of the pieces, whether split or round, general soundness, body or limbwood, and degree of dryness.

LUMBER.

Specifications for lumber deal with quality and size, in addition to kind of wood. Very many wood-manufacturing concerns are now buying their rough stock lumber by grade and dimension where formerly they took the "mill-run" product, or the lumber as it came

[1] For size and contents of standard cord, see p. 16.

from the saw without sorting and classifying. It is not the purpose of this bulletin to take up in detail the subject of grading, because it is rather complicated. Four grades of rough lumber are generally recognized, as follows: First and seconds, a general term for the highest grade; No. 1 common; No. 2 common; and No. 3 common, or culls. The basis for grading is the quality of the lumber as determined by the number and size of standard defects, such as knots, shake, wormholes, dote, and stain; also by the width of the piece. As lumber becomes more valuable, particularly the finished product, the number of grades greatly increases. In the lumber market grades have been more or less standardized for each species by the various manufacturing associations, from which copies of grading rules may be obtained at a few cents each.

UNITS USED IN THE MEASUREMENT OF TIMBER.

The woodlot owner should be familiar with the various units of measure used in the sale of wood, so that he may be able to make an estimate of his standing trees and to measure or scale the timber after it is cut. In regard to his ordinary field crops he is well informed. He knows that hay is sold by the ton, and he can estimate how many tons the grass on a certain field will produce; or, if he has the hay in a barn, he can calculate how many tons there are in a mow of a certain size. He can estimate the amount of his corn or wheat in a similar manner, because he deals with these crops every year. Timber, however, may be sold from a woodlot only once in a generation. It is natural that the farmer, not being as familiar with timber measurements as he is with those relating to other crops, should rely on the estimates of the buyer, who, obviously, is careful to see that his own interests are protected. What the farmer needs, then, is a guide to which he can refer when he is considering selling some of the products of his woodlot.

Wood is sold in a number of different units. The amount may be measured in board feet, in cords, or it may be sold by the piece in the form of ties, poles, posts, or other products. In the latter case it is comparatively easy to determine, if one has the specifications, just which pieces of wood fulfill the requirements; but when logs are sold in the round it is not easy to determine how many board feet are contained in each log.

To enable one to estimate the number of board feet in logs of different sizes log rules are used. A log rule is a statement, either in the form of a printed table or burnt upon a measuring stick, of the estimated number of board feet of lumber which can be sawed from logs of various lengths and diameters. There are over 40 different log rules in use, and the values assigned to logs of the same size by different rules vary considerably. In some States one rule has been made the legal rule and must be used when no log rule is specified in contracts for selling logs, although if buyer and seller can agree to use a different rule no objection is made. In other States, however, it is illegal to use any other rule than the statute rule.

The number of board feet in a log 12 inches in diameter by 16 feet in length, scaled by the different rules, ranges from 62 to 112 board feet. This is a large variation. If the seller had the choice of a rule for measuring logs of this size, he would naturally select the one which gave a large value; and the buyer would, of course, prefer the rule which gave a small value.

TABLE 6.—*Comparison of log rules.*

[The values given are for 16-foot logs only.]

Top diameter of log inside bark.	Scribner.		Doyle.	Doyle and Scribner.	Holland or Maine.	Blodgett or New Hampshire.	Humphrey or Vermont.	Bangor.	Cumberland River.	Square of three-fourths.	Herring.	Champlain.	Tiemann.[1]
	Scribner.	Decimal C.											
	Contents—(board feet).												
Inches.													
4	(10)	(10)	......	......	(3)	13	11	(6)	8	12	(8)	8	9
5	(13)	(10)	1	1	(11)	19	18	(12)	12	14	(12)	14	15
6	18	20	4	4	20	26	24	23	17	27	(19)	22	23
7	24	30	9	9	31	35	32	27	23	37	(20)	32	32
8	32	30	16	16	41	43	43	41	31	48	31	43	43
9	42	40	25	25	52	54	53	54	29	61	43	56	55
10	51	60	36	36	68	65	67	69	47	75	53	70	69
11	61	70	49	49	83	78	80	81	57	91	65	87	84
12	79	80	64	64	105	92	96	100	68	108	77	105	101
13	97	100	81	81	120	106	112	118	80	127	91	124	119
14	114	110	100	100	142	123	131	137	93	147	107	146	139
15	142	140	121	121	161	139	149	158	107	169	124	168	160
16	159	160	144	144	179	157	171	182	121	192	142	189	183
17	185	180	169	169	205	176	192	204	137	217	162	219	207
18	213	210	196	196	232	197	216	228	153	243	183	247	233
19	240	240	225	225	271	217	240	258	171	271	206	277	260
20	280	280	256	256	302	240	267	300	190	300	230	308	290
21	304	300	289	289	336	262	293	334	209	331	256	341	319
22	334	330	324	324	363	287	323	379	229	365	284	376	351
23	377	380	361	361	401	313	352	409	250	397	313	412	384
24	404	400	400	400	439	339	384	444	273	432	344	450	419
25	459	460	441	441	477	367	416	484	296	469	377	490	455
26	500	500	484	484	507	397	451	526	320	507	411	532	493
27	548	550	529	529	556	429	485	566	345	547	447	575	532
28	582	580	576	582	611	457	523	609	372	588	485	620	573
29	609	610	625	609	657	490	560	652	399	631	525	666	615
30	657	650	676	657	705	514	600	697	427	675	567	711	659
31	710	710	729	710	755	547	640	743	456	721	616	761	704
32	756	740	784	736	765	572	681	792	485	768	655	811	751
33	784	780	841	784	818	628	725	842	516	817	703	868	799
34	800	800	900	800	969	656	771	872	548	867	752	923	849
35	876	880	961	876	919	704	816	(920)	581	919	(800)	980	900
36	923	920	1,024	923	1,028	741	864	(1,000)	614	972	(850)	1,078	953
37	1,029	1,030	1,089	1,029	1,059	785	912	(1,050)	649	1,027	(910)	1,097	1,007
38	1,068	1,070	1,156	1,068	1,135	827	963	(1,110)	685	1,083	(960)	1,159	1,063
39	1,120	1,170	1,225	1,120	1,209	870	1,013	(1,170)	721	1,141	(1,020)	1,223	1,120
40	1,204	1,200	1,296	1,204	1,281	914	1,067	(1,230)	750	1,200	(1,080)	1,287	1,179

[1] The Tiemann rule is a good standard for purposes of comparison. It is not in common use, but gives the actual amount of lumber that can be slash sawed from average sound logs by a circular saw cutting a ⅛-inch kerf. This table shows that the Scribner rule underestimates the amount of lumber that can be sawed from small logs, but for those 20 inches and up it comes very close to the truth. The Doyle rule underestimates still further the contents of small logs, but overestimates those of large logs.

Comparison of a few log rules with the Tiemann rule.

Log rule.	For diameters of—				
	6 to 11 inches.	12 to 20 inches.	21 to 30 inches.	31 to 40 inches.	41 to 50 inches.
	Per cent of Tiemann rule.				
Tiemann	100	100	100	100	100
Champlain	101	106	108	109	109
Scribner	76	89	99	99	102
Doyle	45	80	98	107	113
Doyle-Scribner	45	80	97	99	102
New Hampshire	99	86	80	78	77
Maine	97	102	105	107	.....
Vermont	98	93	91	91	90
Bangor	97	101	106	105	.....
Cumberland River	70	66	65	64	64
Square of three-fourths	111	105	103	102	102

Great care should be taken in selecting the log rule. The Doyle rule in particular should be avoided by sellers, many of whose logs are of small diameters. A 6-inch 16-foot log scales only 4 board feet by the Doyle rule and an 8-inch log only 16 board feet.

Table 7 shows how the price per thousand board feet would have to vary with a number of different log rules in order to obtain the same price for any given piece of timber.

TABLE 7.—*Table showing the price which would have to be obtained if 1,000 board feet of logs scaled by the Tiemann rule were scaled by various other rules, assuming a stumpage price of $5 per 1,000 by the Tiemann rule.*

Log rule.	For diameters of—				
	6 to 11 inches.	12 to 20 inches.	21 to 30 inches.	31 to 40 inches.	41 to 50 inches.
	Value of stumpage per 1,000 board feet.				
Tiemann	$5.00	$5.00	$5.00	$5.00	$5.00
Champlain	4.95	4.72	4.63	4.59	4.59
Scribner	6.58	5.62	5.05	5.05	4.90
Doyle	11.11	6.25	5.16	4.67	4.42
Doyle-Scribner	11.11	6.25	5.15	5.05	4.90
New Hampshire	5.05	5.81	6.25	6.41	6.49
Maine	5.15	4.90	4.76	4.67	.....
Vermont	5.10	5.38	5.49	5.49	5.56
Bangor	5.15	4.95	4.72	4.76	.....
Cumberland River	7.11	7.58	7.69	7.81	7.81
Square of three-fourths	4.50	4.76	4.85	4.90	4.90

SCALING TIMBER.

BOARD FEET.

Log lengths can be conveniently measured with a measuring stick 8 feet long. About 3 inches should be added to the nominal length of the log, so that the rough end may be trimmed at the mill. If more than 6 inches of extra length is left, however, carelessness in sawing the tree into logs is indicated. For scaling purposes the average diameter inside bark at the small end of the log is measured. Diameters are rounded off to the nearest inch; that is, 7¼ would be considered 7 and 7¾ would be considered 8.

As soon as each log is scaled it should be marked with crayon, so that there will be no danger of scaling it again. If systematic scaling is to be done, it is desirable to use a special book for the purpose. Number each log in this case instead of marking it with a cross or other mark. When the log is scaled its number is written on the small end.

The scale book should be ruled off into groups of four columns, the first column for the number of the log, the second for its length, the third for its diameter, and the fourth for the number of board feet. Only one kind of timber should be entered on a page.

Form for ruling log scale book.

Log No.	Length.	Diameter.	Scale.	Log No.	Length.	Diameter.	Scale.
	Feet.	*Inches.*	*Bd. ft.*		*Feet.*	*Inches.*	*Bd. ft.*
1........	....	....	....	10........	....	....	....
2........	....	....	....	11........	....	....	....
3........	....	....	....	12........	....	....	....
4........	....	....	....	13........	....	....	....
5........	....	....	....	14........	....	....	....
6........	....	....	....	15........	....	....	....
7........	....	....	....	16........	....	....	....
8........	....	....	....	17........	....	....	....
9........	....	....	....	Etc........	....	....	....

In case no scale stick is available the logs can be measured with an ordinary rule or yardstick and the board-foot values entered later. If the farmer expects to do much scaling he should provide himself with a scale stick. This consists of a strip of hickory about a quarter of an inch thick and an inch and a half wide and long enough to measure the largest logs which he will have to scale. It has burned on it the estimated board-foot contents of logs of different lengths and diameters. The contents of the logs can be read directly from the stick.

The scaling of sound logs is a comparatively simple matter. The question of how much to allow for defective logs is a point which requires years of experience to master; but ordinarily the farmer will not need to bother with the exact amount which should be deducted for decayed places in the logs.

LINEAR FEET.

Some forest products, such as piles and mining timbers, are sold by the linear foot. This simply means that timbers of certain diameters are sold for special purposes, the price depending on the number of linear feet in the stick or the total length of the stick. In this case it is only necessary to make sure that the diameters are those demanded by the specifications and that the lengths are measured accurately. If it is desirable to keep a record of posts scaled by this method, they can be entered in a scaling book and given a number or not as the scaler may think necessary.

BY THE PIECE.

Railroad ties, posts, and some other products are usually sold by the piece. Certain maximum and minimum specifications or sizes are usually given, and then the sticks that come within these sizes are counted. These can be kept track of by numbering or marking with a crayon, one end of each tie as it is counted.

CORDWOOD.

Most farmers are familiar with the measurement of cordwood, but one or two points may be mentioned in this connection. It is customary to pile green cordwood 2 or 3 inches higher than the required 4 feet, in order to allow for shrinkage and settling as the wood dries. The average height and the average length of the pile should be measured in finding the number of cords.

The standard cord is 8 feet long 4 feet wide and 4 feet high. In some localities a long cord, 8 feet by 5 by 4 feet is used. Again, it often happens that sticks 4 feet long are sawed into 16-inch sticks and split fine enough for stove fuel. A running cord of this short wood, that is, a pile 8 feet long 4 feet high and 16 inches wide, equals one-third of a standard cord.

ESTIMATING STANDING TIMBER.

WITHOUT VOLUME TABLES.

Unless the woodlot is large it is desirable that every tree be estimated separately. The procedure is as follows:

A notebook or sheet of paper should be ruled off in squares of a convenient size somewhat as shown in the sample diagram below.

Species.	Butt log.			Second log.			Third log.			Total scale.
	Length.	Diameter.	Scale.	Length.	Diameter.	Scale.	Length.	Diameter.	Scale.	
	Feet.	*Inches.*	*Bd. ft.*	*Feet.*	*Inches.*	*Bd. ft.*	*Feet.*	*Inches.*	*Bd. ft.*	*Bd. ft.*
White oak...	16	16	....	16	14	....	16	11	....	....
Red oak......	12	10	....	12	8	....	....	....	....	....
Sugar maple.	14	15	....	12	12	....	....	....	....	....
Beech........	16	18	....	16	16	....	14	13	....	....
(Etc.)........	....	....	....	....	....	....	....	....	....	....
....	....	....	....	....	....	....	....	....	....	....
....	....	....	....	....	....	....	....	....	....	....
....	....	....	....	....	....	....	....	....	....	....

The estimator looks over the first tree and makes an estimate of how many logs can be cut out of it. Suppose the first tree is a white oak which forks at about 50 feet above the ground. Above that point the branches are too small or too crooked to be used for saw logs. Allowing for the stump, then, the merchantable length of the tree is 48 feet, or three 16-foot logs. By looking at the tree carefully the estimator decides that the diameter, inside the bark, at the top of the first 16-foot log is 16 inches. Sixteen feet farther up the diameter appears to be 2 inches less, while at the top of the third log the diameter is 11 inches. These figures are entered in the proper spaces as shown in the diagram; and, later on, the number of board

F—[illegible]

FIG. 4.—Measuring the contents of a woodlot and marking trees to be cut. (Marking is done by blazing the bark or by the use of white paint.)

feet in each of the three logs can be determined with the aid of the log rule, and the total board-foot contents of the tree found by adding the results.

In some cases it may be desirable to indicate in some way the grade of each log in the tree. The butt logs are generally of the highest grade and the top logs of the lowest. Where higher prices are paid for No. 1 logs, the difference may be enough to make it worth while to separate them from the No. 2 or No. 3 logs. The grade of the logs can be indicated in the upper right-hand corner of the square which is left for the board-foot contents of the log. When the final figures are added up only those which have a "1" in the upper right-hand corner will be added together to get the total amount of No. 1 logs; then are added the values which are indicated by No. 2, and so on.

After each tree is estimated, it should be marked in some way, so that there will be no danger of its being measured again. A piece of chalk may be used or a small blaze can be made with a hatchet. This procedure is continued, the trees being taken as they come, but only those estimated which are big enough to be merchantable.

It is advisable to estimate the trees on an area of fairly uniform width, continuing across the woodlot until the other side is reached, then on the return trip the estimator can proceed on a fairly straight line. This makes it possible to be sure of getting all the trees without having to cover too much ground. The width of the first strip on which the timber is estimated will depend upon the convenience of the operator. With open timber the width can be greater than where the trees stand close together or where there is much underbrush. Under average conditions 50 feet would be a good width for the strip.

This method can also be used in estimating posts or poles or even cordwood. If posts are to be estimated the species or kind of wood, the length, and the top diameter of each are recorded. If the facts are put down in this form, the value of all the posts, or of any particular class, may be easily calculated. Table 8 will be useful in estimating roughly the quantity of material in cords, ties, poles, or sawlogs contained in trees of different diameters.

TABLE 8.—*Quantity of material contained in trees of different sizes.*[1]

Diameter of tree (breast high).	Number of trees of each size required to yield—						Tie and pole product per tree.	
	1 cord.			1,000 feet of lumber.			Number of ties, hardwoods.[4]	Length of pole, hardwoods.[5]
	Hardwoods.		Softwoods.	Hardwoods.		Softwoods.		
	Northern.	Southern.		Northern.[2]	Southern.[3]			
Inches.								*Feet.*
2	.....	179	.....	.....	.....	.....	.....	.....
3	.....	90	.....	.....	.....	.....	.....	.....
4	.....	50	.....	.....	.....	.....	.....	.....
5	33	25	.....	.....	.....	.....	.....	.....
6	20	17	.....	.....	.....	.....	.....	.....
7	15	13	20	.....	.....	.....	.....	.....
8	11	9	13	.....	.....	25	.....	.....
9	8	7	10	85	64	20	.....	.....
10	6	6	8	45	33	15	1	.....
11	5	5	7	28	22	10	1	.....
12	4	4	6	19	13	8	2	25
13	3.5	3.4	4.5	14	11	7	2	25
14	3.0	3.0	3.7	12	9	6	3.3	30
15	2.5	2.5	3.0	8	7	5	3.3	35
16	2.0	2.2	2.6	7	6	4	.....	40
17	1.7	2.0	2.1	6	5	3.1	.....	40
18	1.6	1.8	1.9	5	4.5	2.6	.....	43
19	1.3	1.5	1.8	4	4.0	2.4	.....	45
20	1.2	1.3	1.5	2.5	3.3	2.1	.....	45
21	1.0	1.2	1.4	3.1	3.0	1.8	.....	50
22	.9	1.1	1.2	2.7	2.7	1.7	.....	50
23	.8	1.0	1.1	2.3	2.5	1.6	.....	55
24	.7	.9	1.0	2.0	2.2	1.5	.....	55

NOTE.—Softwoods taken to 4 inches top diameter. Northern hardwoods: Beech, birch, and maple to 4 inches top diameter. Southern hardwoods: Chestnut, oak, hickory, basswood, ash, etc., to 3 inches top diameter.

[1] Bulletin 9, State of New York Conservation Commission (adapted in tie and pole production).
[2] For every thousand feet of lumber about two-thirds of a cord of wood can also be cut from the tops.
[3] For every thousand feet of lumber about three-quarters of a cord of wood can also be cut from the top
[4] For every 10 ties about 1 cord of wood can also be cut from the tops.
[5] For every 10 poles about 1 cord of wood may be cut also from the tops.

A HOME-MADE HEIGHT MEASURE.

An instrument for measuring the heights of trees can easily be made at practically no cost. (Fig. 5.)

Take a piece of half-inch board 7 by 9 inches and plane it smooth on all sides. Draw the line *AB* ⅜ of an inch from the lower edge and parallel to it. Two inches from the left end of the board draw *CD* at right angles to *AB*. Make a mark at *E*, $6\frac{1}{4}$ inches from *D*, and another at *F*, $3\frac{1}{8}$ inches from *D*. Now draw a line *JK* through *F* parallel to *AB*. Start at *D*, lay off inches and quarter inches on *AB* in both directions, marking *D* as zero and putting down the number of inches from *D* to each inch mark. Do the same for the line

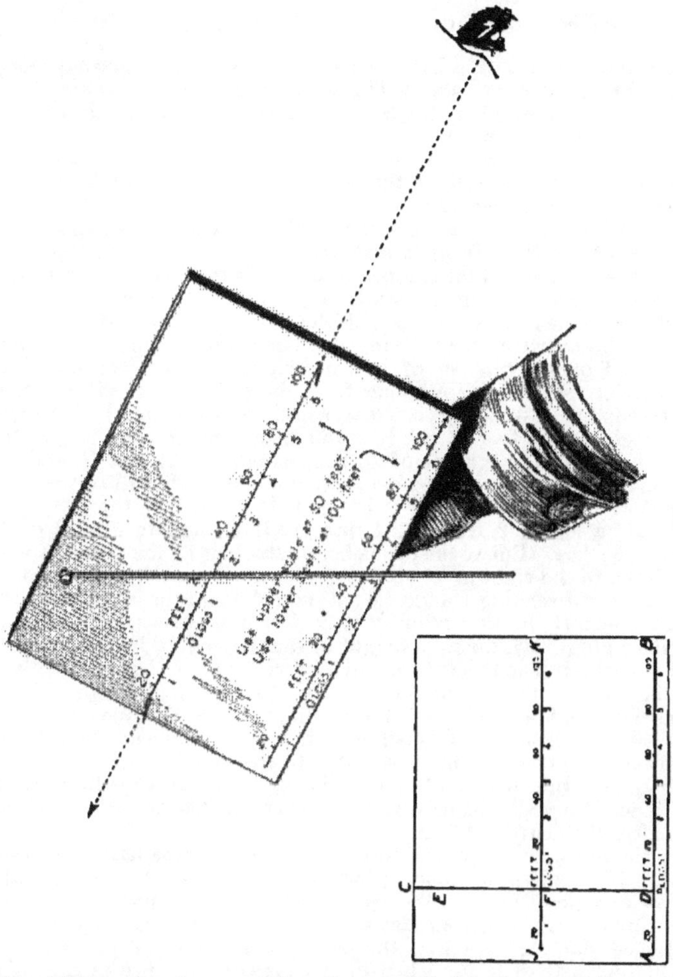

FIG. 5.—A simple home-made instrument for measuring heights of trees.

JK. Take a brad or small nail and drive it in carefully on the line *JK* about an inch from the edge of the board. Drive it in until the point comes out on the back of the board; then pull it out and drive it in from the back until the point sticks out about one-fourth inch from the face of the board. File off or cut off with pliers any part of the brad that projects from the back of the board. In the same way insert another brad near the other end of the line *JK*. These brads are the sights, and it is important that they be straight and true.

Now take a piece of straight, heavy wire 10 inches long, and bend one end of it into a loop about an eighth of an inch in diameter. The center of the loop should be in line with the straight part of the wire thus:  not thus  . Fasten this piece of wire loosely to the board at *E* with a half-inch screw, so that it will swing freely when the board is on edge. The loop should be big enough to fit loosely over the shank of the screw, but small enough so that it will not slip off over the head.

Screw a piece of wood about 6 inches long, 1 inch wide, and half an inch thick to the back of the board to serve as a handle, and the height measure is complete.

How to use it.—To measure the total height of a tree, stand at a distance of 100 feet from it and hold the instrument in the right hand in such a way that the pendulum swings freely but very near the board. Sight along the brads at the top of the tree and let the pendulum come to rest. Then with the left hand press the pendulum against the board without giving it a chance to change its position. Now read off the number of feet in height on the lower scale. If the wire crosses the line 5 inches from the point *D*, it indicates that the tree is five 16-foot logs or 80 feet high above the level of the eye. Now sight at the foot of the tree and take another reading. If the pendulum hangs to the left of *D*, that is, between *A* and *D*, add the amount indicated to the first reading, and the result will be the total height of the tree. Thus, if it hangs half an inch to the left of *D*, add half a log or 8 feet to the first reading, making a total of 5½ logs, or 88 feet. But if the eye is below the foot of the tree, the wire will hang to the right of *D* (between *D* and *B*) and then the amount of the second reading should be subtracted from the amount of the first. Thus, if the first reading is 96 feet and the second is 12 feet (to the right of *D*), the total height of the tree will be 96 less 12, or 84 feet. If the tree is less than about 75 feet high, or if it is difficult to see the top at a distance of 100 feet, the observer should stand 50 feet from the tree, but in this case the readings are on the line *JK*.

When the instrument is sighted the pendulum can be kept in position by tilting the hand slightly to the right. This brings the wire against the board and holds it in place so that a reading can be obtained. Care should be taken, however, so that the wire will not slip after the board is tilted.

In the example given, the total height of the tree has been measured. It is often of more practical importance to measure the height to a point on the tree beyond which there is no merchantable saw timber. This measurement is made in the same way as that described above, except that the instrument is pointed at what will be the top of the last log when the tree is cut, and then at the point where the top of the stump will be.

ESTIMATING WITH VOLUME TABLES.

A volume table gives the same information about a whole tree that a log rule gives about a log; that is, the average number of board feet which a tree of any given size is estimated to contain.

Such tables are made by scaling a large number of trees and finding the number of board feet in each, then grouping those of the same size together and averaging them. The table gives the average number of board feet in trees of the sizes measured. Trees differ in shape, and even those of the same height and diameter will vary a good deal in contents, but when many trees are measured the averages are fairly dependable. A volume table which would give an accurate total if applied to all the trees on a tract might show a result containing an error of from 25 to 50 per cent if applied to only one or two trees.

Since different kinds of trees differ from each other in form, the volume table made for one species does not necessarily apply accurately to another. There is not so much difference between the individual hardwoods or individual softwoods as between hardwoods and softwoods. Table 9 is to be used as a general volume table for hardwoods (broadleaf) and Table 10 for softwoods (conifers). Certain factors are given by which correction can be made so as to produce accurate results for different kinds of trees; for example, the hardwoods table applies to red oak without correction, but for white oak 10 per cent must be added when the trees are over 16 inches in diameter.

Estimating the timber on a tract by means of volume tables is not so accurate as estimating each log in each tree separately; but it can be done much more quickly and is accurate enough under ordinary circumstances.

The trees are tallied in a different manner from that indicated where volume tables are not used. If the table is made to show the volumes of trees of various diameters and log lengths, a tally sheet must be prepared so that the trees may be tallied in the same units. A sheet of this kind, which can be ruled on paper, is shown below. The kinds of trees for which different stumpage prices are paid should be kept separate in order that the correct values can be calculated.

Sample tally sheet for tallying trees when volume tables are available.

ACRE No. ....

Diameter breast-high.	White oak.			Black oak.			Tulip poplar.			Hickory.			Chestnut.			Etc.					
	1-log.	2-log.	3-log.	1-log.	2-log.	3-log.	1-log.	2-log.	3-log.	1-log.	2-log.	3-log.	1-log.	2-log.	3-log.	1-log.	2-log.	3-log.	1-log.	2-log.	[illegible]
Inches.																					
8........																					
10........																					
12........																					
14........																					
16........																					
18........																					
20........																					
22........																					

TABLE 9.—*Contents in board feet of hardwood trees of different diameters and merchantable heights.*

[Stump height, 2 feet. Trees over 75 years old. Scribner decimal C rule.]

Diameter, breast-high.	Number of 16-foot logs.									Diameter inside bark of top.	Basis.
	1	1½	2	2½	3	3½	4	4½	5		
	Volume—board feet.										
Inches.										*Inches.*	*Trees.*
8	20	27	35	43	....	....	....	....	....	6	....
9	20	32	42	53	....	....	....	....	....	6	1
10	20	38	52	64	81	....	....	....	....	6	2
11	21	43	62	78	98	120	....	....	....	6	4
12	23	50	73	93	120	140	180	....	....	6	3
13	25	58	86	110	140	170	200	....	....	7	4
14	27	67	100	130	160	190	230	260	....	7	9
15	30	77	120	150	180	220	260	300	....	8	13
16	34	89	130	170	200	250	290	340	390	8	18
17	38	100	150	190	230	280	320	380	440	9	40
18	43	120	170	210	260	310	360	420	490	9	56
19	48	130	200	240	290	350	400	470	540	10	65
20	54	150	220	270	330	390	450	520	590	10	75
21	62	170	250	300	370	440	500	580	650	11	88
22	69	190	270	340	410	480	550	640	720	11	90
23	77	210	300	380	450	530	610	700	790	12	67
24	85	230	340	420	500	580	670	770	860	12	80
25	93	250	370	460	550	640	740	840	940	13	56
26	100	280	410	510	600	700	810	910	1,020	13	89
27	110	300	450	560	660	770	880	990	1,110	14	68
28	120	330	490	610	720	830	960	1,080	1,200	14	81
29	130	360	530	660	780	900	1,030	1,160	1,300	15	61
30	140	390	580	720	850	980	1,120	1,250	1,400	15	47
31	....	420	630	770	910	1,050	1,200	1,350	1,510	16	45
32	....	450	690	830	980	1,130	1,290	1,450	1,620	16	40
33	....	480	740	890	1,050	1,211	1,380	1,560	1,730	17	49
34	....	....	800	950	1,120	1,290	1,480	1,670	1,860	17	30
35	....	....	860	1,010	1,180	1,380	1,570	1,790	1,990	18	22
36	....	....	920	1,070	1,250	1,460	1,680	1,910	2,140	18	17
37	....	....	....	1,130	1,320	1,550	1,780	2,040	2,280	19	24
38	....	....	....	1,190	1,390	1,640	1,890	2,170	2,430	19	11
39	....	....	....	1,250	1,460	1,730	2,000	2,300	2,600	20	16
40	....	....	....	1,311	1,540	1,820	2,120	2,430	2,760	20	15
41	....	....	....	....	1,610	1,910	2,240	2,570	2,930	21	6
42	....	....	....	....	1,680	2,000	2,360	2,720	3,100	21	3
43	....	....	....	....	1,750	2,090	2,470	2,860	3,270	22	3
44	....	....	....	....	1,830	2,190	2,590	3,010	3,430	22	2
											1,300

Correction factors for different species.

Chestnut, for diameters from 0 to 40 inches, subtract 10 per cent.
Chestnut oak, for diameters from 32 to 40 inches, add 10 per cent.
White oak, for diameters from 18 to 40 inches, add 10 per cent.
Red oak, for all diameters, use the table without change.

It will be noticed that the volume tables which are based on diameter and number of logs (merchantable lengths) use a 16-foot log as a standard, but that additional columns showing half logs are given. In estimating any individual tree, the number of logs and half logs contained in it is estimated and indicated on the tally sheet.

A 16-inch, 2-log tree would be tallied by putting a dot in the square opposite 16 inches and in the column headed 2. The trees may be tallied by fives; that is, four parallel marks and a fifth one across the first four, thus: 𝍸 ; but unless this method is preferred, trees should be tallied in tens, because by this method more trees can be shown on the same amount of space. The first four trees are indicated by dots and the next six by connecting lines. Each complete square with its diagonals indicates ten trees. The different stages by which the tally is built up are shown below:

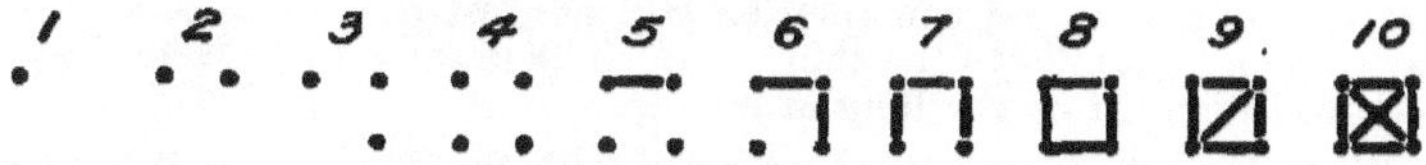

TABLE 10.—*Contents in board feet of coniferous trees of different diameters and merchantable heights.*

[Stump height, 2 feet. Diameter (inside bark) of top, 6 inches. Trees over 75 years old. Scribner decimal C rule.]

Diameter breast-high.	Number of 16-foot logs.							Basis.
	2	2½	3	3½	4	4½	5	
	Volume—board feet.							
Inches.								*Trees.*
8	37	52	66	75	84			12
9	41	58	70	82	93			9
10	47	66	77	92	100	120		12
11	53	74	86	100	120	140		13
12	60	83	97	120	140	160	200	8
13	68	94	110	130	160	190	220	4
14	77	110	120	150	180	210	240	7
15		120	140	170	200	240	270	11
16		130	160	190	230	270	310	20
17		150	180	220	260	300	340	21
18		170	210	250	290	330	380	20
19		190	230	290	320	370	420	34
20		210	260	310	360	410	470	27
21			290	350	400	460	520	33
22			320	390	440	510	570	40
23			360	430	490	560	620	37
24			400	470	540	620	690	37
25			440	520	600	680	740	47
26			480	560	660	740	810	52
27				600	720	800	880	43
28				650	780	870	950	45
29					840	940	1,030	39
30					910	1,010	1,100	47
31						1,080	1,190	40
32						1,150	1,260	44
33						1,230	1,310	39
34							1,420	36
35							1,500	34
36							1,580	29
								840

Correction factors for different species.

Hemlock:
For diameters from 8 to 10 inches, add 10 per cent.
For diameters from 11 to 20 inches, add 22 per cent.
For diameters from 21 inches and up, add 30 per cent.
Red spruce:
For diameters from 8 to 10 inches, add 5 per cent.
For diameters from 11 inches and up, add 25 per cent.
Shortleaf pine:
For diameters from 10 inches and under, add 15 per cent.
For diameters from 11 to 19 inches, add 25 per cent.
For diameters from 20 to 23 inches, add 35 per cent.
For diameters from 24 inches and over, add 40 per cent.
White pine: For all diameters, use the table without change.

The volume tables are based on diameter breast high, which is the diameter outside bark 4½ feet from the ground. This diameter can be conveniently measured by means of tree calipers; but calipers are somewhat expensive, and an ordinary carpenter's steel square can be used.

The square is kept horizontal. Both arms are placed in contact with the tree, the shorter one pointing away from the operator; a narrow strip of wood can then be laid against the opposite side of the tree and parallel to the short arm. The diameter of the tree will then be indicated on the long arm.

When the whole area has been estimated, the operator will have a tally of the total number of trees of each size and kind on the tract. Suppose that there are 12 three-log red oaks 18 inches in diameter and that the volume table for hardwoods indicates that trees of this size contain 260 board feet. The 260 is multiplied by 12. The same thing is done for each of the other sizes for which there is a tally. This gives, then, the total number of board feet of red oak. The same thing is done for other kinds of hardwoods, except that after the total volume has been found it may be necessary to increase it or decrease it for the different species by the amounts indicated in the footnote to the table.

PARTIAL ESTIMATES.

In case the woodlot is so large or the time available is so short that it is not practicable to measure each tree, a partial estimate can be made. One-quarter of the area may be gone over and this quarter considered a fair sample of the whole woodlot. The amount on this sample area may then be multiplied by 4 to get an estimate of the total stand on the whole tract.

Different methods of measuring part of the stand are possible. The simplest of these is to lay out squares or rectangles containing a quarter of an acre, or 1 acre, and to measure all the trees on these plots. If the whole woodlot contains 50 acres and if 10 plots containing an acre each are measured, one-fifth of the area would be covered; therefore the amount of timber found on these plots would have to be multiplied by 5 to obtain the total stand.

There is a tendency in locating plots of this kind to pick out areas where the timber is better than the average. This should be avoided because it leads to too high an estimate of the woodlot. A plot 208 feet square contains very nearly 1 acre, and one 104 feet square contains a quarter of an acre.

If the diameter of each tree is to be estimated and not actually measured and the estimator is working without assistance, he may stand at a given point and estimate all of the trees within 59 feet of him. The area of a circle of this size is a quarter of an acre.

A modification of the sample-plot method is the strip method. Instead of measuring out plots here and there the timber on a strip 66 feet wide is measured. An area of this width and 660 feet long measures 1 acre. At the end of each acre (every 660 feet) a new tally sheet is begun. The timber is estimated in a continuous strip across the tract. When the boundary of the woodlot is reached the estimating crew measures off a certain distance (say, 264 feet) at right angles to the strip, and starting there continues the estimating, this time going back toward the first boundary line, and so on. This results in the gridironing of the tract by these sample areas in such a way that almost invariably all classes of timber are tallied in their proper proportion. (See fig. 6.)

The distance between the center lines of the strips determines what proportion of the tract is covered. If this distance is only 66 feet, all of the tract has been covered; if it is 132 feet, half of the tract; 264 feet, one-quarter of the tract, and so on.

To estimate timber by the strip method it is necessary to have two or more men in the estimating crew. The distance along the strip may be measured with a tape or chain or it may be estimated fairly

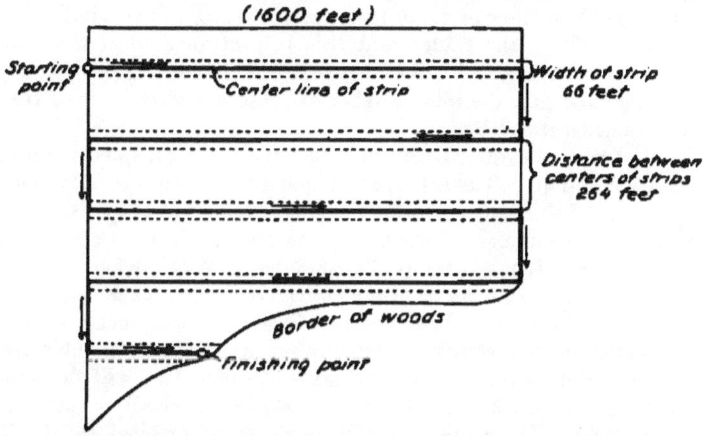

FIG. 6.—Strip method of estimating 25 per cent of a stand of timber.

closely by pacing. The tallyman walks along the center line of the strip and the caliper man or estimator measures or estimates the timber on an area 33 feet wide on each side of the tallyman. If the trees are actually calipered it takes longer, of course, than if the diameters are estimated by the second man. The estimator calls out the species, the diameter, and the height of the tree or number of logs in it; and the tallyman makes the proper entries.

The greater the proportion of the tract which is covered by the strip method the more accurate will be the results; and as a rule at least one-quarter of the area should be included in the strips. This means that the center lines of the strips should be not more than 264 feet apart.

For woodlots of 50 acres or less it is recommended that each merchantable tree be estimated separately. For tracts greater in size either the strip method or the sample-plot method may be used. If only a rough estimate is desired the sample-plot method can be used to advantage in any case, because it is quicker and its accuracy depends on the care with which the plots are located.

ESTIMATING CORDWOOD.

Cordwood can be estimated without volume tables in much the same way as saw timber. The diameter of the stick is measured at the middle outside bark instead of at the small end inside bark. The figures below show the volume in cubic feet of 4-foot sticks of ordinary dimensions.

Diameter of sticks (inches)	2	3	4	5	6	7	8	9	10	11	12
Solid contents (cubic feet)	0.1	0.2	0.3	0.5	0.8	1.1	1.4	1.8	2.2	2.6	3.1

The branches, or that part of the stem which is suitable for cordwood, may be laid off by eye into 4-foot lengths, then the diameter at the middle of each of these is estimated and tallied on a sheet of paper ruled in squares. The total number of sticks of any size is multiplied by the number of cubic feet corresponding to that size, which is obtained from the table; and this is continued until the total volume of each class of sticks has been obtained. These volumes added together give the total number of cubic feet in the tree or trees under consideration.

Though a cord contains 128 cubic feet the space occupied includes both wood and air. The actual solid contents of a cord is only about 70 per cent of this amount, or 90 cubic feet for wood of average size. To obtain the number of cords it is necessary, then, to divide the total number of cubic feet by 90. For small sticks, where the average diameter is 4 inches or less, a converting factor of 80 cubic feet per cord should be used; in the case of larger sticks 10 inches or over in diameter the converting factor may run as high as 100 cubic feet per cord. For ordinary firewood sizes 90 cubic feet will be satisfactory. Crooked rough sticks can not be piled as closely as straight smooth sticks. Therefore a certain quantity of crooked wood will make a greater number of cords than the same amount of straight wood.

There are usually from 500 to 600 board feet in a cord. Cords may be converted into board feet by multiplying board feet into cords by dividing by this number. Thus 10 cords of medium-sized pulp wood, containing 500 board feet per cord, are equivalent to 5,000 board feet. Large-sized wood, however, might contain 600 board feet to the cord, so that 10 cords would be equivalent to 6,000 board feet.

In some cases it may be desirable to know how much the volume will be reduced by peeling cordwood. The thinnest barked trees usually have at least 6 per cent of the total volume in the form of bark and from this it ranges up to 30 per cent.

FINDING THE SALE VALUE OF STANDING TIMBER.

Woodlot owners often sell their timber without having a sufficient knowledge of its market value to protect their interests, and suffer loss in consequence. Such loss can be avoided only by a careful and thorough study of all available markets.

IMPORTANT STEPS.

The following steps may be of assistance in acquiring a knowledge of the sale value of timber:

(1) Take advantage of the experience of neighbors who have recently sold timber or have otherwise informed themselves in regard to good markets and current prices.

Doubtless the preponderance of poor bargains over good ones has something to do with the proverbial reticence of farmers on the subject of their timber sales. It is not unusual to find cases where adjacent farmers have sold approximately the same grade of material at about the same time for widely different prices. In communities where the cooperative spirit is strong stumpage values usually become pretty well known.

(2) Apply to the State forester, the county agricultural agent, or any other available public official or personal agency for sources of information and advice regarding possible markets and timber prices.

(3) Employ the services of some reliable man who has made a special study of market prices of logs and lumber. The saving gained thereby, unless the owner has had much experience along that line, may amount to from 10 to 40 times the cost of the examination.

The opportunity in this field is particularly promising. In most sections where timber has been sold to any extent in the past, men of the necessary qualifications can be found whom such employment by the day or the job would enable to keep up with market conditions and be of very real assistance to owners of timber.

(4) Get into touch, through correspondence, with outside buyers, and thus awaken competition among as many prospective purchasers as possible. A live effort along this line will often succeed in bringing about an open market for standing timber.

(5) Determine the value of the material by reference to current market prices and the total cost of putting it on the market.

STUMPAGE VALUE.

The sale value of standing timber, known as its stumpage value, is of primary importance to the owner. Most woodlot timber sales are based upon the value of timber in the standing tree, rather than on its later value when cut and placed on the market in the form of cordwood, ties, poles, bolts, logs for further manufacture, or lumber.

With a knowledge of the market price and the cost of getting the material from the stump to the market the owner is in a position to ascertain by a simple calculation the value of his standing timber. This is the difference between the value of the product on the market and the total costs of marketing, including a reasonable profit on the operation, which may fairly be placed at from 20 to 25 per cent on the combined investment in timber, labor, and lumbering equipment.

For example, if average mill-run red-oak lumber is worth $24 per thousand feet at a market point and the total cost of logging, sawing, and hauling, including a fair profit on the business, is $11, the value of the standing timber is $13 per thousand board feet. In the same manner the stumpage value of poles, ties, and other primary timber products may be obtained. If a 35-foot chestnut pole is worth $4 delivered at a loading point along the railroad, and the cost of logging and hauling, plus a profit of 20 per cent on the operation, is $2.10, the stumpage value is $1.90. Likewise, if the average value of a No. 2 white-oak tie is 56 cents and the cost of cutting, hewing, and hauling, plus a fair profit, is 29 cents, the stumpage value would be 27 cents. Maple and beech cordwood, selling for $5.60 per cord in a given town and costing $1 for cutting, $3.50 for hauling, and 30 cents profit, a total of $4.80, has a stumpage value of 80 cents per cord.[1]

The value of timber in the tree is affected by its location and accessibility, since these determine largely the cost of production and marketing. The distance, character of the road, and daily hauling capacity of a team and wagon are factors to be taken into account. Through improved methods of logging and transportation, timber becomes relatively more accessible, and the cost of production is reduced, its stumpage value being then increased. Efficiency of labor, teams, and machinery employed in logging, economy in utilizing material and conducting the operation, and skill in securing the best market for the product, whether sold in the log or in a manufactured state, all count as factors in raising the value of standing timber.

TABLE 11.—*Equivalent lumber values of four different sizes of ties sold at various prices.*

[Cost of sawing assumed to be $1 per thousand board feet for 1-inch lumber, and 10 cents per tie. Loss of one-fifth the timber scale by sawing 1-inch lumber as compared to sawing the material into ties.]

Size of tie.	Price received per tie—cents.									
	30	35	40	45	50	55	60	65	70	75
	Value per thousand board feet, 1-inch lumber.									
No. 1: Size, 7 by 9 inches by [illegible] feet; contents, 45 board feet, or 22 ties per M board feet				$13.72	$15.11	$16.50	$17.89	$19.28	$20.60	$22.06
No. 1: Size, 7 by 8 inches by [illegible] feet; contents, 40 board feet, or 25 ties per M board feet			$13.38	14.94	16.50	18.06	19.63	21.19	22.75	24.31
No. 2: Size, 6 by 8 inches by 8 feet; contents, [illegible] board feet, or [illegible] ties per M board feet		$13.[illegible]	[illegible]	17.16	[illegible]	21.40	23.23	25.15	......	......
No. 3: Size, 6 by 7 inches by 8 feet; contents, [illegible] board feet, [illegible] ties per M board feet	$1[illegible]	20.[illegible]	22.7[illegible]	25.88	29.00	......	......	......	......	......

[1] For a detailed discussion of stumpage value and costs of production of hardwood lumber, ties, poles, and cordwood in southern New England, see Forest Service Bulletin 96, "Second-Growth Hardwoods in Connecticut," by E. H. Frothingham. Approximate values for New York are given in Bulletin 9, "Woodlot Forestry," by R. Rosenbluth, State of New York Conservation Commission. Tables of values for white pine will be found in U. S. Department of Agriculture Bulletin 13, "White Pine Under Forest Management," by E. H. Frothingham, and "Marketing White Pine in New Hampshire," by J. H. Foster, Extension Bulletin No. 3, New Hampshire College and Experiment Station.

In determining stumpage values it is only fair to base the calculation upon the product of highest value for which the tree is suited. For example, if white oak is sawed into wagon stock of specified sizes worth $40 per thousand board feet, the return in stumpage value is $28[1] for each thousand feet of lumber sold. It would be only $14.90[2] if the same material had been sawed into ties worth 70 cents each. Allowing a sawing cost of 10 cents each for ties and $4 per 1,000 feet for sawing 1-inch lumber, a given amount of log material will net $15, whether sawed into ties (7 by 8 inches by 8½ feet) and sold at 70 cents each or into inch lumber at $22.75 per thousand feet.[3] Table 11 gives the equivalent returns per thousand board feet of 1-inch lumber for material worked into ties of different sizes and sold at various prices. For example, if No. 2 ties (6 by

F—32367-A

FIG. 7.—Three-quarters of a cord of chestnut wood for extract, on the way to the railroad yards. (The wood is cut 5 feet long, which is the length specified in this region (East Tennessee) by all the acid plants. From 12 to 14 cords make an ordinary carload.)

8 inches by 8 feet) are selling at 50 cents each, the returns are approximately equal to selling the same material in the form of lumber at $19.38 per thousand board feet.

If the owner takes part in the lumbering, his profits from his stumpage value are added to by profits from the operation proportional to the extent to which his labor and capital go into the logging, milling, and marketing the product. Under certain conditions he may be able actually to sell the sawed product of his woodlot. Usu-

[1] Allowing a cost of $12 per thousand for production and marketing of 1,000 feet of lumber.

[2] Allowing $7 for making and marketing 31⅓ ties, the number of 7 by 8 inch by 8½ foot ties derived from the material yielding 1,000 feet of rough lumber, using a saw cutting ¼-inch saw kerf.

[3] One-fifth of the timber scale is lost by saw kerf with the ordinary circular saw, and therefore a tie containing 40 board feet by actual scale would yield only 32 board feet of 1-inch lumber.

ally the farmer is not equipped or experienced sufficiently to accomplish this profitably. He is able, however, in many cases to market his timber direct to the consumer in the form of logs, bolts, poles, piling, and cordwood. In general an advance in stumpage values of all woodlot products has been in progress throughout the country. It would be very profitable for the farmer to make a greater effort to acquaint himself fully with general market conditions and stumpage values and to place a corresponding value on his timber resources before making further sales or even local use of his timber.

MARKETING COSTS.

The principal operations necessary to get the product from the stump to the market are:

(1) Cutting, logging, and roughworking the trees in the woods. This includes such operations as cutting logs and bolts, hewing ties, peeling poles, etc., and often ranking and piling them for convenience. In case the material is worked up in a portable mill on the ground or near by, the short haul to the mill should be included here.

(2) Transporting the product of whatever kind to the railroad, wood-using plant, sawmill, town yard, or other market. The assumption here is that the material is sold and shipped considerable distances, so that it is known to have a certain value at some definite point.

(3) Further manufacture to produce certain kinds of products, such as sawed lumber, sawed ties, etc. Bolts, hewed ties, poles, mining timbers, and other products require no further treatment for their marketing.

Usually local cost figures for logging and roughworking are readily obtainable. The most variable cost is that of hauling and transportation, because of the varying distances, means of transportation, and differences in weight of different kinds of timber in a green and seasoned condition. The third item, the expense of sawing lumber, ties, or other materials before they are considered to be on the market, is probably the least variable of the three different items. The density and weight of the wood has a good deal to do with the transportation and milling items in the marketing costs.[1] Pine and cottonwood, for instance, cost less to haul and cut than oak and hickory.

MARKETS AND PRICES.

The farmer's market will be found at a sawmill, lumber yard, wood-manufacturing plant, railroad station or siding, mining company, electric-light company, traction company, or general contrac-

[1] Average marketing costs, itemized separately for lumber, ties, poles, cordwood, and charcoal in New York will be found in Bulletin 9, "Woodlot Forestry," State of New York Conservation Commission, 1913; also, for white-pine lumber in New Hampshire in Extension Bulletin No. 3, "Marketing White Pine in New Hampshire," New Hampshire College and Experiment Station, Durham, N. H.

tor's office. The market may be local or at some distance. In most regions where supplies are limited and prices high the stationary sawmill, obtaining its raw products by rail and long-haul wagon delivery, is superseding the portable mill. This is particularly true in the regions of oak, hickory, and other more valuable hardwoods. Markets for bolts, billets, posts, piling, and logs of various species may very often be found by consulting the wood-manufacturing industry bulletins and woodlot marketing bulletins, published by various States, containing lists of firms making different commodities. In some of these is given the kind of woodlot material purchased as raw product.

It is well to have clearly in mind the different prices for wood products as they advance successively from the tree to manufacture and market. Thus the stumpage price and the market price, or base price, stand at the two extremities. Local and f. o. b. prices are intermediate prices. By "local" price is often meant that which the buyer would pay for wood material delivered at the railroad or other supply point. The "f. o. b." price is the price of material "free on board" cars at some point designated, as f. o. b. mill or f. o. b. railroad. It equals the base price, or price on the general market, minus the cost of freight from the shipping point to the market point.

Market values of timber products may be learned from local mills and lumber yards, markets and jobbers in the cities, and various lumber journals and other publications devoted to the lumber interests. Some companies or bureaus throughout the country make a business of furnishing actual selling prices in the more important lumber-market centers and listing stock for sale.[1] Through large lumber manufacturers and lumber-selling associations in different parts of the country, base prices at stated points, and sometimes reported mill prices, may be obtained. These base prices show the comparative values of different species, although the current selling prices may in many cases vary considerably.[2] In a number of the northern and central States, woodlot experts are working under the direction of the State forester, to whom applications for information on values and prices in local and distant markets should be directed.

For prices and specifications on crossties, requests should be made to the local railroad agent or direct to the general purchasing agents, whose addresses can be obtained from the passenger-service folders or learned by inquiring at the local stations. Mining companies

[1] The Lumberman's Bureau, Washington, D. C., furnishes such information for the eastern United States. Branch offices are located at St. Louis, Mo.; Memphis, Tenn.; and Hattiesburg, Miss.

[2] The Forest Service compiles quarterly reports of current sales and furnishes averages on species by regions. These general averages, however, are of relatively little use in local sales of small amounts of timber.

furnish similar information in regard to their needs. Poles are purchased by electric lighting and power companies, electric traction companies, telegraph and telephone companies, and others, to whom requests for information should be sent direct. For prices on piling it would be well to look to the railroad and to dock, wharf, bridge, and bulkhead contractors in the larger towns and cities. Cordwood is purchased by brickmakers, bakeries, lime-kiln operators, packing houses, and fuel dealers.

Owners desiring information regarding prices and the location of manufacturing plants will find it useful to communicate with manufacturers' associations throughout the eastern portion of the United States, where the marketing of farm-grown timber assumes special importance.[1] The associations include in their membership makers of cooperage, veneer and panels, vehicles and implements, paper and pulp, and lumber.

F-11188-A

FIG. 8.—Yellow poplar and white oak logs at a veneer plant. (This class of log is worth from $30 to $50 per thousand feet on the yard.)

State foresters are often able to furnish valuable hints and other assistance in locating buyers of rough materials from the farm woodlot, and should be consulted by owners desiring such aid.

SHIPPING BY RAIL.

When a shipment is to be made by rail, obtain from the local railroad agent the freight rate in carload lots for the given commodity between the shipping point and the destination. The rate obtained is then applied to the total weight of the commodity as shown in Tables 1 to 5. This will give the approximate but not exact cost of shipment. Rates for shipments in carload lots are generally quoted

[1] These associations are made up mostly of manufacturers, but include some wholesalers and other dealers. Lists of these associations are made up annually, and, if desired, copies may be obtained upon application to the Forester, Forest Service, Washington, D. C. A large number of dealers' associations exist, but are smaller in membership and more local in character than the manufacturers' associations.

per 100 pounds, with a stated minimum weight for which payment must be made. Shipments in less than carload lots are impracticable because of the very high cost. The following example will illustrate the method. Suppose the freight tariff on "bolts" is 6.3 cents per 100 pounds between two specified railroad points, and a farmer wishes to ship a carload of dry elm bolts to a cooperage plant at the given destination. The material weighs 2,400 pounds per cord [1] and 18 cords are to be loaded on the car. The total weight will be 43,200 pounds and the cost will be $27.22 for the carload, or an average of $1.51 per cord. Since 40,000 pounds is the minimum weight for this class of material on this railroad, the least charge for a shipment by carload rates would be $25.20. Thus if less than 16.7 cords are loaded on a car, the cost per cord will increase in proportion as the total weight of the contents falls below the minimum. The tariff sheet of one railroad lists 58 different commodities under the

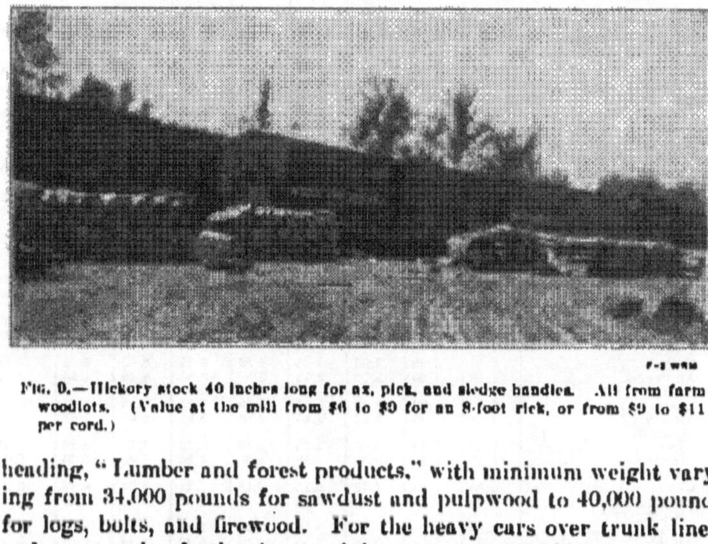

F-3 WAM

FIG. 9.—Hickory stock 40 inches long for ax, pick, and sledge handles. All from farm woodlots. (Value at the mill from $6 to $9 for an 8-foot rick, or from $9 to $11 per cord.)

heading, "Lumber and forest products," with minimum weight varying from 34,000 pounds for sawdust and pulpwood to 40,000 pounds for logs, bolts, and firewood. For the heavy cars over trunk lines, and to certain destinations, minimums up to 60,000 pounds are quoted. Cars may not be loaded in excess of 10 per cent of their marked weight capacity. Usually the rate is about the same for the principal kinds of timber products over the same haul. Tables 12 and 13 show the approximate cost per 1,000 board feet of shipping logs and lumber, both green and air dry, of different species, at rates of from 2 to 10 cents per 100 pounds.

[1] Bolts averaging 12 inches in diameter and 3 feet long, making a short cord 3 feet in width. (See Table 2.)

In selling logs and other products to outside markets it is a good thing to effect the sale at a price for the material delivered at the railroad, either in the yard or aboard the cars. Then, the buyer, rather than the farmer, handles the shipping end of the business. The chances are that by this arrangement the farmer may realize more profit than if he had sold f. o. b. the destination point.

TABLE 12.—*Cost of shipping logs, green and air dry, per 1,000 board feet (Doyle scale), at rates of from 2 to 10 cents per 100 pounds.*

[Costs given are for logs measuring 18 inches in diameter at the small end. For 12-inch logs add 40 per cent and for 24-inch logs subtract 15 per cent of the costs given. Weights used are those shown in Table 1.]

Species.	Rate in cents per hundred pounds.								
	2	3	4	5	6	7	8	9	10
	Cost of shipping 1,000 board feet.								
Ash:									
Green	$1.54	$2.31	$3.08	$3.85	$4.62	$5.39	$6.16	$6.93	$7.70
Air dry	1.36	2.04	2.72	3.40	4.08	4.76	5.44	6.12	6.80
Basswood:									
Green	1.32	1.98	2.64	3.30	3.96	4.62	5.28	5.94	6.60
Air dry	.82	1.23	1.64	2.05	2.46	2.87	3.28	3.69	4.10
Beech:									
Green	1.78	2.67	3.56	4.45	5.34	6.23	7.12	8.01	8.90
Air dry	1.40	2.10	2.80	3.50	4.20	4.90	5.60	6.30	7.00
Birch, yellow:									
Green	1.84	2.76	3.68	4.60	5.52	6.44	7.36	8.28	9.20
Air dry	1.44	2.16	2.88	3.60	4.32	5.04	5.76	6.48	7.20
Cherry, black:[1]									
Green	1.46	2.19	2.92	3.65	4.38	5.11	5.84	6.57	7.30
Air dry	1.16	1.74	2.32	2.90	3.48	4.06	4.64	5.22	5.80
Chestnut:									
Green	1.76	2.64	3.52	4.40	5.28	6.16	7.04	7.92	8.80
Air dry	.98	1.47	1.96	2.45	2.94	3.43	3.92	4.41	4.90
Cottonwood:[2]									
Green	1.50	2.25	3.00	3.75	4.50	5.25	6.00	6.75	7.50
Air dry	.88	1.32	1.76	2.20	2.64	3.08	3.52	3.96	4.40
Elm:									
Green	1.66	2.49	3.32	4.15	4.98	5.81	6.64	7.47	8.30
Air dry	1.20	1.80	2.40	3.00	3.60	4.20	4.80	5.40	6.00
Gum, red:									
Green	1.50	2.25	3.00	3.75	4.50	5.25	6.00	6.75	7.50
Air dry	1.10	1.65	2.20	2.75	3.30	3.85	4.40	4.95	5.50
Hickory:									
Green	2.06	3.09	4.12	5.15	6.18	7.21	8.24	9.27	10.30
Air dry	1.66	2.49	3.32	4.15	4.98	5.81	6.64	7.47	8.30
Maple, sugar:									
Green	1.80	2.70	3.60	4.50	5.40	6.30	7.20	8.10	9.00
Air dry	1.40	2.10	2.80	3.50	4.20	4.90	5.60	6.30	7.00
Oak, red:									
Green	2.06	3.09	4.12	5.15	6.18	7.21	8.24	9.27	10.30
Air dry	1.40	2.10	2.80	3.50	4.20	4.90	5.60	6.30	7.00
Oak, white:									
Green	2.00	3.00	4.00	5.00	6.00	7.00	8.00	9.00	10.00
Air dry	1.54	2.31	3.08	3.85	4.62	5.39	6.16	6.93	7.70
Sycamore:									
Green	1.68	2.52	3.36	4.20	5.04	5.88	6.72	7.56	8.40
Air dry	1.16	1.74	2.32	2.90	3.48	4.06	4.64	5.22	5.80
Yellow poplar:									
Green	1.22	1.83	2.44	3.05	3.66	4.27	4.88	5.49	6.10
Air dry	.90	1.35	1.80	2.25	2.70	3.15	3.60	4.05	4.50
Tupelo:[3]									
Green	2.10	3.15	4.20	5.25	6.30	7.35	8.40	9.45	10.50
Air dry	1.18	1.77	2.36	2.95	3.54	4.13	4.72	5.31	5.90
Walnut:									
Green	1.66	2.49	3.32	4.15	4.98	5.81	6.64	7.47	8.30
Air dry	1.14	1.71	2.28	2.85	3.42	3.99	4.56	5.13	5.70

[1] Silver maple is about the same as black cherry, which may be substituted.
[2] For willow use figures for cottonwood, adding 10 per cent for green and subtracting 8 per cent for dry.
[3] For black gum use figures for tupelo.

TABLE 13.—*Cost of shipping 1-inch lumber, green and air dry, per thousand board feet, at rates of from 2 to 10 cents per hundred pounds.*

[Weights used are those given in Table 1.]

Species.	Rate in cents per hundred pounds.								
	2	3	4	5	6	7	8	9	10
	Cost of shipping 1,000 board feet.								
Ash:									
Green	$0.80	$1.20	$1.60	$2.00	2.40	$2.80	$3.20	$3.60	$4.00
Air dry	.70	1.05	1.40	1.75	2.10	2.45	2.80	3.15	3.50
Basswood:									
Green	.68	1.02	1.36	1.70	2.04	2.38	2.72	3.06	3.40
Air dry	.42	.63	.84	1.05	1.26	1.47	1.68	1.89	2.10
Beech:									
Green	.92	1.38	1.84	2.30	2.76	3.22	3.68	4.14	4.60
Air dry	.72	1.08	1.44	1.80	2.16	2.52	2.88	3.24	3.60
Birch, yellow:									
Green	.96	1.44	1.92	2.40	2.88	3.36	3.84	4.32	4.80
Air dry	.74	1.11	1.48	1.85	2.22	2.50	2.96	3.33	3.70
Cherry, black:[1]									
Green	.76	1.14	1.52	1.90	2.28	2.66	3.04	3.42	3.80
Air dry	.60	.90	1.20	1.50	1.80	2.10	2.40	2.70	3.00
Chestnut:									
Green	.92	1.38	1.84	2.30	2.76	3.22	3.68	4.14	4.60
Air dry	.50	.75	1.00	1.25	1.50	1.75	2.00	2.25	2.50
Cottonwood:[2]									
Green	.72	1.08	1.44	1.80	2.16	2.52	2.88	3.24	3.60
Air dry	.44	.66	.88	1.10	1.32	1.54	1.76	1.98	2.20
Elm:									
Green	.86	1.29	1.72	2.15	2.58	3.01	3.44	3.87	4.30
Air dry	.62	.93	1.24	1.55	1.86	2.17	2.48	2.79	3.10
Gum, red:									
Green	.78	1.17	1.56	1.95	2.34	2.73	3.12	3.51	3.90
Air dry	.56	.84	1.12	1.40	1.68	1.96	2.24	2.52	2.80
Hickory:									
Green	1.04	1.56	2.08	2.60	3.12	3.64	4.16	4.68	5.20
Air dry	.86	1.29	1.72	2.15	2.58	3.01	3.44	3.87	4.30
Maple, sugar:									
Green	.94	1.41	1.88	2.35	2.82	3.29	3.76	4.23	4.70
Air dry	.72	1.08	1.44	1.80	2.16	2.52	2.88	3.24	3.60
Oak, red:									
Green	1.08	1.62	2.16	2.70	3.24	3.78	4.32	4.86	5.40
Air dry	.72	1.08	1.44	1.80	2.16	2.52	2.88	3.24	3.60
Oak, white:									
Green	1.04	1.56	2.08	2.60	3.12	3.64	4.16	4.68	5.20
Air dry	.80	1.20	1.60	2.00	2.40	2.80	3.20	3.60	4.00
Sycamore:									
Green	.86	1.29	1.72	2.15	2.58	3.01	3.44	3.87	4.30
Air dry	.60	.90	1.20	1.50	1.80	2.10	2.40	2.70	3.00
Yellow poplar:									
Green	.64	.96	1.28	1.60	1.92	2.24	2.56	2.88	3.20
Air dry	.48	.72	.96	1.20	1.44	1.68	1.92	2.16	2.40
Tupelo:[3]									
Green	1.10	1.65	2.20	2.75	3.30	3.85	4.40	4.95	5.50
Air dry	.60	.90	1.20	1.50	1.80	2.10	2.40	2.70	3.00
Walnut:									
Green	.86	1.29	1.72	2.15	2.58	3.01	3.44	3.87	4.30
Air dry	.60	.90	1.20	1.50	1.80	2.10	2.40	2.70	3.00

[1] For silver maple use figures for black cherry, since the weights are about the same.
[2] For willow use figures for cottonwood, adding about 20 per cent for green lumber.
[3] For black gum use figures for tupelo, since the weights are about the same.

The amount of forest products of any kind that can be shipped in or on a car varies with both the cubical and weight capacity of the car. The following table shows roughly the amount of different kinds of forest products that can be shipped in the average 60,000-pound-capacity car.

Lumber:	
Rough .... board feet..	15,000 to 18,000
Finished .... do....	17,000 to 20,000
Logs:	
Large, 24 inches .... do....	5,000 to 7,000
Small, 12 inches .... do....	4,000 to 5,000
Bolts or butts .... cords..	12 to 16
Cordwood, 4 feet .... do....	15 to 18
Stovewood, 16 inches .... ranks..	30 to 40
Mine timber (see Posts, Poles, Logs).	
Poles or piling .... pieces..	25 to 40
Ties:	
7" by 9" by 8½' .... do....	300
6" by 8" by 8' .... do....	350
5" by 6" by 5½' (mine tie) .... do....	1,100
Posts:	
4" top, 7 feet	800
6" top, 8 feet	500
Tanbark .... cords..	16 to 18
Sawdust .... tons..	12 to 18

WHEN TO SELL.

Woodlot owners do not always know when to sell standing timber and when to use it for local needs. In some localities it unquestionably pays the farmer better at all times to sell it, particularly the more valuable kinds. For example, in the central hardwood region farmers profitably sell their select yellow-poplar trees and with the money purchase and haul back to the farm for distances of from 4 to 8 miles southern-pine siding for their houses and barns. On the other hand, there are too often instances where one finds choice white oak of the best quality for veneer or furniture stock sawed up into posts for the farm.

The woodlot owner should keep in touch with market conditions in order that he may market his product to the best advantage. With rarely an exception the timber is not dying, decaying, or "going back" by fungous or insect attack at the rapid rate alleged by buyers, who, obviously, desire to buy as cheaply as possible; and, unless it is overmature, it is increasing yearly in volume and value. Cutting during the early period often represents a real sacrifice in financial returns. The approximate age at which trees should be cut in order to secure the highest net money returns per year is very different for different species. Thus cottonwood, ash, and yellow poplar become commercially valuable at much earlier ages than white oak and black walnut.

When other farm work is least pressing the farmer should give attention to estimating, measuring, cutting, marketing, and selling his timber. Spare help and time to supervise the work make the winter a favorable season. It is easier to haul logs on the snow than over ordinary roads, and the logs are less liable than at any other time of the year to deteriorate quickly through attacks of insects or fungi.

HOW TO SELL.

The choice of methods of selling will depend largely upon the kind of timber and the owner's knowledge of its value, his past experience, and the condition of the market. Woodlot products are sold either in the standing tree or in a more or less roughly manufactured condition. Except when sold by the lot or lump, sales are based upon a measure by log scale or lumber tally or upon individual count of units of designated size or character.

SELLING BY LOT OR LUMP.

Timber sold by the lot, boundary, or tract is either "lumped off" to include a designated tract or sold on an acreage basis.

This method has prevailed over all others, particularly in the rougher and less settled districts. As a rule it is strongly favored by the purchaser because in such a transaction his better knowledge of both timber yields and values gives him an advantage over the average woodlot owner. Many examples of the sacrifice by the owner of a large share of the value of the timber can be found in nearly any woodlot region. On account of greater competition among purchasers and an increase in timber values, sales of standing timber by the lot or lump are now being made with better profit than formerly.

In using this method it is very important in advance of the sale (1) to secure a good estimate of the amount, quality, and unit value of each kind of product in the stand; (2) to get bids from as many buyers as possible; and (3) to have an agreement clearly specifying the restrictions in regard to the manner and amount of cutting, so as not to impair the producing power of the forest. The sale may include only trees above a specified minimum diameter limit, or only such trees as have been previously marked by the owner for cutting. Suggestions of conditions which may or may not be included in the timber sale, according to the local conditions and the wishes of the owner, will be found on pages 43 and 44. When safeguarded in the manner suggested above, this method becomes one of the safest and most satisfactory of all methods of selling and should receive full consideration when sales are contemplated.

Selling by lump eliminates the anxiety and misunderstandings attending sales by log-scale measurement. If competition is keen, it is likely that nearly or quite the full value of the timber will be reached in the bids. By this method the owner foregoes the opportunity of profitable employment for himself and his teams which he would have if he logged the material and sold it after hauling it to the mill or shipping point.

Unless restricted by the terms of the agreement, the buyer usually cuts very closely. Selling by the lot is therefore a good method to use where the owner intends to clear the land for other uses. For the same reason, if the land is to be kept in timber, the owner should make provision in the contract of sale to retain sufficient control over the logging operations to protect the young growth and provide for a future crop. The importance of care in cutting, on account of its effect upon the succeeding growth and production of the stand, can hardly be overstated.

SELLING BY LOG SCALE.

Timber is sold at a certain price per thousand board feet, measured in the log.[1] It is sold either "in the tree," in which case the value of the standing timber is all that is considered, or in the log, cut and

FIG. 10.—A black walnut log, 35 inches in top diameter by 12 feet in length, which brought $135 per thousand feet, or $95.85 for the log, at the railroad. (The original owner, a farmer, sold the whole tree, standing, for $50; the buyer felled it, at a cost of $15, and sold it there for $138.20; it was resold without being moved for $164.84, and later sold to a large sewing-machine factory.)

delivered at some designated point, in which case the price is based on the stumpage value plus the labor of cutting and transportation.

The chief concern of the owner in selling his standing timber by this method is to determine in advance the true value and price to be charged per unit of measure. This may be secured as (1) an average or "woods run" for the entire lot, or (2) separated by species and, if desired, by grades under each. The latter is the more accurate and satisfactory method. How to ascertain stumpage values is discussed on page 27. The owner has the choice of selling only selected and marked trees, or all trees above a certain diameter limit and none

[1] In regions where sales are small and values high, it is frequently customary to buy and sell timber by the hundred rather than thousand board feet.

others, or, if he chooses, all merchantable trees. Selling only marked trees gives very good results indeed when the selection is properly done; selling to a diameter limit follows in preference; selling all merchantable trees should not be used in connection with this method, but restricted to sales by the lump or lot, in order to secure full utilization of the lower grades.

Selling standing timber, to be paid for on the basis of the amount determined by scaling up the logs when cut, is one of the most common of methods. A good many sales are made where the owner cuts and delivers the logs to the mill or shipping point. Because the average farmer is not usually equipped to do an extensive business of this character, the method is mostly confined to relatively small sales and often to the higher-priced woods, such as white oak, yellow poplar, white ash, or black walnut. In selling by the log, the owner who measures and grades his timber,[1] even though he does it roughly, has an advantage over one who is obliged to accept without a check the scale and inspection of the purchaser. In case he has not sufficient experience himself, it will usually pay the owner to hire, if necessary, a competent person to give him instruction in the work.

The contents of trees are more valuable when cut into logs and delivered at the mill or on board cars; and by doing this work himself the owner may share the legitimate profit derived from the enhanced value of the commodity. This additional profit can usually be figured as from 20 to 30 per cent of the cost of logging and hauling.

SELLING BY COUNT.

Poles, piling, crossties, small mining timbers, cordwood, etc., are sold by individual count of units of specified sizes.[2] The smaller sizes of bolts, for example, are sold the same as fuel wood by the cord. Because of its simplicity and ease of application, the method has much to recommend it for use wherever it can be applied in woodlot sales.

SELLING BY LUMBER TALLY.

There are two ways of selling timber to be paid for according to the amount of lumber sawed from it in the mill. In the one case, the woodlot owner takes no part in the logging and sawing, but disposes of his standing timber at a stumpage price per thousand feet of lumber actually produced at the mill. This method of sale is desirable where conditions are such that the material can more easily or more reliably be measured and checked after leaving the saw than while in the log. It is more applicable also to stands of timber consisting of only a few species than to a mixture of many different kinds. Since mill scales as a rule show from 15 to 30 per cent overrun in excess of log scales in common use, the owner secures returns on the full amount of the product sold. In the other case the owner personally takes charge of the logging and milling and markets the

---

[1] See p. 14 for scaling and p. 2 for grading. [2] See pp. 7 to 12 for specifications.

manufactured product. If successful in marketing, he secures the full value of his stumpage and, in addition, a share in the profits derived from the operations of logging and manufacturing. Time, knowledge, and experience necessary to supervise the actual operations or contract for parts of it, and capital to finance and carry on the work are requisites.

In this connection it should be clearly recognized that primarily the farmer is a producer and not a manufacturer. His concern, therefore, is in producing and disposing of the raw product, or the timber as it stands in the tree, rather than in logging and milling. However, with teams, wagons, and spare labor available, particularly during the winter months, he can often find profitable employment in logging, or at least in hauling the logs to the mill or shipping point. The sawing must usually be contracted for, because the investment in sawmill and power outfit would entail too great an expense. In milling and selling, the farmer usually works at a great disadvantage, because he must compete with men whose entire time is devoted to the business. Unless the owner has a definite contract before beginning sawing, he is very likely to find himself later on with lumber on his hands for which there is little demand.

EXAMPLES OF MARKETING.

The advantage to be gained through a knowledge of marketing timber is best shown by a few actual examples:

(*a*) A woodlot owner in Maryland received an offer of $1,500 for a tract of timber, which he was inclined to accept as a fair price. Before the sale was made, however, he requested the advice of the State forester as to the amount and value of the timber. As a result the State forester made an examination of the tract, estimated the market value of the timber, and furnished the owner a list of timber operators who might be prospective buyers. The timber was then publicly advertised, with the result that the man who had previously made the $1,500 offer raised his bid to $4,500, and the sale was finally made to another person for about $5,500. Only three months elapsed between the date of the first offer and the final sale. Not only was the original offer increased by nearly 270 per cent, but the woodlot was also left in excellent condition. This was accomplished by having the trees to be cut selected and marked by the State forester with a view to leaving the young growing timber on the ground, together with sufficient seed trees to restock the open places. The contract further called for close utilization by cutting the stumps low and using to small diameters in the tops, the lopping of tops for cordwood, and the scattering of the remaining brush.

(*b*) An 80-acre farm in south central Michigan had on it a 10-acre woodlot, containing about 18,000 board feet of basswood and about 12,000 each of hard maple, soft maple, red oak, soft elm, ash, and beech. The trees were overmature, many of them hollow; and the owner knew he ought to "sell them to save them." Timber on an adjacent 10 acres had previously been sold for less than $100 per acre, or a total of about $1,000. Even this value compares well with incomes commonly obtained from woodlots in southern Michigan. Instead of selling on the first bid made, however, the owner, acting on the advice of an expert attached to a near-by forestry school, wrote to a number of wood-using firms in different cities, from some of whom, after examination of his timber, he secured bids on the different species in his woodlot. As a result of his bargaining, he received for his stumpage sums amounting, in the aggregate, to nearly $2,000. For his red oak, bought for quarter-sawing by a firm outside the State, he received $21 per 1,000 board feet. His other trees were purchased by veneer companies, the basswood re-

FIG. 11.—A mill sawing posts and boards from red cedar gleaned from farm woodlots and pastures.

turning $19 per 1,000 board feet, ash $16, elm and hard maple $14, soft maple and beech $12.

(*c*) An owner in northwestern Ohio received bids of $550 and $600 lump sum for his timber. Following the advice of a relative who had previously run a sawmill, he engaged a portable mill, sawed out, and sold the following at the prices named:

(1) White oak butts, rough lumber for wagon stock, hickory butts for bands, and elm butts for hoops, sold for	$1,350
(2) Barn frame, cut and used on the farm, value	600
(3) 500 railroad ties, sold for	250
(4) Balance, consisting of cheaper poles, "sap timber, cull, and refuse" sold to the buyer who had offered $600 for the standing timber for	350
Gross receipts from timber	2,550
Total cost of operation	1,150
Net for stumpage value and profit	1,400

It will be noted that $600 was the highest bid received for the standing timber, whereas he cleared $1,400.

(*d*) In western Ohio, a woodlot owner who had carefully protected his best timber for many years accepted in 1914 a local buyer's lump sum offer of $260 for the timber on 6.5 acres. The trees were tall, clean, good-sized white and bur oak of high grade. By a careful measurement of the stumps and tops, made just after logging, the writer found that the tract had yielded not less than 14,500 board feet per acre, or a total of something over 84,500 board feet.[1] A fair price for this quality of timber would be $17 per 1,000 feet on the stump. At this rate the timber included in this sale was worth not less than $1,436, or $1,176 more than the farmer received for it. Though this may seem to be an extreme case, mistakes only slightly less striking are common.

TIMBER-SALE CONTRACTS.

The woodlot owner should draw up a written contract covering every sale of woodlot products. Even in small sales much trouble and financial loss have resulted from failure to put the terms of the sale in writing.

The primary aim of the seller should be to make absolutely clear the conditions under which he desires to dispose of his product. The essential conditions to be inserted in the complete form of timber-sale contract refer to (1) description and location of the timber; (2) price and manner of payment; (3) conditions of cutting and removal; and (4) title and means of settling disputes. Under the third heading are put down the provisions regarding the duration of the contract, the marking of the timber, the diameter limits, the method of scaling, merchantability, the degree of utilization, and protection against injury.

As an aid to those unfamiliar with such agreements, a sample contract is given, showing the more important provisions that should be included in a contract for the sale of marked trees to be scaled in the log. Substitute clauses are given for use in other kinds of sales. No single form of contract will suit all classes of sales, but owners of woodlot timber should have no difficulty in adapting this contract to their use.

SAMPLE TIMBER SALE CONTRACT.

TIMBER CONTRACT.

AGREEMENT entered into this 16th day of November, 1915, between James Boyd, of Centerdale, Ohio, hereinafter called the seller, and Thomas B. McCord, of New Albany, Ohio, hereinafter called the purchaser.

WITNESSETH:

ARTICLE I. The seller agrees to sell to the purchaser, upon the terms and conditions hereinafter stated, all the living timber marked or designated by the

---

[1] Allowing 10 per cent deduction for possible further defect than was noted.

seller and all merchantable dead timber, standing or down, estimated to be 84,000 board feet, more or less, on a certain tract of land situated in the township of Centerdale, county of Tompkins, State of Ohio, and located on the farm belonging to the seller, and about one-half mile west of his farmhouse.

ARTICLE II. The purchaser agrees to pay the seller the sum of seven hundred dollars ($700), more or less, as may be determined by the actual scale, at the rate of fourteen dollars ($14.00) per thousand board feet for white oak and white ash, twelve and 50/100 dollars ($12.50) for red oak and hickory, eight dollars ($8.00) for sugar maple and beech, and six dollars ($6.00) for black gum, blue beech, and ironwood, payable prior to the date of removal of material, in installments of two hundred dollars ($200) each.

ARTICLE III. The purchaser further agrees to cut and remove said timber in strict accordance with the following conditions:

1. Unless extension of time is granted, all timber shall be cut, paid for, and removed on or before March 30, 1910.

2. Saw timber shall be scaled by the Doyle log rule, and measured at the small end along the average diameter inside the bark.

3. The maximum scaling length of logs shall be 16 feet; greater lengths shall be scaled as two or more logs. Upon all logs an additional length of 4 inches shall be allowed for trimming. Logs overrunning this allowance shall be scaled not to exceed the next foot in length.

4. No unmarked timber of any kind shall be cut, except black gum, blue beech, and ironwood.

5. Stumps shall be cut so as to cause the least possible waste; stumps of trees up to 16 inches in diameter not higher than 12 inches above the ground, and those of trees above this size at a distance above the ground not greater than three-fourths of their diameter.

6. All trees shall be utilized in their tops to the lowest possible diameter for commercially salable material.

7. Young trees shall be protected against unnecessary injury; only dead trees and the less valuable kinds may be used for construction purposes in connection with lumbering operations.

8. Care shall be exercised at all times by the purchaser and his employees against the spread of fire.

ARTICLE IV. It is mutually understood and agreed by and between the parties hereto as follows:

1. All timber included in this agreement shall remain the property of the seller until paid for in full.

2. In case of dispute over the terms of this contract, final decision shall rest with a reputable person to be mutually agreed upon by the parties to this contract; and in case of further disagreement, with an arbitration board of three persons, one to be selected by each party to this contract and a third to be the State forester or his chosen representative.

IN WITNESS WHEREOF the parties hereto have hereunto set their hands and seals this day of 19 .

Witnesses:

------------------------------ ------------------------------

------------------------------ ------------------------------

The following are specimens of clauses that should be substituted in the contract when other methods of sale are used.

In lump-sum sales substitute in Article I a descriptive clause modeled on this one:

All merchantable living trees, except yellow poplar, white ash, and basswood which measure 13 inches and below in diameter at a height of 1 foot above the ground.

This provision will reserve the basis for a second crop consisting of the more valuable and rapid-growing kinds of trees, and remove all of the inferior and slower-growing trees.

In a sale to a diameter limit the clause should read somewhat as follows:

All merchantable living trees, 14 inches and over, measured at the height of 1 foot above the ground.

The payment clause in lump-sum sales should be varied to read something like this:

* * * the sum of ——— dollars ($———) for said timber, payable prior to the cutting of the material, in installments of ——— dollars ($———) each, payable on or before ———, respectively.

Other clauses which might be included are those requiring that the timber shall be scaled in the presence of the seller or his authorized agent; that the log lengths shall be varied so as best to utilize the timber; that unmarked trees, if cut, shall be paid for at double the regular price; that tops left in logging shall remain on the tract for the use of the seller (or, if desired, shall be utilized by the purchaser).

In selling by lump the other essential change is to omit the provisions, or parts of them, referring to scaling, measuring, and unit prices. The total amount to be paid is very important, while the total estimated quantity of timber is optional.

THE SMALL SAWMILL.

Practically all that has been said in regard to the marketing of lumber by the farmer applies equally to the owner of a small portable sawmill. The small millman's interest is closely related to that of the woodlot owner, since the prosperity, success, and profit of both are dependent upon the millman's ability to manufacture carefully and market to good advantage. If the millman shows good management in handling his business, the farmer who sells him his raw materials is certain in the end to obtain larger prices for his stumpage. In fact, practical assistance in marketing given to the small millmen will undoubtedly prove effective in assisting the small owner to secure the full value of his timber.

It is to the advantage of both the woodlot owner who manufactures his product and the millman who buys and saws the farmer's standing timber to work up the logs into the most salable form. In advance of sawing it is well to secure a definite contract, or at least follow a lumber bill which conforms to standard market requirements of special industries. Advance orders call for stated quantities of material of specified kind, sizes, and grades. The operator of a small portable sawmill is likely to lose money if he saws without due regard for the market requirements in material, sizes, and grades. Investigate the market first, then proceed to cut up the timber. This applies equally to cutting up logs in the woods and running the logs through the sawmill. Great waste, with consequent reduction in profit, results from failure to locate the market before beginning to harvest the crop. Undoubtedly, the present custom had its origin in the customary method of harvesting field crops. The timber crop is, however, essentially different from the field crop

F-[illegible]

FIG. 12.—Portable steam sawmill cutting a log of maximum size for the saw.

in one respect, namely, that there is seldom any necessity for quick harvesting.

COOPERATION IN MARKETING.

There is unquestionably a clear and definite need for cooperation among owners in the selling of woodlot products. The average farmer by himself acts at a great disadvantage, because the whole field of caring for growing timber, selecting trees for cutting, and finding the best market is unfamiliar ground.

Because he has not a carload lot of a particular kind of material and shipment by local freight is absolutely prohibitive, the woodlot owner is obliged in many instances to cut up choice kinds of material into very inferior products; for example, he may find it necessary to turn clear white oak or black cherry into railroad ties and sell his material at a great sacrifice to a local buyer—a middleman. Several farmers acting cooperatively could market their black-walnut logs, basswood, hickory or oak bolts, piling, or other products direct to the wholesaler, manufacturing plant, or user at greatly increased profits over those received from their individual sales.

The services of a reliable and experienced timberman as adviser would be extremely helpful to the majority of farmers. The services of such a man, who is known to be working in the interests of the farmer, are needed:

(1) To estimate the contents and market value of woodlots. The owner will then be in a better position to decide how to sell most profitably.

F-21101

FIG. 13.—A northern woodlot yielding a by-product of much value. (The maple-sirup industry brings good wages to the farmer and his teams during a dull season on the farm.)

(2) To supervise the marketing of timber in carload lots. Because of his superior knowledge such an adviser will be much better fitted to secure current market prices than the average farmer.

In regions where timberwork has been going on for many years men of the necessary qualifications will be quite readily found. They should be selected under the approval of the State forester in States where such an officer is employed. The farmers' timber adviser should be clearly identified with such organizations as the county improvement associations or with the State Extension Service. The farmer might pay a fair price for each piece of estimating and selling, or each county might employ a man whose duty it would be to advise the farmers. Several farmers acting cooperatively could secure the services of the timber agent at relatively small cost to each.

No attempt is made here to work out and recommend a plan of cooperation. This could undoubtedly be effected through the aid of the State and Federal Governments in conjunction with the present farm demonstration and management movement for better buying and selling on the part of farmers. Groups desiring to effect permanent organization can secure assistance and information as to methods and procedure from the marketing and rural organization specialists of the United States Department of Agriculture.

HOW TO PREVENT THE DETERIORATION OF CUT WOODLOT PRODUCTS.

A good rule to follow is to allow as little delay as possible between the felling of the tree and its manufacture into rough products. This means that sales should be arranged for prior to beginning cutting. It is often necessary or desirable, however, to put off the delivery of logs, bolts, poles, etc., until some months after cutting, either in order to allow them to season or because a good sale can not be arranged at once. A great deal of the weight of freshly cut products is due to the water they contain, and a few months' seasoning will often reduce this to a marked degree, the amount of reduction depending, of course, on the climate, the weather, and the exposure to sun and air. At the same time, unless preventive measures are taken, the products are sure to deteriorate through decay, insect attack, checking, or some other agency. A certain amount of deterioration is apt to take place in any case if the delivery is put off for some time; but the amount can be greatly reduced by proper preventive measures.

Logs and other round timber should never be allowed to remain long in the woods after cutting. As soon as possible they should be taken to a dry, well-aired, and unshaded area and placed on skids well off the ground; otherwise the opposite extreme should, if possible, be adopted, namely, of keeping the timber in water. Within a few days after the trees are felled the bark should be removed from poles, posts, and other material which will not be injured by checking or season cracks. The ends of logs should be coated with paint, creosote, or tar. This will not only assist in preventing decay, but will also retard seasoning to some extent and thus keep the logs from checking badly.

Poles should be peeled, and hauled or dragged to a place free from débris or rank vegetation and freely exposed to sun and wind. There they should be rolled upon skidways not less than 18 inches high, so that no part of them will rest on the ground. There should be only one layer of poles on each skidway. When ties are cut, it is usually cheapest and most desirable to haul them, unseasoned, directly to the railroad and there pile them according to the specifications furnished by the tie buyer.

Cordwood should be stacked in loose piles in a sunny, well-aired, and well-drained place free from rank vegetation. Two sticks on the ground running the length of the pile will keep it from contact with the soil and thus prevent decay in the lower layers.

PRACTICAL HELPS IN MARKETING.

The following suggestions may be helpful to the farmer in selling his woodlot products:

(1) Find out from as many sawmills and wood-using industries as possible what prices they offer for various wood products, in order that advantage may be taken of the best market. This applies to sales requiring shipment as well as to local sales.

(2) Before selling, inquire from neighbors who have recently disposed of their timber and use their experience as a guide. Failure to do this has resulted in many instances in not getting the full value of the product.

(3) Thoroughly investigate all local timber requirements and prices, since in many cases local markets pay better prices than outside markets because of the saving of transportation charges.

(4) Advertise in the papers and otherwise secure competition among outside purchasers. The expense will be small and outside buyers will thus learn of chances to bid on timber in competition with local buyers.

(5) Secure bids whenever practicable both by the lump and by log-scale measure. A choice is thus offered and the more profitable form of bid can be accepted.

(6) Consider the responsibility of the prospective purchaser before making the sale, in order to avoid slow payment, costly collections, and losses.

(7) Prior to making sales, secure at least a fairly good estimate of the amount and value of the material for sale. Persons acquainted with the business of measuring or estimating timber can usually be found in every region where timber has been handled in the past.

(8) Market the higher grades of timber instead of using them on the farm for purposes for which cheaper material will prove as serviceable. This should be done in many cases even if it makes necessary the purchasing and hauling of lower priced lumber to the farm. Markets which pay good prices usually buy on grade and inspect closely.

(9) Remember that standing timber does not deteriorate rapidly nor do the uses of wood change greatly within a few years. The owner, therefore, is not forced to place his product on the market regardless of market conditions.

(10) Use a written timber-sale agreement in selling woodlot timber, particularly where the cutting is done by the purchaser.

WASHINGTON : GOVERNMENT PRINTING OFFICE : 1916

The Cornell Reading-Courses

PUBLISHED BY THE

NEW YORK STATE COLLEGE OF AGRICULTURE AT CORNELL UNIVERSITY

Entered as second-class matter at the post office at Ithaca, New York

.. A. STOCKING, Jr., *Acting Director* A. R. MANN, *General Editor*

COURSE FOR THE FARM, ROYAL GILKEY, Supervisor

OL. III. No. 62 APRIL 15, 1914 FARM FORESTRY SERIES No. 4

METHODS OF DETERMINING THE VALUE OF TIMBER IN THE FARM WOODLOT

JOHN BENTLEY, Jr.

Persons who have read the first number[1] of the Farm Forestry Series .f Reading-Course lessons have learned something about the proper anagement of trees in the farm woodlot in order to obtain their est growth; also how to make cuttings in timber so as to improve the .ondition of the remaining trees. The object of all work in forestry is the production of wood and lumber for use. Since this product has a al value, the question may very properly arise: " How can I estimate e value of my timber? "

In many parts of the State it is not uncommon to hear of timber being old by the piece or by the acre, without any reference whatever to the ..nount of lumber or cordwood there is in the woodlot, and regardless of the true value of the product in the market. What takes place usually s this: A portable sawmill outfit passes through the region; a woodlot wner who needs to raise a little ready money hears of it and offers his mber for sale, or perhaps the sawmill owner has noticed a good piece f timber and approaches the owner with an offer. The sawmill owner nows that the majority of farmers have no means of telling exactly hat their timber is worth. As a result the timber is often sold for a um of money much smaller than it is really worth simply because the wner of the woodlot is ignorant of timber values and of how such values re determined. In many cases timber has been sold for less than alf of its true value. It is therefore worth while for the farmer to inquire to the matter of timber values, and before accepting any offer for the imber in his woodlot he should ask himself these questions: " Is the

[1] Reading-Course Lesson for the Farm, Vol. I, No. 12, Farm Forestry Series No. 1, " The improvement of the woodlot."

timber in my woodlot worth $2 a thousand on the stump, or is it worth $10 a thousand?" "How many thousand feet of lumber can a skillful sawyer obtain from my woodlot?" "How much does it cost him to cut the trees, haul the logs to his sawmill, and saw them into lumber?" "Am I getting all that I can get, or should get, for my timber?" A few farmers can answer these questions for themselves, or can seek advice from some one in the neighborhood who has had experience in buying and selling timber, and who knows timber values. But there are many persons in the State who desire definite knowledge concerning the way in which the value of standing timber is determined. It is the purpose of this paper to discuss ways and means of finding out, first, how much merchantable timber there is on a given piece of land; and secondly, how much that timber is worth in the market, under given conditions. The whole subject can be dealt with to the best advantage by a discussion of the following subjects:

- Units of measurement in common use
  - The board foot
  - The cord
  - Standards
  - The cubic foot
  - Poles, posts, railroad ties, and other units
- Reckoning the contents of logs in board feet
  - Log rules: their construction and application
  - Factors affecting the board-foot contents of logs
  - Relations between board measure and cubic measure
  - Relations between cordwood and cubic measure
- Scaling
- Methods of estimating the merchantable saw timber in a woodlot
  - The tree-to-tree count
  - Volume tables
  - Area methods
- Methods of estimating the cordwood in a woodlot
  - Cordwood tables
- How to determine the stumpage value of timber under different conditions
- Summary

UNITS OF MEASUREMENT IN COMMON USE

The board foot

Most lumber is sold by the thousand feet, board measure (M feet, B. M.), and the board foot is by far the commonest unit of measure in use. For example, we may learn by inquiring at the nearest lumberyard that hemlock is selling at "$22 per thousand," or that white pine is worth "$35 per thousand." The meaning in each case is that a thousand feet of lumber of that particular kind is worth the price stated. The price varies, of course, with the many grades of the lumber and with the supply and the demand. A board foot — one of the thousand thus spoken of — is a board one foot long, one foot wide, and an inch in thickness, or its equivalent. Theoretically it should be exactly of these dimensions, or their equivalent, and 12 board feet should constitute a cubic foot; but for several reasons the term "board foot" is sometimes rather loosely applied, and a solid cubic foot of timber never yields 12 board feet in inch boards.

Board-foot measure is applied to lumber other than inch boards; planks, scantling, dimension timbers, and other pieces more than an inch in thickness are also reckoned in board feet. Thus a plank 2 inches thick, 1 foot wide, and 12 feet long, contains 24 board feet; a "two-by-four" 12 feet long contains 8 board feet. The rule for finding the board-foot contents of any regular piece of sawed lumber may be stated as follows:

Multiply the width by the thickness of the board (or other piece) in inches, and multiply this product by the length in feet; divide the result by 12.

Sometimes planks and dimension timbers will be sawed slightly less than the full number of inches called for. Thus, on close measurement, a two-by-four may be found to measure only $1\frac{7}{8}$ x $3\frac{7}{8}$ inches, or the thickness of a plank that is supposed to be the full two inches may prove to be but $1\frac{7}{8}$ inch. This practice is employed by some sawmills, and the contents of the timbers is reckoned as if the full thickness were provided. Again, if inch boards are planed on one or both sides, or if flooring is tongued and grooved, the pieces will be slightly less than the full inch in thickness or slightly less than the specified width; but they are nevertheless reckoned as full size, because in the beginning a board of full size was used to produce the finished, planed board. These slight differences in actual thickness are understood by the purchaser, and there is no intention on the part of the manufacturer to defraud; it is simply customary to reckon in board feet, as if the material were the full size.

A special stick is sometimes used by lumber-inspectors, which shows at a glance the board-foot contents of a piece of lumber when width, thickness, and length are known. Such a stick simplifies the calculation of the amount of lumber in a number of boards when a large shipment of different sizes is being loaded.

The cord

Perhaps the next commonest measure for wood is the cord. Wood intended for fuel, for paper pulp, and the like, is usually measured by the cord, which is a convenient unit for sticks that are too small or too short to be scaled by the board foot. By a "cord" is understood a pile of wood cut into four-foot lengths and stacked so as to be four feet high and eight feet long. It may also be defined as 128 cubic feet of stacked wood. Unless otherwise specified, the full cord, as defined above, is understood. Sometimes wood only 18 or 24 inches in length or, indeed, any other odd length is stacked in piles 8 feet long and 4 feet high, and passes as a cord. It is generally understood, however, that such a pile is a "short cord," and the price of such wood is adjusted accordingly. The factors that influence the actual contents of a cord of wood are discussed on page 142.

Standards

In some parts of the State, notably in the Adirondack mountains, a log 13 feet long and 19 inches in diameter at the small end is spoken of as a "standard." The use of this unit of measurement dates back to the early days of lumbering in the Adirondack mountains; and to a limited extent its use still persists. Since a standard is roughly equivalent to 200 board feet, it is frequently reckoned as "5 to the thousand." In New Hampshire and elsewhere, other standards are in occasional use.

The cubic foot

While common among foresters who are making a careful study of the volume growth of trees, the use of the cubic foot as a commercial unit is not common at the present time, although it may be adopted in the future as timber becomes scarcer and lumber more valuable. Even now, certain tropical woods of great value are bought and sold by the cubic foot. Long-continued usage has made the board foot and the cord the two commonest units, however, and for the reason that everybody is so familiar with them it will doubtless be a long time before the cubic foot will supplant them.

Poles, posts, railroad ties, and other units

Such pieces as poles, posts, and ties are sold by the separate piece. The piece of timber must generally satisfy certain dimensions as to length, width, thickness, diameter, or girth. When different sizes are recognized, the value of the piece is determined by size and quality.

Railroad ties, for example, may be standard gauge ties or narrow gauge ties or ties of special sizes, such as those used under switches or on bridges and trestles. It is also customary to recognize certain grades, or qualities, in ties. According to specifications furnished by the New York Central Railroad, ties are classified as follows:

All ties shall be 8 feet 6 inches (8′ 6″) long and sawed square at both ends. Not more than one inch variation in length, over or under the specified length, will be allowed.

Class A: Pole ties must be 7 inches thick and not less than 7 inches or more than 12 inches wide at any point on the face, and shall be hewed or sawed on two parallel sides. Only one tie shall be made from the section of a tree. Sawed ties must be square on four sides, 7 inches thick, and 9 inches wide.

Class A ties are reckoned as equivalent to 44 board feet each, or 23 to the thousand.

Class B: Ties may be hewed or sawed on four sides to size 6 x 9 inches. Two or more ties can be taken from one section of a tree.

Class C: Ties may be 6 inches thick with face not less than 6 inches at any point (not over 25 per cent shall have this minimum width) and may be hewed or sawed on two sides; or if hewed and sawed on four sides they may be 6 inches thick and not less than 8 inches wide on the face. This class includes also ties with slight splits and other minor defects that do not materially impair the usefulness of the ties, but exclude them from Class A and Class B inspection.

Ties must be piled in accordance with kind and class.

The prices paid in 1914 will be:

	Class A	Class B	Class C
All oaks, except red oak	70 cents each	63 cents	55 cents each
Red oak	55 cents each	45 cents	Not taken
Chestnut	65 cents each	60 cents	50 cents each

Poles may be of any specified length, usually in multiples of 5 feet, as 25, 30, 35, 40, 45, or 50; and they must be 7 inches in diameter at the top. They range in price from about $2 each for 25-foot poles to $9 each for 50-foot poles.

Posts are usually 7 feet long and of a specified diameter or girth at the small end. Values for posts depend on whether they are split or round, and whether of a durable species or a short-lived species. Definite values are hard to give. They may range from 10 to 50 cents each, according to size, species, and quality.

Pieces of small girth are frequently sold by the *linear foot*, or the running foot. This means that the value of the piece is determined by its length alone, no attention being paid to the diameter or the girth.

Other special units of measurement may be met with occasionally, but those named in the preceding paragraphs are the commonest. Since stumpage values are almost always reckoned in terms of board feet, the methods of determining the contents of logs in this unit will first be considered in some detail.

RECKONING THE CONTENTS OF LOGS IN BOARD FEET

Log rules: their construction and application

It is frequently necessary to have some means of determining about how much lumber can be obtained from a sound log when its length and diameter are known. In order to meet this demand, tables have been constructed, some from mathematical formulæ, others from drawn diagrams, and still others from actual mill tallies, which attempt to show the contents in board feet of sound logs of different lengths and diameters. Such tables are called log rules, log tables, or log scales, and may be found

TABLE 1. BOARD-FOOT CONTENTS OF 10-FOOT, 12-FOOT, 14-FOOT, AND 16-FOOT LOGS, 6 TO 40 INCHES IN DIAMETER, BY THE UNIVERSAL RULE AND THE SCRIBNER RULE.

Universal rule*					Scribner rule†				
	Length of log (feet)					Length of log (feet)			
	10	12	14	16		10	12	14	16
Diameter of log at small end (inches)	Board feet	Board feet	Board feet	Board feet	Diameter of log at small end (inches)	Board feet	Board feet	Board feet	Board feet
6	9	11	12	14	6	10	12	14	18
7	14	17	20	22	7	16	18	24	28
8	20	24	28	32	8	20	24	28	32
9	27	33	38	44	9	25	30	35	40
10	36	43	50	57	10	31	40	45	50
11	45	54	63	72	11	40	50	55	65
12	55	66	78	89	12	49	59	69	79
13	67	80	94	107	13	61	73	85	97
14	79	95	111	127	14	71	86	100	114
15	93	111	130	148	15	88	107	125	142
16	107	129	150	172	16	100	119	139	159
17	123	148	172	197	17	115	139	162	185
18	140	168	196	223	18	133	160	187	213
19	157	189	220	252	19	150	180	210	240
20	176	211	246	282	20	175	210	245	280
21	196	235	274	313	21	190	228	266	304
22	217	260	303	347	22	209	251	292	334
23	238	286	334	382	23	235	283	330	377
24	261	314	366	410	24	252	303	353	404
25	286	343	400	457	25	287	344	401	459
26	311	373	435	497	26	313	375	439	500
27	336	404	471	538	27	343	411	479	548
28	364	437	509	582	28	363	436	509	582
29	392	470	548	627	29	381	457	533	609
30	421	505	590	674	30	410	493	575	657
31	452	542	632	722	31	443	532	622	710
32	483	579	676	772	32	460	552	644	736
33	515	618	721	824	33	490	588	686	784
34	549	658	768	878	34	500	600	700	800
35	583	700	816	932	35	547	657	766	876
36	619	742	866	990	36	577	692	807	923
37	655	786	917	1,048	37	643	772	901	1,029
38	693	831	970	1,108	38	667	801	934	1,068
39	731	878	1,024	1,170	39	700	840	980	1,120
40	771	925	1,079	1,244	40	752	903	1,053	1,204

* Printed with the permission of the author, Professor A. L. Daniels.
† Reprinted from the "Manual for Northern Woodsmen" by Austin Carey.

in books dealing with the subject of lumbering and in many books on forestry. There are many different log rules, some of which enjoy wide use, others being restricted to certain territories where they are known to give satisfactory results; still others are used only for certain local units of measurement. The practical value of any log rule depends not only on the accuracy and soundness of the principles by which it is constructed, but also on the skill and discretion of the man using it. Log rules are intended to show the probable contents of sound, straight logs when they are sawed by a sawyer who understands how to make the most of a given log. If defects are present in the log, the scaler must make certain discounts from the rule.

In practice, logs are scaled with the aid of a "scale stick," which is graduated to inches and has printed on it the values in board feet corresponding to the different sizes of logs (both by diameter and length). Thus, the board-foot contents of any given log may be read directly from the stick, which should be applied to an average diameter of the small end of the log, when the diameter and length are known. (For further details, see "Scaling," page 143.) Scale sticks are manufactured for several of the common rules, so that each person may select the stick best adapted to his purposes and locality.

For convenience, two log rules are here given. One, the Scribner, is a very old rule that has been widely used in the northern States. It was constructed from diagrams allowing for a saw kerf of one fourth inch, which is a liberal allowance. The other rule, known as the "Universal," is based on a mathematical formula, and is printed here with the permission of its author, Professor A. L. Daniels, of the University of Vermont. It will be noticed that the values given in this rule increase regularly as the size of the log increases, while those in the Scribner rule are sometimes greater and sometimes smaller than are the corresponding values in the Universal rule. This is because the Scribner rule is not based on a mathematical formula.

If a comparison is made of several of the standard log rules in use, such as the Doyle, the Scribner, and the Maine, it will be found that the greatest relative differences occur in the small-sized logs. The Doyle rule,[3] for example, gives an extremely small scale for logs of small diameter, and a good sawyer can always saw out more board feet than this scale gives. For large logs, however, it gives too large a scale. The rule is really accurate only for logs of medium size, or for those of about 20 to 36 inches. The Maine rule gives best results when used with logs of short length. Many of the rules will be found to be adapted to the timber in certain parts of the country, while in other regions, where the trees attain different forms, they will give very poor results.

[3] The Doyle rule is very widely used, but it is inaccurate for logs of small diameters and for very large logs. It is based on the following formula:

$$\textit{Board feet} = \left(\frac{D-4}{4}\right)^2 \times L,$$

in which D equals the diameter of the small end in inches, and L equals the length in feet. The rule is inaccurate because it allows a uniform factor for slabs and saw kerf (the 4 inches which is deducted from the diameter) regardless of the size of the log. It is evident that this amount of loss differs with the size of the log, and it is a fact (not too widely known) that the Doyle rule gives values too small on logs up to about 20 inches. Since there is always a large proportion of small logs in any quantity of them, it follows that the mill cut overruns the scale by 10 to 20 per cent if the logs are sound.

It has been said that certain rules have been constructed from the results of actual work in the mills. In several instances in which a large number of logs have been followed through the mill, the product actually obtained has been found to agree very closely with the Universal log rule, and it is presented in the belief that its use will prove satisfactory.

Factors affecting the board-foot contents of logs

Besides the size of the logs, there are several other factors that materially affect the contents of logs in board feet. They are as follows:

The width of the saw used.— There are many different styles of saws used in the mills of to-day, such as circular, or rotary, saws, band saws, and gang saws. These vary considerably in form and thickness, and it is easily seen that the amount of wood taken out by the saw in passing through the log, technically known as "saw kerf," will affect directly the

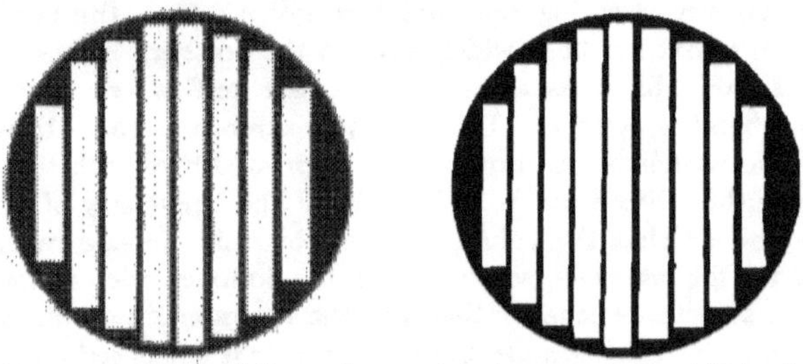

FIG. 77.— *Left-hand figure shows a $\frac{1}{4}$-inch saw kerf; the right-hand, a $\frac{1}{8}$-inch saw kerf*

amount of the lumber that can be obtained. Thus, a band saw taking out a kerf only $\frac{1}{8}$ inch in thickness wastes only half as much as a rotary saw taking out a kerf of $\frac{1}{4}$ inch, and the final product may be 10 to 20 per cent greater in actual board feet.

In Fig. 77, the left-hand figure shows how eight boards 1 inch thick and not less than 6 inches wide may be obtained from a perfect log 12 inches in diameter, if a saw kerf of $\frac{1}{4}$ inch is taken out. Under these conditions a log 16 feet long of this diameter will yield 96 board feet. The right-hand figure shows how nine boards 1 inch thick and not less than 6 inches wide may be obtained from a log of the same size, if a saw kerf of only $\frac{1}{8}$ inch is taken out. Under these conditions the log will yield 108 board feet, or a gain of 12 per cent, due entirely to the saving in saw kerf. Since no logs are perfect, but exhibit some irregularities in form, it is seldom possible to obtain the full number of board feet as indicated above. Log rules, therefore, properly make allowances for these irregularities.

The width of the smallest board that can be considered merchantable.—If no boards less than 6 inches in width are considered as merchantable, it is apparent that much good lumber will be lost toward the outer part of the log next the slabs. This loss increases with small logs, as is shown in Fig. 78. From these drawings it will be seen that the product of a log is affected by the width of the board which may be considered merchantable. The saw kerf is ¼ inch in both cases, but in the left-hand figure only eight boards 1 inch thick can be obtained, if none less than 6 inches wide is considered merchantable; in the right-hand figure, nine boards 1 inch thick can be obtained if a board three inches wide is considered merchantable. In the first case, a log 16 feet long and 12 inches in diameter would yield 96 board feet; in the second, 104 board feet. Modern log rules allow for narrower boards than do the older log rules.

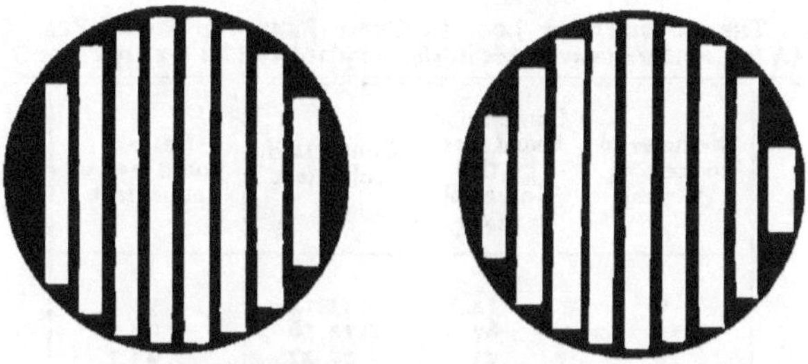

FIG. 78.—*Left-hand figure shows result when nothing less than a 6-inch board is considered merchantable; right-hand figure, when 3-inch boards are considered merchantable*

The straightness and soundness of the log.— If the log is crooked or if there is a defective spot in it, there is sure to be a loss in the number of board feet that can be produced from it. If the crook is slight, there may be a chance of obtaining short boards from the log, but even then there is certain to be some loss. In unsound logs the cause of the loss is very apparent.

The skill of the sawyer.— If the sawyer is careful to turn the log so as to take advantage of slight irregularities in form, which are common in almost every log, it is possible to make the log go farther and yield a greater number of board feet than if it is cut through and through without regard to its form and shape.

The efficiency of the machinery.— Well-kept and well-regulated machinery, sharp, carefully filed saws, attention to the little details of mill-adjustment, and like considerations will do much towards increasing the quantity and quality of the output. The efficiency of the machinery is a most important factor.

The thickness of the boards themselves.—If dimension stuff is being sawed from logs, there will be a larger scale than if inch-boards are sawed, because there is less loss in saw kerf.

It is apparent, therefore, that no one log rule can be expected to give uniformly accurate results under all conditions. Due allowance must be made for the factors just mentioned.

Relations between board measure and cubic measure

It is practically impossible to find any constant ratio between the cubic contents of logs and the number of board feet that they will yield. This ratio depends chiefly on the size of the logs, as will be seen by an inspection of the following table, which includes logs of only a few sizes for the purposes of illustration:

TABLE 2. THE CONTENTS OF LOGS IN CUBIC FEET AND BOARD FEET COMPARED
(A few representative sizes in the standard 16-foot log are chosen)

Diameter of 16-foot log (inches)	Contents in board feet, by the Universal rule	Contents in cubic feet	Ratio of board feet to cubic feet
6	14	3.14	4.5 : 1
12	89	12.56	7.0 : 1
18	223	28.27	7.9 : 1
24	419	50.27	8.3 : 1
30	674	78.54	8.6 : 1
36	990	113.10	8.7 : 1

When it is desirable to obtain an approximate equivalent between board feet and cubic feet, the figures given in the above table can be used as a guide. It must be remembered, however, that these values will not apply if a log rule other than the Universal is used.

Relations between cordwood and cubic measure

The actual number of cubic feet of wood in a cord of stacked wood varies from about 60 to 100, depending on the length of the sticks, the diameter of the sticks, the method of piling, whether the sticks are split or round, and whether they are green or dry. The straightness of the sticks also affects very strongly the amount of wood in a cord. In this respect, it is nearly always true that there will be less solid wood in a cord of hardwood sticks than in a cord of sticks from coniferous trees, as pines, spruces, and the like. A safe average factor to use in computing the actual number of cubic feet in a cord of wood is 70 per cent. This gives approximately 90 cubic feet for each cord of full size (8 x 4 x 4 feet).

SCALING

Scaling, or determining with the aid of the scale stick the contents in board feet of a given log, can be learned only through actual practice. It is almost impossible to give any hard and fast rules for scaling. The knowledge of how to allow for the defects that occur in nearly all logs is acquired by practice and observation; but although the art of scaling cannot be learned from books, the following points may prove helpful:

(*a*) Remember that the scale stick shows the contents of straight, sound logs, according to diameter and length; it is taken for granted that the sawyer is skillful enough to get the most out of a log. Even in sound, straight logs, loss may be caused by too thick slabbing, by cutting material too thick or too wide at the main saw, by poorly regulated machinery and dull saws, by waste in edging and trimming, and the like. Such loss is due to a lack of skill on the part of the sawyer and poor workmanship on the part of other operators, for which the scaler is not to blame.

(*b*) For certain visible defects, which are here explained, allowances can be made by the scaler. The more common terms used in defining defects are as follows:

Checks. These are cracks, or splits, or seams, running lengthwise which are developed in the course of the seasoning of the log.

Dote. This is the general term used by lumbermen to denote decay or rot in timber. The condition may be spoken of as "dote," or the part of the log decayed may be said to be "doty." Another term meaning the same is "dozy."

Cat-face. This term is applied to partly healed scars on the stem of a tree caused by fire or mechanical injury. As a rule, cat-faces do not cover a very large part of the tree and do not constitute a serious defect unless they have caused rot to develop.

Shake is defined as a crack in timber, due to the action of frost or wind, which usually results in the separation of the annual rings of growth, so that the continuity of the timber is broken. When "shaky" logs are sawed, the lumber resulting from them appears split and cracked. If the cracks follow the annual rings all the way around the tree, the defect is known as circular shake, and it results in a very large loss in the lumber.

The following suggestions, summarized from "The National Forest Manual" of the U. S. Department of Agriculture, may also be of some assistance:

Among the points which must be considered are the size and shape of the logs, the quality as affected by various kinds of defects, the size and location of the defect, and the requirements and limitations of markets. . . .

Measurement of diameters

All diameters will be measured inside the bark at the top end of the log. If logs are not round, scalers will average the greatest diameter inside the bark at the top end of the log with the diameter at right angles to this. The necessary reduction in diameter will be made for swelling at the scaling end of a log when no lumber can be produced from it.

Defects in logs

The following defects are most common:

Uniform center or circular rot, circular shake, pin dote, ground or stump rot, cat-face, dote at side of log extending to the bark, burns or defect caused by lightning extending along side of log, defect caused by lightning extending along the log in spiral form, punky or soft sap, deep checks or seams, dote appearing in knots, curve, or sweep, crooks, crotches, and blue sap.

Merchantable material

In general, a log containing sufficient sound material to saw out salable lumber equal to one third of its contents as given by the scale rule is termed "merchantable." This will be varied in accordance with the character of the timber and local market conditions. The term "sound material" is here used to signify such material as will produce lumber commonly merchantable in the markets supplied.

Center or circular rot

For loss caused by uniform circular rot, the following rules are given:

For uniform defect 3 inches or less in diameter deduct 10 feet b. m. in logs up to 16 feet in length.

For defect 4 to 6 inches in diameter add 3 inches to actual diameter of rot, and deduct from the full scale of the log an amount equal to the contents of a log of the resultant diameter.

For defect 7 to 12 inches in diameter add 4 inches to diameter of rot and deduct an amount equal to the contents of a log of the resultant diameter from full scale of log.

In measuring the diameter of this type of rot the scaler should measure it at the end of the log showing the greatest area of defect, since the saw cuts in straight, parallel lines.

Shake

Circular shake may, in general, be allowed for as in center rot.

Dote

If the visible area affected by pin dote amounts to 4 inches in diameter, or more, it should be allowed for as in circular rot.

Cat-face

Cat-face may be allowed for in the following manner: Consider what proportion of the length of the log is affected; find the contents of this section on a scale stick, then determine the proportion of the section that will be lost in sawing, and deduct this amount.

Side defects

The percentage of loss caused by defects located at the side of a log is much less than when they occur near the center, since in the former case much of the defect will come out in slabbing. This is especially true of the butt of the first log where the flare or swell is considerable at the point of cutting.

Since they do not usually run deep and can be mostly removed in slabbing, defects caused by lightning extending spirally along a log do not affect the scale.

Spiral checks

Where deep spiral checks are found, the scaler will measure the diameter of the portion of the log included within the largest circle that can be described on a cross section without being materially affected by the checks, and class as defective all that part of the log outside the area defined by the circle.

Unsound sap

Where a shell of unsound sap occurs, only the sound heartwood will be measured.

Unsound knots

Where dote appears in the knots, it indicates that the area of rot increases in the portion of the log near the knots, and deductions should be from 10 to 50 per cent greater than when it appears at the ends alone.

Curve or sweep

The percentage of a log affected by sweep or curve varies according to the diameter of the log. An amount of curve that might cull a very small log would not necessarily cause the rejection of a larger log. The scaler should, when possible, sight along curved logs, noting where the saw would square the log, sufficiently to enable boards to be cut on both sides affected by the curve, thus determining the amount of loss caused by the sweep. It should be remembered that boards sawed near the slab are always narrower and contain fewer board feet than those sawed from the balance of the log.

METHODS OF ESTIMATING THE MERCHANTABLE SAW TIMBER IN A WOODLOT

In all cases when standing timber is bought or sold, it is desirable to have some means of telling approximately the amount of merchantable timber that can be obtained from the trees on a given tract of land. It is necessary to know the amount of timber in order to determine the value of the timber, which may be reckoned according to the thousand feet (M feet) board measure (B. M.), or the cord. The value of standing timber is frequently spoken of as *stumpage value*. The term means the value of the timber on the stump, that is, of standing timber. The work of thus determining the amount of lumber or other manufactured wood product that a given body of standing timber will yield when cut is called *timber-estimating*. It is also spoken of as *timber-cruising*. It consists of reckoning, either by means of some mathematical calculation or by the aid of past experience in judging timber, the amount of merchantable timber that exists on a particular piece of land.

Years ago, when timber was plentiful and the value of lumber was comparatively low, timber-cruisers would often guess at the amount of lumber that could be produced from a specified piece of land, arriving at their estimate by a process in which arithmetic played a very small part and practical experience a very large part. They had seen many bodies of timber cut; they knew how many acres were cut over and they knew how many logs were taken out; they knew how much lumber the mill had been able to produce from those logs. This experience gave them some idea as to how the timber in that part of the country might be expected to run. They also knew how much to allow for in the way of damage, defect, and unmerchantable material, so that their results were fairly accurate. They usually erred on the safe side, and estimated low rather than high. The method was good when stumpage values were very low; but with the increasing scarcity of timber and the rising value of lumber it has become necessary to have something more reliable than a mere guess, for a large amount of money is often at stake. Modern sawmills are expensive to set up and maintain, and modern methods of logging employ many men and costly equipment; it is therefore necessary to calculate rather closely on stumpage values and the cost of operations before venturing into the lumber business. Lumbermen want to know within about ten per cent the amount of lumber that their timber lands will yield when cut.

Although the amount of money involved is not large, it is just as important that the farmer who owns a woodlot of 5, 50, or 100 acres shall be able to tell within ten or fifteen per cent what his timber will yield. Even if he does not intend to sell his timber, he should know how much there is of it in order to avoid overcutting and mismanagement, which in the absence of definite figures are almost sure to follow, with a consequent depreciation in the value of the woodlot.

If any degree of accuracy is to be obtained in making estimates of standing timber, at least two figures are required: first, the average stand to the acre (or the stand of an average acre), and secondly, the number of acres in the tract under consideration. The only exception to this rule would be in the case of a very small woodlot in which a tree-to-tree count including every tree might be possible. In this case the area of the woodlot would not be required, but the estimate would be based on the count. If the number of acres in the woodlot and the stand on an average acre are known, the contents of the whole stand may be reckoned. Then, if necessary, certain allowances may be made for diseased, defective, or unmerchantable timber. Allowances of this kind can usually be made to best advantage when they are based on observations made at the sawmill, where logs can be watched in order to determine how they saw out, that is, to see what proportion of the lumber from the logs is unmerchantable.

Two methods of timber-estimating will be described: The first is based on the principle of a tree-to-tree count and is intended either for use on small areas only, where every tree can be counted, or for single trees. The second method is intended for larger areas, where only a small percentage of the trees can be counted.

The tree-to-tree count

Naturally, this method is the most accurate of all, for each tree is inspected and the contents is estimated separately. It thus becomes possible to allow for the irregularities of form and the varying degrees of taper that are exhibited by all trees, especially the hardwoods. In applying this method, one should first determine the breast-height diameter[3] of the tree to be estimated, and tally this in the column marked "Trees," as shown below in the sample tally sheet, Table 3. If possible this breast-height diameter should be measured accurately with a pair of tree calipers[4] (Fig. 79), because with a knowledge of the exact diameter at breast height it becomes much easier to judge the top-diameters of the logs above. If calipers are not convenient, a circumference tape may be used or the diameter may be judged by the eye. To do this accurately, however, requires considerable skill and practice. If an ordinary tapeline, graduated to inches, is used in getting the circumference, the measurement may be reduced to diameter by multiplying by $\frac{7}{22}$.

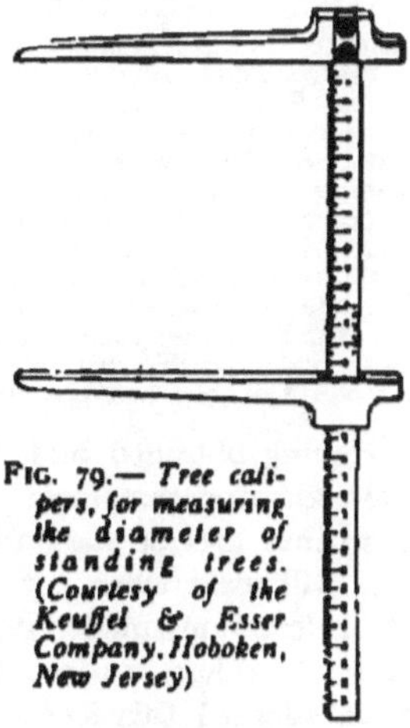

FIG. 79.— *Tree calipers, for measuring the diameter of standing trees. (Courtesy of the Keuffel & Esser Company, Hoboken, New Jersey)*

TABLE 3. SAMPLE TALLY SHEET FOR TIMBER ESTIMATES

Plot No........................ Locality..........................

Date.................................... ....

(16-foot logs)

Diameter breast-high (inches)	Pine		Oak		Maple		Hemlock		Total		
	Trees	Logs	Trees	Logs	Trees	Logs	Trees	Logs	Logs	Scale	Board feet
6		·						::	7	14	98
7		·						::	6	22	132
8		··						·	5	32	160
9		···						·	6	44	264
10		··						··	6	57	342
11		··						··	5	72	360
12		·	·					··	6	89	534
13		·						··	4	107	428
14		··	·					:	7	127	889
15		···					·	·	5	148	740
16									2	172	344
17								·	2	197	394
18								·	3	223	669
19						·		·	1	252	252
20								·	1	287	282
21							·				
22			·		·		·				
Totals	5	17	5	15	3	9	9	25	66	....	5,888

The form of tally sheet here shown is convenient for recording trees and logs on a small plot. In such a tally sheet the first column, designated "Diameter," should

[3] The diameter of standing trees is measured at a point 4 feet 6 inches from the ground, a distance designated as "breast height." The use of this standard height is to be preferred to the stump height, which is too variable.

[4] Tree calipers, instruments for measuring the diameter of standing trees, may be purchased from Keuffel & Esser Company, Hoboken, New Jersey, at a cost of $4.50 each for the 36-inch size.

contain numbers from 6 up to the diameter of the largest trees to be found in the woodlot. To the right of this column are columns for each of the species of trees that are to be estimated. These columns in turn are subdivided into two, the first for trees and the second for logs. The separate trees are tallied by breast-height diameter, and the several logs by diameter inside bark at the upper end. Thus, the first tree inspected on a plot might have been a pine whose diameter was 20 inches. According to the system of tallying used[1] a dot would be placed in the column marked "Trees" under "Pine," and opposite the 20 in the inches column. Then if this tree contained four merchantable logs whose top diameters were 16, 13, 11, and 8 inches, respectively, a dot would be placed in the column marked "Logs" opposite the corresponding diameters, 16, 13, 11, and 8. This process is repeated for every tree on the plot. After all the trees and logs are tallied, the totals may be read from the sheet. The logs are totaled in the column marked "Logs" under "Total," and the scale of a single log of that size is indicated in the column under "Scale." (This value is taken from the Universal log rule, page 138.) The product of the number of logs by the scale of each one is indicated for each diameter in the column marked "Board feet." The sum of all the values in this column gives the total number of board feet on the plot, which is the object of the whole operation.

Having obtained and recorded the breast-height diameter of a tree, the estimator next looks up the trunk of the tree, mentally divides the stem into logs of standard length, and decides just how many logs the tree will yield when cut. The work of estimating logs in the tree and the calculations made later will be easier if only one standard log-length is used. Thus, 16-foot logs are very common, and many estimators have adopted this length as their standard in estimating. In order to accommodate this length to trees that may have more or less than an even number of 16-foot logs, some estimators recognize half-logs, that is, 8-foot lengths, in their work. Any standard length may be chosen, of course, but the use of two or more standard lengths complicates both the tallying of the logs and the scaling of them later.

If the trunk of the tree that is being judged is straight and clear, with an even taper, the work of estimating the number of logs and their respective sizes will be a simple process; but if the trunk is irregular, or forked, or shows an excessive taper, the task will be more difficult. It is precisely at this point, however, that the accuracy of the method becomes apparent, because proper allowance can be made for such defects as crook, forks, or excessive taper. The next step to be taken is to decide at what points on the stem of the tree the tops of the successive logs will come, and to judge the diameter of the stem at these points. Allowances must be made for bark, and in each case the diameter of the several logs, inside the bark at the top end, is recorded in the column marked "Logs" on the tally sheet. Estimating the top diameters of logs in the tree is not easy

[1] The system of tallying used is called the "dot-and-dash" system. The following symbols show the values corresponding to them:

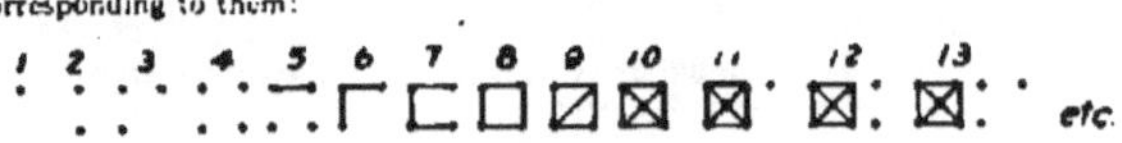

This method is economical of space and time, and, by its use, it is possible to record a large number of trees on a single sheet. Being arranged in blocks of ten, the tally is quickly and easily read.

to do, first, because trees do not taper uniformly and, secondly, because the thickness of the bark varies considerably not only with the species of tree but also with the size, the age, and the height of the tree and the locality in which it is growing. With the help of the suggestions in the next paragraph and a little practice, however, the timber-estimator will rapidly gain confidence. If one has an opportunity to observe the taper of logs and the thickness of bark on logs as they are cut in the woods or decked at the mill, it will not take long to acquire considerable skill in estimating the size of logs in the tree. This method of work is so much more likely to be accurate than any other that it is recommended here as the most practicable method for owners of woodlots to follow.

Most trees grown in the forest where they attain good form will taper 2 to 4 inches for every 16 feet in height. The taper in tall trees is less marked than it is in short trees that break up into branches at a relatively low point on the stem. The first, or butt, log and the last, or top, log will frequently show more taper than do the intermediate logs of a tree. Measurements on a large number of white pines show the following average taper for trees yielding four 16-foot logs:

	Taper
From diameter breast-high to top of first log	2 to 2½ inches
From top of first to top of second log	1½ to 2½ inches
From top of second to top of third log	2 to 3 inches
From top of third to top of fourth log	3½ to 4 inches

Each species of tree has its own characteristic form and taper, which must be observed and studied before great accuracy can be expected in judging tapers. The hardwoods are more irregular in taper than are the coniferous trees (pines, spruces, firs, and hemlocks).

The thickness of the bark is also a variable quantity. It depends not only on the kind of tree but also on the diameter of the tree at different ages and heights. Since it is necessary to make due allowances for the thickness of the bark in judging logs, the following table (Table 4) has been prepared. This table shows, for different species of trees, the approximate allowance that must be made for bark at different heights.

With the trees recorded by breast-height diameter and the logs recorded by length and top diameter inside bark, as shown on the sample tally sheet, Table 3, it is now possible to apply any desired log rule and scale the logs on paper. Thus, it was found that there were ten 16-foot logs of 8-inch diameter scaling 32 board feet each by the Universal rule, or a total of 320 board feet. Of the 9-inch logs, there were eight scaling 44 board feet each, or a total of 352 board feet. Each diameter class is calculated separately, and the total for that size is entered in the last column of the tally sheet. By adding all the values in this column, the total estimate for the trees of all sizes is found. The reason for recording the logs and the trees separately and keeping the number of trees by their breast-height diameter is to determine on how many trees the estimate is based. After a few reliable estimates have been obtained, other estimates in the same region may be checked by making comparisons of the number of trees.

TABLE 4. AMOUNT IN INCHES THAT MUST BE DEDUCTED FROM TOP DIAMETER OF LOGS OUTSIDE BARK, IN ORDER TO OBTAIN DIAMETERS INSIDE BARK

Size of 16-foot logs	Trees with thick bark (A)	Trees with thin bark (B)
On logs 24 inches and over	Deduct 3 inches	Deduct 1 to 2 inches
On logs 12 to 24 inches	Deduct 2 inches	Deduct 1 inch
On logs 6 to 12 inches	Deduct 1 inch	Deduct 1 inch*

(A) Trees with thick bark: oaks (especially chestnut oak and black oak), pitch pine, chestnut, walnut, butternut, ash, tulip poplar, cottonwood, locust, and hemlock.
(B) Trees with thin or medium bark: white pine, spruce, balsam fir, beech, hard maple, soft maple, birches, hickories, sycamore, cherry, basswood (except in old trees).

* Fractions of inches are not considered in scaling, and it is therefore useless to make smaller deductions.

As an aid in determining how many logs of standard length may be cut from a certain tree, it is well to measure the height of a few trees until the eye becomes accustomed to judging heights accurately. Methods of measuring the height of a standing tree are described on page 98 of the "Woodsman's Handbook,"[1] Bulletin 36 of the Forest Service, U. S. Department of Agriculture. The simplest of these methods is to compare the shadow of the tree with the shadow of a pole of known length, set perpendicular to the earth. Multiply the length of the shadow of the tree by the length of the pole, and divide the product by the length of the shadow of the pole. The result will give the height of the tree.

An instrument called a hypsometer, for the purpose of determining the height of trees, is made in a simple form as is shown in the accompanying illustration (Fig. 80). In order to use this instrument the operator should stand at a known distance from the base of the tree, and sighting in turn at the top and at the bottom of the tree he should observe the readings, as shown by the little pendulum. The readings are graded so as to give percentages of the base line. For example, a man standing 100 feet from the base of a tree sights to the top of the tree; the pendulum swings to 75. This indicates that the top of the tree is 75 per cent of the base line, or 75 feet above the level of the eye. When he sights to

[1] This publication may be purchased from the Superintendent of Documents, Government Printing Office, Washington, D. C., for twenty-five cents. (Do not send stamps, for they will not be accepted.)

the bottom of the tree, the pendulum swings to 5 on the opposite side of the zero mark. This indicates that the foot of the tree is 5 per cent of the base line, or 5 feet below the level of the eye. Adding these two readings, we obtain 80 as the total height of the tree. Any convenient distance may be chosen as a base line, and the principle is always the same — the sum of the readings represents the height of the tree in terms of a percentage of the base line.

The best results are obtained when a base line of at least 100 feet is used. Full directions for using this instrument accompany it.

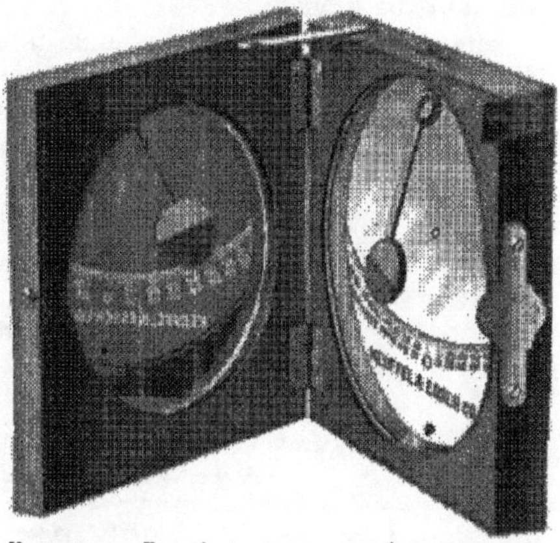

FIG. 80. — *Box hypsometer, an instrument for determining the heights of standing trees. (Courtesy of the Keuffel & Esser Company, Hoboken, New Jersey)*

Volume tables

Instead of going through the process of mentally dividing trees into logs and scaling them on paper, as described in the tree-to-tree count, it is sometimes possible, by the help of reliable volume tables, to shorten the work and obtain the estimate by measuring only the diameters and the heights of the trees. The contents in board feet can then be read directly from volume tables. Volume tables are, therefore, tables from which the board-foot contents of a tree can be determined when the breast-height diameter and the height are known. They are constructed from measurements taken on a large number of felled trees. These measurements are then averaged and compiled in the form of a table, a sample of which is shown on page 152. Since the values given in volume tables are the results of averages, it follows that they give satisfactory results only when applied to a large number of trees, or when the trees are known to be of average form. Furthermore, a volume table should be used only in a locality where conditions are practically the same as those that prevailed in the locality where the volume table was constructed. That is, it would not be wise to use for white oak in western New York a table which had been constructed from measurements of white oak grown in North Carolina. Neither would it be wise to use for white oak grown in a rich, moist bottom land, a table that had been constructed from the measurements of trees grown on a dry, rocky hillside, even though not far distant. The conditions, both general and local, must be similar.

Therefore, while the use of volume tables is often very convenient and time-saving, it is safe to use them only when a large number of trees is being estimated and when a table can be found that is known to have been constructed from trees growing under the same general conditions which prevail in the locality in question. Unfortunately there are but few reliable volume tables in existence at the present time. The "Woodsman's Handbook" contains a few tables that are fairly reliable. One of these is shown below in order that the form of a volume table may be understood by the reader. When good volume tables are available, this method will be a safe one to use.

TABLE 5. SAMPLE VOLUME TABLE FOR WHITE PINE IN NEW HAMPSHIRE

(From the "Woodsman's Handbook," Table No. 12.)

Breast-height diameter (inches)	Height of tree (feet)											Basis (trees)
	30	40	50	60	70	80	90	100	110	120		
	Volume in board feet											
5	8	12	15	...	...	...	...	.....	.....	.....	.....	7
6	13	20	23	27	29	...	...	.....	.....	.....	.....	41
7	18	28	34	39	44	...	...	.....	.....	.....	.....	75
8	24	36	45	53	62	...	...	...	.....	.....	.....	118
9	32	44	56	69	81	93	...	.....	.....	.....	.....	156
10	41	53	70	85	102	119	138	.....	.....	.....	.....	177
11	..	63	84	103	126	147	168	.....	.....	.....	.....	164
12	..	73	100	125	151	177	200	228	245	.....	.....	116
13	..	84	117	148	180	210	238	270	293	.....	.....	137
14	...	95	137	173	210	243	277	312	348	.....	.....	91
15		105	158	200	241	282	321	362	406	.....	.....	61
16			181	230	277	323	370	415	470	.....	.....	88
17			209	261	313	368	421	471	540	.....	.....	70
18			238	297	352	411	475	531	610	688	.....	68
19			270	336	393	460	530	598	682	763	.....	44
20			303	379	436	506	583	660	750	840	.....	35
21			...	425	480	553	634	720	830	918	.....	23
22				...	522	597	681	779	887	990	.....	16
23				...	566	639	727	834	958	1,065		19
24				...	...	674	769	889	1,030	1,135	.....	9
25					...	706	809	943	1,105	.....	.....	12
26					...	737	846	994	1,180	.....	.....	11
27						...	...	1,046	.....	.....	.....	....
												1,578

The volume given is actual saw cut. Sixty per cent was round-edged, and forty per cent squared; seventy per cent, one-inch boards, and thirty per cent, 2½-inch plank.

Area methods

The quarter-acre circle method.—In this method it is assumed that a careful count and estimate of the trees on a part of the whole area (perhaps 10 per cent) may be used as an average figure for the entire tract; and that the estimate for an average acre, multiplied by the total number of acres, will give us an accurate estimate of the timber in the entire stand. One way in which this method may be applied is to make a careful estimate of the trees on a circle, the area of which is one quarter of an acre. The method is as follows: Select a part of the stand in which average conditions as to the number of trees, the height of trees, and the diameters of the trees are represented. Count and tally the logs in the trees on this quarter-acre as described in the tree-to-tree method. In order to be sure that you have an area of exactly one quarter of an acre select some tree, rock, stump, or other mark as the center of the circle and then count all trees that are found within a radius of 59 feet from the center. This 59-foot radius should be measured with accuracy since the estimate obtained on this quarter-acre is to be multiplied by a large factor in order to obtain the estimate for the whole stand, and a difference of only a foot or two in one direction or another may make a large difference in the result. If you cannot judge the 59-foot distance accurately by stepping or pacing,[7] this distance should be measured with a tapeline. Be sure to count all trees on the area once and only once.

After the trees have been tallied according to the number of logs and their top diameters, as already described, these logs may be scaled exactly as before, and the total contents of the plot may be determined by adding together the number of board feet in each log.

This method has much to recommend it: One man can do all the work unassisted. If the sample areas have been carefully selected and the work of estimating is carefully done, there is no reason why this method should not lead to fairly accurate results. In using this method the important thing to be remembered is that the sample plots chosen should represent average conditions. They should be neither too good nor too poor. It is often a temptation to select a plot that has very good timber on it — better in fact than the average — with the result that too large an estimate is obtained.

If the estimator feels unable to make a fair choice of sample plots, they may be taken at regular intervals along a compass line. This will eliminate the element of choice in the location of plots. The compass lines should be run in a direction that will insure crossing the different types, qualities, or age-classes; and the sample plots should be taken at regular intervals, perhaps every 20 or 40 rods, regardless of the density of the stand. Only in this way will an impartial estimate be obtained.

The number of plots selected should be sufficient to include representative parts of the stand. If conditions are variable, more plots will be

[7] The average man cannot step a full yard at one stride without a conscious effort, and to do this in the woods is tiresome work. It is recommended that, when measuring distances by pacing, a natural step be adopted; such a step is about 33 inches for a man of average height and is equivalent to six steps to the rod, or about 21½ steps for the 59-foot radius of the circle.

necessary than if the stand is uniform throughout. As a general rule it may be stated that, when conditions are uniform, an estimate based on 5 or 10 per cent of the total area will be accurate enough. If conditions are variable, however, plots covering as much as 20 or 25 per cent of the total area may be necessary in order to be sure of accuracy.

Rectangular-measurement methods.—In applying area methods, by which the trees on only a part of the entire tract are actually counted and estimated, it is not necessary that a circle method be used. Plots may be square or rectangular, so long as the exact area that they cover is known. When running long strips through the woods, acres are frequently measured 40 rods long and 4 rods wide. The essential point is to have a plot the area of which is known definitely. Plots that are square or rectangular, however, are usually more difficult to measure than are circular plots, and rectangular measurements should rarely be attempted unless two or more men can do the work together. Long strips through the woods, to be run to the best advantage, require the services of at least three men. For the owners of small woodlots, or for those who wish to do the work alone, the quarter-acre circular plot is recommended as the least difficult and the most practical method.

METHODS OF ESTIMATING THE CORDWOOD IN A WOODLOT

Trees that are too small to produce saw logs are best estimated as individual poles of specified lengths or else as cordwood. After the saw logs have been removed from large trees, there is often considerable

TABLE 6. SAMPLE FORM OF TALLY SHEET FOR ESTIMATING CORDWOOD

Species: Red, black, and scarlet oak   Area: 10 acres

Breast-height diameter (inches)	Number of trees, by height — Height of trees (feet)						Reduced to cords, by Table 8
	30	40	50	60	70	80	
4	25*	40	30	......	......	......	2.60
5	8	30	10	......	......	......	1.81
6		60	65	......	......	......	7.15
7	......	20	15	30	......	......	5.22
8	......	5	42	60	......	......	11.27
9	...	......	18	52	......	......	9.37
10	......	......	8	41	......	......	8.06
11	...	....	2	36	4	......	9.20
12		......	......	2	18	......	5.80
13		......	......	1	9	......	3.52
Total cords			......	......	......		64.00

* In the woods, the trees are tallied by the dot-and-dash system, described on page 148. For simplicity, numbers are given in the sample.

material suitable for cordwood left in the tops. While it is difficult to give either suggestions or tables that will help in the work of estimating the cordwood in the tops of trees, it is possible to give tables that will enable one to estimate the amount of cordwood obtainable from trees of small diameter, provided the height is known (page 150). In order to make this kind of timber-estimating possible, Tables 7 to 11 inclusive,

TABLE 7. AMOUNT OF CORDWOOD CONTAINED IN ONE CHESTNUT TREE, BY HEIGHT

Height of tree (feet)	30	40	50	60	70	80
Breast-height diameter (inches)	Cords	Cords	Cords	Cords	Cords	Cords
4	.016	.021	.028	......	......	......
5	.024	.032	.042	......	......	......
6	.030	.043	.056	.067	......	......
7	......	.059	.071	.083	......	......
8	......	.071	.089	.109	.125	......
9	......	.091	.111	.132	.153	......
10	......	.115	.137	.159	.183	.196
11	......	.139	.166	.192	.222	.244
12	......	.164	.196	.227	.256	.294
13	......	......	.227	.263	.294	.333
14	......	......	.263	.303	.357	.385
15	......	......	.303	.344	.400	.455
16	......	......	.344	.400	.455	.525

TABLE 8. AMOUNT OF CORDWOOD CONTAINED IN ONE BLACK, RED, OR SCARLET OAK TREE, BY HEIGHT

Height of tree (feet)	30	40	50	60	70	80
Breast-height diameter (inches)	Cords	Cords	Cords	Cords	Cords	Cords
4	.020	.027	034		...	...
5	.031	.037	.045	......	...	......
6	......	.052	.062	.071	....	....
7	......	.067	.077	.091	.100	
8	......	.083	.100	111	.143	......
9	......	.100	.125	.137	.167	.200
10	......	.111	.152	.167	.200	.250
11	......	.149	.185	.217	.256	.294
12	......	.189	.222	.256	.294	.333
13	....	.238	.278	.312	.357	.385
14		286	.322	.370	.416	.455
15	......	.345	.385	.435	.475	.500
16	......	......	.455	.500	555	.588

have been prepared. They include the material in the trees of the several species down to a limit of two inches in diameter in the tops. The trees should be counted and tallied according to diameter and height, as indicated in the sample form of tally sheet, Table 6. The appropriate tables should then be applied to reduce the number of trees to cordwood.

TABLE 9. AMOUNT OF CORDWOOD CONTAINED IN ONE TREE OF WHITE OAK OR CHESTNUT OAK, BY HEIGHT

Height of tree (feet)	30	40	50	60	70	80
Breast-height diameter (inches)	Cords	Cords	Cords	Cords	Cords	Cords
4	.020	.027	.034	......	......	......
5	.031	.038	.047	......	......	......
6	......	.053	.062	.077	......	......
7	......	.071	.083	.091	.110	......
8	......	.091	.105	.125	.149	......
9	......	.111	.133	.161	.192	.227
10	......	.133	.161	.196	.233	.270
11	......	.156	.188	.233	.270	.313
12	......	.185	.227	.270	.313	.370
13	......	......	.263	.312	.370	.416
14	......	......	.303	.357	.416	.476
15	......	......	......	.400	.475	.555
16	......	......	......	.475	.555	.625

Cordwood tables

For a few of the common species of trees found in our eastern woodlots, Tables 7 to 11 inclusive, show the approximate amount of cordwood contained in trees of different diameters and heights. These tables have been constructed from various sources; the volume in cubic feet has been used, and a converting factor has been applied that gives the contents directly in cords.[a] In using the tables:

Multiply the value given in the appropriate table for a specified height and diameter by the number of trees of that size. Do the same for all diameters and heights, and add the results together.

For example: In the tally sheet, Table 6, it will be found that the 25 trees, 4 inches in diameter and 30 feet high, yield .50 cord of wood (25 x .02 in Table 8). The 40 trees, 4 inches in diameter and 40 feet high, yield 1.08 cord (40 x .027). The 30 trees, 4 inches in diameter and 50 feet high, yield 1.02 cord (30 x .034). The total number of cords for

[a] The converting factors for chestnut and the oaks were taken from Bulletin 96 of the United States Forest Service. For the other species, bulletins 73 and 80 were consulted. While not constructed from trees growing in New York, these tables should give approximately accurate figures.

all trees 4 inches in diameter is therefore the sum of these three values, or 2.60, which is placed in the last column. The same method is followed for all diameters. The sum of the values in the right-hand column gives 64, the total number of cords on the area.

TABLE 10. AMOUNT OF CORDWOOD CONTAINED IN ONE MAPLE, BIRCH, OR BEECH TREE, BY HEIGHT

Height of tree (feet)	30	40	50	60	70	80
Breast-height diameter (inches)	Cords	Cords	Cords	Cords	Cords	Cords
4	.023	......	......	......	......	......
5	.031	.037	......	......	......	......
6	.040	.055	......	......	......	......
7	.047	.062	.077	......	......	......
8	......	.071	.091	.112	......	......
9	......	.091	.117	.147	......	......
10	......	.117	.141	.192	......	......
11	......	.139	.161	.222	.256	......
12	......	.161	.185	.256	.303	......
13	......	......	.227	.294	.357	......
14	......	......	.263	.345	.416	......
15	......		......	.400	.500	......
16	......	......	......	.455	.555	......
17	......	......		......	.588	.625
18	......		......	......	.666	.714

TABLE 11. AMOUNT OF CORDWOOD CONTAINED IN ONE HICKORY TREE, BY HEIGHT

Height of tree (feet)	30	40	50	60	70	80
Breast-height diameter (inches)	Cords	Cords	Cords	Cords	Cords	Cords
4	.016	.020	......	......	......	......
5	.025	.027	.040	......	......	......
6	.034	.040	.055	.071	......	......
7	.042	.055	.071	.091	......	......
8	.053	.077	.100	.111	.143	......
9	......	.096	.122	.149	.182	.222
10	......	.120	.153	.182	.222	.263
11	......	.149	.185	.222	.263	.312
12	......	.178	.217	.264	.312	.357
13		......	.256	.312	.357	.416
14		......	......	.357	.416	.476
15		......	......	.416	.476	.555
16		......	......	......	.555	.625

HOW TO DETERMINE THE STUMPAGE VALUE OF TIMBER

After it is definitely known how many thousand feet of lumber or how many cords of wood a given tract of land will yield, there still remains the problem of determining the sale value of the stumpage. This is a problem into which a great many factors enter, such as the cost of team-hire and labor, the distance of the timber from the nearest mill and market, the ease with which the trees can be felled, cut into logs, and hauled to the mill. There is such a wide variation in the cost of labor in different parts of the country, and so much depends on the relative accessibility of the timber, that the most satisfactory way of handling this question is to see how stumpage values are determined under a given set of conditions and then adapt the figures so as to apply to a particular case.

First of all, it may be assumed that the timber is so located that a haul of one mile is required to reach the mill, and that the mill is located in a town which has railroad shipping facilities. If at the same time the logging conditions in the woods are not difficult, the conditions are most favorable for the easy marketing of the timber; stumpage values should therefore be the highest. The necessary costs of operations in one typical case were as follows:

	Cost per thousand feet
1. Felling	$0.50
2. Trimming and sawing into logs	1.00
3. Skidding and loading	1.25
4. Hauling logs, a mile	.40
5. Sawing at mill	4.00
6. Piling, transferring, and the like	1.00
7. Loading and hauling lumber to cars, a mile	.35
Total	$8.50

This probably represents the most favorable conditions under which lumber can be produced. It assumes favorable conditions in the woods, moderate labor costs ($2.00 per day), and nearness to the mill and the shipping point. The difference between the total cost of operations ($8.50) and the local market price of the mill run of the species cut, minus an allowance for the operator's profit of 15 to 25 per cent, should be approximately the value of the timber on the stump. By "mill run" is meant the average of all the grades of lumber produced from the logs, just as it comes from the mill. Most woodlots will produce relatively small quantities of the better grades of lumber; therefore the mill run values will not be very high. For example, the mill run of hemlock lumber in a town in eastern New York sells at $18 to $20 a thousand feet, according to the location of the mill. The stumpage value can then be determined by the following rule:

Divide the selling price by 1 plus[1] *a fair percentage of profit; from this, subtract the cost of operations; the remainder is the stumpage value.*

Taking the figures given above for hemlock at $18 a thousand, and allowing a 20 per cent profit on operating costs, the operator will find that this rule works out as follows, giving a stumpage value of $6.50 a thousand.

$$\frac{\$18}{1.20} - \$8.50 = \$6.50, \text{ stumpage value}$$

Since the conditions outlined above are exceptional in that the timber is not far from the mill and the mill is situated at the shipping point, it may be fairer to assume that conditions are somewhat harder. Less favorable conditions might mean not only rougher, steeper ground in the woods, but also greater distances from the woods to the mill and from the mill to the shipping point. It may therefore be assumed that a haul of three miles from the woods to the mill is necessary, and that a haul of similar distance is necessary from the mill to the shipping point. The cost of operations in a typical case under these conditions was as follows:

	Cost per thousand feet
1. Felling trees	$0.75
2. Trimming and sawing into logs	1.25
3. Skidding and loading	1.75
4. Hauling logs, 50 cents a mile for 3 miles	1.50
5. Sawing at mill	4.00
6. Piling, transferring, and the like	1.00
7. Hauling lumber to shipping point, 40 cents a mile for 3 miles	1.20
Total	$11.45

It will be seen at a glance that these figures, which represent more nearly the average conditions of to-day, bring the cost of operations to a much larger figure, and that the difference between local market values for the mill run of the lumber and the cost of operations is much smaller. It follows that the stumpage value for all kinds of timber rapidly decreases as the distance from the mill and from the market increases, and also that the stumpage values decrease rapidly if the conditions under which the logging must be carried on are not favorable. In these days much of our timber is located in rather inaccessible places, so that the foregoing figures represent more nearly the average conditions.

[1] The selling price is divided by "*1 plus a fair percentage of profit*" not only in order to cover all actual costs of operation, but to insure against losses arising from unexpected sources and to allow the operator some margin of profit to which he is justly entitled, because he assumes some risks.

In determining the cost of operations, each owner should estimate his labor at a fair price, and the cost of his team at a price that he would be able to get if he were hiring it out by the day. This is only fair because work in the woods is not easy, and it is always attended with some risk, both to equipment and to the horses employed. The following diagram presents in a graphic way how the costs in lumbering are distributed, and it may be of some help to those who are trying to determine the value of their timber on the stump:

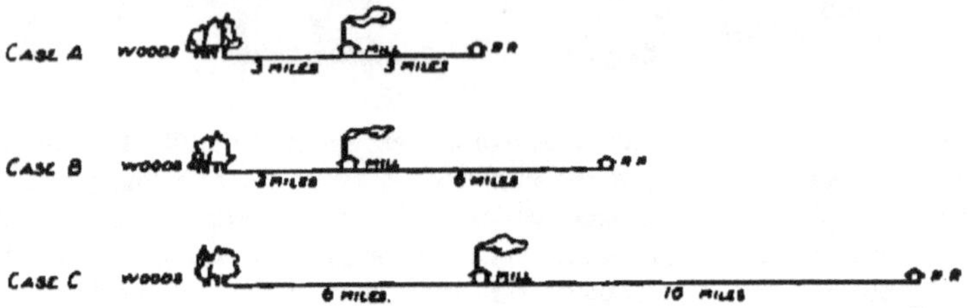

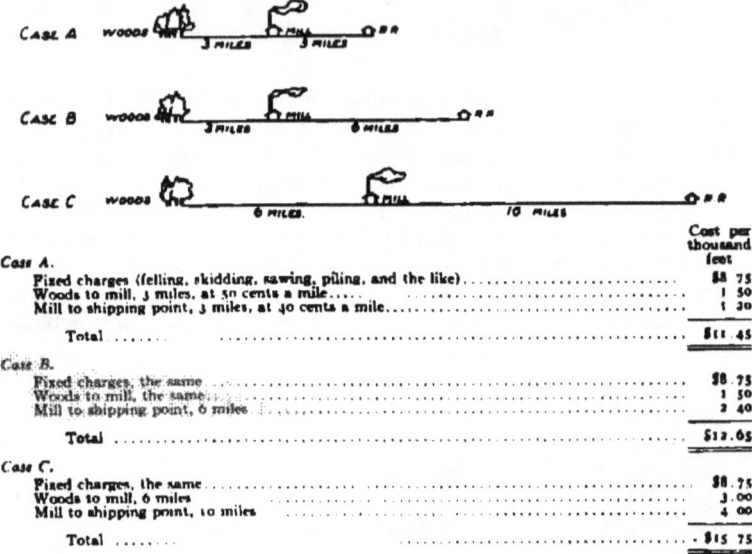

	Cost per thousand feet
Case A.	
Fixed charges (felling, skidding, sawing, piling, and the like)	$8 75
Woods to mill, 3 miles, at 50 cents a mile	1 50
Mill to shipping point, 3 miles, at 40 cents a mile	1 20
Total	$11 45
Case B.	
Fixed charges, the same	$8 75
Woods to mill, the same	1 50
Mill to shipping point, 6 miles	2 40
Total	$12.65
Case C.	
Fixed charges, the same	$8 75
Woods to mill, 6 miles	3 00
Mill to shipping point, 10 miles	4 00
Total	$15 75

In each of the foregoing cases, the stumpage value may be determined by applying the formula already given. If the allowance for profit be placed at 20 per cent and the mill run be valued at $18 a thousand (a fair value for hemlock), the following results will be obtained:

Case A.

$$\frac{\$18}{1.20} - \$11.45 = \$15 - \$11.45 = \$3.55 \text{ a thousand, stumpage value}$$

Case B.

$$\frac{\$18}{1.20} - \$12.65 = \$15 - \$12.65 = \$2.35 \text{ a thousand stumpage value}$$

Case C.

$$\frac{\$18}{1.20} - \$15.75 = \$15 - \$15.75 = \text{a negative value}$$

In Case C a negative value is obtained. This indicates that unless the operator is satisfied with a smaller percentage of profit, it will not pay him to attempt the manufacture of lumber under the conditions given. If a selling price of \$24 a thousand could be obtained, as might be the case with white pine instead of hemlock, he could still afford to operate under the conditions given, for the formula would then show the following results:

$$\frac{\$24}{1.20} - \$15.75 = \$20 - \$15.75 = \$4.25 \text{ a thousand, stumpage value}$$

In determining the stumpage value of cordwood, much the same process may be followed out; the cost of getting the material to the mill (which in this case would probably be a small power-mill operated by the woodlot owner) would be perhaps a little larger than it would be in the case of saw logs because small pieces, such as are used for cordwood, are more expensive to handle than logs are. On the other hand, there is less expense in handling cordwood after it has been brought from the woods because the market is nearer, and the cost of piling and transferring to the shipping point is eliminated. A good cordwood market is very desirable, because parts of trees that would otherwise be unmerchantable can be worked up into cordwood and sold at a profit. In some parts of the State, cordwood brings as much as \$5 a cord wholesale, for mixed woods, and as much as \$6.50 a cord for special kinds, such as hickory, which makes the best fuel. When retailed, or sold delivered in the cities and towns, the price is much higher than this.

In certain parts of the State, woods of a particular species bring a very good price because they are used in the manufacture of some article of trade for which there is a great demand. For example, basswood or maple may be much in demand for veneers; or poplar, which in some places is almost worthless, may be in great demand for pulpwood. The presence of a plant that is engaged in the production of wood alcohol, acetic acid, and the like, may give a greater value than is usual to such species as beech and birch; or the presence of a local charcoal industry may in the same way afford a greater value to certain woods of the region. Local markets should always be studied carefully, and advantage taken of them. If cordwood brings a good price, the management of timberlands on a profitable basis becomes a relatively simple matter, because nearly all the product of the woodlot can be utilized and no special treatment is necessary. If the market for lumber is good locally, and there seems to be a steady demand for timbers of saw-log size, it will require a longer time to produce the material but it will bring a better price in the end. Clear, straight timber will produce lumber of higher grade and greater value than crooked, limby trees, and a little attention to the growth of the timber when it is young and vigorous will be repaid by the production of a greater proportion of clear, first-grade lumber.

SUMMARY

In conclusion it may be said that the value of timber, on the stump, depends chiefly on three things:

(1) The species, or kind, of timber.

(2) The operating costs, that is, the total cost of cutting, hauling to the mill, sawing, and transferring to the shipping point.

(3) The market conditions, that is, the supply and the demand.

The last of these three factors is particularly variable, and should be watched closely so that advantage may be taken of a good market.

In estimating the amount of merchantable timber in a piece of woods, two methods are open to the owner. In the case of small woodlots the trees may be counted individually, and the logs that they will yield may be tallied, so as to be scaled later. When the area to be covered is large, a certain proportion only is estimated in detail, and care should be taken to select stands that represent average conditions.

Unless the owner of woodlands can rely on contractors to do careful, honest work, with as little damage to young trees as possible, it will be better to supervise the work in the woods very carefully, or, better still, to do it for oneself. Careless woodsmen are likely to do unnecessary damage, and this source of loss should be avoided.

THE CORNELL READING-COURSE FOR THE FARM

The Cornell Reading-Course for the Farm aims to assist those who desire to read reliable agricultural literature. It provides an opportunity for those who are unable to leave their work to receive in their homes consecutive instruction on subjects of particular interest. The course is conducted by means of printed lessons dealing with practical agricultural problems. Certain lessons discuss fundamental principles which should be understood by those who wish to farm most successfully; others contain concrete suggestions or give detailed directions for the best practices. Below is given a list of available lessons showing the arrangement by series. The number of lessons available is increased by the publication of a lesson each month, which is added to the appropriate series. The new lessons are sent to readers as issued. Enrollment in the course is by series. Each lesson is accompanied by a discussion paper which contains questions on the important points in the lesson. If the discussion paper is returned it is read carefully, and a personal reply is made when information is requested. Another Reading-Course lesson in the same series is sent on the receipt of a discussion paper whether the questions are answered or not, as the return of a discussion paper indicates the reader's desire for further instruction. It is hoped that the discussion paper not only will assist the reader, but also will bring the College and the individual farmer closer together.

Often the most benefit from the Reading-Course has been derived by the organization of study clubs. When groups of persons discuss Reading-Course lessons together, there is an added interest and an opportunity for the exchange of ideas which results often in mutual helpfulness among members of the group.

AVAILABLE READING-COURSE LESSONS FOR THE FARM, ARRANGED BY SERIES

Residents of New York State may register for one or more of the series mentioned below by addressing The Cornell Reading-Course for the Farm, College of Agriculture, Ithaca, New York.

SERIES		LESSONS
The soil	42	Tilth and tillage of the soil
	50	Nature, effects, and maintenance of humus in the soil
Poultry	6	Incubation — Part II
	10	Feeding young chickens
Rural engineering	8	Knots, hitches, and splices

SERIES		LESSONS
Farm forestry	12	The improvement of the woodlot
	28	Recent New York State Laws giving relie from taxation on lands used for forestry purposes
	40	County, town, and village forests
	62	Methods of determining the value of timbe in the farm woodlot
The horse	14	Horse-breeding to increase the farm income
	46	Feeding and care of the horse
	56	Practical horse-breeding
Dairying	16	Practical dairy problems
	32	Composition of milk and some of its product
	54	The dairy herd
	60	Farm butter-making
Fruit-growing	18	The renewal of the neglected orchard
	22	The culture of the currant and the gooseberry
	36	Culture of red and black raspberries and of purple-cane varieties
	48	Culture of the cherry
	52	Culture of the blackberry
Farm crops	20	Alfalfa for New York
	24	The rotation of farm crops
	66	Meadows in New York (in press)
Stock-feeding	26	Computing rations for farm animals
Vegetable gardening	30	Hotbed construction and management
	34	Home-garden planning
	58	Planting the home vegetable garden
Plant-breeding	41	Improving plants by selection or breeding
	38	Principles and methods of plant-breeding
	44	Methods of breeding oats
Country life	64	The farm home and the rural school (in press)

The above list is correct to June 15, 1914. The demand may at any time exhaust the supply of particular numbers. Requests will be filled as long as the supply lasts.

THE APPLICATION OF RECONNAISSANCE DATA TO THE PROBLEM OF MARKING TIMBER FOR CUTTING

By Richard H. Boerker

The object of this study is to inquire into the number of trees to the acre, the density, the representation of age classes and the contents of trees and stands in our Western Yellow pine forests, with the idea of securing data that might be of use in the management of these stands. About 60 per cent of the merchantable timber on the Lassen Forest is Yellow pine; the largest and most continuous stands are found in the eastern and central parts of the Forest.

This study is confined to pure Yellow pine stands, *i.e.*, stands in which Yellow pine represents 80 per cent or more of the merchantable timber. The data used were taken from the forms made out in the reconnaissance work of the last two years. Owing to the fact that these data include only those trees above 5 inches D.B.H. the study involves only trees above that diameter. Investigations have shown that on the basis of the number of trees per acre the average Yellow pine stands are composed about as follows:

Other species	10%
Yellow pine:	
Under 5 inches	10
Over 5 inches	80
Total	100

The stand on each form, representing two acres—usually a fair average of the entire forty—, was classified into 5 diameter groups, namely: 6–10", 11–20", 21–30", 31–40", and over 40". This was done with 350 forties. These were taken by groups of sections and were representative of the pure Yellow pine stand in 17 townships. These data represent 700 acres actually calipered, and if we assume that the ordinary strip taken through the center of a forty is fairly representative of the entire forty, then this study is based on 14,000 acres.

The Average Number of Trees Per Acre

After the stands had been classified into the 5 diameter groups mentioned before, it was found that the 700 acres in question contained from 5 to 80 trees per acre. Upon closer examination, it was noted that 28 trees per acre was the dividing line, so to speak, between the average and the maximum, for only 14 acres out of the total 700 contained more than 28 trees per acre. Below 28 inches the stands were divided as follows and the entire 700 acres classified:

TABLE 1

Class	*No. Trees per Acre*	*No. Acres Measured*	*Per Cent of Total*
I Very open	5– 9	222	32
II Open	10–15	220	31
III Medium	16–20	148	21
IV Dense	21–28	96	14
V Very dense	28–80	14	2
Total		700	100

From this table it will be seen that a large majority, in fact 84 per cent, of our Yellow pine stands contain 20 trees or less per acre. If distributed evenly over an acre, these trees, young and old, would be about 50 feet apart. This condition immediately reflects the conditions of soil exposure, drouth and brush. which, as a matter of fact, are present.

The various density classes were found to conform very closely to various sub-types in the Yellow pine region. It seems only natural that the density of a stand should be closely related to the site which that stand occupies. In general, the lower the altitude and the drier the site, the more open the stand; and the higher the altitude up to a certain limit, the greater the amount of soil and atmospheric moisture available, the greater is the tendency towards a mixture with other species, the denser is the stand and the better the forest conditions. The description of these classes is as follows:

I. *Very open.*—(5–9 trees per acre.) Usually pure, but occasionally mixed with Lodgepole pine of poor quality. Soil: light volcanic ash. Site: poor, open, dry, sage-brush flats. Elevation: 5400 to 5700 feet.

II. *Open.*—(10–15 trees per acre.) Usually pure, but occasionally mixed with White fir; on lava flats with heavy undergrowth of manzanita and snow-brush. Soil: volcanic ash with loam and clay. Elevation: 5400 to 5700 feet.

III. *Medium.*—(16–20 trees per acre.) Sometimes pure, but often mixed with White fir and Lodgepole pine; on lava flats with light to medium cover of snow-brush and manzanita. Soil: volcanic ash, with considerable loam and clay. Elevation: 5400 to 5700 feet.

IV. *Dense.*—(21–28 trees per acre.) Humid slope type mixed with White fir, also cedar, Douglas fir, Sugar pine and Lodgepole pine. Soil: rich, sandy loam with gravel and disintegrated shales and slates in mixture. Elevation 4500 to 5800 feet.

V. *Very dense.*—(Over 28 trees per acre.) Humid slope type like above, usually about 5500 feet.

Having determined these density classes, the next step was to ascertain the relation of these classes to the diameter groups spoken of before. Accordingly, the average number of trees per acre for each class and each diameter group was determined and compiled into the following table:

TABLE 2

AVERAGE NUMBER OF TREES PER ACRE

Diameter Groups	*Very Open*	*Open*	*Medium*	*Dense*	*Very Dense*	*Average*[1]	*Maximum Acre*
6–10 inches	0.63	3.0	3.4	5.3	9.2	2.8	48
11–20	0.9	3.8	4.6	8.0	11.2	3.7	15
21–30	1.2	2.7	5.3	8.4	13.5	3.8	15
31–40	2.4	3.1	3.3	3.5	4.7	3.0	1
Over 40	1.7	1.8	1.3	0.9	1.1	1.5	1
Totals	6.8	14.4	17.9	26.1	39.7	14.8	80

Probably the most striking result of this table is that the average number of trees per acre above 5 inches D.B.H. is only 14.8. The maximum acre given above is the acre in Class V that had the greatest number of trees on it. It is interesting to note here how the average compares with the best we have. Another feature of this table is the poor representation of the lower diameter groups and the large percentage of trees over 20 inches in diameter. It is likewise interesting to note that as the density of the stands increases, the lower diameter groups are better, and the upper diameter groups more poorly represented.

Density of Stands

It is by no means an easy matter to obtain figures on the density of all-aged stands. Considerable time was spent in trying to arrive at a method of determining this factor. It was of no avail to try to compare our stands with German stands of Scots pine, principally because of the great difference in sizes and age of the two species and on account of the fact that stand and yield tables are in most cases made for even-aged stands under careful management. It was concluded that all the literature written would not be of as much use as a few hours spent in

[1] Properly weighted on basis of acreage.

the field. Quite a few crown measurements were taken during the last two summers and this fall a new method occurred to me. In riding through these Yellow pine stands after a light snowfall, I noticed that the open spots underneath the trees (that were free from snow) corresponded very nearly to the projected crowns of the individual trees. This observation resulted in a very easy way of measuring crown diameters and the areas of the crowns as projected on the ground. The following table shows the results of these observations:

TABLE 3

Diameter Group	*Average Diameter Breast High Inches*	*Area of Projection of Crown Sq. Ft.*
6–10 inches	8	100[1]
11–20 inches	15	348[2]
21–30	25	1038
31–40	35	1536
Over 40	..	1925

Applying these figures to the various classes of stands based upon number of trees per acre, we get the density of our Yellow pine stands in tenths based upon an ideal acre.

TABLE 4

Density Class	*Total Trees per Acre All Diameters (From Table 2)*	*Total Area Projected Crowns Sq. Ft. per Acre*	*Crown Density in Tenths Based upon Ideal*
I	6.8	8,581	.23
II	14.4	12,652	.36
III	17.9	15,014	.42
IV	26.1	19,141	.55
V	39.7	28,168	.81
Average	14.8	13,107	.38
Maximum	80.0	29,050	.83
Ideal	....	34,848	1.00

The ideal acre is an acre (43,560 sq. ft.) of Yellow pine, in which 10 per cent, or 4356 sq. ft. is allowed for the young stuff below 5 inches D.B.H., and an additional 10 per cent, or 4356 sq. ft., is allowed for "other species," the remaining 80 per cent, or 34,848 sq. ft., being taken up by the Yellow pine over 5 inches D.B.H. considered in this study. This assumes that the trees utilize every square foot of sunlight, there being no overtopping. This is largely true in the case of Yellow pine, on account of its intolerance. The projected crown area of the

[1] Average area per tree, fifty-year Scots pine No. 1, diameter 8 inches, is 94 square feet.

[2] Average area per tree 120-year Scots pine No. 1, diameter 16 inches, is 283 square feet.

ideal acre, therefore, represents the maximum amount of crowns that can be crowded on one acre and still have each tree enjoy the maximum of direct sunlight. There is, undoubtedly, under normal conditions considerable overtopping, and for this reason the ideal acre on the basis of total crown space is conservative, for it does not take this into account. On the basis of the ideal acre 84 per cent of our Yellow pine stands have a crown density of less than 0.42 or are less than half stocked.

Such a basis of comparison as the one above is fairly indicative of the degree of density of the Yellow pine stands. There is a relative comparison between our poorest and best stands, if nothing else. It is safe to say that the ideal is by no means the best that can be grown, for reasons mentioned above. For this reason these densities are probably high.

The Representation of Age Classes

By consulting the latest growth tables on Yellow pine, the following relation appears to exist between the diameter groups mentioned above and the age of the trees:

Diameter Group	*Age*
6–10 inches	40–55 years
11–20	55–100
21–30	100–150
31–40	150–270
Over 40	Over 270

For the purposes of this study only three age classes will be considered, as follows:

TABLE 5

Diameter Group	*Age*
6–20 inches	40–100 years
20–30	100–150
31 inches and over	Over 150

The following table gives for each crown density class the representation of the three age classes in per cent:

TABLE 6

Crown Density Class	*Trees Per Acre All Ages From Table 2*	*Representation by Age Classes Years* 40–100	100–150	150 and over	*Total Per Cent*
		From Tables 2 and 5			
Very open I	6.8	22%	18%	60%	100%
Open II	14.4	47	19	34	100
Medium III	17.9	45	30	25	100
Dense IV	26.1	50	32	18	100
Very dense V	30.7	51	34	15	100
Average	11.8	44	25	31	100
Maximum Acre	80.0	79	19	2	100

Contents of Stands and Trees

If we apply a Yellow pine volume table to the trees in the various density classes, we get some interesting results:

TABLE 7

Class	*Trees per Acre, All Diameters From Table 2*	*Total Volume All Trees*	*Average Volume per Tree*
Very open..............I	6.8	12,142 Bd. Ft.	1785 ft.
Open..................II	14.4	15,385	1070
Medium..............III	17.9	15,839	885
Dense.................IV	26.1	17,374[4]	665
Very dense.............V	39.7	24,595	620
Average..................	14.8	14,813[4]	1000[5]
Maximum acre...........	80.0	19,490[6]	

To show how the volume of the stand is distributed in the various age classes and to give an idea how much of our merchantable timber is in the form of mature and over-mature trees, the following table is offered:

TABLE 8

	Total Stand per Acre	*Stand per Acre by Age Classes Years* 40–100 (6-20 *inches*)	100–150 (20–30 *inches*)	*Over* 150 (*over* 30 *inches*)
Very open...........I	12,140	100	750	11,290
	100%	1%	7%	92%
Open..............II	15,385	450	1745	13,190
	100%	2%	11%	87%
Medium..........III	15,840	500	3230	12,110
	100%	3%	22%	75%
Dense.............IV	17,375	930	5460	10,985
	100%	4%	32%	64%
Very dense.........V	24,595	1330	9100	14,165
	100%	5%	35%	60%
Average.........	14,815	450	2100	12,265
		4%	14%	82%

[4] This corresponds very nearly to the average figures secured in the reconnaissance computations.

[5] This would make the average Yellow pine for the area examined 28 inches D.B.H., with five logs, and from this we can figure that the logs in the Yellow pine type run on the average of 5 per M ft. B.M.

This is based on 10,360 trees calipered.

[6] It is very evident that this table does not show a true condition of affairs. It is based on the number of trees per acre and a large number of trees per acre does not necessarily mean a heavy stand. But here, as elsewhere, it is significant that young growth from 6–20 inches is the most important factor that determines the density of stands.

Results of the Study

Number of Trees per Acre:

1. Average number of trees varies from 5–80 per acre.
2. Average number per acre for 700 acres of 14.8 trees.
3. About 84% of the stands have 20 trees or less per acre.
4. Only 16% of the stands have more than 20 trees per acre.

Density of Stands (based on ideal acre):

1. Crown density varies from 0.23 to 0.81.
2. About 84% of the stands have a density of from 0.23 to 0.42, and are therefore only ¼ to ½ stocked.
3. Only 14% of the stands have a density of 0.55 or about ½.
4. Only 2% of the stands have a density of 0.81.
5. Average crown density of Yellow pine stands is 0.38, and therefore they are less than ½ stocked.

Representation of Age Classes:

1. In our Yellow pine stands from 15–60% of the trees are over 150 years old and over 30" in diameter. The average percentage of over-mature trees is 31%.
2. The more open the stand the less the representation of young timber below 20" and the greater the representation of the old trees above 30".
3. In going from the very open to the very dense stands the percentages increase from 22% to 79% in the case of the young timber and decrease steadily from 60% to 2% in the case of the mature timber.
4. Our stands do not obey the law of the number-of-trees-per-acre-age curve which shows that the representation in the younger age classes should be much greater than that in the older age classes.

Contents of Stands and Trees:

1. The more open the stand the greater the average contents of a tree.
2. Volume per acre increases with the density of the stand.
3. The average Yellow pine tree for large areas contains 1,000 board feet, is about 28" D.B.H., and contains 5 logs, which would indicate that this timber runs 5 logs per M ft.
4. From 60–92% of the merchantable timber is over 150 years old and over 30" in diameter.
5. The amount of merchantable timber over 150 years old decreases as the density of the stands increases.
6. Most of cutting will have to be done in the class that is over 150 years old.

7. The very open and the open stands have the greatest amount of mature timber in them and unfortunately are the ones that can stand cutting least of all.

8. A comparison of tables 6 and 8 is valuable in that it shows the relation of the proportionate volume in each age or diameter class to the number of trees in that class. For example, if all the timber above 30" in diameter is marked for cutting in the average stand this would remove only 31% of the trees, but 82% of the volume.

CALIFORNIA
STATE BOARD OF FORESTRY

BULLETIN No. 5

A Discussion of Log Rules

Their Limitations and Suggestions for Correction

BY

H. E. McKENZIE

CALIFORNIA
STATE PRINTING OFFICE
1915

18022

CALIFORNIA STATE BOARD OF FORESTRY

Hiram W. Johnson .... Governor
Frank C. Jordan .... Secretary of State
U. S. Webb .... Attorney General
G. M. Homans .... State Forester

OFFICE OF STATE FORESTER

G. M. Homans .... State Forester
Alexander W. Dodge .... Deputy State Forester
J. Diehl Schoeller .... Assistant State Forester
H. E. McKenzie .... Forest Engineer
W. J. Moodey .... Secretary
J. A. Harney .... Clerk

PREFACE

THE lumberman is beginning to realize the necessity for standardizing the methods employed in handling his industry. We recognize the problem of standardization as a broad one and feel that the following discussion of log rules is an appropriate contribution to the solution of a problem which influences both the commercial handling of lumber and the scientific study of forest products. There is an unquestionable need for a standard rule for the accurate determination of the volume of logs of various lengths and diameters, and the amount of manufactured lumber possible to produce from such logs. There are many log rules in use throughout the United States, some more accurate than others.

The following discussion has been prepared by Mr. H. E. McKenzie, Forest Engineer with this department, and was suggested by the result of a mill scale study (to be issued as a separate publication) in which the statute rule of California, the Spaulding Log Rule, was found to show a marked discrepancy between the log scale and the amount of lumber sawed out. This discrepancy led to the further investigation embracing all of the log rules in use in the United States, with the view of determining what rule, if any, is universally applicable or to devise such a rule.

G. M. HOMANS,
State Forester.

CONTENTS

ILLUSTRATIONS

DISCUSSION OF LOG RULES

INTRODUCTION

IT is customary among the lumbermen of this country, when buying or selling logs, to base their calculations upon the value of the lumber the logs will produce when sawed rather than upon the total volume. The by-products, such as slabs, sawdust, and loss by normal crook, which accompany the manufacture of lumber from logs of various sizes, are therefore ignored in the valuation, and tables have been compiled which aim to show the volume of lumber in units, known as board feet (1"x 12"x 12"), after the elimination of by-products has been made. Such tables are called "log rules."

It is the object of this publication to discuss many of the different log rules now in use, to show the principles upon which they are based, and wherein they are defective; to introduce a new log rule, based upon mathematical principles, and designed to be flexible to the varying conditions, both in milling operations and in the character of the timber to be sawed. Also, to show relations, where they exist, between any two rules or any number of rules, such that a transformation from one rule to another can be accomplished, and to reduce the various rules, wherever possible, to a definite form, in order that comparisons by formulæ may be easily made, and the allowance for slabs, sawdust, etc., by each rule readily ascertained.

2—18022

CONSTRUCTION AND UNDERLYING PRINCIPLES OF LOG RULES.

LOG RULES IN GENERAL.

About forty-five log rules have been devised within the last seventy-five years for the measurement of sawed lumber from logs of different sizes, and the values shown by these different rules cover an enormous range. It is safe to say that 90 per cent of them are so constructed that at best they are of value only under the conditions of the locality where they were first employed, and there is no means whereby they can be intelligently corrected for other conditions. Such is the case with all log rules based upon diagrams showing the amount of lumber in logs after allowances have been made for slabs, saw-kerf, etc. Such is the case with all log rules obtained by correcting these rules or combining them for others. Also rules resulting from actual experience at saw-mills have the same objections. They bear the prints of local conditions and, due to the method whereby they came into existence, they can never be anything more than local, and can only be applied to milling conditions similar to those existing at the mills where they were first constructed.

The only logical way of constructing a log rule which will be flexible and which will adjust itself to universal conditions, is to so construct it that the underlying, fundamental principles are so segregated as to make them independent of one another, and to have them so worked together as to give the aggregate result of all factors, which will be in all cases proportional and equal to the volume of the manufactured product. There are several distinct principles underlying the measurement of lumber which logs of different sizes will produce, which cannot be overlooked in any rule that is destined to become a correct universal measure. Such a rule must embody the principle that the slabs which cover the material, or part of the log which is to become the finished product, should be allowed for by making the allowance proportional to the barked area of the log. The slabs are the covering, as it were, which necessarily has to be removed in order to get to the part of the log that produces lumber, and they should not be, and are not, cut any thicker from large logs than from small ones. The best material contained in the log usually lies nearest to the bark, and it is greatly to the advantage of the millman not to waste any of his best grades.

Several log rules in most common use today do not embody the above principle. The Spaulding Log Rule, which is the statute rule of California, does not adhere to it. The Scribner Rule, which is the official rule of the Forest Service, U. S. Department of Agriculture, and of several states, does not take it into consideration, and instead of having the volume of slabs proportional to the barked area of the logs, they have them proportional to the total volume, as will be shown further on.

It would not be any more absurd if one tried to figure the number of board feet necessary to side up a house by figuring the volume of the house instead of its lateral surface. A definite per cent cannot be given as indicating the relation of slabs to trees of different volume, any more than a definite per cent can be given as indicating the relation of all lateral surface to the volume of houses of different dimensions. The Spaulding, Scribner and all other log rules with a waste allowance for slabs varying directly as the volume of the log are mathematically incorrect, since there is no reason for cutting any thicker slabs from large logs than from small ones.

Another principle underlying the measurement of lumber contained in logs of different diameters and lengths is the relation of the allowance for sawdust to the size of the log. Since the waste allowance which should be allotted to slabs should be proportional to the barked area, it can be met by reducing the diameter of all sized logs a constant amount, and the remaining volume can then be considered as lumber plus sawdust. It is very evident that the sawdust allowance depends upon the dimensions of the lumber to be sawed and upon the width of the saw used. It is also evident that, for any specific width of saw-kerf and dimensions of lumber to be sawed, the allowance for sawdust should be a definite per cent of the total volume of all logs, not including slabs. A sawdust factor which fulfills these conditions is as follows:

$$\frac{k\,(w + t + k)}{(w + k)\,(t + k)}$$

Where k = width of saw, in inches.
w = average width of lumber to be manufactured, in inches.
t = average thickness, in inches.

This factor shows what fractional part of the log minus allowance for slabs should be allowed for sawdust.

$$\left[1 - \frac{k\,(w + t + k)}{(w + k)\,(t + k)}\right]$$

represents the fractional part of the log after slab allowance is made, which becomes lumber.

Log rules which ignore these principles can not be any more than local rules, applying to conditions existing at very few mills.

There are several other considerations to be taken into account in constructing a log rule, which are not of such vital importance as the two principles cited above. They are allowances for taper, shrinkage, normal crook and excessive taper in small logs. All of these factors depend largely upon the character of the timber, and should be adjusted accordingly for the different species, and for the same species growing under different conditions.

THE THREE RULES MOST COMMONLY USED.

The Spaulding Log Rule.

The Spaulding Log Rule is the statute rule of California, having been adopted by an act of the legislature in 1878. It is constructed from diagrams, and the following comments upon it were published by its author:

"Each sized log has been scaled so as to make all that can be practically sawed out of it, if economically sawed. Each log to be measured at the top of small end, inside of the bark, and if not round, to be measured two ways—at right angles—and the average taken for the diameter. Where there are any known defects, the amount to be deducted should be agreed upon by the buyer and the seller, and no fractions of an inch to be taken into the measurement.

"In the foregoing table I have varied the size of the slab in proportion to the size of the log, and have arranged it more particularly for large logs by taking them in sections of twelve feet and carrying the table up to 96" in diameter. As there has never been any in use for scaling over 44", it has been my purpose to furnish a table for the measuring of logs that can be implicitly relied upon for correctness by both the buyer and the seller; and to do so, I have spared no pains to render it perfect."

This rule has been very carefully prepared, and all values given are very consistent with the principles upon which it is constructed. These principles are clearly shown in the graphic analysis made of the rule in Fig. 1. They are as follows: (a) The sawdust allowance varies

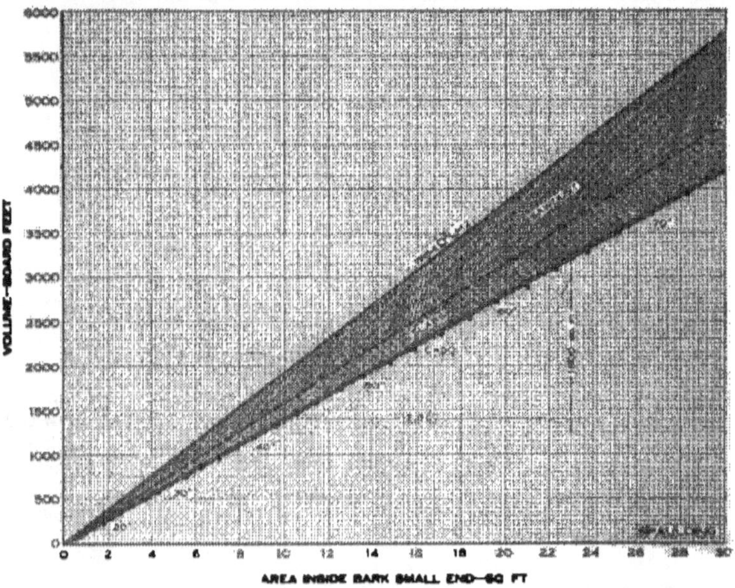

FIG. 1. A graphic analysis of the Spaulding Log Rule, based upon area in square feet inside bark at small end of logs. This diagram shows the following: (*a*) Top curve, total contents in board feet of logs of different diameters 16′ long with no allowance made for taper. (*b*) Curve "k," volume in board feet remaining after 18% of the total volume has been allowed for sawdust (this allowance is about right for ¼″ saw-kerf). (*c*) Curve passing through origin and drawn parallel to bottom curve. (*d*) Bottom curve located by plotting volumes in board feet for 16′ logs of even inches in diameter inside bark, as given by the Spaulding Log Rule. The formula indicated by this analysis is as follows: $(.048D^2 - 2)L$ = B. M. = volume in board feet.

directly with the volume. (b) Slab allowance varies directly as the volume plus a constant. (c) No allowance made for taper. (d) No allowance made for normal crook. (e) Total waste allowance remains constant, regardless of the width of saw-kerf.

The big disadvantage of such a rule lies in the fact that it is not flexible to conditions existing at mills in different localities where it might be used, or to the character of the timber sawed. It is unaffected by taper, normal crook, width of saw-kerf and excessive taper in small logs, and such corrections can not be properly made due to the diagram

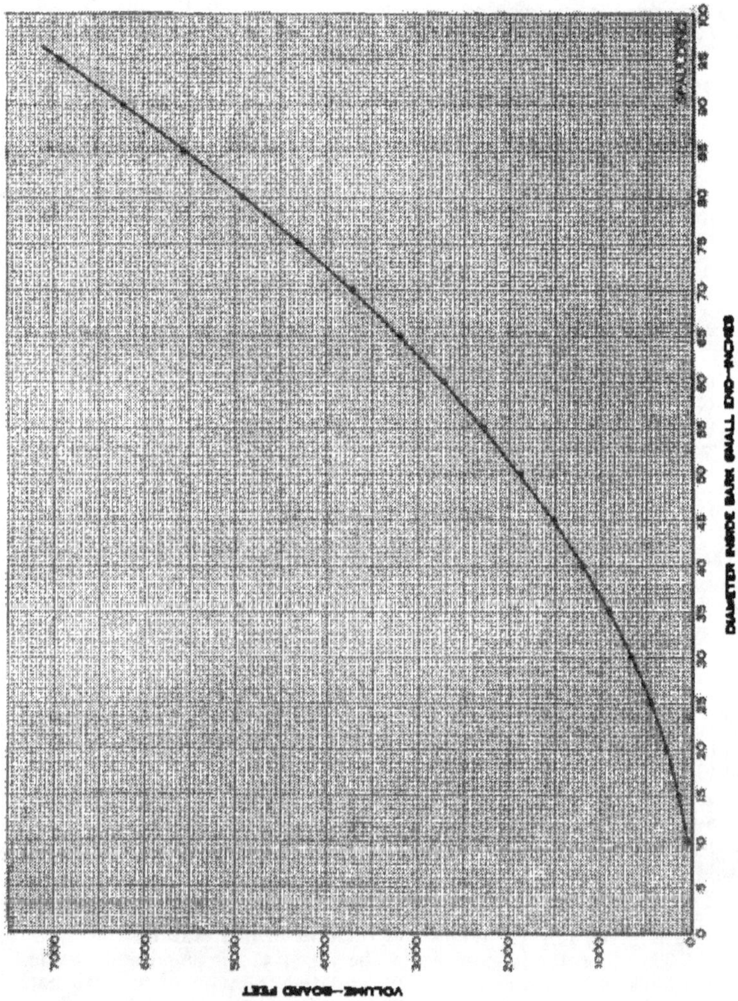

Fig. 2. The curve shown in this figure is a graphic representation of the formula $(.048D^2 - 2)L = $ B. M., when $L = 16'$. The points on the curve are plotted independently from values given by the Spaulding Log Rule, the object being to show how closely the formula fits the rule.

method used in first constructing the rule. Fig. 1 indicates the following formula: $(.048D^2 - 2)L = $ B. M. = volume in board feet, which very closely fits this rule as shown in Fig. 2.

Small logs will invariably over-run this scale, due to the constant "2" shown by the formula. Intermediate logs will hold up the scale, fall below, or go above, largely depending upon the width of saw-kerf and the average dimensions of the lumber sawed. Large logs will generally run higher than the intermediate sizes, due to the fact that the slab allowance varies directly with the volume plus a constant. The following deduction shows the total waste allowance of the Spaulding Log Rule expressed in per cent of the rule:

$(.048D^2 - 2)L = \text{B. M.} =$ total sawed out as shown by Spaulding Log Rule.

$$\frac{.7854D^2}{12}L = \text{total contents} = .0655D^2L$$

$$.0655D^2L - (.048D^2 - 2)L = \text{waste} = [(.0655 - .048)D^2 + 2]L = (.0175D^2 + 2)L.$$

$$100\frac{(.0175D^2 + 2)L}{(.048D^2 - 2)L} = \%\text{ waste based on total sawed out as shown by Spaulding Log Rule.}$$

$$= 100\frac{.0175D^2 + 2}{.048D^2 - 2}.$$

When $D = 10''$, the waste allowance based on the total sawed out as shown by the Spaulding Log Rule = 134%.
When $D = 20''$, the waste allowance = 52.2%.
When $D = 30''$, the waste allowance = 43.1%.
When $D = 40''$, the waste allowance = 40.1%.
When D = diameter in inches of very large logs, waste allowance = 36.5%.

The Scribner Log Rule.

The Scribner Log Rule is the oldest rule in general use, and is the statute rule of Idaho, Minnesota, Oregon, Wisconsin and West Virginia. Also, it is the official rule adopted by the Federal Forest Service.

It was constructed from diagrams the same as the Spaulding Log Rule, and the following description was published by its author in 1846:

"This table has been computed from accurately drawn diagrams for each and every diameter of logs from twelve inches to forty-four, and the exact width of each board taken after being squared by taking off the wane edge and the contents reckoned up for every log, so that it is mathematically certain that the true contents are here given, and both buyer and seller of logs will unhesitatingly adopt these tables as the standard for all future contracts in the purchase of saw logs where strict honesty between party and party is taken into account. In these revised computations I have allowed a thicker slab to be taken from the larger class of logs than in the former edition, which accounts for the discrepancy between the results given in these tables and those in former editions.

"The diameter is supposed to be taken at the small end, inside the bark, and in sections of 15′, and the fractions of an inch not taken into the measurement. This mode of measurement, which is customary, gives the buyer the advantage of the swell of the log, the gain by sawing into scantling, or large timber, and the fractional part of an inch in the diameter. Still it must be remembered that logs are never straight and that oftentimes there are concealed defects which must be taken as an offset for the gain above mentioned. It has been my desire to furnish those who deal in lumber of any kind with a set of tables that can implicitly be relied upon for correctness by both buyer and seller, and to do so I have spared no pains nor expense to render them perfect; and it is to be hoped that hereafter these will be preferred to the palpably erroneous tables which have hitherto been in use. If there is any truth in mathematics or dependence to be placed in the estimates given in diagrams, there cannot remain a particle of doubt of the accuracy of the results here given."

This log rule gives practically the same results as does the Spaulding. It is not as carefully prepared, however, since the values given are not as consistent with the underlying principles of the rule. A graphic

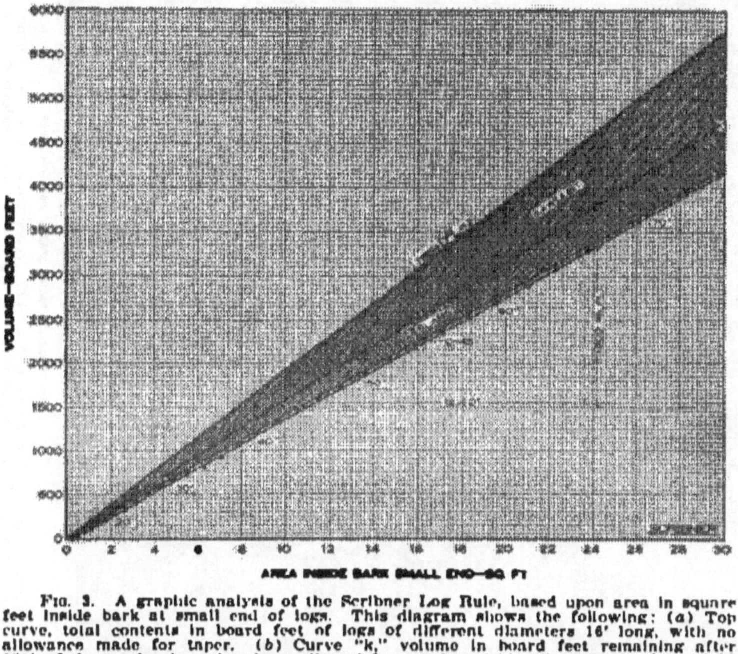

FIG. 3. A graphic analysis of the Scribner Log Rule, based upon area in square feet inside bark at small end of logs. This diagram shows the following: (*a*) Top curve, total contents in board feet of logs of different diameters 16′ long, with no allowance made for taper. (*b*) Curve "k," volume in board feet remaining after 15% of the total volume has been allowed for sawdust (this allowance is about right for ¼" saw-kerf). (*c*) Curve passing through origin and drawn parallel to bottom curve. (*d*) Bottom curve located by plotting volume in board feet for 16′ logs of even inches in diameter inside bark as given by the Scribner Log Rule. The formula indicated by this analysis is as follows: $(.048D^2-3)L$ = B. M. = volume in board feet. This formula is almost identical with the one obtained for the Spaulding Log Rule. It does not apply, however, to diameters below 14" or above 75". No formula can be written for the Scribner Log Rule that will fit all values given, due to the inconsistency of the individual values of the rule.

analysis of it is given in Fig. 3, which shows the fundamental principles upon which it is based, and which are the same as for the Spaulding rule. The formula indicated by the analysis shown in Fig. 3 is $(.048D^2-3)L$ = B. M. = volume in board feet, which is practically the same as for the Spaulding Log Rule, the only difference being in the constant "3". Fig. 4 shows how closely this formula fits the rule.

Small logs will invariably overrun this scale, and to a slightly greater extent than for the Spaulding Log Rule, since the constant shown by the formula is "3" instead of "2". Intermediate logs will hold up the

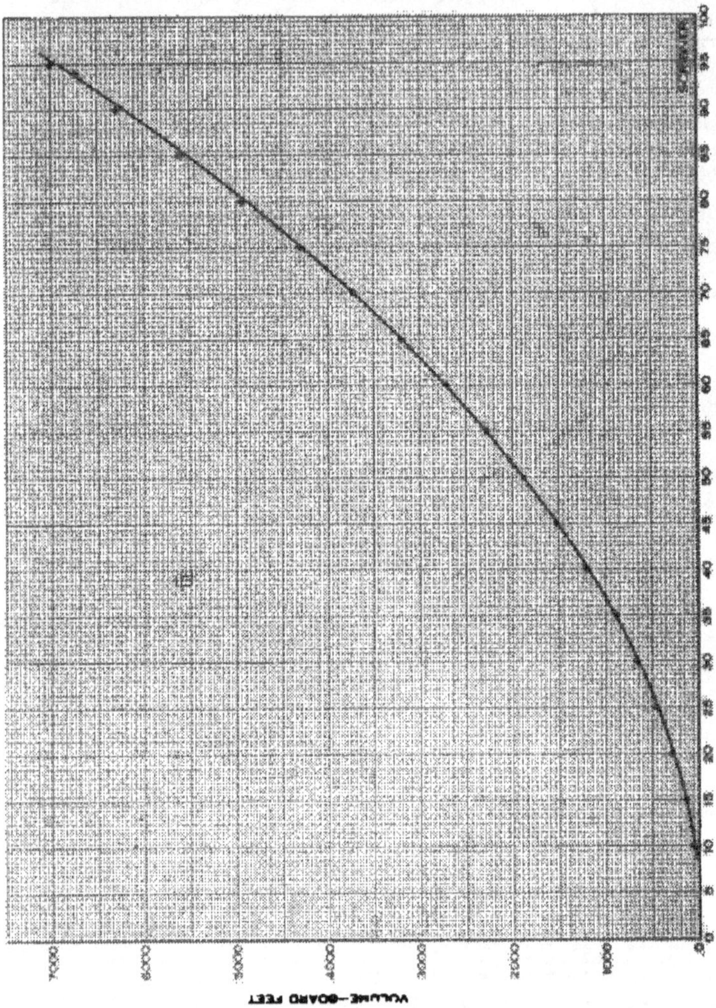

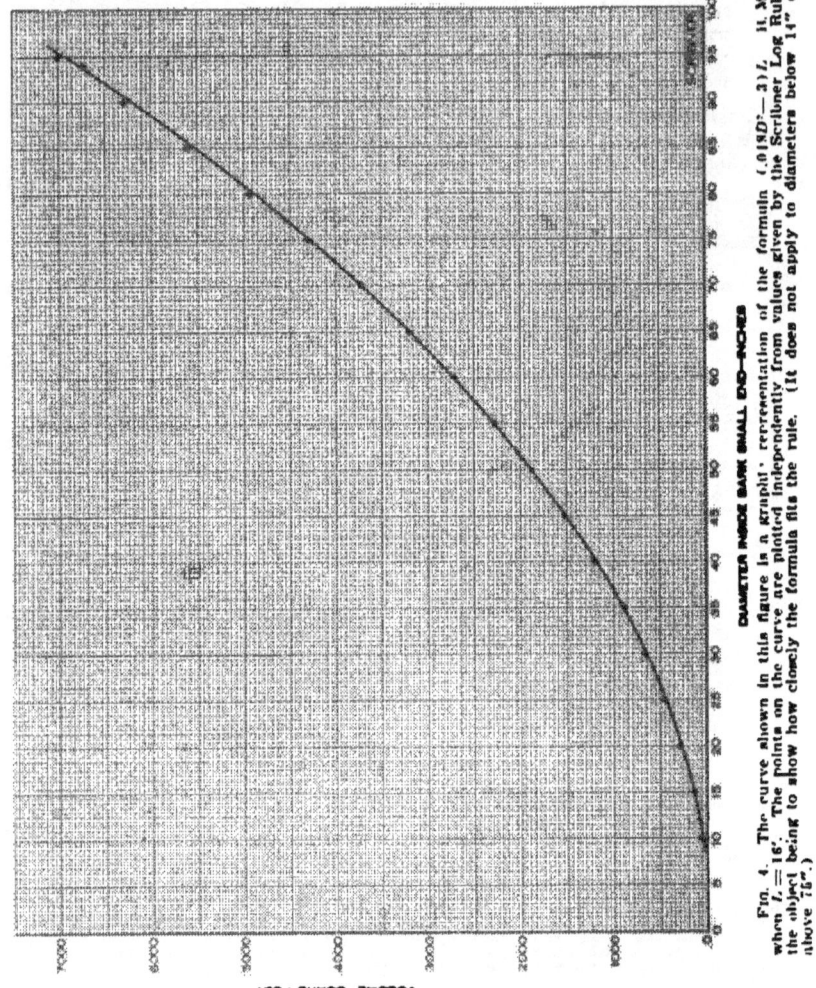

FIG. 4. The curve shown in this figure is a graphic representation of the formula $(.018D^2 - 3)L$ B. M., when $L = 16'$. The points on the curve are plotted independently from values given by the Scribner Log Rule, the object being to show how closely the formula fits the rule. (It does not apply to diameters below 14" or above 75".)

scale, fall below or go above, largely depending upon the width of the saw-kerf and the average dimensions of the lumber sawed. Large logs will run higher than the intermediate sizes, due to the fact that the slab allowance is directly proportional to the volume plus a constant. The following deduction shows the total waste allowance of the Scribner rule expressed in per cent of total sawed out, as shown by the rule:

$(.048D^2 - 3)L = $ B. M. = Total sawed out as shown by the Scribner Log Rule.

$\frac{.7854D^2}{12}L = $ total contents $= .0655D^2L$

$.0655D^2L - (.048D^2 - 3)L = $ waste $= [(.0655 - .048)D^2 + 3]L$
$= (.0175D^2 + 3)L$

$100\frac{(.0175D^2 + 3)L}{(.048D^2 - 3)L} = $ % waste based on total sawed out as shown by Scribner Log Rule.

$= 100\frac{.0175D^2 + 3}{.048D^2 - 3}$.

When $D = 10''$, the waste allowance based on the total sawed out as shown by the Scribner Log Rule = (Formula does not apply below 14").

When $D = 20''$, the waste allowance = 61.8%.
When $D = 30''$, the waste allowance = 46.7%.
When $D = 40''$, the waste allowance = 42.0%.
When $D = $ diameter in inches for very large logs, waste allowance = 36.5%.

The Doyle Log Rule.

The Doyle Log Rule is used throughout the entire country and is the statute rule of Florida, Louisiana and Arkansas. It is constructed from the formula $\left(\frac{D - 4}{4}\right)^2 L = $ B. M., which is stated as follows: Deduct 4" from the diameter of the log as an allowance for slabs; square one quarter of the remainder and multiply the result by the length of the log in feet. No mention is made in this rule of a sawdust allowance. If four inches from the diameter of the small end is the slab allowance, the sawdust allowance must be the difference between the solid contents in board feet remaining after the slab allowance has been made and the contents shown by the rule. The determination of sawdust allowance follows:

$\left(\frac{D - 4}{4}\right)^2 L = B.M. = $ volume in board feet, as shown by the Doyle rule, of log D inches in diameter at small end inside bark and L feet long.

$\frac{.7854(D - 4)^2}{12}L = $ volume in board feet of log D inches in diameter inside bark at small end L feet long with waste allowance for slabs but none for sawdust.

$\frac{.7854(D - 4)^2}{12}L - \left(\frac{D - 4}{4}\right)^2 L = $ sawdust allowance for log D inches in diameter and L feet long.

$\dfrac{\frac{.7854(D - 4)^2}{12}L - \left(\frac{D - 4}{4}\right)^2 L}{\frac{.7854(D - 4)^2}{12}L} \times 100 = $ sawdust allowance for log D inches in diameter and L feet long expressed in per cent of volume in board feet left after slab allowance has been made

$= \frac{.295}{.0655} = 4.5\%$

Therefore, the sawdust allowance for the Doyle Log Rule = 4.5% of the total volume left after 4" has been deducted from the diameter as an allowance for slabs. This sawdust allowance is correct in principle, since it is a definite per cent of the total volume after slabs have been accounted for. It is, however, entirely too small. The thinnest modern band saws take away at least 10% of the volume of the lumber sawed unless the product be large timbers, and the allowance of 4.5% is not one-half as large as it should be for even one of these saws. The

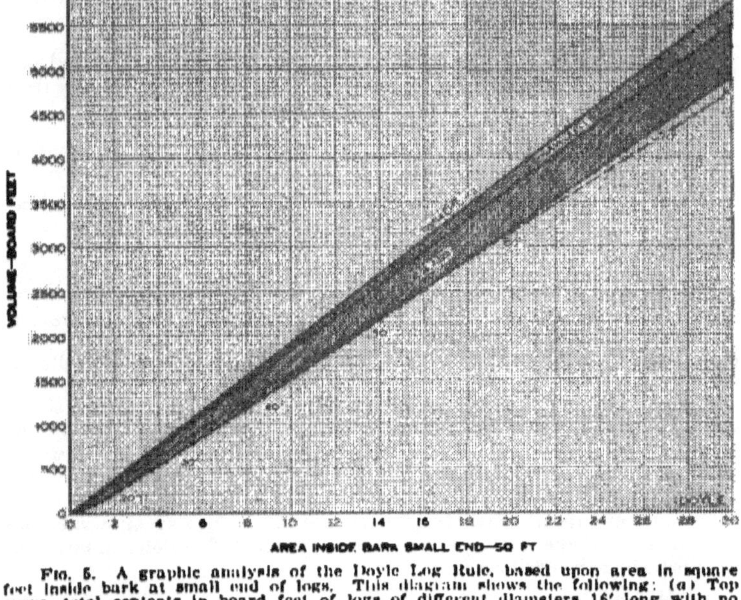

FIG. 5. A graphic analysis of the Doyle Log Rule, based upon area in square feet inside bark at small end of logs. This diagram shows the following: (*a*) Top curve, total contents in board feet of logs of different diameters 16' long with no allowance made for taper. (*b*) Next lower curve, volume in board feet remaining after an allowance of 4.5% has been made for sawdust. (4.5% of the total volume of logs, after slab allowance has been made, is the only portion of the waste allowance of the Doyle Log Rule that varies directly as the volume. Therefore, it is the only part of the formula that varies directly as the amount of sawdust.) (*c*) Curve "k," values for volume in board feet after an allowance of 18% for sawdust has been made. This curve intersects the log rule at about 56", showing, that, at this point and above, the waste allowance which should cover slabs and sawdust is not sufficient to even cover the sawdust. The Doyle Log Rule, however, is correct in principle, but its values are ver" poorly chosen.

principle upon which the Doyle Log Rule is based is correct, however, since the slab allowance is proportional to the barked area and the sawdust allowance is proportional to the total volume left after the allowance for slabs has been made. But the allowance for slabs is absurdly large and that for sawdust is absurdly low. In short, the principle of the rule is correct, but the values are very poorly chosen. Fig. 5 shows a graphic analysis of the rule.

A log rule was used long before the Doyle rule came into existence, which gave the same results, and was stated as follows: Deduct 4" from the diameter for slabs, then, squaring the remainder, subtract one-fourth for saw-kerf and the balance will be the contents of the log 12′ long, from which the others may be obtained by proportion. It would appear from this that a generous allowance for sawdust had been made, but as a matter of fact the apparent sawdust allowance is a part of the allowance already made for slabs. This is clearly illustrated in figures 6 and 7, when the above rule is applied. (Deduct 4″ from the diameter for slabs and in Figures 6 and 7 we have $D-4=AB$. Then, squaring the remainder $(D-4)$, we have $(D-4)^2=ABCD$. Subtract $\frac{1}{4}$

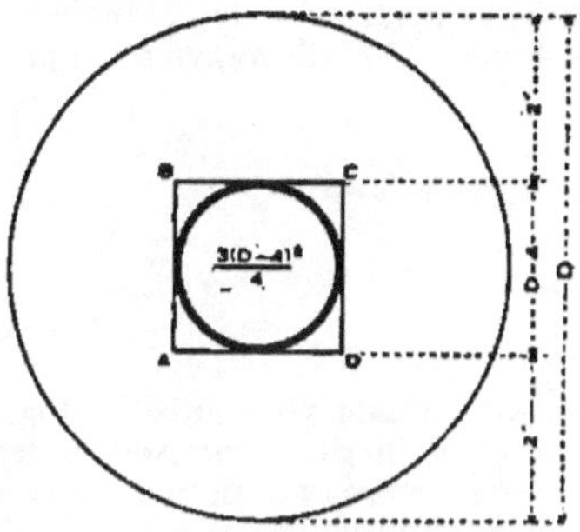

FIG. 6. The Doyle Log Rule as applied to a 6″ log.

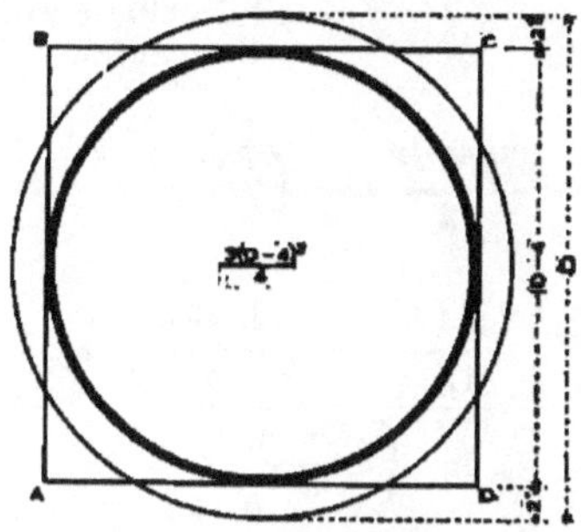

FIG. 7. The Doyle Log Rule as applied to a 30″ log.

for saw-kerf, giving $\frac{3}{4}(D-4)^2$, which is the inside circle. The inscribed circle outside of this is equal to $.7854(D-4)^2$. It is apparent from this that $.7854(D-4)^2-\frac{3}{4}(D-4)^2$ is the only true portion of the diagram which could represent sawdust.) This rule amounts to the same thing as the Doyle Log Rule, but in statement is misleading and ambiguous.

The sawdust allowance as shown by Figures 6 and 7 in per cent of total contents after slab allowance has been made is as follows:

$$\frac{.7854\,(D-4)^2-\frac{3}{4}\,(D-4)^2}{.7854\,(D-4)^2}\times 100=$$

$$\frac{.0354\,(D-4)^2}{.7854\,(D-4)^2}\times 100=\frac{3.54}{.7854}=4.5\%$$

which is the same as shown by the Doyle Log Rule formula.

The following deduction will show the total waste allowance of the Doyle Log Rule for logs of different sizes expressed in per cent of total sawed out, as indicated by the rule:

$$\left(\frac{D-4}{4}\right)^2 L = B.M. = \text{volume in board feet of log } D \text{ inches in diameter at small end inside bark and } L \text{ feet long.}$$

$$\frac{.7854\,D^2}{12} L = \text{total volume in board feet contained in log } D \text{ inches in diameter and } L \text{ feet long. (No allowance for taper.)}$$

$$\frac{.7854\,D^2}{12} L - \left(\frac{D-4}{4}\right)^2 L = \text{total waste allowance.}$$

$$\frac{\frac{.7854\,D^2}{12} L - \left(\frac{D-4}{4}\right)^2 L}{\left(\frac{D-4}{4}\right)^2 L} \times 100 = \text{total waste allowance for log } D \text{ inches in diameter and } L \text{ feet long expressed in per cent of used volume.}$$

$$= \frac{.003\,D^2 + .5\,D - 1}{.0625\,D^2 - .5\,D + 1} \times 100.$$

When $D = 10''$, the waste allowance based on the total sawed out as shown by the Doyle Log Rule $= 191\%$.

When $D = 20''$, the waste allowance $= 63.8\%$.

When $D = 30''$, the waste allowance $= 39.5\%$.

When $D = 40''$, the waste allowance $= 29.4\%$.

When $D = 50''$, the waste allowance $= 23.8\%$.

This waste allowance is obviously too high for small logs and too low for large ones. This is due to the fact that the slab allowance is too generous and the sawdust allowance too small. Small logs will invariably over-run the scale; intermediate logs will usually scale about right, since the large slab allowance makes up the shortage for sawdust; large logs will invariably under-run the scale, because the combined slab and sawdust allowance is too small for waste, though the actual slab allowance is too large for slabs alone.

The McKenzie Log Rule.

The McKenzie Log Rule is based on mathematical principles and is designed to cover all conditions encountered in the manufacture of lumber from logs of various diameters and lengths. All factors influencing the total volume sawed out have been taken into consideration and treated separately, thus making the rule flexible to the varying conditions, both in milling operations and in the character of the timber.

The following factors which affect the mill output from logs of different sizes have been included:

(*a*) Slabs.
(*b*) Normal crook.
(*c*) Saw-kerf.
(*d*) Average dimensions of lumber sawed.
(*e*) Taper.
(*f*) Excessive taper in small logs.

The mathematical principles underlying the rule are as follows:

(*a*) The slab allowance is a function of the barked area and varies directly with it.

(*b*) Normal crook is also a function of the barked area, and varies directly with it the same as slabs.

(*c*) The sawdust allowance is a function of saw-kerf and average dimensions sawed at mill, and for any given saw-kerf and average dimensions the sawdust allowance should vary directly as the volume minus the slabs.

(*d*) Taper allowance equal to e'' in f'. (f not to exceed 16′.)

(*e*) Excessive taper in small logs offset by a constant.

Let D = diameter in inches inside bark at small end.
Let L = length of log in feet.
Let k = width of saw-kerf, in inches.
Let w = average width of lumber sawed, in inches.
Let t = average thickness of lumber sawed, in inches.
Let C = constant.
Let a = constant.

then $(D - a)$ = diameter of log after an allowance for slabs and normal crook has been made. (Since slabs and normal crook both vary the same, they can be accounted for by the same constant, a.)

$\frac{\pi (D - a)^2}{4}$ = area in square inches of small end of log after the slab and normal crook allowance has been made.

$\frac{\pi (D - a)^2 L}{4}$ = volume in units of 1″ × 1″ × 12″ contained in log L feet long and D inches in diameter after the slab and normal crook allowance has been made. (Taper allowance to be made later.)

$\frac{\pi (D - a)^2 L}{4 \times 12}$ = volume in units of 1″ × 12″ × 12″ or board feet in log L feet long and D inches in diameter after slab and normal crook allowance has been made.

No allowance has, as yet, been made for sawdust. This allowance depends upon the width of saw-kerf and the average dimensions of lumber to be sawed. The saw-kerf from one side and edge of an average board bears the same ratio to that board as the total sawdust from all boards does to the total volume after slab allowance has been made. This is true of all volume becoming sawdust, excepting saw-kerf amounting to $2k(D - a)$, which should be considered as part of the slabs since it varies directly as the barked area, and is the sawdust formed in cutting the slabs.

$$k(w + t + k)\frac{L}{12} = \text{volume of wood forming sawdust from each average board.}$$

$$(w + k)(t + k)\frac{L}{12} = \text{volume of sawdust plus volume of average board.}$$

$$\frac{k(w + t + k)\frac{L}{12}}{(w + k)(t + k)\frac{L}{12}} = \frac{k(w + t + k)}{(w + k)(t + k)} = \text{fractional part of wood, necessary to make average board, becoming sawdust.}$$

This ratio of sawdust to average board plus sawdust holds for volume of logs minus allowance for slabs.

$$\left[1 - \frac{k(w + t + k)}{(w + k)(t + k)}\right] = \text{fractional part of log, after slab allowance is made, which becomes lumber.}$$

Therefore, $\left[1 - \frac{k(w + t + k)}{(w + k)(t + k)}\right]\pi\frac{(D - a)^2}{48}L$ = volume in board feet of lumber of average dimensions from log D inches in diameter at small end inside the bark and L feet long, when saw-kerf is k inches wide.

A constant C = to a few board feet, when added to this formula has a compensating effect for the excessive taper in small logs. Since most small logs sawed are the top logs from medium or large sized trees, they have an excessive taper which can not be accounted for by a uniform taper allowance applied to the whole tree. Therefore, this constant, which in all cases will be very small (not exceeding 10 board feet) is applied and its effect on large logs is negligible, but on small ones it will play an important part in eliminating an accumulative error in total sawed out at the mill.

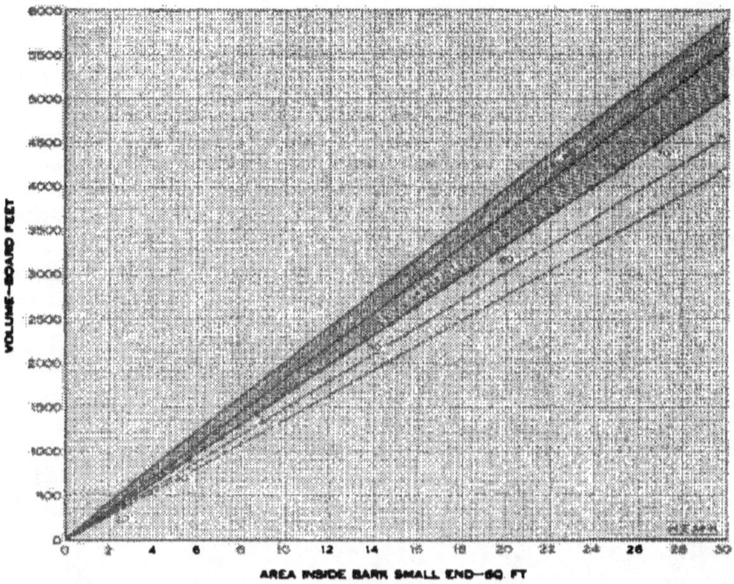

FIG. 8. A graphic analysis of the McKenzie Log Rule, based upon area in square feet inside bark at small end of logs. This diagram shows the following: (*a*) Top curve, total contents in board feet of logs of different diameters 16′ long with taper allowance of 1″ in 8′. (*b*) Next lower curve, volume in board feet remaining after an allowance for slabs has been made. (*c*) The log rule curve for ¼″ saw-kerf, showing volume in board feet after an allowance for slabs and sawdust has been made. (The allowance for slabs in this rule varies directly as the "barked" area, and that for sawdust directly as the volume minus slab allowance.) (*d*) Curve "k," position that the log rule curve takes when the saw-kerf is ⅛″ instead of ¼″. (*e*) Curve "k′" shows position of the log rule curve for a ⅜″ saw-kerf. The formula for this rule is as follows:

$$\left[1-\frac{k(w+t+k)}{(w+k)(t+k)}\right]\frac{\pi(D-a)^2}{48}L+C=\text{B.M.}$$

k = width of saw-kerf, in inches.
w = average width of lumber, sawed, in inches.
t = average thickness of lumber sawed, in inches.
π = 3.1416.
D = average diameter inside bark, small end, in inches.
a = constant.
L = length of log, in feet.
C = constant included to compensate for excessive taper in small logs.

The formula is:

(not making any allowance for shrinkage and surfacing; the complete formula with this allowance made is shown on page 52.):

$$\left[1-\frac{k(w+t+k)}{(w+k)(t+k)}\right]\frac{\pi(D-a)^2}{48}L+C=\text{B.M.}$$

with a taper allowance of t'' in f' to be applied when compiling a table. The section used should not be taken over 16′ long: 8′ is better.

Its Application.

The above formula when applied to conditions existing at the Red River Lumber Company's mill in Lassen County, California, gave results shown in the following table. The value of *a* determined at this mill is extremely small, due to the fact that slabs were cut very thin and edgings were graded as moulding stock, also to the fact that short lengths were cut from logs where taper was great enough to permit it. The formula was first applied to 16′ logs, thus getting the taper in 16′ included with the slabs. Volumes in board feet of logs of other lengths were then figured with a taper allowance of 1″ in 8′.

TABLE 1. The McKenzie Log Rule, based upon the following formula:

$$\left[1 - \frac{k\,(w + t + k)}{(w + k)\,(t + k)}\right] \frac{\pi\,(D - a)^2}{48} L + C = \text{B.M.}$$

Where k = saw-kerf = $\frac{1}{8}$″.
Where k = average width of lumber = 12″.
Where t = average thickness of lumber = $\frac{3}{4}$″.
Where D = average diameter of log inside bark, small end, in inches.
Where a = 1″.
Where L = length of log in feet.
Where C = 2 = constant allowed for excessive taper occurring in small logs.
Where B. M. = volume in board feet.
Where π = 3.1416.

With these values substituted, the formula becomes $.942(D - 1)^2 + 2$ = B. M. for 16′ logs.

Table based upon 16′ logs. Taper allowance of 1″ in 8′ made for other lengths.

TABLE I.

Length in feet	4	5	6	7	8	9	10	11	12	13	14	15	16	Length in feet
	DIAMETER IN INCHES — BOARD FEET													
8	4	7	10	15	21	27	35	43	53	63	74	87	99	8
9	5	8	12	18	24	31	40	50	61	72	85	99	113	9
10	6	9	14	20	28	36	46	56	69	81	96	112	127	10
11	7	11	16	23	31	40	51	63	76	91	106	124	141	11
12	7	12	18	25	34	44	56	69	84	100	117	136	155	12
13	8	13	19	28	38	49	62	76	92	109	128	149	170	13
14	9	14	21	31	41	53	67	83	100	118	139	161	184	14
15	10	16	23	33	44	57	72	89	108	127	150	173	198	15
16	10	17	25	36	48	62	78	96	116	137	161	186	214	16
17	11	19	28	39	52	67	84	104	125	148	173	200	230	17
18	12	21	30	43	57	73	91	112	131	159	185	214	246	18
19	14	23	33	46	61	78	98	120	144	169	198	228	262	19
20	15	25	35	50	65	83	104	127	153	181	210	242	278	20
21	16	26	38	53	70	89	111	135	162	191	223	257	294	21
22	18	28	41	56	74	94	118	143	171	202	235	271	310	22
23	19	30	44	60	79	100	124	151	180	213	247	285	327	23
24	21	32	46	63	83	105	131	159	190	224	260	300	343	24
25	23	35	49	67	88	112	139	168	201	236	274	316	361	25
26	25	37	53	72	91	118	147	178	212	249	288	332	379	26
27	27	40	56	76	99	125	155	187	223	261	302	348	397	27
28	29	42	59	80	104	131	162	196	233	274	316	364	415	28
29	30	45	61	85	110	138	170	205	244	286	331	380	433	29
30	32	48	66	89	115	145	178	214	255	298	345	396	451	30
31	34	50	70	94	121	151	186	224	280	311	359	413	470	31
32	36	53	73	98	126	158	194	233	277	323	374	429	487	32

TABLE I—Continued.

Length in feet	17	18	19	20	21	22	23	24	25	26	27	28	29	Length in feet
	DIAMETER IN INCHES — BOARD FEET													
8	114	129	144	162	180	199	219	240	261	283	307	332	358	8
9	130	147	164	184	205	226	249	273	296	321	348	377	403	9
10	146	165	185	207	230	254	279	305	332	360	390	421	454	10
11	162	183	205	230	253	281	309	338	367	396	431	466	501	11
12	178	201	225	252	280	309	339	370	403	436	473	511	550	12
13	195	219	245	275	304	336	369	403	438	475	515	556	598	13
14	211	237	266	297	329	363	399	436	473	513	556	600	645	14
15	227	255	286	319	354	391	429	469	509	552	597	645	693	15
16	243	273	307	342	378	417	457	499	544	590	638	688	739	16
17	261	293	330	367	406	447	490	531	582	631	683	736	790	17
18	279	314	352	392	433	477	522	570	621	673	727	784	841	18
19	297	334	375	417	460	507	555	605	659	714	772	831	893	19
20	315	354	397	442	487	537	587	640	697	756	817	879	944	20
21	333	374	419	466	515	567	620	676	736	797	862	927	995	21
22	351	395	442	491	542	597	653	711	774	839	906	975	1046	22
23	369	415	464	516	570	627	685	746	813	880	951	1025	1096	23
24	387	435	487	541	597	657	718	782	851	922	996	1070	1150	24
25	407	457	512	568	627	690	753	820	892	966	1045	1120	1205	25
26	427	480	536	595	657	722	788	858	934	1010	1090	1175	1260	26
27	447	502	560	623	687	754	824	897	975	1060	1140	1225	1315	27
28	468	525	584	650	717	787	859	935	1020	1110	1185	1275	1365	28
29	488	547	608	678	747	819	894	974	1060	1160	1235	1330	1420	29
30	508	570	632	705	777	852	930	1010	1100	1205	1285	1380	1475	30
31	528	592	656	733	807	885	965	1050	1140	1255	1330	1430	1530	31
32	550	615	685	760	836	916	1000	1090	1180	1280	1375	1480	1585	32

TABLE I—Continued.

Length in feet	30	31	32	33	34	35	36	37	38	39	40	41	42	Length feet
	DIAMETER IN INCHES / BOARD FEET													
8	383	410	438	469	498	528	561	594	627	604	698	734	774	8
9	434	465	497	531	564	598	635	672	710	752	790	831	876	9
10	486	520	556	594	630	668	710	751	793	839	882	929	1130	10
11	537	574	614	656	696	739	783	829	876	926	973	1024	1080	11
12	588	629	673	718	762	808	858	908	959	1015	1065	1120	1180	12
13	639	684	721	781	828	879	932	986	1040	1100	1155	1215	1280	13
14	690	739	790	843	894	949	1005	1065	1125	1185	1250	1315	1380	14
15	742	792	848	906	960	1020	1080	1140	1210	1275	1340	1410	1485	15
16	793	846	907	968	1025	1090	1155	1220	1290	1360	1430	1505	1585	16
17	848	907	969	1035	1095	1165	1235	1305	1375	1455	1530	1610	1690	17
18	903	965	1030	1100	1165	1235	1310	1385	1465	1545	1625	1710	1800	18
19	957	1025	1095	1165	1235	1310	1390	1470	1550	1635	1720	1810	1905	19
20	1010	1085	1155	1230	1305	1385	1470	1530	1640	1730	1820	1915	2010	20
21	1065	1140	1220	1300	1375	1460	1545	1635	1725	1820	1915	2015	2120	21
22	1120	1200	1280	1365	1450	1535	1625	1720	1810	1910	2010	2115	2225	22
23	1175	1260	1345	1430	1520	1610	1705	1800	1900	2005	2110	2220	2330	23
24	1230	1320	1405	1495	1590	1685	1780	1875	1985	2095	2205	2320	2435	24
25	1280	1380	1470	1565	1660	1760	1865	1970	2080	2190	2305	2425	2550	25
26	1330	1440	1535	1635	1735	1840	1950	2060	2170	2285	2410	2530	2670	26
27	1405	1495	1605	1705	1810	1920	2030	2145	2260	2385	2510	2640	2770	27
28	1465	1565	1670	1775	1885	1995	2115	2230	2355	2480	2610	2745	2890	28
29	1525	1630	1735	1845	1960	2075	2195	2320	2445	2580	2715	2850	2995	29
30	1585	1690	1800	1915	2030	2155	2280	2405	2535	2675	2815	2960	3105	30
31	1640	1750	1865	1990	2105	2230	2365	2495	2630	2770	2915	3065	3215	31
32	1700	1815	1935	2055	2180	2310	2445	2580	2720	2870	3015	3170	3325	32

TABLE I—Continued.

Length in feet	DIAMETER IN INCHES													Length in feet
	43	44	45	46	47	48	49	50	51	52	53	54	55	
	BOARD FEET													
8	812	852	890	932	978	1020	1065	1110	1155	1200	1250	1300	1345	8
9	919	963	1005	1056	1105	1150	1200	1255	1305	1355	1410	1465	1520	9
10	1025	1075	1125	1175	1230	1285	1340	1395	1455	1510	1575	1635	1695	10
11	1130	1186	1240	1300	1360	1415	1480	1540	1605	1670	1735	1805	1870	11
12	1240	1295	1355	1420	1485	1550	1615	1685	1755	1825	1900	1970	2045	12
13	1345	1410	1475	1540	1625	1685	1755	1830	1905	1980	2060	2140	2170	13
14	1450	1520	1590	1665	1740	1815	1890	1975	2056	2140	2225	2310	2395	14
15	1560	1630	1705	1785	1865	1950	2035	2120	2205	2290	2385	2475	2570	15
16	1660	1740	1820	1905	1990	2080	2170	2260	2355	2445	2545	2643	2745	16
17	1773	1860	1945	2035	2000	2220	2315	2410	2515	2610	2715	2820	2925	17
18	1885	1975	2065	2160	2200	2360	2460	2560	2670	2770	2880	2995	3105	18
19	1995	2090	2190	2290	2390	2495	2605	2710	2825	2935	3050	3170	3285	19
20	2105	2210	2310	2420	2525	2635	2740	2850	2980	3095	3220	3345	3470	20
21	2220	2325	2430	2545	2655	2775	2885	3010	3135	3260	3380	3520	3650	21
22	2330	2440	2555	2670	2790	2910	3040	3160	3295	3420	3565	3695	3830	22
23	2440	2555	2675	2795	2920	3050	3180	3310	3450	3585	3725	3870	4010	23
24	2560	2673	2800	2925	3055	3190	3325	3460	3605	3745	3890	4046	4195	24
25	2670	2795	2925	3060	3195	3335	3475	3620	3770	3915	4065	4225	4380	25
26	2785	2920	3050	3190	3330	3480	3625	3775	3930	4080	4240	4405	4570	26
27	2900	3040	3180	3325	3470	3625	3775	3930	4090	4250	4415	4585	4755	27
28	3020	3160	3305	3460	3610	3765	3925	4085	4255	4415	4590	4765	4945	28
29	3135	3285	3435	3590	3745	3910	4075	4240	4415	4585	4765	4950	5135	29
30	3250	3405	3560	3725	3885	4055	4225	4400	4580	4755	4940	5130	5330	30
31	3365	3530	3690	3855	4025	4200	4375	4555	4740	4925	5115	5310	5510	31
32	3485	3650	3815	3990	4165	4345	4530	4710	4905	5090	5290	5495	5695	32

TABLE I—Continued.

Length in feet	Diameter in inches: 56	57	58	59	60	61	62	63	64	65	66	67	68	Length in feet
	Board feet													
8	1400	1460	1505	1560	1615	1665	1725	1780	1840	1900	1960	2020	2080	8
9	1580	1640	1700	1760	1830	1880	1945	2010	2075	2145	2210	2280	2350	9
10	1760	1825	1895	1960	2035	2095	2170	2240	2315	2390	2465	2540	2610	10
11	1945	2015	2090	2165	2240	2315	2390	2470	2550	2635	2715	2800	2885	11
12	2125	2200	2285	2365	2445	2530	2615	2700	2790	2880	2970	3060	3150	12
13	2305	2390	2475	2570	2655	2745	2840	2930	3030	3125	3220	3320	3420	13
14	2485	2580	2675	2770	2865	2960	3060	3160	3265	3370	3475	3580	3690	14
15	2670	2765	2865	2975	3075	3175	3285	3390	3500	3615	3730	3840	3960	15
16	2850	2950	3060	3170	3280	3390	3500	3620	3735	3855	3975	4100	4230	16
17	3035	3145	3265	3380	3495	3615	3730	3855	3980	4110	4235	4370	4500	17
18	3225	3340	3465	3585	3710	3835	3960	4090	4225	4360	4495	4640	4775	18
19	3415	3535	3665	3795	3920	4050	4190	4325	4470	4615	4755	4905	5050	19
20	3600	3730	3870	4005	4145	4280	4420	4570	4715	4865	5015	5175	5325	20
21	3790	3925	4070	4210	4360	4505	4650	4810	4960	5120	5275	5445	5600	21
22	3975	4130	4275	4420	4575	4730	4880	5045	5205	5370	5535	5710	5880	22
23	4165	4315	4475	4630	4790	4950	5110	5280	5450	5625	5795	5980	6150	23
24	4355	4510	4675	4835	5005	5170	5340	5520	5695	5875	6055	6245	6430	24
25	4545	4710	4885	5045	5225	5400	5580	5765	5950	6135	6325	6520	6715	25
26	4740	4915	5090	5265	5450	5630	5815	6010	6200	6395	6590	6795	7000	26
27	4935	5115	5300	5480	5675	5860	6055	6255	6455	6655	6860	7075	7285	27
28	5130	5315	5510	5695	5895	6090	6290	6500	6705	6915	7130	7350	7570	28
29	5325	5520	5715	5915	6120	6320	6530	6745	6960	7175	7395	7625	7855	29
30	5520	5720	5915	6130	6345	6550	6765	6990	7210	7435	7665	7900	8140	30
31	5715	5925	6125	6345	6565	6790	7005	7235	7465	7695	7935	8180	8425	31
32	5910	6120	6345	6560	6785	7010	7240	7480	7715	7960	8200	8455	8705	32

TABLE I—Continued.

Length in feet	DIAMETER IN INCHES 69	70	71	72	73	74	75	76	77	78	79	80	81	Length in feet
	BOARD FEET													
8	2145	2210	2280	2340	2405	2475	2540	2610	2685	2755	2825	2900	2970	8
9	2430	2495	2515	2640	2706	2795	2865	2945	3000	3110	3185	3270	3355	9
10	2695	2780	2865	2940	3025	3115	3195	3285	3375	3460	3550	3645	3735	10
11	2965	3055	3155	3245	3335	3430	3520	3620	3720	3815	3910	4015	4115	11
12	3250	3330	3430	3545	3645	3745	3845	3955	4065	4165	4275	4385	4500	12
13	3525	3630	3740	3845	3955	4055	4170	4290	4410	4520	4635	4755	4880	13
14	3800	3915	4035	4145	4265	4385	4500	4620	4755	4875	5000	5130	5260	14
15	4075	4200	4325	4445	4570	4700	4825	4960	5100	5225	5360	5500	5640	15
16	4350	4480	4610	4745	4880	5020	5150	5290	5440	5580	5720	5870	6020	16
17	4635	4775	4915	5055	5200	5350	5490	5635	5796	5945	6090	6255	6415	17
18	4920	5065	5215	5365	5520	5675	5825	5980	6150	6306	6465	6636	6806	18
19	5205	5360	5515	5675	5835	6000	6160	6325	6500	6670	6835	7015	7195	19
20	5490	5650	5815	5985	6150	6325	6495	6670	6855	7030	7206	7400	7585	20
21	5775	5945	6115	6295	6470	6656	6830	7010	7206	7395	7575	7780	7975	21
22	6060	6235	6415	6605	6790	6980	7165	7355	7560	7756	7950	8160	8370	22
23	6345	6525	6715	6910	7105	7305	7500	7700	7910	8115	8320	8540	8755	23
24	6630	6820	7020	7225	7425	7636	7840	8045	8265	8480	8690	8926	9150	24
25	6925	7125	7320	7540	7750	7970	8180	8400	8625	8866	9076	9315	9550	25
26	7215	7425	7640	7860	8075	8306	8525	8755	8980	9225	9455	9705	9950	26
27	7510	7725	7950	8180	8400	8640	8870	9105	9350	9595	9836	10100	10350	27
28	7800	8025	8260	8495	8730	8975	9215	9460	9715	9970	10200	10500	10750	28
29	8090	8325	8570	8815	9055	9310	9560	9810	10100	10350	10600	10900	11150	29
30	8385	8630	8880	9130	9380	9646	9905	10160	10460	10700	11000	11250	11550	30
31	8680	8930	9190	9450	9710	9985	10250	10500	10800	11100	11350	11650	11950	31
32	8965	9230	9495	9770	10050	10300	10600	10900	11160	11454	11750	12050	12356	32

TABLE I—Continued.

Length in feet	82	83	84	85	86	87	88	89	90	91	92	93	94	Length in feet
	DIAMETER IN INCHES — BOARD FEET													
8	3060	3130	3205	3285	3365	3445	3525	3605	3690	3775	3856	3940	4030	8
9	3415	3530	3615	3705	3795	3885	3975	4070	4160	4253	4350	4445	4515	9
10	3835	3930	4025	6125	4225	4325	4425	4530	4630	4735	4845	4950	5090	10
11	4225	4330	4435	4545	4655	4765	4880	4985	5105	5220	5335	5455	5570	11
12	4615	4730	4850	4965	5085	5205	5325	5450	5575	5700	5830	5955	6090	12
13	5010	5135	5230	5390	5515	5650	5775	5905	6050	6185	6323	6460	6600	13
14	5400	5535	5670	5810	5950	6085	6230	6370	6520	6665	6815	6965	7120	14
15	5790	5935	6080	6230	6375	6530	6680	6835	6990	7150	7306	7470	7630	15
16	6180	6335	6480	6650	6810	6965	7130	7295	7460	7630	7800	7970	8145	16
17	6580	6745	6910	7080	7250	7420	7590	7765	7945	8125	8305	8485	8670	17
18	6960	7155	7330	7510	7690	7870	8055	8265	8425	8613	8810	9000	9200	18
19	7380	7565	7756	7940	8130	8320	8515	8710	8910	9110	9310	9515	9725	19
20	7785	7975	8170	8370	8570	8770	8975	9180	9390	9600	9815	10030	10250	20
21	8190	8385	8595	8805	9015	9220	9435	9650	9870	10100	10300	10550	10800	21
22	8590	8800	9015	9235	9455	9675	9900	10100	10360	10600	10850	11050	11300	22
23	8985	9210	9435	9665	9895	10120	10350	10600	10850	11100	11300	11550	11850	23
24	9385	9620	9855	10100	10330	10570	10800	11050	11300	11600	11850	12100	12350	24
25	9795	10050	10300	10550	10800	11050	11300	11550	11800	12100	12350	12600	12900	25
26	10200	10450	10700	10950	11250	11500	11750	12050	12300	12600	12850	13150	13400	26
27	10600	10900	11150	11400	11700	11950	12250	12500	12800	13100	13350	13650	13950	27
28	11050	11300	11600	11850	12150	12400	12700	13000	13300	13600	13900	14200	14500	28
29	11450	11700	12000	12300	12600	12900	13200	13500	13800	14100	14400	14700	15050	29
30	11850	12150	12450	12750	13050	13350	13650	13950	14300	14600	14900	15250	15600	30
31	12250	12550	12850	13200	13500	13800	14100	14450	14800	15100	15450	15750	16100	31
32	12650	13000	13300	13600	13950	14250	14600	14950	15300	15600	15950	16300	16650	32

TABLE I—Continued.

Length in feet	95	96	97	98	99	100	101	102	103	104	105	106	107	Length in feet
	DIAMETER IN INCHES — BOARD FEET													
8	4115	4205	4295	4385	4490	4570	4665	4735	4855	4960	5045	5145	5240	8
9	4610	4740	4810	4935	5060	5135	5200	5305	5470	5580	5680	5800	5910	9
10	5170	5260	5350	5615	5620	5740	5855	5970	6000	6210	6330	6435	6575	10
11	5700	5800	5940	6075	6190	6320	6445	6580	6705	6840	6975	7110	7245	11
12	6220	6330	6465	6685	6765	6900	7040	7185	7330	7470	7600	7765	7915	12
13	6745	6885	7023	7195	7355	7480	7640	7785	7945	8095	8280	8420	8560	13
14	7270	7425	7590	7755	7906	8070	8235	8400	8565	8730	8900	9073	9245	14
15	7800	7955	8140	8315	8480	8650	8820	9005	9155	9360	9545	9730	9910	15
16	8320	8500	8680	8865	9045	9235	9425	9610	9800	9995	10200	10400	10600	16
17	8860	9050	9240	9435	9630	9830	10030	10230	10430	10630	10830	11030	11250	17
18	9395	9600	9800	10000	10210	10400	10650	10850	11060	11300	11500	11700	11950	18
19	9930	10150	10350	10600	10800	11000	11250	11450	11700	11900	12130	12400	12650	19
20	10470	10700	10900	11150	11400	11600	11850	12100	12340	12560	12800	13050	13300	20
21	11000	11250	11500	11700	11960	12200	12450	12700	12960	13200	13450	13750	14000	21
22	11550	11800	12050	12260	12535	12800	13050	13300	13600	13850	14100	14400	14650	22
23	12100	12350	12600	12850	13150	13400	13650	13950	14200	14500	14800	15050	15350	23
24	12600	12900	13150	13450	13700	14000	14250	14550	14850	15150	15420	15700	16050	24
25	13150	13450	13750	14000	14300	14600	14900	15200	15500	15800	16100	16400	16700	25
26	13700	14000	14300	14600	14900	15200	15500	15800	16150	16450	16750	17100	17400	26
27	14230	14550	14850	15200	15600	15800	16150	16450	16750	17100	17450	17750	18100	27
28	14800	15150	15450	15750	16100	16400	16750	17100	17400	17750	18100	18450	18800	28
29	15350	15700	16000	16350	16700	17050	17350	17700	18000	18400	18750	19150	19500	29
30	15900	16250	16600	16950	17300	17650	18000	18350	18700	19050	19450	19800	20200	30
31	16450	16800	17150	17500	17850	18250	18600	18950	19350	19760	20160	20500	20900	31
32	17000	17350	17750	18100	18450	18850	19200	19600	20000	20400	20750	21150	21550	32

TABLE I—Continued.

Length in feet	DIAMETER IN INCHES													Length in feet
	108	109	110	111	112	113	114	115	116	117	118	119	120	
	BOARD FEET.													
8	5345	5445	5545	5650	5750	5860	5965	6070	6175	6285	6395	6505	6615	8
9	6025	6140	6250	6370	6485	6605	6700	6840	6960	7080	7205	7330	7460	9
10	6705	6830	6955	7080	7215	7350	7500	7615	7745	7880	8025	8100	8300	10
11	7385	7520	7660	7810	7945	8085	8250	8385	8530	8675	8835	8985	9140	11
12	8065	8220	8370	8525	8680	8840	9000	9135	9320	9480	9645	9815	9980	12
13	8745	8910	9075	9250	9415	9585	9750	9910	10100	10250	10430	10645	10800	13
14	9425	9600	9780	9970	10150	10350	10500	10700	10900	11050	11250	11450	11650	14
15	10100	10300	10500	10700	10900	11100	11300	11500	11650	11850	12100	12300	12500	15
16	10800	11000	11200	11400	11600	11800	12050	12250	12450	12700	12900	13100	13350	16
17	11500	11700	11950	12150	12350	12600	12800	13050	13250	13500	13700	13950	14200	17
18	12150	12400	12650	12850	13100	13350	13550	13800	14050	14300	14550	14800	15050	18
19	12850	13100	13350	13600	13850	14100	14350	14600	14850	15100	15350	15650	15900	19
20	13550	13800	14050	14350	14600	14850	15100	15400	15650	15950	16200	16500	16750	20
21	14250	14500	14800	15050	15350	15600	15900	16150	16450	16750	17000	17300	17600	21
22	14950	15250	15500	15800	16100	16350	16650	16950	17250	17550	17850	18150	18450	22
23	15650	15950	16250	16550	16850	17100	17450	17750	18050	18350	18650	19000	19300	23
24	16350	16650	16950	17250	17550	17900	18200	18550	18850	19200	19500	19850	20200	24
25	17050	17350	17650	18000	18300	18650	19000	19350	19650	20000	20350	20700	21050	25
26	17750	18050	18400	18750	19100	19450	19800	20150	20500	20850	21200	21550	21900	26
27	18450	18800	19150	19500	19850	20200	20550	20900	21300	21650	22050	22400	22800	27
28	19150	19500	19850	20250	20600	21000	21350	21700	22100	22500	22850	23250	23650	28
29	19850	20250	20600	21000	21350	21750	22150	22500	22900	23300	23700	24100	24500	29
30	20550	20950	21350	21750	22100	22500	22900	23300	23750	24150	24550	25000	25400	30
31	21250	21650	22050	22500	22900	23300	23700	24100	24550	24950	25400	25850	26250	31
32	21900	22400	22800	23200	23650	24050	24500	24900	25350	25800	26250	26700	27150	32

A COMPARISON OF THREE DIFFERENT TYPES OF LOG RULES.

There are three distinct types of log rules now in general use. They are as follows: (a) Rules with a waste allowance varying directly as the barked area of the log and the volume of the log after the barked area allowance is made. (b) Rules with a waste allowance varying directly as the total volume of the log alone. (c) Rules with a waste allowance varying directly as the total volume of the log plus a constant.

When $D =$ diameter at small end inside bark in inches.
When $L =$ length of log in feet.
When $a =$ constant (in inches).
When $\pi = 3.1416$.
When $c =$ constant with limits of 0 and 1.
When B. M. = volume in board feet of manufactured product,
the three types may be expressed by these formulæ:

$$\text{(a)} \quad (1 - c)\frac{\pi (D - a)^2}{4 \times 12} L = \text{B.M.}$$

$$\text{(b)} \quad (1 - c)\frac{\pi D^2}{4 \times 12} L = \text{B.M.}$$

$$\text{(c)} \quad \left[(1 - c)\frac{\pi D^2}{4 \times 12} - b\right] L = \text{B.M.}$$

NOTE: The above formulæ are special cases of

$$\left[(1 - c)\frac{\pi (D - a)^2}{4 \times 12} - b\right] L = \text{B.M.}$$

In formula (a) the constant b equals zero, and the constant a has a positive value. Therefore, the curve $(1 - c)\frac{\pi D^2}{4 \times 12} L$ has been moved in a horizontal direction a units to the right of the origin.

In (b), $a = 0$, and $b = 0$, or the curve maintains its normal position.

In (c), $a = 0$, and b has a positive value, or the curve has been moved in a vertical direction b units.

None of the log rules analyzed had values for both a and b such that one of them could not be easily eliminated. The Universal Log Rule, for instance, reduces to the following formula:

$$\left[(1 - .20)\frac{\pi (D - 1.591)^2}{4 \times 12} - .1325\right] L = \text{B.M.}$$

The constant $b = .1325$ is so small that its effect upon the log rule is negligible. $(1 - .20)\frac{\pi (D - 1.6)^2}{4 \times 12} L = \text{B.M.}$ gives values for this rule within 2 board feet, and is the formula listed below.

The following is a comparison of log rules which may be expressed in the form:

$$(1 - c)\frac{\pi (D - a)^2}{4 \times 12} L = \text{B.M.}$$

NOTE: The constant c is the fractional part of the log becoming sawdust after an allowance of a inches from the diameter has been made for slabs. It can be expressed in per cent by multiplying by 100, or moving the decimal point two places to the right. $(1 - c)$ in like manner is the fractional part allowed for the manufactured product.

Champlain:

$$(1 - .20)\frac{\pi (D - .8)^2}{4 \times 12} L = \text{B.M.}$$

Boughman Rotary Saw: (Original values slightly erratic)

$$(1 - .19)\frac{\pi (D - .87)^2}{4 \times 12} L = \text{B.M.}$$

Boughman Band Saw: (Original values slightly erratic)

$$(1 - .10)\frac{\pi (D - 1)^2}{4 \times 12} L = \text{B.M.}$$

Wilson: (Original values slightly erratic)

$$(1 - .193)\frac{\pi (D - 1)^2}{4 \times 12} L = \text{B.M}$$

Carey: (Original values slightly erratic)

$$(1 - .193)\frac{\pi (D - 1)^2}{4 \times 12} L = \text{B.M.}$$

Baxter:

$$(1 - .338)\frac{\pi (D - 1)^2}{4 \times 12} L = \text{B.M.}$$

Click: (Original values slightly erratic)

$$(1 - .236)\frac{\pi (D - 1.25)^2}{4 \times 12} L = \text{B.M.}$$

British Columbia:

$$(1 - .273)\frac{\pi (D - 1.5)^2}{4 \times 12} L = \text{B.M.}$$

Universal:

$$(1 - .20)\frac{\pi (D - 1.6)^2}{4 \times 12} L = \text{B.M.}$$

International:

$$(1 - .16)\frac{\pi (D - 1.62)^2}{4 \times 12} L = \text{B.M.}$$

(Applied to 4′ sections with taper allowance of 1″ in 8′, and constructed for ⅛″ saw-kerf.)

Preston:

$$(1 - .20)\frac{\pi (D - 1.75)^2}{4 \times 12} L = \text{B.M.} \quad \text{(Small logs)}$$

$$(1 - .20)\frac{\pi (D - 1.5)^2}{4 \times 12} L = \text{B.M.} \quad \text{(Large logs)}$$

Doyle:

$$(1 - .045)\frac{\pi (D - 4)^2}{4 \times 12} L = \text{B.M.}$$

McKenzie:

$$\left[1 - \frac{k (w + t + k)}{(w + k)(t + k)}\right] \frac{\pi (D - a)^2}{4 \times 12} L + C = \text{B.M.}$$

Where k = saw-kerf in inches.
Where t = average thickness of lumber sawed, in inches.
Where w = average width of lumber sawed, in inches.
Where a = constant.
Where C = constant included to compensate for excessive taper in small logs.

To be applied to 8′ sections with taper allowance of e'' in f'.

It will be observed that of the above rules the Doyle and the Baxter are the two extremes. The Doyle rule has an enormous slab allowance with extremely small allowance for sawdust, (4.5%); where the Baxter rule has a small slab allowance and a very large allowance for sawdust, (33.8%).

Log rules of this form are correct in principle, and can be adapted to conditions existing at different mills, and to the character of the timber in different localities. The sawdust allowance, however, should not be fixed, but should depend upon the width of saw-kerf and the average dimensions of the lumber. The slab allowance should also be flexible, and should be determined by the timber to be sawed. Allowances for taper, excessive taper in small logs, shrinkage, etc., can be applied when making up a table based upon

$$(1 - c)\,\frac{\pi\,(D - a)^2}{4 \times 12}\,L = \text{B.M.}$$

This type of log rule can be represented diagramatically by drawing concentric circles of diameters D and $(D - a)$ respectively. The difference between the two rings will represent slab allowance. Draw a sector of the small circle with angle equal to $c \times 360°$. This will represent the sawdust allowance.

The following is a comparison of log rules which may be expressed in the form:

$$(1 - c)\,\frac{\pi\,D^2}{4 \times 12}\,L = \text{B.M.}$$

Constantine:

$$(1 - 0)\,\frac{\pi\,D^2}{4 \times 12}\,L = \text{B.M.}$$

Saco River: (Original values slightly erratic)

$$(1 - .276)\,\frac{\pi\,D^2}{4 \times 12}\,L = \text{B.M.}$$

Derby: (Original values slightly erratic)

$$(1 - .279)\,\frac{\pi\,D^2}{4 \times 12}\,L = \text{B.M.}$$

Square of Three-quarters:

$$(1 - .283)\,\frac{\pi\,D^2}{4 \times 12}\,L = \text{B.M.}$$

Partridge: (Original values slighty erratic)

$$(1 - .312)\,\frac{\pi\,D^2}{4 \times 12}\,L = \text{B.M.}$$

Vermont:

$$(1 - .363)\frac{\pi D^2}{4 \times 12} L = \text{B.M.}$$

NOTE: This rule gives the solid contents in board feet of the largest square timber contained in a log D'' in diameter inside bark at small end, and when divided by 12, becomes the formula for the Inscribed Square Rule, which actually gives the cubic contents of the largest square timber that can be sawed from a log of known length and diameter.

Stillwell: (Original values erratic)

$$(1 - .368)\frac{\pi D^2}{4 \times 12} L = \text{B.M.}$$

Ake:

$$(1 - .376)\frac{\pi D^2}{4 \times 12} L = \text{B.M.}$$

Square of Two-Thirds:

$$(1 - .435)\frac{\pi D^2}{4 \times 12} L = \text{B.M.}$$

NOTE: This formula, when divided by 12, is supposed to give, but does not give, the number of cubic feet of square timber that can be sawed from a log D'' in diameter at middle point inside bark. After the division by 12 is made, it is called the Two-Thirds Rule.

Orange River:

$$(1 - .491)\frac{\pi D^2}{4 \times 12} L = \text{B.M.}$$

Cumberland River:

$$(1 - .548)\frac{\pi D^2}{4 \times 12} L = \text{B.M.}$$

It is obvious that the Constantine rule has no allowance for either slabs or sawdust, and that all log rules which can be expressed in this form have a total waste allowance which is directly proportional to the total volume of the log, (taper not taken into consideration). The two extremes are the Constantine and the Cumberland River. The former with no allowance for waste whatever and the latter with an allowance of 54.8%.

There can not exist for different sized logs a constant ratio between volume sawed out at mill and volume in board feet as shown by a log rule of the above form. The principle is incorrect.

$(1 - c)\frac{\pi D^2}{4 \times 12} L = \text{B.M.}$ can be represented diagramatically by drawing a circle diameter D and then a sector of that circle with angle at center equal to $c \times 360°$. The area of the sector will represent the total waste allowance and the remaining area the lumber product.

The following is a comparison of log rules which may be expressed in the form:

$$\left[(1-c)\frac{\pi D^2}{4\times 12}-b\right]L=\text{B.M.}$$

Bangor: (Original values slightly erratic)

$$\left[(1-.258)\frac{\pi D^2}{4\times 12}-.5\right]L=\text{B.M.}$$

Boynton: (Original values erratic)

$$\left[(1-.350)\frac{\pi D^2}{4\times 12}-.67\right]L=\text{B.M.}$$

Parsons: (Original values erratic)

$$\left[(1-.246)\frac{\pi D^2}{4\times 12}-1\right]L=\text{B.M.}$$

Warner: (Original values erratic)

$$\left[(1-.466)\frac{\pi D^2}{4\times 12}-1\right]L=\text{B.M.}$$

Spaulding: (Original values slightly erratic)

$$\left[(1-.266)\frac{\pi D^2}{4\times 12}-2\right]L=\text{B.M.}$$

Hannah: (Original values very erratic)

$$\left[(1-.266)\frac{\pi D^2}{4\times 12}-2\right]L=\text{B.M.}$$

Applies approximately to logs from 12″ to 42″ in diameter. This rule is very poorly constructed.

Wilcox: (Original values erratic)

$$\left[(1-.340)\frac{\pi D^2}{4\times 12}-2\right]L=\text{B.M.}$$

Finch and Apgar: (Original values very erratic)

$$\left[(1-.280)\frac{\pi D^2}{4\times 12}-2.5\right]L=\text{B.M.}$$

Ropp:

$$\left[(1-.236)\frac{\pi D^2}{4\times 12}-3\right]L=\text{B.M.}$$

Scribner: (Original values very erratic)

$$\left[(1-.266)\frac{\pi D^2}{4\times 12}-3\right]L=\text{B.M.}$$

Applies approximately to logs from 14″ to 75″, inclusive, in diameter. This rule is very poorly constructed.

Favorite: (Original values erratic)

$$\left[(1-.285)\frac{\pi D^2}{4\times 12}-3\right]L=\text{B.M.}$$

Maine: (Original values slightly erratic)

$$\left[(1-.222)\frac{\pi D^2}{4\times 12}-.67\right]L=\text{B.M.}$$

(For small logs, 6″ to 15″, inclusive.)

$$\left[(1-.222)\frac{\pi D^2}{4\times 12}-2\right]L=\text{B.M.}$$

(For logs 16″ to 48″, inclusive.)

Herring: (Original values slightly erratic)

$$\left[(1-.392)\frac{\pi D^2}{4\times 12}-1\right]L=\text{B.M.}$$

(Small logs up to 30″.)

$$\left[(1-.313)\frac{\pi D^2}{4\times 12}-5.5\right]L=\text{B.M.}$$

(For logs from 30″ to 42″, inclusive.)

Dusenbury: (Original values slightly erratic)

Practically the same as the Herring Log Rule.

Rules of this form will usually give a large per cent of mill overrun for small logs, due to the presence of the constant b. Intermediate logs will run below, hold up the scale or overrun, all depending upon the value of c in the rule used and the width of the saw-kerf. The effect of the constant b becomes small for intermediate sized logs, and is practically negligible for large ones. Large logs will run higher in per cent of mill overrun than the intermediate, since the slab allowance in this type of log rule increases directly as the volume of the log plus a constant. The principle is incorrect.

$\left[(1-c)\frac{\pi D^2}{4 \times 12} - b\right] L =$ B.M. can be represented diagramatically by drawing two concentric circles, the larger one with diameter D and the smaller one with diameter sufficient to allow for b board feet; then drawing a sector forming an angle of $c \times 360°$ at the center. The area of the sector and the small circle will represent the waste allowance for slabs, sawdust, etc., while the remaining area will be the lumber product.

MISCELLANEOUS LOG RULES.

The Chapin, Northwestern, White and Ballon log rules have no definite underlying principles.

The Drew and the Forty-five were found to be of the form

$$\left[1-(c-cD)\right]\frac{\pi D^2}{4\times 12}L = \text{B.M.}$$

Where c = constant less than 1 and greater than 0.

Where c = constant much smaller than c and greater than 0.

Their formulæ are as follows:

The Forty-five rule:

$$\left[1-(.496-.00763D)\right]\frac{\pi D^2}{4\times 12}L = \text{B.M.}$$

The Drew Rule:

$$\left[1-(.450-.003D)\right]\frac{\pi D^2}{4\times 12}L = \text{B.M.}$$

In these rules the allowance for total wastage when expressed in per cent of the total contents of the log, taper not considered, decreases uniformly as the diameter increases. When $cD = c$, there is no allowance for wastage whatever. The Forty-five Log Rule allows for no wastage in logs 65″ in diameter and shows more volume for logs over 65″ than they actually contain. The Drew rule also shows a uniformly decreasing per cent of wastage, and for logs 150″ in diameter the waste allowance becomes zero. The principle of these rules is absolutely incorrect.

LOG RULES BASED ON STANDARDS.

Any log rule, constructed to show volume in board feet of lumber contained in logs of various lengths and diameters, which is based upon definite principles, may be reduced to what is called a standard log rule. The only difference between the ordinary log rule and its unlimited number of standards is in the unit of measure. A log of any specified dimensions may be chosen as the unit of measure, and so long as the underlying principles of both the standard and the rule expressing values in board feet are the same, there will always exist a definite relation between them and the one may be expressed in terms of the other by multiplying by a constant.

When d = Diameter in inches of the standard log and
l = Length in feet of the standard log,

log rules of the form $(1-c)\dfrac{\pi (D-a)^2}{4 \times 12} L = \text{B.M.}$

become $\dfrac{(D-a)^2 L}{(d-a)^2 l} = V$, in standards.

Log rules of the form $(1-c)\dfrac{\pi D^2}{4 \times 12} L = \text{B.M.}$

become $\dfrac{D^2 L}{d^2 l} = V$, in standards.

Log rules of the form $\left[(1-c)\dfrac{\pi D^2}{4 \times 12} - b\right] L = \text{B.M.}$

become $\dfrac{(D^2 - s) L}{(d^2 - s) l} = V$, in standards.

All standard log rules now in use are based upon $\dfrac{D^2 L}{d^2 l} = \text{Vol.}$, in standards. Therefore, any one of them may be reduced to the form $(1-c)\dfrac{\pi D^2}{4 \times 12} L = \text{B.M.}$, since $\dfrac{D^2 L}{d^2 l} \times \text{Const.} = (1-c)\dfrac{\pi D^2}{4 \times 12} L$. Furthermore, it is evident that all standard rules of the same form bear a constant relation the one to the other, and any number of units of a certain standard rule may be reduced to units of any other standard of the same form by multiplying by the proper constant. For example, the Nineteen Inch Standard Rule, $\left(\dfrac{D^2 L}{19^2 \times 13} = V, \text{ in standards}\right)$, may be applied to a large number of logs of different sizes, and the aggregate scale of these logs then given in 19″ standards, may be reduced to Blodgett, cube standards, etc., or to any of the following log rules expressing results in board feet: Constantine, Saco River, Derby,

Square of Three-quarters, Partridge, Vermont, Stillwell, Ake, Square of Two-thirds, Orange River, or Cumberland River, by multiplying the aggregate by the proper constant. The result in every case will be precisely the same as though the logs were scaled separately by each of the rules. If, however, it is desired to reduce the aggregate scale of these logs now expressed in standards or in board feet, as the case may be, to board feet as shown by the Doyle Log Rule, for instance, the problem is impossible. There is no way of making the reduction. The logs will have to be scaled in accordance with the principles of the Doyle Log Rule in order to get such results. If only a single log were in question instead of a number of different sizes, it would be very easy to make such a reduction, but since there is no common ratio existing between the Doyle Log Rule (also other rules of that form) and the Nineteen Inch Standard (and others of its form) for logs of all sizes, the reduction can not be applied to more than one log or set of logs of equal diameters.

It is folly to compare results obtained by two logs rules of different forms as applied to logs of various sizes. It is evident that a comparison of the formulæ of such rules would reveal a great deal more. Values shown by log rules of different forms are not comparable, since their underlying principles are different. Any comparison made of such values only lead to confusion and really do more harm than good.

The following will illustrate how the Nineteen Inch Standard Rule may be reduced to other standards and also to any log rule giving values in board feet which is of the same form:

Given: The Nineteen Inch Standard Rule $\frac{D^2 L}{19^2 \times 13} = V$, in 19″ standards, and given: The Blodgett rule $\frac{D^2}{16^2} L = V$, in Blodgett standards, to find the common reducing factor c:

$$\frac{D^2 L}{19^2 \times 13} \times c = \frac{D^2 L}{16^2}$$

$$\frac{c}{19^2 \times 13} = \frac{1}{16^2}$$

$$c = \frac{19^2 \times 13}{16^2} = 18.33$$

Therefore, if a log or any number of logs of different sizes have been scaled by the Nineteen Inch Standard Rule, the results may be expressed in Blodgett standards by multiplying by 18.33, which is the number of Blodgett standards contained in a Nineteen Inch standard. The ratio holds constant regardless of the size of the logs.

In like manner, the reducing factors for all other standard rules may be obtained.

Given: The Nineteen Inch Standard Rule $\frac{D^2 L}{19^2 \times 13} = V$, in standards, and the Vermont rule $(1 - .363) \frac{\pi D^2}{4 \times 12} L =$ B.M. in board feet.

To find how many board feet as shown by the Vermont rule are equivalent to a standard of the Nineteen Inch rule:

$$(1 - .363)\frac{\pi\, 19^2}{48} \times 13 = 195.5$$

Therefore, 195.5 board feet as shown by the Vermont rule equals one standard of the Ninteen Inch Standard Rule. This relation holds for all sized logs. In like manner, reducing factors for the Constantine, Saco River, Derby, Square of Three-quarters, Partridge, Stillwell, Ake, Square of Two-thirds, Orange River and Cumberland River rules may be obtained. All rules of the above form have definite reducing factors which apply to all logs, regardless of size, and to any aggregate scale representing any number of logs.

Given: The Nineteen Inch Standard Rule $\frac{D^2 L}{19^2 \times 13} = V$, in standards, to find a log rule equivalent to it when one standard = 200 board feet:

$$(1-c)\frac{\pi\, 19^2}{4 \times 12} \times 13 = 200$$

$$1 - c = \frac{200 \times 48}{\pi \times 19^2 \times 13} = .650$$

$$c = .350$$

Therefore: $(1 - .350)\frac{\pi D^2}{4 \times 12} L =$ B.M. is an equivalent rule for the Nineteen Inch Standard when a standard unit is equal to 200 board feet. In like manner equivalent rules for other standard rules may be obtained when the value of the unit is given in board feet.

For instance, the Blodgett rule allows 10 board feet for the equivalent of one standard, and the resulting rule which is equivalent to the Bodgett under these conditions is

$$(1 - .405)\frac{\pi D^2}{4 \times 12} L = \text{B.M.}$$

$(1 - .423)\frac{\pi D^2}{4 \times 12} L =$ B.M. is the equivalent for the cube rule when its standard unit = 12 board feet.

It must be borne in mind that log rules of the form

$$(1 - c)\frac{\pi D^2}{4 \times 12} L = \text{B.M.}$$

are very poor rules for measuring the number of board feet of lumber that can be sawed from logs of different sizes, and that the three distinct types of rules discussed under the heading "A Comparison of Three Different Types of Log Rules" can have no common reducing factor for logs of different sizes, since the underlying principles are not the same. In the case of the standard rule based upon $\frac{D^2 L}{d^2 l} = V$, V is directly proportional to the square of the diameter of the log and also directly proportional to its length, whereas a log rule based upon correct principles has the volume in board feet vary directly as the diameter minus a constant squared, and directly as the length, with a taper correction applied to at least 8′ sections.

Standard log rules based upon $\frac{D^2 L}{d^2 l} = V$ are, however, excellent rules where a measurement proportional to the total contents of the log is desired. Such measures are applicable to logs which are to be made into pulp or whenever the total contents of the log is to be used. These rules do not take taper into consideration. They can be reduced to cubic feet by multiplying by a constant.

THE TRANSFORMATION OF VOLUME TABLES BASED UPON A GIVEN LOG RULE TO VOLUME TABLES BASED UPON OTHER RULES.

Volume tables constructed to show the number of board feet contained in trees of different merchantable lengths and diameters breasthigh, and based upon a log rule of the form

$$(1-c)\frac{\pi(D-a)^2}{4\times 12}L=\text{B.M.}$$

can be transformed to tables based upon other rules of the same form where the value of the constant a is the same. If the value of a is different in the rule to which the values are to be reduced, there is no way of accomplishing the transformation. For example, tables based upon the Baxter rule can be transformed to tables based upon the Boughman Band Saw rule by dividing each value in the former table by (1 — .338) and multiplying by (1 — .10). But tables based upon the Baxter rule cannot be transformed to ones based upon the Doyle rule, or on any other rule of that form where a is not the same as in the Baxter rule, or to forms where a does not enter, unless the average diameter of all portions of the bole is known thus making it possible to find the value of D for all logs in the tree.

Volume tables based upon rules of the form $(1-c)\frac{\pi D^2}{4\times 12}L=\text{B.M.}$ and also upon the form $\left[(1-c)\frac{\pi D^2}{4\times 12}-b\right]L=\text{B.M.}$ can be easily transformed from the one to the other. For example, a volume table based upon the Spaulding Log Rule, showing the average volume in board feet of trees of different diameters breasthigh and merchantable lengths can be transformed to a table based upon the Ropp rule by adding twice the average merchantable length shown in the table to each average value, and then dividing by (1 — .266) and multiplying by (1 — .236) and subtracting from each value thus obtained three times the merchantable length. The resulting table will then be based upon the Ropp rule, and the values therein will be the same as though the Ropp rule had been used for scaling the individual logs instead of the Spaulding rule. In like manner, any volume table based upon a log rule of the form $\left[(1-c)\frac{\pi D^2}{4\times 12}-b\right]L=\text{B.M.}$, can be transformed to a volume table based upon any other log rule of that form.

Again, a volume table based upon a log rule of the above form can be transformed to a volume table based upon any log rule of the form $(1-c)\frac{\pi D^2}{4\times 12}L=\text{B.M.}$ by adding to each value in the table $b\times$ the merchantable length, and then dividing by $(1-c)$ of the log rule upon which it is based and multiplying by the value of $(1-c)$ of the log rule to which the transformation is to be made. For example: A volume table based upon the Spaulding Log Rule showing average volume in board feet of trees of different diameters breasthigh and merchantable lengths can be transformed to a table based upon the Vermont rule by adding twice the average merchantable length to each of the values shown in the table, and then dividing the values thus obtained by (1 — .266) and multiplying by (1 — .363). The resulting table will then be based upon the Vermont rule. Should it be desirable to further transform the table to values in cubic feet of the Inscribed Square rule, divide all values by 12. This last reduction will show the volume in cubic feet of the square timbers that can be sawed from trees of different merchantable lengths and diameters breasthigh.

The total number of cubic feet inside bark contained in logs of trees measured for the original volume table based on the Spaulding Log Rule can be obtained by adding twice the average merchantable length to each value in the table and then dividing by (1 — .266) and dividing by 12. This reduction gives the volume in cubic feet of the total logs in each tree, without the taper of the various logs originally measured being taken into consideration.

To recapitulate: All volume tables based upon

$$(1-c)\cdot\frac{\pi\,(D-a)^2}{4\times 12}L = \text{B.M.}$$

can be reduced to any other table based upon the same form of log rule where the constant *a* is the same as in the rule originally used in compiling the table.

All volume tables based upon rules of the form

$$(1-c)\,\frac{\pi\,D^2}{4\times 12}L = \text{B.M., or } \left[(1-c)\,\frac{\pi\,D^2}{4\times 12} - b\right] L = \text{B.M.}$$

can be reduced or transformed to volume tables based upon any log rule of either of these forms, and in all cases the resulting tables will be the same as though the individual rules had been applied to the original data.

Any volume table based upon one of the following rules can be transformed to a volume table based upon any of the other rules here given: Constantine, Saco River, Derby, Square of Three-fourths, Partridge, Vermont, Inscribed Square (which is the Vermont rule divided by 12), Sillwell, Ake, Square of Two-thirds, Two-thirds rule (which is the Square of Two-thirds Rule divided by twelve), Orange River, Cumberland River, Bangor, Boynton, Parsons, Warner, Spaulding, Wilcox, Ropp, Favorite, Nineteen Inch Standard, New Hampshire (or Blodgett), the Cube Rule, Twenty-two Inch Standard, Twenty-four Inch Standard, Seventeen Inch Rule.

NOTE: The Hannah, Finch and Apgar, and Scribner rules have been omitted in the above list since their original values appear too erratic to be included. The Maine, Herring and Dusenbury also have been omitted, since each of these rules have separate formulae for small and large logs.

In like manner any volume table based upon

$$(1-c)\,\frac{\pi\,(D-a)^2}{4\times 12}L = \text{B.M.}$$

can be transformed to other volume tables of the same form, provided the constant *a* is the same in rules under consideration.

The following tables illustrate how the transformations described above may be made:

TABLE 2. Average volume in board feet, as shown by the Spaulding Log Rule, contained in merchantable portion of immature western yellow pine trees of different merchantable lengths and diameters breast high.

TABLE 2.

Diameter breast-high in inches	Merchantable length (feet) 70	80	90	100	110	120	130	Diameter inside bark top log, inches	Height of stump, feet	Basis, number of trees
	Volume, based on the Spaulding Rule (bd. ft.)									
20	300	370	465	550	....	....	....	6.6	1.2	11
21	325	405	495	580	....	....	....	6.7	1.2	
22	350	435	530	630	730	....	....	6.7	1.2	39
23	380	475	570	680	780	....	....	6.8	1.2	
24	415	510	620	730	840	....	....	6.9	1.3	67
25	450	560	670	785	905	....	....	7.0	1.3	
26	490	605	725	845	975	1100	....	7.1	1.3	92
27	....	655	780	915	1060	1180	....	7.1	1.3	
28	....	710	845	980	1130	1270	1415	7.2	1.3	100
29	....	....	910	1060	1210	1365	1560	7.3	1.3	
30	....	....	980	1140	1300	1460	1630	7.4	1.3	65
31	....	....	....	1225	1395	1565	1750	7.5	1.3	
32	....	....	....	1310	1400	1675	1870	7.6	1.4	57
33	....	....	....	1400	1585	1780	1990	7.7	1.4	
34	....	....	....	1495	1695	1900	2125	7.8	1.3	29
35	....	....	....	....	1800	2020	2255	7.9	1.3	
36	....	....	....	....	1910	2140	2400	8.0	1.4	27
37	....	....	....	....	....	2265	2550	8.2	1.4	
38	....	....	....	....	....	2395	2700	8.5	1.5	7
39	....	....	....	....	....	2525	2850	9.0	1.5	
40	....	....	....	....	....	2660	3005	9.6	1.5	8
Total number of trees										502

This table is based upon the original measurements of 502 trees.

TABLE 3. (A transformation of Table 2.) **Average volume in board feet, as shown by the Ropp Log Rule, contained in merchantable portion of immature western yellow pine trees of different merchantable lengths and diameters breasthigh.**

TABLE 3.

Diameter breast-high in inches	Merchantable length (feet) 70	80	90	100	110	120	130	Diameter inside bark top log, inches	Height of stump, feet	Basis, number of trees
	Volume, based on the Ropp Log Rule (bd. ft.)									
20	245	322	402	481	....	....	....	6.6	1.2	11
21	271	348	433	512	....	....	....	6.7	1.2	
22	300	390	469	564	650	....	....	6.7	1.2	39
23	331	421	511	616	710	....	....	6.8	1.2	
24	358	458	563	668	772	....	....	6.9	1.3	67
25	401	500	615	725	841	....	....	7.0	1.3	
26	436	566	672	787	913	1006	....	7.1	1.3	92
27	....	618	730	861	992	1118	....	7.1	1.3	
28	....	662	796	929	1076	1211	1353	7.2	1.3	100
29	....	....	874	1011	1159	1310	1463	7.3	1.3	
30	....	....	938	1045	1232	1410	1578	7.4	1.3	65
31	....	....	....	1182	1350	1560	1702	7.5	1.3	
32	....	....	....	1271	1450	1632	1820	7.6	1.4	67
33	....	....	....	1355	1550	1745	1952	7.7	1.4	
34	....	....	....	1464	1663	1868	2091	7.8	1.3	29
35	....	....	....	....	1771	1985	2230	7.9	1.3	
36	....	....	....	....	1880	2190	2378	8.0	1.4	27
37	....	....	....	....	....	2248	2585	8.2	1.4	
38	....	....	....	....	....	2380	2690	8.5	1.5	7
39	....	....	....	....	....	2520	2850	9.0	1.5	
40	....	....	....	....	....	2630	3010	9.6	1.5	3
Total number of trees										502

This table was obtained by transforming the values in Table 2, based on the Spaulding Log Rule, to values shown here based upon the Ropp rule. The transformation was made in accordance with the underlying principles of both rules, and was accomplished as follows: To each value shown in Table 2 twice the merchantable length indicated at top of table was added. The new values thus obtained were divided by (1 — .266) and multiplied by (1 — .236), and three times the merchantable length subtracted. The resulting table is based upon the Ropp rule, and does not include any logs under 10″ in diameter, since logs below this size have been automatically discarded by the Ropp rule formula, which gives small negative results for logs under 8″ and small positive results for logs between 8″ and 10″. The negatives below 8″ and the positives between an 8″ and 10″ will about neutralize, thus giving a table which does not include logs below 10″ in diameter.

TABLE 4. (A transformation of Table 2.) Average values in board feet, as shown by the Vermont Log Rule, contained in merchantable portion of immature western yellow pine trees of different merchantable lengths and diameters breasthigh.

TABLE 4.

Diameter breast-high in inches	Merchantable length (feet)							Diameter inside bark top log, inches	Height of stump, feet	Basis, number of trees
	70	80	90	100	110	120	130			
	Volume, based on the Vermont Rule (bd. ft.)									
20	382	469	560	651	....	....	....	6.6	1.2	11
21	404	491	587	677	....	....	....	6.7	1.2	
22	428	517	617	721	825	....	....	6.7	1.2	39
23	452	552	652	764	868	....	....	6.8	1.2	
24	482	582	695	807	922	....	....	6.9	1.3	67
25	512	625	738	855	977	....	....	7.0	1.3	
26	547	665	785	908	1039	1164	....	7.1	1.3	92
27	....	708	834	969	1108	1232	....	7.1	1.3	
28	....	756	890	1025	1173	1311	1454	7.2	1.3	100
29	....	....	954	1094	1242	1395	1546	7.3	1.3	
30	....	....	1008	1163	1320	1478	1641	7.4	1.3	65
31	....	....	....	1238	1408	1568	1746	7.5	1.3	
32	....	....	....	1312	1488	1663	1850	7.6	1.4	57
33	....	....	....	1390	1568	1754	1964	7.7	1.4	
34	....	....	....	1471	1663	1860	2072	7.8	1.3	29
35	....	....	....	....	1754	1962	2182	7.9	1.3	
36	....	....	....	....	1850	2068	2310	8.0	1.4	27
37	....	....	....	....	....	2175	2440	8.2	1.4	
38	....	....	....	....	....	2287	2572	8.5	1.5	7
39	....	....	....	....	....	2400	2706	9.0	1.5	
40	....	....	....	....	....	2520	2835	9.6	1.5	8
Total number of trees										502

This table was obtained by transforming the values in Table 2, based upon the Spaulding Log Rule, to values shown here based upon the Vermont Rule. The transformation was made in the following manner: To each value shown in Table 2, twice the merchantable length indicated at top of table was added to each of the values. Each of the new values thus obtained was divided by (1 — .266) and multiplied by (1 — .363). The resulting values form the above table, and include all logs contained in the merchantable lengths. This table is the same as would have been obtained had the results been based directly upon the woods measurements.

TABLE 5. (A transformation of Table 2.) Average values in cubic feet as shown by the Inscribed Square Log Rule contained in the largest square timbers that can be sawed from the merchantable portion of immature western yellow pine trees of different merchantable lengths and diameters breasthigh.

TABLE 5.

Diameter breast-high in inches	Merchantable length (feet)							Diameter inside bark top log, inches	Height of stump, feet	Basis, number of trees
	70	80	90	100	110	120	130			
	Volume, based on the Inscribed Square Rule (cu. ft.)									
20	31.8	39.1	46.7	54.3	....	....	....	6.6	1.2	11
21	33.7	40.9	48.8	56.4	....	....	....	6.7	1.2	
22	35.5	43.1	51.4	60.0	68.7	....	....	6.7	1.2	[illegible]
23	37.6	46.0	54.3	63.6	72.3	....	....	6.8	1.2	
24	40.2	48.5	57.9	67.4	76.8	....	....	6.9	1.3	67
25	42.7	52.1	61.5	71.8	81.4	....	....	7.0	1.3	
26	45.6	55.4	65.5	75.7	86.5	97.0	....	7.1	1.8	98
27	....	59.0	69.5	80.7	92.0	102.7	....	7.1	1.3	
28	....	62.9	74.2	85.5	97.7	109.3	121.1	7.2	1.3	100
29	....	....	79.4	91.2	103.6	116.2	128.8	7.3	1.3	
30	....	....	84.0	97.0	110.0	123.0	136.8	7.4	1.3	65
31	....	....	....	103.2	117.0	130.7	145.4	7.5	1.3	
32	....	....	....	109.3	123.8	138.7	154.0	7.6	1.4	57
33	....	....	....	115.8	130.7	146.1	162.8	7.7	1.4	
34	....	....	....	122.6	138.7	155.0	172.5	7.8	1.3	29
35	....	....	....	....	146.2	163.5	182.0	7.9	1.3	
36	....	....	....	....	154.2	172.3	192.5	8.0	1.4	27
37	....	....	....	....	....	181.2	203.2	8.2	1.4	
38	....	....	....	....	....	190.8	214.0	8.5	1.5	7
39	....	....	....	....	....	200.0	225.3	9.0	1.5	
40	....	....	....	....	....	210.0	236.0	9.6	1.5	8
Total number of trees										502

Values in this table are indirectly based upon the measurements necessary for a compilation of Table 2. They were obtained by dividing values shown in Table 4 by the constant 12.

THE TRANSFORMATION OF THE SCALE OF A NUMBER OF LOGS IN THE AGGREGATE, BASED UPON A GIVEN LOG RULE, TO THE SCALE OF THE SAME LOGS IN THE AGGREGATE, BASED UPON ANOTHER LOG RULE.

The total volume of a number of logs of various sizes as shown by a log rule of the form $(1-c)\frac{\pi(D-a)^2}{4\times 12}L=$ B.M. can be transformed to the volume as would be shown by another log rule of that form where the constant a is the same. For example: Should it be required to know the total volume in board feet of a trainload of logs of various sizes as would be shown by the Boughman Band Saw Rule when the aggregate scale based upon the Baxter Rule is known to be 320,000 board feet, the following steps are necessary: Divide 320,000 by $(1-c)$ of the Baxter rule, which is $(1-.338)$, and multiply by $(1-c)$ of the Boughman Band Saw Rule, which is $(1-.10)$. The result thus obtained which will be 435,000 is the same as would have been obtained had the Bowman rule been used for the original scale. Such transformations can not be made where the constant a in the two rules in question are not the same. Had the trainload of logs been scaled by a rule of the form $(1-c)\frac{\pi D^2}{4\times 12}L=$ B.M. it would not be possible to make such a transformation, but it would be possible to transform the total scale to a new total based upon another rule of the same form. For example: If a trainload of logs should scale 300,000 board feet by the Square of Three-quarters rule, and it should be required to find the aggregate scale according to the Inscribed Square rule, the following procedure is all that is necessary: Divide 300,000 by $(1-.283)$ and multiply by $(1-.363)$ and then divide by 12. The final result, 32,000 cubic feet, is exactly the same as would have been obtained had the Inscribed Square rule been used for the original scale. In like manner, a transformation could have been made to a number of other rules of similar form.

Had the trainload of logs been originally scaled by a log rule of the form $\left[(1-c)\frac{D^2}{4\times 12}-b\right]L=$ B.M., such as the Spaulding rule, a transformation to another rule of that form where b is the same could be accomplished by dividing by $(1-c)$ of the formula used and multiplying by $(1-c)$ of the formula to which the transformation is to be made. But, in cases where the value of the constant b is different in the log rules in question, no reduction can be made, unless the sum of the length of all the logs in the trainload be known. If the sum of all log lengths is known, it would then be possible to transform the total scale to other total scales based upon $\left[(1-c)\frac{\pi D^2}{4\times 12}-b\right]L=$ B.M. or $(1-c)\frac{\pi D^2}{4\times 12}L=$ B.M. whether the constant b is the same or different in the rules in question. Had the trainload of logs been originally scaled by the Spaulding Log Rule, or any other rule of similar form, where b has a value greater than 0, the transformation of the total scale to a total based on a log rule of the form $(1-c)\frac{\pi D^2}{4 \times 12}L = \text{B.M.}$ would be impossible unless the sum of the lengths of all logs in the trainload be known. Suppose, for example, the aggregate scale of a trainload of logs was 250,000 board feet by the Spaulding Log Rule, and the sum of all log lengths in the load was 12,000 linear feet, and it was required to know the total scale when based upon the Square of Two-thirds rule, the following operations are all that would be necessary: Add to 250,000 twice the sum of all log lengths, which would be 24,000, divide by (1 — .266) and multiply by (1 — .435). The resulting aggregate scale of the trainload of logs based on the Square of Two-thirds rule would then be 211,000 board feet, which is the same as would have been obtained had the Square of Two-thirds rule been originally applied.

SUMMARY.

No log rule will give an accurate measure of the lumber content of logs of various sizes that fails to properly combine all the factors encountered in converting logs into lumber. These factors are the same for all species under all milling conditions. The value of the factors alone increases or decreases according to the species and method of sawing, but the number of factors remain constant. As a result of failing to recognize the factors that must be combined in devising a properly constructed log rule, by failing to employ all of them, or by combining them improperly, there is no accurate log rule in use applicable to variable milling conditions. Any log rule capable of becoming a standard measure and susceptible of correction for certain variable factors must recognize a slab allowance proportional to the barked area of the log, and a sawdust allowance expressed as a definite per cent of the total volume of all logs, not including slabs. The per cent for sawdust is dependent upon the width of the saw-kerf and average dimensions of lumber to be sawed. Other factors to be taken into account are taper, shrinkage, normal crook and excessive taper in small logs, but these are of less importance than the two cited above.

The following log rules are constructed with a total wastage allowance proportional to the total volume of the log, regardless of size—taper not considered:

Constantine, Saco River, Derby, Square of Three-quarters, Partridge, Vermont, Stillwell, Ake, Square of Two-thirds, Orange River, Cumberland River. These rules are incorrect in principle, therefore no correction is possible.

Another group of rules is derived by substituting a waste allowance proportional to total volume, plus a constant for logs of different sizes—taper not considered. It would seem as though some effort had been made to correct the inaccuracy of the preceding group by adding a constant to compensate for waste occasioned by sawing logs of different sizes. The underlying principles of these rules are incorrect, however, and consequently their values cannot be properly adjusted. Such rules are the following:

Bangor, Boynton, Parsons, Warner, Spaulding, Hannah, Wilcox, Finch and Apgar, Ropp, Scribner, Favorite, Maine, Herring, Dusenbury.

Log rules with slab allowance varying directly as the barked area of logs of different sizes and with sawdust allowance directly as the volume after the slab allowance has been made are correct in principle, but are not necessarily correct measures. Rules of this type are as follows:

Champlain, Boughman's Rotary Saw, Boughman's Band Saw, Wilson, Carey, Baxter, Click, British Columbia, Universal, International, Preston, Doyle, McKenzie.

Of the preceding rules the Champlain, Universal, International and McKenzie are the only ones that are at all flexible to milling conditions and character of timber to be sawed. The Champlain and the Universal are the same, with the exception of the slab allowance, which in the case of the Universal is twice as great as for the Champlain. The sawdust allowance for both rules is made by allowing $\left(100 - \frac{100}{1+k}\right)$ per cent of the volume of the log (taper not included) for sawdust. This factor is correct for a gang saw with saws k'' thick and 1″ apart, but does not apply to any other milling conditions. Taper is not taken into consideration by either of these rules. Both rules have a fixed slab allowance, and the sawdust factor is affected by saw-kerf alone.

The International Log Rule also has a fixed slab allowance, and the sawdust allowance is unaffected by the dimensions of the lumber to be sawed. The value of this factor has been worked out for different gauge saws, and is the same regardless of dimensions of the manufactured product. The rule has a fixed taper allowance of ½″ in 4′, and tables compiled in accordance with the rule are based upon 4′ sections.

Since the analysis proved that no log rule now in use is universally applicable, a rule has been prepared and designated the McKenzie rule, which may be made to apply accurately to any set of conditions and at all times be susceptible to proper corrections made necessary by modifications of local methods employed.

This rule, with no allowance made for shrinkage and surfacing, is shown on page 19, and for convenience may be written:

$$\left[1 - \frac{(w + k)\ (t + k)\ - wt}{(w + k)\ (t + k)}\right] \frac{\pi\,(D - a)^2}{4 \times 12} L + C = \text{B.M.}$$

With an allowance for shrinkage and surfacing included, the rule complete becomes:

$$\left[1 - \frac{(w + c + k)\ (t + b + k) - wt}{(w + c + k)\ (t + b + k)}\right] \frac{\pi\,(D - a)^2}{4 \times 12} L + C = \text{B.M.}$$

Where b and c in inches, represent these allowances in thickness and width, respectively.

APPENDIX.

How to Adjust the McKenzie Log Rule to Conditions Existing at Any Mill.

This can best be shown by assuming a set of conditions and then reducing the rule from its general form to a special form in accordance with whatever the limitations imposed may be. For example, assume the following:

Mill output for period of three months:

150,000 bd. ft. of	1" × 3"	cut	1 1/16" × 3 1/8"
120,000 bd. ft. of	1" × 4"	cut	1 1/16" × 4 1/8"
180,000 bd. ft. of	1" × 6"	cut	1 1/16" × 6 1/8"
225,000 bd. ft. of	1" × 8"	cut	1 1/16" × 8 1/8"
700,000 bd. ft. of	1" × 12"	cut	1 1/16" × 12 1/4"
550,000 bd. ft. of	1" × 14"	cut	1 1/16" × 14 1/4"
300,000 bd. ft. of	1" × 16"	cut	1 1/16" × 16 1/4"
270,000 bd. ft. of	1" × 18"	cut	1 1/16" × 18 1/4"
180,000 bd. ft. of	6/4" × 8"	cut	1 9/16" × 8 1/8"
275,000 bd. ft. of	6/4" × 10"	cut	1 9/16" × 10 1/8"
500,000 bd. ft. of	6/4" × 12"	cut	1 9/16" × 12 1/4"
300,000 bd. ft. of	6/4" × 14"	cut	1 9/16" × 14 1/4"
275,000 bd. ft. of	6/4" × 16"	cut	1 9/16" × 16 1/4"
240,000 bd. ft. of	6/4" × 18"	cut	1 9/16" × 18 1/4"
600,000 bd. ft. of	2" × 4"	cut	2 1/8" × 4 1/8"
450,000 bd. ft. of	2" × 6"	cut	2 1/8" × 6 1/8"
225,000 bd. ft. of	2" × 8"	cut	2 1/8" × 8 1/8"
175,000 bd. ft. of	2" × 10"	cut	2 1/8" × 10 1/8"
200,000 bd. ft. of	2" × 12"	cut	2 1/8" × 12 1/4"
210,000 bd. ft. of	3" × 3"	cut	3 1/8" × 3 1/8"
270,000 bd. ft. of	3" × 6"	cut	3 1/8" × 6 1/8"
250,000 bd. ft. of	3" × 12"	cut	3 1/8" × 12 1/4"
300,000 bd. ft. of	4" × 4"	cut	4 1/8" × 4 1/8"
150,000 bd. ft. of	4" × 6"	cut	4 1/8" × 6 1/8"
375,000 bd. ft. of	5" × 8"	cut	5 1/8" × 8 1/8"
180,000 bd. ft. of	6" × 6"	cut	6 3/16" × 6 3/16"
120,000 bd. ft. of	6" × 8"	cut	6 3/16" × 8 3/16"
275,000 bd. ft. of	7" × 9"	cut	7 3/16" × 9 3/16"
250,000 bd. ft. of	8" × 8"	cut	8 1/4" × 8 1/4"
200,000 bd. ft. of	8" × 12"	cut	8 1/4" × 12 1/4"
375,000 bd. ft. of	8" × 16"	cut	8 1/4" × 16 1/4"
100,000 bd. ft. of	12" × 12"	cut	12 1/4" × 12 1/4"

Width of saw kerf = 1/8″

Average taper (not including butt logs or top logs) = approx. 1/2″ in 8′

Average thickness of slabs and edgings at small end of logs = 5/8″

To determine a special form of

$$\left[1-\frac{(w+e+k)\,(t+b+k)-wt}{(w+e+k)\,(t+b+k)}\right]\frac{\pi\,(D-a)^2}{4\times 12}L+C=\text{B.M.}$$

which will conform to the above milling conditions and character of timber.

(*a*) The determination of the average value of

$$\left[1-\frac{(w+c+k)\ (t+b+k)-wt}{(w+c+k)\ (t+b+k)}\right]\quad (A)$$

For 1" × 3" lumber cut 1 1/16" × 3 1/8"

$w=3,\quad c=1/8=.125,\quad k=1/8=.125$

$t=1,\quad b=1/16=.0625$

$(w+c+k)=3.+.125+.125=3.25$

$(t+b+k)=1+.062+.125=1.187$

$(w+c+k)\ (t+b+k)=3.25\times 1.187=3.86$

$wt=1\times 3=3$

$$\text{Then } (A)=1-\frac{3.86-3}{3.86}=1-.223=.777$$

Therefore 150,000 bd. ft. represents 77.7% of the original material, or 22.3% has been forfeited to sawdust, shrinkage and surfacing in manufacturing 1" × 3" lumber, cut 1 1/16" × 3 1/8" when saw kerf = 1/8"

$\frac{150{,}000}{.777}$ = 193,000 = the volume in bd. ft. of material actually used in producing 150,000 bd. ft. of 1" × 3" lumber (not including slabs and edgings).

With similiar determinations made for all other dimensions of lumber cut, we have:

150,000 bd. ft. of	1" × 3" cut	1 1/16" × 3 1/8"	requiring 193,000 bd. ft. of solid material.
120,000 bd. ft. of	1" × 4" cut	1 1/16" × 4 1/8"	requiring 151,000 bd. ft. of solid material.
180,000 bd. ft. of	1" × 6" cut	1 1/16" × 6 1/8"	requiring 222,000 bd. ft. of solid material.
225,000 bd. ft. of	1" × 8" cut	1 1/16" × 8 1/8"	requiring 276,000 bd. ft. of solid material.
700,000 bd. ft. of	1" × 12" cut	1 1/16" × 12 1/4"	requiring 857,000 bd. ft. of solid material.
550,000 bd. ft. of	1" × 14" cut	1 1/16" × 14 1/4"	requiring 672,000 bd. ft. of solid material.
300,000 bd. ft. of	1" × 16" cut	1 1/16" × 16 1/4"	requiring 364,000 bd. ft. of solid material.
270,000 bd. ft. of	1" × 18" cut	1 1/16" × 18 1/4"	requiring 327,000 bd. ft. of solid material.
180,000 bd. ft. of	6/4" × 8" cut	1 9/16" × 8 1/8"	requiring 209,000 bd. ft. of solid material.
275,000 bd. ft. of	6/4" × 10" cut	1 9/16" × 10 1/8"	requiring 317,000 bd. ft. of solid material.
500,000 bd. ft. of	6/4" × 12" cut	1 9/16" × 12 1/4"	requiring 570,000 bd. ft. of solid material.
300,000 bd. ft. of	6/4" × 14" cut	1 9/16" × 14 1/4"	requiring 346,000 bd. ft. of solid material.
275,000 bd. ft. of	6/4" × 16" cut	1 9/16" × 16 1/4"	requiring 316,000 bd. ft. of solid material.
240,000 bd. ft. of	6/4" × 18" cut	1 9/16" × 18 1/4"	requiring 275,000 bd. ft. of solid material.
600,000 bd. ft. of	2" × 4" cut	2 1/8" × 4 1/8"	requiring 718,000 bd. ft. of solid material.
450,000 bd. ft. of	2" × 6" cut	2 1/8" × 6 1/8"	requiring 529,000 bd. ft. of solid material.
225,000 bd. ft. of	2" × 8" cut	2 1/8" × 8 1/8"	requiring 261,000 bd. ft. of solid material.
175,000 bd. ft. of	2" × 10" cut	2 1/8" × 10 1/8"	requiring 202,000 bd. ft. of solid material.
200,000 bd. ft. of	2" × 12" cut	2 1/8" × 12 1/4"	requiring 232,000 bd. ft. of solid material.
210,000 bd. ft. of	3" × 3" cut	3 1/8" × 3 1/8"	requiring 246,000 bd. ft. of solid material.
270,000 bd. ft. of	3" × 6" cut	3 1/8" × 6 1/8"	requiring 304,000 bd. ft. of solid material.
250,000 bd. ft. of	3" × 12" cut	3 1/8" × 12 1/4"	requiring 279,000 bd. ft. of solid material.
300,000 bd. ft. of	4" × 4" cut	4 1/8" × 4 1/8"	requiring 340,000 bd. ft. of solid material.
150,000 bd. ft. of	4" × 6" cut	4 1/8" × 6 1/8"	requiring 169,000 bd. ft. of solid material.
375,000 bd. ft. of	5" × 8" cut	5 1/8" × 8 1/8"	requiring 405,000 bd. ft. of solid material.
180,000 bd. ft. of	6" × 6" cut	6 3/16" × 6 3/16"	requiring 190,000 bd. ft. of solid material.
120,000 bd. ft. of	6" × 8" cut	6 3/16" × 8 3/16"	requiring 131,000 bd. ft. of solid material.
275,000 bd. ft. of	7" × 9" cut	7 3/16" × 9 3/16"	requiring 297,000 bd. ft. of solid material.
250,000 bd. ft. of	8" × 8" cut	8 1/4" × 8 1/4"	requiring 277,000 bd. ft. of solid material.
200,000 bd. ft. of	8" × 12" cut	8 1/4" × 12 1/4"	requiring 210,000 bd. ft. of solid material.
375,000 bd. ft. of	8" × 16" cut	8 1/4" × 16 1/4"	requiring 402,000 bd. ft. of solid material.
100,000 bd. ft. of	12" × 12" cut	12 1/4" × 12 1/4"	requiring 202,000 bd. ft. of solid material.

9,000,000 bd. ft. is manufactured from............................10,310,000 bd. ft. of solid material, not including the wastage necessary for slabs and edgings.

10,510,000 — 9,060,000 = 1,450,000 bd. ft. required for sawdust, shrinkage and surfacing.

$$\frac{1{,}450{,}000}{10{,}510{,}000} = .138$$ = fractional part of the logs, after slab allowance has been made, which becomes waste.

(1 — .138) = fractional part becoming lumber.

Therefore the average value of (A) becomes (1 — .138) for the above milling conditions.

(*b*) The determination of slab allowance or surface wastage:

This allowance is provided for in the formula by the constant "a", which represents twice the average thickness of the slabs and edgings coming from the small end of logs, regardless of their length. The value of "a" can be closely estimated at any mill by watching the logs being sawed into lumber. If the character of the timber being sawed is such that a waste allowance, additional to that made for slabs and edgings is necessary, to correct for losses due to crook, such an allowance should be made by increasing the value of the factor "a" to a sufficient amount to offset losses caused by such defects.

For the milling conditions under consideration here, the value of "a" is assumed to be 5/8″ × 2, or 1.25. Substituting this value and the average value of (A), already determined, in the general formula, we have the following special form:

$$(1 - .223)\frac{\pi (D - 1.25)^2}{4 \times 12} \cdot L + C = \text{B.M.}$$

for logs L feet long with no allowance made for taper.

For 8′ sections this form becomes:

$$(1 - .223)\frac{\pi (D - 1.25)^2}{6} + C$$

or

$$.407 \, (D - 1.25)^2 + C = \text{B.M.}$$

The constant C is included in the formula to counteract excessive taper in small logs, and its value should never be over 10 board feet. It can be definitely determined for a certain class of timber, by first ascertaining the mill overrun for small logs when $C = o$, and then making the value of C great enough to correct for the overrun. Large logs will be affected a negligible amount by the addition of this small quantity.

With $C = 3$ board feet, we have for the final reduction of the general rule:

$$.407 \, (D - 1.25)^2 + 3 = \text{B.M.}$$

to be applied to 8′ sections with a taper of 1/2″ in each 8′.

A volume table based on the above rule with a taper allowance of 1/2″ in 8′ should be compiled as follows:

Length in feet	Diameter in inches: 6	7	8	9	10	11	12	13	14	16
	Board feet									
8	12	16	22	28	34	42	50	59	69	80
9	14	18	25							
10	16	21	28							
11	17	23	31							
12	19	26	34							
13	21	28	38							
14	22	30	41							
15	24	33	44							
16	26	35	47	59	72	98	104	123	144	
17	28	38	50							
18	30	41	54							
19	32	43	57							
20	34	46	61							
21	36	49	64							
22	38	51	68							
23	40	54	71							
24	42	57	75	90	114	148	168	192	224	

Values for 8′ sections of different diameters are first determined directly from the formula. Then 16′ logs are considered as being made up of two 8′ sections, the one being one-half inch in diameter greater than the other; 24′ logs as three 8′ sections, one of them being the measured diameter at small end of log, another one, one-half inch greater than this, and the third, one inch greater. Thus, 26 board feet, which is the volume given in the above table for a log 16′ long and 6″ in diameter, was obtained by adding 12 board feet, which is the volume given for an 8′ section of same diameter, and 14 board feet obtained by averaging twelve and sixteen. (The average of 12 and 16 board feet gives volume for 8′ section, six and one-half inches in diameter.) The volume of the 24′ log of six inches in diameter shown in the table was obtained by adding 26 and 16. Twenty-six board feet being the volume of the first two 8′ sections contained in the log and sixteen board feet being the volume of the third or largest section. Other values may be obtained in a similar manner.

If the taper allowance were 1″ in 8′ instead of 1/2″ in 8′, a 16′ log 6″ in diameter at the small end would scale the same as two 8′ sections; the one 6″ in diameter and the other 7″. A 24′ log 20″ in diameter would, in like manner, scale the same as three 8′ sections; the first 20″, the second 21″ and the third 22″ in diameter. If this log were 22′ long instead of 24′ the scale would then be equal to that of the first two sections plus three-quarters of the third. By similar computations, all values composing a complete volume table for logs of different diameters and lengths can be compiled.

Log rules determined as explained in this Appendix apply to average conditions existing at the mills where they are made and are average rules which do not measure the fluctuations encountered in individual logs.

o

www.ingramcontent.com/pod-product-compliance
Lightning Source LLC
Chambersburg PA
CBHW020857130726
47900CB00014B/952